SO-AAE-135

YESTERDAY . . .

A man conceives a formula for a horrifying super-weapon that can mean death and enslavement for millions. This incalculable force for evil lies dormant. Until now.

TODAY . . .

His son inherits the key to Armageddon in a final legacy. It is the Caesar Code. To crack it is to unleash more terror than ever imagined by man or woman.

THE CAESAR CODE

"FIVE STARS . . . an engrossing story . . . if it doesn't end up as a blockbuster movie, it's Hollywood's fault."　　　　—*West Coast Review of Books*

JOHANNES MARIO SIMMEL is one of the world's most widely read authors. Born in Austria in 1924, he published his first book of short stories at age seventeen. Since his first big international bestseller, *The Monte Cristo Cover-Up* in 1963, he has produced instant European bestsellers and sales that total over 60 million copies. His novels have been translated into 26 languages and many of them have been made into films.

THE CAESAR CODE

Johannes Mario Simmel

Translated by Andrew White

WARNER BOOKS

A Warner Communications Company

WARNER BOOKS EDITION

Copyright © 1970 by Droemersche Verlagsanstalt Th. Knaur Nachf.,
Munich/Zurich

Authorized translation of the work *Und Jimmy ging zum Regenbogen*
by Johannes Mario Simmel

This Warner Books Edition is published by arrangement with
Droemersche Verlagsanstalt

Cover photograph by Dan Wagner

Warner Books, Inc.
666 Fifth Avenue
New York, N.Y. 10103

A Warner Communications Company

Printed in the United States of America

First Warner Books Printing: February, 1986

10 9 8 7 6 5 4 3 2 1

The events of this novel are based on true incidents which occurred in a major West German city between 1934 and 1965.

To protect the innocent, the action has been transferred to another period, 1938 to 1969, and to a different city, Vienna, remote from the actual happenings. The police precincts, courts, offices, authorities, secret and legal associations and all other religious or secular institutions are given their proper names, but were never in any way connected with the real events. Their representatives in this work are purely imaginary and without exception products of the author's invention.

Laws, paragraphs, decrees, memorandums, reports, and speeches, together with snatches from BBC broadcasts, have been reproduced verbatim.

All real events, persons, and names have been changed in such a manner as to make their identification impossible.

The author would like to express his sincere thanks to all those who helped him in the reconstruction of those events.

This leaf from an Oriental tree,
Transplanted to my garden's soil,
The secret sense does decree,
For the knowing man to uncoil.

Is it but one living soul,
That in itself has split to two?
Or is it the two do form one whole,
Each chosen part to the other true?

To solve the labyrinthine quest
I spun out the thread guiding me best:
Did you feel the sense in the tale I told,
That I'm not just one but double-souled?

Goethe: *Ginkgo biloba* from
'*The West-East Divan*'

THE SECRET

This leaf from an Oriental tree,
Transplanted to my garden's soil,
The secret sense does decree,
For the knowing man to uncoil.

1

The contract was for a neat job. A bullet in the head. So they had sent for Clairon. Neat bullets through the head were his specialty.

I don't know what Manuel Aranda has done, Clairon was thinking. They never tell you that. All I know is they want Manuel Aranda dead, and quickly. Once it's done I can go back home to Janine.

Janine was Clairon's daughter, five years old. He loved her more than anything else in the whole wide world. His wife was two years dead. He thought of his child and a smile lit up his face.

They had pointed Manuel Aranda out to him several times: striding from the portals of the Ritz Hotel on the Kärtner Ring into a plush, blue, rented Mercedes; entering the offices of the Institute of Forensic Medicine on the Sensengrasse; walking along various streets; standing in front of the Security Bureau offices at Police Department Headquarters in the Berggasse. They had shown him photographs and films of the fingered man, color movies taken with hidden 8mm cameras, so that he could study at leisure what his victim looked like, how he walked, the way he moved, the exact shape and size of his head. The films and the photographs had arrived on the same plane as Manuel Aranda himself. Clairon was an experienced hit-man, but never before on any contract had there been pressure, such a hectic, nervous, runaround. Every hour Manuel Aranda was permitted to stay alive seemed to intensify some deadly threat. The guy must have done something real bad, Clairon mused. They've never played it quite so rough and wild before.

It was January, and in Buenos Aires the heat was suffocating. The films shot in Manuel Aranda's hometown showed him strolling along the streets, always wearing a Panama hat. In Vienna, he had changed his headgear to a fur cap: no doubt he felt the cold as much as Clairon did. Clairon had bought himself a fur hat as soon as he had arrived.

11

So it'll have to be a bullet through the headgear as well as the head. Well, okay, I've dealt with hats before. Caps, too, and even a steel helmet. It always worked out. Just have to be a bit more accurate, that's all.

The blue Mercedes turned into the sideroad crunching over the ice-encrusted cobbles. In a brief one-and-a-half seconds Clairon focussed his gunsights on the car's front license plates. He checked the numbers carefully: yes, it was the right car. Clairon had become an ultra-cautious operator ever since he had been sentenced to death, cautious, and conservative. Clairon was using a German rifle, a 98k; he set its range at 175 yards, supporting the barrel on the left foot of a weeping angel.

2

At that moment in time, 14.43 hours on Thursday January 16, 1969, the Civic Cemetery of Vienna, opened in 1874, was composed of 329,627 graves spread over an area of 27,454,-588 square feet. Clairon had called up City Hall to inquire, for he was curious to know the size of the place where the deed was to be done. A huge number of graves had been vacated and re-occupied two, three, or four times since the turn of the century. One hour from now the grave count would have risen to 329,629 because two burials were scheduled for the afternoon. The ground was frozen solid; pneumatic drills were necessary to start the digging.

It was Clairon's first time on the scene, but already he knew it like the back of his hand. A descriptive brochure and a pocket map of the cemetery had been of help and so had the garrulousness of the woman who sold them to him. And he had carefully paced and inspected the whole area as soon as he had arrived; it was well marked. Clairon had learned the day before of Manuel Aranda's intention to visit the graveyard. At 16.55 hours, in a back room of the French travel bureau 'Bon Voyage' on the Schwarzenbergplatz, the message had come in over the short-wave transmitter.

"Come in, Olympus. come in. Olympus, Number Eleven calling."

"Receiving you, Number Eleven, state your message."

"Aranda has come back to the hotel. He told Zero that he wants to go to the cemetery tomorrow, and asked him to show him the way."

Reception was loud and clear. The set-up in Vienna was pretty cosy. The travel bureau was a front for an effective HQ, the number of active agents was surprisingly high, and they had five automobiles, all of which had built-in two-way transmitters outfitted with scrambling and unscrambling devices. Eavesdroppers would hear only an incomprehensible mess of sound. The car they wanted to give Clairon was fitted with this equipment.

"Where are the keys?" asked the man who had just been working the transmitter. Altogether there were five men in the windowless back room, including the chief, Jean Mercier, who ran the travel bureau, and Clairon. The question caused noticeable agitation in everyone except Clairon, who had no idea what keys were being asked for.

"They're in the box."

"Idiot! Where's the box?"

"In the morgue, where else? At the Institute of Forensic Medicine. I mean."

"Are you sure, completely sure?"

The boss himself now spoke into the microphone. Jean Mercier was a big man, pale, with dark shadows beneath his eyes, long eyelashes and hair streaked with gray. He had been running the Vienna HQ for five years. Beautiful women were his favorite pastime, and if what Clairon had heard was true, he still could, at fifty-five, get any woman he wanted.

"Yes, I'm sure, absolutely. Aranda complained to Zero that they wouldn't release the box. He can only get it with the corpse, and he won't get the corpse until tomorrow morning at ten." Some static crackled in the transmitter, but the man's voice came through loud and clear.

"You don't suppose Aranda smelled a rat and was lying to Zero?"

"Listen, boss, we had someone on Aranda's tail all day. Didn't let him out of his sight for a second. And he came out of the examiner's office *without* the box."

"So what—couldn't he have had the keys in his pocket?"

"No way."

"You know what's on the line. If the guy turns up with the keys now, it's curtains for us."

"Relax, boss. Cool it. We asked. Those medics follow the

13

book. Aranda couldn't get a thing out with him, not even a shoelace. Our whole plan is based on them sticking to the rules, right?"

"Yes. You're right." Mercier loosened his necktie.

"Okay. Aranda gets the keys tomorrow morning, but he'll have to go right on to the air freight office and arrange to have the body taken away. That'll take him until noon, for sure. Then he'll come back to the hotel and eat, and afterwards he'll drive to the cemetery."

"But what if he *doesn't* drive out to the cemetery? Then he's got the keys—and what if he says, Okay, open up, quick?"

"Zero's sure Aranda really intends to go to the cemetery. Aranda isn't even thinking of those keys. He's hardly aware of them. *He doesn't know a damn thing.* Zero is absolutely sure Aranda will have the box brought up to his apartment and not give it a second look—at least, not before going out to the cemetery. But that's the risk you knew we were taking all along: that short time between the moment when Aranda gets the keys and when he's liquidated."

I wish I knew what keys they're talking about, thought Clairon. Oh, to hell with it, I don't want to know. His eyes met Mercier's. Mercier spoke.

"So it has to be the cemetery. Understood?"

"Understood."

"Your man must not return from the cemetery."

Clairon nodded. Mercier continued to talk into the microphone.

"Where is Aranda now?"

"In his apartment. He can't go to the cemetery any more today, it's too late. After four-thirty they don't let anybody in. And he has to go to his embassy to get some papers for the casket."

"Hello, Number Three, come in, Number Three."

"Number Three reporting, Olympus." Another man's voice came from the transmitter.

"Were you listening?"

"Yes, boss."

"Have you got a good view of the hotel entrance?"

"Yes."

"You can see the coffeehouse exit, too?"

"Yes, boss." There was a large café in the hotel.

"When you see Aranda leaving for the embassy, follow him. Keep on his tail wherever he goes. Report his move-

14

ments to us. We'll have to keep twenty-four hour surveillance. Number Nine will relieve you in two hours . . ."

Clairon had left the travel bureau and bought a pocket map and descriptive brochure of the cemetery. The main roads were broken at infrequent intervals by small circles, from which roads branched out in every direction. Diminutive whitewashed buildings were scattered along the sides of the roads. Clairon visited two of them. There were an enormous number of comfort stations at the Civic Cemetery.

It's a good thing I have snow-chains, Clairon thought. It had been snowing heavily for days, and, while the principal roadways had been cleared, the side roads and pathways were all under two feet of snow. In the main roads, snowploughs had pushed the snow to the sides, creating small white mountains. The going was tough for pedestrians and drivers alike. Long stretches had not been salted and were slippery and treacherous.

"Olympus calling Number One . . . Olympus calling Number One."

"Number One receiving you, Olympus. Come in!"

"Aranda has just left the restaurant and went into the coffee house. He's having coffee there. Let's synchronize watches now, please."

"13.34."

"13.34."

Here we go again, thought Clairon. God-in-Heaven, I've just about had enough.

Back in 1961, I was with the OAS, the terrorist organization as it was called. Well, okay, I guess we weren't too fussy about the way we did things. But that's where I learned what I know today. And besides, de Gaulle wasn't too fussy, either, about what he did to the French settlers in Algeria. They caught me blowing up a movie house. I really love kids, I'd no idea there was a children's matinee on just then. I was condemned to death and put against a wall to be shot. But just as they had blindfolded me, some filthy scum comes up to me and says, we won't shoot you if you'll work for us from now on, and I'm no hero, I'm not that dumb, so I say it's a deal, and I've been hitting for them ever since. In Vienna this time.

The swine, Clairon thought bitterly. When will I be rid of them? *Never!* And now my wife's dead, too. If it weren't for Janine . . .

The thought of his small daughter cheered Clairon. Maybe

things were not so bad with him after all. He had a child, a house, a good income. As cover they had set him up as director of a French import firm in Casablanca.

While driving around the cemetery, he had encountered less than a dozen people and only four cars. Thank God for that. The heavy load of snow dropped from the sky had broken down branches and whole trees. The white mass covered hedges and bushes, beech trees and elms, weeping willows, elders, plane trees, acorn and chestnut trees, soaring spruce and cypress trees, graves and gravestones, wrought-iron gates and tiny chapels. Busts and figures in sculptured stone were grotesquely refashioned. One lifesize sandstone sculpture of a woman in mourning by the side of a grave now seemed to portray a woman in the ninth month of pregnancy; the curly-haired head of a young boy grimaced a drunken grin. The snow was lord of the graveyard, and its vassals were the crows. They squatted by the thousands in the crowns of trees, big, fat, and repellent, all packed together in a dense mass; their hoarse croaking shattered the air.

"Olympus calling Number One ... Olympus calling Number One ..."

Clairon responded.

"The time is now five minutes before two o'clock. They've just got Aranda's car out of the garage and he's about to leave the hotel."

"Okay," said Clairon. He drove across the cemetery and stopped beside an ancient elm near Groups 56, 57, 58, 59, 71 and 72. There was no sign of another living being. Clairon quickly called in to HQ:

"I've arrived and am getting into position."

"Very good, Number One. Number Two is following Aranda. In case Aranda changes direction and doesn't drive to the cemetery as expected, Number Two will call Number Twelve, who will inform you. But I think we can rely on Aranda. He'll show up on schedule."

"Let's hope so," said Clairon, and turned off his radio and engine. He got out of the car.

A man of forty-eight, Clairon looked older. Narrow, aquiline features, tight-lipped. He was wearing a dark-green, waterproof poplin coat lined with lamb's wool, a new black fur hat, a woollen scarf, ski trousers, and fur-lined boots. He kept the 98k under his coat and cautiously made his way toward Group 73—a longish and difficult walk on ice as smooth as glass. The pathway to Group 73 was deep in snow,

16

and before stepping into it Clairon took two felt rags out of his coat pocket and tied them around the soles of his boots. Then he jumped over a snow bank at the edge of the road, and sank over his knees into snow.

Slowly and carefully he let his eyes take in the details of Group 74. In a few seconds he had picked out the details he was looking for. They had not shown him all those pictures of the gravesite for nothing.

Keeping one eye constantly on the gravesite in Section F74, Clairon now went about the task of choosing the most suitable gravesite in his immediate vicinity. It did not take him long. After wading about a little while he found the ideal site: a grave in Section L73, property of the Reitzenstein family. Four dead—two men and two women—were already at rest here, under a gray marble slab nearly as tall as Clairon himself. Hewn into the stone and gilded were their names, eroded partially by the weather.

On top of the massive marble gravestone was a pedestal about a foot high, also marble, supporting a kneeling figure of a weeping angel, sculptured in gray marble, lifesize, wings outspread, with flowing robes and long hair falling down his back. His hands were clasped over his face. The handle of a marble torch was fastened to his right thigh, its crown resting on the pedestal. A flame of stone blazed out from it. The chalice of the torch lay at one end of the heavy block, the angel's left foot at the other. On the front end of the pedestal, in large capital letters, were these words:

EST QUAEDAM FLERE VOLUPTAS

As he stood there before the awesome tomb Clairon instinctively and automatically translated the inscription in the correct rhythm: *weeping out sadness makes the body feel whole.*

Moved, he repeated the text to himself while connecting the wires to his leather gloves: special gloves that could be heated by running wires up his jacket sleeves to two batteries in his breast pockets. It was essential for his fingers to remain warm.

A hood of snow about a foot-and-a-half high crowned the angel's head; his wings, the pedestal, the gravestone, the whole grave, were equally snowed-under. Clairon cushioned himself back into the snow: it was really the perfect hideout. It was impossible for anyone to see him from the roads.

Under the angel's bent left knee the folds of his flowing robe left a triangular opening blocked by snow which Clairon

17

quickly cleared away to provide his spyhole. Then he cleared a portion of the pedestal about six inches wide between the angel's big toe and the spot where his right knee completed the triangle. Now Clairon had an embrasure for his 98k. He slid the barrel into the peephole until it was nicely held by the angel's marble big toe. The gun poked out directly above the gilded 'U' in the word VOLUPTAS.

3

14.43 hours.

The barrel of the 98k swivelled slowly as Clairon followed the approaching blue Mercedes through the telescopic sights. It was a long drive from the Ritz, on the Ring, out to the cemetery, and he had had a long wait for Aranda. But now at last the victim was in sight. Clairon's hands were warm, but the rest of him felt frozen stiff.

He kept his weapon aimed with a featherlight touch. His eyes glued to the telescopic sights, he let his gaze drift upwards from the car's license plate over the radiator and across the hood to the windscreen. The reflections from the glass were so blinding that Clairon was unable to make out anything specific.

The Mercedes made agonizingly slow headway, no doubt because of the icy conditions, and Aranda was probably looking out for the right turn-off to Group 74 and the gravesite; all the little signposts were buried under the snow, making his task even more difficult. So much the better. The gun barrel inched around, bit by bit. Resting on the angelic big toe it was easy to keep it steady and controlled as it moved.

A dull, thunderous roaring rolled over the landscape from above.

It was not the first time. Clairon had heard it several times since embedding himself in his hideout. He glanced at his watch.

14.45 hours.

That must be Pan American Flight 751 to Rome, Beirut, Karachi, Calcutta, and Hongkong, he thought automatically.

Just taking off. Schwechat, the international airport, was southeast of this spot, not too far away. All planes flew over the cemetery as they climbed after takeoff. The din they made was so terrific that any other noise would be drowned out—including the sound of a shot. Even the crows would stop their croaking when a plane passed overhead. What a break to have the takeoff runways pointing right at the cemetery! This lucky twist of fate had even coaxed a smile of satisfaction from Clairon's normally sour-faced and jumpy boss.

The Mercedes got closer and closer. The roar of the jets swelled to a deafening clamor as the lower-lying clouds bounced the noise around as in an echo chamber. Clairon felt the air begin to vibrate. He pressed himself against the back of the large gravestone. No vibration there. Clouds of powdery snow were swept off the trees and the grave mounds, while whole lumps fell from the branches. The Boeing was close now, would be overhead in a few moments. The clouds were too low for it to be seen. The Mercedes stopped. Thank God, Clairon thought.

The invisible Boeing droned, whined, and whirred overhead, howling as though about to burst apart. Thus was the peace of this giant resting-place of the dead disturbed again and again from before dawn till well past midnight.

A lump of snow plopped down from the head of the weeping angel.

Clairon narrowed his eyes to slits. An inhuman quiet came over him, as always in such moments. The Mercedes was parked right opposite him, about a hundred yards away. Clairon raised the barrel a tiny bit to the right, bearing in mind the short distance. Now he had the left-front side window of the car in his telescopic sights.

Come on, get out. Just get out of the car, my friend. Not too slow, not too fast. And stop—just for a second, that will be enough. What a break, to have that devilish din up above. This man Manuel Aranda, whom I don't know, about whom I know nothing, this man whom I must kill—he'll have it all behind him soon. Me, too. Come on now, man, come on out. The car door opened. A figure appeared. But it was not a man. It was a woman.

19

4

"What was the dead woman's name?"

"Steinfeld."

"Valerie Steinfeld?"

"You know the name?"

"Oh, come on, it's been in the papers often enough. I've been following the story. It's a real spooky one too. Nobody knows . . ."

"Where's the grave?" Manuel Aranda put the question impatiently. He was tall and slender, and looked down from his height on the gatekeeper, a small, elderly man in a dark uniform, a cap and a walrus moustache stained with nicotine. He was on duty at the main entrance.

"Are you from the police?" The tiny gatekeeper blinked up at Aranda.

"No, I'm not from the police."

But you're a foreigner! Look at that brown skin!

The gatekeeper cocked his head a little to one side. "You're a relative of the Steinfeld woman—Frau Steinfeld, I mean?"

"No relative, either!" Aranda said loudly, almost shouting, his fingers clenched to a fist inside the pockets of his camelhair coat.

"Excuse me," the gatekeeper mumbled, his feelings hurt. "I was just curious. Especially in a case like this . . ."

"Where's the grave? *The grave!*"

"Well, you know, I can't tell you just like that off the top of my head. She was buried yesterday, right?"

"On Tuesday, yes."

"I'll call the office, wait here a moment." The gatekeeper went inside his little lodge.

Manuel Aranda waited. Inside the collar of his camelhair coat he was wearing a cashmere scarf. He had on furlined half-boots, gloves, and a fur cap. He felt cold. His face, oval in shape, was deeply suntanned. His eyes were gray, his nose straight, his lips full and bluish from the cold.

He gave the impression of a man confused, dazed, angry, and afraid. He was twenty-six. In his little lodge the gatekeeper was talking excitedly into the telephone.

"What kind of a mess is this? I said, V-a-l-e-r-i-e S-t-e-i-n-f-e-l-d! Day before yesterday! Surely to God you haven't already forgotten where you buried her!"

Manuel Aranda felt a wave of vertigo. He had been experiencing such bouts of dizziness ever since his arrival in Vienna. They passed quickly, but invariably left him feeling totally helpless, angry, and alone. He felt like a man on the verge of a serious illness. He imagined himself in a labyrinth, fumbling his way ever-deeper into the darkness and clamminess of its depths. It was the secret that made him so weak and ill, he thought, the secret . . .

He turned his head, which made his dizziness worse for a moment, and caught sight of the blue Mercedes he had rented, parked just a few paces away.

Fly back home, the Police Commissioner had said. But I won't fly home. Not under any circumstances. I made him understand that. He gave in. I have to know how it happened, why she did it, who gave her the job of—

"Hello there!"

Aranda turned quickly, felt a sudden onrush of giddiness again, a fear of falling. The old, good-natured gatekeeper was standing in the entrance to his little lodge.

"That's the second time I've . . ." He swallowed. "Are you all right? You look pale. Would you like some brandy?"

"No, thanks. You found it?"

"Yes, now I have it." The gatekeeper blinked, his bloodshot eyes streaming. "Frau Steinfeld is buried in Section F74. They shovelled the snow away when they buried her the day before yesterday, but there's been a lot come down since then. So everything'll be under deep snow again, that's for sure. F74's quite a ways away, almost right at the other end, a good half-hour's walk."

"I have a car. Is it permitted to . . . ?"

"Only on the main roads! And you have to pay five schillings."

Aranda pressed a 20 schilling note into the man's outstretched hand.

"Thank you, your Highness." The gatekeeper tore off a page from a block. "When you get to 74—oh, excuse me just a moment." The gatekeeper's face had lit up as he caught sight of someone behind Aranda. His voice took on a more cheerful tone. "At last! I was beginning to think something had happened!"

"Well, first I didn't get away on time, then my car broke down about a mile from here." It was a woman's voice.

This time Manuel Aranda was careful to turn his head slowly in order to avoid the dizziness. Behind him stood a woman, perhaps thirty years old and of about his own height. Aranda found himself looking at a face with even features and a serious expression—small nose, beautiful mouth, chestnut hair flowing out from under a tightly knotted headscarf. The young woman had put on far too much powder and make-up. Her eyes were invisible behind outsized dark glasses with round frames. Her boots and coat were sealskin. "Good afternoon," said the young woman. Aranda nodded silently.

"What was the trouble with the car?" the gatekeeper asked. The young woman was a favorite of his; somehow he felt himself to be on the same wavelength. A couple of days before she had come into his lodge to ask for a glass of water. She wanted to take some pills she was carrying with her, and they had talked for a few minutes while she was waiting for the pills to take effect.

"It's the fuel-pump," she answered. "I had to have the car towed away. You have to wait ages before anybody gets to you out here. Then I took the tram." The young woman hunched her shoulders and nodded with her chin toward the opposite side of the street. "I found the stone-mason's shop closed with a notice to ask here."

The gatekeeper, red-nosed, offered a polite bow. "Herr Ebelseder had to go into the city. But he left it with me in case you came. He said you've paid for it already." He paused. "The only thing is, it's far too heavy to carry such a long way."

"I'll take a taxi. There are some over there."

"That should be okay"—the gatekeeper's deeply lined face lit up again—"or perhaps the young gentleman would be kind enough to take you with him. He's driving over to the same spot."

"Where to?" The young woman's voice sounded suddenly unsteady.

"To the same grave as you, what do you think! Strange, perhaps, but true! Do you know each other, perhaps?"

The young woman looked Manuel Aranda carefully up and down through her dark glasses.

"No," she said, but her voice had a nervous edge.

Aranda's curiosity was aroused, he felt excited.

"You must be Irene Waldegg," he said.

"How do you know——" She stopped. He watched her beautiful mouth close tightly.

"I was shown some photographs."

"By the police?"

"Who else?" he answered shortly.

She stared at him.

"My name is Manuel Aranda. Does it sound familiar?" His tone was aggressive.

"Yes," Irene Waldegg said. They exchanged hostile glances.

The gatekeeper noticed nothing unusual. "How about that!" he said in a jovial tone. "You do know each other after all! I have the thing inside. I——"

A car horn honked three times. A white Lincoln with blue-tinted windows stopped outside the front gates. The man at the wheel had a square face, protruding jaw, freckles, blonde hair, crew-cut. A small, swollen scar ran across his forehead. He wore a rusty-brown duffle-coat. He was gesticulating impatiently at the gatekeeper, a 100-schilling note between his fingers. "Quick," said crew-cut. "Make it snappy!" He spoke with an American accent. His teeth were large, white and uneven, and as he sat waiting he chewed heavily on a piece of gum.

Irene Waldegg and Manuel Aranda were still staring at each other, totally oblivious of the surroundings. A jet passed overhead with a deafening roar, shattering the air, but the young man and the young woman saw and heard only themselves. The noise died. The woman spoke:

"I beg your pardon?" He had not caught the words.

She repeated them. "A strange place for a rendezvous."

"I did not choose it."

"Nor did I," said Irene Waldegg, her lips suddenly quivering as though she were about to cry.

"But you did know that I was in Vienna?"

"Of course. Don't look at me like that! It wasn't my fault."

"What do I know?" said Manuel Aranda.

"What is that supposed to mean?" Her voice rose in anger.

"It's supposed to mean that I know nothing at all," he replied.

"Why didn't you call me? Why didn't you come to see me? How long have you been in Vienna?" Her tone was aggressive.

"Two days."

"So you've had time. Why didn't you?"

"I had to go through a lot of formalities to get the body released. I didn't have time. Not yet."

The gatekeeper gave the American his change. The Lincoln screeched through the gate and into the cemetery. "Five miles an hour speed limit!" the gatekeeper shouted after him angrily. Then he strode back, mumbling, "It takes all kinds! So, Miss, I'll get it for you now, you've been waiting long enough." He disappeared into his lodge.

"So you didn't have time," she said bitterly, "but you do have time to come out here."

"I want to see the grave."

"Why?"

"Because . . ." He stopped, feeling faint again, lonely, and sad. "I want to see everything and talk to everybody who had any connection with the whole affair."

"Except me!" The hostility in her voice was plain.

"I would have come to see you in time, you can bet on that," he retorted sharply.

"I'm no criminal," she said, almost shouting. "You were with the police, and with Commissioner Groll."

"True. So what?"

"Does Groll say I'm a criminal?"

"No."

"Does he say it was my fault?"

"No."

"Does he say I'm under suspicion?"

Goddammit, Aranda thought, what is this? What right does she have to talk like that? He answered more calmly:

"Groll has not said the slightest thing against you. Still, you must understand——"

Irene Waldegg interrupted him bitterly, "I understand, all right! I'm not to be trusted. I have a chemist's shop, after all, it's easy for me to get at poisons. So I'm a prime suspect. Better not talk to me yet, better make inquiries first, keep a watch on me, see how I check out, maybe I did do something after all!"

"I never said that!"

"But you thought it! Let me tell you what I think. I think your behavior is most unfitting, Mr. Aranda. You're not the only one who's suffering, you know."

The gatekeeper emerged from his lodge, beaming and talking: "There you are, Miss! Everything to your liking? Personally I find it a very lovely piece. Herr Ebelseder's a real

24

artist, don't you think?" The piece the doorman handed to Irene Waldegg was fashioned in wrought-iron, in the shape of a half-open pair of calipers, about two feet long and fitted with a crosspiece at the open end. Attached to the narrow end was a small metal frame, behind which a card edged in black and printed with black letters was on display under glass.

Irene Waldegg took the large black iron calipers into both hands. Aranda read the words on the memorial paper:

VALERIE STEINFELD

6th March 1904–9th January 1969

Beneath the inscription was a cross.

"The ground's frozen solid, of course. But now you've met your friend, you'll have some help. I mean . . ." The doorman seemed put out. "Did I say something wrong? Maybe I'd better call a taxi?"

"No!" Aranda spoke up quickly. "No taxi." He turned to Irene Waldegg. "Please forgive my behavior. Let's drive over together. I—I have a lot to ask you . . ."

She stood there without a word, a pathetic figure, the wrought-iron sculpture in her hands and the dark glasses covering her eyes. After a seemingly endless time she nodded, yes.

The gatekeeper rushed over. "Let me help!" Without more ado he relieved Irene Waldegg of the temporary gravestone and put it into the trunk of the Mercedes. Aranda asked Irene Waldegg. "What kind of car do you drive?"

"A Mercedes too. But a different model."

"Perhaps you wouldn't mind driving then? You know your way around here better than I do."

"Be glad to." Her hand reached towards her glasses, as if to remove them, but then she didn't. She got into the driver's seat of the car. The gatekeeper slammed the trunk shut and followed Aranda around the car to the other side.

"The lady all right?" he asked in a whisper.

"Perfectly," answered Aranda.

"I guess it hit her hard."

"Of course."

"Ah, well, death," the doorman said philosophically, bowing deeply as he slipped another banknote from Aranda into his pocket.

Slowly Irene Waldegg put the car into gear. The car turned into the wide road which lead to the Dr. Karl Lueger

Church. It was a bumpy ride over the ice. Irene Waldegg kept her eyes fixed on the road.

"There must have been a reason!" Aranda said.

"There is none."

"Or we haven't found it yet. Groll maintains your aunt was completely sane."

"Completely."

"Well, then," said Manuel Aranda, "there absolutely must have been a reason for Valerie Steinfeld to poison my father."

5

Crows, crows, crows all around—screeching, screaming, croaking.

"No!" Irene Waldegg said, steering the car slowly and carefully. "There's not a single clue. You can go out of your mind just thinking about it. There's no explanation or motive I can fathom. Not even something outlandish or wildly improbable. It's all terribly unreal . . ."

"Except that Valerie Steinfeld is dead," said Manuel Aranda. "And my father is dead. There's nothing unreal about that. Valerie Steinfeld poisoned my father. Then she poisoned herself. According to the police, there's no doubt at all about those two facts."

"Groll is a clever man with a lot of experience," answered Irene Waldegg, "and he has a lot of specialists working for him. Doesn't he have any idea about a motive? At least some tiny clue?"

Careful, Aranda thought. I gave Groll my word of honor not to say anything. During his short time in Vienna Aranda had had a number of conversations with the high-ranking police official. By now he knew a lot about a lot of people. You don't even have an inkling about the things I know, thought Aranda as he eyed the girl surreptitiously. But I'm not going to tell you any of them, I'd be a louse if I did, because Groll trusts me. I don't trust you, I'd be mad to trust any of you!

"No, he doesn't have the faintest clue," Aranda lied.

Irene Waldegg drove around a funeral chapel. Its roof was buried in snow, and huge icicles hung down from it.

"Since when have you known Groll?" Aranda asked.

"Since . . . that night. He had his men pick me up and take me to the bookstore. I had to identify my aunt, then go to the station for questioning." The woman hunched her shoulders. A shudder ran through her body. "It was horrible. They both looked dreadful. The poison had—"

"Enough, enough," he interrupted quickly. "But you were able to identify your aunt?"

"Immediately."

"And my father?"

"I never knew your father, Mr. Aranda."

"Are you sure?"

"Quite sure." She lied like a born liar, if she was lying.

"Did your aunt ever mention his name?"

"Never, I'm quite sure of that, too. I tell you, it's enough to drive you crazy!"

You said it, he thought to himself. A bit too often.

"Were you sharing an apartment with Frau Steinfeld?" Aranda kept his gaze fixed on Irene Waldegg. A beautiful face, he thought. An open face. Except I can't see her eyes. What sort of eyes does this woman have?

"I'm beginning to think I really would have been better off with a taxi," the woman replied calmly.

"What's that supposed to mean?"

"It means I've had enough of your questions. You know everything anyway! Groll told you everything, didn't he? Do you think you can catch me in some lie? You still think I'm guilty. It was stupid of me to fall for your lousy apology."

Got to cool it, he thought. The woman's no fool. I'm the one who's behaving like an idiot. Aloud he said, "My apology was sincere, I assure you. Let me tell you what I know, what Groll told me. You were living with your aunt, Frau Steinfeld. It was her apartment, in the . . . oh damn, I've forgotten the name of the street."

"Gentzgasse."

"Right, Gentzgasse. You're a pharmacist. You own the pharmacy in the Lazarettgasse. It used to belong to your uncle, you worked for him, and he left it to you when he died three years ago." That's better, Aranda thought. I'll never get anywhere if I fight her.

"You do have snow tires, don't you?" Irene Waldegg asked.

"Yes." Knocked a little off his stride, he frowned in irritation before continuing. "Frau Steinfeld was not your only rela-

27

tive. I know that, too. Your parents are alive. Somewhere in southern Austria, in . . ."

"Villach," she said, "in Kärnten. I came to Vienna to study."

"Groll told me. And Frau Steinfeld worked in the Landau Bookstore in the Seilergasse."

"Have you been there yet?"

"I haven't been anywhere yet. I haven't had time, I told you. But I intend to go there later today. First, though, I wanted to see Frau Steinfeld's grave."

"Groll's men talked to the bookdealer Martin Landau and his sister by telephone that very same evening. But neither one had ever seen your father before, or ever heard his name from my aunt or anyone else. Is that the same information you have?"

"Yes, it is. But Frau Waldegg . . . can we try to be a bit more friendly toward each other from now on? As you can see, I'm really making an effort to be fair and nice to you . . ."

She said nothing, but nodded her head.

"I know your aunt had been working in the bookstore for a very long time. But for how long exactly? I don't know honestly."

"An eternity." For the first time her voice was gentle and without edge. "She was already working there when I was born, and I'm thirty-one. Valerie started there in 1938."

"Valerie?"

"I always called her Valerie. She preferred it. She felt it made her younger." Irene Waldegg turned into a new side road, which stretched straight ahead without break. Not a soul was to be seen anywhere.

"Valerie started as a salesgirl, I think. She became sales manager after the war, and for the past twelve years she was a bookkeeper there."

"And what about the day . . . what happened, exactly?"

Irene paused to shift into low gear at the edge of a huge patch of ice. Not a word came from her, and her silence immediately aroused Aranda's old mistrust and suspicion. Was she trying to think up some plausible lies? "Well?"

"On the day it happened . . ." Irene began and stopped.

"Go on! Just a week ago today, remember?"

"Valerie and I left the house together that morning. Just as we always did. I took her to the bookstore in my car before driving to the pharmacy. I've been doing that ever since I've had the car. Except when I have night-duty, like tomorrow."

"What about tomorrow?"

"Tonight I'm on night-duty, so tomorrow I can't drive Valerie to the——" She stopped. "Oh my God, I can't get used to the fact she's dead."

She drew her hand across her forehead. The gesture touched Aranda. She, too, has lost someone she loved, he thought. Now she's in despair, just as I am; confused, frightened, angry, lost, just like me. No, she's not playing games with me. Can it be I've found a person I can trust? Can it be?

"Valerie was so cheerful that morning," she continued.

"Why was that?"

"She had just won a color television in some newspaper contest. She entered every competition she could find. She always said you're bound to hit it lucky once in a lifetime!"

"You're bound to hit it lucky once in a lifetime." He thought, I heard Frau Steinfeld say that once before. In quite different circumstances.

Once again the woman shuddered.

"Your aunt never came home that evening. Didn't you get worried?"

"Not at first. She often got home late. Sure, when she still was not home by nine o'clock I did begin to feel uneasy. There was a real blizzard outside. I thought maybe she'd had an accident. I was just about to call the bookstore when the doorbell rang. It was the police, come to fetch me."

"So you didn't speak to your aunt on the phone at all that evening?"

"No."

"But Valerie Steinfeld did have a telephone conversation."

"Yes," Irene Waldegg answered. "I've heard it."

"So have I," said Manuel Aranda. "Three times."

6

"Killed him . . . killed him . . . poison . . . poison . . . look at him on the floor . . . you're bound to . . . you're bound to hit it lucky once . . . once in a lifetime . . ." It was a female

29

voice gasping and gulping the words, screaming them, muttering them.

Wolfgang Groll depressed a button on the tape-recorder that stood on a small table. The reels whirred to a stop, and the only sound left in the speakers was the hum and crackle of static. A green glow came from the magic eye.

"You were listening to the voice of Frau Steinfeld," said Groll. "Three witnesses have identified it and are prepared to swear to its authenticity, Mr. Aranda."

"How did you happen to record this?" Aranda asked.

He was wearing a dark-blue suit, white shirt and black tie. For the last hour and a half he had been sitting in Commissioner Groll's office, in the Security Branch of Police HQ in Vienna. During that time Groll, whom Aranda knew from two transatlantic telephone calls and a number of telegrams to police HQ in Buenos Aires, had once more gone over the details of the mysterious crime. He had recounted to Aranda the known events of that evening, and given him the names and exact descriptions of everyone—witnesses and relatives—connected with the crime in any way. Commissioner Groll had taken an instant liking to Manuel Aranda, and was genuinely concerned about the young man, who by now had a harried and exhausted look. The clock read almost midnight. Aranda had arrived in Vienna at 21.50 hours. He had taken a taxi to the Ritz, a luxury hotel on the Kärtner Ring where his father had been staying.

The foyer of the Ritz was resplendent with light from three massive candelabras. Marble pillars gleamed, antique tapestries hung from rosewood panelled walls. The floor was marble covered with expensive carpets. Aranda kept his taxi waiting as he walked over to the reception desk. A man of about forty-five hurried towards him.

"Señor Manuel Aranda?"

"Sí."

"Bienvenido en Viena, Señor Aranda!"

A slim, elderly man with white hair came out of the large open office behind the reception desk. His voice was soft and heavy with sympathy:

"Buenos noçes, Señor Aranda. Reciba mi mas sincera condolencia . . ."

"Thank you. I can speak German," said Aranda.

Whereupon the two gentlemen welcomed him to Vienna

once more, in German, and offered him their renewed condolences for the tragic loss he had suffered. The younger man was deputized as Head of Reception: he introduced himself as "Pierre Lavoisier, sir, at your service." Lavoisier then introduced the older, white-haired man:

"Count Romath, our Director."

Count Romath looked as though he could have stepped from the pages of a British men's fashion magazine. He held himself very straight, and he wore an elegant black suit, a silver tie with a pearl tiepin, and a white silk shirt with soft collar.

A small group in evening dress, men and women, strolled by, laughing.

Count Romath greeted them, and seeing other guests approaching turned quickly to Aranda and said, "I suggest we go into my office, Mr. Aranda. Just for a moment."

He led the way, a trifle unsteady on his feet: he was well past sixty. His office was at the end of a short corridor behind the reception area. The furnishings were tasteful: a floor lamp next to an antique coffee table, brocaded armchairs, priceless Chinese scatter-rugs over red carpeting, heavy red damask curtains, panelled walls and a magnificent reproduction of Adolph Menzel's 'Supper at the Masked-Ball,' a painting Aranda knew well. Flickering gold, burning red, luminous purple and black were the dominant colors of the picture, framed in slate-gray and roughly fifteen inches by eighteen inches in size.

A tall, slender copper vase on the writing-desk contained flowers that resembled orchids: brownish-white spotted with bright yellowish-gold.

"It's terrible, really terrible, my dear sir," began the Count, fingering the pearl in his tie. "Nobody understands it. Nobody can explain it."

"Did you see my father again—after he was dead?"

"Yes. I . . . I was called to the bookstore to identify him. Your father was carrying a passport, but they needed someone who had known him personally. He was a wonderful man, your father. A real gentleman. We had a few talks together."

"What about?"

"About Argentina. I had some property over there, you know. I lived there for five years before the war." The Count ran a hand through his white hair. "We received your telegram. Do you really want your father's suite?"

31

"Yes," Aranda said. It was here in this office that he first felt the dizziness that was to attack him again and again.

"As you wish, of course." The Count played with the pearl on his tie. "The police searched the suite, but didn't take anything away, and we have tidied everything up again since the search."

"Then I'd be grateful if you would have my bags taken up."

"At once." The Count led the way. "May I show you the rooms personally?"

"I have to leave again immediately."

"Right away?"

"Yes. I have a taxi waiting. Is it far to the"—Aranda fumbled in the pocket in his camelhair coat and pulled out a scrap of paper—"Berggasse?"

"Berggasse?"

"Police headquarters. I telephoned Groll between planes from Paris. He said he would see me today no matter how late. I had asked for an interview. You can imagine how urgently I . . ."

"I can indeed," replied the Count. "My only concern is that the Commissioner himself is facing a big mystery. But your anxieties are completely understandable. If I were in your place I couldn't go to bed without at least having . . . forgive me, the Berggasse is about fifteen minutes by car."

"Would you be good enough to call the Commissioner and tell him I am on my way?"

"Mr. Lavoisier, would you see to that immediately, please?"

"Yes, sir." Pierre Lavoisier stepped over to the door and held it open for Manuel. "After you?"

The Count nodded a gracious farewell. Once alone in his office, he waited a short minute, then locked the door, strode rapidly over to the picture on the wall, felt for and found a hidden catch on the underside of the frame, and pressed it. A small section of the moulding opened up to reveal a box about the size of a pack of cigarettes in the hollowed-out interior of the frame. A miniature radio transmitter with a range of roughly a mile and a half. The receiver was in a car parked in a sidestreet about three-quarters of a mile from the Count's office.

Romath pulled out the antenna on the transmitter and started speaking in a calm voice: "Calling Sunset . . . Calling Sunset . . . This is Able Peter, Able Peter . . ."

"Go ahead, Able Peter," said a man's voice over the transmitter's tiny speaker.

The Count continued in English. "Our new guest is about to depart in a taxicab parked in front of the hotel for the Berggasse, to see Groll."

"Thank you, Able Peter. Over."

"Over," said Romath. He replaced the transmitter into its hiding place and touched the hidden catch again. The section of the moulding slid back into place. It was a carved, ribbed frame, and the movable section was invisible to the naked eye. The Count unlocked the door.

Meanwhile, Manuel Aranda was being escorted to the waiting taxi by Lavoisier, who was almost exaggeratedly solemn and courteous. One of the five pages on duty in the lobby opened the glass doors for them, while a bulky doorman held open the taxi door. The cab drove off immediately. The doorman stayed out in the open, while the page, a slender and handsome youth of about twenty, decked out in a gray uniform, returned to the foyer with Lavoisier and stayed by the reception desk while Lavoisier went behind it and began leafing through a telephone directory.

"I feel sorry for Aranda," said one of his colleagues who was standing by him.

"Yes, it's a tragedy," Lavoisier answered, running his finger down the names in the book.

"There it is," he murmured half to himself. "Security Branch, Vienna Police Department HQ, Section Two, Berggasse, Telephone number 34 55 11 . . ." He reached for a telephone and dialled. "And such a courteous young man," he added. "His father was the same," said his colleague. Lavoisier, speaking into the telephone, could be heard asking for Groll, who came on the line without delay. The deputy Head of Reception identified himself, then announced Manuel Aranda's imminent arrival.

The page straightened out the fringe on one of the rugs, then walked slowly past his fellow pages, across the entire entrance hall to a corridor at the far end behind the main coatroom which led into an adjoining coffeehouse. Here, there were six telephone booths, built into the red, damask-covered wall. They were really a part of the coffeehouse, but the coffeehouse belonged to the hotel. It was possible to enter and leave the 'Ritz' through the café.

Opposite the telephone booths were two doors leading to washrooms and toilets for ladies and gentlemen. The page went into the first booth, deposited a schilling and dialled. He had a slight Viennese accent: "Weigl here. He left two minutes ago for the Berggasse, to see Groll."

"I'm glad you called." The answering voice was without accent. "The idiots went and lost him at the airport."

"Assholes! The number of the taxi is W 471 546. Got it? A Mercedes 200 Diesel, black."

The voice at the other end repeated the details.

"I'll put them through to HQ right away. How are things over where you are?"

"Everything fine. The receptionist is on holiday still, Lavoisier is taking over for him while he's gone. I'm standing in myself for a fellow who's down with flu. The boss is coming back in a couple of days now. It'll have to be all over by then."

"It will be. Easily. Let's leave it at that. Take care."

The Mercedes 200D, license plate W 471 546, drew up in front of Police HQ in the Berggasse and stopped. Opposite, in the Hahngasse, two men were sitting in an Opel Kapitän. One of them palmed a microphone to his mouth and spoke into it softly, in French: "Come in Olympus . . . come in Olympus . . . Number 8 calling . . ."

"Receiving you, Number Eight."

"The taxi just arrived," said the man into the microphone. "Aranda is getting out . . . paying the driver . . . walking up to the building . . . talking with the guard . . . he's been let through . . . he's going in . . . now he's inside, can't see him any more."

"Stay where you are, you two. When Aranda comes out again—it can't be very long—follow him. Check with me every fifteen minutes! Over."

"Over," said the man in the Opel Kapitän, and put the microphone down. He took a cigarette out of the pack his colleague offered to him.

"What do you think is up? That was the big boss again, in person. Do you think he works around the clock?"

"Yes."

"Well, he's never done that before! Have you any idea why we're on No. 1 alert just because this guy's here?"

"B," replied his companion.

"What?"

"B. What do you suppose 'B' stands for, any ideas?"

"You've been drinking too much. Are you drunk?"

"Don't be ridiculous! *B!* It has to mean something, this B."

34

"Now come on . . ."

"I happened to be in HQ when the courier from Paris got here; I just picked up a few words before he disappeared with the boss. I heard him mention something about B."

"What about B?"

"I didn't get it clear. But I did understand the B. And I could tell that what could happen is just about the worst."

"The worst?"

"Yes, the worst. B. I heard it loud and clear. What do you say to that?"

Thirty yards behind them a big black American Ford was parked. In it sat two men. During the last few minutes one of them had been frantically turning the knobs of a receiver about the size of a portable radio. The set was fitted with hypersensitive microphones capable of picking up conversations within a radius of fifty yards, even when they were taking place behind walls or inside automobiles. All that was required was to set the directional antennae. The man holding the radio on his lap suddenly looked up, uttered a curse in a heavy American accent, then said: "Nothing to be done."

"They've got all their cars sealed off," his companion said.

"I give up," said the first man. "Maybe the Russians can make it work."

"Probably not."

"Maybe just. They've got some fantastic people working this kind of job. And better instruments than ours."

"The Russians won't hear anything either," said the second man, "not this time, not in a 'B' case."

The first man let out another curse, then grabbed for his microphone again . . .

7

Aranda's voice was quavering. Groll's expression, as he looked at the harried and exhausted youth, was fraught with concern. The clock read almost midnight. Groll spoke in an especially calm tone of voice:

"Your father was murdered five days ago, Mr. Aranda, on the ninth of January. On that evening—"

"I would have been here much quicker if we hadn't had an airport workers' strike in Buenos Aires right up until yesterday!"

"I know that. Please keep calm. On that evening, the ninth of January, a woman telephoned the midtown police precinct four times between 19.24 and 19.39."

"How can you be sure it was the same woman every time?"

"All the calls came into the guard room, and the duty officer claims to have recognized the voice each time. It was apparently not difficult: the woman was so excited she could only just stammer the words out . . . and then she always said the same thing: 'Killed him! Killed him!' "

"But on the tape recording . . ."

"The first three times she didn't say anything else, Mr. Aranda, and then she always hung up. Perhaps she was too weak to continue. Perhaps she was scared. The voice was more blurry each time, and in fact the autopsy showed that Frau Steinfeld had consumed a large amount of alcohol. She must have been drinking between calls."

"I see."

"When the second call came, we got our experts to try to trace the call, and the inspector also turned on the tape recorder that's attached to our telephone. He recorded what Frau Steinfeld said when she called for the fourth time, and that's the tape we have here."

"How did the inspector know it was Frau Steinfeld?"

"At the time, he didn't. The only reason I mention her name is that we have, as I said, three witnesses prepared to swear that the voice belongs to Frau Steinfeld—the owner of the bookstore, Martin Landau, his sister Ottilie, and Frau Steinfeld's niece, Miss Irene Waldegg."

"So after the fourth call the woman didn't hang up?"

"No. The fourth call went on for quite a while. I assume Frau Steinfeld was pretty drunk by then and not really conscious of what she was doing. She wanted to talk, had to talk. The inspector was clever, and held her on the phone."

Wolfgang Groll was fifty-nine years old, tall and corpulent. He kept his silver-gray hair combed back above a broad face with bushy gray eyebrows and sparkling gray eyes. Groll liked to laugh loud and often. His mouth was large. The war had robbed him of one lung, and he suffered occasionally from circulatory disturbances; nevertheless, there was nobody in the bureau who could equal his energy. He was in his office every morning at eight o'clock, and could work the night through without seeming to tire.

He was, indeed, a man who needed very little sleep, and when he was not working he busied himself with researches in the natural sciences. His lifelong wish had been to be a biologist; his large apartment in the Porzellangasse housed a huge library of books on the natural sciences, philosophy and history, encyclopedias, specialized reference works, index-card files and an archive all his own.

What very few people knew was that for many years Wolfgang Groll had been working on a book entitled *New Man—New Cosmos.* He had planned the book as a popular work which would present a summary of all that modern astronomy, physics, chemistry, biology, psychochemistry and other specialized branches of science had contributed towards the creation of a *new* cosmos and a *new* man. To summarize and diagnose the practical use of new knowledge for the new man, for his perspectives and behavior in the world, was the innermost wish and ambition of this lonely criminologist, whose first fascination had been the natural sciences.

The pressed leaf of a gingko tree, a particularly beautiful sample, lay beneath the glass top of his desk. Groll's whole way of life and thought centered around this mysterious tree. Somehow the gingko tree had always been there at the important moments of his life: in the park at Schönbrunn on the day he decided to devote his life to the natural sciences; in the garden of the university institute on the day he had had to give up his studies; in the ancient palace garden, where he had first met his wife Olga, with whom he had lived happily until her death nine years ago; at the entrance to the hospital to which he had brought her, and which she was never to leave again; on the day of their wedding; on the day he became a soldier; in front of the Ukrainian country mansion which housed the army hospital to which he had been taken after his injury; in the gardens of the sanatorium where he convalesced years later, recovering from lung surgery. The operation had given his life back to him . . . a new life actually had begun for him in that park . . . Again and again, always at critical turning-points in his life, Groll had encountered the gingko tree, singly or in groups.

The gingko tree can grow up to one hundred twenty feet tall. When young, the tree's crown is slender and round; later, it becomes uneven, and not infrequently the tree is wider than it is high. Although a member of the pine family, the gingko looks like a broad-leaf tree, and in the fall its wonderfully resplendent golden leaves drop to the ground. Groll of course knew Goethe's poem 'Gingko biloba,' a love-poem, but expressive of a phenomenon Goethe had described again and again: the polarity of the universe, of this world, of all life, and of all forms of existence.

Goethe had reflected time and again on such polarities: Inhalation-Exhalation. Health-Disease. Happiness-Unhappiness. Systole-Diastole. Ebb-Tide. Day-Night. Man-Woman. Muscle flex-Muscle relax. Earth-Heaven. Life-Death. Darkness-Light. Negative-Positive. Good-Evil.

8

"It goes without saying," continued Groll, "that the Precinct Inspector was careful not to disturb Frau Steinfeld's drunken raving. He did not want her to panic and slam down the receiver again as she had done three times before. Listen again, Mr. Aranda. The man's voice belongs to the Inspector."

Groll gently pushed a button of the tape recorder. The reels began to turn, the loudspeakers hummed.

"What sort of capsule?"

"Cyanide, what do you think? ... What kind of policeman are you ... I kept myself under control this morning ... took all my strength ..."

"This morning?"

"That's when he first came in ..."

Manuel Aranda felt dizzy. He tightened his grip on the arm of the tattered old leather sofa and held on. It was unreal. Fantastic. Horrible. Here was the voice of a woman who had been buried just a few hours ago, on the afternoon of January 14. Here was this voice, now dead, buried, nonexistent, speaking about his father, also dead, equally nonexistent, a body in the morgue of the Institute of Forensic Medicine.

"Ehrlich's great portfolio ..."

"Ehrlich?"

"Yes, Ehrlich!" Suddenly the woman's voice was a scream, shrill. "Old Viennese engravings . . . he wanted to have them . . . nothing else would do . . . Albert Ehrlich . . ."

"Oh, yes, of course. Albert Ehrlich."

"The inspector had to keep the technicians in mind," Groll interjected softly. With his right forefinger he traced tenderly over the contours of the large, greenish-silver gingko leaf, following the curves of the deepest notch. "They needed *time!* Time to trace where the call was coming from." Aranda nodded. Below, a patrol car zoomed away with siren wailing.

"The shop was full of customers . . . it was impossible . . . we did have the Ehrlich, of course . . . I can get it for you if you like . . . how soon, he asks . . . it must be today, tomorrow he's leaving, by air . . ."

"That's right!" said Aranda, looking up. "My father was due to fly to Paris early on January 10 and then on to Buenos Aires. The International Congress here ended on the seventh." He looked hard at Groll. "Why didn't he fly on the eighth? What was he doing in Vienna those three days?"

"What indeed?" asked Groll. He was thinking: if we could find it out and tell you, would it make you happy or unhappy? Groll's finger caressed both sides of the gingko leaf. Or is it that the two do form *one* whole, each chosen part to the other true? All of us are known as one whole, Groll thought, and yet we are split into day and night. You, young man, know only the day side of your father. The night side is unknown to you. You cannot even imagine its existence. How will you react if I talk to you frankly? I must proceed with caution, Groll thought, and answered: "I really have no idea what kept your father in Vienna." There goes a lie, he thought.

Meanwhile Valerie Steinfeld's voice continued: ". . . he'd have to call back later, but not before seven o'clock . . . that's what I told him . . ."

"Not before seven? But you close the shop at six-thirty!" It was the inspector speaking.

"Well, that's the reason, God help me!" A pause. Noises in the speaker sounding like a glass being hastily filled and drained. "The salesgirls can never get away fast enough . . . five minutes after the half hour they're all gone . . ."

Aranda sat hunched up, staring fixedly at the tape-recorder on the coffee table.

Poor devil, Groll thought. So young and helpless, so lost.

And there's nothing I can do to help. Nobody can, and nobody will. Quite the opposite. That's the trouble!

". . . just Martin and his sister . . . they stay on for a while quite often," it was Valerie's voice again, continuing, ". . . I tell them they can go, I'll finish up everything . . . do the day's books . . . and so on . . . and lock the shop . . ."

"Go on."

"Suddenly I'm afraid he won't come . . ."

"I get it."

"Five past seven . . . he comes in . . . covered with snow . . . wonderful for me, of course . . ." The voice became buoyant, Valerie Steinfeld pitched into a drunken laugh. It sounded horrible, like nothing on earth. That voice is laughing, Aranda thought, and the woman who owned it is already under the sod.

"How do you mean, wonderful?"

"I was going to give it to him in a glass of cognac, see . . . because of the taste . . . and the acidity . . . I'd thought of everything . . . so I say, take your coat off, yes, you must, just for a moment, and have a drink . . . you'll be catching your death . . . your *death*—hahahahaha!"

Manuel Aranda sat up straight, with a sudden movement. He flexed his arms, clenched his fists and took a deep breath. It's aggression, Groll thought. Brought on by her laughter.

As Manuel Aranda remained transfixed in his new pose, Valerie's voice went on: ". . . now let's have a quick drink then I'll get you a taxi . . . he was thrilled . . . said, enchanting, truly enchanting, real Viennese charm . . . kissed my hand . . . hello, hello . . . are you still there?"

"I'm listening. Go on."

"He looked at the book . . . I went into the little tea-room."

"Into the tea-room."

"For glasses, brandy snifters . . . the bottle . . . then one of the capsules . . . please God, let the poison work. . ."

"What sort of capsule was it?"

"Glass . . . they're all glass . . . sealed . . . she told me sealed glass capsules would preserve the poison for years . . . many years . . . she gave me a file, too . . . in case I had to pour the poison into anything . . ."

"*She?*" Aranda looked at Groll, who was sitting in semi-darkness. "Who is *she?*"

"I don't know," answered Groll.

". . . filed one corner off . . ." the woman's voice was fading. There came four short, high-pitched whistling sounds.

40

"What was that?" asked Aranda.

Groll pressed the button again, and stopped the tape.

"A signal for the inspector. The experts had traced the call: it was coming from the Landau Bookstore in the Seiler-gasse. A patrol car with police and special agents was despatched immediately. Meanwhile the Inspector was trying to keep the conversation going as long as possible, to hold the woman on the line."

The reels were turning again. ". . . the cyanide in the glass . . . call him into the tea-room . . . he comes in . . . unsuspect-ing . . . doesn't recognize me . . . says thank you once again!" Again Valerie Steinfeld broke into hideous laughter. "Swal-lows it . . . in one big gulp . . . then . . . then . . . then" . . .

"I understand. Who are you? Where are you calling from?"

"Kemal could take a chance and ask now," said Groll.

"I . . .," the woman's voice was wheezing now. "I . . ." Then a click, and the low hum of the speaker.

"That's where she hung up," Groll said. He stood up and turned off the machine, spilling cigar ash over his shirt and vest as he did so. "A few minutes later the police broke down the bookstore door and rushed in." Groll walked over to the half-open window.

Slowly he breathed in the fresh cold air. He was thinking: here I'm the liaison man to the State Police. Even if I knew more than we already suspect, I couldn't tell you anything, not a thing. And what I do know they've forbidden me to say, those Federal big shots. Big shots and top brass, Groll thought, and the poor soul sitting here is a nobody from the other end of the world, with not one single friend around to care about helping him or saving his neck. Groll thought of the frightening strength of the strong, the oppressive power of the powerful, and the terrifying helplessness of the helpless, thought how everything was a vicious circle, how each class and condition of man multiplies and perpetuates its own kind. He swung round, and spoke:

"The police found two persons dead in a small back room of the bookstore, the tea-room: your father, Raphaelo Aranda, and Valerie Steinfeld. She must have taken cyanide right after she had hung up the phone. By biting on a cap-sule. The police doctor found small slivers of glass in her mouth. The two corpses were lying close to each other on the floor . . ." Groll flicked some ash from his cigar. "Their hands were touching."

Manuel Aranda stayed silent.

"I'm sorry," said Groll, "but that's how it was. Would you like a drink?"

"No, thank you."

"A whisky? Cognac? Slivovitz? Vodka?"

"No, nothing, really. I . . . I would like . . ."

"Yes?"

"I would like to hear the tape again," said Manuel Aranda.

9

"They say your father was a chemist?"

Irene Waldegg was steering the car carefully along the road between Groups 73 and 75. At the last roundabout she had noticed a single parked car.

"Yes, a chemist and a biologist." Manuel Aranda said, nodding. Both now kept their voices low, and spoke somewhat diffidently, as though ashamed of their earlier behavior. "He owned a factory in Buenos Aires, the *Quimica Aranda*."

"For making medicines?"

"No. The *Quimica Aranda* is one of Argentina's biggest manufacturers of pesticides and insecticides."

"It must be a big factory."

"Yes, very big. That's why my father was invited to represent his country at the Congress. There were experts from all over the world here."

Irene Waldegg drove skilfully over a patch of slick ice. It was very warm in the car now.

"Are you a chemist, too?"

"I'm still a student. One semester to go. But of course I've worked in our laboratories, during vacations."

Irene Waldegg turned into a drive between Groups 73 and 74. She drove slowly and carefully.

"It's up ahead there somewhere. The section starts here."

"The crossway, the watchman said."

"The fifth, right. Hard to find in the snow. Day before yesterday the pathway had been cleared. But it's all snowed under again now."

A plane, just taking off from Schwechat, was lumbering thunderously up into the sky toward the cemetery.

"That's the second path . . ."

"Right," Aranda said. "You aunt—was she ever married?"

"Yes," she replied. "Her husband was killed in the war."

"Where?"

"I'm not sure. Valerie didn't like to talk about it. There's the third path . . ."

The roar of the jet overhead was deafening now.

"Children?"

"One son. But she didn't get on with him. Too bad, really. He was not yet twenty by the end of the war. Heinz was his name. I saw some photographs of him once. Nice-looking young man. But he just couldn't get along with Valerie!" She had to shout the last words over the din of the aircraft.

"In 1947 he went to Canada, where they had started a new emigration program. Twelve months later he was killed in a car accident in Quebec. That was the fourth path. And there's the fifth, right in front of us!" Irene let the Mercedes roll to a gentle stop. The jet was right on top of them now, its engines roaring, howling, whining, revving to such a crescendo it seemed the airplane must burst. Irene stopped the car, put on the hand-brake and turned off the motor. She opened the door on her side, and climbed out.

God in Heaven, Clairon thought. He had Irene's head in the sights of the 98k. Who's the dame? How'd she get here? What a mess! Fucking wiseguys! Look what a foul-up you've made now! Where's Aranda? He's not there at all! Oh, yes he is, *behind* the car. And what's he got in his hands?

"Here is where we have to go in," said Irene.

"The snow is very deep here."

Manuel heaved the iron grave ornament over a snow bank, stuck it into the soft snow beyond and jumped over the bank. He instantly sank in over his knees, and stretched out his arms to help Irene. She jumped, but clumsily, slipped, and for a moment she was in his arms, held tight to save her from falling. Their faces brushed against each other. Quickly, she extricated herself. He stepped back.

"I'll lead the way, you step in my footsteps," he said.

"But, your shoes . . ."

"I'll be all right. But your boots have slippery soles. I don't want you to take a real fall. Step carefully. Just tell me which way to go."

"Straight ahead as far as that spruce tree, then make a left."

What piece of junk is Aranda dragging along, Clairon wondered. The barrel of the 98k swivelled slowly on the angel's toe as Clairon kept the pair carefully in his sights. He had a close-up of Irene's back, then for a split second, one of Aranda's shoulders, then a small section of his fur cap. The thunder of the Boeing 707 still rolled along the sky, but more distantly. The crows resumed their croaking.

Good God, thought Clairon, what do I do now? I don't know who the dame is, but she sure is keeping Aranda covered up. I could knock her off, too, of course. But that's not in my orders. And what if Aranda throws himself down when he hears the shot? And gets away? I'm not in a shooting-gallery here. I've got to hit him first. *He's* my target, not the woman. I'll get her, too, right afterwards, if I can before she dives for cover. I can't take chances. Boy, oh, boy, what a mess! Well, I'll just have to hang on and wait.

"To the left! Let me help you carry that thing!"

"No, thanks, it's okay."

"Nonsense!" Irene took three large strides, caught up with Manuel, and was beside him when he turned left between two rows of graves.

I don't believe it, Clairon thought. Now she's covering him *again!* And *how!* The thing they're carrying must be for the grave. What a shitty mess!

"Make a half-right at the black stone," said Irene. "There it is right in front of us, between the two weeping willows."

"We have still got quite a ways to go," he said.

"You speak German well. Have you been in Germany or Austria before?"

"Never. But we always spoke German at home. I spoke German as a small child."

"Are your parents from Germany?"

"No. My mother has been dead eight years. Both my parents were born in Argentina. So was I."

Side by side, they continued trudging through the snow.

"Who came to the funeral?" he asked.

"My parents came up from Villach. Martin Landau and his sister were there, too." Irene looked hard at Manuel. "And a woman we didn't know."

"What do you mean, a woman you didn't know?"

"None of us knew her."

"Strange."

"Yes, strange. We talked about it."

"What did this woman look like?"

"I couldn't tell. She wore a veil."

"A veil?"

"Yes. A long veil. And she cried a lot. She came by car, and was already here when we arrived. And she was the first to leave at the end. It looked almost . . . as though she didn't want to be recognized . . ."

"Was she old? Young?"

"Hard to say with the black veil. Early forties would be my guess." Irene Waldegg paused to take a deep breath. Manuel stopped, too. "Just for a moment . . ."

"Perhaps we'd better not talk."

"It's just my boots. They feel so heavy . . ."

Clairon, behind the massive pedestal and beneath the huge angel, was shifting from one foot to the other. He had thick woollen socks on, but his toes were beginning to freeze. He kept the two people in his sights, but they were getting further and further away. Nothing to be done, Clairon thought. I'll just have to be patient. I've had plenty of practice at that! If my chance comes up before 15.10 hours, I'll risk it even in the quiet, and get the hell out of here. It would be good if I could do it when Air France is making a lot of noise. There's a Sabena taking off at 15.20 hours. And a Swissair at 15.30. If there's no other way, if they're going to get back into the car and I have no choice, I'll shoot the woman first.

So here it is, thought Manuel, suddenly quite calm, drained of emotion. The grave of the woman who murdered my father. I wanted to see it, first thing, today. I've imagined all sorts of things: what I would feel when I saw it, how I'd stand it. And here it is, a clump of earth, frozen over, and covered with snow in a blizzard. That's the grave of the murderess. I'm standing on it. And what do I feel?

Nothing. Nothing. Nothing.

"Whatever she did—she was the most wonderful person I ever knew . . ." Irene said staring at the grave. She was speaking to herself, not to him. Her voice was toneless, she spoke as if in a trance. ". . . Valerie was such an intelligent woman; she never got angry, always ready to forgive—no matter what . . . she never bore a grudge. She would always find some excuse, some explanation. 'Put yourself in the other person's place'—how often have I heard her say that . . ."

But the woman speaking on the tape was different, Manuel thought. Quite different.

"She never lied. She was . . . so honest, so honorable. Never let anyone down. In all the years we lived together there was not one quarrel, not one unkind word . . . and the

45

trips we made together . . . to the North Sea, to Lugano, to Capri, to Normandy . . ." Beautiful! Manuel thought. A eulogy for a murderess.

"Valerie . . . I . . . I loved her so much . . ." Irene's voice dropped to a whisper. "More than any other person . . . yes, even more than my mother . . . I am fond of my mother, truly fond . . . but since I've been in Vienna *Valerie* has been my mother . . . more than my real mother . . . more and more . . ."

15.01 hours, Clairon thought. Nine more minutes.

"Now she's dead! And I'm alone, all alone. What am I going to do?" Irene's voice was the voice of an unhappy child.

Manuel thought: And what about me? Where was I yesterday morning?

10

"One shirt."

How I loved you! Your humor, your kindness, your wisdom. You offered your friendship so freely, without forcing it on me! My friends envied me for having such a father . . .

"One undershirt."

I could always confide in you, about anything, when I was a little boy, and later, too. You had understanding for everything. You were always ready to help when I needed you, as long as I can remember . . ."

"One necktie."

You worked hard, but you always had time for your family! When I was on vacation, you took a holiday, too, and the three of us, Mama, you, and I, went to Mar del Plata. It was there you taught me to swim, and later went fishing with me, just the two of us . . .

"One pair of gold cufflinks. One gold tiepin."

You took me duck hunting in the Tandil hills, gave me my first gun on my fifteenth birthday.

"One pair of socks with garters."

The man reciting the list was an employee in the Medical Examiner's office. His face was hollow-cheeked, and his glasses were so thick and sparkled so much that it was impossible for Manuel to see his eyes. The man wore a gray tunic. Carefully and punctiliously he was placing on a table every piece of clothing and personal effects that had been found on Manuel's father at his death.

Here, in the basement of the Institute, the walls were of white tile, there were no windows, only electric light, and there was a pervading smell of disinfectant. Turning round, Manuel could look through the open door across a corridor and into a huge hall. There were a few tall, white, empty tables standing on the polished floor. One wall consisted of steel, locker-type doors, closing off the compartments in which the corpses were kept. Manuel's father was still behind one of those doors. Manuel was not permitted to see him. ("Sir, what do *you* think? An autopsy was ordered. Your father was . . . he's no longer . . . well, anyway, you cannot see him, *no matter what*.") You built a wonderful house for us in Olivos, the most beautiful suburb of Buenos Aires, right by the river, right by the Rio de la Plata. A wonderfully big house, a wonderfully big park, where I played tennis and cricket . . .

"One briefcase. Inside it one passport, five photographs . . ." Pictures of Mama and myself, I know them . . .

". . . some foreign papers—what is this one?"

"Driver's-license and identification card."

"Driver's-license and identification card . . ." The gray-clad man's spectacles flashed like magnifying glasses, bright, silvery.

". . . various banknotes . . ."

He counted them in a mutter, moistening two fingers. "It comes to 25,860 schillings in bills, and there was another 1,540 schillings in bills and 60 groschen in coins in the pockets of his suit and overcoat . . . please don't pull such a sour face, sir, don't get impatient, we have to have proper records here, I have to enter everything into the books, and afterwards you'll have to sign for them . . . then there's 865 American dollars in bills and 74,500 pesos, also in bills. What are those you're holding, please?"

"Traveller's checks."

"Aha. Would you mind counting them and telling me how much it comes to, and spelling it for me, too, please?"

I'm a rich man now. But everything I own *you* earned, *you* worked for, built it up. And now you're dead. Everything belongs to me. I'd give it all away, every bit of it, just to have

47

you come back to life again, you, my father, laid out on a slab behind one of those doors, dead five days and autopsied. Seeing you is forbidden . . .

"One key-ring with one, two, three . . . six keys . . ."

The man in gray finished at last. He had packed everything into a large cardboard box—the overcoat rolled up, the suit, the shoes—the box was closed and secured with strong copper wire. Manuel signed the lists. He could hear water running somewhere. Men walked along the wet corridor carrying stretchers with sheet-covered corpses.

"If the gentleman would be good enough to go upstairs to the administration office now," said the man in gray with a polite cough.

Upstairs they were expecting him. They were all very solemn and very courteous. It was not their fault that his father had been murdered. They had their job to do. They handed Manuel some forms to fill out. Next, one of them sat down at a typewriter and began to fill out other forms with information supplied by Manuel. It turned out that certain police documents had not been obtained, without which they could not release the body. An argument ensued. But Manuel soon saw it was useless to argue. He had never in his life felt so miserable, so downtrodden. "What you have to do now is go over to the Berggasse and get all the documents I've written down for you here, then come back to us. But before three o'clock. We close at three. No, wait, you have to leave the box here, sorry."

"But—"

"*Regulations*, sir! You need an authorization from the police to take away your father's property. And the regulations say we can release the property *only together with* the body."

"When will that be?"

"Well, if you can get back here with all the papers we need before three o'clock, then we'll have everything ready for you tomorrow morning."

"Not till tomorrow morning?"

"There's a lot to be done, you'd be surprised. We've got to get a coffin that's the right size. We've got to get the body out of the cooler. Then we need a second coffin, an airtight one, for transportation. It's not all that simple. Tomorrow at ten, yes, we'll be ready. Now don't start that again, Mr. Aranda, we're only doing our job. You'd better be leaving for the Berggasse."

So he drove to the Berggasse (with Clairon following him

in the Kapitän), where the officials told him they would have the papers ready the next day.

"It's 12.15. We close at noon. And we're not open in the afternoons."

Manuel lost control and began to shout to keep from bursting into tears.

"Hey you, we don't stand for shouting around here, understand?"

Turning his back on the officer, Manuel went to see Groll, who received him immediately. There were three secretaries sitting in his front office. Groll was friendly and calm as always. He made a quick telephone call.

"You'll have your papers in twenty minutes," he said.

"Thank you. I appreciate it. Now I'll be through with everything tomorrow. I'll get my father's things, too. I want to see them again. I can pick them up in the car."

"Why do you need a car in Vienna?" Groll asked, although he knew the answer.

"Because you said the case was closed as far as you're concerned."

"I also told you why. In homicide cases where there can be no doubt who the murderer was, and where the murderer has killed himself after committing the crime—"

"—no further investigation is necessary, according to Paragraph 224 of the Austrian Penal Law," Manuel said, finishing Groll's sentence for him.

"That's the law."

"So you're not interested in *why* the murder was committed! The case is closed . . ."

"I didn't say that. I said that according to the law no further investigation is *necessary* . . ."

"I won't leave Vienna until I know why this woman killed my father!" Manuel shouted. "And I won't let anyone get in my way! There's an Argentinian embassy here. I'll get them to help me if you try to stop me."

Groll looked at him. The young man's face was dark red. "Red fury," Groll thought. He always noted this symptom in his visitors, one of the ancient mechanisms of color change brought on by rage, to which man has been subjected since the days of his earliest ancestors. The "red fury" is not the most dangerous, Groll thought.

"*I* won't try to stop you," he said. His voice was calm.

"What do you mean by that? Then, who *will*," Manuel's voice faltered. "*Who* will?"

At least I have to give it one more try, Groll thought. Without looking at Manuel he said: "Fly home, my dear Mr. Aranda. Take your dead father home, and try to forget what has happened."

"You're asking me to forget that my father was murdered?"

Here is the second symptom, the second warning, thought Groll. The young man had gone white as chalk. He could now *explode* any moment. From time immemorial, the "white fury" has been the more dangerous symptom. And nothing has changed since then. What *hubris* for men to think they have achieved progress just because of a few technological achievements. Good God, Groll thought, progress.

Aranda's next words came in a whisper: "You're really asking that of me? Commissioner! You know something and you're not telling me! What is it? Talk! Look at me!"

Right, Groll thought, you've asked for it, you're going to get it.

"Your father's death was a complete mystery to us at first, also."

"And now?"

"Now we know at least one thing: there were foreign powers interested in your father, powers that are fighting their battles right here in our country."

"You mean . . . *espionage?* That's ridiculous!"

"Far from it. Agents from several countries were in touch with your father," said Groll.

"So you think my father was involved in some kind of spy plot?" Manuel's voice was suddenly relaxed again.

"Yes."

"But that's absurd! My father was a perfectly normal chemist, and biologist."

"Yes, he was," said Groll.

"An ordinary businessman."

"Yes," said Groll.

"A scientist who concerned himself with the most harmless thing on earth! Cropdusting! *Pesticides!*"

"Yes," said Groll.

"Why do you always agree with me?"

"Because you're right in everything you say," Groll answered, pulling a cigar out of a leather case, then preparing it and lighting it with great care.

"Commissioner," said Manuel, breathing hard, "what power, what secret service, what organization could have had an interest in murdering my father? Tell me, please, I beg you!"

"I don't know," Groll said. I've got to stop right here, he was thinking.

"You know something! You know something!"

"No, I don't, Mr. Aranda."

"What can my father have done, what can he have known, to have been killed?"

"I don't know," said Groll, and thought: Only half a lie. I really don't know. Not *exactly*.

"I think you're lying. I think you know a lot more than you're saying. I think—" Manuel broke off. "Forgive me, I'm all confused. On edge. I'm not being fair, forgive me. Of course you'd tell me more if you knew more."

"Of course," answered Groll, his face motionless. There are times when I hate my job, he was thinking.

"But that this Frau Steinfeld did it . . . *she* couldn't have been working for some . . . or could she? Or *could she?*"

"Why not?" said Groll. I can't imagine it either, he thought. But what other explanation is there?

"Yes, why not?"

"Mr. Aranda," said Groll. "Vienna is a very big city . . ."

"Not as big as Buenos Aires!"

"No, it's not, that's true. But it's also not the city the world believes it to be . . ." Groll sat down at his desk, and gazed absentmindedly at the gingko leaf.

"What do you mean?"

"This city has a bright side," said Groll, covering one half of the leaf with his hand, "and a dark side." He covered the other half of the leaf. "It's been like that ever since the Turkish wars. Longer—ever since the Romans were here. Vienna was a frontier city for centuries, and wars were fought both openly and secretly on its soil. And Vienna still is a frontier city. A frontier city. The past is present here. Nothing has changed. I know Vienna is the city of the Blue Danube, the Spanish Riding School, art collections, museums, for many foreigners. The city of Schönbrunn, the Belvedere, and the Prater! The city of Johann Strauss, city of gaiety and frolicking, of singers and fiddlers, music and wine out in Grinzing . . . but have you any idea of the number of foreign agents we know for sure to be in Austria? *Fifty thousand.* Those are the ones we *know* about. The ones we don't know about are probably even more numerous. Agents from the East, from the West, they all work here, in Vienna, gay, singing, swinging Vienna. And do you know how many police officers we can afford to put into the field against them? Four hundred!"

"How many?"

"Four hundred. You heard right the first time," Groll said, all the time thinking: *and how sure are we even of these four hundred?*

Manuel Aranda was almost shouting: "Why four hundred? Why not four thousand? Why don't you set your house in order here? Why don't you put an end to this state of affairs?"

"Mr. Aranda, our country is neutral. The Allies granted us a State Constitution, and withdrew their troops. How long do you think it would take for them to send the troops back in again? How long do you think we'd stay in their good graces if we started meddling in their affairs? Austria is small, very small. They knew what they were doing when they picked our country for their theatre of operations. You don't have a choice when you're so small. When you're small, you keep quiet."

"Because you're afraid."

Groll looked hard at Manuel, smiled and asked: "You think we're cowards, despicable cowards?"

"No," Manuel said. "No, not that."

"We have to act the way we do, in order to protect ourselves. That's top priority."

"Which means that certain state agencies here are trying to find out why my father was killed?"

"Right," said Groll. "But none of these agencies, nor any individual, not even myself, can give you any official help. You understand?"

"Yes."

"Which doesn't mean I'm not on your side."

"Thank you."

The telephone rang. Groll picked it up and spoke briefly. Then he said: "Your papers are ready. You can collect them now."

"Thank you."

Groll walked Manuel to the door. Placing one hand on his shoulder, he said:

"Be careful."

11

"It'll stay now," said Manuel Aranda. With Irene Waldegg's help he had pushed the temporary grave ornament into the frozen ground. It had been hard work. They had taken turns throwing their whole weight against the sides of the crosspiece, pushing the pointed ends of the large calipers deeper and deeper into the soil. Now they were both out of breath. The dull roar of an aircraft sounded in the distance, coming closer. The crows were silent. Trying to straighten up, Irene lost balance, slipped, and gave a low, startled cry. Quickly, Manuel grabbed her. Irene's head struck his chest and her dark glasses fell into the snow. He held her close, steadying himself.

Clairon blinked.

For the first time he had a clear view of Aranda's head.

Clairon raised the barrel of the 98k gently till he had Aranda's head in the sights. Easy does it, he thought, easy . . . Now's your chance. Don't waste it. Careful . . .

The roar of an Air France jet became louder. It was 15.11 hours. Snow was swept upwards from the graves, lumps of it dropped from the trees.

"I . . . I . . .," Irene stammered, looking up at Manuel. Now he could see her eyes. They were brown, like her hair, and red and swollen from crying.

"It's all right now," he said. "Please calm down."

Suddenly her whole body went limp, her knees buckled, and he had to hold her more tightly. "I feel so awful! Somehow I'd been keeping a grip on myself, I . . . I thought it would be all right . . . but now . . . now . . . it just hit me for the first time that she . . . that she is never coming back. . . . Valerie, Valerie! Why, why did you . . ." Tears were streaming down her face, Manuel could no longer make out her stammered words, overhead the roar of the Boeing had reached a deafening pitch, and so they stood, he with his arms around her, her head on his chest, like a pair of lovers, tragic young lovers. Manuel looked at the woman sobbing in his arms. No, he thought, she can't be guilty.

Now the jet was directly above, in the clouds, on its way to Paris and New York, its engines screaming and howling.

Clairon's eyes were slits. Leaning gently against the marble slab he felt drained of emotion, as always. This is it, he thought. A wonderful chance. Couldn't be better. He had a perfect view of Aranda's head, was lining up the profile in the telescopic sights. I'll plug him through the temple, he thought, using Manuel's right ear, to take aim. Yes, through the temple. That always works,

The Boeing passed over the cemetery with ear-shattering noise. Clairon's finger began to squeeze the trigger.

The shot was barely audible. Without a sound Clairon pitched forward into the snow. He was dead.

12

On the edge of Section 55, in a locked cubicle of the men's toilet, a man stood on the lavatory seat. The barrel of his rifle was poking through the small window at the back of the cubicle. It was an American Springfield, model 03, 7.62-mm caliber, bullet length 75 mm, rifle length 1250 mm, ten-round magazine, telescopic sights. Altogether, the gun weighed only ten pounds.

The man wore a rust-brown duffle coat and heavy shoes. His face was square, his jaw broad, a short, swollen scar ran across his forehead, freckles spotted the rest of his face. His blond hair had been clipped into a crew cut. The old gatekeeper had noticed the crew cut when the man had asked for change of a hundred-schilling note then raced like a madman into the cemetery in his white Lincoln. The man had slowed down very quickly to the approved speed of 5 miles an hour, because the last thing he wanted was to be conspicuous. But his need for urgency was extraordinarily great. Luckily, he knew the cemetery well, from previous visits. The man's cheeks had grown red. He looked younger than his forty-one years.

He was a veteran of the Korean war. On the night of April 25th 1951, during an attack by the North Koreans at

Munsan-ni, his company commander, Lieutenant Charles J. Deeping, had been killed by a shot in the head. The bullet had come from an American Springfield rifle, model 03. Sergeant First-Class Howard Kane was suspected, court-martialed, convicted of murder in the first degree (motive: revenge) and, according to the report in the army paper *Stars and Stripes*, executed. But three days before the news item appeared in the paper, brown-haired, freckle-faced Howard Kane found himself in Washington, where he had a series of conversations with various people. Immediately after the last of these talks he was on his way to New York, free of ties, without dependents, calling himself David Parker and carrying papers in that name, his curly brown hair now transformed into a blond crew cut. Formerly an electrician's mate in Chicago, he had a new profession now.

Former Sergeant First-Class Howard Kane, alias David Parker, travelling salesman, took one last look through the telescopic sights on his Springfield rifle. The bullet had hit Clairon in the right temple before he had had a chance to fire his own weapon. Half his face had been torn away.

Those 7.62 slugs do a lot of damage. Blood was gushing out into the snow from what remained of the left side of Clairon's face. David Parker took a good, long look at Clairon. He had seen a lot of dead men in his life.

Satisfied, he climbed down from the wooden toilet seat, stuck the rifle under his duffle coat and left the little building. He walked quickly down the path between the Sections 55 and 56 to where the white Lincoln was parked. He opened the trunk and hid the rifle under a pile of old rags. He locked the trunk, got behind the wheel, turned on the ignition and a built-in transmitter, and as he drove slowly away picked up a microphone and spoke:

"Calling Stardust . . . Calling Stardust . . . This is Charlie Baker . . . Charlie Baker here . . . over."

A man's voice came in over the transmitter: "Okay, Charlie Baker, this is Stardust, I can hear you, over."

The conversation continued in English.

"Mission completed. Dead."

"Sure?"

"Dead sure! Got him right through the head. I'm not coming back into town. I have a change of clothing with me . . ."

13

". . . and another pair of shoes and a suitcase full of clean underwear in the car," said the voice. It was coming through the loudspeaker of a strong transmitter housed in a gray box and standing on a long, chromium-and-steel table. Like the transmitter in David Parker's car, this one was equipped with scrambling and decoding devices. The room in which it stood was full of new fenders, headlights, signal lights, rear lights and windshield-wipers. The room was on the ground floor of a huge warehouse. It looked like a miniature city: boxes and crates piled as high as buildings; narrow lanes running between them. It was the warehouse of a firm called AMERICAR, which carried spare-parts for practically every type of American automobile. In the canyons formed by crates men worked with winches and hoists. Electric carts raced back and forth.

The managing director of AMERICAR was Gilbert Grant, a tall, heavy-set, lively man of fifty-two, with ruddy face and blue watery eyes blood-shot like the eyes of an alcoholic.

The steel door of the room which housed the transmitter was electronically controlled and soundproof. Fresh air came in through a ventilator. Only Grant, his American aides, and sometimes his guests, were permitted to enter that room; the workers were convinced that all the company records, checkbooks, and operating cash were kept there. But they were well-treated and handsomely paid, and so kept their noses out of everything that did not concern them directly. Gilbert Grant had chosen them for that reason.

Two young Americans serving at the transmitter had stepped to one side. Gilbert Grant was now sitting at the microphone. His jet-black hair shone under the powerful lamp that hung from the ceiling.

"Okay, Charlie Baker," he said. "Drive straight out to the airport. When does your plane leave?"

"In about two hours," replied David Parker. "Over."

"Fine. Leave the car in parking lot 3, as agreed. Locked. We'll collect it this evening. Many thanks, and have a good flight! That's all, over."

"Okay. Thanks to you, too. Till next time. Over and out."

"Over and out." Gilbert Grant leaned back in his adjustable chromium-and-steel chair, swivelling it around as he did so. A fourth man was seated next to him. He was of the same height as Grant though a trifle younger, slim and aristocratic in appearance. He was Fedor Santarin, President of the "Society for Austrian-Soviet Student Friendship," which had its seat in an old palace in the center of the city. Both Grant and Santarin spoke fluent English, French, German, and Russian.

"I don't need you two right now, why don't you go look around outside," said Grant to the two young Americans. With his great bulk, he looked very much like Orson Welles.

"Alright, Mr. Grant." The two walked over to the electronically controlled steel door.

"Just a moment!" Fedor Santarin was smiling. With an elegant movement—all his movements were elegant, in contrast to the sluggish clumsiness of his colleague—he drew a long, slender, gold-wrapped box from an inside pocket of his immaculate suit. The box contained an expensive assortment of candy from Demel, a famous confectioners' in Vienna. Santarin always carried such boxes around with him, and loved offering them around. He opened the box and held it out to the young men.

"May I offer you something?"

The two were familiar with the ritual. Each of them took two pieces of candy, thanked him, and left through the steel door. Grant had taken a large glass and poured bourbon into it until it was half-full. He drank it without water, drained it in one long gulp, expelled a jet of air, then refilled the glass to the half-way mark. He seated himself on a crate of headlights and put his feet, in their knobby shoes, on another crate. He looks like some thick-headed Ukrainian peasant, Santarin thought, who himself resembled an English aristocrat.

"To Clairon," Grant raised his glass. "May he rest in peace." He downed a hefty portion of the drink.

"Amen," said the Russian, popping a chocolate ball into his mouth. He was fiddling with the gold wrapping. He wore a diamond ring on his left hand.

"I couldn't tell Parker, of course, nor the two boys," said Grant.

"Of course not." Fedor Santarin picked out a piece of nougat.

"But it really is a fucking shame that Parker got Clairon before the guy had had a chance to knock off Aranda." Grant's tone was angry.

"It's not your fault, Gilbert. We sent Parker out so late that it didn't seem humanly possible for him still to have a chance."

"He's such a damned good man," said the American, gloomily. "Tough shit. Nobody else would have brought it off." He burped, then took another drink. "I nearly talked my mouth off with my bosses. Get rid of Aranda! Get rid of him, it's the only way! And if the French do it for us, all the better! We've got to get rid of him no matter what. But no dice! These goddamn motherfuckers always know better." Gilbert Grant sounded bitter.

"Same here," said Santarin. "I begged my supervisor. This Aranda fellow is pretty damned dangerous, he said to me. Not for the French alone—for everybody. And what happens? My top brass gets together with your top brass, Gilbert, and we get orders to get rid of Clairon before he can get rid of Aranda! That's what I call logic, how about you?! He's pretty damned dangerous, but we've got to keep him alive at all costs!"

"Calling Stardust, calling Stardust ... Noble George here ..." said a voice over the loudspeaker.

The American slid down from the crate, walked over to the table, glass in hand, and answered.

"Still another car full of detectives has arrived at the Ritz, Stardust. They all went into the hotel."

"How many detectives were there?"

"Three."

"Okay, fine, stay where you are, Noble George. Over and out." Grant sat on the desk. "There you are: you heard it yourself. Everything's going according to plan, just as we wanted it."

"And just as we planned it."

"You're right: just as *we* planned it! You and I," said Grant, pointing at the Russian with his forefinger. "We're the ones who do all the work, not the big boys. And how about that for a plan? Got the whole goddamned police force into the hotel. Everything blown wide open. And meanwhile, Clairon bumps off Aranda. They should have let him do it, the shitheads! Then a little visit to the right person—by my boss or yours—the Austrians would have shit in their pants like they always do when our big boys yap at them, and either handed the stuff over or destroyed it, and we could have closed the case. But no, goddammit, Manuel Aranda isn't to be touched, he's got to be protected, for God's sake!" He imitated another man's voice: " 'I hold you personally responsible for removing Clairon in time.' " Sliding off the table, he walked over to the cabinet and tipped up his glass again. " 'That's an order!' Order my arse."

"If we had disobeyed a direct order in a B-case, that would have been the end for us, you can bet on that."

"I'm no gambler," said Grant, laughing bitterly. "At least, not with my neck. Christ, what a life!" He was inclined to depressions.

"It's not very nice," said Santarin, "but quite comfortable. Chin up, Gilbert, we'll manage to deal with the living Aranda." He looked at his Swiss wristwatch. "There's still time. We'll have to get over to my place in the Wollzeile before long. I asked Nora Hill to come. We'll have to explain to her exactly what she has to do—now that Aranda is going to stay alive."

"Nora Hill," Grant repeated, with a rapt expression. "What a woman—if we didn't have her . . ."

"But we do, and she's worth her weight in gold," Santarin remarked with a contented smile.

14

In a back room of the Bon Voyage Travel Bureau several men were desperately trying to make radio contact with Clairon. "Something's happened," said Jean Mercier, barely able to control his nerves. "Clairon should have reported in long since. Number Zero, too! Long since! Something's gone wrong . . ." Mercier began to pace the room. But what? And how? This waiting is driving me crazy!

It had taken a long time for Irene Waldegg to recover her composure. Arms around Manuel, supported by him, she had wept in racking sobs at Valerie Steinfeld's grave. Manuel let her cry, he knew he could do nothing else. He hugged her securely and patted her back as she sobbed and trembled, twice wailing out the name of the dead woman. After what seemed a long time she finally let herself by led back to the Mercedes. She found it hard to keep her balance in the deep snow.

"Where are my glasses?" she asked when they were in the car.

"In my pocket."

"Let me have them, please." He handed her the glasses, and she put them on.

"I can't run around without them, my eyes are too swollen. You saw them yourself."

"Yes," said Manuel. He touched her hand. She looked at him through the dark glasses. "If you want . . ."

"If I want what?"

"If you want . . . I mean, if you don't mind . . . that is . . ." He began to stutter. "I . . . I didn't trust you at first . . . I . . . I don't trust anyone here, you can understand that, can't you?"

She nodded.

"But now . . . now I'm not suspicious of you any more. I'm sure you loved your aunt as much as I loved my father. I . . . I believe now that they were *both* good people . . . your aunt and my father. It makes their death all the more mysterious."

Irene said nothing.

"Shall we try to find the truth together?"

"Yes," Irene replied, softly.

He stroked her arm.

She took her hand away and gazed out into the twilight. A long silence followed. Manuel kept his own eyes fixed straight ahead, too. Then suddenly he felt her fingers gently touch his. He did not turn his head, and she did not move hers.

15

The black fur of the Baribal bear was shamefully ragged, even completely worn away in some spots. The animal stood over six feet tall, holding in its claws a large basket full of books with bright, colorful jackets. Manuel picked one from the top of the pile. Its title was *The Happy Lion*, and the cover showed a portrait of one, drawn in dazzling colors.

The giant bear growled, deep, loud, and long. Manuel put the book back in the basket. The bear let out another growl. If what Groll told me is true, then this bear is over a hundred years old, and has a small lever in its back for winding up the growling mechanism inside the stuffed animal. For more than a hundred years now this mechanism has been wound up at the start of every business day. How many children have been clawed by it through the years, Manuel thought . . .

The Baribal bear stood right next to the shop entrance, a large glass door hung with an ageless velvet curtain, on top of which was a glockenspiel. Every time the door was opened or closed the silvery bells played the first two lines of the song "Take joy in life while your lamp still burns . . ." in festive tones. The glockenspiel had been playing for more than 158 years. It graced the entrance to one of Vienna's oldest bookstores. Manuel had seen the shop sign through the swirling snow of the evening storm. It said, in old fashioned letters:

LANDAU BOOKSTORE. RARE AND SECONDHAND BOOKS
FOUNDED 1811

Inside, the store was a good sixty feet long and forty-eight feet wide, with very high ceilings. Street noise could be heard faintly, muffled.

"Good morning. Can I help you?"

The question roused Manuel from his thoughts. A young salesgirl had approached him. There were two other girls and two men, one young, one elderly, working in the store. There were a number of customers in the shop.

"I would like to speak to Mr. Landau," he said, "my name is Manuel Aranda."

"Mr. Landau is on the telephone at the moment. I'll tell him you're here. One moment, please."

The girl hurried off.

Manuel looked around in the shop. Oak bookshelves covered the walls from floor to ceiling. Books lined the shelves: two sections of new books, two of rare works. There were several giant ladders with rungs covered in worn velvet, which, hooked on to iron rails along the ceiling, could be pushed back and forth. There were tall, antique lecterns where books, especially folio editions and other outsize works, could be examined at leisure. Two ancient rocking-chairs were also part of the décor. The floor was made up of long, dark planks. Through the years hundreds of thousands of feet had trodden these planks, wearing them down, covering them with pockmarks. The heavy, nickel-plated cash register at the check-out counter must have been a good eighty years old . . . how many different kinds of currency it must have counted and recorded during those years . . .

"Martin Landau," Groll had told him, "runs the store exactly the way his father did, and his father's father, and his great-grandfather before that. He doesn't change anything in the store unless he absolutely has to. Anything novel or different makes him feel uneasy. When you go and see the bookstore you will be visiting a corner of the old Vienna as it once was and has long since ceased to be, a museum of the past. Naturally, Landau's flair for preserving the past is what gives the store its charm, especially for foreign visitors. Ah well, the old Vienna!"

The old Vienna, ah!

It's true, Manuel thought, this shop does exude a magic of its own, even the lighting. Large, round, glass shades, yellowish and opaque, hung from the ceiling on long bronze rods, shedding a warm, cosy light.

"You wished to speak to me, sir?" asked a low, quiet voice.

Manuel saw a man bowing nervously. "I am Martin Landau," the man said. He was of medium height, had the face of a scholar, delicate features, pale skin, gray hair, long fingers, and extremely small feet. According to Groll, Martin Landau was sixty-six years old. He looked older. Very thin, he seemed almost wasted. Dressed immaculately, though in an oddly old-fashioned style, he looked at the world through gray, perpetually frightened eyes. He seemed hypersensitive. His left shoulder was high, and his head slightly inclined to the left. His pale lips were stretched into an anxious smile.

"The man *is fear personified,*" Groll had said. "You'll see. He's afraid of everything, real or inspired, afraid of everything around him, of the present, the future, and of practically all of mankind. The hunched-up shoulder and the crooked head and the perpetual smile are mere tics. He's got others, too. For instance, he washes his hands about twenty times a day, according to what one of the salesgirls told us."

"Is he mad?"

"Not more than we all are. A bit strange perhaps."

Martin Landau rubbed his hands together as he watched Manuel, an anxious smile on his lips. He doesn't even need soap and water for his obsession, Manuel thought, then said softly:

"I guess you can imagine why I'm here. My father—"

Landau broke in at once. "Please, not here," he stammered anxiously. "So many people around, you can see. If you would be good enough to follow me . . ." And already he was leading the way, nodding and bowing to the customers, rubbing his hands.

Manuel followed him through the shop to a corridor leading off one of the book-lined walls into the storeroom. The storeroom, too, was very old, with small, beamed archways to permit passage and loftier, high-flung ones supporting the ceiling. At the end of the short corridor to the right was an opening in the wall without a door. The wall was two feet thick, and black with age. Beyond the opening, Manuel saw a small room, into which Martin Landau now turned, swiftly and silently.

"Please come in, Mr. Aranda," he murmured smiling, his shoulder hunched, his head bent.

For a moment Manuel felt himself go numb when he saw this backroom.

"It's the "tea-room," he thought.

Just one week ago his father had been murdered in this room.

16

Tearoom . . .

Many shops had back rooms like this one. They were used for making telephone calls, receiving friends, making coffee, for resting and reading.

The tea room was rather cramped. A windowless room, its walls were covered with bookshelves. The spines of many volumes shone in the glow of a green-shaded reading lamp that stood on an old writing-desk; they shone red and blue, gold and brown, green, silver, and white.

Next to the writing-desk was a worn old leather sofa, on which were cushions and a folded blanket. A clumsy-looking old radio stood on a small table at one end of the sofa. The only modern object in the whole room, as far as Manuel could see, was a compact black telephone on the writing desk. It had probably been forced on the nervous man after the telephone company had insisted on dismantling the old equipment.

The carpet in the tearoom was threadbare. My father lay here, Manuel thought. In his death throes. Foaming at the mouth. Fighting for his life, in vain. The poison was stronger than he was. My father lay here where I am standing now, he thought—and had to catch hold of a bookshelf, overcome by dizziness.

There was an old armchair in front of the desk. Valerie Steinfeld sat here, Manuel thought, while the room spun around his head. That's where she sat, my father's murderer, drinking cognac and telephoning the police. And then she took poison herself. And then she lay down on the carpet, next to my father . . .

"Please have a seat," said Landau. Manuel sat down on a shaky rocking-chair with a ragged wicker backrest. Landau slid into the armchair by the desk. He did it soundlessly.

"Oh, how tactless of me! I should have said so before! My deep sympathy with your terrible loss." Landau spoke softly and almost without moving his lips, head bent, his perpetual smile still on his face. He looked ghastly.

Manuel merely nodded.

"We still can't quite accept what happened," said Landau. He spoke very softly and indistinctly: "I had known Frau Steinfeld since 1921. That's forty-eight years, after all, just imagine that. I thought I knew her as well as my own sister. And now . . . now she goes and does something like this . . . something so terrible, so senseless . . ."

"It can't have been senseless," Manuel said.

"I beg your pardon?" Manuel's remark had given Landau quite a jolt.

"Frau Steinfeld was not out of her senses. So what she did cannot have been senseless. There must have been a reason. But what was that reason?"

"I don't know!" Martin Landau said. His hands began to tremble violently.

"But even if you don't know why she did it, you must have wondered about it?"

"Of course." Landau's hands were still trembling. Why? Manuel thought. He remembered Groll saying: "This Landau

64

fellow knows something. They all know something. But nobody's talking, nobody's talking . . ."

I'll get him to talk—the old coward. Even if I have to break every bone in his body, he'll talk to me.

"Of course you did. And . . .?"

"We think about it night and day, Mr. Aranda. After all, we—"

"Who's 'we?' "

"My sister and I. We live together. In my parents' house in Hietzing. Just the two of us . . . we talk and think of nothing else. Why did Valerie do it? But we can't find a reason, not a trace of an explanation, not a shadow of suspicion . . ."

"Mr. Landau, you say you've known Frau Steinfeld since 1921. She worked here from 1938 on—for thirty-one years. Do you mean to tell me you have no idea at all why she did what she did, that you and your sister can't come up with even a shadow of an idea?"

"No, I'm telling you, we can't!" Landau replied in a hoarse whisper. "Do you think I wouldn't tell you if I knew anything?"

"No I don't think you would tell me. I think you know a lot and are not saying everything. Why not, Mr. Landau?"

"Now listen, after all . . ."

"Why are you lying to me? Why did you lie to the police? What are you hiding, Mr. Landau?"

"Not so loud, not so loud! They'll hear you in the store!" the bookseller begged. The helpless smile still played on his lips, he simply could not erase it, he had been smiling helplessly all his life, now he had to go on smiling until he died. "I can understand why you're so worked up about it, but I've no idea at all about the motive, I swear to you!"

"If you're swearing that you have no idea, then your oath is a *lie!*"

A wild rage at the weak-kneed lump of misery before him suddenly seized Manuel, and he leaned over to talk directly into Landau's face, forcing the old man to cringe as far back into his chair as he could. "You know *everything* about Valerie Steinfeld!"

"I—"

"You know her life! You know what she did with her life. Or do you deny that?"

"No! Yes, I mean! Yes, that's what I mean! I *don't* know. Valerie worked for me, but after all . . . her private life was not my business."

65

Manuel pressed on harder and harder. "You knew her a long time before she started working for you. Seventeen years! How did you get to know her?"

"She . . . was one of our oldest regular customers."

"Did you know her husband?"

"No."

"Frau Steinfeld was a customer here for seventeen years, and you never saw her husband in the shop?"

"Oh, sure, he came sometimes, of course, but . . . but you can't call that knowing the man, after all!"

"You're lying again! You were friends!"

"You can't prove that." Landau's face began to change color, it was turning yellow and he coughed and gulped for breath. Manuel gave him no rest.

"Why did Frau Steinfeld start working for you?"

"She . . . she . . . she . . ."

"Well?"

"She just wanted to work!"

"Had she studied the book trade?"

"No . . ."

"Why did you take the trouble to teach her the business yourself? Why didn't you just hire some professional help?"

"I wanted to do her a favor!" Landau drew a trembling hand across his mouth.

"So she *asked* you to do it?"

"No, she just wanted very much to . . ."

"What? What did she want very much to do?"

"Work in a bookstore."

"Why? Was her husband out of work?"

"No . . ."

"What was his profession?"

"I . . . I don't know . . ."

Manuel straightened up. Landau let out a soft cry. Manuel bent back down over him.

"You don't know Herr Steinfeld's profession?"

"Wait, yes, I do know it . . . he was a newscaster at Radio Vienna."

"And he let his wife work for you?"

"Yes! *Yes!*" Landau was fighting for breath. I'll break him down, Manuel was thinking, I'll break him down. I've almost got him where I want him.

"In which drawer were the poison capsules?"

It worked.

66

Gasping and retching Landau leaned over sideways and pointed to the bottom left-hand drawer of the desk.

"So you knew it!"

"I asked her a hundred times, a thousand times, to throw those capsules away! She wouldn't do it . . ."

"Why didn't *you* do it?" shouted Manuel, a wild feeling of triumph welling up inside him. Just one more minute, one more minute, and he will break. "Why didn't you? Answer me!"

"Listen, I am not supposed to get excited. I'll have another heart attack. I must ask you—"

"*Why did you not* throw the poison away?"

"I couldn't . . ."

"Why not?"

"That particular drawer has a complicated lock. Valerie took the key one day and never returned it . . . after all—"

Grabbing Landau by his jacket lapels Manuel hissed: "What was the name of the woman who gave Valerie the poison?"

"The woman . . ."

"Yes, the woman! What was her name? Give me her name, quick! Or I'll ram your teeth down your throat!"

"Don't, you're hurting me—"

"I'll hurt you a damn-sight more. Give me her *name!*"

"The . . . name . . ." Landau swivelled round on his chair, Manuel kept a tight grip on his lapels. The old man was breathing very shallowly, and his lips were changing color. "I can't. I'm not allowed . . ."

"You're not allowed to mention the name?" hissed Manuel, half out of his mind with rage. He was bent low over Landau. But in the next moment he felt his shoulder seized, and was sent crashing into the rocking chair. A woman stood before him, wearing a Persian lamb coat and a Persian lamb hat with mink trimming. Her hair was gray but her face was unlined and flushed from the cold. Manuel noticed her expressive dark eyes and thin-lipped mouth.

"Get out of here, this minute, or I'll call the police," said the woman. Snow was melting on her hat and on the shoulders of her coat. She wore black suede boots. Her voice was firm and self-confident. She sounded like someone accustomed to giving orders.

"Good evening, Miss Landau," said Manuel. It's his sister, he thought. Christ, why did she have to show up just now.

"Get out!" said Ottilie Landau.

Her brother, in his armchair, gasped: "This is Mr. Aranda, Tilly."

"I know," she said grimly. "I heard he was here. I seem to have come just in time. Go on, get out of here!"

"Miss Landau, there has been a murder here if I were you I'd watch my words."

"Don't trouble yourself wondering what you would do in my place. Have you ever heard of harrassment and illegal entry?" Removing her fur hat she pushed Manuel to one side, walked over to the writing-desk and picked up the telephone. "My brother has a heart condition. Look at him. If anything happens to him, you're to blame." Ottilie Landau began to dial.

No sense in pushing any further, Manuel thought. I can't afford to get involved with the police. And that woman is really going to call the police. She'll do anything to protect her brother—probably has protected him all her life.

"Put down the phone," he said. Then he turned on his heel and left the tearoom.

Tilly filled a glass with water, took two small red pills from a box on the writing-desk, and held them out to her brother.

"Take these," she said, and this time there was motherly tenderness and concern in her voice. "Here is some water with them."

He did as he was told, obedient as a small child. Water ran down his chin; Tilly wiped it away with her handkerchief.

"I was so terrified," he yammered. "I thought I'd have a heart attack any second. I no longer knew what I was saying. My head is still throbbing!"

"You didn't give her name away," she said, stroking his hair back into place. "There's nothing he can do to us, nothing at all."

"You didn't see him . . . he is relentless . . ." Landau's hands started to tremble again. "He digs and keeps on digging. Tilly, oh, Tilly, why didn't I listen to you while there was still time? You were dead against it—"

"You bet I was!" she said, bitterly.

"But you went along with it after all."

"We had to, Martin. It was our duty. It was I who told you then and I'm telling you now, there will be terrible things happening yet. Terrible things." He nodded in despair. Tilly went on talking, pressing his head against her bosom as if he were her son.

"What's done is done! We can't undo it." She stroked him gently, but her voice hardened. "Let the son-of-a-bitch poke his nose in here as much as he likes! He won't find out from us why Valerie killed his father. We don't know why, we don't have the least idea. That's our story, even if he comes a hundred times. Even if they all come a hundred times. We don't have the faintest idea. They can ask till they're black in the face."

"Oh, Tilly," the old man said in a whining tone, and put his arm around her hips. "If I didn't have you, I'd be lost, completely lost. What am I saying, *lost?* I'd be *dead!* They'd have bumped me off long ago, if it hadn't been for you!"

17

"Mr. Aranda, would you care to follow me, please?" No sooner had Manuel Aranda set foot into the brilliantly lit lobby of the Ritz than one of the reception clerks, his face pale and twitching, hurried over to him. Manuel, with snow all over his overcoat and speckling his hair, still furious from his clash with the Landaus, gave the man a hostile stare.

"What's the matter now?"

"Not so loud, Mr. Aranda. Please, I beg you, keep your voice down," the clerk groaned, while a page helped Manuel out of his overcoat and bore it off to the cloakroom. Manuel had seen this particular clerk several times, but had never spoken with him. Behind the reception-desk stood a second man, staring at Manuel. All three porters were staring, too, their expressions full of concern. The lobby was almost empty, but the hall beyond was teeming with people. The hotel's little orchestra was going through a romantic if somewhat wobbly rendering of "You're a Hit with the Girls, Bel Ami." The reception clerk had gripped Manuel by the elbow and was leading him with discreet force.

"Don't touch me. I don't like it."

"So sorry, Mr. Aranda. The Manager would like to see you in his study."

Manuel shrugged, and accompanied the clerk, a young,

balding man, across the priceless carpets in the foyer, past marble pillars and wall-sized tapestries, beneath the gigantic candelabra flashing every color of the spectrum, and down the short corridor behind the reception desk which led to the Manager's study. The clerk opened the outer half of a double door and knocked, then opened the inner door and motioned Manuel into the office, which Manuel had seen once before. From behind the antique writing-desk a white-haired, slimly built man rose in greeting. It was Count Romath.

"At last!"

The clerk left, and the doors closed behind him.

"A thing like this has never happened before in the entire history of this hotel! We are in your hands. If your understandable indignation should make you break your silence, the hotel is finished!"

"You're absolutely right," said Groll. Manuel wheeled around, and once again the nauseous pressure of giddiness assaulted him. The police chief had been waiting in a brocaded armchair by the door. Now he stood up.

"Good evening, Mr. Aranda. I was getting rather worried about you. Where were you from 14.00 hours until now?"

"I don't understand what that—"

"Answer me, please!" There was urgency in Groll's voice.

Manuel shrugged and gave an account of his afternoon and evening. The Count let out a groan. Groll's voice was expressionless when he spoke:

"They were just a hair's breadth away from pulling it off, and there would have been no suspects."

The Count began to pace in his rather mincing way—from the red damask curtains to the floor lamp with the silk shade, and back again. He was coughing; he seemed to be suffering from a cold.

"What's happened?" Manuel asked.

"Before I can answer that," said Groll, lighting up a cigar and puffing out clouds of blue smoke, "before I can answer that I myself must ask a question." The Count was coughing angrily and ostentatiously. Groll gave him a placid look. Romath shrugged and resumed his pacing between the window and the lamp. Groll contemplated his cigar with an air of self-satisfaction.

"When they released your father's personal effects to you at the Sensengasse yesterday, was there a set of keys among them?"

"No. Or rather, yes, yes, there was. The keys were in the cardboard box with all the other things."

The Count coughed, sighed, paced up and down.

"When did you get the box?"

"This morning at ten o'clock. With the coffin."

"What did you do with the box?"

"I put it in the trunk of my car. Listen, this whole—"

"How long was the box in the trunk?" Groll's tone was calm and friendly.

"Until I came back from the shipping office ... until noon."

"And then?"

"Then I asked a page to carry the box up to my suite. I just went up for a moment to wash my hands before lunch."

"And the page brought the box up while you were doing that?"

"No. I met him in the hall ... can you tell me now—"

"In a moment. Did you go back to your rooms after lunch before you drove out to the cemetery?"

"No. I just went into the Café next door. I'd put my overcoat in the cloakroom."

"So, the last time you saw the box with your father's effects was shortly before noon, in the hall on your floor."

"Yes."

"That's the end," Count Romath groaned, coughing. "The absolute end."

"Very cleverly done," said Groll admiringly, as if he had not heard the Manager at all.

"What about the box? Has it been stolen?" shouted Manuel.

"It's in your suite. The lead plugs used to seal the copper wire have been ripped off and the wires untwisted. If everything had gone according to plan they'd have twisted the wires together again and plugged them. You'd never have noticed anything."

"What do you mean, I'd never have noticed anything? Has the box been opened?"

"I thought I'd just made that clear," Groll said. He seemed to take pleasure in needling the Count, and puffed a cloud of cigar smoke right into his face. The hotel Manager looked at Groll, his whole body shaking, turned away and walked quickly back over to the damask curtains by the windows. He was mumbling half to himself "If I'd had any suspicion ... oh, my God, if I had had the slightest suspicion!"

"But you didn't have any at all, is that it?" The Count paced around.

"Look here, if you're implying that I—²

"I'm not implying anything. Don't get excited, Count. There's going to be plenty of time for that soon," said Groll. He was being deliberately provocative. Romath stared over at the corpulent chief-of-police, then mumbled something incomprehensible and began to pace the room again. He's like a caged animal in a zoo, Groll thought. It can't just be the hotel he's worried about. I'll find out what's eating at him sooner or later. I have a pretty good idea already.

"Why was the box opened? Please tell me!" Manuel's voice was loud and angry.

"To take something out that was wanted, Mr. Aranda."

"What?"

Groll fumbled in the jacket pocket of his flannel suit. "That," he said, placing a key-ring on the Manager's desk. Manuel looked from one man to the other uncomprehending. "Your father's key-ring that was returned to you in the Sensengasse. That's the one, isn't it?"

"Yes, that's the one. I recognize it by the leather covering."

"It is your father's key-ring," said Groll, "but not all the keys on it belonged to your father. This one for instance . . ." said Groll, holding up a bizarrely cut Yale key, ". . . this one did not belong to your father. It belongs to the hotel. I was just in time to prevent its being used to cause a major disaster."

"A major disaster? What are you talking about? Why are you here? What made you come?"

"I got a call from an old friend . . ." said Groll.

18

"Nora Hill speaking." It was a woman's voice, low-pitched and sounding almost hoarse through the telephone Groll held to his ear.

"Lovely to hear from you, a real pleasure. High time you were thinking of me again! You haven't shown a sign of life since that Yugoslav was carted off in October—"

"Listen, this is urgent. You know Manuel Aranda?"

"Yes. What about him?" Groll looked at his watch. It was 13.15 hours.

"Aranda will be leaving the Ritz at two o'clock. Make sure you and a few of your officers are in the hotel lobby at that time, and watch what the deputy Reception Clerk does."

"The deputy Reception—"

"Yes. The Chief Clerk is on vacation. His deputy is forty-five years old, tall, slim, and has graying hair. He's a Frenchman called Pierre Lavoisier. Has striking bright eyes. When he goes into the vault, follow him, whatever happens!"

"Why?"

"You will see. It has to do with the Aranda case. Very much so. The big haul is planned for this afternoon." Nora Hill's voice sounded perfectly controlled. "If you and the State Police want to get anywhere in this affair, do what I say."

"Madam, our agents have observed Gilbert Grant and Fedor Santarin entering your place in the country very often lately. Can I assume that you are speaking in their behalf?"

"You can assume what you like, Commissioner. Hasn't our collaboration always been excellent?"

"Always," Groll confirmed.

"And have you not always received first-class information from me?"

"That's true, certainly." Groll cleared his throat. "So, we have Russians and Americans working together once again. Must be something big."

"It's very big."

"And the common enemy is France?"

"Don't act so innocent. You've had your suspicions for a long time."

"Suspicions, yes, madam. But what I've always wanted is proof. I guess you don't know what it's all about."

"No. And that's the truth. Even I am not told everything. You know that."

"I know. I thank you, dear lady. And if ever I can do something for you again, you know I'm always at your service."

At seven minutes to two Groll was seated near the entrance in the lobby of the Ritz, pretending to be immersed in a newspaper. Four inconspicuous men who had arrived before him were scattered about the place, sitting in armchairs, leafing through magazines at the newsstand, buying cigarettes.

Shortly before two, Groll saw Manuel Aranda come from the café into the lobby, hand in his room-key at the reception-desk, and leave the hotel wearing an overcoat. He climbed into a blue Mercedes that had been driven up to the hotel entrance by a garage-hand.

Five minutes passed. Ten minutes. Lavoisier, whom Groll had recognized immediately from Nora Hill's description, was working behind the reception-desk together with two other men. Three new guests signed in. Lavoisier talked with all of them, and seemed perfectly cool and collected. At 14.26 hours Groll saw a tall, good-looking page whom he had noticed before stroll across to the reception-desk and stop near the open counter. Something fell out of his hand, and Lavoisier and the page bent down towards it simultaneously. They straightened up again as one man. About two minutes later Lavoisier went into the large, open office behind the reception-desk and opened a small wall safe. His two colleagues were not watching him. Groll and his men were observing his every move. Groll saw a number of small Yale keys in the safe, and also one large key with a long neck. Pierre Lavoisier took the large key out quite calmly, and returned to the desk. He said something inaudible to his colleagues, then walked towards a corridor that ran parallel to the one in which Romath's office was situated.

Groll heaved himself slowly out of his chair and wandered without haste across the lobby. He saw Lavoisier descending a flight of steps in the corridor. A door was opened, light went on, and the door remained ajar.

After that, everything happened very quickly. Two men who had been waiting in the lobby followed Groll. Two other men who had been loitering by the newsstand rushed over to the good-looking page, who turned his back on them. He swung around as they grabbed him by the arms. His face had gone ash-gray, the color of his uniform. Without a word he let himself be taken to the elevator. There were only a few hotel guests in the lobby, and they noticed nothing.

Meanwhile, Groll had reached the door at the front of the short flight of stairs. He opened it without a sound. He was in the hotel vault; built into the walls were safes, large and small. An electric light was burning. Lavoisier was stooped in front of a large safe, which he had opened with a skeleton key and a Yale key that were clipped to a key-ring in a leather case. He was in the act of extracting a small,

74

flat, leather attaché case from the steel safe when Groll, thinking "Good old Nora!" said in a loud voice: "Oh, I beg your pardon!"

The Frenchman wheeled around. He gripped the attaché case in his left hand. In his right he had a pistol pointing at Groll.

"Get your mitts up!" he hissed. "Against the wall ... over there ..."

Groll put up his hands and took a few slow paces.

"Faster! Are you going to move or do you want a hole in your stomach?" Lavoisier croaked. Groll stepped quickly over to the rear wall of the room, his head bowed, eyes lowered, shoulders slack.

Keeping his gun on Groll, Lavoisier backed towards the door. "Don't move or you're dead ..."

Groll stood perfectly still.

With the hand holding the attaché case Lavoisier fumbled behind him for the doorknob, heard a sound and whirled around. One of Groll's men who had been waiting by the door gave Lavoisier a powerful karate chop on the neck, across the jugular. Lavoisier crashed to the floor, the attaché case and the gun falling from his grasp. Groll's men rushed him, yanked him to his feet, and handcuffed his hands behind his back almost before he regained consciousness. One of Groll's men took off his own overcoat and draped it around Lavoisier's shoulders.

"Much obliged," said Groll, calmly. He picked up the black attaché case. "Bring him to the elevator and go down into the lower-level garage. From there take him up into the courtyard. We have a delivery van there, from a champagne company. The page will be in it already. The two of them must not communicate with each other. Put one in the front seat and lock the other up in the back. There are more men by the car."

"I demand that you notify my Embassy at once! I am a Frenchman! I demand a lawyer and a representative from my Embassy."

Groll did not even look at him.

"Arrest him. Grand larceny and armed resistance against Federal officers. We'll keep the page for questioning as an accomplice."

Lavoisier exclaimed in outrage, "You can't do that! You have no warrant!"

"We'll get it at the prison. The two of you were caught in

the act. And you can forget about your Embassy. We're taking you in for a criminal offense, not a political one. That's why we're putting you in the police jail in Rossauer Street." I hope Hanseder will be happy with that arrangement, Groll was thinking. I really cannot play it down any further. His people will just have to make the trip to Rossauer Street to interrogate the fellow. But he won't say anything, I know the type. The page might talk, he's younger, and scared. Only did it for the money, in all probability. Lavoisier looks for all the world like one of those damned fanatics who do it out of conviction. Too bad. He must know a whole lot more than the page.

"Send Horn and Gellert here," said Groll. "They have taken the boy into the courtyard. You two go with them to the prison. The rest of us will take another look around here. I'll take care of the attaché case myself . . ."

19

". . . until Mr. Aranda comes back. He and only he will be permitted to open it, I said." Groll finished his report, puffing on his cigar. "So I stayed here. You've been keeping me waiting long enough."

"Where is the attaché case?" Manuel asked tensely. With a speed and grace astounding in so large a man Groll bent down and produced a small, flat, crocodile leather case from behind the desk.

"Here. I didn't let it out of my sight."

Manuel jumped to his feet.

"What's in it?"

"We'll soon find out." ,

"What do you mean, soon? Why not now?"

"Let me tell you the full story and . . . let me just check up on one thing, Mr. Aranda. Please do what I ask: I have my reasons. Okay?"

Manuel shrugged his shoulders wearily.

"Thank you," said Groll. "After Lavoisier and the page had been taken away I looked around in your suite. Later I called three of my men over. They were parked in front of the Ritz; I wanted them to be seen by anyone keeping the hotel under surveillance. I didn't want anything else to happen before you came back. The men in the hotel. We have reconstructed the whole chain of events. The page—he's Viennese, incidentally, name's Karl Weigl—and Lavoisier are not talking, as I expected. But Weigl's bawling already, and he'll sing before the day's over."

"He'll do what?" Manuel asked.

"Unload. Spill the beans. Tell us what he knows. He won't have much to sing about. But maybe he'll tell us the name of his contact men to the French HQ." Groll sighed. "We've known who that is for many years." They were alone now in the handsome office. Blue cigar smoke filled the room. Count Romath had excused himself, coughing. Groll was standing at the antique writing-desk, staring at the tall, slim, copper can containing the flowers that looked like orchids. Their petals were covered with white, brown, and golden-yellow spots.

"What's the matter *now?*" asked Manuel, more annoyed than ever. "Please, Herr Groll, what are you thinking about?"

"About this Inca lily here."

"What?"

"That is an Inca lily," Groll declared, completely absorbed in contemplation. He bent over. *"Alstroemeria aurantiaca.* Probably the "aurea" variety. It's the species that's supposed to have this yellowish-gold coloring."

"Herr Groll!"

"I'm an idiot," continued Groll. "This bright gold. And now it is here, before my very eyes . . ."

"What are you talking about?"

"I have my little eccentricities, you know! I'm really crazy about colors. I was wondering all this time where he's hiding it. I couldn't really ask him, could I? So I smoked Romath out with my cigar. It was just careless of him to put these Inca lilies here, that's all. I've got such a thing about colors . . . so let's see . . ."

Groll walked over to the reproduction of the "Masked Supper" on the wall. The dominant color in the painting was a translucent gold that shone with unreal brightness. Manuel looked at it uncomprehendingly. Groll placed his ear to the wood of the frame and tapped with his knuckles. "Hm," he said. "Hm." He kept tapping. "There it is," he said suddenly. He ran both hands along the bottom spar of the frame. He soon found what he was looking for. He pressed the hidden catch until a section of the frame moved downward, revealing a little hollowed-out space, containing a small metal box. Groll took it out and nodded with satisfaction.

"What's that?"

"A transmitter, Mr. Aranda. There just had to be one here."

"Why?"

"Somehow the Count had to convey the information to his superiors that you would leave the hotel at 14.00 hours. Telephoning would have been much too risky. Telephones can be tapped." Groll sighed.

"No point in *my* talking into this thing. I don't know the call numbers. Nobody will answer."

"Are you trying to say . . . that the Count . . ."

"Of course. He knew about Lavoisier. My contact had been tipped off about him, and tipped me off in turn."

"Who is your contact?" Manuel asked.

"Somebody who's running a very risky business. But a very lucrative one. Too lucrative. If the circumstances were different he would have been in the clink long before now. But this is Vienna. We've come to terms. He gives me information, and I leave him alone."

"So the Count is working for the Americans, too?"

"For the Americans *and* for the *Russians*. Interesting, don't you think? No doubt you thought the American and Russian secret services only worked *against* each other."

"Yes."

"You were quite wrong, then. But it probably takes years of experience in Vienna to find that out. Mr. Aranda," said Groll, replacing the transmitter and sliding the frame back over it, "if I might give you a piece of advice, please remain in the Ritz and go along with the Manager's request for discretion. You're safer here than anywhere else in Vienna. Here you have the Americans and the Russians to protect you, if we play it right."

"What do you mean, play it right?"

"I'd rather explain that to you somewhere else," Groll said. "The room here could be bugged, I can't be sure. And the Russians and the Americans are not all *that* eager to protect you. Let's go." He picked up the attaché case.

20

The black attaché case lay on the green felt cover of **a** large billiard table in one of the game rooms of the Café next door to the Ritz. Groll handed the key-ring to Manuel.

"Please."

Manuel opened the attaché case with the smallest key. Inside was a sheaf of papers clipped together. Groll lifted them out, looked them over briefly, then placed them on the billiard table. Manuel stared fixedly at the top page of the manuscript. It was covered with evenly spaced groups of letters written in ink with a broad pen. Manuel glanced at the first lines.

EIOXS RFSTR LUCTX MNCRY EYBSX NLGZQ VTRKD RWRET WHVEM GAJGX . . .

Groll read along over Manuel's shoulder.

"It's in code," said Manuel.

"Yes, a damned tough one to crack, I'm afraid," said Groll.

"What do you mean?"

"I was a decoder during the war for two years. I could be mistaken, of course, but this one seems to be a very long 'Caesar.' That's a technical term."

"I know. My father's favorite hobby was codes."

"Oh, my God!" Groll sent a red ball across the billiard table. It bounced off two corners and angled back at him. "That's just dandy. He knew about codes, then?"

"Yes. He had a friend with whom he corresponded in that way. They made bets, because my father liked to use quotation codes, those are codes which—"

"—are keyed to a quotation. I know. Is that his handwriting?"

"Definitely. I recognize his Ns and Ms, which are written the wrong way round, and the Hs, like two pillars with a crossbeam."

"Well, if it is a quotation code, it's almost certainly impossible to crack without knowing the quotation."

Manuel leafed through the manuscript. "Thirty-six closely written pages. A gigantic message. My father was able to compose in code very quickly. But what could have been the point of these thirty-six pages, a real monster of a job?"

"That, my dear friend, is the whole secret."

"What sort of secret?"

Groll cleared his throat, ran his fingers through his silver hair, and lowered his voice. "Your father was a very cautious man. By now you know so much about Frenchmen, Americans, and Russians—it couldn't be helped—that I'd better tell you more. Your life is at stake, Mr. Aranda, your personal safety! From what we know, and we are far from knowing everything, your father was in touch with the French, the Russians, and the Americans, no doubt in the hope of selling them something."

"What?"

The Commissioner pointed to the manuscript.

"That."

"That?"

"That."

"Then why is it still here, under lock and key?"

"As we see it, your father made a deal with the Americans and the Russians. They presumably have a copy of the manuscript. But the negotiations with the French were not yet complete. Your father wanted to cover himself from all angles—lock the manuscript up in one place, the money in another, the decoding formula somewhere else."

"So my father was very cautious; but not cautious enough, as it turned out. The code didn't prevent him from being murdered."

"No. But the murder obviously prevented the deal from going through."

"Does that mean you think the murder was organized by the Americans and the Russians?"

"I don't think anything. My only concern is for *you*, Mr. Aranda. You're the one who has the manuscript now. I don't want you to be murdered, too."

"But you were just saying I would have the Americans and Russians on my side now, and they're the stronger party. That's why you wanted me to stay in the Ritz."

"What I said was, the Americans and the Russians will protect you *if we play it right*," Groll reminded him. "That doesn't mean these gentlemen are your friends. In fact, I'm convinced they're deadly enemies of yours, just as much as the French. What they would prefer most is for you *and* the manuscript to disappear. They don't want anything to become publicly known. It really is a big thing you're involved in now, and a dangerous one, and believe me, Mr. Aranda, I know what I'm talking about—we do have a few people who care about what's going on in our country."

Groll had taken a small Minox camera out of his pocket and was photographing the manuscript page by page. The first ten pages done, he picked up the second ten. Finally he had copied them all. "I'll have to take this to our specialists. And to the Feds. I don't think we can crack the code. But I have an idea. I really don't want anything to happen to you, I would feel . . . really bad."

They looked at each other. Their eyes met and held.

"Thanks," said Manuel at last, while Groll was thinking, if I had a son, he would be just the same age . . .

The commissioner walked over to the big sliding door of the billiard room, opened it and looked out into the Café. He gave a brief nod, and a sad-faced young man wearing a dark suit and horn-rimmed glasses immediately came into the room. Groll slid the door closed behind him and introduced him. The sad-faced young man's name was Schäfer.

"Listen to me, Schäfer," said Groll.

21

A short time later, at 19.43 hours, Wolfgang Groll and Manuel Aranda left the Ritz through the front entrance. Groll was carrying the black attaché case. Two large, powerfully built men walked on each side of the pair, keeping constant watch in every direction. The four trudged through the swirling snow and a howling east wind which whipped particles of ice into their faces. A large car was parked in front of the main entrance. They climbed in. One of the men took the wheel, started the car, drove around the hotel, and steered the vehicle up the Ringstrasse. In spots, the road was covered with snow and snowploughs were in action; cars were slipping and skidding on icy patches and on freshly fallen snow. Traffic was still heavy and moving slowly. Manuel and Groll sat in the back seat, the two bodyguards up front. Groll now had the small attaché case on his knees. The round lamps on both sides of the Ringstrasse hung like long strings of pearls under the white-mantled trees. They passed the Museum of Natural History, the huge monument to the Empress Maria Theresa, the Heroes' Gate, the entrance to the Hofburg, all enveloped in snow . . .

"Looks pretty, doesn't it?" said Groll.

Manuel nodded.

"That's one aspect of this city. The other—" Groll broke off, and asked the driver, "Are we being followed?"

"Yes," said the man. "By a Chevrolet and a Buick."

"Good," said Groll. "Make sure you don't lose them by mistake."

"They'd been waiting for hours outside the hotel," said the man at the wheel. "The French are in the Buick. I recognize one of them."

"Then the others must be in the Chevrolet," said Groll.

"Shit!" the man next to the driver of the Buick was at that moment speaking into a hand microphone. "Excuse my language, boss, but it's enough to make a man throw up. We're at the Bellaria now. If some miracle doesn't happen, they'll have the stuff at Police HQ in a moment." Through a lot of static Jean Mercier's voice came over the loudspeaker inside the Buick: "For God's sake don't lose them, Number Five. I have to know exactly where the object is being taken."

The cars continued along the Ring past the parliament building, which was completely snowed in, then past the Burgtheater. The amber candelabra flanking the floodlit building wore tall hats of snow. On the other side of the park the floodlit façade of the Rathaus loomed into view. The snowflakes were coming thick and fast now. Pedestrians moved slowly and cautiously. All sound was muffled by the snow; an eerie quiet pervaded the traffic-jammed streets. The car carrying Manuel and Groll, and the two other cars, moved past the darkened university and the Schottenring intersection, then made a left turn into Währingerstrasse.

In the Chevrolet a young man was speaking into a microphone in Russian. "Calling Lesskov ... Calling Lesskov ... this is Gorki ..."

"Receiving you, Gorki. Come in, Gorki." The voice coming from the loudspeaker in the car was also Russian.

"We're on our way up the Währingerstrasse, to Police HQ, I presume. The attaché case is in the car."

"Excellent," said Fedor Santarin, President of the "Society of Austrian-Soviet Student Friendship." He was sitting, as immaculately dressed as ever, next to Grant in an old palace in the Wollzeile, in a room that could not be opened except with special keys. Priceless pieces of antique furniture, walls hung with fine engravings, a large carpet covering the entire floor, and a modern short-wave transmitter built into one of the four-foot-thick walls, were all illuminated by a warm, indirect light. Two soberly dressed men were seated beside the metal box, one at the microphone.

"Keep your receiver open, Lesskov, keep your receiver open ..." said the voice coming over the speaker.

"Understood, Gorki," said the man at the microphone.

"Now," said Santarin in English, "it's all going wonderfully according to plan, don't you think, Gilbert? It really doesn't make any difference where they take the attaché case—the French won't ever see it again, no matter what happens. And everything can then proceed as discussed with Nora Hill."

"What luck!" Grant, spare-parts dealer for American automobiles, took a sip from a hip-flask.

"Well, yes, of course, it's a very lucky thing that Romath works for us so devotedly and single-mindedly," said Santarin, carefully tugging at his trousers to protect the creases. "Here in Vienna we have *only* absolutely first-rate people, I swear it by the Holy Mother of Novgorod. What a blessing that Graf Romath likes to make it with young boys. Sometimes the boys are too young."

"And you're the ones who despise the aristocracy!"

"What do you mean? After all, Tolstoi was an aristocrat. And a religious man, like myself!"

"Come in, Lesskov, please come in, Lesskov, Gorki here."

"Receiving you, Gorki. What's up?"

"We made a mistake," Gorki said. "Aranda and the Commissioner are not going to Police HQ. They turned left into Nussdorferstrasse, and are now heading west in the direction of Döbling, Sievering, and the western suburbs!"

22

As these events were taking place, a serious looking man of about thirty left the Ritz Café and, with his hat pressed down over his forehead and his coat collar turned up, he walked along the Ring as far as the Opera House, where he turned into the Kärtnerstrasse. Through the thick, swirling snow he could see a profusion of brightly colored electric signs. Inspector Ulrich Schäfer was a highly talented police officer who enjoyed the respect and friendships of his colleagues at Police HQ. His young wife, however, was slowly dying from multiple sclerosis. Her tragic affliction was the cause of Schäfer's perpetual sadness.

Several paces behind him, four men were walking on both sides of the street. They were members of Schäfer's team, and they never let him out of their sight for a second.

Schäfer walked past the display windows of a jeweler's shop glittering with diamonds and gold and precious stones. Carla's father was a jeweller, too, Schäfer thought sadly. After his wife's death he sold his business and died a well-to-do man. Now his fortune was being devoured by Carla's illness. The rest home in Baden, where Carla was hospitalized, cost enormous amounts. There was still some money left, but it would not last forever, no, not even very much longer. Multiple sclerosis is a terrible disease. It can take years to kill its victims. They hardly ever survive, but sometimes take a horribly long time to die. What would happen if Carla lived longer than the money lasted? Such were Inspector Schäfer's unhappy thoughts.

He turned into the Kohlmarkt, and walked past the Demel Confectionery, where Fedor Santarin was a regular customer. Schäfer's guards stayed at a discreet distance. He came to an old house, black with age, with a large, green portal into which a smaller, open door had been cut. To the right was a secondhand antique dealer, to the left a laundry. Over the door was a sign advertising an "Imperial-Royal Shirtmaker." Schäfer stepped into the wide courtyard of the ancient house;

it was cold and smelled of smoke. He walked quickly across the cobbled pavement to the opposite end of the courtyard, where a second door similar to the first barred the way into an inner quadrangle. To the right and left of it, were narrow worn, winding stairways. There were nameplates of business firms and doctors, and lawyers along the walls. Choosing the stairway on the left, Schäfer climbed to the second story, past floors marked as usual in Vienna apartment houses "Hoch-parterre" and "Mezzanine."

Finally he stood opposite a door fitted with both a Yale lock and a standard lock. A brass nameplate by the door said: Drs. Rudolf Stein and Heinrich Weber, Attorneys at Law. Schäfer gave three short rings and one long. Instantly he heard steps approaching.

A man's voice asked, "Who is it?"

"Inspector Schäfer."

"Put your I.D. into the letter-box."

Schäfer did as he was told.

A few seconds went by, then a human eye appeared in the spy-hole of the door, and scrutinized Schäfer for a long time. Then the door was unlocked and opened. Inside stood a tall, broad-shouldered gray-haired man smoking a cigar.

"Where is it?" he asked.

"Under my shirt," replied Schäfer.

23

"There'll be wine galore,
And we'll be no more.
There'll still be girls around
When we are in the ground . . ."

The wine merchant Ernst Seelenmacher was singing the old song in a low voice. He was seated at a small table and he plucked the strings of a zither delicately. Seelenmacher wore a gray-green Tyrolean costume and a white shirt open at the neck. His face was weatherbeaten, his hair short, thick, and gray. Ernst Seelenmacher was a big, strong man, sixty years old and brimming over with good health. He, his wife and two daughters ran a small "Heuriger," a place where new wine is served in Grinzing, well out of the way of the large, fashionable Heuriger.

The place had four rooms, all whitewashed. Each one led into another through arch-shaped openings. Seelenmacher's guests sat at old tables on long benches. In the summer months they sat outside, under the big beautiful chestnut trees.

The wine was served in "siphons." A siphon is a glass globe ending in a tube and resting on a decorative iron stand. Wine flows from the globe and through the tube when the bottom of a wine-glass is pressed gently against a nozzle at the end of the tube.

Ernst Seelenmacher and Wolfgang Groll had known each other for many years. They talked for hours on end about the cultivation and improvement of different kinds of wine and the many strange creatures to be found in a vineyard. Seelenmacher was a collector of things he dug up from the fertile earth of his vineyard—fossils, Roman coins, bits of swords, fragments of Roman vases and vessels with inscriptions and drawings. He would often give his friend some of the fossils, but kept the Roman coins and potsherds. His grand passion was the study of the ancient Romans, their history, culture, art, religion, literature, and law. He spoke and wrote Latin fluently, and the two friends often had conversations in Latin. Seelenmacher had been educated in a Catholic seminary because as a young man he had ardently desired to become a priest. But his parents had died, and he had had to take over the vineyard. And so the two friends had one important aspect of their lives in common: their youthful dreams had not been fulfilled, yet neither one had ever ceased to dream. Seelenmacher only sang when a customer asked him. Requests usually came from some young people in love but on this evening, with Grinzing under a pall of snow, it was an elderly married couple. The two were sitting close together on a bench, drinking, listening, holding hands, and watching Mr. Seelenmacher.

High up in the wall, above Seelenmacher's head was a large, crescent-shaped window. It gave onto a room on the first floor which was furnished with antique peasant furniture and served as the wine-merchant's office. The room contained a large oaken desk covered with bills and files. Beside the telephone lay a yellowed copy of Seneca's tragedy *Medea* in Latin. The book was open . . .

"You have understood everything I said?" asked Groll. He was standing at an open window that looked out over the garden.

The car in which he and Manuel had been riding was parked in front of the inn. Two detectives were seated inside it, staring, like their boss, into the swirling snow. A short way down the little street a Buick and Chevrolet were parked.

Manuel was sitting behind the desk in Seelenmacher's office. "Yes," he said. "I understand. Everything."

He looked through the crescent-shaped window at Seelenmacher playing his zither, and at the elderly married couple sitting there holding hands. The gentle strains of the song wafted up to him. Groll had introduced Manuel and Seelenmacher on arrival at the pub. Seelenmacher had offered Manuel a glass of wine while Groll made a telephone call. Afterwards Manuel had climbed the stairs to the first floor.

"Now I will give you the names and descriptions of the Russian, the American, and the Frenchman with whom you are dealing in this affair." He did so, then continued, "These men are your personal enemies. The Heads of the Vienna Residencies, as they like to call themselves. But, of course, they're not the top of the heap yet! The hierarchy is pretty complicated. These people are dangerous all right, but they get their orders from somebody above them. And that somebody is responsible to somebody else again. That's how it goes. Our friends are high up on the ladder, proud men, and jealous of their positions. One of my people has taken the camera with the photos of your father's manuscript to the State Police. But I'm afraid that even their specialists won't be able to break the code. As for you, I'd like to suggest . . ." Groll had explained his plan and Manuel had agreed to cooperate.

"Fine," said Groll, walking from the window to the desk. "Let's get started." He picked up the telephone, dialled the number of Police HQ, and asked the operator who answered to connect up a conference line. He gave her the numbers of the French travel-agency *Bon Voyage*, the spare-parts firm AMERICAR, and the "Society for Austrian-Soviet Student Friendship."

"Say that Mr. Manuel Aranda would like to speak to Monsieur Mercier, Mr. Grant, and Comrade Santarin." He waited.

The operator came back on the line: "Mr. Grant is not there, sir, they say."

"Then just connect us with the other two," said Groll. And to Manuel: "Grant seems to have left his HQ. Ask Santarin if he's with him."

Manuel nodded, and took the receiver.

After a short wait a relaxed, velvety voice at the other end said: "Santarin here."

Almost simultaneously another voice, this one edged with anxiety, spoke: "Jean Mercier speaking. What's all this about? I don't know you, Mr.—"

"Yes, yes, all right," said Manuel Aranda. His voice was steely. "Mr. Santarin, is Mr. Grant with you?"

"He certainly is, Mr. Aranda."

"Do you have an extension phone? Can he listen in, too?"

"Certainly, my dear Mr. Aranda."

"Would you perhaps enlighten me as to what's going on?" It was Mercier's voice.

"Of course. That's why I called you. Gentlemen, you must have been wondering why I drove so far out of Vienna to Grinzing. The people you had following me must have been wondering, too. Well, I did it to gain time."

"I don't know what you're talking about," the Frenchman interjected.

"Oh, be quiet, Mercier," Santarin said. "Time for what, Mr. Aranda?"

"You all know what happened this afternoon at the Ritz. You know that I have in my possession the attaché case with my father's manuscript." Manuel looked over at Groll, who nodded as if to say: Good! Keep it up! Manuel continued: "You know—or perhaps you don't know—that the text of the manuscript is in code. Mr. Mercier knows that."

"I haven't got the slightest notion! I don't even know why I am listening to you!"

"A good point, Mr. Mercier, why are you? Now, the text is in code, but I found the key to the code in the attaché case," said Manuel, lying as per Groll's instructions. "I have decoded a small part of the text. I know what it's all about just as you do." He was saying what Groll had told him to say: "And I know that one hell of a scandal is going to break loose when I tell the world about the contents of this manuscript and what you all are up to, gentlemen." Manuel stopped.

One of the men who had been listening to him suddenly seemed to have trouble breathing. I'll bet that's Mercier, Manuel thought. Groll had told him exactly what to say. He

88

must know much more than he has told me, Manuel thought. Whatever it is that my father has in common with these men, I'll drag it out into the open somehow, *myself!* Manuel spoke on: "You and your governments will be compromised beyond precedent throughout the world if just one little iota comes out about the transaction you were conducting or planning to conduct with my father.

"It was very unwise of you to have Mr. Groll and me followed out here," Manuel continued.

"Who followed you? What are you talking about?"

"For God's sake, Mercier, keep quiet!" said Santarin.

> *"If you will be my sweetheart,*
> *Oh, do it secretly . . ."*

Seelenmacher's voice came up from the bar below. The elderly couple were sitting there solemnly, holding hands and drinking toasts to each other.

"You probably think that the Austrian authorities could not risk publicizing the contents of the manuscript and the circumstances of my father's death because of the political repercussions. Well, it may well be that the Austrian authorities cannot risk it. *But I can, and I will.* I'm an Argentinian, a private citizen, I don't need to take any diplomatic precautions. And I do not have to save face. For that reason I have sent the manuscript, together with a report on everything that happened, to an attorney. The messenger who delivered it slipped past your people. I guess you don't have the most open-eyed crew, gentlemen, thank goodness. The manuscript is in the care of this attorney. In a safe with a seven digit combination . . ."

Groll, standing at Manuel's side, nodded again.

"This attorney expects a telephone call from me every day. If twenty-four hours go by without a call from me, he is authorized to hand over all the materials to the Swiss Embassy, which will make them public at an international press conference. After that the countries you represent will be condemned by the whole world—and I don't like to think what your personal fates will be."

Groll had told him what to say, word for word. Manuel had protested at first: "But you're implying that my father was involved in some kind of dirty deal, something unspeakable!"

"As matters stand right now, that possibility cannot be excluded!"

"I don't believe it! I'll never believe it!"

"Perhaps your father was being blackmailed, put under heavy pressure, who knows?" was Groll's answer.

Now Manuel was thinking, the men at the other ends of the phone are quiet. So I must have hit a bull's eye with Groll's words. But what was it my father did? What? Please God, what? Then he said, purposely making his voice cold and hard: "I assume you have all understood now that the worst thing for you would be if anything happened to me."

"Really, sir ... Mr. ... what was your name again? I really don't know why I'm still listening ..." said Mercier's voice.

"If you don't know, who does?" asked Manuel, his tone icy. "Hang up. Go on, hang up!" The line stayed open.

"Perhaps we could clear up the misunderstanding if we could sit down together sometime," said Mercier.

"No way," replied Manuel. "You've been warned now, all of you. You know what will happen if I don't call my attorney every day." With that he hung up.

"Excellent," said Groll.

Inspector Schäfer, sad-faced and young, wearing horn-rimmed spectacles, came into the room. Silver flecks of snow came floating in through the wide open window.

"Everything okay?" asked Groll.

"Yes. Dr. Stein is waiting for your call, Mr. Aranda. You have to call his partner as well, Dr. Weber. At their home number. Here are all the telephone numbers." Schäfer handed Manuel a small card. "Stein suggests you call every day between 15.00 and 18.00 hours at his office, and ask for either him or Weber. On weekends, call one of the home numbers. Each day give one code word as the *fourth* word in the first sentence you speak. The word for this evening is "blizzard." Stein will answer you: listen for the *seventh* word in *his* first sentence. The seventh word is always the code-word for the following day. Stein and his associate have worked that out to avoid complications. That way nobody can fool them by imitating your voice. And of course you must always make your calls from public telephone booths."

"Well done, Schäfer," Groll said. The inspector nodded and left the room, as downcast and worried-looking as ever.

"What's wrong with him?" Aranda asked.

90

"His wife is very ill, poor devil. Call my friend Stein, he's waiting."

Manuel looked at the small card, dialled and immediately afterwards heard a man's voice: "Stein!" Manuel spoke in measured tones: "It's quite a blizzard tonight, is it not, Doctor? This is Manuel Aranda speaking. How are you?"

Stein answered immediately, "I'm afraid I'm getting a bad cold, I feel really down." He was speaking slowly and clearly. So "cold" is tomorrow's codeword, Manuel thought. They talked on for a while about a fictitious court-case, then said their farewells.

"Now the partner," Groll said.

Manuel called Weber. The procedure was repeated: Weber, too, thought he was going to catch a bad cold, and the word "cold" was the seventh of his first sentence.

Once these conversations were over, Groll filled two beautiful old glasses with wine from an old stone pitcher. The sounds of Seelenmacher's zither-playing drifted up from below as Groll spoke.

"I think we have done everything we can now to prevent you from meeting the same fate as your father."

"Mr. Groll," said Manuel, "I am very happy to have met a man like yourself."

A telephone call came in for Groll from his homicide squad.

"What's happened?"

"Just listen to this, Sir," said a police officer who was obviously speaking from an interrogation room. Groll jerked the receiver away from his ear hastily as the sound of loud, harsh shouting came through, strong enough for Manuel to hear, too, and to recognize the angry voice of some other police official.

"The knife was on the table! You grabbed it and attacked him with it!"

The reply came from a high-pitched male voice:

"It was self-defense! He had his filthy hands on me and was going to rape me, the dirty dog!"

"Bullshit!," the detective shouted at the top of his voice. "*You* were after *his* balls! You wanted to suck him off, you foulmouth! And when he didn't go for it, you took the knife and stuck him like a pig!"

"I'll be right over," said Groll into the phone, and hung up. Then he turned to Manuel and said: "We have nice,

91

simple, straightforward murders in Vienna, too ..." He took his coat. "I have to get back on the job. Come with me. I'll have my driver bring you back to your hotel."

Manuel said nothing.

"What's wrong?"

"I hope you won't mind if I just stay here for a while," Manuel answered. "Do you think your friend will let me?"

"Of course. Are you not feeling well?"

"No, it isn't that. It's just that everything ... was a bit too much for me all at once. I'd like to be alone, and think ..."

"I understand," said Groll. "Let's meet again tomorrow. Stay as long as you like. Seelenmacher will get you a taxi when you want to go back home." He shook Manuel's hand. "Chin up," he said.

"I will."

"A stupid piece of advice, I know," Groll said. He looked at the young man helplessly, placed his hand on his shoulder for an instant, then walked out of the room. The zither music and soft singing of the wine merchant could still be heard from below.

Manuel emptied his glass and refilled it. He stared through the open window at the falling snowflakes until he began to feel dizzy again. So many flakes, he thought. So many mysteries. A woman has poisoned my father. My father was involved in some murky business. I must come to terms with that fact. Perhaps it will turn out that my father was not guilty after all, that he was an innocent victim and not a perpetrator. But what of the coded manuscript? What could be its significance? *Could* it be something good? I am a chemist. I have a science-oriented mind. I'm not in the habit of living with uncertainties, puzzles, and doubt. I need facts, reasonable facts, to shed some light on all the darkness. Don't I have enough facts? Two people dead. Secret agents. An affair of state, if Groll is right. The manuscript. Yes, those are facts, but nevertheless incomprehensible facts! Manuel felt desperate. He thought, human existence is a fact. But it would be incomprehensible if we were not here. We are here, and it is still incomprehensible. Father, he thought, father, whom I love, can I still believe you were the wonderful man I knew?

"She was a wonderful woman ..." That was what Irene Waldegg had said about Valerie Steinfeld this afternoon at the snow-covered grave.

A wonderful woman.

And my father was a wonderful man.

Is it possible we are both right? Or am I deceiving myself? Is Irene deceiving herself? Irene! Manuel's thoughts suddenly went out to Irene. She is on night-duty at the pharmacy tonight. I'll go and see her. I have to tell her what has happened. I have to talk with her. He felt a great longing to see Irene Waldegg again, but his legs were like lead. Five minutes more, he thought. Just one more glass of wine. As he was lifting the pitcher, the door opened and Seelenmacher came in.

"Telephone for you," he said. "A woman."

"Did she give her name?"

"No. She just said it was urgent."

Manuel lifted the receiver. "Aranda speaking. Who is it? What's so urgent?"

"Extremely urgent, Mr. Aranda. I've been told you're in Grinzing." The woman's voice was dark. Manuel thought of the cars that had been on their tail.

"Who told you?"

"My place is a long way out of town, and hard to get to from Grinzing. It's easier from the hotel, and you have a car there, I understand. I'll give you exact directions how to get here from the Ritz. Go back there in a taxi and get your Mercedes."

"Who are you?"

"You will not be sorry if you come. I have what you are looking for."

"Listen—I want to know who you are!"

"My name is Nora Hill. I am the woman from whom Valerie Steinfeld got the cyanide capsules."

24

"Yvonne has been a bad girl. She has to be punished. Which of you gentlemen would like to give her the whip?" asked Nora Hill in a rough, low-pitched voice. She was not speaking loudly, yet the words seemed to echo in the vast stillness of the circular hall dimly lit by blue light. Manuel had been let in by an athletic-looking man in a dinner-jacket. He was now standing at the back of the hall, almost in the dark. Nora Hill stood in the center, under a spotlight. Manuel knew it was Nora Hill. The athlete had said: "Madame is busy at the moment. But she told me you were coming. I'll tell her you're here. Please wait here a moment."

The athlete had led Manuel into a small salon furnished with antiques. A variety of sounds and music penetrated from elsewhere in the house. Then came silence, followed by the harsh, strong voice of a woman giving orders. Manuel had ignored the athlete's request, his curiosity was too great. He wanted to see the busy lady at work. He tiptoed out of the salon and along a deserted corridor until he reached the hall. There he saw the lady of the house. . . .

Next to Nora Hill, sharing the spotlight with her, was a young girl with flaming red hair. Nora Hill's evening gown was ankle-length silver lamé. She had black hair, big, black eyes, a large mouth, and wore heavy make-up. A fascinating woman, Manuel thought. Her age? Forty, at the most. She wore large pear-shaped emerald ear-rings, an emerald necklace with a great many stones, and an emerald ring. The jewels sparkled. Nora Hill was supporting herself on two light metal crutches, with upholstered leather pads fitted to her elbow joints.

She held a whip in her right hand. The whip had a short handle and many narrow brown thongs. Looks like leather, Manuel thought. Nora Hill raised her right hand, while leaning heavily on her left crutch, and swung the whip high through the air, thongs whistling.

"Well, then, gentlemen! Yvonne has to get her punishment. Now. Whoever wants to can whip her till she loses consciousness."

The girl was stark naked. She was trying to cover her pubic hair and breasts with her hands. "Hands away!" Nora Hill snapped.

The girl hesitated.

Nora Hill cracked the whip across her back. The girl squealed.

"Hands away!"

Yvonne let her arms drop to her sides. Now she stood there completely exposed, the triangle of her pubic hair as flaming red as the hair on her head.

"Don't tell me you're shy! Come on, gentlemen!"

Nora Hill never raised her voice. She laid her right crutch

94

against an armchair, leaving her right hand completely free to swing the whip. With her left arm she was leaning heavily on the second crutch. There must have been at least twenty men and a dozen girls sitting around in the bluish half-darkness on armchairs and couches in front of small tables laden with glasses, bottles, and champagne buckets. Manuel could barely make out the silhouettes of young and older men, some in dinner-jackets, some in suits. The girls all seemed to be young and pretty. Some were light-skinned, some dark; there was one negress. Some sat next to their men, some on their laps, few were totally dressed, most were in various stages of undress, some in nothing but shoes and a bit of underwear.

In a clever and practiced manner Nora Hill balanced herself on the one crutch and whipped the leather thongs across the white stomach of the red-haired girl. Yvonne had very pale, white skin. She screamed again and doubled over. In a flash Nora struck again, this time across the girl's buttocks. The thongs cracked and slapped against the flesh.

"So, what are you waiting for, gentlemen? Isn't this fun? What's the matter with you?" Nora Hill spoke precise German, without a trace of Austrian accent, Manuel suddenly noticed. "Isn't there any man among you who wants to whip Yvonne? Not one?" There was absolute quiet in the hall. Manuel caught the sound of someone breathing heavily.

"Then Gloria will have to do it," Nora decided, and continued without raising her voice: "Gloria!"

"Yes, ma'am."

A second girl popped up out of the darkness, Manuel could not see from where. This girl was also naked, except for a pair of snugly fitting, soft knee-high leather boots. The girl was a swarthy type, with bluish-black hair.

"Gloria, you will whip Yvonne!"

"Yes, ma'am." Gloria curtsied.

Nora Hill lowered herself into the armchair. Her movements were very smooth. She kept the second crutch in her hand. "No holding back! Otherwise you'll get a few yourself! Twelve strokes!"

"Yes, ma'am."

"Yvonne, you will count them, is that clear?"

"Yes, ma'am," whispered the redhead. The nipples of her large breasts had large pink halos.

Nora Hill struck the floor with her crutch.

"The rope!"

A rope snaked down from the darkness of the high, vaulted ceiling.

"Raise your hands!" the woman in the silver gown commanded.

Gloria tied Yvonne's hands in such a way that she had to hold them high above her head. The rope was given a sudden tug upwards. Yvonne was now on tiptoe. Nora Hill struck the floor again.

"First on her back!"

The whip swished through the air.

The girl cried out. Her body swayed and turned sideways.

"Count!"

"One . . ."

"Louder!" The crutch struck the floor.

"One!" shouted the blonde girl.

"Go on!" called Nora Hill. "On her ass this time!"

The whip's thongs whistled.

Yvonne screamed again.

An uneasy feeling spread through the hall.

The crutch hit the floor commandingly.

"Count! I'm not going to say it again!"

"Two . . .," sobbed Yvonne.

"On her backside! In between! Right in the crack!"

The tips of the thongs cracked. Yvonne turned.

"Three . . ."

The crutch struck the floor.

"Her breasts!" Nora Hill ordered.

Crack!

Yvonne screamed with pain.

"What do you say?"

"Fo . . . Four . . ." she sobbed.

"Now the tits again!"

"Aaaaaouououh!" Yvonne was swaying wildly by now.

"Fi . . . Fi . . . Five," she managed to groan.

"Now go for her cunt. And hard!" said Nora Hill.

Yvonne was yelling with pain, her red hair flying, her body jerking in spasms.

Manuel saw the athlete in the dinner-jacket go up to Nora Hill and whisper in her ear. She gave a brief nod. The whipping ceremony continued.

"Now her belly!"

"Oh, my God, six . . ."

Manuel sat down. The scene aroused in him a mixture of revulsion and excitement. The excitement he felt annoyed him. He stared at Nora Hill. What sort of nightmare have I got myself into now, he thought?

"The thighs, at the front!"

"Aaaaaaoouuh!" Yvonne screamed.

The house must have been built by a mad architect or commissioned by some rich madman. It was circular in shape, not only inside, but outside as well. Two stories high, it looked like an artfully designed tower. In the dimly lit garden, Manuel had just been able to make out some elegant art nouveau stone ornaments along the outside walls.

Nora Hill's house was situated at the western boundary of the city. Driving west from the Ring, Manuel had found his way without too much difficulty. He had passed a number of snowploughs. The deserted road leading up to Nora's villa had already been cleared.

The countryside thereabouts was largely open and undeveloped. Magnificent villas stood in large gardens, with untouched woodlands stretching out behind them. Nora Hill's round, tower-like house stood in an old, wild park. It was surrounded on all sides by a tall fence made of sharply pointed iron rods. A gardener's cottage stood by the main gate. When Manuel rang, a huge man emerged from it all muffled up and asked Manuel's name and business. He then slunk back into the little house, muttering, "Got to call up first!"

He returned after a few moments to open the wings of the massive gate.

"Keep going straight on. There's a parking lot up front."

The parking lot was large and cleared of snow. Manuel counted fourteen cars parked there, all luxury vehicles with foreign plates. When he climbed out of the Mercedes he was almost knocked down by the force of a howling east wind which hurled icy crystals in his face until he smarted and tingled.

"Good evening, Mr. Aranda."

Manuel wheeled around.

Behind him stood a man in a dinner-jacket. The man looked like a free-style wrestler. He was holding an open umbrella.

"May I have the pleasure of escorting you to the house . . ."

This house . . .

"Whip her ass again!" Swoosh! The whip hissed into the soft flesh. Gloria, black-haired, leather-booted, was breathing hard now as she wielded the whip, her breasts heaving and sinking, her face distorted. Yvonne, dangling from the rope, was screaming with pain, her body arched.

"Eleven ..."

"On her belly again!" Nora Hill ordered, stumping her crutch. The tips of the whip-thongs sang through the air, snapping loudly as they bit into the white flesh.

This time, the girl only moaned.

"Twelve ..."

Then her body flopped forward, as if she had fainted. Manuel saw figures moving like shadows on the chairs and sofas. The air hung heavy with the scent of cigar and cigarette smoke, perfume, perspiration, excitement, and women.

"Get her out of here!" Nora Hill said.

The rope suspended from the darknesses of the ceiling was lowered. Red-haired Yvonne collapsed in a heap and lay motionless. Gloria untied her hands, and Yvonne's arms dropped to the ground. She didn't move. Two waiters in black trousers, white shirts, and short red jackets sprang into the spotlight and dragged the girl out into the dark between them. Gloria stretched herself once more, her legs spread open, her belly stuck out. But when the lights came up she was gone.

Half-naked girls slung their arms round their men, touching them, kissing them, stroking them. Manuel saw that there was a mixture of races among the men, too, as well as among the women.

The moment the brighter yellow lights went on, a gaunt man with high Slavic cheekbones and very pale skin walked over to Manuel. The man was wearing a dinner-jacket and had a small moustache. His black hair shone with oily dressing.

"Mr. Aranda?"

"Yes."

"My name is Enver Zagon," said the man, speaking with a heavy Eastern European accent. He seemed in a terrible hurry. "I have to talk to you. About your father's death ..."

"What do you know about it? Who are you?"

"I know that ..." He broke off suddenly. "Quick! Light my cigarette! Fast!"

"But ..."

"Not now! Later."

Manuel struck a match, and the man who called himself Enver Zagon bent down to light a cigarette in a long holder with a broad mouthpiece. Then he bowed and returned to his armchair, in which he had been sitting by himself, away from the others.

Manuel could not understand what had alarmed him so suddenly. Uneasily he looked around the large room with its fully inlaid floor. He saw half-drunk men, girls in their slips, panties, and silk stockings, waiters in black, red, and white uniforms scurrying between the tables bringing champagne buckets, glasses, and bottles. Then he saw her, Nora Hill. The jewels on her body flashed and sparkled, the silver dress glowed red, and she was coming toward him with rapid, practiced, rhythmic movements of her two crutches.

The crutches were now making almost no sound. Nora Hill put her whole weight on them, as he could see from the strain showing through her smooth-skinned, young-looking face. Obviously she could not take a single step without these crutches. Yet Nora Hill was able to smile. She displayed flashing white teeth.

"I'm glad you came, Mr. Aranda." Her voice, accentless, low-pitched, and smoky, sounded calm and relaxed, not in the least out of breath. Manuel bowed. The woman raised her hand, with crutch, high enough for his lips to touch the skin. The skin was cool and dry. What beautiful hands, he thought. And what eyes! Beautiful eyes, yes, but how much cynicism, coldness and hatred of mankind showed through them.

"I was really expecting to receive you in the salon."

"Yes, but . . ."

"But you are a very inquisitive young man, well, all right. So you've seen me in action . . . What did that man want from you?"

"Which man?"

"Oh, please, Mr. Aranda!" Her voice had become metallic.

"Oh, that one. Nothing at all. He just needed a light for his cigarette."

"He wouldn't get the chance to ask for anything else." Abruptly Nora Hill lowered her voice, an expression of disgust, which Manuel was going to see often, crossed her beautiful face, and she said as she looked at her clientèle: "Just look at that. Men! They're all hot or bothered now and can hardly wait to get at my girls. It's as simple as that. And, of course, it's all a fake, a charade."

"How do you mean?"

"Yvonne didn't feel a thing, not a thing."

"But the whip . . ."

"The thongs are soft nylon. It doesn't hurt, not a bit. Did you see any stripes on the girl? Any blood?"

"No."

An Englishman staggered past them, very drunk, a girl on his arm.

"Come on, baby, now I'll fuck you."

"See? It's working already." Nora Hill's lips curled. "Every human being on this earth is a sadist. You are. I am. We all are. Something is acted out in front of us, we react. No, Yvonne didn't feel a thing. Yet you and the others didn't notice the difference! You didn't notice there was no blood, nor any stripes! Do you think I could really afford to have one of my girls whipped senseless? Yvonne is the best chick here. We need her tonight still. If someone really wants to see blood, well, all right, we can provide that too. People—aaah!"

"You despise people?"

"Not any longer. It's too exhausting. There are only two kinds of people, you know, young man, bad people and stupid people." She flashed her bright smile at him again. "I prefer the bad ones," she said.

"Let's go upstairs to my room," she said. This is going to be rather a long talk."

She swung between her crutches toward a broad staircase which ran along the circular inner wall to a landing on the first floor. Manuel, following behind her, found he had to quicken his steps to keep up with the lame woman because she propelled herself with such speed. He turned around and saw that the gaunt man was still sitting in his armchair. He seemed to be watching Manuel worriedly.

25

"Swine," said Nora Hill. "Dirty, greedy swine. That's what people are, in my experience. Naturally I include myself. Along with my father and mother."

"Your parents, too . . ."

"And how! I'm not from around here, as you must have

100

noticed by my accent, young man. I was born in Essen. In 1915."

"In 1915? So you're . . ."

"Fifty-four. I'm well-preserved, I know. My father was an officer in the army, my mother a dancer in a variety show. She went through a lot of men. Until the lieutenant came on the scene. She was in love with him—aaah, sickening! He got her pregnant. Promised to marry her. Then, to his immense relief, the First World War broke out and he disappeared for good. As for me, my dear mother handed me over to some farmers the minute I was born. I was in her way, she wanted to enjoy herself with men. When I was five the farm family told me she had died. She had gone into hospital with a simple case of flu, and died of pneumonia. When my foster parents told me my mother had gone to Heaven, I couldn't stop laughing. No, to this day I've never met a single human being I could love or respect, or want to imitate." Her voice softened. "With one exception. There is someone I admire still from the bottom of my heart, whom I look up to and revere. Someone I'd be proud to be like, but never will be."

"And who is this person?"

"The person I'm talking about," said Nora Hill, "was Valerie Steinfeld."

The beautiful lady of the house was sitting in a chintz-covered armchair in front of a large fireplace set in the middle of a living room furnished with antiques. It formed part, as Manuel had discovered, of an ingeniously designed large apartment consisting of a bedroom, dressing-room, bathroom, and balcony. There was a small bar in the living-room, and book shelves along the walls, with built-in stereo and TV. The fireplace was surmounted by a huge chimney to catch the smoke. The athletic-looking man in the dinner jacket, whom Nora Hill called George and who in her absence seemed to combine the functions of servant, associate, and head of the establishment, had arranged a stack of big logs next to the fireplace. The fire crackled. Curtains covered the large windows, which were incessantly being scraped and tapped upon by the twigs of the trees outside. George had brought in a bucket of ice, glasses, soda siphons, and a bottle of whisky. The light metal crutches lay beside Nora on her chair. She was smoking a cigarette in a long silver holder. Laughter and music drifted up from the floor below, as did the drone of voices talking and shouting. It was a solidly built

101

house. With visible pride Nora Hill had shown Manuel around a little as they were coming up . . .

The stone banister on the first floor—with the rope Yvonne had hung from still attached to it also ran around the entire hall. The house had a huge diameter.

"I'll show you a few of the rooms," Nora Hill had said, swinging herself along ahead of Manuel hurriedly, energetically, and without a trace of embarrassment. Along the walls between doors Manuel saw large and expensive prints of the Forty-nine positions of love as described by Aretino and painted by Giulio Romano. Above each door was a small lamp with opaque glass, as in a hotel. Nora Hill hastily opened each room in turn. Everything Manuel saw took his breath away by its beauty, taste, or outlandishness. "Every room is individually furnished. And we've got a swimming-pool and a movie-theater on the ground-floor. The rooms cost me a fortune. Look at this one, for instance, the Chinese room . . ." There was also a room furnished in French Rococo style, hung with etchings of the period; an Indian room, a Greek room, a harem room. Then there was a room furnished like a monastery cell, another like a prison cell, yet another decorated and furnished completely in black. There was a medieval torture-chamber with all the accoutrements and engravings from the works of the Marquis de Sade. One room had mirrors covering the walls and ceiling. Two doors Nora passed by quickly. The little lights above these doors were on.

"Every room will be occupied in a short while," said the woman with the beautiful cynical face.

"Where do you get the girls from?"

"Some of them live here, others live in the city. Whenever I need more, or a specific one, I call up. I have a share in a few night clubs. George picks them up in the car."

"George?"

"The manservant. My lover—you thought so—didn't you? You didn't? Strange. It's been six years now. He's one of the bad people. I couldn't stand a stupid one for long. He serves me marvelously well, believe me. And is crazy about me. Of course, built the way he is and looking the way he does, he's had everything. The only thing he hadn't had was a woman with two gamey legs and a lot of dough. Now *that's* something special . . ." She opened another door. It was furnished in heavy turn-of-the-century style. A large oil painting on the wall depicted a young man kneeling before an older man.

Both were naked. The younger man was making love to the older man.

"We cater to this sort of thing, too," said Nora Hill. "I don't have many customers who ask for it, but some do. And my boys are absolutely dependable. That's important. Most of those types are into blackmail, but not my boys. They earn too much here. Of course, I charge more than for the other stuff. And boys have never given me any trouble. Girls have, a lot. But name me one profession that doesn't have its headaches?" And she had hurried on . . .

"Cheers!" said Nora Hill, raising her glass. She was sitting in front of the crackling fire, opposite Manuel. Both were drinking.

"Well then: I knew Valerie Steinfeld. I knew her well. I am in a position to tell you what she was involved in. It's like something from the *Arabian Nights*. A tough, dangerous story. What's the matter?"

"What do you mean?"

"The look in your eyes. You're thinking: this woman isn't going to tell me anything for nothing!" Manuel hesitated. "Of course that's what you were thinking! And you're right."

"I understand," said Manuel, putting his glass down. A log on the fire cracked with a sound like a gunshot.

"No, my dear young friend, you don't understand. No blackmail. No money. I have enough. And not your documents, either."

"What documents?"

"Mr. Aranda!" She looked at him with an ironic smile.

"You know . . ."

"Of course. But I'm telling you, I don't want the manuscript."

"What is it you want then?"

"I'll tell you everything I know about Valerie Steinfeld. I'll help you clear up the mystery of your father's death. The only thing is, you must not . . .

". . . rely on me alone. You won't hear Valerie Steinfeld's story complete tonight. Not because I'm trying to tease you, but because I want you to have the chance of checking out the truth of what I tell you bit by bit."

"She's doing a magnificent job," said Gilbert Grant.

"She's a treasure," replied Fedor Santarin, fiddling with the diamond ring on his finger.

The American and the Russian were sitting in a room that looked as though it had been furnished for a little girl. Teddy bears and dolls lay around the room, as did toys, pretty little dresses, baby-doll nighties, colored hair-ribbons, and children's shoes. Grant had his feet up on a coffee-table. In one hand he was holding a hip-flask full of bourbon, from which he took occasional swallows. His face was as red as ever, his eyes watery as usual. Santarin had shaved again during the evening, and was sitting on the small bed. He was talking English again, as a courtesy. Grant wiped his mouth and asked, "But can she keep it up?"

"She *has* to, Gilbert, so don't worry. In Austria the statute of limitations does not go into effect for twenty years in cases of murder. We have a few years time yet."

Meanwhile, Nora Hill, who was sitting just three rooms away from the two men, had continued speaking. Her voice was coming over a loudspeaker that hung from a nail above the bed directly beneath a picture of Snow White and the Seven Dwarfs.

". . . I want you to convince yourself that what I am telling you is the truth."

"How do I do that?" Manuel Aranda asked.

"By going to all the other people involved in this case and getting them to tell you *their* versions."

"They won't tell me anything. I've tried already."

"Maybe, but if you go to them knowing what I'm going to tell you this evening, they'll talk all right, all of them."

"And all that will take time, lots of it," Grant murmured. "If anything should happen to Aranda now ..."

"I asked Jean Mercier to come here."

"Here?"

"Yes. He'll be arriving later. In about an hour. I told him we're all in this together now, however grotesque that might seem."

"I'll ask you for something only after you have heard the whole story from me and tried it out on all the others," said Nora Hill in her dark, low voice. "You're thinking of the B-Project, of course, but I—"

"What project?"

"Here it comes!" Fedor Santarin, who was playing with one of the dolls, straightened up.

"I don't understand," said Nora Hill.

"The B-Project—what is that?"

"No idea."

"But you just mentioned it!"

"You must have heard wrong, my friend."

"I certainly did not! And I don't understand—"

"You *did* hear wrong. B-Project? What's that supposed to be?"

"I have no idea."

"Oh, let's drop it. It's silly."

"I'm sorry. What was it you said, then?"

"Can't remember. You've rattled me."

"She's magnificent, isn't she!" Santarin beamed. "Did you hear how she slipped that in! He really *doesn't* have any idea. Which means I was right: he was lying to us, he does not have the key to the code."

"Maybe he's bluffing," said Grant.

"Never! That was real. He was bluffing when he lied to us. Well, he can go on bluffing Mercier. Let Mercier go on believing Aranda has the key to the code. I never believed it. You doubted it. That was why I asked Nora to test him out. Are you convinced now?"

"Yes," said Grant.

"What a woman!" said Santarin.

"What a tragedy a woman like that has to be a cripple," Grant sighed, sentimentally.

"Tragedy? It's a stroke of luck! There's nobody smarter than someone physically deformed," Santarin replied.

"And what will you ask of me?" came Manuel's voice.

27

"It will be in the nature of a request," Nora Hill answered. "Our glasses are empty: could you mix us two more drinks, please?"

"And you don't even have to fulfill the request," she said as he refilled the heavy whisky glasses. "You can refuse it." I hope the microphone in the chimney is working, she thought. What I'm doing here has been approved by their masters in Washington and Moscow. It was Santarin's idea: he's the smarter of those two miserable pigs blackmailing me. What can I do? Nothing. Got to do what they ask. It takes twenty years for a murder case to be shelved.

Manuel said nothing, twirled his glass around in his hands. The sounds of the music and voices below reached him again.

"Do you want to hear my story? Do you accept my suggestion?" Nora Hill asked.

"Yes," said Manuel. "If at the end, I'm really free to decide for myself whether or not to fulfill your request, I'd like to hear what you have to say."

"It's a deal."

"When did Valerie Steinfeld get the cyanide capsules from you?"

Nora Hill raised the silver cigarette holder to her mouth and blew smoke-rings, slowly and contemplatively.

"Twenty-six years ago."

28

Monday, October 4, 1942, 9 A.M.

Nora Hill entered the quiet Seilergasse from the Neuer Markt-Opernring end. The weather was cold and gray; it was the sort of day that never really lightens. Nora Hill had just arrived from the south, and was shivering in the cold despite her leopardskin coat. Under the coat, she wore a corn-colored wool dress with a suede sash. A black turban was wrapped around her head. She had beautiful legs. Her feet were clad in black suede Italian shoes with wedge-shaped heels. Over her right arm dangled a crocodile-leather handbag, in which she carried the pistol Jack Cardiff had given her. Nora Hill was twenty-six years old. Her walk was provocative, sexy. Heavy make-up gave her a foreign look—"the German woman uses no make-up" was the party line. Nora Hill had huge, dark eyes with long lashes, a large mouth made to look even larger with the aid of lipstick, and black, silken hair protruding from under the turban. She had stripped off her suede gloves. Her long fingernails were painted red to match her mouth. Around her right wrist she wore a wide platinum bracelet set with diamonds, and on the third finger of the same hand she wore an unusual ring studded with red, green, blue, and white stones. Women who met Nora Hill turned to look her up and down with hostile eyes; men would turn their heads to get a second look.

Don't stare like that! thought Nora Hill. She had been ordered to dress and make up like that . . . by the Germans. The reasoning for it seemed logical enough: outside Germany an elegant, beautiful, and sophisticatedly dressed woman was not too conspicuous, whereas in Germany she would be extremely noticeable, making it easy to shadow her. Hence the jewelry: Nora Hill had smuggled it out of Germany and deposited it in a bank safe in Lisbon, where she had a whole stash of it still. The bracelet and the ring were back in Germany now, because Jack Cardiff had said: "When you go to visit Valerie Steinfeld you must look as conspicuous as possible. Even the most thick-headed Gestapo man on your tail must be convinced you would not have chosen such a get-up if you were plotting against the regime . . ."

To hell with this woman Valerie Steinfeld, Nora Hill thought bitterly. I don't know her. I'm not interested in her. She's not my responsibility. I have enough to do to save my own skin. But Jack had said: "You've got to go to her. You've got to help her. I beg you."

And there's the rub, Nora Hill thought, I'll do anything Jack asks me to do. I love him. So you see where love gets you . . .

ENTRANCE TO THE CATACOMBS read the notice next to the

107

door. The catacombs, a centuries-old labyrinth of underground corridors and tunnels extending beneath almost the entire center of the city, were frequently being used as official air-raid shelters. To the right of the entrance was a leather-goods shop, with a lot of cheap items on display, and next to it was the shop Nora was looking for. Above the windows, which were half boarded up with wooden slats, was a longish metal shield, which once might have been bright green in color but was now darkened with dirt. It said, in old-fashioned script:

LANDAU BOOKSTORE. RARE AND SECONDHAND BOOKS.
FOUNDED 1811.

The knob on the entrance door was rusty, and could be turned only with difficulty. Nora wheeled around and carefully eyed the people in the short street. Women. Children. Soldiers. A few civilian men. A man on a bicycle pedalled by, puffing under a load of boxes. No, Nora thought, I wasn't followed. The man in the Homburg hat and blue overcoat, who had been tailing her since her arrival at Langenlebern airfield had just managed to jump back behind the corner of a house at the end of the Seilergass. He was looking at the big clock in the center of the Neuer Markt.

9:06 A.M. The man in the Homburg hat lit a cigarette. He had the feeling that whatever it was Nora Hill had to do in the bookstore was going to take her a long time. And his feelings seldom deceived him. "Take joy in life while your lamp still burns . . ." the ancient tune struck his ear as Nora opened the door and entered the shop. Electric light was burning in the store. Opaque glass globes hung from the ceiling on long, steel rods. At the bottom of each globe that had a light in it, one could see a layer of dirt and insects that had gathered there. The steel rods were stained. A huge, tiled stove stood at one end of the salesroom.

Nora Hill closed the door behind her, the stiff hinges scraped and squeaked, the glockenspiel melody started up once again. On her left she saw a stuffed bear, at least eight feet tall, black, its fur worn, standing upright. It was a Baribal bear of the species living in North America. Seeing it there put Nora Hill into a somewhat better mood for the first time that morning.

29

Dear Jack! Beloved Jack!

For a moment Nora allowed her thoughts to dwell on him, with profound gratitude. Seeing the stuffed bear had been a huge relief. Jack Cardiff had told her to expect the bear.

"The bear stands there holding a basket full of books. It has a mechanism that makes it growl. If you take a book out of the basket you set it off," he had said.

The bear really was holding a basket in its paws. In it were a few books. Nora took one out, and the bear let out a long, low growl. The title of the book was *The Wonderful Life of the Small Boy Who Became Our Führer*. Nora put the book back. The sad bear with the shabby fur growled again.

Nora let her eyes sweep around the room. Everything was as Jack had described it.

"Hello!" she called out.

Nothing moved.

"Hello!" she called out again, louder this time. A man stepped out from between the rows of bookshelves. His thin face was that of a scholar, his hands were slender and fine, his feet very small. He was immaculately if eccentrically dressed in old-fashioned style. His eyes, soft and gray, twitched nervously. It's him all right, thought Nora, feeling reassured. Jack had described Martin Landau precisely, and everything fitted. Landau always keeps his left shoulder slightly hunched up, Jack had said, his head slopes a little to the left, and his pale lips show a perpetual smile, a nervous smile. He wears a party badge in his left buttonhole.

"Beware especially of this fellow Landau. He's the weakest link in our plan."

That was what Jack had said. At least he had not tried to hide anything, or to lie to her in order to give her a false sense of security. Jack never lied, and that was why Nora loved him.

It's a good start, Nora thought. But now I've got to make sure, fast. I have to know how big a coward this Landau is.

So she remained silent, and fixed Landau with her eyes. Immediately he evaded her gaze. Good heavens, Nora thought, you're going to have to stand up to a lot more than a woman's eyes, man. If you don't, it's going to be curtains, and not just for you.

This man is thirty-nine, Jack had said, and he's never had a woman in his arms. I can see that myself, I don't need Jack to tell me that. This man at thirty-nine goes home every night like a good boy to his sister and crawls into some corner to jerk off. They don't need to find any Gestapo to bully this fellow. "The weakest link in our plan . . ."

Christ Almighty, Nora thought, what could Jack have had in mind? How could you save someone's life with the help of a wet rag like Landau?

Aloud Nora said: "Good morning!"

Landau started, as though someone had just kicked him in the pants. He stepped back two paces, shot his right arm up and forward, and with head and one shoulder sloping, answered, softly, anxiously, and indistinctly: *"Heil Hitler!"*

Ah, well. That's Mr. Martin Landau. Party member Martin Landau.

"I happen to be passing through Vienna," said Nora, watching the miserable coward's scared reaction to every word. Jack sure had given her quite a job this time! "I'm looking for a certain work on Greek mythology, secondhand," she said.

Landau's lower lip began to tremble.

"Greek mythology," repeated Landau mumbling. "Well, you know . . ."

"Yes?" said Nora, stepping forward a pace.

Immediately he retreated one step, while managing to stutter, "Well, mythology, you know, after all . . . there's quite a lot here on Greek mythology . . . Curtius, Meyer, Droysen . . . on Greek culture, too . . . language, music . . ."

Nora looked straight at him again—but was unable to hold his gaze—and said clearly and emphatically, "What I need is *Faith of Hellas*." At that he seemed to cave in completely, and cast his eyes down to stare at his shoes.

"Well?" Her voice became louder and louder, she was growing increasingly angrier at the thought of what might lie before her with such a man as her accomplice. She felt helpless. "Do you have *Faith of Hellas*?"

His lips moved, his head remained bowed.

"I can't hear you!"

110

He jerked his head up quickly and hissed, as though he had lost his mind: "I said I don't know!"

"Well, couldn't you take a look?" Nora was talking very loudly now. She felt like hitting him over the head. On the other hand, she knew that she had put him into a difficult position. One must be fair.

"I'd be glad to take a look, of course," Landau mumbled mournfully. "Would you follow me please . . ." He hurried on ahead. "Through this corridor here . . . we're just in the middle of rearranging things, you know . . . it's a terrible mess . . . we use the quiet period before the Christmas rush to organize ourselves a little. I was in the stacks, that's why I didn't hear you at first, please excuse me . . ."

The corridor ended in the first of the stackrooms. There was no light on. On the right was the doorless entrance to a small but comfortable study with a green-shaded lamp. A stove roared, overheated. The lamp threw a weak light over the nearest corner of the stacks, revealing thousands of books piled on large tables, on the floor, and on shelves. Most of the room remained in complete darkness.

SAVE ELECTRICITY! admonished a notice on the wall. Landau stopped.

"We've put Greece right at the back now . . . there's hardly any demand for it these days. I hope you will excuse the untidiness . . . there's so much to do, and so little help . . . my three salesclerks have been drafted . . . I only have one left . . . must be somewhere in the stacks . . ." He called out, "Frau Steinfeld!," and when an answer was slow in coming he shrieked hysterically: "Frau Steinfeld, make it snappy!"

30

"Coming!" a clear, young voice called out.

A woman in a black calico smock came through an archway from another part of the stacks where electric light was burning. With an automatic gesture she turned a light switch, and the dim glow behind her went out. Now there was only the light from the green desk-lamp in the little room beside them.

Valerie Steinfeld was slim and tall. Nora had seen photographs of her; still, she did not recognize the woman right away. The photos had been made years earlier, and had shown a beautiful young woman laughing happily and with shining blonde hair cascading in gentle waves down her back. Valerie's hair had remained the same, but her face had changed. It's the eyes, Nora thought, and the mouth. These blue eyes and this full mouth have not laughed for years, nor even smiled. The eyes are still beautiful, but the expression in them is frightening. These eyes will never laugh again, Nora thought. They cannot, and they can no longer cry either. Valerie Steinfeld has no more tears.

"Yes, Mr. Landau?" Valerie Steinfeld looked at the palefaced man without changing her expression, just as she had looked at Nora without expression. Valerie had very pale skin.

"The lady is looking for—" Landau began, his voice quavering, then was interrupted by the tinkle of the glockenspiel in the store.

Tremendously relieved, Landau bowed; as he did so the swastika on his party badge flashed in the light from the lamp in the small study.

"Excuse me, Miss. Customers." He hurried away. Both women stood tensely, looking at each other: Valerie solemn, her eyes measuring and evaluating Nora, Nora increasingly agitated.

She's thirty-eight years old, Nora thought. Eleven years older than I! I'll stare her down, damned if I won't. But it's not easy! Jack, forgive me, but I'm in the wrong camp. This just isn't the place for me. Desperate, unhappy people are not my cup of tea. I'll have to get through this as fast as possible. Then I'll disappear and I'll never see Valerie Steinfeld again.

"I'm looking for *Faith of Hellas*," said Nora.

"Aha," said Valerie Steinfeld. That was all she said. And she continued to stare at Nora, matter-of-factly, politely, and in absolute control of herself.

Nora felt anger rising inside her, anger against herself and the irrationality of her feelings. She had cursed Landau for his cowardice; she should have been grateful to Valerie Steinfeld for her cool and collected bearing. Instead, she found this Steinfeld woman unbearable. Her face was too serious, but otherwise she was quite pretty . . . a somewhat dusty Cinderella. So there was that, too! Nora Hill had never had a girlfriend in her whole life.

Up to now, Nora thought, all the women I've had anything to do with have either despised me or been afraid of me. Now I seem to have found someone who feels neither fear nor contempt. But that will change when I tell her what I've come here to say; let's see if she'll keep her self-control.

"There are two works on that subject. One by Levy, one by Trockau," said Valerie Steinfeld. The two women looked each other in the eyes. There followed a kind of question and answer game.

"The Trockau, of course. The Levy is forbidden."

"Yes, of course. The Trockau . . .," said Valerie. "There's the one-volume edition published in 1929——"

"It's in two volumes."

"I beg your pardon?"

"You're mistaken. The first edition was in two volumes. But I need the second edition, which came out in 1931, edited by Merian and Stähelin."

Valerie Steinfeld went into the study at a leisurely pace, turning her back on Nora Hill. She seemed to be looking through the shelves—she would have given that impression to anyone standing behind her. In reality, she was holding her eyes tightly closed and her hands were gripping the arms of an old easy chair in front of the crowded old desk.

"Merian and Stähelin . . .," repeated Valerie Steinfeld, slowly. Her back twitched with tension. Nora noticed it, and thought, so, you're no superwoman after all. "Those volumes had been ordered by someone several months ago. I got them out of the stacks and put them somewhere here, ready to be picked up. But the customer never came back for them. Now where can they be?" And she looked around, her eyes open again. Nora Hill stepped into the little room after her. So that's the "tearoom" Jack spoke of, she thought.

"Let me think," Valerie said in a monotone, her eyes running the lengths of the shelves. "Where was it I put those volumes?"

And so the performance continues, Nora thought. It has to. It would be quite possible that some total outsider should ask for that particular edition of *Faith of Hellas*. Perhaps it had happened already, and that was why Landau was so jittery, even though he knew that there were a number of safeguards.

"It's not here . . . nor here . . ."

Valerie had been pulling individual volumes out of the shelves, sometimes bending low, sometimes standing tiptoe.

113

Now she looked at Nora as though trying to say: let's get it over with, *talk!*

"On this side, perhaps?" Nora asked.

Valerie pretended to continue her search.

Nora looked around the small room once more. That's the worn-out carpet Jack told me about, and over there's the shaky rocking-chair. There's the little stove in the corner, glowing red. What a lot of noise it makes! Jack didn't tell me anything about the desk. Nor anything about the shortwave radio on top of it. A "Minerva 405." Nora knew that type of radio. Seven tubes, first put on the market in 1940, the most powerful and best radio available at the present time. Jack couldn't possibly have known about it, of course. You could get London on that type of radio even in daytime . . .

"I really don't know where else to look . . . the books must be here, they were never picked up," Valerie said. "But they're not here."

The moment had come.

"Yes, they are," Nora said.

"Where?" The question came weaker this time. Valerie was at the end of her strength. Nora looked around with a smile and gave no answer.

"Where?" asked Valerie a second time. Her voice had suddenly lost all its firmness and was quavering. Her eyes were imploring now: they had lost that brave stare. They were saying: Please! Please!

Well, all right, Nora thought.

She spoke slowly and very distinctly. "The books are right in front of you. On the fifth shelf from the top, to the left of the couch. The twelfth and thirteenth book, counting from the corner." And with a quick movement she stepped forward and pulled two heavy tomes from the shelf. "There's volume one, and there's volume two," she said, looking at Valerie again.

"I'm very glad you found them," said Valerie, showing no emotion. "May I take a quick look at the price?"

Nora froze.

One second. One second.

I must have done something wrong. She did everything right. But I . . .

"Wait!" Nora grabbed Valerie's arm. Her confused state of mind and the stuffy air of the room made her feel boiling hot.

"Yes?" Valerie asked politely, raising an eyebrow. Nora

felt desperate. What had gone wrong? What did I ... Then she remembered. And the moment she remembered what she had forgotten, admiration for Valerie Steinfeld surged through her. Angry at herself and her own arrogance, and angry at the woman she couldn't help admiring, Nora opened her handbag and took out a scrap of yellowish-blue paper with some lettering on it. On one side the paper had been ripped off along a bizarre, zigzag line. The printed letters read: HELLER'S LEM-

Valerie Steinfeld knelt down, pulled out the left-hand bottom drawer of the desk and rummaged around in it, while Nora kept thinking: *two* recognition signals had been agreed upon, not just one! I forgot the second one; but *she* did not forget it, in spite of her excitement.

Valerie had found what she was looking for. She got up. In her hand she was holding a similar scrap of yellowish-blue paper. Both women smoothed out their pieces of paper, and Nora laid her half on the crowded desk top. Very slowly, Valerie moved her half closer to Nora's. Her fine hands were dusty from the stacks. She moved her piece of paper back and forth until the torn part fitted exactly against the torn edge of the other half. Joined together, the two pieces now formed a candy wrapper. The words HELLER'S LEMON DROPS—A DELICACY! could now be read across the entire piece.

"Forgive me," said Valerie in a quiet voice.

"What's there to forgive? It was my fault. And congratulations. You don't panic easily!"

"I hope not," said Valerie calmly. Then she opened the door of the little stove and threw both pieces of paper into the fire. "What is your name, Miss?"

"Hill. Nora Hill."

Valerie closed the stove door. A sudden feeling of faintness made her sit down quickly on the ancient sofa. Its springs creaked. Valerie looked up into Nora's face. Her eyes were radiant now, like the eyes of a young girl in love. A smile lit up her beautiful face. It was like a sunrise.

In a strangled voice Valerie Steinfeld asked: "Is he well?"

31

"When I left this city some years ago," shouted Adolf Hitler, "I carried in my heart the same unshakable faith that fills my heart today!"

He was standing before a cluster of microphones on the balcony of the ancient Town Hall in the city of Linz. The square beneath him, swarming with thousands upon thousands of people, was bathed in the glare of searchlights. Hundreds of torches were burning. The windows of every house were lit. The additional illumination had been requested by a broadcaster who had described the huge excitement of the masses, the overwhelming joy of the Austrians to have been brought "home" into the Reich, speaking breathlessly and as though carried away by the orgy of jubilation.

The news of Hitler's triumphal entry into Austria was broadcast on the evening of the 13 March, 1938, throughout Austria and Germany and overseas by short-wave transmission. Hitler's voice reverberated across the entire greater German Reich through loudspeakers strategically placed at road junctions, airports, railroad stations, wharfs, warehouses, restaurants, and market places:

"I want to share with you my profound emotion at having my faith confirmed after so many long years!"

Vienna's main railroad station, Vienna West, resembled a giant ant-heap. On that evening of March 13, 1938, the railroad stations of Austria swarmed with hurrying, scurrying, pushing, weeping, cursing, and hysterical people, trying to get out of Austria as the beautiful spring day with its balmy air and velvet blue sky, drew to a close.

People! People!

". . . Providence had called me from the heart of this city to be the Führer of the German Reich, and laid upon me a holy mission!" Hitler's voice, heavily amplified, rolled like thunder across the platforms of the Vienna West station. Paul Steinfeld put his lips to his wife's ears in order to make himself understood.

"The Führer and you," he said, "the best that Austria ever produced!"

Valerie, who had been fighting back her tears for hours, gazed at her husband through clouded eyes. They had been married for fifteen years. She knew that what her husband had just said was the sad and bitter joke of a man who had to flee to save his life—it was his way of declaring his love for her at such a moment. Tenderly she stroked his hand. He pressed his lips to her ear and kissed it. They were standing next to a train that was ready to leave, amid a throng of pushing, shoving, and shouting people. Paul Steinfeld waved to a man who was trying to keep his hot-dog cart from being trampled. The man nodded and began pushing his way along the platform through the crowds.

". . . and that mission," Hitler's voice blared, "was to return my dearly beloved homeland to the German Reich!"

"One People, One Reich, One Führer! One People, One Reich, One Führer!" For minutes the chanting of the crowds in Linz blasted out over the loudspeakers. Valerie pressed herself close to her husband. Their bodies touched, as they had just two hours before in the large bed of their quiet bedroom in their Gentzgasse apartment . . .

They had been alone. They had made love, wildly, desperately, both knowing it was the last time for a long while, neither saying so. They had made love without a word, then lain side by side on their backs, silent, until Paul Steinfeld said, "Time to get dressed, darling."

Valerie was wearing a blue and white checked suit and a small blue cap over her blonde hair that shone like gold under the strong arc-lamps of the station. It fell over her shoulders in long waves. She looked very young, slender, and pretty, more like a teen-age girl than a woman of thirty-four. Her skin was clear and pale, her blue eyes suffused with love and grief as she looked at her husband.

Paul Steinfeld was wearing a brown suit with a fine white pinstripe. He was tall and slender. His abundant hair was the same color as his eyes—black. He was swarthy-skinned. An aquiline nose emphasized his strong profile, and high cheekbones gnarled his rugged face. Black eyebrows slanted upwards toward a broad forehead above a narrow face, giving him a permanently skeptical expression. His voice was deep, warm, and pleasant.

"*Heil Hitler*, what would the gentleman like?" The man with the hot-dog cart had reached them. He also sold beer, lemonade, rolls, candy, and small tin swastikas with pins. Steinfeld bought a large bag of lemon drops.

"... I had faith in this mission, lived my whole life for it, and I believe I have now fulfilled it!" The clamor that broke out after these words was deafening. The loudspeakers crackled with the strain. "Führer, we thank you! Führer, we thank you! Führer, we thank you!"

Surreptitiously Paul Steinfeld opened the bag and emptied its contents into his pocket. Valerie watched him uncomprehendingly as he tore the paper bag slowly and carefully in two, along a bizarrely zigzagged line. The din all around them was deafening, he spoke directly into her ear: "Take a look. I will keep the top half, you take the bottom part. If anyone comes claiming to have news from me, he must identify himself by showing you the top half. And it has to fit exactly with the half you have. So keep your piece safely."

"But we already agreed on *Faith of Hellas.*"

"*Sieg Heil! Sieg Heil! Sieg Heil!*"

"*One* sign of identification is not enough. I've been thinking about it. Who knows what the situation is going to be? If someone does come to you from me, you have to be sure of him. Just as I have to be sure."

"You?" She was talking directly into his ear also. Around them people were pushing, shoving and shouting. "How do you mean, you?"

"It's possible you might find someone who can get to me. In that case, you give him the scrap of paper."

"That means you will have only *one* identification sign."

"But I'll be in England by then, I hope. You're staying here, so you'll be in a much more dangerous spot than I. Valerie, don't, please! Please, sweetheart, don't cry ..."

"I'm trying not to," she sobbed. "It—it just came ... I can't help it! It's so terrible. I'm so frightened for you ..."

He hugged her to him. Do you think I'm not scared for you? he thought. I've never been so afraid for a person in my life as I am for you, my love, left behind, all alone and helpless, and I can't help you, nobody can help you, that's what the man from "Gildemeester" told me.

Using Dutch money and brave collaborators, the "Organisation Gildemeester" had for years been helping persons whose lives were threatened by the Nazis to escape into other countries. The collaborators had passports, visas, and official stamps, and could deliver forged papers overnight if need be. That had been the case with Paul Steinfeld. Not only had he been the chief newscaster of Radio Vienna, he had also worked for many years as First Political Correspondent. The "Organization Gildemeester" knew that he was on the Nazi's list of people to be arrested, and were getting him out of the country as fast as possible.

But only *him* ...

"We can do nothing for your wife and son," the man had said. "Passports are in short supply, and we have to save them for people in danger of their lives. Your wife and son are not in any such danger. They will be kept under constant surveillance, your wife will be interrogated, her passport will be revoked and letters from other countries confiscated—but nothing worse than that will happen to her, at least not for the time being. It's regrettable, but you can't send for your wife later, nor for your son. The Nazis will never allow them to leave the country, because they will hope to learn something about your whereabouts. But please be careful about every line you write. The best thing would be not to write at all. It's hard, I know. But we just don't have enough passports. Please explain to your wife ..."

Paul Steinfeld had explained to Valerie.

And now she says she's frightened for me. For me! And I must not show her how frightened I am for her. I must not show her how little courage I have left.

"Frightened?" Steinfeld grinned. "Nothing will happen to me! *Ubi bene, ibi patria.* Which means in free translation: my country is where my legs are!"

She had to smile, through tears.

Now *I* feel like yelling, he thought, and whispered into her ear: "You must not forget how to laugh! I want to see your laughing face when I come back!"

"When you come back ..."

Hitler's voice ranted and raved. "With burning heart and fanatical determination I have toiled at my great purpose of bringing the Ostmark, this blooming garden, home into the community to which it has rightfully belonged for immeasurable centuries ..."

The loudspeakers were straining again. *"Sieg Heil! Sieg Heil! Sieg Heil!"*

"Of course I'm coming back," Paul Steinfeld whispered into Valerie's ear. "What else did you think? I'll be back soon." Will I really? Will I ever come back? There'll be a war, he thought. I'm forty-three years old. In 1914, when I went in as a volunteer, they were all shouting, at a railroad

119

station like this one, "We'll be home by Christmas!" Home by Christmas. How long will this new war last? Steinfeld spoke to her tenderly:

"So don't forget how to laugh, whatever happens. Otherwise I'll ask for a divorce, understand?" Valerie nodded, smiling through her tears. She pressed her body against his once again.

"God the Almighty made my dream a reality! And so I can, in the face of history,—"

"Sieg Heil! Sieg Heil! Sieg Heil!" Even Hitler's voice was drowned out by the jubilant cheers of the crowds in Linz.

The train let out a long, high-pitched whistle, then a second and a third—they were inaudible. A porter brusquely separated Valerie from her husband.

"All aboard! Something wrong, sir? The train is leaving!"

It was a fact: the train was slowly pulling out. The exasperated porter guided Steinfeld onto the runningboard of a coach as it glided by, gave him a push up, jumped in after him and slammed the door. A moment later Steinfeld had pulled the window down and was stretching his hand out toward Valerie. She grabbed it and began to run. We didn't even have a chance to kiss, she thought.

The platform was crammed with waving, screaming, crying people. Valerie bumped into many of them, hurt herself, stumbled and would have fallen under the wheels if Steinfeld's big, strong hand had not held on to her with an iron grip.

"And so, in the face of history, . . .—"

"Führer, lead us and we'll obey! Lead us, Führer, we will obey!"

Valerie could see that her husband was shouting something.

"I can't hear you!" she shouted back.

He leaned out of the window, yelling with all his might.

"I can't hear a word!" she shouted desperately. The train was picking up speed, the end of the platform was coming up.

Paul Steinfeld shouted as loudly as he could. But all Valerie could hear was: ". . . do . . ."

"Do what? Do what?"

". . . in the face of history, I can declare: my beloved Ostmark—"

"Heil! Heil! Heil! Heil!"

Valerie lost a shoe. Steinfeld noticed. In a flash he let go of

120

her hand. Inches before the end of the platform Valerie, staggering wildly, recovered her balance. When she looked up she saw her husband, a long way off now, waving still and shouting. She waved back.

"My beloved Ostmark has come home—"

"Sieg Heil! Sieg Heil! Sieg Heil!"

The last of the coaches slid by. Valerie could no longer see her husband. The long train was gliding along in a wide curve between a labyrinth of tracks and a host of white, red, and green lights. Its taillights disappeared. Valerie hobbled back to where her shoe lay. She bent down to slip it back on.

". . . come home to the German Reich!"

Another roar from the crowd.

"One People, One Reich, One Führer! One People, One Reich, One Führer!"

Valerie straightened up. Clenched in her left hand was the torn scrap of paper. It depressed her that she had been unable to hear the last words her husband had tried to call out to her. It depressed her throughout the next four years.

32

The little oven in the tea room rumbled like thunder.

"Your husband is well, Frau Steinfeld," Nora said.

Valerie shut her eyes for a second, bowed her head, and bit into her lower lip. When she spoke she kept her gaze fixed on the ground, and her voice shook: "Four years, four years I've waited for this moment . . ."

She raised her head and looked at her visitor with blue eyes glistening with tears and so bright with happiness that Nora felt sick to her stomach. "I am grateful to you. Thank you . . . Thank you . . ." Several times over she repeated the same words of gratitude, with Nora feeling more and more ill at the thought of what she had to tell this woman. Why me, she thought bitterly. I'm not good at such things. It's enough to make me throw up.

"Why do you look so angry?" Valerie asked, puzzled.

I'm losing control of myself, Nora thought, furious with

121

herself, and answered, "Angry? What nonsense! Why should I be angry?"

"Or is there something wrong with Paul? Is he ill? His liver! He always had problems with his liver! Please tell me the truth! I—"

"Stop! You must believe what I tell you. It's the absolute truth. If you don't want to believe me—"

"I do, I do!" Valerie brushed a strand of her hair out of her eyes that had fallen across her forehead. "Please, Miss Hill, you have to understand. It's four years since I heard from him. I haven't had a single line. Everything he wrote was confiscated."

"I understand. Have you had to go through a lot?"

"It hasn't been easy. House searches. Interrogation by the Gestapo at the "Metropole." They took my passport away, just as my husband had predicted. And I kept having to go to the "Metropole" for interrogation, questions and questions—and I didn't have the answers. I really didn't. They must have noticed I wasn't lying, and let me go time and again. They never really did anything to me, nor to the boy." Valerie suddenly asked: "How do you know about my husband and myself?"

"I'm—in the diplomatic corps, a courier," Nora answered. "I fly back and forth between Vienna and Lisbon. In Lisbon I had some business with an English colleague. We became friends. He told me he had just met your husband in London. That's how the connection started."

Valerie nodded.

"You're in love with that Englishman, aren't you?"

"Yes," Nora said.

"Dear me, what's going to happen with you two?"

"We intend to marry as soon as the war's over. Are you sure nobody can hear us in here?"

"Certain."

For a moment Nora felt happy and free from the sordidness of the war. "Yes, Jack and I plan to get married. And live in England. He's inherited a pub there, in the country. On the Sussex coast, near Hastings. I've seen photographs of it. Big, big trees all round, on a country road with rows and rows of poplars—" She broke off. "But what's all that to you? I'm here to talk about your husband!" Valerie was hanging on Nora's every word. "He wanted to write to you, but my friend dissuaded him. It would have been too dangerous for me to have tried to smuggle in a letter, you understand?"

122

"Of course."

"And so *I'm* your husband's letter. Do you trust me?"

"Yes," Valerie said, and wiped her eyes with the back of one dusty hand. "I trust you."

"Good. Your husband has a small apartment in London, at 30 Eaton Mews South. First he had to go to the Isle of Man, like all refugees. Then he needed to get residence and work permits. He got them more than three years ago. People with his experience were in demand. Now he's working as a newscaster in the BBC's German Service."

Valerie's face lit up with a smile.

"So he really made it! I thought so! I thought so! And it really was his voice I heard!" Valerie pressed a hand to her temples. "I didn't know what had happened to him, not even whether he had managed to get out. I had to wait such a long time without any news at all. I thought perhaps he might be working as a broadcaster in London—*if* he had managed to get as far as London. But how was I to find out? With the old radio I have at home you get the BBC only at night—and that's too dangerous."

"Because of the boy?" Nora asked.

"Because of Heinz, yes. Then the "Minerva 405" came on the market." Valerie pointed to the large radio set. "I bought one right away. And I prayed to God to let me hear his voice, please God. A few days later I did hear a voice that sounded like his. And the more I listened to it, the more it sounded like Paul. In the end I felt *almost* completely sure. And happy. So very happy!"

"Mr. Landau allows you to listen in to London from here?"

Valerie shook her head. "He nearly dies in his shoes every time. He's so terrified I think he'd like to kill me, that's how scared he is. It's forbidden after all, and he's a Party member."

"So I noticed."

"He was too afraid not to be. He's one of the best persons in the world, Martin—Mr. Landau, I mean. We've known each other for a long time, that's why I call him Martin. When we're alone."

"I know."

"His sister Tilly wouldn't let me listen in if she knew! But Martin doesn't give me away! I hear the midday broadcasts every day, you know. I cook something for him and myself for lunch here in the tea-room—sometimes I bring something from home—then I hurry him a bit so as not to miss the beginning of the broadcast. The store closes for lunch, you know. I clear the things away and wash the dishes, then I take that"—Valerie pointed to a large, colorful woollen blanket on the old sofa—"and cuddle up next to the radio with the blanket over my head and over the radio, and I listen to London. I often ... I often hear him. Yesterday was the last time ..."

"When?"

"Yesterday. In the evening."

"Yesterday ..." Nora Hill repeated. She was thinking, This woman believes she heard her husband's voice yesterday, but Jack told me Paul Steinfeld was on holiday this week. So it can't have been his voice.

"Naturally, she's bound to believe she recognized her husband's voice," Jack Cardiff had said to Nora. "Let her believe it. It will make her happy. Even if she's always wrong."

"But how come?"

"According to what Steinfeld has told me," Jack Cardiff had said, "the broadcasters are not actually trained to adopt a uniform intonation, but the voices do tend to develop a likeness to each other, just as in a large family. They have a certain rhythm in common. Even the broadcasters themselves over there can't always say which one of them is talking at any given moment. And anyway, it's always difficult to distinguish between voices—all the more so over the radio, with all those jammers interrupting. Maybe Frau Steinfeld had her doubts sometimes, too ..."

Yes, the woman had had doubts sometimes, in the early days. But now she could hear the voice of her beloved husband, and her uncertainties had disappeared. Listening to the voice meant everything to her now.

So that is happiness, Nora Hill thought. It's one definition of it anyway. What a dirty world we live in. And now it's my job to break the news to her. Let's get it over with quickly!

"The noise was pretty terrible the day you went with your husband to the station to see him off, was it not?"

"Yes."

"Hitler was giving a speech. Your husband shouted something to you from the train, but you couldn't hear him."

"How do you know? Oh, of course!"

"Your husband told my friend, and he told me. What your husband was shouting was, 'You've got to do everything, everything to protect the boy!'" Valerie sprang to her feet, her face ashen, her eyes agitated again.

"Protect him? Is he in danger then, Heinz?"

"Yes," said Nora. I've got to be blunt, she thought. There's no way to spare her feelings. That's why I'm here.

"Miss Hill, listen to me, the boy is all I have left! If anything should happen to him—"

"Nothing will happen to him."

"But you said he's in danger!"

"Yes, he is in danger. But nothing will happen to him if you do exactly as I say—which is what your husband asked me to say. It's just a precaution."

"What do you mean, precaution?"

"Frau Steinfeld, your husband is a Jew. You are an Aryan, as they call it. So that makes your son a so-called First-Degree Half-Caste." Sweat began to break out on her brow—there was somebody standing outside in the darkness of the stacks.

He had crept in silently under cover of the darkness, and had been standing there for only a few seconds. Nora had an especially fine ear. She caught the sound of short, quick-drawn breaths.

From where I stand, she thought, he's to the right of the entrance to this little room, on the side leading to the stacks. Martin Landau is in the store, and the store is off to the left. I kept my eyes on the opening the whole time, and Landau did not pass it. So it can't be Landau who's hiding in the stacks to the right of the door, eavesdropping on us. It's a trap, Nora thought. I've walked into a trap. I know exactly what to do. We're trained to deal with situations like this one. The training usually turns out to have been childishly simplified. It's experience that counts. If you don't learn from experience, you die. I'm still alive, and intend to stay that way. Frau Steinfeld or no Frau Steinfeld, I'm not going to give up my life for anybody.

Nora's feelings hardened. Gone the pity, the sentimentality. She was thinking and acting now with ice-cold precision. She had got to her feet without a sound as soon as she had heard the breathing outside. Valerie was staring at her. What if that Mr. Landau gave me away because he was so terrified? What if he notified the police, the Gestapo? What if some such swine is standing outside there, just a few feet away, getting ready to arrest me and the Steinfeld woman—to hell with the Steinfeld woman, it's *me* I'm worried about. But I won't be

125

arrested if I can just get out of here. All I need is to get as far as my chief, Carl Flemming. He's a real big shot: his sister married Kaltenbrunner's adjutant, and Kaltenbrunner likes Flemming. If I can get to Flemming, the lousy dog, I'll be safe from the Gestapo.

I won't shoot the guy behind the door just knock him down with the butt of my pistol. That way they'll never be able to prove it was my gun that did it.

She coiled herself and jumped. Valerie had turned the light off in the passageway outside when they had entered the little room. Nora could barely make out anything except a bright smudge in the darkness: the man's face.

The white smudge was all Nora had to judge her aim by. Holding Jack Cardiff's pistol by the barrel she let go a blow as hard as she could muster, aiming for the side of the temples. That was the surest spot, she had found that out twice already. Now she confirmed it for the third time. The white smudge dropped from sight. There was a gurgling sound and the thud of a fall. Then a scream from Valerie Steinfeld. Afterwards, dead silence. Nora Hill ran like mad, up the passageway and into the store, the pistol at the ready in her hand in case there was a second man to deal with. She was running so fast she couldn't pull up before colliding with the old bear at the entrance. He swayed, almost toppled. Nora had reached the door, jabbed the handle down. The door would not open, however hard Nora rattled. It was locked and barred.

33

"What's the matter, George? I said I didn't want to be disturbed!" Nora Hill had sat up straight in her armchair with an angry movement, and was glaring at her lover who, after a cursory knock at the door, had entered the living-room of her apartment, interrupting her story in midstream. Manuel had risen, too.

Nora Hill's manservant, confidant, and lover twiddled at a button on his dinner-jacket, embarrassed. "I'm very sorry,

Madame. I would never have dared to disturb you, but the Flying Dutchman is here." Nora Hill laid her long, silver cigarette-holder on an ashtray over the open fireplace.

"Good Lord!" she said. "The Flying Dutchman. I'd completely forgotten him. Drunk again, I suppose?"

"And how, Madame. He's running amok. I've tried everything to——" The athletic man in the dinner jacket did not get the chance to finish his sentence. He was shoved to one side by a large man who came bustling into the room. Voices, music, and singing came into the room as the door was opened. The big, strong man had blonde hair and a ruddy, round face. He was indeed very drunk. Manuel kept expecting him to fall down, but his movements were agile and graceful.

"At last, Madame!" Reaching Nora, he bent over and kissed both her hands. Even that did not cause him to lose his balance, although he swayed a little. "I've just arrived from the Hague. Freshened up a little and changed my clothes. And this so-and-so here didn't want to let me in to see you, a regular old customer like me." He straightened up and glared over at George.

"Don't be angry with him, my dear." Nora stroked one of his pudgy, red hands. "I'm in the middle of a discussion." She pointed to Manuel. "Mr. Aranda, Mr. de Brakeleer." The man called de Brakeleer took no notice whatever of Manuel.

"Do you have the new feathers? You told me you would have them by today. For goodness' sake, Madame, don't disappoint me! I was so excited during the flight over, I just had to keep drinking. If you'll tell me that you don't have——"

"Of course I have the new feathers."

"From a *bird of paradise?*"

"From a bird of paradise. They're the most beautiful you can imagine."

De Brakeleer could not contain his pleasure. He clapped his hands and did a little jig on the spot. "Birds of paradise!" he exclaimed. "Oh, oh, birds of paradise!"

"A friend of mine sent the feathers."

"Where are they?" the ruddy Dutchman shouted, quite beside himself.

"George will give them to you." Nora turned to her man-servant. "They're in the Maria-Theresa cupboard in the bottom drawer."

De Brakeleer clapped his hands again. "I can feel it

127

already," he shouted. "I can feel it already, it's going to be just tremendous today."

"That's for sure," said Nora. "The mirror-room, as usual?"

"Yes, of course."

"And Yvonne?"

"As always, yes."

"George, tell Yvonne, please."

"Yes, Madame."

"You're an angel, Madame, a true angel. A thousand thanks."

Nora gave George a signal. The manservant bowed to de Brakeleer and escorted him out of the room.

"Please excuse the interruption." Nora lifted herself out of the armchair and swung on her crutches over to the bookshelves with the built-in TV. "I'll go on with the story in a moment. I just want to see how things are going. He's one of my most difficult customers, that Flying Dutchman."

"Why do you call him the Flying Dutchman?"

"You'll see in a moment," said Nora, opening the small doors of the TV set. Manuel observed that the set had an unusually large number of knobs.

"To hell with that Dutchman!" Grant was saying in the child's room. "Nora was just going strong."

"She can't neglect her business," replied Fedor Santarin, who had lain down on the bed underneath the loudspeaker. "We've got time. We have to wait for Mercier anyway ..."

Nora had switched on the set and pressed one of the control buttons. To Manuel's surprise the mirror-room came up on the screen, complete, filmed from a point halfway up one wall.

"You have closed circuit TV?"

Nora focussed the picture. "Did you think it was just an ordinary set? Do you think I have time to watch television? Every room has a corner with a shower, washbasin, and bidet. You've noticed that, haven't you?" There was pride in her voice.

"Yes."

"Very well. And every room has a small, built-in TV camera also. Hidden, of course. Pretty complex set-up. Cost me a fortune, too. But I do have to know what's going on in the rooms any time I want, don't you agree?" She was thinking: And there's a video-tape machine here, too, behind the TV. I can record every scene that takes place in this room on

128

film and tape, and play it back as often as I like on a screen. But you needn't know about that, my friend.

"The girls' profession is not without its risks," Nora said. "If they think they're in danger, they only need to press a button. Then their room number lights up on this board over here. I can switch the set on immediately to see what's going on, and if necessary send George and a few other men in to help."

Manuel looked towards the wall by the window. He saw a small black box with a glass face, like the ones used in hotels for summoning waiters or maids.

"Here they are now," Nora said.

Manuel looked at the screen, and saw the Dutchman entering the mirror-room. He had one arm around the redhead Yvonne, who was now wearing a black cocktail dress. In her hand she had a bundle of apparently magnificent, colorful feathers, every single one of them at least two feet long, very thin, and lined with fine hairs.

"Tonight," de Brakeleer's voice could be heard to say, "I'm going to fuck you so hard, my soft little chicken, that you'll go blind and deaf."

"Yes, darling, yes," said Yvonne. The two disappeared behind a screen.

"It'll take a moment until they're both undressed and he's been prepared," Nora Hill said. She swung over to the fireplace on her crutches, took the cigarette holder and her whisky glass, and hobbled back to the TV set. "Just a few minutes more, then I'll go on with my story." The TV screen now showed only an empty room. The sound of voices could be heard indistinctly from behind the partition.

"How did you become a secret agent?" Manuel asked.

Nora shrugged her shoulders. "My foster parents were killed in an accident—a truck drove straight into their hay-wagon. Both died on the spot. I was put into an orphanage. I stayed there six years. I was very precocious and developed early. The Director of the orphanage was crazy about me—in fact, I made him crazy about me. He raped me when I was twelve years old, because I wanted to be raped. But he didn't realize that. I blackmailed him, of course. He was married and had three children. He was the first man I ever black-mailed. Not for very much, he didn't have much. But he did arrange for me to go to Berlin on a scholarship to St. Cecelia High School. He had a sister who lived in Berlin. He arranged for me to move in with her. Well, come on, get on with it," she said to the TV set.

"And how did it go on?"

Nora took a sip from her drink, then blew some smoke rings. "How did it go on! At fifteen I was the mistress of a banker, Arthur von Knichtlein. A despicable jerk. Married. I milked him all right: my own apartment, my first mink, my first jewels . . . I milked all my men, except one . . ."

"Yes, darling, yes," said Yvonne. The two disappeared behind a screen.

"Jack Cardiff."

"Jack Cardiff." She nodded, pulled on her cigarette, and took a big swallow from her drink. "He was the only one. But otherwise . . . Herr von Knichtlein had a good friend in the Ministry of the Interior. On the day he had his stroke— Herr von Knichtlein, I mean, it happened in the bank—I lost no time in becoming the lover of the man from the Ministry. I was seventeen then. And beautiful, too—I suppose I can allow myself that little boast now. I was constantly changing lovers, and soon I was *the* talk of Berlin. At twenty-two I was a rich woman. A villa in Grunewald, a car, a bank account. And jewelry galore!"

Nora laughed. "That was my big obsession: jewelry and precious stones. In 1942, when I got dragged into this Steinfeld affair, I already had a veritable fortune in jewelry and precious stones in a bank vault in Lisbon."

What a fantastic story, Manuel thought, keeping his eyes on the woman on crutches, a truly fantastic story.

"I picked men up, dropped them again, passed from one to the next—why shouldn't I talk about it? I was the Queen of the Foreign Office. When the war broke out and things became serious—it looked as though I might have to go to work in a factory—I started to look around for an interesting man. It turned out to be Herr Flemming, whose sister had married Kaltenbrunner's adjutant. When I was twenty-five Herr Flemming sent me on my first mission abroad, to Lisbon, as a courier. His department was working out of Berlin in those days. Later everything was decentralized and we ended up in Vienna. But at that time, when Germany was still going from victory to victory, I always started out from Berlin." Nora gave a hoarse laugh. "Well, anyway, as long as we were victorious I worked for the Germans. Then later, when we weren't so successful, I became a double agent."

"And in 1942?"

"In 1942 I met Jack Cardiff. We fell in love. From that moment on I worked only for the British, and the information I fed back to my chief Flemming was always either false or valueless. And I delivered correct and important information about the Germans to Jack. After all, I got it all directly from Flemming. He was almost as good in bed as Jack, by the way. I couldn't help thinking that if that were the only criterion we would win the war. Everybody was delighted with the job I was doing, the Nazis *and* the British. Jack was very clever at giving me dummy information. And because Flemming had assigned me to Jack officially, it was safe for me to be seen anywhere in Lisbon with my lover . . ."

Yvonne had emerged from behind the partition, stark naked. She hopped into the room in a bent-over position, clucking like a hen: "Quaaa, quaa, qua-quaa! Quaaaa, quaa, quaa, quaaaa!!"

Manuel sat bolt upright.

Next, the Dutchman appeared on the screen. He was completely naked also, big and massive, and with the entire bundle of paradise-bird feathers stuck into his behind. Willem de Brakeleer marched behind Yvonne like a cockerel, arms flaying, Yvonne's ass in front of his nose, her feet shuffling across the floor, her cackling resounding through the air. "Cock-a-doodle-doo!" Brakeleer hooted. "Cock-a-doodle-doooooo!"

"Charming, don't you think?" said Nora. Surreptitiously she pressed a button next to the TV set. Manuel did not notice it, because she stood so that her body was in front of the button which switched on the videotape machine. The machine would now run automatically for fifteen minutes, filming and recording everything, then switch itself off automatically. Nora Hill felt immense satisfaction. It was one of your colleagues who asked for this recording, you swine, you dirty blackmailers who think you can listen in and watch everything and then put the screws to me. But you don't know everything. You're in a for a big surprise.

"Quaaaa, quaaa, quaaa!" Yvonne shuffled and hobbled, her fanny outstretched. Willem de Brakeleer pranced along behind her, the magnificent feathers spreading from his arsehole like peacock feathers, his breath coming in short, heavy gasps, cackling out loud: "Cock-a-doodle-doo! Cock-a-doodle-doooo!"

"I often wish," said Fedor Santarin, listening to the sounds coming through the loudspeaker above his head, "I could be

131

as perverse as you Westerners. It makes me quite nervous. We Russians are much too normal."

"Don't be sad," Grant said to him consolingly. "You've got the top reputation internationally in rape!"

"Ah, yes, rape," Santarin sighed. "But that's a perfectly normal activity!"

On the TV screen the Dutchman was still strutting up and down cackling loudly, while Yvonne, in front of him, also kept on cackling. She hopped onto a bed, and crouched down with her backside high in the air. De Brakeleer stalked up to her.

"Cock-a-doodle-dooooooo!" he croaked, but suddenly didn't sound too happy.

"Quaaaaaa, quaaaaa, quaaaaa!" cackled Yvonne, reaching behind her but finding nothing much in her hand.

"Can't get it up again!" said Nora. "Why does he always drink so much beforehand?" Manuel watched Yvonne doing her best to help the Dutchman using her hand, mouth, and voice. The Dutchman was angry now, and stamping on the ground.

"Quaaaaa, quaaaaa, quaaaaa!!"

"Cock-a-doodle-doooo, dammit! It's got to work sometime, keep doing that, more, harder!"

"Quaaaaaa, quaaaaaa!"

Nothing helped.

"Poor man," said Nora. "He must be desperate. I can't tell you how often he's tried. And with all sorts of feathers! He always wants new ones, more beautiful than the last. Try getting them! Costs him a fortune."

"And all for nothing."

"As you can see. He managed to get an erection with heron feathers once for about half a minute, then it went all squashy again." Nora Hill sipped her drink. "Just look at Yvonne. She really tries hard. A girl can't try any harder than that, can she?"

"No, I guess not."

"Quaaaa, quaaaa, quaaaaa!" cackled Yvonne, busy at her endeavors. "What's the matter, sweetie, don't you like me?"

"Cock-a-doodle-doooo!" the Dutchman croaked, tears in his eyes. I just hope it's all getting onto the tape, Nora thought. Aloud she said, "That's enough, I think."

Switching off the TV set she swung back over to the fireplace and let herself glide slowly into her armchair. "Excuse

132

the interruption, but business is business. Where was I when ... Oh, yes, the shop door had been locked. I was rattling at the handle ..."

34

She rattled the handle of the locked door. It didn't make sense. Why was it locked? The deathly silence in the store made her feel suddenly frightened.

Turning round, Nora Hill raced back along the passageway to the stacks. The light was now on in the first rows. Valerie Steinfeld was leaning over the prostrate figure of a man, half covering him. Nora gripped her pistol tightly—this time the right way round. I'm going to get out of here, she thought, I'm going to get out of here. Even if the guy down there is still unconscious, he won't be for long. She took three steps forward. Martin Landau was no longer unconscious. *Martin Landau!*

Nora had not been thinking of him at all during the last exciting seconds. But there he was stretched out on the dusty floor, eyes open, groaning softly, with a handkerchief pressed to his right temple. The handkerchief was already soaked with blood, and blood was dripping onto the floor and staining his suit. The scene did not shock Nora, nor cause her to feel any sympathy for Landau. Her uppermost emotion was anger.

"What sort of idiotic games do you think you're playing?" she hissed at him.

He raised his eyes. "You—you—" Martin Landau began.

"Do you have any bandages?" Nora asked, turning to Valerie.

"In the tearoom."

"Go and fetch what you have."

"It's bleeding!" Landau moaned. His voice stuck in his throat. "I can't stand the sight of blood."

"I'll put a bandage around your head and then you won't see any more blood. I'm really sorry, but what were you doing creeping around there like that? How did you get over to this side of the tearoom anyway?"

133

"The Gestapo—"

"*What?*"

He swallowed some blood that had run into his mouth and looked at Nora.

"What do you mean, the Gestapo? Talk!"

"A man . . . must have been from the Gestapo. I kept watch through the door while you were here. He was standing there the whole time . . . never let the shop out of his sight."

"There's no one standing there now," said Nora.

"There was."

"Where?"

"Over there, directly opposite, on the corner of Neuer Markt."

"What did he look like?"

"Tall, thin, blue overcoat, blue Homburg—"

"A Gestapo man wearing a Homburg? Have you ever seen a Gestapo agent?" Nora's tone was ironic. But the seed of doubt had already been planted in her heart. What if this coward was not just imagining things? What if I really am being watched? A blue Homburg—perhaps the man *was* tailing me? And maybe he *was* a Gestapo agent? Wearing the blue Homburg as a cover! I mustn't get too clever. Perhaps he's someone quite different. Everybody's spying on everybody else these days. Who knows who it was? Who knows who it is? I'm scared. Very scared. Maybe it's not this fellow Landau's fault. Maybe he's telling the truth.

"I'm sorry," said Nora Hill, contrition in her voice. "Forgive me, please. I'm really sorry."

"I was only trying to save you. And that's the thanks I get! I have a weak heart, that's why I wasn't drafted . . ."

Valerie returned carrying a tin box marked with a red cross on a white circle. Nora opened the lid.

"Good," she said. "Now some water. Cold. To wash the blood off." Valerie hurried back into the tearoom. Nora got to her feet. "I'll be right back!"

She ran into the store and up to the main entrance. With her eyes directly above the top edge of the green curtain, she looked carefully up and down the length of the Seilergasse scanning every doorway as far as the corner of the Neuer Markt. Then she ran back to Landau, who lay there still moaning. Valerie was kneeling by his side, a basin of water next to her.

"Sit up straight," said Nora. He did as she told him, groaning. "There's no one there in a Homburg and a blue over-coat."

"Yes, there is."

"No, there isn't, for God's sake!" It was fear that made her react so sharply.

"Then he's hiding. I couldn't stand his staring any more. So I hung the sign 'Back Soon' on the door, went outside, locked the door behind me, and—"

"Take that handkerchief away!"

He took it away. The wound was superficial, but large. Nora began to apply iodine liberally. He whimpered with pain.

"Get hold of yourself!"

"What then? What did you do then, Martin?" asked Valerie, softly. She had gone pale.

"I walked down the Seilergasse—ouch!"

"Don't be such a baby! And then?"

"And then the man in the Homburg hat stood still and watched me, followed me with his eyes."

"Sit up." Nora began winding the bandage round his head. He groaned with pain.

"Get out of here! Get out! Out!" he suddenly started shouting, beating the ground with clenched fists.

"Martin, Martin, please! We weren't finished. Miss Hill still has something to tell me, something very important."

"But not here!"

"It's news from Paul!"

"Then you get out with her, dammit!"

"But where to? Where to, Martin? In broad daylight!"

"That's your worry, I don't care!" He grabbed the blood-stained handkerchief and threw it away, then picked up the old-fashioned telephone.

"Martin!" Valerie shouted. "You wouldn't—"

"You bet I will! And right now! I'm not going to throw my life away for that bitch!"

Nora and Valerie looked at each other.

"It's no use," Nora said.

"But you can't! You must tell me." Valerie was holding on to her. "I have an idea!" Valerie took a deep breath. "The Church of St. Stephen! Less than two minutes from here!"

"That's a good idea," said Landau, taking his hand away from the telephone. "Go there, it'll be quite empty at this time. It's dark, too. Go across the Hof and the Spiegelgasse. When you've gone, I'll take another look around and open up the front door again. And if the man with the Homburg comes looking for you—"

"He won't come, don't worry, Mr. Landau."

"Lie down, Martin," Valerie said. "Don't open the shop again for the moment. Wait till I get back. It won't be long. Then we can always say we were both out, and that you fell and *I* bandaged you up."

"I hate you," said Martin Landau in a low voice to Nora Hill. "I hate you—"

"You go on ahead," Valerie broke in hastily, speaking to Nora. "Here, here is a flashlight. You don't even know where the shelters are! Go out through the back entrance to the stacks, there's only one way. Do you know where to go when you get to the Spiegelgasse?"

"Yes."

"Sit down in the church somewhere where it's very dark," Valerie said.

"Yes."

"I'll follow in a few minutes."

"Yes," said Nora, and left. She had to cross four large warehouse floors, pistol in her right hand, flashlight in her left. Her crocodile-skin handbag hung from her left forearm. There was a musty smell, like old leather. Mountains of books everywhere. Nora had to shine the flashlight all over the place, and had some difficulty finding the way through. At last she reached the iron door. She switched off the flashlight and put it down on a table. Then she clicked back the safety-catch on her pistol. She was in the grip of cold panic, but felt completely devoid of scruples. They won't get me alive, she thought. Dear God, please! Sweat broke out on her forehead. She pushed down the handle of the iron door, heaved it open, then quickly pressed her back to the wall next to the door frame. Turning her head to one side she looked out into the open. Just an old courtyard full of rubbish. A barren chestnut-tree in the middle of it. But not a living soul. All quiet. Absolute quiet. Nora took a step forward. Another. Another. Now she was framed in the doorway, looking over the entire courtyard. It was deserted.

But maybe somebody's hiding behind the garbage pails, behind the rubbish, she thought. I've got to get out of here. Out! She stepped out of the doorway, gun at the ready though half-hidden by her handbag. Two steps. Three. Nothing. Her legs were like jelly as she crossed the courtyard. Any moment she expected to be called from behind. Then she

136

would have to whirl around and—no, better to do what the man asked first—bullshit! Hands up, he would say! Drop the gun! Drop it! No, her only chance was to shoot first. Then run, run . . . One step. Another step. Another.

Nothing.

As Nora neared the entrance to the house leading on to the Spiegelgasse she could feel her back soaking with sweat. There was nobody in the courtyard. And in the Spiegelgasse? She moved quickly out through the entrance. She felt surer of herself now. A look to the right, a look to the left. No blue Homburg, no blue overcoat. A few passers-by only. Nobody took any notice of her.

I knew it, Nora thought, slipping the pistol back into her pocket, this Landau fellow sees ghosts, ghosts! Let's get the hell over to Carl Flemming right away. Then forget the whole scene. I'm not crazy! Risk my life for others?! The pair of them in there are irresponsible, the man anyway. As for the woman—what is she to me, what's her boy to me?

Nora Hill began walking down the Spiegelgasse with a quick, energetic stride.

I've had just about enough, she was thinking. Even Jack will have to see there was nothing more I could do to help in there. He loves me, after all, and wouldn't want to lose me. As for going into St. Stephen's Cathedral! Not me. I'm not about to go to the Cathedral, Frau Steinfeld, I'm not going to have anything more to do with this crazy game, not on your life. You'll be looking for me in vain there in the church, Frau Steinfeld. Sorry. Very sorry. Go to hell, Frau Steinfeld.

35

"Deus indulgentiarum Domine: da animae famuli tui Alois Zwerzina, cujus anniversarium depositionis diem commemoramus . . ." The gaunt old priest chanted the words in subdued tones from the Chapel of St. Catherine out into the massive nave of St. Stephen's Cathedral. The Chapel of St. Catherine was one of the numerous side chapels in the Cathedral.

137

The outside walls of the Cathedral were gray; inside, the atmosphere was dark and gloomy. The only light came from a few clusters of candles. The medieval stained-glass windows behind the main altar had been removed, as had the most precious of the paintings and statues, relics and triptychs of St. Stephen. They were now deep under ground in various locations in the Greater German Reich, "stored," as the designation went, in the dry air of salt mines. This was to protect them in case the Cathedral was hit by bombs.

Shadows moved through the vastnesses of the church. Shoes scraped. Men and women wandered about, stood still, bowed deep in prayer. They seemed mere silhouettes. Only St. Catherine's Chapel was warmly illuminated from the light of many candles. There were flowers in front of the altar, the scent of incense wafted across, and the lean, old priest, assisted by an eager acolyte with a pimply face, was reciting a prayer. A woman dressed in black sat in the front pew of the chapel.

". . . refrigerii sedem, quietis beatudinem . . ."

That's a mass *"In Anniversario Defunctorum,"* Nora thought. She had been raised a Catholic by her foster parents. The priest was commemorating the death of a certain Mr. Alois Zwerzina. The woman in the pew must be the widow, or perhaps the sister or mother of the dead man. I'm damned if I know why I came here, she thought. I was determined never to see Valerie Steinfeld again. I'd got as far as the Graben, I'd even turned left to go and see Carl Flemming, then suddenly I turned around and ran over here. I'll be damned if that doesn't make me a fool who deserves all that's coming to her, Nora Hill thought angrily.

Some distance away, on the opposite side of the center nave, the man in the blue overcoat stood motionless in the shadow of some scaffolding. He had removed his blue Homburg. His eyes were fixed on Nora's back. Now they moved sideways. A second woman, wearing a gray coat and a headscarf, who had been wandering round the interior of the church for some time, seemed to have found what she was looking for. She walked with soft and deliberate steps towards Nora Hill, slid into the same pew, and sat down next to her. The man in the blue coat had a lean, hungry-looking face, piercing dark eyes, eyebrows that met above the nose, and dark hair cut short. He stepped back still further into the shadow of the scaffolding. His eyes narrowed to slits as he watched the two women start to whisper to each other.

36

"Thank God," whispered Valerie. "I couldn't find you . . . looked through the whole church . . . was beginning to be afraid you'd changed your mind. But no, you kept your word. You are a good person, I know you are. What is it you have to tell me, Miss Hill?"

"No *names!* First there's something I must know."

"Of course. Ask whatever you like. Please."

Horrible, Nora thought. Now that she's afraid she looks like a whipped animal. Where's her courage now, her self-control, her arrogance? Oh well, Nora thought, we are none of us heroes! She whispered in reply, "How old is your son now?"

"He'll be seventeen in May."

"Where does he go to school?"

"First he went to the academic high school. But the Director wanted his school to be for Aryans only. Heinz was the only half-caste. He was not a particularly good student. So when he was in fourth grade they told me they would fail him, or give him a good reference on condition that he leave the school."

"Then what?"

"I spoke with him and asked him what he wanted to do— there are all kinds of professional schools, I expect you know that?"

"*. . . et quia considerabat, quod hic, qui cum pietate dormitionem acciperant . . .*"

"Yes."

"Then he said his ambition was to become a chemist."

"A chemist?"

"Yes. He was tremendously interested in that subject. The State Institute is on the Hohe Warte. The course used to be six years. Now, with the war on it is only four. Chemistry graduates are needed badly in industry right now. Very badly. Aryans have the right to go to the university after the State Institute. They all get a graduation certificate and a diploma. Heinz is not permitted to go to the university, but he will be able to take a job as a chemical engineer in two years' time. He has suddenly become a good student. One of the best! Just imagine! No complaints any more, no headaches, everything's going smoothly—touch wood!"

Nora bent forward. "One more question, a very important one. Does Heinz hate his father?"

"Yes, he hates him, dreadfully," Valerie answered sadly, her head bowed. "For a long time he never suspected he was a half-caste. He even joined the Hitler Youth."

"What?"

"All his friends were in it. And he wanted to be with them so very much. I thought it safer that way. Everything went fine, until they asked for the Aryan I.D. in the school. Then I had to tell Heinz—"

"Why are you crying?"

"I remember the day they kicked him out of the Hitler Youth . . . he cursed his father. We had a job calming him down, Agnes and I . . . Agnes Peintinger . . . she used to be his nurse. She worked for us before he was born, now she does the housework for us."

"I know all about Agnes."

"My husband must have talked about her, of course! Well, Heinz was terribly upset. And furious. He swore at me for having married a Jew—" Valerie covered her face with her hands. "It was terrible, terrible! He felt like a criminal, rejected and despised like the lowest of the low—and all my fault! Agnes tried to talk some sense into him for months on end. Finally he began to forgive me; he hasn't completely done so to this day. But he hates his father like the plague. Is that not awful?"

"Awful? It's wonderful."

37

Nora Hill lay on the ruffled bed completely naked, eyes shining, hands clasped behind her head. It was a large bed in the bedroom of Jack Cardiff's elegant apartment on the wide

Avenida da Liberdade, near the large Praça do Marquês de Pombal, which had a lofty monument to the Marquês in the middle of the square. The Marquês had been Prime Minister under King Joseph the First, and a great reformer. Sunlight blazed into the room, sounds of cars and people came up from the streets below. It was a sultry day in Lisbon on the afternoon of October 3, 1942. Nora's plane was due to leave that evening. But there was still some time, she still had a few hours left. Her bags were already packed in the Hotel Aviz, where she always stayed.

Jack Cardiff came out of the living-room. He had put on a gray silk dressing-gown, and was pushing a small bar cart before him. He was a tall, slim man with bright eyes and a sunburnt face. Nora gazed at him happily. She loved him; a few moments earlier she had been in his embrace, locked to him on the bed, panting with desire and lust. She loved him, oh, how she loved him, his voice, his body, everything about him! A smile on her face, she watched him as he expertly mixed two gin-and-tonics. He handed her a glass.

"To a happy reunion, my darling," Jack said.

"To a happy reunion," Nora Hill echoed. After taking a drink she said, "Each time I think of Germany I am scared, terribly scared, that something will happen to separate us, take us away from each other—"

"Nothing is going to happen," he said. "I'm just as sad everytime I have to go to London. But we always come back together again, darling, and always will, right to the day this war ends."

"And then we can be together forever," she whispered. "You're my love. My only love. And you will always be my only love."

"And you mine, darling," Jack Cardiff said, pulling a heavy gold cigarette case from the pocket of his dressing gown and lighting two cigarettes with a gold lighter. "You've memorized everything I want you to tell Mr. Flemming?" He slid the cigarette case and the lighter—gifts from Nora—back into his pocket.

She nodded as he walked over to the bed, placed one of the cigarettes in her mouth, then kissed her nipples. He sat down on the bed and began stroking her thighs tenderly.

"Everything, I have it all by heart," said Nora. His hands were so soothing. "I have a lot to tell Flemming."

"If things don't happen that way, he will simply assume we've changed our plans. And that we might try to land in

Sicily. Or Greece. We can keep this up for a long time," said Cardiff.

"Is it really going to go on for a long time?"

"I'm afraid so, darling. Don't be sad. The day will come when we will beat the Germans . . ."

"What's wrong?" Nora looked anxiously at the only man she had ever loved. A certain tension in his voice and face had made her uneasy. "There's something worrying you!" The warm light of the midsummer afternoon slanted across the bedroom.

"Yes, Nora, there is. I didn't want to tell you about it at first. But I promised. And so I just put it off, till the last minute."

"Why?"

"Because it might put you in danger."

"I've been in danger for years. Tell me! You have to—you promised! Yes, *there*, stroke me there. Slowly, very slowly. To whom did you make the promise?"

"Paul Steinfeld," he replied.

"What does Steinfeld want?" Nora asked. Jack had already told her about this Austrian refugee in London, and about his wife Valerie and son Heinz, and about Steinfeld's anxieties concerning the welfare of his family.

"Listen," said Cardiff, taking a puff at his cigarette. "You know the BBC has simply fantastic intelligence, especially the German service. These people get the latest information out of Germany time and again—it borders on magic. Lately they've been getting reports that have worried Steinfeld a lot. He's a full-blooded Jew, though he was baptised a Protestant. His wife is Aryan. I can't stand that word, so help me! The son, who means everything to Steinfeld, is therefore a first-degree half-caste. If his father were only half-Jewish, the boy would be a second-degree half-caste; in that case, Steinfeld wouldn't be feeling so anxious about him—"

"Your hand. Put your hand here, please."

"Up to a short time ago the Nazis were leaving the first- and second-degree half-castes alone. Half-Jews were permitted to study, to join the army—"

"Only until the beginning of this year," Nora said.

"Exactly. Only until the beginning of this year. Since then, Himmler's radicals have begun to gain ground against Goebbels, who had wanted to put off the whole problem until after the war. First, all soldiers who were half-Jewish were sent home. Then all sorts of harassments started. They got worse.

First-degree half-castes, especially those with Jewish fathers, and all the more if those fathers had *emigrated*, were arrested, thrown into jail, and sent to labor camps. And Steinfeld says it's going to get even worse very soon. They have their sources of information. He knows what he's talking about."

"Well, so what?" Nora asked, taking Cardiff's hand in hers.

He was puffing nervously at his cigarette. "Steinfeld says the Nazis are preparing a new law according to which first-degree half-castes—with the exception of the Nazi big-shots and their relatives—will be treated as Jews. The war is going badly. Some distraction, some excitement is necessary to take people's minds off it. Hence, the new wave of terror. Naturally there's been a reaction among those concerned. Steinfeld told us they had learned of a whole spate of paternity suits mushrooming in Germany. They go something like this: the mother of a half-Jew, whose father's whereabouts are unknown, goes to court and swears her child is the offspring of an adulterous relationship with an Aryan man, disqualifying her own husband as the natural father."

Nora let go of Cardiff's hand and held out her glass. "Make me another one, please," she said. And while he fixed two more gin-and-tonics she remarked: "I hadn't heard of anything like that."

"The participants keep it quiet, naturally. The judges, too. It's not supposed to get any publicity. But the BBC has documented several dozen definite cases. And already some attorneys are specializing in these suits, which are quite complicated. The woman must find an Aryan man willing to swear on oath that he is the natural father. Steinfeld has been thinking for his own case of an old friend of his for whom his wife now works, the book dealer Landau. He's the only one Steinfeld can think of. Then there have to be witnesses! And a whole lot of other paraphernalia! I tell you, without a specialized attorney it's not possible. Steinfeld knows an attorney in Vienna who might be able and willing to do it, a staunch anti-Nazi! He would definitely take the case . . ."

"... *quia descendi de caelo, non ut faciliam voluntatem meam* ..." chanted the old priest in the cold, dark cathedral of St. Stephen. The sweet scent of incense mingled with Nora Hill's provocative perfume. Nora had told Valerie Steinfeld everything that Jack Cardiff had asked her to tell, had told the story as hastily and briefly as possible. Even a dark church was not an entirely safe place.

"The attorney you're to go to is called Forster, Otto Forster. His offices are in the Rotenturmstrasse."

No reply.

"Frau Steinfeld!"

No reply.

Nora nudged Valerie. Slowly Valerie raised her head. She suddenly seemed years older.

"Please don't look at me like that! Please, Miss, don't be angry with me! I ..." Valerie was gasping for breath. "I ... I have to think about it ... and talk it over with Martin ... nothing's happened to us yet, because we've been so quiet and humble ..."

Nora Hill felt the urge to get to her feet. I can't stand any more, she thought, I've got to get out of here. I don't want to see this woman again. It's up to her now. I've done what I came to do.

She felt Valerie gripping her arm with both hands. "No ... please don't go ... if he were *your* boy, would you go running to this Dr. Forster without thinking about it first?"

"... *qui videt Filium et credit in eum* ..."

"Think about it as much as you like. Whether you do it or don't do it is all the same to me. Do you hear me, it's all the same to me!" Nora Hill hissed at the ashen-faced woman, trying at the same time to loosen the iron grip of the woman's hands.

"What you're asking of me ... is ... monstrous ... *inhuman* ... I'm supposed to go and say ... swear to it, too! And other people have to swear to it as well. And he was the only man I ever loved, Paul ... *he* is Heinz's father!"

"Not so loud, dammit!"

"Of course, he is," Valerie whispered, in a strangled voice. "I never betrayed my husband. We loved each other! And I'm supposed to swear that Martin and I—"

Using all her strength Nora managed to break away.

"Let me out. I'm going."

"When will you come again?"

"Never. In six weeks I'll be flying back to Lisbon. I'll telephone you before I leave. I'll just ask questions. You simply answer yes or no." And Nora stood up, pushed Valerie's legs aside roughly and clambered out of the pew. She sank down on one knee, crossed herself, and walked quickly towards the exit.

Valerie watched her. Then she gulped a deep breath and turned her gaze towards the soft light from the candles in front of her on the altar. Her face remained motionless, set like stone.

The man in the Homburg hat, watching her, was thinking:

I'll know more about you too, soon. Then he left the church, as hurriedly as Nora Hill. Valerie Steinfeld looked as if she had just died.

39

"Get up on the desk!"

"Carl, you're crazy!"

"Yes! Crazy about you! It's been two months I haven't seen you. Come on, spread those legs! Spread your legs, I said!"

"But I feel terrible! All your people, the secretaries—"

"The hell with them! Let them think what they like. Just let them dare show what they think! So come on, come on!" The Director of "Flemming HQ" slid back into an armchair. Grabbing Nora Hill's legs beneath the knees he pressed her feet against the arms of the chair. She was sitting opposite him on a large desk, still wearing stockings, bra, a black headscarf, and her jewelry. Her baby leopardskin coat, her shoes, the gray woollen dress, the handbag in crocodile leather, and her underwear lay scattered about the office. Flemming had practically torn them from her body.

"Don't! Please don't!"

"Don't talk! What a beautiful perfume ... beautiful! What is it?"

Nora had to laugh in spite of herself.

"*Fleurs de Rocaille*, by Caron." At least she had had a chance to freshen up in Flemming's bathroom after she arrived. He had allowed her that much.

"It's a new perfume ... you never had that one before," he gasped, burying his head between her thighs. True, Nora thought, it is a new perfume. Jack Cardiff gave it to me.

"Yes ... yes ... that's wonderful ... it'll be wonderful for you too in a moment ..."

Nora felt herself being aroused by the situation, by what he was doing. I'm a whore, she thought. A lousy whore. Only yesterday I was in Jack Cardiff's bed, and now look at me! A whore! Well, okay. Even a whore has a man she really loves. I love Jack. This jerk here, this Nazi swine, I need him, I'm dependent on him, he protects me, and I need protection. He's convinced I'm sleeping with Jack, of course, but never mentions it. Maybe the thought excites him. Jack never asks me what I do with Flemming, either. Seems to be a tacit understanding between the three of us. Moral? Oooooah—*morality!* Survival, plain survival, that's the name of the game here. And then I can stay with Jack and be faithful to him for ever. He's quite a guy, this Carl Flemming.

"Is that good?"

"Yes ... yes ... a bit ... further up ..." Nora Hill was breathing more heavily. Flemming's office was on the third floor of the old building Am Hof, opposite the main office of the National Bank. The house had been confiscated. There were still a few shops on the street level. But the stairway to the mezzanine and the entrance to the elevators were sealed off with wire fences. No unauthorized person could get through.

The "Flemming HQ" had a staff of three dozen aides of varying ranks working in the house, and many more agents on the job in the field. When Flemming took over a modern telephone exchange had been installed, and a large radio station. High antennas were planted on the roof. Radio operators occupied the top floor. Specialists were constantly at work evaluating reports and keeping in contact with Berlin, monitoring foreign and secret transmissions around the clock, sending coded messages by short-wave transmitters to couriers already en route. Typewriters clattered, telex machines rattled, and men and women hurried along the hallways busily, in civilian dress . . .

"Good? Is that good?" Flemming was panting for breath.

"Yes . . . yes . . ."

"More? Shall I stay . . . or do you want . . ."

"No! Stop, or . . . come, now I—"

He jumped to his feet, letting his trousers drop to the ground. He slammed into her, and they enveloped each other, Nora squeezing her thighs around his back. He held her tight, kissing her shoulders, her breasts and sucking her nipples.

"*Now!*" She moaned, all her senses going wild. "Now . . . oh . . . oh . . ." She was not acting now. Quite a man, this Carl Flemming. A Nazi swine, but oh, yes, quite a man.

An hour and a half later Nora Hill drove home. Home meant Flemming's villa. He had told her he would follow as soon as he could get away from the office. Nora was in the backseat of Flemming's car. Albert Carlson, Flemming's chauffeur, was at the wheel. He drove carefully and well, was a model of courtesy and spoke only when Nora addressed him first. Soon they were out of the city and had reached the western periphery of the city by the Lainz Zoo. Here, in its own park, was the villa where Flemming lived: a massive, round structure resembling a tower, decorated with stone ornaments in *Art Nouveau* and also with blue, red, and yellow mosaic patterns. The house had been built in the '20s by an eccentric Viennese banker. The banker had emigrated in 1937, and since then the house had changed hands several times, finally being bought by the Foreign Office. It would have been far too big for Flemming alòne. It had been assigned to him, with a large house staff, but was used simultaneously as a pied-à-terre for couriers, agents, spies, bigshots from Berlin, and undercover figures of various nationalities. Albert Carlson brought the car to a gentle halt on the gravel drive in front of the main entrance, then with a great show of courtesy helped Nora Hill to climb out. He was wearing a gray uniform with a peaked cap.

"I'll bring your bags right away."

Nora nodded and walked up the three steps to the entrance. The door opened immediately; she did not have to

wait. A butler bowed. He had been notified of her arrival by
the guard at the main gate, over the house telephone.

"It's a real pleasure to see you again, Miss Hill!"

"A pleasure to be here, Konrad." Nora walked past him
into the spacious, circular hallway of the house. Antique furnishings stood all around. In the center was a fountain, water
playing. Rare fish swam around the basin. Daylight slanted in
through a glass roof. Nora Hill climbed the spiral staircase to
the first floor, where her apartment was situated. Oh, for a
bath, she thought, a long, hot bath. She stood still for a moment on the staircase.

"Is anything wrong, Miss?" the servant asked, behind her.

"No, nothing at all," Nora answered, continuing her climb.
She had just thought to herself: will Valerie Steinfeld be able
to persuade herself to bring that lawsuit? And if not, would
anything happen to her son? And what if she did proceed
with the lawsuit, and something still happened to the boy?
Oh, my God, Nora thought, as she went up to her apartment,
Valerie's in for a bad time. She'll need a lot of luck to get
herself and the boy through. But everybody needs a lot of
luck, she thought, suddenly indifferent to the fate of Valerie
Steinfeld.

The chauffeur in the gray uniform had taken two suitcases
of black crocodile leather out of the trunk of the car. A blue
overcoat and a blue Homburg lay in the trunk. Albert
Carlson, chauffeur, a man with a lean, hungry face, piercing
eyes and eyebrows that came together in a straight line, carefully covered the hat and coat with a blanket, then locked the
trunk. Good that I always have that outfit with me when the
boss sends me out to fetch Nora Hill, he thought. I knew I'd
catch her in something one day. Now I've caught her . . . almost. I have to know more. And then . . .

40

"Of course, at the time I really had no idea that Albert
was tailing me in that overcoat and Homburg hat," Nora Hill
said. "I only found out about that later, much later—the

148

shit." She finished the drink that Manuel had refilled twice during her recital, then squashed a cigarette in the ashtray. The fire in the fireplace was burning with long, tongue-like flames. Sparks sprayed out all over whenever a log split.

"But what's the use of calling him a shit—he was human, that's all," she said, a youthful woman in her fifties, wearing a silver gown.

Manuel asked quickly, "What happened with the chauffeur? And . . . with the others?"

Nora Hill smiled, revealing beautiful teeth. "My friend, this is where I stop for the moment."

"What do you mean? Now listen—"

"I'm sorry, but I've reached the point where it's important that others fill in a gap in my story. What happened to me in the six weeks that followed is of no interest. But a lot happened to Valerie Steinfeld in that time about which I know nothing, even to this day. And it's Valerie Steinfeld's story you want, is it not?"

"Of course."

"Well, I simply don't know the *whole* story. But I can tell you that it's no Arabian Nights fairy tale. It's a pretty rough story. Other people played important parts. Now those people should tell you what they know, just as I am doing. I do know a little more, and will tell it to you—later. But first you have to find out what happened during those six weeks after I met her."

"She's putting on a terrific show," said Fedor Santarin in the little girl's room.

"Yeah, terrific," Gilbert Grant grunted. "And what do we do while Aranda is putting the jigsaw pieces together trying to get at the truth?"

"He *has* to get at the truth, Gilbert, don't be a fool," the Russian said calmly. "It's the only way he'll fulfill Nora's request."

In Nora's living-room Manuel was saying, "What makes you feel that Valerie Steinfeld went through a lot during those six weeks?"

"Facts," said the woman with the game legs. "Before I flew back to Lisbon I telephoned Valerie Steinfeld, as we had agreed. We had another rendezvous in the Cathedral of St. Stephen. Yes, she said, she had decided to go through with the suit, and had already been to see Dr. Forster. Things had begun to roll."

"But did she tell you what made her decide to do it?"

149

"I asked her, but she didn't want to say. I'm sure it had to be something very serious. Perhaps she was afraid of upsetting her husband. She wanted him to learn from me and Jack Cardiff that she was doing what he had asked. She wanted him to feel reassured." Nora looked away. "She was a wonderful person," she said softly. "The only real human being I ever met . . ." Nora poured herself a straight shot of whisky and drank it down in one gulp. "You must find Dr. Forster, my friend. And you have to talk to Martin Landau. Then it will be my turn again." She smiled again, looking like a young woman. But her smile seemed strangely rigid.

"You say you gave Frau Steinfeld the cyanide capsules twenty-six years ago?" Manuel asked.

"Yes, in the summer of 1943. The situation had become much more dangerous then, and she had asked me for some. I got the cyanide and gave it to her. Valerie wanted poison for herself and the boy in case of a serious emergency. A strong poison that would work quickly and without risk of failure. I'm sorry."

Manuel shook his head. "No need to be. I appreciate your frankness. But . . ." Suddenly he had difficulty in talking. ". . . but then why did she kill my father and herself with those capsules?"

"I don't know, Mr. Aranda."

"And what happened to her husband? And to the boy?"

Nora shrugged. "I was very ill after the war, for a long time. That was when it happened . . ."

Manuel looked quickly at her crutches, then looked away.

"I didn't see Frau Steinfeld again until March, 1948. I went to see her, in the bookstore. And of course I asked her how things had gone for her. We had met quite often before the end of the war, but then we had lost touch."

"And what did she say?"

"She was miserable and sad. Almost distraught. She told me her husband had divorced her and her son had accepted an offer to study and work in the United States. He was living in Los Angeles."

"She told somebody else," said Manuel, confused, ". . . her niece . . . that her husband had been killed in the war and that her son had emigrated to Canada because they couldn't get along with each other. Which shows that the niece knows nothing about the whole story. Frau Steinfeld lied to her."

"Perhaps she lied to both of us," said Nora Hill.

"But why?"

"Maybe she had her reasons."

"If what she told *you* is the truth, then it should be possible to find her husband, if he's still alive—or at least her son Heinz!" Manuel's voice rose. "If what she told you is the truth, it would mean at least that she won her lawsuit!"

"Not necessarily. Heinz might have escaped some other way. What she told me need not have been the truth. She was distraught, as I said. When I asked her how the lawsuit had gone, she said it had never been completed." Nora raised a hand. "What happened, what really happened, is still a mystery. For me, too, to this day."

"If the son is living in America—why didn't he come to Vienna for his mother's funeral?"

"Why not, indeed, Mr. Aranda?" Nora Hill raised herself up on her crutches. "You're at the beginning of a very long journey. I'll help you along as much as I can. But the final puzzle is for you to solve . . ."

"First-class," Fedor Santarin said, contemplating an artificial penis painted with forget-me-nots. He had found it in a toy chest. "Nothing will keep him from following the tracks now. He has hunting fever, thanks to Nora. Drink a toast to her, Gilbert!"

"It's late," Nora said to Manuel. "You must be tired."

"I have to go," said Manuel, who had thought of something at that moment.

Together they left the apartment. Nora Hill swung herself down the hall steps at Manuel's side. New guests had arrived, and the party had become very loud. They were drinking, talking, and dancing with the girls to jazz music blaring out of the loudspeakers. Waiters hurried back and forth. Nora greeted all the new arrivals. Manuel felt sick; people repelled him. Suddenly the manservant, George, was standing in front of them. He whispered something into Nora's ear, and she nodded, then turned half-around to speak to him. At the same moment Manuel felt someone touch him. He looked up. Right next to him, in a nylon lace cape and high-heeled shoes, was the redhead Yvonne, dancing with a colored man. Her naked body showed through the cape. Yvonne's fingers ran nimbly across Manuel's jacket. Then she was gone in the crowd. Manuel reached into his pocket. His hand touched a piece of paper.

"I'll come to the door with you," Nora Hill said. He wheeled around. She was looking at him gravely. Had she noticed anything? George, her manservant, was striding across the hallway towards a door, through which he disappeared.

"The snowstorm is over," Nora Hill said as Manuel was putting on his overcoat in the cloakroom. She held a hand out to him. "As soon as you've spoken with the others, come and see me again." She remained standing in the open entrance, watching him walk over to his car. He turned and waved. Nora Hill lifted a crutch and waved back.

A short time later Manuel was driving through a quiet, snow-covered residential area toward the city. There was not a living soul to be seen. Manuel took out the scrap of paper Yvonne had placed in his pocket. He switched on the light above the dashboard and read these words, in the nervous, fancy handwriting of an intellectual:

"I may be able to help you. Am on call in the villa till Sunday, after that I'm free. Telephone me Sunday around noon at 86 57 41. Then come over to my place. Your father came, too. Yvonne Werra."

41

"But you were her sister! You must know whether it's true or not, Good God! Is it true?"

"I ... Look, Irene, please understand!" It was thirty years ago, a third of a century, all long finished and past! And we're supposed to drag the whole story up again? You were so unhappy, so worked up, we didn't want to upset you even more ..."

"So it's true!"

Silence.

The telephone line crackled.

"It's true!" Irene Waldegg shouted, beside herself.

"Yes ..." Her mother's answer came softly, and sounded hesitant and unhappy.

"Why was I never told? By you, or father, or Valerie? After all, it's no longer a crime to have been married to a Jew and to have had a half-Jewish son!"

"True, today it's no crime. But in those days! And you were just a child then, you wouldn't have understood."

152

"But what about later? After the war?"

"It wasn't possible."

"Why not?"

"Valerie forbade us to say anything. She didn't want to talk about it herself. What she'd gone through had been too big a shock for her. And she lived in fear that such a regime might come back. The persecutions—it was a constant nightmare for her."

"What do you mean, it was a nightmare? What happened to Heinz then? Did she bring the lawsuit or not?"

"Yes . . ." The far-off voice quavered.

"And did she win it or lose it?"

"Neither one, nor the other. It was never decided."

"What do you mean?"

"Don't shout so loud, please! Now you've woken your father—it's nothing, Hans, nothing important. Irene's calling from Vienna. I'll tell you about it later. Go back to sleep . . ." In a whisper: "My God, you have to remember, he's had one stroke already!"

"What happened with—"

"Don't shout! I've had just about enough! It's all that foreigner's fault, that chemist's, Aranda!"

"His son's listening in, Mother. On the extension."

"I'm sorry. It's not your fault, Mr. Aranda. Your father got himself involved in a very dangerous game. Valerie, too."

"Valerie, too?"

"Yes, Valerie, too!" The voice from Villach became shrill. "She had her secrets, from you, from us all!"

"Mother, you don't believe that yourself!"

Irene's mother now spoke very fast. "I beg you, Irene, don't start snooping around or something terrible will happen again . . . And you, Mr. Aranda, as long as you're listening: I ask you to leave my daughter in peace and not to bother her with your investigations."

"But I *want* him to bother me with them!" Irene shouted. She was sitting at the desk in her office, at the Möven Pharmacy. She was wearing a white apron over her dress. A sofa which had been opened out to a bed was in the room. The store itself was half in darkness. Glittering bottles and flasks and hundreds of different kinds of medicine in shiny packages were lined up all along one wall. Light slanted into the pharmacy from the powerful streetlamps that had been installed all around the new buildings across the street. When Manuel had arrived at 1:30 A.M. he had seen the modern

153

towers reaching into the sky. A large part of the block was still under construction. An enormous hospital was being built there.

Manuel had told Irene, who kept her large, dark glasses on to cover her swollen red eyes even at night, everything that had happened to him. Irene, who was wearing no makeup and looked pale and tired, had listened to his story with mounting excitement. He had been unable to talk her out of calling up her parents in Villach right there and then. Her mother had come to the phone. Manuel noted grimly that her voice became more and more anxious as the conversation went on.

"But why? You know everything now, thanks to Mr. Aranda's snooping!"

"Mother, he's listening!"

"On the extension, yes, I know, you told me! Leave my daughter alone, Mr. Aranda! I'm sorry about what happened to your father, but why must you insist on tarnishing the memory of a dead woman?"

"What do you mean, tarnishing her memory?" Irene asked. "His father was killed by Valerie. Surely that gives him some right to ask a few questions!"

"Oh, my God," sighed the voice from Villach. "Oh, my God, what can I say?"

"Well, for instance, you could start by telling us what happened to Valerie's husband and to the boy. I've asked you that already!"

"Heinz went to Canada. He was killed in an accident there," answered Irene's mother quickly. "And Paul Steinfeld died during the war."

"But he was in England!"

"He . . . he . . . was killed in an air-raid on London. Valerie was terribly unhappy . . . never wanted to talk about it. Can't you understand that?"

"No, mother, I don't understand it, and I won't rest until I do! Everything! And—"

"Irene, my little dear, my darling, I beg—"

"—Mr. Aranda won't rest either! I'm sorry I got you out of bed. Good night." And Irene Waldegg hung up. With trembling hands she pulled a cigarette out of a pack. Manuel lit it for her. She stood up, a young woman with brown hair and a beautiful, serious face, walked over to the washbasin, filled a pan with water, then went over to an electric hotplate. Her movements were jerky and nervous as she busied herself.

"I shouldn't have come," said Manuel helplessly. "But I thought I had better tell you everything at once—"

"You did right! I'm all right again now. I'm making us some strong coffee."

"—seeing that your interest in it is as great as mine."

"Of course, it is. I'm grateful for your trust in me. One thing is sure: that Nora Hill woman did not lie to you. And I thought I knew Valerie. I have to know what happened! I won't rest!"

"Nor will I," said Manuel. He stood up, walked over to Irene, and stroked her back gently. "Tomorrow I'll talk with Landau. Then I'll have to find the attorney, Forster. Let's hope he's still alive. If only it were not all so long ago, if only so much time had not gone by already!"

"I think my mother's lying," said Irene, abruptly.

"So do I," said Manuel, embarrassed.

They looked at one another, not knowing what to say. A snow plough rumbled past outside. After a pause Manuel spoke.

"So the boy wanted to be a chemist. My father was a chemist."

"A coincidence," said Irene. The coffee was ready. She brought a sugar-bowl, condensed milk, cups and saucers. She poured two cups.

"By the way, that woman with the long veil who came to Valerie's funeral and cried so much telephoned."

"What did she want? Did she give you her name?"

"Bianca Barry. Wife of a painter. She knew Heinz when they were both young, she said. She heard that we were trying to discover what happened."

"Who did she hear that from?"

"From Martin Landau. He called her up to warn her."

"*Warn* her?"

"About us. Especially you. Landau asked her what good it would do for anyone if everything came out. She was talking in a big hurry. She said her husband agreed with her that if we want to know exactly what was going on and what happened, then we should be told. She asked us to visit her tomorrow morning. I have her address. At eleven o'clock. Her husband will be there, too. I said we would come. After doing night-duty I can always take the next morning off and—"

The doorbell of the pharmacy rang shrilly. Irene went into the front shop. Manuel heard her scream and ran after her. Outside, in front of the door, a man lay face down in the

155

snow beneath the light of the lamps from the new hospital buildings. His limbs were twisted under him, and he was not moving.

42

AND LOT WENT UP OUT OF ZOAR, AND DWELT IN THE MOUNTAIN, AND HIS TWO DAUGHTERS WITH HIM: FOR HE FEARED TO DWELL IN ZOAR: AND HE DWELT IN A CAVE, HE AND HIS TWO DAUGHTERS
Genesis, 19; 30.

The words were projected in large capital letters onto the screen, white against a black ground. After a while the subtitles flicked off the screen, and there followed pictures of a cavernous landscape and of a cave, before which a very old man with a long stick, white locks, and shaky movements, together with two pretty girls, one blonde and one dark-haired, were making themselves at home. A second subtitle appeared:

AND THE FIRSTBORN SAID UNTO THE YOUNGER, OUR FATHER IS OLD, AND THERE IS NOT A MAN IN THE EARTH TO COME IN UNTO US AFTER THE MANNER OF ALL THE EARTH:
COME LET US MAKE OUR FATHER DRINK WINE, AND WE WILL LIE WITH HIM, THAT WE MAY PRESERVE SEED OF OUR FATHER.
Genesis, 19; 31-32

Wild music accompanied the film. An orchestra played to a crescendo. As soon as the subtitles had gone, the situation revealed itself as totally changed. The old man Lot lay on the ground in front of the cave, heavily intoxicated. Empty flasks scattered around indicated that the two girls had converted the intentions of the elder sister into action. They were shown dancing together lasciviously, then stripping off their robes until they were naked. Their bodies were full and beautifully formed. The orchestra was whipping itself to a frenzy. Now the two creatures, freed of inhibition, fell on the old man and lifted his robe. The huge organ of a young man was revealed, still at rest. The daughters of Lot took to playing with the primary sexual member of their father, caressing it, massaging it, until it swelled into a mighty erection. Lot regained consciousness. He wanted to rest, but his daughters did not let him.

The blonde daughter got down on her hands and knees, her bottom stretched high into the air. The dark-haired daughter helped Lot rise and pushed him behind her sister. She tore his robe from his body, revealing that this old man was in fact a muscular youth, wearing a wig and make-up.

"FATHER, IT HAS TO BE! THINK OF OUR PROGENY! YOU ARE ALL WE'VE GOT!"

Lot, finding this argument seemingly irresistible, nodded his head, seized his kneeling blonde daughter around the haunches, thrust his supermember between her thighs, and applied himself as best he could. His dark-haired daughter lent her help. It didn't work.

"WAIT! I'LL PROP IT UP!"

And prop it up she did, the dark-haired lass. Now the father rammed like a bull. Close-ups and pan-shots depicted his activity and the faces of his daughters, distorted with lust. Lot's jaws champed. His blonde daughter twisted, jerked and bit into the sandy soil. The orchestral accompaniment reached a thunderous climax.

"So we're agreed," Fedor Santarin said, offering the two other men a long, open bag of gold-colored paper filled with Demel candy. Grant declined with a wave of his hand, and refilled his glass with bourbon. Mercier took a piece of candy.

"From now on we're working together. Grant is chief of all operations. I'm his deputy. And you, Mercier, are my deputy."

Lot was going at it full speed, his body whamming away, as was his young daughter's kneeling before him. The older daughter had crawled beneath her sister's body and was stimulating herself with the fingers of one hand, and fiddling with her sister's nipples with the other. It was the third filmstrip the three men had watched in Nora Hill's private screening room, which was as large as a regular movie theater and elegantly furnished with carpets and seats. They had secluded themselves in this room as did all visitors to the establishment who had important things to discuss and wished to be sure there were no hidden microphones picking up their conversation. Recorded music formed the accompaniment to every film.

Everything had its price at Nora's. That applied also to the use of the screening room, no matter what the purpose of such use might be. One showing cost eight-hundred schillings. Drinks were served beforehand, and were charged for separately. The film ran anyway, whether or not anyone watched. Nora Hill insisted on that. She wanted everything at her house to have the appearance of a decent private brothel.

"What's the matter with you, Mercier? Have you changed your mind again?"

"How could I change my mind?" said the Frenchman angrily. "I don't have any other choice."

"Exactly," said Gilbert Grant. "You're really up shit creek this time, Mercier. Get used to the idea."

"If only you had not bumped off Dr. Aranda before I—"

"Stop harping on that!" the Russian interjected sharply. "And don't start on it again, ever! Dr. Aranda is dead. We made a deal with him. You didn't. That's your bad luck. But that's why our situation is no rosier than yours."

"I'd call is rosier," said Mercier. The three agents were conversing in German.

"Yes, as long as Aranda's son is alive and the documents are in the safe," said Grant. "If anything goes wrong and the papers are brought out into the open, then it's curtains for all three of us. Maybe that's some consolation for you."

The camera moved in slowly on the younger daughter, as her body bobbed up and down, Lot holding on tightly to her buttocks, his grand organ rhythmically stabbing deep and sweeping out again in a wide arc.

"THAT'S GOOD, FATHER!"

"What's this wild music called?" Grant asked.

"Mazeppa," Santarin answered.

"What?"

"Mazeppa, Symphonic Poem No. 6, by Franz Liszt. You really have no education, Gilbert. You don't know *Mazeppa?"*

"Never heard of it."

Lot and his daughters seemed slowly to be approaching a climax. The young woman was pounding the sand with her fists, her mouth wide open, her breath coming in gasps under her father's ravaging assault. The elder daughter, greatly aroused, was alternately rubbing her pussy and squeezing together her younger sister's breasts, which hung directly over her head.

"You're a barbarian, Gilbert," said the Russian.

"Don't you know the piece either, Mercier?"

"No, I regret . . ."

Lot meanwhile had hoisted himself from behind onto his younger daughter's back, and holding on to her shoulders was licking the nape of her neck, then he stretched his head high into the air and plugged away like a machine.

"MORE. . . MORE . . . YES, LIKE THAT . . . LIKE THAT . . ."

"So that's the cultured West," Santarin said. "Mazeppa was a cossack, an Ukrainian notional hero. Your countryman Victor Hugo, Mercier, wrote a poem about him. And Liszt set it to music."

"A man can't know everything," said the Frenchman, irritated.

Lot and his younger daughter were working themselves up to a tremendous finish. Drums rolled, trumpets blared.

The scene on the screen had reached its climax. The young daughter had an orgasm, Lot ejaculated with violent spasms, his face contorted to a grimace.

"NOW . . . NOW . . . NOW!"

The blonde girl sank to the ground, exhausted, Lot on top of her. The dark-haired daughter lay on her back, legs spread wide, rubbing away like mad. *Mazeppa* had reached a climax, too.

"Nora chose the record especially for me," Santarin said, showing off. "Herbert von Karajan and the Berlin Symphonic. She has a large record collection."

"And how long are the papers going to be in the safe?" asked Mercier. "Forever?"

"Of course not. We . . . I mean Santarin has a plan."

"What sort of plan?"

The Russian leaned forward in his armchair and whispered something into the Frenchman's ear. Mercier's eyes lit up.

"My compliments. That's really something!"

The elder daughter was squeezing her breasts and rolling around in the sand. She kept her legs spread wide. Lot had disentangled himself from the younger girl and was stiffened for action again. The elder daughter seemed unable to contain herself from sheer excitement.

"NOW ME, FATHER! ME, TOO! SOME WOMEN CANNOT CONCEIVE. WE MUST NOT TAKE CHANCES!"

Lot the Father tossed himself upon his elder daughter. The younger girl assisted him, guiding his organ home. The old man began slamming away again like a man possessed. The dark-haired girl's temperament was livelier: her legs kicked wildly high in the air, she pounded her father's back with her arms, bit his shoulders, and writhed like a snake under his glistening body.

"DEEPER, FATHER! DEEPER! STILL DEEPER!"

"The only thing is, I'll never get the papers then," said Mercier. He had been drinking champagne, and was a little groggy. Only Santarin had abstained from alcohol.

"Never, you're right," Santarin said. Mercier's fleeting smile escaped his notice. "We're the ones who hit the bull's eye this time, my dear friend . . ."

Liszt's Symphonic Poem was mounting to another crescendo, as were the events on the screen. The dark-haired girl carried on more energetically than her younger sister. She was raging like a wolf—and like the strings of the orchestra.

"AAAAH! I'M DYING! I'M DYING! DO IT, FATHER, DO IT!"

There was a loud knock at the door.

Santarin got up and opened it. Nora Hill swung in on her crutches. A man in a fur-lined leather coat, his face red from the cold, followed behind her.

"What's up?" Santarin asked the man in the leather overcoat. He spoke in Russian.

"We got a call from Gogol," the young Russian answered, staring transfixed at the screen. "We got a call from Gogol. We got a call from Gogol—"

Santarin jabbed him in the ribs.

"Take your eyes off the screen, you idiot!"

Nora lifted a hand and signalled to the projection-room. The film stopped, the music, too. Lights flared up in the little theater. Grant and Mercier stepped over to the others.

160

"What sort of call? Where are you anyway?" Santarin asked, in German this time.

"Two streets from here." The young man spoke German also. "Gogol tailed Aranda, you know that, Comrade."

"Yes. Where did they end up?"

"In the Ninth District."

"In the Ninth . . . that's where that Waldegg woman's pharmacy is!" Mercier shouted.

"Yes," the young man said. "Gogol presumes he's on his way there."

"So what next?" Grant asked.

"Gogol reports that a gray Skoda overtook him and Aranda. License-plate number, W 453 579. That's the Albanian's car—"

"Zagon?" Mercier blurted out, agitated.

"Yes, Zagon," the young man replied. He was still rather confused.

"Zagon must not be allowed to get to Aranda, whatever happens. If he tries, you know what to do. Quick, to your cars! And send some of your cars to the pharmacy, right away!" Santarin turned to the young man in the leather overcoat: "Inform Gogol. Möven Pharmacy. The boys know what they have to do if they see the Albanian. They'll get reinforcements. Tell them that."

"Yes, Comrade."

"I just hope it isn't too late," Mercier said.

"Come on, let's move!" said Santarin. The four men rushed out of the theater.

43

Irene Waldegg hurried back from the office. She had a Yale key in her hand and used it to unlock the pharmacy door. Together with Manuel she burst out into the cold air outside. The street was deserted, lit up by the streetlamps for the new hospital. Parked cars lined the street, Manuel's blue Mercedes among them, quite close by.

"Is he just unconscious or . . ." Manuel, who was bending

over the motionless man in the snow, got no chance to finish the sentence. The man sprang suddenly to his feet and ran hell-for-leather into the shop.

Manuel had recognized him. It was the man who had approached him at Nora Hill's house, and who had shut up as soon as he had seen Nora coming towards them.

"That's incredible!" Irene ran back into the shop.

"Stop!" Manuel shouted, but he was too late. He saw Irene suddenly raising both arms above her head. He plunged in after her. Silhouetted in the open door to the office, the man who had been lying in the snow said in fluent German with a heavy Slavic accent, "You too, Mr. Aranda! Get your hands up, quick!" He held a gun in his hand, and was coming towards them. Irene backed away. Manuel raised his arms. The unwelcome guest slammed the shop door, locked it, and gestured with his gun. "Into the office!"

He made Irene and Manuel go ahead of him. Now they got a good look at him—tall, lean, with pale skin, high Slavic cheekbones, a small moustache. His black hair glistened under the light. His bow-tie was awry, his overcoat full of snow and dirt.

"Stand still!" Quickly and expertly the Albanian frisked Manuel, looking for a gun but finding none. He looked over at Irene questioningly.

"Where's your gun? Don't lie to me. I know you have one when you do night-duty. Where is it?"

"In the chest beside the desk," she replied. "In the top drawer." Her eyes wide with fear, she watched the man yank open the drawer. What he saw there seemed to satisfy him.

"Sit down at the desk. Both of you. Hands on top!" He waved his gun. They did as he had ordered. He turned a chair round and sat down himself, elbows on the back of the chair, gun at the ready.

"I'm not going to hurt you, I give you my word. I just have to be careful. So don't try anything stupid."

"What is it you want?" asked Irene. Her voice quivered.

"I have to talk to Mr. Aranda. He and I have met already." The Albanian gave a slight bow from his sitting position. "I must ask you to forgive me for this intrusion, Miss Waldegg. My name is Zagon, Enver Zagon."

"What do you think you're playing at, Mr. Zagon? What's all that ringing the doorbell and pretending to be dead in the snow supposed to mean?"

162

"Would you have opened the door otherwise, Miss Waldegg? There—you see? No pharmacist opens his door at night to a stranger. And I had to get inside somehow. Let me assure you I'm here as a friend."

"Then put the gun away," Manuel said angrily.

Zagon thought for a moment, then slid the gun into his coat pocket.

"What is it you want?" Irene asked again, this time in a voice suddenly sparked with fury.

"I want to help Mr. Aranda. He knows that, don't you, Mr. Aranda? I told you so at Nora Hill's house."

"Yes. You know something about my father."

Enver Zagon nodded. "Everything."

"What do you mean, everything?"

"I mean I know everything there is to know. But let me explain something first, so that you know you can trust me: Albania is fighting a bitter war against that criminal imperialistic, revisionist clique of traitors in the Soviet Union, who are betraying all the aims and goals of Marxism and Leninism. Our allies are the heroic sons of the People's Republic of China. The world is divided between Washington and Moscow. So—"

"Listen, it's almost two o'clock in the morning. Can't you spare us all this claptrap, Mr. Zagon?"

"I prefer not to call a spade a spade in this affair. You know what I'm talking about," said Zagon, then lowered his voice to a whisper. *"Or do you not know?"*

Manuel started, and hoped the man did not notice. I've got to keep playing the game, he thought to himself, then said, "Of course I know."

"Good. You have read your father's papers. Did you not feel horrified, did your skin not freeze over with goosepimples, when you realized what—please excuse me for speaking so frankly, but I'm sure you appreciate my emotion, you must have had similar feelings yourself—what your unscrupulous, unprincipled, criminal of a father, yes, *criminal*, agreed upon with the Americans and the Soviets, what sort of deal he made with them?"

Irene's eyes behind the dark glasses had filled with shock and fixed themselves on Manuel. He tried to speak, the words stuck in his throat, he nodded his head and stayed silent. If only I had some idea what that man is talking about, he thought. Groll said some similar things, though not so cruelly. What did my father do? *What did my father do?*

163

"And it's typical that he made a deal with the Americans *and* with the Soviets. The comradeship between these two gravediggers of the world we live in depends on this kind of double-dealing. The balance of fear between the two has to remain stable, always, on all fronts. Why don't you answer?"

"I'm listening to you."

"You can't find anything to say, that's it! You're horrified, shattered. I can understand that! But Mr. Aranda, if you just accept this crime, if you tolerate it, if you stay silent out of fear, then you're just as great a criminal as your father was! Worse, perhaps! Don't interrupt me! Your father committed evil. That is bad. You *know* that he did. If you do not apply your best efforts to combat this evil, then you are worse than he was!"

A pause.

"What did your father do?" Irene asked.

"Aha!" Zagon exclaimed triumphantly, before Manuel could answer. "So you haven't told her! Very good. And a good thing that I was cautious. So you've had pangs of conscience. And like us, you're convinced your father more than deserved his death here in Vienna!"

Forgive me, father, forgive me, Manuel thought, and nodded.

"The killing was typical, too, was it not? He was used and then removed before he could make a deal with the third nation he was negotiating with—"

"France . . ."

"Correct."

"And the Americans and the Soviets had him . . ."

". . . liquidated, of course. The usual procedure. You see how these gangster nations operate. They have no scruples!"

"If you're trying to say my aunt was acting for the Americans and the Soviets when she—" Irene's voice sounded angry.

"No. No. You are not informed. And should not be. You have a better chance of staying alive that way." Zagon turned to Manuel. "Where are the papers?"

"In a vault. Very safe."

"Excellent. That puts those two iniquitous countries in the palm of your hand. It gives you a unique chance to rip the masks off their faces!"

"How?"

"By working for us."

"Who is 'us?' "

"The Albanian People's Republic and the People's Republic of China. We will protect you."

"You're not in a position to do that."

"Oh, aren't we! If you agree, we get the papers under the strongest possible guard—and in a few hours we can be in Tirana by plane. And from Tirana you tell it all to the world over radio and television and through the newspapers, describing what happened in Vienna and publishing the text of the original documents! Nothing will happen to you, we will guarantee that! The peoples of all nations will rise in anger and horror against these tyrants of the earth—"

The telephone rang. Irene moved towards it.

"Let it ring."

"I can't! I mustn't! I'm on night-call! I can lose my license if I don't pick up the phone! A doctor's trying to reach me, perhaps ... or maybe somebody needs some medication urgently, and wants me to make it up!"

"Just leave the receiver on! Do as I say! Lose your license, dammit! We've got other things at stake here. A doctor! Suppose it's the Russians or the Americans trying to track me down?"

"And what if it's your own people with some important message?" Manuel asked.

Zagon hesitated.

"All right," he said at last. "Pick it up."

Irene spoke into the phone, then handed it to Zagon. "It's for you."

The Albanian listened, then began speaking into the phone in his own tongue, choppily and at tremendous speed. After a short while he slammed the receiver back down and leapt to his feet. He had the gun in his hand again.

"I was right," he said, gulping for breath. "The Americans and the Soviets! And the *French,* too! All on my tail. They're outside already, my people say ..." He hurried into the shop, pressed himself against the wall by the entrance door, and peered outside. He noticed Manuel coming up behind him.

"Watch out! Stay where you are! There's one ... and another ... over there. I know their cars, dammit. Four cars! And my car's on the other side of the block. I should get out of here, but I'll never get out this way!" He ran back into the office, Manuel behind him. "Give me the key to the back-door," he shouted.

"The back-door's been walled up," Irene answered.

"What?" Zagon's face went ashen. "When? Why?"

"Just a few days ago. The owner is building garages there."

"How about the windows to the courtyard?"

"All barred," said Irene.

"Hell! What am I going to do now?"

"Calm down," said Manuel. "What can they do to you here?"

"You'll see that in a moment. The fireworks'll be starting any moment now."

"A shoot-out, you mean?"

"What were you thinking? They'll be in here! The door's only glass. One or two shots and they're in the shop. Another couple of shots and I'm a dead man."

"Take it easy, take it easy," Irene said. "Vienna is not Chicago."

"Oh, no? Just you wait!" Zagon's hand with the gun was trembling.

"But that's ridiculous!" Irene was growing angry. "Here we are in the middle of a city in a neutral country." Zagon gave an uneasy laugh. "If what you're saying is true, then there's only one thing to do—get the police!" And she reached for the phone. Zagon pushed her back against a wall.

"No way!"

"No police?"

The Albanian laughed, grim-faced. "What are you going to tell them?"

"The truth, of course!"

"Don't you know the Austrian police? They'll shit in their pants! If they come at all they'll get here too late, or they'll let the dogs out there get me anyway. I'm only some filthy Albanian to them!"

"Stop it," Manuel said. "You're making me sick." He pulled a small notebook out of his pocket and leafed through it.

"What are you going to do?"

"Telephone."

"Who?"

"The police," said Manuel.

The next instant he felt the muzzle of the revolver pressing into his stomach.

166

44

"The natural sciences cannot tell us anything about God. We have known that since Immanuel Kant, if not longer. But if, in the search for valid perspectives on the world, man allows himself to straddle the boundary between science and ideology, then the following thought is worthy of consideration: God created this world not as a cosmos well-ordered from the very beginning, but as an unending play between trial and error, chance and necessity."

The words were written in a tiny, neat hand on a white sheet of paper that lay before Commissioner Groll. His massive, antique desk was a jumble of manuscripts and open books. An old table-lamp with a parchment shade shone down on the chaos. The rest of Groll's study was in darkness. The walls were covered with bookshelves. One window was half-open, and fresh, cold, night air streamed into the room. An old samovar stood on a small table, a telephone on another.

Groll had the receiver to his ear.

For three minutes he had been listening to Manuel's story. From time to time he took a sip of tea. He always consumed large quantities of tea when working into the night, and he had been at his desk working for some hours now. The homosexual murderer had broken down after an interrogation of barely two hours and confessed everything. Groll's staff was taking care of the necessary follow-up details. Groll himself had driven home and made himself comfortable—slippers, an old dressing gown, his tie removed. Thus he sat looking at a manuscript page from his life's work page-number *713*. There would be at least as many pages again before the work was finished. A small, gilded frame was propped against the heavy pedestal of the old lamp. It contained, behind protective glass a yellowish-gold gingko leaf. Groll kept it always before him when he worked through those night hours he loved so much.

". . . Zagon rammed a gun in my stomach when I said I was going to call the police," Manuel's voice said over the telephone. "He does not trust the Austrian police—but I told you that already."

"Yes, you told me that, Mr. Aranda. A clever man, your visitor."

"He let me use the phone only after I told him I was going to call you directly. He knows you, of course. What's going to happen, Commissioner? What can we do? I know you are not in a position to do much, but Zagon needs help—and quick!"

Groll replied, "I think I have a solution. An Austrian solution . . ."

45

Sirens blaring, blue warning-lights flashing, three dark-green police cars screeched into the Lazarettgasse from the Spitalgasse, skidding round the corner on the snow-covered, icy road.

A few seconds later an ambulance sped into the street, blue light flashing and siren blaring. The cars slid to a stop outside the Möven pharmacy. Three men jumped out of the ambulance. Nobody left the policecars.

Lights went on in a few windows of the houses round about, shutters were thrown open, and people appeared silhouetted in the squares of bright light. The sound of shocked voices could be heard.

Manuel, who had been waiting with Irene on the other side of the glass door, unlocked it hastily.

"Dr. Bernard," one of the three men from the ambulance said. "Police doctor. You called the Precinct about a man."

"Yes."

"Where is he?"

Manuel pointed to the lighted office. The doctor and two attendants in gray uniforms—one elderly and thin, the other young and thick-set, both shivering in the cold—hurried through the pharmacy into the small office at the back. Enver

Zagon was cowering there in the far corner, foaming at the mouth, eyes rolling, eyebrows twitching, outstretched hands trembling violently. Commissioner Groll had given a few instructions over the phone for Manuel to pass on to Zagon . . .

"*Help me,*" the Albanian was yelling. "*Help me! Help Me! Help me!*"

The two ambulance men moved forward quickly and gripped him under the armpits. The police doctor knelt down and examined him carefully.

"Easy now . . . easy . . . we're your friends . . ."

"Friends," Zagon howled. ("It'll look good if he makes as much noise as possible," Groll had said.) "You, my friends! You're disguised! Do you think I can't see that? Leave me alone! Leave me alone! I'll do anything you say, but please don't kill me! Don't kill me . . ." He twisted and turned in the grip of the ambulance men, his eyes rolling.

"Take him to the psychiatric ward right away," the police doctor ordered, getting to his feet. The two ambulance men dragged Zagon to his feet with a struggle. He resisted violently, kicking, spitting and shouting. All in vain.

Outside in the cold a crowd had gathered, watching with fascination as the man in the dinner-jacket and dirt-spattered overcoat was dragged struggling into the rear of the vehicle. Zagon shouted desperately for help. The onlookers stared open-mouthed, columns of frozen breath rising from their lips. A man with a thick overcoat over his pyjamas asked one of the policemen who had climbed out of his patrol car, once the situation was under control, what was going on.

"A madman," the policeman said, simply.

"Where are they taking him?"

"Over to the psychiatric ward, of course."

A baby's penetrating whine drifted across to them from somewhere.

A man in a duffle coat emerged from the crowd and strode a few paces down the street to a black Lincoln. The man at the wheel of the Lincoln also wore a duffle coat.

"Shit," said the first man, climbing into the front seat next to the driver and slamming the door. "Wait till they've all gone, then turn the engine on and get moving. I've got to tell HQ what's happened." He was speaking English with a broad American accent.

Verse Two

THE QUESTION

Is it but one living soul,
That in itself has split to two?
Or is it the two do form one whole,
Each chosen part to the other true?

1

It was a cheap envelope of poor quality, gray paper. The address had been written with an old, shaky typewriter:

> To:
> Frau
> Valerie Steinfeld
> Gentzgasse 50 A
> Vienna XVIII., Austria

Beneath the address, underlined, were the words: PLEASE FORWARD! On the back of the envelope, typed across the long edge, was: Sender: Daniel Steinfeld, A1. 17 Maja 7/51, Warsaw.

Manuel Aranda was turning the envelope over and over in his hands and looking at Irene Waldegg. She returned his gaze with a shocked expression in her eyes, which were still bloodshot, but no longer swollen. She had taken her dark glasses off, but she was still heavily made up in order to camouflage the grief and exhaustion in her face. She wore a black suit with a gold pin on one lapel, black nylon stockings, black shoes.

Manuel had been awakened by her at 7:30 that morning, in the pharmacy. He had been sleeping deeply until then, and it took him a moment to remember where he was. Irene had dropped off to sleep for a short time at the desk. The night bell had not rung again ...

"You'll have to get up and leave before my staff arrives, Mr. Aranda."

He had got to his feet still half-asleep, and pulled on his shoes and jacket.

"If you'd like to wash ... I'll be making some coffee in the meantime."

He ran his hand over his unshaven face and shook his head. "I'd better get back to the hotel. I'm sorry, I just fell asleep."

"I was very ... very happy that you spent the night here, Mr. Aranda."

He had looked at her for a long time. She had taken off her glasses and met his gaze.

"I'll pick you up at ten-thirty to go to see this Frau Barry." He had become self-conscious.

"Good."

"I'd be happy to drive you home. Your car is still being repaired."

"No, thanks. I have to wait till my people come. Then I'll take the tram. It isn't far."

Manuel Aranda drove back to the Ritz. His suite in the hotel was elegantly furnished. In one corner of the salon was the cardboard box that had been broken into, and which contained everything Manuel's father had had on him at his death—with the exception of the key to the safe, which had been stolen. Manuel thought he caught a whiff of lysol as he walked past the box and into the bathroom, where he turned on the hot-water tap. What am I going to do with all that stuff, he thought. Keep it? Send it on ahead to Argentina? Throw it away? He couldn't make up his mind.

He felt better after his bath. He ordered some breakfast, and to his amazement found he was hungry. Some strong coffee restored him completely. At about 8:15 the telephone rang. Manuel picked it up and heard a woman's voice which he thought he recognized, speaking hurriedly.

"Mr. Aranda? Thank God I've reached you. Your father used to stay at the Ritz, so I thought I'd try there. This is Martha Waldegg, Irene's mother."

"Good morning, Frau Waldegg. What can I do for you?"

"The conversation last night, when my daughter called me. You heard it."

"Yes."

The voice of Irene's mother began to quaver. "That was a terrible tragedy that happened, Mr. Aranda, really terrible. And I'm afraid some other terrible things might happen . . ."

"Frau Waldegg, excuse me, but my father was murdered—by *your sister!* Think of that."

"I do think about it, all the time. I didn't want to hurt your feelings or insult you, I really didn't. I just wanted to ask you, as a mother afraid for her child, not to continue your inquiries."

"Do you know what you're asking?"

"Yes. But I ask you just the same."

"Why are you afraid for your child?"

"I . . . I can't tell you that now. I'm making the call from the Post Office. I didn't want my husband to hear me."

"Why are you afraid for Irene?"

Manuel heard the woman at the other end begin to sob.

"Frau Waldegg, you know a lot your daughter and I do not know, and things that many others don't know, either, including your husband. Am I right?"

Sobs.

"Am I right, Frau Waldegg?"

"Yes, yes. It would be . . . it would be a catastrophe if Irene and my husband found out. The happiness of my family is at stake, the future of three people!"

"And you think you can stop me making any more inquiries by telling me that?"

"I'm begging you!"

"It's absurd, Frau Waldegg. I intend to do everything in my power, everything, to find out the truth. I can't hold back for anyone, not even for you."

The woman in the Post Office in Villach was crying now. Manuel let her cry as long as she wanted. He knew she would begin talking again. Finally, between sobs, she said, "Very well, then. I see your point. I'll tell you everything . . . on one condition."

"What's that?"

"That you don't say one word to Irene about this phone call. Not one word!"

"Agreed," Manuel said. It really must be something terrible that Irene's mother is keeping secret, he thought.

"Thank you. Then you'll have to come out to Villach to see me, without Irene's finding out. I can't get away . . . come . . . next week sometime."

"Why not before?"

"Because my husband must not be here when you come. And next week he's going to Vienna for a day to see our solicitors. We have some property in Vienna that we're selling—"

"What day is he coming in?"

"That's not certain yet. But I'll call and let you know in good time. If you're not in the hotel I'll leave a message."

"All right, Frau Waldegg. I'll wait then. But no longer than a week. After that I'll come without notice."

She gave a soft cry.

"I'm sorry, but I have to know what really was going on with Frau Steinfeld! Good-bye for now, Frau Waldegg."

175

There was no reply. The sound of unchecked weeping came over the telephone, then came a click as the connection was broken. Manuel sat there motionless, staring at the cream-colored receiver. Slowly he placed it back on the hook.

2

"Dr. Forster, I am Manuel Aranda. I'm the son of—"

"Yes, I know. I've read a lot about the case. Your father was poisoned by that Frau Steinfeld, right?" His voice sounded old and refined. "What brings you to me, Mr. Aranda?"

"Many years ago, in 1942, you represented Frau Steinfeld in an unusual lawsuit."

"Not Frau Steinfeld. Her son."

"But—"

"It's rather complex. Yes, I knew both of them, son and mother. And I did handle the case. What happened upset me a lot—even though an attorney should be accustomed to all sorts of things don't you agree? And when I read about Frau Steinfeld, how she died and what she had done, I was horrified, and nothing made sense any more. I assume you want me to tell you what happened way back?"

"If you wouldn't mind, Dr. Forster. I would have called you at your offices, but—"

"My son has been in charge there for the last eleven years now. I'm retired."

"Yes, so I was told. I was given your home number and address in the Sternwartestrasse. May I visit you there?"

"Of course, I'd like to help you if I can."

"Today is Friday. May I come tomorrow?"

"If you hear nothing to the contrary, you can assume we found the files. Come and have afternoon coffee with me, about four o'clock. By then I'll have read the papers through again and refreshed my memory ..."

3

"Mrs. Landau, it is—"

"Aranda! You're Aranda, I recognize your voice." The bookdealer began to gasp. "What do you want this time?"

"The situation has changed. I'm not going to let myself be scared off a second time. From now on you're going to tell me all you know—about Valerie Steinfeld and the paternity suit, and about—"

"Paternity suit?" Landau squealed.

"You know exactly what I'm talking about."

"But how did you find out?" Landeau's voice was shaking.

"From Nora Hill."

"Oh, my God!"

"Oh, my God, right. I know a lot already, Mr. Landau. If you don't come clean now and tell me every single thing you know I'll see that you are involved in the affair. It's a pretty dangerous affair, I think you've seen that already—two people have died in it up to now and there could be more." Got to get him scared, the coward, Manuel thought, and continued, "You could very well be number three. Nora Hill is on my side now. I think you know what that means for me—*and for you!*" The last remark was a shot in the dark.

It found its mark.

"Don't threaten me . . . my heart . . . my heart, you know! I'll tell you everything that happened, but you know most of it already it seems, but *Tilly!*"

"Then let's get on with it," Manuel said. "But this time you come to me."

"At the Ritz?"

"Yes. We can talk in my room without being disturbed. I'll expect you this afternoon at three o'clock."

4

That had been an hour and a half ago.

Now Manuel was standing at Irene's side, turning the cheap envelope around in his fingers.

She was watching him, puzzled.

"Do you understand it? From Warsaw? Daniel Steinfeld? Who is that? What does it mean?"

"When did the letter come?"

"This morning."

They were in a large, elegant living room. The sound of a vacuum-cleaner could be heard from next door. An elderly woman wearing a headscarf and an apron had opened the door to Manuel. As far as he could judge, the apartment was very large. Doors led off a panelled hallway into a number of rooms. The windows in the living-room looked out over a large, quiet courtyard where three old chestnut trees displayed their bare snow-covered crowns.

Valerie Steinfeld's apartment was on the third floor of a dark, well-kept house with an ancient, creaky, jolting elevator. The room housed a large collection of books, many fine cabinets and cupboards, silver candelabra, graceful chairs and floor lamps.

"I beg your pardon?" He had not heard what Irene had said.

"I said: perhaps it was some relative of Valerie's, or of her husband's. Not that I know of any such relatives. I always thought Paul Steinfeld didn't have any. I'll call my mother!"

"No, don't!" He grabbed her arm. "Wait. Let's read the letter first. It might tell us something."

"Read it? But it's addressed to Valerie!" The vacuum next door was humming loudly and monotonously. "Whoever it was wrote the letter had no idea that Valerie was dead!"

"Perhaps that's why it will help us to know what is in the letter!"

They looked at each other. After a few seconds Irene said, "Open it!"

Manuel tore it open. He unfolded the coarse yellowish sheet of paper inside, and read aloud what was written on it in faltering typewriter script. *"Warsaw, June 6, 1969—*Frau Steinfeld was still alive then!"

Irene nodded. She was pressing her hands together. He read on:

"My dear Valerie. Forgive me for turning to you after so long a time. It's been a little eternity since we were last in touch. And please, please, try to forget that your husband and I couldn't stand each other. If only we'd been good brothers, perhaps everything would have turned out differently. But probably not, when I think about it. Now he's dead, and you and I have had no personal contact since 1948. But I know you were fond of me even though we saw each other so seldom. It's—"

"Saw? Does that mean he was in Vienna? When? Only in 1948? He writes that they saw each other several times, even though at infrequent intervals . . . how come he went to Warsaw?" were Irene's interpolated questions.

"Perhaps Frau Steinfeld was in Warsaw a few times and saw him there."

"No, she never—" Irene broke off. "Or maybe? I really don't know anything important about her."

Manuel read from the letter again.

"Now a situation has come up that I never dreamed of. I need your help, urgently,—please don't be afraid . . ."

"Oh, my God, and she's dead, dead, dead!" Irene wiped her hand across her forehead.

"Perhaps you can already imagine what it's all about. I do not know whether any news from here has reached you. Hence the urgency of this request: a good friend of mine, Jakob Roszek, will arrive at Vienna East with his family on Tuesday January 21 at 7:40 a.m. on the "Chopin Express." He has a wife and a very pretty fifteen-year-old daughter. Roszek is tall, powerfully built, wears a pair of thick glasses and has a broad, very pale face. He will be wearing a fur hat, his wife and daughter fur coats. Daughter and mother both have blonde hair and blue eyes. The two women will be wearing silk scarves over their hair, and Roszek will carry a large, fat book bound in leather under his arm. "Shakespeare's Collected Works in Polish." Irene sank into a chair while Manuel read on. She kept her eyes fixed on him.

"You will certainly recognize my friend, Valerie, because he will stay on the platform until someone speaks to him.

179

And if anything goes wrong, he will have you paged over the loudspeakers. Whatever happens, please, please *be at Vienna East next Tuesday at 7:40 a.m.* and listen to what Roszek has to tell you. He will explain everything to you precisely. Thanking you in advance for your kindness, I am, dear Valerie, your old friend, Daniel."

Manuel looked up and into Irene's eyes. "Don't," he said hastily. "Don't cry, please don't cry again."

"It's all so, so uncanny! What am I going to do?"

"Go to the East railway station, of course," answered Manuel. "Let's hear what this Roszek has to say."

"You want to—"

"Of course. Why not? Oh, excuse me. Would you rather go alone?"

"Oh, no," Irene said, her eyes glistening with tears. "I'd be grateful if you'd go with me, I'm grateful to you anyway for standing by me, Mr. Aranda."

"And I'm grateful to you," he said softly.

5

Sixteen colorful carousel horses were standing around in the rooms, in the corridors, and upon the stairs. There were four barrel organs, each one at least eight feet wide and just as high. There were life-size dummies—a drowned man in evening dress, a flower girl with a basket full of wax flowers, a chimney sweep, a butcher, a policeman, a barman, a barmaid and bargirls—all standing around in the various rooms or sitting on priceless chairs. Hundreds of wonderful seashells, stones, and costume dolls from all over the world were on display in wall cabinets in every room and around the staircase. Alongside the *objets d'art* a magnificent collection of kitsch was on display: knickknacks, dogs, cats, birds, and shepherdesses, all in porcelain; a collection of pipes and of large and small Buddhas; brilliantly colored butterflies arranged in fantastic patterns under protective glass. Glass balls the size of oranges, some with strange contents, lay around on tables in huge numbers.

The villa was very spacious, two stories high, with steep flights of stairs, a labyrinthine confusion of rooms and corridors with walls covered to the ceiling with bookshelves. One room had a giant ostrich carved in wood, painted white with a red beak. There was a collection of old clocks, a collection of bottled ships, a collection of grotesque, garish posters from France, America, Japan, and India—posters for exhibitions, theater premières, famous silent movies, night clubs, the *"Grand Guignol."* It was a veritable museum, the house through which the painter Roman Barry was conducting Irene and Manuel—a museum that seemed more like a dream than reality.

Roman Barry was a big, strong man in his middle forties, with a cheerful, ruddy face, a short black beard, and a black crew cut. He was wearing velvet corduroy trousers, sandals, and a loose, gray, flannel shirt. There were spots of paint on his hands and clothes.

"Bianca will be here in a moment, she's just on the phone with my dealer. She takes care of the business side."

Manuel was at first so enchanted by the house that he momentarily forgot the reason for his visit, while marveling at the innumerable treasures which filled the house to the point of overflowing.

Then the door opened, and Bianca Barry entered the room. She was wearing a sports skirt and a high-necked pullover, a long coral necklace and a ring with a colorful enamel seal. She wore no make-up; her skin was pale, her hair cut short and brunette, her mouth full and red, her eyes gray. She had the slim, beautiful figure of a young woman. She welcomed them warmly and the relaxed, open atmosphere of the house and its owners quickly transferred itself to Irene and Manuel. Soon they were sitting around a table nibbling pastries, eating canapés and drinking vermouth or campari soda. Roman Barry drank wine and smoked a big, magnificent Savinelli pipe.

"So, out with it, Bianca, our guests are waiting."

The woman who looked so young bent over. "Fine. Let's begin then. I am forty-three—"

"No!" Irene said.

"—and going on forty-four. My husband is forty-five. We have a fifteen-year-old daughter, Barbara, who is at school. We have been married for nineteen years. My first great love was Heinz Steinfeld. Please help yourself to what you feel like—crackers, drinks. Everyone helps himself in our house.

181

Yes, Heinz ..." She looked over to her husband, blinking. "Roman is still jealous of Heinz."

"Not a bit," Barry said.

"Oh yes, you are," Bianca said. "It's all right, dear. At least we don't have any secrets from each other, do we?"

"Thank goodness," said the painter, taking an immense swallow from his wine.

"That's why I asked you to come here: to tell you what happened with Heinz at that time ... I was sixteen, so help me! And he was six months older than I. We had been going together for two years—that's what we say in Vienna, Mr. Aranda. And *how* we went together! With what innocence! Oh, it was the most innocent love in the world, I do believe ..." Bianca crossed one leg over the other, clasped her hands around her knee and smiled. She spoke quickly and self-confidently.

"I was living with my parents in Döbling, near the Hohe Warte. My school was there, a girls' high school. And right next door—with just a fence and a few trees in between— was the State Institute for Chemistry, where Heinz was a student. He had classes every day until four in the afternoon, because they had to do lab work every day. We girls were through at half-past one every day at the latest. Then, if Heinz was in the labs and not at some lecture, we used to signal to each other through the windows—secretly and carefully, of course."

"As a half-Jew he was not supposed to have a girlfriend— is that so?"

"Yes, that's true. And besides ..." Bianca stopped.

"Go on, say it," said her husband, egging her on. He was drinking a lot of wine and smoking continuously.

"Well, there was another boy in love with me, very much in love. But I didn't want to have anything to do with him. His name was ... Peter Haber. Terribly jealous, he was, and really furious about my going with Heinz. He spied on us. We used to meet in the afternoons and on Sundays, and during vacations. We took a lot of precautions and were pretty careful not to be seen—so we thought. In reality we were terribly foolhardy ... just children ... it had to end the way it did. On the October 21—I remember the date exactly, it was just two days after my birthday. Yes, it was on the October 21, 1942 ..."

6

Coming out of the building, Heinz turned left into a quiet side street and walked towards the fenced-in football-field. As he walked he occasionally looked over his shoulder. The street was deserted. Heinz had taken off his white lab uniform and was wearing knee stockings, half-shoes, short pants, and a tweed jacket. He had never worn long trousers and did not own a real suit.

Heinz Steinfeld was a slender youth, very tall for his age. He had his mother's narrow face, blue eyes, and blonde hair. And freckles. He was wearing a broad, soft collar and no tie. He couldn't stand ties.

He kicked a stone with his left foot as he walked towards the football field. Although he had no real friend at school, many of the boys liked him and were friendly and kind towards him. They treated him as one of themselves, although they all knew his father was a Jew. One of the teachers who was hostile to Heinz had one day loudly announced this fact to the whole class. But in general Heinz could not complain about his teachers. True, there were a few 150 percent Nazis who alternately ignored and tormented him, or tried to humiliate him with snide remarks. Among his classmates, too there were a few real stinkers. Nothing really bad had happened, but Heinz always felt miserable, helpless, and dishonored when he was attacked. There was nothing he could do to defend himself He would have been only too happy to have handed out beatings to his tormentors—but he could not permit himself such a luxury. The Director of the Institute, Professor Dr. Karl Friedjung, had made that perfectly clear to him.

"You are very privileged to be here, Steinfeld. Your conduct must be above reproach at all times. I will not tolerate any irregularities."

The old windbag, thought Heinz, and climbed through a hole in the wire fence. The playing field belonged both to the Institute and to the girls' high school. At the far end were bushes and undergrowth, through which Heinz made his way to a dilapidated barn in which all sorts of tools and assorted rubbish were kept. The tools must have been lying there for ages, because they were all, without exception, rusty and rotten. The little hut seemed to have been forgotten. Heinz had discovered it about a year ago. Now he took one of his shoes and gave three short and two long knocks on the wooden door, then opened it. A moment later Bianca was standing before him, wearing the white blouse he liked so much, a black skirt, and a black jacket. Her schoolbag lay on a crate. Heinz closed the door behind him. Now the light in the hut, which penetrated through cracks and opaque window panes, was dim. There was a smell of leather, soil, and old wood.

"Heinz, hello!" Bianca smiled radiantly at him.

"Hello!" They shook hands like boys. "I got here as quickly as I could. Have you been here long?"

"Just a few minutes."

Bianca sat down on an old bench. "Come over here. I've brought you something . . ." She offered him a large, shining, red apple.

He did not want to take it. No matter what! But he had to.

Finally they divided it, each eating half. Something was troubling Heinz, Bianca could sense it. She was as tall as he was, and had the body of an adult woman. Her breasts curved softly under her silk blouse. He'll tell me everything sooner or later, Bianca thought, he always does—then asked him between chews:

"If you go to America, will you take me with you, promise?"

"I can only go to America if we lose the war."

"Well, we're going to lose it—you said so yourself!"

"You can't win a war against four fifths of the world, that's for sure. And terrible."

"Terrible? But if we won, we could never . . ."

His face contorted with hate. "Right! Thanks to my father, the Jewish pig!"

She recoiled from him. "Heinz!"

"Well, it's true! Look at me! What am I, because of him? Tolerated, just tolerated. We can't even let ourselves be seen together in public. I'm not allowed to go to the university. I have to keep my mouth shut, always. All because of him *that*—"

"*Heinz!* I'm going home if you say that word again! You promised me you wouldn't talk like that about your father

184

ever again. It's not his fault after all. Could he choose who his parents were?"

"Did my mother have to marry him?" Heinz hurled the apple core into a corner. "She has no feeling at all, no instinct for what simply isn't done! And I'm the one who has to suffer from it."

She stroked his hair. "It's not so bad ... you can manage ... many people are nice to you. And look, you don't have to be a soldier."

"But I'd like to be a soldier!"

"And I'd be dying every day thinking what might happen to you! I want you alive, I want to be with you forever," she said, snuggling up close to him. He sat there, stiff and embarrassed. "Because I like you more than all the other boys I know put together." She continued to speak without interruption, trying to take his mind off his gloomy thoughts. "Hauswirth has given us homework again and I don't understand a word of it. Will you help me with it this afternoon?"

"Of course!"

She gazed at him tenderly. She was very close to him now. "I told you about Siegler and Mach and the Pertramer girl, didn't I?"

"Yes. What happened?"

"The rumor is they had a big fight because Mach saw Pertramer and Siegler kissing. Have you ever done that?"

"What?"

"Kissed a girl?" she said, looking him straight in the eyes. "Never!"

Whereupon she threw her arms around him and kissed him tenderly on the mouth. For a moment he felt petrified, then he, too, raised his arms and pressed them around her back. Their kiss would not end. Heinz let one hand slide down and touched Bianca's breast. She sighed happily. He pressed his lips to hers.

At that moment the door of the shed flew open, and a tall, slim man entered. Behind him was a boy who turned and ran away. But Bianca, who had disentangled herself promptly from Heinz, had recognized him. It was Peter Haber, her jealous admirer.

"He's ratted on us!" the realization flashed through Bianca's head. That's the Director of the Chemistry Institute, what's-his-name, Friedjung, and he's very strict, Heinz says, oh, my God!

Professor Dr. Karl Friedjung, who wore the Nazi party badge on his left lapel, was relishing the situation. He said nothing, rocked back and forth on his toes, kept his hands in his jacket pockets, and looked at them without a word. For at least two minutes he did not break the silence. Bianca looked at Heinz. Heinz was staring at the ground.

"So," said Friedjung at last, in a cold, hard voice. "So you've nothing to tell me, no explanations, eh? You've lost your tongues, eh? Fine, very fine. My congratulations, Steinfeld. You, of all people. A person like you should be taking care not to attract attention in any ... hum! ... *disagreeable* way. And you, little lady, what's your name?"

He took a writing pad and a pencil from his pocket. Bianca gave him her name.

"From the high school next door?"

"Yes."

"Which class?"

"6A."

"You, my lady, are going home immediately. I will inform your headmistress. And as for you, Steinfeld, who was allowed to study here by special dispensation, you have misused our trust shamefully, you wretch, you scum, and you can expect to be dealt with severely.

"Please, Dr. Friedjung," said Bianca in despair. "Please try to understand! We love each other and—"

"You love each other!" Friedjung's revulsion was so great he had to step back a pace. "Have you no trace of honor in your body? Don't you know that what you're doing is almost a crime against the race? What am I saying, 'almost?'" He was screaming the words out now, in a fury. "You *are* committing a race crime! In broad daylight! I was blind! I trusted you! I thought you would be a responsible citizen!"

"If Peter Haber had not brought you here—" Bianca began, but Friedjung shouted her down.

"Shut your mouth! The boy only did his duty as a good German! But I'm going to make an example of you, Steinfeld, you can bank on that! You'll be trembling jelly before I'm finished with you! Get up, you're coming back with me to the Institute to pack your things, empty your desk and get out of the school for good. You are expelled! You and an Aryan girl ... or are you not Aryan, either?"

"Yes, I am."

"Incredible! Fornicating! On the grounds of the Institute!

186

That's something we've never! And Steinfeld, you can be sure it's never going to happen again, you shameless, miserable little half-Jew! You're finished!"

7

"Jew whore!" Egmont Heizler screamed, crashing a massive slap across his daughter's face. She staggered back against the cupboard door. The blow stung hotly and brought tears to Bianca's eyes. Once again Egmont Heizler, philologist, Germanist, author of well-known works on German literature, Party comrade and official speaker—he of the mellifluous voice and dramatic talent for public speaking—slammed his daughter across the face. "You swine! You haven't one iota of dignity in your body!"

"But his mother called you up!" Bianca stammered. She had just got home. "Heinz spoke with her and she told him I should go home at once, and in the meantime she would call you up and talk to you!"

He gave a scornful laugh. His breath smelled of schnapps. "Yes, she telephoned, that . . . that fine lady! Shameless bitch! You can bet I told her what I thought!"

"You quarrelled with her?"

"*Quarrelled?* That's good! I gave her what's what till she was speechless and couldn't get a single word out . . . eh, Mommy?"

"Yes, Daddy," a small, gray-haired woman confirmed in a sorrowful voice. She was almost half-hidden by the massive frame of her husband.

"Your ulcers—"

"You and I," Egmont Heizler roared thunderously. "You and I have a score to settle now, that's what I told her. Not just Director Friedjung and you! No, *you and I as well!* Your son seduced my daughter! You're going to hear from me! You can"—he belched loudly—"count on that, my dear, good lady!"

"But Heinz and I never—"

"I don't want to hear you pronounce the name of that dirty Jew!"

"He's not a Jew! He's only half-Jewish!"

That earned her a third clout.

"Daddy," her mother exclaimed. "Please, Daddy! Don't get so worked up! Your ulcers—"

But the historian, critic, and interpreter of modern German literature disregarded his ulcers. "Be quiet, Mommy! You don't realize what consequences this might have for us! *For me!* An official speaker has to set an example! In every respect! And his family, too! Instead, what does this rotten bitch do?" He raised his hand to beat her again. Bianca recoiled. He pursued her around the room. "This rotten bitch befouls our name. While millions are fighting a heroic battle for the future of our Reich, she's out smooching with some Jewish pig—don't contradict or you'll get another one— Jewish pig I said, disgusting, repulsive *pig!*"

"But we only—"

"Shut your trap! I'm doing the talking, get that? You're going to get what's coming to you! You'll see!"

8

". . . well, anyway, and so I gave my word of honor never to see Heinz again," said Bianca Barry. She paused to sip at her Campari. Throughout the recital her face, smooth-skinned and without make-up, had remained friendly and controlled, her voice even. "Ah, well," she said, then, "it was all so long ago . . . so very, very long ago. Every step I took was watched. Once I managed to telephone Heinz. He too had given his mother his word of honor not to see me. Both of us were very frightened. My father and Friedjung were moving Heaven and Hell. I got to feel it . . . and how. Poor grades in school. Loss of rank in the League of German Girls. I had been a Group Leader."

"In the what?"

"In the League of German Girls, Mr. Aranda. The female version of the Hitler Youth. I was chastised and warned what to expect if I ever again . . . and so on."

"What happened to Heinz?"

"I didn't find that out for a long time. Nobody knew. Then a girl from my class told me she'd seen him. Riding a bike. She'd talked to him. He was very scared. Was working as a reel man."

"As what?"

"Between movie-theaters. A film is made up of eight or ten reels, I believe. If there are several movie-houses showing the same film, then the reels have to be carried from one to the other, so that one print can do for two or more theaters."

"So he never got back into the Institute?"

"*Never*," said Bianca. "Friedjung made sure of that, aided and abetted by my fine father."

"And you? Did you never see each other again?"

Irene could sense Frau Barry's growing nervousness, and her strenuous effort to keep it under control.

"Yes, just *once* . . . I simply couldn't stand it any more and waited for him on the street he had to ride down every evening on his bike." Bianca lowered her head. "It was terrible. He looked pale and miserable. And very neglected. Clothes full of holes. Dressed in shabby overalls with an old leather jacket on top. We said hello and talked a bit. But miserably, hurriedly, and without really saying anything. I was far too afraid to talk normally with him for any length of time, or even to meet him. My father was still threatening me. The League of German Girls was threatening me. My teachers were threatening me. And the other boy, Peter Haber, followed me, wherever I went . . ."

Manuel had noticed that the bearded painter had been sucking at his pipe unhappily for some time. Suddenly he spoke out aloud. "I'm sorry . . . I'm really terribly sorry."

"Why?" asked Manuel, baffled.

"My wife is trying to spare my feelings. I don't deserve it. I behaved like a pig in those days. The only excuse I have, if it is one, is that I was so much in love with Bianca that I didn't quite realize what I was doing. There never was a Peter Haber. Bianca invented that name. That Peter Haber was *me. I* am Peter Haber!"

9

During the silence that followed, Roman Barry refilled all the glasses without asking, and everyone drank without a word. A while passed before Bianca said, softly, "You can't understand why I married him, of all people, can you?"

"You must have had your reasons," Manuel said politely.

"Many of them, it's true," said Bianca nodding. "My parents were dead, killed in an air raid, our house was destroyed. And Heinz was dead."

"What?" chorused Manuel and Irene.

"Yes, dead. Killed in an air-raid, too."

"In an *air raid?*"

"His mother told me herself. It happened in February or March 1945—I can't remember the exact month. He had been called up to do war-work as a laborer in a factory on the Danube. Bombing was heavy there—"

The painter interrupted. "It will be on my conscience to my dying day that I behaved as I did towards Heinz. I ruined his education—"

"Don't talk nonsense," Bianca said. "It was *Friedjung* who ruined that!"

"But *I* was the one, *I, I,* who brought Friedjung to the shed in the garden! I started it all! That's why it's my fault that Heinz had such a miserable life. But at least his death wasn't my fault. I can't do anything about American bombs, can I?"

"He's always asking that question," Bianca said softly.

"But it's true, isn't it?" Roman Barry's voice implored.
Manuel nodded.

"Yes, of course it is," Irene said. "And besides, you were not much more than a child in those days. I can understand everything perfectly, even your marrying each other when you met up again . . . two people, both feeling alone and lost . . ."

"And what about the Director of the Institute?" asked Manuel. "Friedjung? What became of him?"

"No idea," said Barry. "They say he fled when the Russians came."

Manuel looked up in astonishment and asked, "Where to?"

"To the West, of course. Must have had a very incriminating record, that fellow. But what became of him after that . . ."

Manuel became excited. "Would you recognize him if you saw him again?"

"Today? After so many years? I don't know . . ."

"Take a look at that!" Manuel had taken out his wallet, and extracted a photograph from it. "Look at this picture, please!"

"Who is it? Your father?"

"Yes. Please take a good look at the photograph. Is that Karl Friedjung?"

The Barrys bent over the color photograph. It depicted a burly, thick-set man of medium height, laughing, his face suntanned, dressed completely in white, on the deck of a small yacht. His hair was gray and thinning. Raphaelo Aranda was holding a pipe in one hand, and waving with the other.

"This picture was taken last year," said Manuel. His face had become blotchy with excitement. "Do you see any resemblance? Is it him? Could it be?"

"It's twenty-five years since I last saw Friedjung," Bianca said helplessly. "But still . . . no, that's not him!"

"How about you?" said Manuel, turning to the painter. "You were in the school! You saw Friedjung much more often than your wife did! I don't have any earlier photos, unfortunately. But my father could have been Friedjung, theoretically. The timing is right. If he fled to Argentina at the end of the war . . ."

"He *could* be Friedjung," said Barry, speaking slowly. "With lots of reservations. It's been twenty-five years. It's a photograph. A man changes a lot in a quarter of a century. But that forehead . . . and the nose . . . the mouth, too . . . it *could* be him . . . could be, could be, it could. But it's impossible, if all you're saying is true."

"The papers he had were perhaps all forged?" said Manuel, his voice catching. "Perhaps—"

"Please, Mr. Aranda, don't get excited!"

"If it really were him—it all sounds fantastic, I know, I know—but if it really were him, then Frau Steinfeld would have had a genuine reason for killing him! He had destroyed her son! Ruined his chances of becoming a chemist! Heinz had had to work as a reel-man because of Friedjung—"

"And in the factory on the Danube!" Bianca added, nodding.

"Where he was killed in the end! Frau Steinfeld must have blamed him for that, too." Manuel took back the photograph as Barry reached it over to him.

"Do you know whether this Friedjung was ever married?" Irene asked.

"No, I don't," said the painter.

"Nor do I," said Bianca. Irene noticed that she was growing more and more nervous.

"Any relatives?"

"No idea." Barry puffed out a cloud of tobacco smoke. Irene touched Manuel's arm. Her woman's instinct had told her that Bianca's nervousness was reaching a critical point.

She said, "We really must go now. We've disturbed you long enough."

"Disturbed us? Nonsense! You must stay to lunch! Let's cast our minds back a bit more and—" Barry stopped, as Irene was already on her feet, and Bianca had risen also.

"Well, if you really do want to leave," the painter said. "But please call us sometime and come again any time. If you have any questions at all, if we can help you further in any way . . ." He walked out of the room at Manuel's side. The two women had already gone out and were descending a staircase flanked by walls from which hung marionettes, Chinese scrolls, and wooden cabinets containing dozens of tiny vases, cups, goblets, and talismans.

Bianca helped Irene into her Persian lamb coat which had been laid across a rocking-horse. As she was doing so she whispered quickly into her ear, "I have to talk to you again, alone, without my husband. I couldn't tell the whole truth in front of him. I was lying, it's true! Everything happened quite differently, but I had to ask you to come, for his sake. You'll hear from me . . ."

"When?" Irene asked.

The men were coming down the stairs.

"I can't say yet. It's hard for me to get away. I'll call you or Mr. Aranda. I . . . I still love Heinz . . . he was the only one I ever loved . . ."

The two men went into the cloakroom.

Bianca Barry immediately smiled at her husband—warmly and openly, and full of sincere affection.

10

"So she was lying!"

Manuel was driving down the Herbeckstrasse toward the city. After Irene had told him of Bianca Barry's closing words he had become very agitated.

"Was she lying all the time?"

"Most of the time, anyway. I had that feeling while I was listening to her."

"And there's nothing we can do except wait for her to call—*if* she ever does!"

Manuel arrived at the dirty structure of the old elevated tram line, and made a right turn. After he had crossed through an underpass he said, "And what about her husband? Was he lying, too?"

"Impossible to tell. You mean when you showed him your father's photograph?"

"Yes. I'm going to call up Commissioner Groll. Perhaps he can find out what became of Friedjung. Or at least whether he has any relatives still living. Martin Landau's coming to see me this afternoon. I'd like to tell you right away what I get out of him. May I . . . do you think we could have dinner together?"

She looked out into the sunshine and the veil of snow the east wind was blowing through the air.

"Tonight I can't, I'm afraid, I don't have time. I have a date."

"A pity." Manuel felt suddenly disappointed and alone. You idiot, he said to himself, what were you thinking about? What made you think such an attractive young woman would not have a boy friend?

"Are you insulted? I made the date several days ago. I'd no way of knowing—"

"I'm behaving like a fool, forgive me," he said. "What right have I to intrude in your private life?"

"Oh, you could have plenty of reasons! We've become real companions in this short time."

"By force of circumstance only. I hope your boy friend is not angry."

"He isn't," said Irene, suddenly short and cool.

11

"Mr. Aranda! At last! There's a man waiting in the foyer for you—he's been there a good half-hour already. I told him I didn't know when you would be back." Count Romath had hurried up to Manuel as he entered the hotel.

"Where is the gentleman?"

"Over there on the right, in the corner."

"Thank you." Manuel handed his overcoat to a page and walked swiftly into the lobby. A small man with hairy hands, black, curly hair, and olive skin rose from an armchair.

"How do you do, Mr. Aranda," the small man said in fluent Spanish. "My name is Gomez, Ernesto Gomez." He took out his passport. "Please . . ."

"I believe you. Why should I look at your passport?"

"Because I have an important message for you, and want to be sure you know with whom you are dealing. As you see, I am a member of the Argentinian legation."

"So I see. Why don't we sit down? Would you like a drink, Mr. Gomez?" Manuel said in Spanish.

"No, thank you. Mr. Aranda, we would like to ask you, in your own interests, to break off your investigations here in Vienna and return to Buenos Aires immediately."

"One moment," said Manuel, taken aback. "How do you know I am conducting any investigations here in Vienna?"

"We know."

"Can you force me to return home?"

"Not if you behave as you have been doing."

"Then I will stay in Vienna."

The man's face showed no emotion. Lowering his voice, he said, "In that case, Mr. Aranda, the Embassy must declare itself unable to ensure your protection or guarantee your safety, nor can we undertake to tender any help in the event you come into conflict with Austrian or other foreign authorities."

"What's going on?" Manuel had been feeling irritated and aggressive since leaving Irene. "What's all that supposed to mean? Are you trying to intimidate me?"

"Not at all."

"Or is it of some importance to the Embassy that I do *not* find out what my father was doing here?"

"The Embassy is interested only in your well-being. It has no other interest in this affair."

"But I could well imagine some other interest after all I've been finding out."

"Mr. Aranda, we cannot, of course, have any influence upon your imaginings. You speak of your father. We warned him, too—urgently and often. He ignored all our warnings and preferred to gamble with his life, as you are doing now. Your father—my condolences, by the way—lost his life here in Vienna. The same could very easily happen to you."

Manuel seized the short, bulky man by the arm. "What are you talking about?" he asked gruffly. "How much do you know? Come on, out with it! Why don't you tell me the real reasons why you came here?"

Displaying astounding strength, the little man freed himself and stood up. He made a formal bow.

"You already know the answers to those questions, Mr. Aranda. I fear we cannot help you. Too bad. Good day to you." And with that he strode off into the foyer and over to the cloakroom. He took his hat and coat and walked out of the hotel without a backward glance.

12

". . . then Kröpelin says Erika, his youngest daughter, has had a baby, but doesn't have the faintest idea who the father is. I don't know what to say to that, so I scratch my head and say 'Well, that's sad your daughter's had such bad luck, Kröpelin, but it happens a lot these days. Everyone has to make sacrifices," a man's good-humored homely voice boomed out of the loudspeaker of the "Minerva 405."

With the colorful, woollen blanket over her head and over

the radio, Valerie Steinfeld sat crouched beside the set, twiddling with its knobs. Turn it down, turn it down, that is too loud! And get it right on the station! Above the man's voice was a constant whine from a number of German jamming stations, but at that hour of the evening the reception was good. The announcer, imitating in masterly fashion the harmless, seemingly obedient tones of a little private, continued:

". . . and Fritz Ziegenbart comforted Kröpelin too. 'That's how we won in the Upper Caucasus!' Kröpelin gaped at him for a whole second, as though he wants to say something, but keeps his mouth shut and hands me a letter. In the letter his wife tells him that his son has had both legs blown off in North Africa. And when I've finished reading I don't know what to say, and Fritz Ziegenbart is mumbling away embarrassed-like: 'In North Africa, now there we're holding fast at El Alamein . . .' "

Valerie felt her hands clamming up and a cold shudder running up her spine. That was her husband talking, Paul, her beloved Paul—*that was his voice!* It was disguised, cleverly and intentionally, in order to reproduce the right intonation for "Private Adolf Hirnschal," a spiritual buddy of the good soldier Schweik. But she recognized in it the voice of her husband, the husband she longed for with every fibre of her body. It was Paul's voice, Paul's voice!*

At the rear of the stacks in the bookstore, Martin Landau was uttering curses to himself, softly and feebly. He was full of resentment that Valerie was doing what she was doing in the tearoom even though she knew how much it upset him, and even though she knew that in the darkness of the evening hours it was impossible for him to take a walk round the block as he did during the lunch hour. It was the 21st of October, 1942.

Landau was sitting among the musty stacks, thinking with a large dose of self-pity: I should forbid her to do it. Yes, that's what I should do, forbid it! But I'm too good-natured.

---

*It was *not* the voice of Paul Steinfeld. Inquiries by the author to the Chief Librarian of the BBC resulted in the information that all the "Hirnschal" letters were read by a refugee German actor. Valerie Steinfeld confused the voice of this actor, who also worked as a newsreader, all through the war with the voice of her husband, which she failed to identify correctly even once. Experts described to the author a number of persuasive reasons, of a technical and psychological nature, for this phenomenon.

Martin Landau really was good-natured. And weak. Very weak in fact, an aesthete, a dream-walker!

He could talk for hours about lost civilizations, for instance. But if you asked him at the end of a day what the turnover had been for the day, how much he had sold and taken in, he would shrug his hunched left shoulder, incline his head, smile, and rub his hands. He had not the slightest idea. That was why he needed Valerie Steinfeld. She simply knew everything and took care of everything that had to do with the business side of things.

Of course, Martin Landau's interest in empires and civilizations of the past was merely an attempt to flee from everything his own time was forcing upon him. All his closer acquaintances recognized this facet in his personality immediately.

And everything had been so noble and inspiring at the beginning. For after all . . .

After all!

That was Martin Landau's favorite expression. After all, when Hitler had marched into Austria, the little country had had more than six-hundred-thousand unemployed, ten per cent of the population. After all, hardly anyone was buying books any more, and business was terrible. The plebs ruled the streets in many localities, and there was a real danger after all that Bolshevism would overrun the country. And after all, Austria had been a part of German-speaking Europe from the days of antiquity, and her "annexation" by Germany was an act that Martin Landau had at first welcomed warmly and sincerely.

He had stood on the Ringstrasse as the men from the "Austrian Legion," National Socialists who had fled to Germany, marched back into their homeland. They were dressed in elegant new uniforms, shining boots, and helmets neatly strapped under their chins. They paraded along, men who had borne many years of exile for the sake of their beliefs, brandishing bells, flags, and banners, singing the 'Song of the young Vienna Workers':

> *"On all the roofs the whistle blows,*
> *For today our work is over . . ."*

and it was left, right, left, right, one, two, one, two, with a training, and a discipline, and an order, left, right, left, right, one, two, one, two, and the cheering from the crowds, and

197

the emotion, left, right, left, right, left, right, left, and the pride was endless:

"Keep the flag up high and close your ranks . . ."

left, right, left, right, left, and many an eye was damp, left, right, left, right, left . . .

If anyone had told Martin Landau then what was to happen not very much later, he would have laughed. And after all, he was not the most stupid of men, he was a man who believed in the noble and the good, and in the beginning of a new era! *After all!*

Then came the first shock, the first terrible moment of horror, when he discovered that his old and good friend Paul Steinfeld had fled the country, with good reason and in the nick of time. Then five days later the world-famous historian of past civilizations, Egon Friedell, who had lived in the Gentzgasse, not far from the Steinfelds, jumped to his death from the window of his apartment after stormtroopers had forced their way in. And yet another shock followed immediately when Martin Landau witnessed how elderly Jews were forced to clean the streets with lye, gaped at, spat upon, and taunted by Viennese children and people (with legendary hearts of gold), their hair and beards twisted and pulled, their legs and bodies kicked by the stormtroopers.

My God, oh, my God!

He had wept. For days afterwards he would burst into tears without warning, and even the combined efforts of Valerie and Tilly did not suffice to comfort him. No, no, it was too horrible. People were disappearing by the thousands into prisons and concentration camps. Hitler invaded Czechoslovakia and Poland. War was declared. And as for what was happening to the Jews . . .

But what could one do?

Leave the Party?

Landau almost died with fear when he thought of the consequences of this alternative. For a long time he had no longer thought of himself as a National Socialist. He helped people wherever he could, though he was constantly afraid. Coming to Valerie's help and giving her a job had been a matter of course. Even Tilly had had no objections.

Martin had known Valerie since 1921, when she was eighteen. In those days he had been very interested in art history, just like Valerie, who was taking courses at night school. He had run into her time and again during his frequent visits to the Albertina, the museum near the Opera House which harbored a world famous collection of drawings and lithographs. He had made friends with her in his shy, inhibited way, the only way in which Martin Landau could make friends with other people. Then Valerie had married Paul Steinfeld, who at that time was the political correspondent for a major newspaper. He changed to radio in 1930. Valerie had introduced the two men to each other, and all three had met often in the Steinfelds' apartment. Martin was very close to them at the time their son was born, and as the years went on the friendship became more and more intimate.

It was a matter of course that he helped them in the terrible year 1938. And when Valerie begged him to help others who were being persecuted, he did it just as spontaneously, even though timorously. But his self-reproaches intensified, and his nervous strength disintegrated more and more. By the time Nora Hill appeared on the scene, he was a nervous wreck.

Her visit frightened him terribly. But what Valerie had to report to him when she returned from her conversation in the cathedral with Nora frightened him still more. And he heaved a sigh of relief when Valerie said, "I won't do it. I could never go through with such an insane lawsuit. *Never!*"

Never! Thank God.

Hear nothing, see nothing, say nothing—that's how Martin Landau tried to live his life from that moment on, and for that reason would never even allow Valerie to tell him what she had heard on the radio. Once, when she tried, he broke out into a rage. "No! No! No!" he had shouted, his voice cracking. "I don't want to hear it! What's happening is bad enough, after all . . ."

Then Valerie had felt a wave of sympathy for him, and said, "Forgive me. I won't try to tell you anything ever again." And she never did . . .

". . . is ended. We will return with the twelfth German broadcast of today at 8 P.M. tonight over 1600 and 1800 meters on long wave, 285, 340, 398, 415, and 450 on medium wave, and 18, 20, 24 and 28 on short wave—"

The telephone rang.

Valerie started. Tearing the blanket from over her head and throwing it on the sofa, she switched off the radio. The black metal box with its rusty hook, from which a heavy, old-fashioned receiver with a rusty mouthpiece hung down vertically, rang insistently once more. Valerie lifted the receiver. "Landau Bookstore."

The next instant a barrage of words from her son hit her.

"I tried calling you at home, Mommy, but Agnes said you weren't there yet. Something terrible has happened, I'm really sorry! He caught us ... please don't be angry, don't be angry!" Valerie, who was wearing her black calico shop tunic, dropped into the armchair in front of the crowded desk.

"Stop! Start all over again Heinz, but slowly this time, and tell me everything in order."

In a trembling voice he told her what had happened, in fairly chronological order. He sobbed as he finished, "and after that we didn't dare come home!"

Valerie put her head down onto her hand. I knew it, she thought. I saw it coming.

"It was Roman Barry, you know who I mean. He followed me and then went and told the Director ... What will he do now, Mommy? I'm a half-Jew!"

She recoiled as if under a blow, but managed to keep her voice firm and calm. "Now stop that. Will you do what I say?"

"Yes, Mommy, that's why I'm calling. We have to do something, we can't just keep on walking all over Vienna. Bianca's feeling sick already, and Agnes said Bianca's mother called to ask if she's with me—"

"I'll call her immediately, and explain to her what happened ... gently, I don't want her to get too upset. I'll get everything straightened out."

"You will, Mommy? Yes? You think you can?"

"We'll talk about it. But you two have to get home now as fast as you can. "I'm finished here for the day and will come home, too. So please hurry!"

Martin Landau, pale and distraught, crept into the tearoom with scarcely a sound. He had heard the telephone ring, then Valerie's voice. Valerie looked up at him, and seeing his horrified look, smiled at him reassuringly. But it did no good.

Landau rushed over to the radio, tuned it quickly to the wavelength of the Vienna Radio, then growled, "You left it on London again! How often do I have to tell you—"

"I was going to change the station!"

"You might have forgotten!" he shouted, his voice suddenly reedy. "Have you any idea what would happen to us, *both of us*, if we were caught doing that? Do you know—"

200

Valerie screamed at him, "Shut your mouth! Can't you think of anyone but yourself, you coward!"

He let himself sink onto the sofa from sheer fright and surprise. The springs creaked loudly, and he stared at Valerie open-mouthed.

She ran her fingers through his lustreless hair. "Forgive me, please. I don't know what I'm doing. Something has happened to Heinz ..."

13

"She told me the whole story and calmed down a little while talking," Martin Landau said.

It was 3:35 in the afternoon, and the bookdealer was sitting opposite Manuel in an armchair in Manuel's hotel suite. Between them was a teawagon, on which a waiter had placed two large pots of tea and a small selection of pastries. Manuel had greeted his guest at the elevator. Landau, his head and shoulder at a slant and smiling apologetically as always, had been wearing a fur-lined coat and a strangely old-fashioned hat. He was in a state of panic.

"You blackmailed me! You know that, don't you? You told me that if I didn't come you would involve me in this espionage affair!"

"That's not what I said. And anyway, how do you know that it's an espionage affair?"

"Why do you think I'm so afraid? It *is* espionage, Tilly and I are convinced of that! Who knows what kind of double life Valerie may have been leading. All we want is to keep out of it—"

"That's no longer possible, I regret to say, Mr. Landau. Now, please be reasonable and do what I say."

Landau had calmed down a little once the tea had been served; he had begun to talk about that fateful evening of October 21, 1942, and about himself—at first mainly about himself. He seemed to feel the need to justify his attitudes and actions so as not to appear a wretch and a coward. What he said impressed Manuel, who suddenly found himself taking a liking to Landau. Poor creature. A man with lots of faults, but basically decent. At least, so it seemed . . .

Graf Romath was in his office standing in front of Adolph Menzel's "Masked Supper." He had locked the door, pressed the catch on the frame to open the secret compartment, and was now speaking into the transmitter, the antenna of which was pulled out.

"Landau is telling Aranda what happened to the Steinfeld woman and her son in the war," he was saying in English. On the desk, next to the vase containing the Inca lilies with their yellowish-brown petals flecked with yellowish-gold, was a miniature black loudspeaker small enough to fit in a jacket pocket. Its short wire was plugged into the telephone. A hypersensitive microphone was hidden in Manuel's suite above the door to the bedroom. Only the initiated knew about it.

Commissioner Groll seemed to be one of the initiated. On the day they had taken the papers out of the black attaché case in the billiard room at the Ritz he had said to Manuel, "You can be sure your room is bugged. And Count Romath will have his orders to keep tabs on you. So whenever you're talking to someone up there, bear in mind that the Director or somebody else is listening in. There's nothing can be done about it. The Count works for the Americans and the Russians in the Ritz—that is, for the stronger side, which evidently came to terms with your father. My advice is for you to stay in the Ritz. With the plan I have in mind, nothing will happen to you."

Count Romath had already listened in to a great many discussions that had taken place in the drawing-room of suite 432—discussions held by Manuel's father. Now he was eavesdropping on the son's conversation . . .

"Okay, Able Peter," came a voice through the tiny transmitter. "Continue!" The voice belonged to a man who had parked his car in a side-street about half-a-mile from the office.

"But it's of no interest—"

"You have your orders—carry them out, understand?" The voice sounded sharp. "Or have you had enough? Do you want to back out? Just say the word, Able Peter—"

"Stop it, Sunset! I am in your hands, I know."

"Report back when Landau has left or when you hear something important. We're always here. Over."

"Over," replied the Count, pressing the antenna back into the transmitter and putting the set back into its hiding-place behind the picture frame. His face was as white as his hair and his lips were quivering. Will this go on forever? he wondered despairingly. Are they never going to leave me in peace? Never again? I'll never stick it out. I can't. I won't. But I don't want to go to prison either. So what am I going to do? I'll switch the microphone back on ...

14

"Couldn't she have thought about whom she was marrying? Couldn't she have thought about who she was making a baby with?"

"Heinzi! Heinzi! Don't talk about your mother like that!"

"Why not? Who's got to clear up the mess she's made? I didn't have a chance to pick my father! And because of him I've got to run around like some sort of sub-human!"

"Heinzi! That's, that's ... sinful, what you're saying! Your good father! A loving, kind man! He was always a wonderful person ..."

"Oh, come on. He was a stinking Jew!"

"Just cut out that kind of talk! This minute! I knew your father before you were born. And I'm telling you, he was a wonderful man!"

The loud voices could be heard from the quiet stairwell as Valerie stepped out of the shaky elevator with Martin Landau and opened the door to her apartment.

"Oh, fine, very fine," Landau murmured, growing pale.

"We'll soon stop that," said Valerie, furious. They quickly hung their coats in the closet and entered the spacious living-room where Heinz was arguing with Agnes Peintinger.

Agnes, who had been Valerie's housekeeper for twenty years, was a small, determined woman of forty-four. She had come to Vienna as a young girl, and had worked for the Steinfelds from the very first, remaining loyal to them through good and bad times. She had admired Paul Steinfeld sincerely. Now she stood there shouting at Heinz, whose face was red with rage. Agnes had a peasant woman's face with a beak-like nose, a broad mouth and dark hair that was turning gray and was tied in a bun at the back. Her hands were rough and red from housework and extraordinarily large. She had small feet. In spite of her delicate build, she was extremely strong and indefatigable.

Her private life was a carefully guarded secret. She never spoke openly about what must have been a terrible experience she had suffered as a young girl. She hinted at it on rare occasions. In all the years Valerie had known her, Agnes had never had a male friend and had never wanted to marry. She had become an old maid; some man figuring in the distant past of her life had, according to the rare hints, done something terrible to her. But what? Had she been raped? Had some farm boy, some farmhand, or even some big farmer made her his mistress, then betrayed her, sent her away, or left her in the lurch?

The village pastor in Leonfelden, where she was born, had obviously helped her to get over her unhappy love affair, instilling her with renewed courage; the little woman time and again spoke with gratitude of the Reverend Ignaz Pankrater, who had her whole heart and trust.

Many years after Agnes had moved to Vienna, Ignaz Pankrater had also come to Vienna too, to take charge of a small church in the Sixteenth District, the Ottakring, a bleak part of the city where only poor people lived. Agnes had been overjoyed at his arrival, and without a moment's hesitation had abandoned the church in the neighborhood of the Gentzgasse in order to pay regular visits to Reverend Pankrater in his modest house of God, to pray there, say confession, and have private audiences with the good pastor at which she told him of her personal needs, fears, and anxieties. And the forty-nine-year-old former country pastor, whom fate had moved to the city, proffered his advice and comfort time after time . . .

Valerie and Martin Landau were now standing in the living-room. Heinz looked at them angrily. Agnes was ringing her work worn hands.

"Am I glad to see you, ma'am! Heinz has been saying really terrible things! I've been getting so upset, I—"

"It's all right, Agnes. Listen, Heinz, have you gone out of your mind? We could hear you outside in the hallway!"

"So what? Let people hear me! I don't give a shit!"

"Don't shout," said Valerie, forcing herself to speak calmly. She thought to herself: my God, how he must suffer, the poor boy! Aloud she said, "Now let's talk everything over calmly. Uncle Martin has come with me to help us decide what to do."

Heinz went into a paroxysm of rage and despair, shouting, "I'm a dirty half-Jew! There's nothing we can do about that! Nothing! I just have to keep my mouth shut, and crawl in a corner, and wait to see what the others do! And they'll do something all right! My fine father—"

"Stop that," Martin Landau called out unhappily.

"You seem to have forgotten whose fault it was that these things happened today!" said Valerie, stepping closer to him.

"I haven't forgotten one thing!" the boy screamed, beside himself. "I think of nothing else! Your husband, my father, that filthy Jew, it's his fault!"

Valerie slapped him across the face, as hard as she could. He staggered back. His face burned red where her hand had struck, but he did not cry. Mother and son stood facing each other, both out of breath.

The doorbell rang.

They all stood transfixed, as though a running film had suddenly been halted.

The doorbell rang again, several times, impatiently.

"I'll get it," said Valerie.

The others stayed behind, not looking at each other, not speaking. The voices of Valerie and a man could be heard from the door.

Martin Landau was thinking desperately: it's the police, or the Gestapo. It's all over. The end. And here am I, right in the middle. Caught right in the middle. Oh, my God.

The door was closed. Valerie returned to the room with an envelope in her hand.

"An express letter," she said, opening the envelope and taking out a folded sheet of paper. The paper bore the letterhead of the State Institute for Chemistry Studies in the upper left-hand corner, and on the right the date, October 21, 1942. The text began without any formal address. Valerie read it quickly to herself, then leant back against the door for support.

"What is it, ma'am?" Agnes called out.

"Who's the letter from?" Martin Landau asked, softly and unhappily.

Valerie read the letter aloud in a monotone: " 'This is to inform you that your son Heinz Steinfeld, Jewish half-caste of the First Degree, is hereby suspended from the Institute on my order, for serious moral turpitude and for disruption of the National Socialist community spirit. I have already brought the case to the attention of the Regional Commandant and Reich Governor of the Province of Vienna, who will proceed with appropriate steps against your son. (Signed) Professor Dr. Karl Friedjung.'"

A deathly silence reigned in the room as Valerie read the final words. No one moved. No one looked at anyone else. Only Agnes's lips were flickering imperceptibly. Agnes was praying.

15

Valerie walked slowly across the room to a window. Behind her the deathly silence remained unbroken. Valerie took a deep breath. Then she turned around and said in a firm voice, "All right then, if there's no other way! There's no need for you to be afraid, Heinz, none at all." She had to swallow before she could continue. "Nothing will happen to you, nothing."

"But Friedjung says he's already notified Schirach!" Heinz was no longer shouting. He was sitting on a linen-box, hunched up, pale and scared-looking.

Valerie swallowed again; the lump kept coming back into her throat. "Schirach won't do a thing. Because you're not really a half-caste."

"What?" Heinz whispered. "What am I *not?*"

"You are not a half-caste Jew of the First Degree." Every word cost Valerie an effort. She pressed her hands behind her onto the window sill for support. I'm committed now, she thought, I have to go through with it. Yes, I have to do it, and quickly.

"But if my father's a Jew—"

"The man I'm married to is a Jew," said Valerie Steinfeld slowly, the words sticking in her throat. "But that man is not your father."

"Jesus, Maria, and Joseph!" Agnes called out.

Heinz had risen to his feet. He gaped at his mother, and stammered out, "Not my father ... but how... what do you mean ... it can't be—"

206

"Yes, it can," said Valerie, and now her voice was suddenly under control and the words came effortlessly from her lips, though they sounded flat, cold and strange, almost inhuman. Her face too had suddenly hardened; it, too, had become cold, strange and inhuman.

"Of course it can, Heinz. I've never spoken about it, because it's anything but pleasant for me to talk about ... but now I have to. There's no alternative. I was unfaithful to my husband."

"Now after all—" Landau began, resentfully.

"You be quiet, Martin, do you mind?" Valerie looked at him. He stopped speaking. Agnes crossed herself.

"I never got on very well with my husband. I was unfaithful to him very soon after we married. The other man is your father, Heinz, not my husband. And the other man is Aryan." Valerie's voice sounded like a gramophone record. "So you are not a half-caste, you're an Aryan, a pure-blooded Aryan!" Valerie had to take a deep breath, it was an effort, pains were stabbing her breast. "And now I'll make a public announcement of that fact. In court. You can imagine that I wanted to avoid it as long as possible, the time has come to do it."

The three people listening to her did not move. The faces of the adults were contorted and glazed with fright. The boy's face was twitching. Breathlessly he asked, "Is that really true, Mommy?"

"It's really true, Heinz."

"But ... but ... but who's my real father then?"

A second went by, two seconds, three seconds. Heinz was looking from face to another.

"Who, Mommy? Who?"

"Can't you guess?"

"Uncle ... Uncle Martin?" The boy stammered out.

Valerie nodded.

Heinz raced over to Martin Landau. His breath was coming in deep gulps, an expression of infinite bliss was spreading across his face.

"Is that true? Is that true, Uncle Martin?"

It's *infamous*, Landau thought, the worst infamy imaginable. He felt weak, was trembling with rage, torn between a boundless anger and a boundless pity as he looked into the child's damp, begging, inquiring eyes. It's the worst infamy in the world! Valerie could at least have talked with me about it and asked me if I agreed. What's Tilly going to say? Oh, my

God, it's terrible. And if Valerie starts that lawsuit now . . . oh, it's awful, *awful!* Why did it have to happen to me? What have I done to deserve it?

"Uncle Martin, is it true?"

At that moment, when he heard the pleading voice of the boy, a great transformation took place within the cowering, eternally jittery Martin Landau. He drew himself up to his full height. His face took on a determined and serious look. His voice was firm and kind. "Yes, my boy, it's true."

"God Almighty in Heaven, help us!" Agnes mumbled.

Then Landau felt himself embraced by Heinz and kissed on both cheeks. He hated to be embraced, hated being kissed. Oh, what a situation!

"I'm so happy!" Heinz exclaimed. "So happy! I knew it! I always knew it!"

"What?" asked Martin Landau, backing away as Heinz let go of him.

"That something was wrong! That I couldn't really be a half-Jew! That I had to be an Aryan!" Heinz ran over to Valerie. He threw his arms around her and kissed her, stammering:

"Forgive me, please forgive me, Mommy, for shouting like that, for everything I said . . . there was no way I could know! Oh, Mommy, Mommy, this is the most wonderful day of my life! Thank you for telling me, thank you for telling everyone in court . . ."

Valerie felt herself getting excited, she was breathing hard, words came pouring out, she had to get them off her chest quickly, right away, before she changed her mind.

"I'll tell it all in court, Heinz. And I'll let that idiot Friedjung know, too, he's going to get a real surprise!"

"The idiot," Heinz repeated, laughing happily. "Agnes, did you hear, were you listening? I'm not a half-Jew! I'm an Aryan! And Uncle Martin is my real father, not that Jew! Oh, Mommy, Mommy, I love you so much!" Heinz staggered away from her over to the door. He passed Landau and said, ". . . and you, Uncle Martin . . ." Sobbed. *"Father!"* Then he was gone. A few moments later the three adults heard the door of his room slam shut. Valerie met the eyes of Landau and Agnes. The lean bookdealer was biting his lip and looking about to burst into tears. But he kept silent, clenching his fists.

The silence remained unbroken.

"Agnes!" Valerie said, after a while.

"Yes, ma'am?"

"What do you think?"

Agnes hesitated. Then her voice sank to a whisper. "It's not true, is it, ma'am? Is it, Mr. Landau? I always say what I think, you know that, ma'am. And now I say, what you just told Heinz, that *can't* be true! You and the Master were so happy together, I know that, I was here all the time! I'll never believe it, it *isn't* true!"

"No," said Valerie, also in a whisper. "No, Agnes, it isn't true. Of course not."

16

Agnes Peintinger blinked and shook her head. She came closer, and asked in a low voice: "Then why did you say it, ma'am?"

"Yes," Landau broke in, losing control, "when after all you—"

"*Wait!*"

He fell silent beneath Valerie's gaze.

"Because I want to save the boy's life, Agnes, that's why I said it. Because I *have* to save him! I have to go through with the lawsuit, Agnes. It's the only way I can protect Heinz from those Nazi murderers, the only way I can pull him through! Do you think it's going to be easy to do and say what I shall have to do and say? But there's no other way! And Paul, my husband, the master you revere so much, is with me in everything I'm doing. He wants it, has wanted it for a long time now!"

"How do you know that, ma'am?" the little housekeeper asked uneasily.

"I got a message from him—but don't ever talk about it! I'm going to go through with it, and you two have to help me!"

"Oh, my God," Landau stammered.

"Why did you say yes, that you're the real father?"

"Because . . . if you're going . . . after all, there was no other . . . Heavens above, what else *could* I say?"

209

"Nonsense! You said it because you are a good man. And you, Agnes, you're a good person, too, we all know that. You will help me, won't you?"

"Of course, ma'am, if you think it has to be, then of course I'll help you, only ..." Agnes stopped, sighed and looked at the ground.

"Only what?"

Her eyes bowed, Agnes replied in a whisper, "If you start a lawsuit, ma'am, will I have to answer questions in court?"

"Naturally. You'll be a very important witness."

"And I'm supposed to answer to make it look as though you really did betray the Master with Mr. Landau?"

"Yes, of course! You *have* to answer that way."

"But if I do, I'll be telling a pack of lies!"

"But you'll be lying to the Nazis, Agnes, those Godless swine, to save Heinz's life. That's honest lying. That's ..."

Agnes raised her head slowly, then said very softly, seriously, and deliberately, "I'm only a stupid old woman from the country, ma'am, but there's one thing I do know: before the Almighty there's no such thing as lies and lies. There's only one kind of lie!"

"Lying's necessary sometimes!"

"They'll have me swear everything on oath, ma'am! What was that? Heinzi's door? No. I'm hearing things already! They'll have me swear to everything! And *perjury* is never necessary! Perjury is a deadly sin!"

"Agnes, be reasonable! A human life is at stake here! And you don't want to help me?"

"I do want to! I do want to!" Agnes whispered anxiously. "But first I have to talk to my Father Confessor and tell him everything!"

"All right, go to your priest. Tell him everything. Of course you must discuss it with him if you can't make up your mind yourself."

Agnes rubbed her hand across her eyes, then said quietly, "What times we're living in, what horrible times, dear God. Hitler, that dog! And the Master so far away ..."

Martin Landau turned away suddenly with a groan.

"What's the matter?" Valerie asked him.

He did not answer.

"Martin, what's wrong?"

His words came out in gasps, indistinctly, "And me a Party member ... and Tilly ... I ... now *I* daren't go home!"

17

Ottilie Landau's voice was shrill with anger, "Let you out of my sight once, and what do you go and do? What were you thinking about? What sort of mess do you think you're getting into? Martin, are you out of your mind?"

Martin Landau and Valerie Steinfeld had needed almost an hour and a half to get to the Gloriettegasse. After listening to their story, Tilly had stood for a while without saying a word, her arms folded, then had let go a torrent of words at her brother, who was sitting on a leather-covered armchair with an anxious and helpless expression.

". . . if Valerie wants to tangle with the Nazis, let her go ahead, that's her look-out! It's her son. She must know what she's doing! But a man like you! A man who gets the willies when the alarm goes off at seven in the morning!? Have you any idea what these Nazis are like, the swine? Do you know what they'll do to you?" Tilly paced up and down in the entrance-hall. "I'm a real anti-Nazi! I hate the whole dirty lot of them! But—" and her voice softened suddenly as she continued—"but you're no match for those filthy rats, you haven't a prayer against them, my poor, dear Martin. Once they start interrogating you and roughing you up a bit—and they will, you can rely on that—you'll break down in no time!"

Then turning to Valerie she said, "They're criminals, those Nazis, the biggest criminals in all history! Murderers, pigs, rogues, vagabonds—but they're not *stupid!* Not stupid at all! And you, one lone woman, do you want to take on that pack of animals single-handed?"

"Yes," Valerie replied.

"You're only bringing misfortune on yourself and Heinz and everybody else who gets dragged into it!" Martin's sister wailed. "There's going to be a tragedy, I know it. Martin is my responsibility, I promised our mother I would look after him, always. You know him. You know how he is." She was speaking as though her brother were not present. "He's com-

211

pletely naive and helpless. And what do you do? You don't care! You drag Martin into your madness. You want him to commit perjury, to lie for you, you you . . ."

Slowly Martin got to his feet. His eyes gazing into space, he said quietly and distinctly, "There's not going to be any lying, Tilly. And no perjury. It's all true. *I really am Heinz's father.*"

Tilly staggered back against a cupboard. "What . . what?" she croaked out.

He's rebelling against the way she's dominated him all his life, Valerie thought. She's told him once too often now that he's unfit for life, lost and helpless without her. He doesn't want to hear that any more. He intends to prove he's capable of doing something *without her!* Oh God, what a stroke of luck!

"Yes," Martin Landau shouted, suddenly self-assured and resolute. "Yes, I am Heinz's real father! I deceived Paul with Valerie!"

"You . . ." Tilly held her hand before her mouth.

"*Betrayed* him!" Her brother shouted triumphantly. "Paul was away a lot the year before Heinz was born. We had been in love for a long time—"

"*You* were in love with Valerie?"

"Yes, I was. And she loved me. When she became pregnant we both knew I *had* to be the father! But Valerie had a lot of trouble allaying Paul's suspicions. She never did quite succeed. Paul had his doubts right up to the time he fled. He told her about them often ..." Martin Landau improvised wildly.

Both women were staring at him now.

My God, Valerie was thinking, do we ever really know another person?

Martin was shouting into his sister's face, "Heinz is my son! And I'll swear to it in court! And I'm swearing to it now, so that you know! And I want you to know something else: I'm not going to have you telling me what to do in this affair, you've nothing to say, *nothing!* I owe that much to Heinz! This affair concerns Valerie and myself and the boy, and nobody else! Understand?" He sank into an exhausted silence, but there was an expression of wild determination on his face.

Ottilie Landau went pale. Is this really Martin, my fearful, timorous, neurotic brother? Could this really be him?

"Martin—" Valerie began, but he interrupted her sharply.

"Be quiet! Tilly had to know sometime. Now she knows. And she knows what I intend to do. She'll just have to come to terms with it. I'm going to fight with you for our son—*yes, for our son*. And I'll fight till we've won . . ."

Suddenly he pressed a hand to his heart, staggered back into his chair, and collapsed into it. "My medicine," he gasped. "Quick!"

18

"Just a heart attack," Martin Landau said. "It passed, of course. I'd had so many already. I'm sure I almost died at least a hundred times. You get used to it." He glanced at his watch. "Ten past five. I'm sorry, Mr. Aranda, but I have to get back to the bookstore. Right away. You know . . . Tilly . . ."

"Of course." Manuel got up with him. The sun had gone down, and the light in the drawing-room of the hotel suite was growing dim. The east wind had died down; scattered snow flakes were falling.

"I thank you for coming, Mr. Landau."

"Quite all right. This is a good meeting-place," the book-dealer said as Manuel helped him into his coat. "I'll come back and continue the story."

"When?"

"Well, let's see: tomorrow's Saturday, that's no good, and Sunday's out, Too. But Monday would be all right. How about Monday, at the same time?"

"Fine," said Manuel, putting his hand on the shoulder of the slim little man. "I owe you an apology, Mr. Landau."

Landau laughed. "For thinking I was a coward? Don't apologize. I *am* a coward! It's only that then . . . yes, those were the best days of my life, with that lawsuit. For once, just *once* in my life, I was a different person!" he said, adding softly, "For Valerie's sake! Oh, my God, were we naive!"

"Naive?"

"We didn't have the slightest idea how such a lawsuit was conducted. We hadn't the faintest notion what we were letting ourselves in for—but I have to go now, really!"

"Certainly. But just tell me one thing: did Frau Steinfeld win the suit or lose it?"

Laudau's shoulder hunched up very high, his head slanted over deeply to one side:

"She won it *and* she lost it."

"What do you mean?"

"I can't explain now. You'll have to hear the whole story."

"Very well, then. But there's something else you can perhaps tell me now: what happened to Heinz?"

Laudau's answer came softly: "He didn't get on with his mother any more. Their relations became worse and worse. He survived the Nazis. But then the Canadians started an immigration program in 1947. He applied at once and went to Quebec. A year later he drove head-on into another car, and was killed on the spot."

"And Paul Steinfeld?"

"He died shortly after the end of the war, in England."

Lies again, Manuel thought. Whenever I ask these questions, all I get is lies. Why? Will I never get to know the truth?

That evening, Manuel Aranda stayed in the hotel. He had dinner in the dining-room, spent an hour in the bar, then returned to his rooms.

Shortly after eleven o'clock his telephone rang. Groll was at the other end.

"Yes . . . yes, Commissioner?" Manuel sat up in bed.

"Were you asleep already?"

"No."

"We've found something that will interest you."

"Is it about Karl Friedjung?" Manuel asked breathlessly.

"Yes."

"Do you know where he is?"

"Yes, we know where he is," said Commissioner Groll.

19

"Where is Friedjung?" asked Manuel, out of breath. He was standing in Groll's office, his coat collar turned up, and had just greeted the Commissioner with a quick handshake. A third man wearing horn-rimmed spectacles, with a sad, resigned expression on his face, was standing behind Groll. Inspector Ulrich Schäfer was holding a bundle of papers in his hands.

"Tell Mr. Aranda, Schäfer," said Groll to the sad-faced Inspector, one of the most capable men in his department.

"Ettinghausenstrasse number 1," said Schäfer dismally.

"Ettinghausenstrasse 1. Where is that?" asked Manuel quickly.

"In the Nineteenth district, by the Kaasgraben. We traced Friedjung's wife to Ettinghausenstrasse number 11. I've been there and spoken with her. She's an elderly lady, seventy-two years old, but still in good health and lively," said Schäfer resentfully. His wife Carla was twenty-eight.

"And Friedjung . . . have you spoken with him?" Manuel's words came out choppily.

"No."

"Why not?"

"Because dead men don't talk," said Groll. "Take your coat off, Mr. Aranda. Just throw it over the couch." He was smoking another of his cigars.

"He's dead?" Manuel sank down on a chair by the desk.

"Yes."

"But you just said he was living at Ettinghausenstrasse number 1!"

"No, Inspector Schäfer didn't say that. He said that's where he *is*."

"What's that mean?"

"Ettinghausenstrasse 1 is the address of a church. There's a cemetery there. It's been closed for a long time—fully occupied. The only room left is in the family graves. The Friedjungs lived at Ettinghausenstrasse 11 for three generations, and have a family grave behind the church—'Our Lady of the Sorrows' it's called—and so Frau Friedjung was able to arrange for his burial there, right close to where she lives."

"When was that?" asked Manuel.

"On February 27, 1945."

"On the . . ." Manuel could not speak.

"You heard correctly," said Groll.

"Thank you," said Manuel. His head was whirling. Somehow he had allowed himself to get used to the idea that Friedjung had fled to Argentina before the end of the war, and was his father. You idiot, he thought to himself, you stupid idiot! So it's a pure case of espionage after all. And Valerie Steinfeld killed my father. Acting for *whom?* The Americans? The Russians? The French? The Albanians? The Chinese? I'll have to be careful, or I might lose my mind!

"On February 25, 1945, towards noon, there was an air raid by American bombers," said Schäfer's voice. Manuel pulled himself together. The Inspector was spreading papers before him on the desk, and pointing out dates, names, times, and various notations written out by hand or with a typewriter. "The Second, Twentieth, and Twenty-First Districts were especially badly hit. There was damage also in the interior of the city, and in the northwest suburbs. The State Institute for Chemistry Studies was destroyed totally . . ."

The Barrys had mentioned that, Manuel remembered.

"There were thirty-five dead—twenty-eight students and seven faculty members, including Karl Friedjung. The bodies were badly mutilated."

"How could they be identified?"

"By the personal papers found on them, and by relatives. Here is the police report, and here is the doctor's report. According to the police report, Frau Friedjung was the one who identified her husband. And there were papers on the body . . . I asked Frau Friedjung again today. She had no doubts then and still has none. Her husband was buried on February 27, 1945, behind the church of 'Our Lady of the Sorrows.' Here is a picture of the grave."

It was a very good photograph. Even the small inscriptions on the headstone were clearly legible. They gave Karl Friedjung's birthdate as April 2, 1904. Which meant he was forty-one years old at his death . . .

And my father was born in 1908, Manuel thought. On August 25. That's when we always celebrated his birthday. Of course, if he had been living with false papers ... stop right there, Manuel said to himself. Your father was not Friedjung, that's definite.

"That will be all, Schäfer," Groll said. "You did a good job. Thanks. You can go home now, you must be tired."

Inspector Ulrich Schäfer left his chief's office and drove home in a Volkswagen. He lived in the Seventh District, in the Seidengasse near the Neubaugasse. Two-thirds of the houses in Vienna are more than a hundred years old. The house in which Schäfer lived was one of these time-honored but hopelessly old-fashioned buildings. There was no elevator and no central heating. Schäfer had been living there for a long time now, without Carla ...

On this night he unlocked the door to the apartment, stepped into the freezing hallway, bent down to pick up his mail, which had been slipped through the letter-slot and was lying scattered on the floor, and glanced through it. Bills and more bills. From specialists. From the laboratories for blood and serum tests, from the sanatorium in Baden (he did not feel up to open them right away). Then there was the colorful brochure of a company offering luxury bungalows on the Costa Brava at low prices. And a cheap, blue envelope bearing neither address nor stamp. Somebody must have pushed it through the letter-slot in person. Schäfer thought for a moment, then tore open the envelope and unfolded the gray, thin sheet of paper he found inside. The message it contained had been written with the aid of letters snipped from a newspaper:

yOU HaVe a LOt of WoRriEs A sIcK WIfE
aND nOt MuCh MoRE MONey wHAt aRE yOU
goINg TO dO? We WILL HElp YoU If You
WiLL HeLP Us IF YoU WaNT to KnOw MOre
PUt The FollOWinG Ad IN The 'KuRieR'
PeRSoNaL COlUmN NeXt TUEsdAY:
   orCHestrA MuSIcIAn GiVeS PRiVaTE
   VIOlIn LeSSoNs in YoUr HoME AppLY
   'pAGaniNi 500' cArE Of THiS PaPEr.
YOu WiLL ThEn HeAr FrOM Us AgAIn If YoU
CoNTaCt The PoLicE oR anY tHiRd PaRTY YoU
WILL ReGREt iT.

Inspector Ulrich Schäfer walked quickly into his spacious living-room, still in hat and coat, his gloves still on his hands, switched on the light and picked up the phone to inform Commissioner Groll at once of the anonymous message. After dialing three digits he stopped, stared at the message once more and replaced the receiver slowly. He stood there in the stark light of a ceiling lamp, apparently unable to take his eyes off the paper with the pasted-on letters.

20

"It looks more and more as if your father had been involved in an espionage case, and was murdered for only that reason," said Groll to Manuel.

"By an old woman?" Manuel shouted. He put his hand to his brow. "I just don't understand it! I can't believe it!"

"It could well be that Frau Steinfeld really *did* have some secret—her sister in Villach wants to tell you what it was," Groll said. "But one thing is clear to me now: the espionage case and the lawsuit that Frau Steinfeld conducted are two completely different and unconnected things. Don't let yourself be misled: they have nothing to do with each other. The lawsuit goes back a quarter of a century, and God knows what importance it still has today, if any. There might be some, I don't want to dispute that. But the stories and confessions we have about the suit are all second-hand—what assurance do we have that they're true? But on the espionage affair, we've got *facts*, first-hand facts! We know what's what in that affair."

"Are you trying to tell me the connections are all just coincidence? The stories we have on the paternity suit and the information on the espionage case complement each other. Is that supposed to be coincidence? And how about what happened to me and to Miss Waldegg—is all that just coincidence? So many coincidences just aren't possible, Commissioner."

"One moment! Often we confuse the coincidental and the

completely irregular. But coincidence, Mr. Aranda, has its own laws. Coincidence and necessity," Groll declared, "free will and compulsion—these opposites are inseparably intertwined to form an inner unity . . ." The thick-set, modest, lonely Chief of the Homicide Squad bowed his head and gazed down upon the glass covering of his desk and the leaf pressed beneath it, as though afraid of the future and what it might bring.

21

The *Thermopylae* was built in Scotland in 1868, and sailed the China route as one of the fastest vessels in the service of the tea-trade. A model of it decorated a bookshelf in the hobby-room which the seventy-four-year old attorney Dr. Forster had set up for himself in the loft of his ivy-covered villa. He lived on the upper floor, his son and his son's family on the two lower floors. The house, built in 1890, was large. It stood in a neglected garden among a forest of ancient trees. Snow-covered trees also lined the edges of the Sternwartestrasse, in a quiet residential part of Vienna.

Forster had led Manuel into his hobby-room first. It contained a large desk and windows opening out in every direction. The *Thermopylae* was forty inches long, and modelled after the original on the scale of one to ninety-six. Forster showed it off proudly. He was a man of astonishing energy for his years, tall, slender, with beautiful hands, a narrow face, and gray eyes. His gray hair was thinning, and he had only one ear, the left one. The right side of his face was a mangled mess, badly scarred and red. Forster must have had a bad accident. Where the right ear had once been there was now a fat, swollen, cleft scar. ("I can hear very well, Mr. Aranda, as long as I'm talking with just *one* person and there are no other noises, voices, or music in the background. If that's the case, then you have to sit on my left . . .")

There was a knock at the door.

A fat, chubby-faced housekeeper in a black dress and

219

white apron stepped into the room. "I've put the coffee in your room, Doctor."

"We're coming!" The old attorney declared. "Anna's a good person! She has to clean up in here now and again."

22

A table in the living-room had been charmingly set. The attorney poured the coffee, praising Anna's pastries as he did so. Manuel looked uneasily at Forster's shockingly disfigured face.

"Those are cottage cheese pastries, one of Anna's specialties. She made them specially for us. Please, help yourself! Let's enjoy ourselves first, then I'll tell you all you want to know. Or at least I'll make a start. You have time, don't you?"

"Certainly," Manuel said. All the time in the world, he thought sadly. That morning he had driven over to the Möven Pharmacy, to see Irene and tell her about the recent developments. She had been very nervous and harried. It was Saturday morning, the shop was very busy, and she had constantly had to rush out of the little back-room office to wait on customers. Her eyes were clear and large again, and she was not using so much make-up, but she seemed extraordinarily irritated to him. She apologised to Manuel after each interruption, but he had the feeling she was not really listening to what he was saying. In the end her distracted mood had rubbed off on him a little.

"We really can't talk here. When can I see you somewhere else? This evening perhaps?"

She shook her head. "I'm sorry, but I can't."

"Your boyfriend again?"

"It's ..." she hesitated. "It's my fiancé," she said slowly and earnestly. "We have to meet tonight. Please understand, Mr. Aranda—"

"But of course," he replied, and felt a wave of quite illogical anger rising within him. Why shouldn't Irene have a fiancé, dammit? A beautiful, young woman! It would be unnatural if she didn't.

"It's not that I don't *want* to see you! I'm terribly anxious to hear everything! But it just happens that this evening—"

"Of course."

"But we really *must* get together!"

"Whenever you have time."

"Now you're angry."

"Me? Not at all. Why should I be?"

"Yes, you are! You're angry, I can tell! But this evening's out, it really is impossible for me. Tomorrow evening perhaps ... I can't say yet ... you could come over to my place. No one would bother us there. But I can't say for sure yet. Can I call you?"

"Any time, of course." Then he left. The farewell was brief and formal. Watch it, he had thought as he climbed into his car, I've got to stay cool and keep my head with that girl. No emotional involvements—forget that nonsense about sharing a sense of loss and all that. For Irene Waldegg I'm just another stranger, and that's it, period. I'll make a fool of myself if I start imagining there's more to it than that ...

The coffee session at Dr. Forster's was over. Anna had cleared the table and covered it with a brocade tablecloth. The attorney brought in a portfolio and sat down again.

"There you are," he said. "Take a look." He passed the thin file across to Manuel. On it stood, in large capitals, VALERIE STEINFELD. Under the name, in smaller letters, was written: *Begun: 24th October 1942.*

The outsides of the folder were stained. It was beginning to get a little mouldy along the edges. Manuel noticed that there was something written beneath the word '*Begun,*' and by peering closely was able to make out: '*Ended,*' followed by a colon. But there was nothing after the colon.

"No date for when it was ended?" Manuel asked.

"No date, no." Forster turned his head a little to one side, so that his left ear faced the front.

"Was the lawsuit not concluded, then?"

"Not by me," said Forster. "I ... I was detained during the final phase. So I can't tell you how it all ended. But I can tell you a lot about the case. What you see here is only a small portion of my papers on the case. My girls unfortunately could find only this one portfolio in the archives. The rest of the documents must be in some other files relating to the Steinfeld case. We'll get them all together in the next few days, and you'll have to visit me again ..."

"With pleasure."

Forster looked at Manuel. "And when you know exactly what happened and why—are you planning to fly back to Argentina then?"

"Yes. of course."

"I envy you," the attorney said. "You are free to leave Vienna." He cleared his throat. "I read through these papers we had managed to find. Now I remember Frau Steinfeld distinctly. Poor woman! She was absolutely distraught when she came to me, although trying her best to be brave and calm." Forster picked up a sheet that had yellowed with age; it was closely covered with lines of type from an old typewriter. He read aloud: "24th October, 1942, 10 A.M. Frau Valerie Steinfeld, born May 6, 1904 in Linz, married, Roman Catholic, resident in Vienna at Gentzgasse 50A, Vienna XVIII, came to my office and stated . . ."

23

". . . a good many years ago now I deceived my husband with a certain Martin Landau. My son, Heinz, was the product of this relationship. I would like you to represent me, Dr. Forster, when I go to court with a paternity suit."

Valerie sat facing Dr. Otto Forster in his office at the lower end of the Rottenturmstrasse. Through the window one could see the Danube canal and one of many bridges. It was a Saturday morning, and there was a lot of traffic on the Bridge of Our Lady. A seemingly endless military convoy was rumbling past a gigantic, bronze statue of the Virgin. Soldiers with unsmiling, tired, listless faces sat jammed together in army trucks.

Nobody imagined that a little more than two years later all the bridges across the Danube Canal would be blown up by the retreating SS in the battle for Vienna. Otto Forster, tall, slender, thin-faced, with gray eyes and well-shaped ears that lay close to his head, interrupted the flow of Valerie's words with one rapid gesture of his beautiful hands.

"Your husband's name is *Paul Steinfeld?*"

"Yes."

"I used to know a Paul Steinfeld." Watch it! "A—hum!—good, former client of mine . . . worked with a newspaper. Afterwards he became a broadcaster, I believe . . ."

"That is my husband," said Valerie, and had to bite her lip quickly to prevent herself from adding: that's why I came to you, he sent me!

That wouldn't do, of course not.

The attorney had to believe that what she was telling him was the truth. Valerie was sitting up straight in her chair. She was wearing a brown suit, a jacket with well-padded shoulders, and a fashionable bell-shaped hat of brown felt. Her blonde hair curved from under its brim.

"He's Jewish, is he not?"

Valerie swallowed.

"Yes," she said, adding, as she had agreed with Martin, "One of the reasons, probably, why we couldn't get along with each other almost from the very beginning of our marriage. I didn't want to believe it. My parents had warned me! They said—"

Forster gestured to her to stop.

"What happened to your husband, Frau Steinfeld?"

"He emigrated to England right after the Anschluss."

"I understand." Forster's face remained expressionless. He had to play the same game as Valerie.

"Have you any contact with your husband?"

"Now? In the war?"

"It's not likely, I know, but it could be. Have you?"

"Of course not!" (Martin had told her to say that!)

"I understand," he said for the second time, and thought to himself: Another of those cases. He asked, "And your husband? Have you told him that he . . ." " . . . is not Heinz's father! No, I never admitted that to him! Even though he was always accusing me of being unfaithful . . ." Of course, Forster thought. " . . . and although he was continually making scenes . . ." Of course, Forster was thinking. ". . . I denied it with all my strength right to the end!"

"Right to the end, hm." Forster observed that Valerie was tugging at a small lace handkerchief out of sheer nervousness. He helped her—a quick and direct approach was the only way in this case.

"That means that your son—how old is he, by the way?"

"Sixteen-and-a-half."

"—is not a half-caste."

"That's why I want to go through with the lawsuit! I am

223

deeply ashamed, but I have to do it!" How familiar it all is, Forster thought sadly. "I have to do it now."

"Why do you have to, Frau Steinfeld?" Forster always addressed his woman clients as 'Frau'. He never used the greeting 'Heil Hitler,' either in person or in his correspondence, signing his letters always with 'Yours sincerely,' or 'with kindest regards,' sometimes with 'I kiss your hand' if writing to a woman, but always avoiding the "German Salute".

Valerie already felt complete confidence in this man, whose face, voice, and eyes gave the impression that he had never known fear. She told him what had happened to Heinz in the Institute for Chemistry Studies, saying at the end; "That is why I cannot remain silent any longer. And that's why I came to you. You have the reputation of being a specialist in such cases."

"Is that so?" said Forster, thinking to himself: So word gets around.

"Yes. At least, that's what a friend of mine, a woman, told me. And so I would very much like you to represent me. I have to go through with it. You agree, don't you?"

He nodded. "Yes, I'm afraid so, Frau Steinfeld. If Schirach has been notified already ... besides the situation of half-castes may soon change . . . for the worse."

So it's true, Valerie thought, it's true what Nora Hill said. So Paul knows more than we know here.

"But as long as the suit is running, your son is safe."

"And afterwards? What are the chances of winning such a suit?"

"That depends on a lot of things."

"How many have you won already?"

"One," he said, adding when he saw her start, "but I have others running still, and that's the main thing."

"I don't understand . . ."

"They're always pretty complicated affairs. There's no way you could have known that, Frau Steinfeld. The first thing you must understand is that you're not the one who can bring the suit, Frau Steinfeld."

"I'm not? Who then?"

Forster tugged at his right ear lobe—right at the very spot where Manuel Aranda, in January, 1969, would see a big, ugly scar.

"Only your son can bring suit, Frau Steinfeld."

"Heinz?"

"Yes, Heinz. He has to bring suit for the purpose of having his legitimate birth revoked in favor of blood descent. That's the technicality. But wait, take it easy! Since he is still a minor, he needs a guardian. You will be the guardian. Your first step will be to go to the County Court at Währing and have yourself appointed as your son's guardian. I can represent you only as the guardian of your minor son who is bringing the suit." Forster laughed out loud when he saw Valerie's startled face. "Just a lot of legal nonsense! And there's more. As in every lawsuit, in these cases, too, there's a sort of District Attorney acting for the State whose job it is to try and have the suit dismissed—even though he's the party against whom the suit was brought."

"But that's crazy! The Court appoints an attorney to try and prove that Heinz is the son of a Jew and not an Aryan?" Valerie was getting more and more frightened.

"It's not crazy at all, Frau Steinfeld. If there were nobody there to cast doubt, contradict, and play the role of devil's advocate, these lawsuits would be child's play and we'd be doing three of them an hour—which would please the mothers, of course."

"Heinz *is* the son of an Aryan, and not my husband's!" Valerie cried. "Don't you believe me?"

Forster tugged at his ear. "If I didn't believe you, I couldn't take your case." He looked at Valerie with an expressionless face. "Does that reassure you?"

He doesn't believe me, but he's taking the case, and that's precisely why he's taking it, Valerie thought, her mood vacillating between despair and hope. She said, "Of course, it does, Dr. Forster."

"Good. As soon as I've notified the Court of the suit in which I represent the boy's guardian, the case will be heard at the Courthouse. By a single judge."

"Just one judge? Are there several who handle these cases?"

"Yes, unfortunately," said Forster. "And they're all quite different. You have a difficult time ahead of you. Frau Steinfeld, a very difficult time. The mere statement that you were unfaithful to your husband will, of course not be enough. The first thing I will need from you is a comprehensive written statement which can be used in court as the basis for the case."

"What sort of statement?"

"About your failed marriage, which you entered against

your parents' will, and which was unhappy from the very beginning. I suppose you must have had quarrels, fights, scenes?"

"Yes," said Valerie. In our entire married life we did not quarrel once, she thought.

Forster nodded, and continued in a monotone. I have to give the poor woman a few hints, he thought. If I don't like the statement when she brings it to me I'll have to help her write it again. Aloud, he said, "I assume it was only after the marriage had been consummated that you discovered that you and your husband were incompatible?"

"Yes," said Valerie, recovering her composure. (She and Martin had thought about this point together.) "All my husband ever thought of was his newspaper, and politics, politics, politics!"

"Typical," said Forster, thinking to himself, She's catching on, good.

"And you, Frau Steinfeld?"

"I was interested in more artistic pursuits. I've been actively interested in the history of art. I have taken courses, but I had to give them up at my husband's insistence."

"Was that a great disappointment to you?"

"Yes, it was. And he . . . made fun of my interests, laughed at me and teased about them!" Valerie cried.

She's catching on, thought Forster, and said, "It shows, once again, that race makes a difference, Frau Steinfeld. A crass materialist, your husband, that's how I remember him, too." They looked at each, neither of them batting an eye. "And, of course, your marriage didn't have much chance of success after he'd started deceiving you, treating you badly, neglecting you . . . would you agree?"

Paul never deceived me, never, Valerie thought, he always loved me and I loved him, but the boy's life is at stake now and I must say these things.

"Yes," she said aloud. "All those affairs with other women. It was terrible."

She's going to tear her handkerchief any moment, Forster thought, and anyone can see she's the kind of woman whose feelings are clean, healthy, straightforward. Perhaps I'd better suggest the angle to her with which my colleague in Frankfurt had so much success. Besides, it's important for me to know how much she can take and just how much can be expected of her. Aloud he said, "Did your husband deceive you because you—forgive me, Frau Steinfeld, but I have to ask

226

you this question—because you refused to let him indulge in certain unnatural sexual practices?" Valerie felt the blood rising to her face. She could not bring herself to answer.

"The court will want to know still more intimate things. It's important for you to prepare yourself for that. You are a lady from a respectable, solid, family background. Many of the questions the judge will ask you would be painful, embarrassing and humiliating even for a less decent woman than yourself. You will have to answer—there's no way around it." He went on as though she had answered his question. "Unnatural sexual wishes, I see, I suspected as much . . ."

His voice seemed to fade a little as she thought, He's trying in his own way to show me how I must behave and what's in store for me. He's trying to tell me that I'm going to have to lie, lie, lie, throw dirt on Paul's name, slander him and make him look like a pig, and Martin Landau's going to have to do the same. He wants to see if I can stand it. I'll stand it somehow. Please, God in Heaven, help me. It's all for the boy, You know that. Have mercy. Paul wants it. Let everything go well. And help Martin not to break down . . .

"The statement I have asked you for, Frau Steinfeld, must give *precise information*: names, dates, places, descriptions of what happened. Everything you say must be consistent with the data pertaining to the birth of the child. And we need witnesses to back up everything you say."

"I have a witness: Agnes Peintinger, our housekeeper. She worked for us even before my son was born. She saw everything, and can confirm what I say." (If the Reverend Pankrater permits her to, Valerie thought, and her knees began to tremble.)

"One witness is very little."

"Then there's the father's sister. She was close to it all, also . . . but she doesn't want to say anything in court."

"Why not?"

"She's afraid . . . doesn't want to have anything to do with law-courts . . . doesn't want to get involved . . ."

"That's regrettable, but understandable. Quite understandable. A lawsuit like this one is dangerous. And under certain circumstances—if you are caught in an outright lie, for instance—it might become mortally dangerous."

Oh, my God, if Martin hears that, if he hears we might be risking our lives, what will he do then, please God, what will he do?

"And the court has the right, through the agency of the

227

Public Prosecutor who is defending the legitimate birth, and is therefore our opponent, to subpoena witnesses and require them to testify."

"But Tilly—that's the father's sister—will not testify."

"That's bad," said Forster.

"Why is it bad?"

"Because if she makes use of her right to refuse to testify, the court will naturally draw its own conclusions. There must be other witnesses who are willing to—" My God, I almost said 'help' you, Forster thought, annoyed with himself "—I mean, to confirm in court from their own observation that you and the real father are telling the truth. We need someone like that, absolutely."

Valerie's face had gone gray. Her hands were clenching and unclenching all the time. Forster noticed it. It's ugly, he thought, very ugly, but what am I supposed to do? Send the woman away, with the letter from that swine of a director already on Schirach's desk? What would happen to the boy then? We've got to give it a try, we've always got to try in the fight against the Nazi swine.

Valerie looked up. "In 1923, when we got married, there was a terrible shortage of apartments in Vienna. We had to stay for a year with a woman called Hermine Lippowski. In Dornbach, outside the city. She sublet one floor in her villa to us."

"Would Frau Lippowski act as a witness on your behalf?"

"I really don't know—"

Forster flew into a rage. "And just what had you imagined, Frau Steinfeld? Did you think you could just come to me and say: my child is not the son of my husband, he has a different father, now you know it, please see that he's declared an Aryan!? What were you thinking of? Do you think the Naz—the courts like these suits?"

Valerie answered in a trembling voice, "I'll go to see Frau Lippowski today and talk to her. I'm beginning to understand."

"No, you're not beginning to understand at all. A lawsuit of this kind is no better than Russian roulette, even if you have a perfect set of witnesses, even if everything you say is true, and even if you happen to get a sympathetic judge!"

"What else has to be done?" Valerie stammered.

"There'll be a comprehensive anthropological examination," Forster said. "That is, an examination of the physical and mental properties of the boy, yourself, and the father, within the framework of the racial laws. Then there'll be an examination of Herr Steinfeld—"

"But he's in England!"

"—using photographs, as far as that's possible. The court will appoint professors to prepare the reports. Then there'll be tests to determine blood-groups. Those results will be decisive."

"I don't understand . . ." Valerie's breath came faster.

There was a ripping sound.

Now she's torn her handkerchief, Forster thought, and said, "Easy, Frau Steinfeld, easy. The point is, the child's blood-group *presupposes* certain blood-groups on the part of the parents. Various combinations are possible."

Valerie raised her head.

"But according to Mendel's researches, *certain* combinations of blood-groups on the part of the parents *exclude* certain specific blood-groups in the child."

Valerie bowed her head again. "In other words: if the child's blood-group falls into this kind of category, the blood-group combination of the parents could make it possible to say *with absolute certainty* that the man purporting to be the father of the child could not *under any circumstances* be the real father."

At these words a thunderous silence descended on the room. The dull roar of the heavy army trucks crossing the Danube Canal Bridge was audible through the closed windows.

"There's no need for you to be afraid, Frau Steinfeld, if you're quite sure the man whose name you're going to have to give me, and not your husband, is the father of your child. You are sure, aren't you?"

"Quite sure!" said Valerie quickly.

"So it's all right, then!" Poor woman. Forster was thinking. Damn that Nazi pack. "Then the blood-group tests will serve to confirm it."

"That is . . ." Valerie was stammering now, her face flushed red, her eyes jumping wildly. "That is . . . I'm as sure as I can be . . ."

"How do you mean? Are you trying to say—excuse the question, Frau Steinfeld—are you trying to say there was *a third man?*" It's always the same mess, the attorney thought, always the same.

"Yes . . . no . . . yes . . ." Valerie was close to tears. "There was another man, once . . . but it can't have been him. Defi-

229

nitely not ... I mean ... I can't imagine it was ... I'm sure it was ..."

I can't tell Martin about the blood tests, Valerie thought, terrified. He'll collapse. A man like him! A Party member!

"Even if you're not absolutely sure," Forster said, "it could happen that everything will *nevertheless* work out favorably, even if it should turn out that the man you name is not in fact the father of your child. This result would occur if the real father has the same blood-group as your husband, or if his blood-group falls within a category that could have produced the boy's when combined with yours."

"It *will* come out right! It must!" said Valerie, excitedly. "But the long wait, it's going to be a big strain on the nerves ... Would it not be possible for us to go to a doctor before the suit begins and have our blood-groups determined? Just for the sake of our peace of mind! You understand, I hope—"

"I understand," said Forster sadly. "No, Frau Steinfeld, that's not possible."

"But why not?"

"Because a test of this kind has to be done in a serological laboratory. And according to government regulations all doctors and institutes that do such tests have to report them at once to the Reich Office for Racial Purity, giving names and all other relevant details. And the first thing the court does in suits such as the one you're planning is to make a routine inquiry at the Reich Office for Racial Purity to see if there have been such tests made. If the court finds that tests have been made it tends to look to them as though—I'm sure I don't need to say any more."

"No," said Valerie. "No, you don't." Then she asked, in subdued tones: "And what if the tests show that the man I named as the father—because of the third man, I can't imagine it, but I have to know—cannot possibly be the real father. What happens then?"

"Well, then," replied Forster, and felt a stab at his heart, "then the situation would be very unpleasant, not impossible to save, but very difficult, very difficult, indeed. But possible, so don't despair. The only thing is, you would have lost the suit. So what do you want to do? I had to tell you all the pitfalls in advance, you understand. Do you still want—" He stopped as the telephone on his desk started to ring, and lifted the receiver. "Yes?" Then he called out, in a pleased voice, "Klever? Could you ask him to wait a moment in the

230

conference room?" He listened. "But I'm in the middle of an important meeting! It's going to take another half-hour, at least." He paused to listen again. "Well, all right, if that's the case, I'm coming." He replaced the receiver and got to his feet. "Please forgive me, Frau Steinfeld—a visitor who wants to see me urgently and can't wait. Will you excuse me a moment?" Valerie gave no reply.

24

The silver badge of the "League of National Socialist Lawyers" shimmered against the offical brown uniform. Party Comrade Dr. Peter Klever, Council to the Cabinet, a big man with a broad face, short, wiry hair, and bushy eyebrows, looked even bigger in his uniform, with the black sword-belt, the red swastika on his left sleeve, riding trousers and stiff knee-boots.

"Otto!"

"Peter!"

Forster walked quickly towards his visitor. The conference room was furnished with a long table and a number of chairs. Klever had removed his flat, peaked cap. The two shook hands warmly and slapped each other on the shoulders affectionately. Klever, who spoke with a strong Prussian accent, was beaming.

"Good to'see you again, my friend!"

"My pleasure, Peter, my pleasure! Have a seat!"

"I don't have time. As I told your secretary, a car's waiting for me downstairs. I came directly from the station. I have a big meeting with some bigwigs from the Vienna Bar Association."

Peter Klever was an attorney, like Forster. He had studied in Berlin, then in Vienna. As a member of the German "Socialist Students' Union" he had had guest privileges at the Austrian organization of the same name, and had met Forster there. They had become good friends. The German club was outlawed in 1933, the Austrian in 1938. Both were dissolved, but personal contact between members was kept up, and the

231

ties of friendship and loyalty strengthened. A few of them purposely took key positions in the Party in the areas of economics and politics, fully aware of the possible consequences for the future, with the aim of using the "inside" information they gained to help their friends "outside" in as safe, sure, and efficient a manner as possible. Among those who had taken this daring step was Peter Klever, who occupied a high office in the HQ of the "League of National Socialist Lawyers" in Berlin.

The Council to the Cabinet spoke in a cynical tone. "Your colleagues here are a fine bunch of swine, old buddy! Congratulations!"

"So they're not calming down?"

"Calming down?" Klever laughed sardonically. "The Vienna Bar Association is swamping us with memoranda, denunciations, and requests to start proceedings against you—more than ever!"

"What's eating them now? Are they getting all het up about the paternity suits I've been taking on?"

"That's the latest! You're getting to be more and more suspicious. But the main trouble is still with the lawsuits you conducted before 1938."

Before 1938 Forster had defended Communists and Socialists accused of high treason and subversive activities.

"I'm doing what I can for you in Berlin, believe me, old buddy. But you really can't go on the way you have been doing here. You're making those shits see red! Paternity suits! Leave them alone, I beg you! Keep quiet and stay out of the limelight for a while, and take a few Nazi clients for a change. You've got to do it! You're in danger, my friend! Will you promise me to be reasonable, and at least stop taking any more paternity suits?"

Forster tugged at his right ear, looked at his old friend, blinked, and said smiling, "I promise . . ."

"You're the limit!" The lawyer from Berlin groaned.

"What do you mean? I just promised!"

"But you were smiling! And you winked!"

"I did? Just a reflex action," Forster said. "I don't feel like smiling or winking . . ."

Five minutes later he was alone in the conference room. Klever had left, promising to keep him informed and to warn him in time if a crisis were brewing. He had hurried away deeply concerned about Forster's stubbornness. For a few minutes the attorney remained alone in the room with the large table and the many chairs. I have a wife and a son, he thought. I am responsible for them. If anything happens to me, they are defenceless. I should stop taking paternity suits, Peter said. Frau Steinfeld is all I need with her shaky, made-up case, all a pack of lies. If only they were good lies. But the poor woman has no idea. She's helpless, completely helpless. And should a woman like that be sent away when she asks for help? Forster walked slowly back to his office. Valerie looked up as he entered. She was still clasping the torn handkerchief in her hand.

"Well," the attorney said, suddenly feeling worn and exhausted. "Have you made up your mind, Frau Steinfeld?"

"Yes, I want to go through with the lawsuit," Valerie answered, her voice quavering. "Whatever happens. Why are you looking at me like that? Don't you want to take my case?"

The attorney sat down behind his desk. It's not *possible* to turn a woman like that away, he thought. It's not *right*.

"Of course I will take it," Dr. Otto Forster replied.

25

"There you have everything I dictated at the time to my secretary in Frau Steinfeld's presence, about her first visit to my offices," Dr. Forster said, twenty-seven years later, to Manuel Aranda. He was an old man now, whose hobby was building model ships and who longed to get out of Vienna, to live as far away as possible. The thick scar where Forster's right ear had once been was now glistening, white as wax.

"Of course, I didn't put anything about my conversation with Dr. Klever into the record."

"Of course not."

"But I remembered it when I was looking over the file again. That's always the case: one detail can touch off memories of all the rest."

"But you don't know how the suit ended, is that so, Doctor?"

"No. I landed in a concentration camp. After July 20,

1944 all hell broke loose for my friend Peter Klever. He was arrested and executed. All his friends were arrested, too. They got me three weeks later."

"On what charge?"

"In those days such things just happened. I was never told the precise charge. The Nazis just cited some old cases I'd done prior to '38. I ended up in Mauthausen." The attorney stroked his hand over the terribly scarred and disfigured half of his face and over the spot where his right ear had once been. "That all happened in Mauthausen. An unfortunate accident."

"An *accident?*"

Forster laughed bitterly. "Just imagine that! A watchdog went mad one evening, tore away from his leash and jumped on me. The guard tried to get the beast off, but couldn't. As you see ... The SS man managed to shoot the dog at the last moment—really at the last moment, otherwise I wouldn't be alive telling the tale. The SS man apologized to me afterwards."

"He *what?*"

"Apologized! Really! 'I'm really sorry, you asshole,' he said, 'and you weren't even doing anything to deserve it'— that's what he said," Forster said. "It was the last thing I heard before I lost consciousness." Forster shrugged. "The guard was young and rather stupid. What can you do? They no longer had the kind of guards they had in 1938. I had a lousy time, and was more dead than alive when we were liberated."

"And you don't know what became of the boy and his father either, I suppose?"

"No, I don't, unfortunately. I was in a hospital for a long time. Then I had to work very hard to get my practice going again so that I could provide for my family. We were as poor as church mice when the war ended. There were strangers living in our house here. I have to be honest: I didn't even give Frau Steinfeld another thought. I'm sorry, Mr. Aranda," the old man went on. "We—all of us—forget too easily and become preoccupied with living our own lives, and our fellowmen are not our brothers and sisters, as they should be ..."

26

Yvonne took a thin, gold-plated steel pin with a large head out of the red velvet box and carefully pierced the crumply skin of the man's balls, pushing the pin through by gently tapping the pinhead with a small gold hammer. It was already the second pin. The flabby, naked man stretched out on the rack in the torture-chamber of Nora Hill's villa moaned.

"Oh, Oh, Oh! That hurts! But I won't talk! I'm not giving any names away!" Then, in a normal voice, he went on, "One more! Put in one more!"

Yvonne was wearing a see-through lace leotard, a broad-brimmed straw hat with a pointed top, and sandals. Her eyes had been made up to give her an Oriental, slanted look. Yvonne's client was wearing shoes and socks. Dutifully she tapped at the pinhead. The pin had pierced the skin and was pinning the scrotum to a small board covered with red velvet that had been placed under the man's balls. The man—who had been introduced to Yvonne as Director Pfitzner—gave another groan. He spread his legs still further apart; he was breathing hard now.

"Torture me! Hurt me! You're not going to get one word out of me!" Then, in his normal voice, "Get the next pin in, *quick!*"

Mechanically Yvonne reached for another pin. It was Saturday night, she was tired after two nights on duty, and she was resentful that she was always the one chosen by guests like this one. Why not Coco for once, or Christine, or Isabel? Why me every time? I get the best pay, so that's all right. But what is it that attracts these fellows? They always want me, always me. She tapped the third pin through the skin and into the tiny board. The worthy Director Pfitzner gave a loud howl. He had an impressive erection by now.

"I'm no traitor, you lousy little blue Mao ant!" Pfitzner yelled. Then he whispered, "It's never been better!" He gripped the leather straps of the rack. He rolled his eyes, ground his teeth. A red light glowed in the torture chamber, which was fitted out with an Iron Virgin, lances, axes, rods, sticks, thumb-screws, gallows, pincers, lead balls, whips, and chains.

"I won't talk, you yellow-skinned slant-eye, you won't get me to talk! Down with China!" the Director screamed.

"Shut your mouth you corrupt, Western pig!" Yvonne shouted back at him, starting on the fourth pin.

"Oh, how she can rage, how she tortures me!" The fifth or sixth pin should do it, she thought, expertly contemplating the man's throbbing penis. Nora Hill had spoken to her especially about Director Pfitzner.

"Take a lot of trouble with him, will you please, Yvonne? Special trouble. The Director's here for the first time. Madeleine sent him." Madeleine was the head barmaid at one of the night clubs in the city from which Nora Hill got her girls when she needed them. "He's German, from Frankfurt. A real big shot in the export business. He confided in Madeleine and told her what he wanted. He has everything with him, in a box. You have a blue leotard, and a straw sunhat."

"But why me again, Madame?"

"Madeleine told the Director about you, what you look like and so on—and he said: 'I want her and nobody else!' So what can I do? It's an easy job, Yvonne. Be reasonable. And I've got another idea, I think the Director will go for it . . ."

And Nora explained what her idea was.

She reminded Yvonne of a certain Mr. Stahl from Duisburg, who had visited them a few months earlier. The man had brought a small suitcase with him, opened it, and given Yvonne (Yvonne again, of course) precise instructions.

"Here is the uniform of a woman Captain in the Soviet army. I want you to put it on: trousers, boots, blouse, belt, cap, everything."

"Where did you get it, darling?"

"Don't call me 'darling!' Call me 'fascist swine!' "

"Where did you get it, you fascist swine?"

"At a theatrical supply house. Here is a gramophone record. The German national anthem. We need a record player."

"We've got one, you fascist." Yvonne was catching on quickly.

"Wonderful. And here's a razor. I'm going to take off all my clothes and lie down on this Procrustean bed. And then . . ." He gave Yvonne further instructions.

Yvonne was supposed to call him names, spit at him, and slit long, fine lines across his breast with the razor. Thin trickles of blood oozed from the cuts. Yvonne's cursings became louder and louder, and Mr. Stahl from Duisburg became more and more aroused.

"Never," he shouted. "You Bolshevik criminals will never win!"

Whereupon Yvonne dealt him, by special request, a massive clout across the ears, then continued her gentle, careful slicing of the man's hairless chest. Blood was already flowing profusely.

"Now!" the man whispered.

Yvonne quickly pressed on a button which turned on a record player built into the wall of the torture chamber. The strains of the German antional anthem blasted out from two loudspeakers in the ceiling, text by Hoffmann von Fallersleben, music by Joseph Haydn. The national anthem of the Federal Republic of Germany began with the words *"Deutschland, Deutschland über alles"* ("Germany, Germany, over all"), but ever since the war had ended in defeat only the third verse was permitted to be sung on festive occasions, even though very few people knew the text.

The man from Duisburg, Mr. Stahl, had brought an old recording, a 78, and asked to have the first verse played, with its outlawed words.

And so a large mixed chorus was heard solemnly singing *"Deutschland, Deutschland über alles, über alles in der Welt ..."* and a split second later a fantastic ejaculation had gladdened the hero from Duisburg . . .

"We still have the record," Nora Hill had said to Yvonne. "He forgot to take it with him. Director Pfitzner is from Germany. Frankfurt, Duisburg, it's all the same. For him you're a Chinese woman who tortures him. That's what he wants. I think it will be a special treat for him if you switch the record on just before he . . ."

Yvonne tapped the fifth pin into place. Only another few seconds, she thought, watching attentively.

"Not one word," the naked, pot-bellied Director Pfitzner moaned. "You're not going to get one word out of me! I'm not going to give anyone away! Never!"

"Oh, yes, you are, you're going to betray them all, you miserable Imperialist! You bag of shit! You damned warmonger! Where are those counterrevolutionaries, those murderers hiding? Come on, out with it!" Yvonne shouted. She gave an extra hard tap on the pinhead to drive the sixth pin through his balls. Let him have his money's worth, she thought, as Director Pfitzner screamed with pleasure.

Hi-ho, here it comes!

In a flash Yvonne switched on the hidden record player with the record from Duisburg. The anthem came, loud and clear, from both loudspeakers: *"Deutschland, Deutschland, über alles . . ."*

How about that? Yvonne thought, turning to Director Pfitzner, how about that?

". . . über alles in der Welt . . ."

A bestial roar split the air.

Director Pfitzner lunged upwards from the rack, kicking Yvonne sharply in the stomach with his right shoe. She screamed, fell backwards, and gasped for breath sickened by the pain. The straw hat had fallen off her head.

". . . wenn es stets zum Schutz and Trutze . . ."

Director Pfitzner had raised himself to his full, massive height. His hair stood wildly on end. His pot-belly flopped up and down, and so did the little board between his legs.

"Turn it off! Turn that damned song off!"

The Director began groping all over the room, in his rage scattering whips, thumb-screws and other devices around the floor. He could not find the record player, nor reach the loudspeakers, even though he tried jumping up towards them.

"Turn that shit song off! Turn it off, turn it off! Are you going to do it, you filthy whore?" And the Director stormed over to where Yvonne was stretched out on the ground and started to kick her viciously. She screamed at the top of her voice.

Director Pfitzner was beside himself with rage. What's gone wrong, Yvonne thought, in a panic. Has he gone out of his mind? Pfitzner dragged her to her feet and started to pummel her with his fists. She staggered back against a wall. He followed her, fists flying, cursing: "Turncoat! Swine! A disgrace! You won't get away with that! I'll have the police on you! Take that, you filthy swine, and that . . . and that!"

". . . from the Maas to the Memel . . ." The words of the anthem thundered across the room.

Yvonne was now too far from the button she could have pressed to turn off the record. Quickly she pressed the emergency button. In Nora Hill's living room and in four

238

other places in the house the number of Yvonne's room showed up in the little black call boxes.

". . . from the Esch to the Belt . . ." A host of female voices . . .

Director Pfitzner was yanking at Yvonne's hair and beating her with his fists all over her body. The blue leotard was ripped to shreds. Yvonne screamed and tried to get away from him, but he blocked her way, his arms flailing like windmills.

"You damned whore," he shouted. "Are you trying to make fun of me?" He was in pain himself: the board was pulling at his balls. In addition to everything else.

"I . . . but how . . ."

"Whore! Think I'm a joke, eh? I'll teach you!"

"*. . . Deutschland, Deutschland über alles . . .*"

The door flew open.

George in a dinner-jacket, stormed in, behind him another manservant. They leaped at the raging man from behind, twisting his arms behind his back and pushing him away from Yvonne, who sank to the ground sobbing.

"Let me go, you dogs! Let me go, you Austrian swine!"

"Please calm down, Sir, please, calm down," George shouted, while he and the other manservant held their prey in an iron grip. He twisted Pfitzner's arm behind his back. The Export Director roared with pain.

"Are you going to be a good boy now?" George asked softly.

Nora Hill swung into the room on her crutches, slamming the door shut behind her. She was wearing a long, dark-blue evening gown and glittering jewelry.

"*. . . über a-alles in de-er Welt!*" The anthem had reached the climactic line. The orchestra came in with an ear-shattering crescendo.

"What's been going on here?" Nora Hill shouted.

"Something not to your satisfaction?"

The flabby man whirled around.

"*Satisfaction?*" he screamed, struggling to loosen himself from the grip of the two men, causing the board which hung from his scrotum to swing and send jabbing pains through him. His penis had long since shrivelled down to the flaccid state. "Satisfaction? I don't like being laughed at!"

"Laughed at?" asked Nora Hill, unable to understand.

"The anthem! That goddammed anthem! You did it on purpose. It was an intentional insult!"

"Nothing of the sort! It's true, we got the anthem out especially for you——"

"Aha!"

". . . but only to do you a special favor!"

"Favor?"

"You're German, aren't you? From Frankfurt? So we thought we'd——"

"Yes! Yes! Yes! I come from Frankfurt," Director Pfitzner shouted, beside himself with rage, the velvet-covered board bouncing up and down. "But it's *Frankfurt-on-the-Oder* I come from!"

27

". . . from the German Democratic Republic, from East Germany. And we idiots played the West German national anthem for him," said Yvonne Werra, concluding her account.

Manuel laughed.

"I would laugh myself if I weren't still so sore all over," the beautiful redhead said plaintively. "Madame keeps saying she kick herself. No more anthems in her house! I think that anthems cause a lot of grief, anyway."

Yvonne was lying on a wide couch in the ultra-modern living-room of her large apartment. Manuel had called her as agreed around noon, and Yvonne had asked him to visit her without mentioning her mishap. When he rang the doorbell Yvonne appeared draped in a short dressing gown over a baby-doll set, bent over and pressing one hand to her side.

"What's the matter, for God's sake?"

"Come in. I have to lie down."

She walked quickly ahead of him into the living-room, where she slipped under the blanket on the couch after taking off her dressing-gown. "It's not serious, but it's painful. It'll be all right tomorrow, the doctor says. He was here this morning. The same one as last night."

"Last night?"

"Madame's house-doctor. He's always on the spot. Does

240

everything for her and for us girls. Everything, if you know what I mean."

"I understand. But what happ—"

"Just a second. I'll tell you in a second. I really caught it this time. Professional risk. Could have been much worse, the doctor said. Look!" She lifted the blanket and one of the bandages around the right side of her body. Manuel recoiled a step when he saw the black, red, and green whirls on her white skin: a huge, severe bruise as big as a dinner plate.

"How did it happen?" Yvonne told him.

Then she stretched, moaning.

"George had to sock the Director a couple of times before he was back to normal. Can you imagine that? In the meantime, Madame had rushed off to fetch the doctor. He's always prompt, he's a real darling. I've had all sorts of things happen to me before now, but never anything this bad. George drove me home, of course, in Madame's car. She has no idea you're here, by the way."

"I'd thought so. Otherwise you wouldn't have been so secretive with your note. I assume Madame Hill doesn't like her girls to have private guests."

"That's true, but there's another factor in your case." Yvonne pulled a face. "Oh, my God, it hurts! That pig of a masochist!"

"What's the other factor?"

"Your *father*, what do you think? I may be able to help you. As I told you in my letter, your father was here, in this very room."

"When? How often?"

"Four times. Always when I was free. The last time was two days before he died."

"Where did you meet him?"

"At the Ritz."

"What?" Manuel looked at her, unbelieving. "It's true! One evening—I'd just finished work and was on my way home—Madame gave me a letter for your father, and asked me to deliver it to the Ritz."

"What was in the letter?"

"I've no idea. All I know is that Madame got it from the American. Grant, his name was."

"I know him. His voice, anyway. I talked to him over the phone once."

"Well, she got the letter from him. They had whispered together for a while—the Russian was with them, too. San-tarin."

"I've heard about him, too. But why were you chosen to deliver the letter?"

"Madame said the men wanted me to. It was urgent, and I would be the least conspicuous messenger. There must have been some deal going on between the American, the Russian, and your father."

"It would seem so."

"Your father *never* came out to the villa, not once. I don't know where he met with those two men. But *I* met him at the Ritz." Yvonne smiled. "We had a drink at the bar and talked a bit. Then when he heard I was free the next day he asked if he could visit me." Yvonne noticed Manuel's look. "He never tried ... I never ... we never slept together, I swear! He was just fond of me. And I liked him, too. He was an interesting man. And more generous than all the other guys put together!" said Yvonne, a depressed look coming over her face. "But he was scared stiff."

"*Scared stiff?* What of?"

"Of being murdered," replied Yvonne Werra.

28

"Did he ever say *who* he was scared of?"

"No, never. I asked him once. He just shook his head. He couldn't talk about it. But he believed he would never get out of Vienna alive. He said it more than once."

"And you didn't do anything about it?"

"What could I have done?"

"Tell the police."

Yvonne Werra raised a hand. "I didn't tell anyone. First because he asked me not to tell a soul he was so scared. And then, because ..." She hesitated.

"Yes? Then what?"

"Look, I see so many peculiar men in my profession. Your father was normal. But perhaps not quite, I used to tell my-self. Maybe his fear of being murdered was *his* thing. At least, that's what I thought. What an idiot I was! But I couldn't have saved him, even if I had gone to the police, or . . . ?"

"I don't think so. Don't blame yourself." Manuel stepped over to a window.

"But I wanted to tell you. Perhaps it will help you. You are trying to find out what happened, aren't you?"

"Yes, I am."

"Well, one thing is certain: your father knew someone was trying to kill him."

Yvonne spoke pure high German, without a trace of an accent. "He was scared. And when it happened, it couldn't have been completely unexpected."

"But if he was scared . . ." Manuel broke off.

"Yes?" Yvonne asked, pressing against the bandage on her stomach with her hands on top of the blanket.

"Nothing. He had no idea, of course, where the murder might be committed, or how. Or did he?"

"He said once, 'If it happens, they're going to arrange for it to come suddenly, in a completely nonsensical place, so that it looks like a totally incomprehensible act.' "

"He said that?"

"Yes. And I said he ought to go to the police! Yes, I *did* tell him that more than once. But he always just smiled and said the police couldn't help him. Nobody could. That's when I began to think maybe it was just his particular crazy thing . . ."

Manuel turned around.

He looked at Yvonne without speaking.

Then he let his gaze wander about the room.

I'm pursued by books, he thought, truly, I'm pursued by books! Even in Yvonne Werra's apartment there is one whole wall covered with books. Manuel walked over to the shelves. Not many novels, he thought. A lot of philosophical, political, sociological works. And alongside them, strangely enough, poetry! Volumes of English, German, French, Italian poetry as well as translations of Indian, Japanese, Russian, Polish, and Portuguese poetry.

"How old are you, Yvonne?"

"The same age as you, I think—twenty-five."

"I'm twenty-six."

"So, I'm almost the same age. Why? Oh, of course. Now comes the big question."

"What question is that?"

243

" 'What's a girl like you doing in a house like Frau Hill's?' That's what you were going to ask, isn't it?"

He nodded.

"The only way to fight the establishment is from the inside."

"What sort of nonsense is that?"

"It's not nonsense!" She sat up. "Ouch! I said that to your father. too. He understood what I meant."

"What?"

"Why I gave up my studies of philosophy, and became first a barmaid. then a girl at Madame's."

"I don't understand. Why did you?"

"Disgust." Yvonne said. "Disgust and revulsion."

"At what?"

"At the society we live in. At the establishment. I have a boy-friend, you know. For four years now. He studied in Vienna first, architecture, high-rise and medium-rise buildings. Now he's at the Munich Institute of Technology. We plan to marry, Robert and I, as soon as he has his degree and can begin practicing. He comes to visit me once a month, whenever he can. He's a member of SDS, which keeps him very busy."

"Member of what?"

"SDS. 'Students for a Democratic Society.' German branch."

"Oh," said Manuel. "So he's an angry young man. Strikes and demonstrations and sit-ins and walk-outs and teach-ins and take-overs of administration buildings and protest marches and fights on the streets. I know."

"There's no need for you to make fun of it! Robert—" Yvonne sat up and pressed a hand against her painful liver.

"Better stay down!"

But she was not listening to him. Passionately she shouted, "Just look at the world around you! A pigsty! And who do you think has all the power in this world? Who is it who has influence and money, who's responsible for wars and catastrophes, who governs and oppresses and enslaves people, who makes deals and breaks them, who lies and betrays and murders? I see it all the time! Nobody could have a better close-up look at these people than I get!" Yvonne had talked herself into a rage. "All the régimes that have brought the world to the brink of catastrophe—the Church, Communism, Fascism—all of them achieved their aims by sex taboos. Every erection was a sin! Sexual instincts had to be sublimated into serving the Party or dying a heroic death for the Fatherland. The result? Well, what do you think? A bunch of impotents, masochists, queers, fetishists, addicts, all screwed-up, depraved, embittered, evil souls! A mob of crazies rotting alive: Madame's guests. Diplomats! Bankers! Army officers! Artists! Psychiatrists! Industrialists! Churchmen! Spies! Double-agents, triple-agents, quadruple-agents! Intellectuals! Demagogues! Politicians! The ruling-class, the whole caboodle! Take your pick! And what they want is to be whipped and beaten and have their balls pricked and their chests slashed and be hung upside down and have feathers stuck up their arseholes and be clawed and scratched and tickled and spat upon. And you can bet they'll ask for the "Cowls" and the "Sawteeth" and the "Five-on-One" and the "Hare and Hedge-hog" and the "Sandman" and the "Water-nymphs" and the—"

"Ask for what?" Manuel interjected, baffled.

"For ....oh, hell, how can I explain all that stuff to you!? It's always the same complicated pigsty business, there's no other way to satisfy jerks of their sort! That's the society we live in! I see it night after night at Madame's!" Yvonne fell silent, breathing heavily.

"But you make a good living and from all that don't have to work hard like other young girls, and you have a car and a beautiful apartment—"

"And give half of what I earn to the SDS!" she shouted.

"Good Lord!" said Manuel. He collapsed laughing onto a stool behind him, unable to contain himself.

Yvonne had a sense of humor, too, and laughed along with him, so hard her liver began to hurt.

"Ouch!" she said. "That's funny all right. Terribly funny. Just like life." Her expression became serious. "Now you've laughed, just like your father. It amused him very much too when I told him. And because I noticed it took his mind off other things, I kept telling him stories, and sometimes I exaggerated ... I could see he enjoyed it a lot."

"Yvonne," said Manuel, "you're a good girl."

"Oh, come on," she replied. "Cut that out." Then she smiled suddenly and said, "Thanks."

Manuel smiled too and went to look over the bookshelves once again.

"Poems," said Yvonne. "I really love poems. So did your father."

"I know,"

"He was thrilled when he saw my collection of lyric poetry. He often had me read poems to him."

"What sort of poems?"

"All sorts. A complete mixture. I know English, French and Italian, and he knew those languages too. My Spanish is very bad. We had a little game . . ."

"I read the poems in the original language, and then we would try to translate them into German. The winner was the one with the more beautiful translation. It was nice. There was just once he . . ."

"What?"

"Oh, a stupid little thing. Not worth talking about."

"What were you going to say, Yvonne?"

"Really, Mr. Aranda, it's not important."

"Please tell me anyway!"

"All right, if you insist." She lay down again. "I like Kipling a lot. Not so much his nationalistic poems, but all the others."

"Same here," said Manuel. "My father was very fond of Kipling, too."

Yvonne nodded. "That's why I often read to him from Kipling. In English. "The Ballad of East and West," "Gentlemen-Rankers"—you know them—"Damned from here to Eternity," "Mandalay," "Bolivar," "Tommy," "Tomlinson." And so on. And then one time we had a little bit of a disagreement. I only remember it because it was the only time I ever saw your father annoyed, upset, really worked-up!"

"What was the occasion?" Manuel asked, trying to hide the excitement welling up inside him. "Oh, it all concerned a few lines out of "The Light that Failed." Right at the beginning. You know them perhaps: *And Jimmy . . .*"

"I can't remember them off-hand . . ."

"Oh, surely!" Yvonne went on quoting:

> *And Jimmy went to the rainbow's foot,*
> *because he was five and a man.*
> *And that's how it all began, my dears,*
> *and that's how it all began.*

"And? What happened then?"

Yvonne shrugged. "It was stupid, I tell you, the whole thing was stupid! We were seeing who could translate this verse best. Into German. My version went: *Und Jimmy ging nach dem Regenbogen, weil er schon fünf war und ein*

246

Mann. Und so fing alles an, meine Lieben, und so fing alles an."

Manuel could feel his heart beating hard and loud. He sat down on the edge of the couch.

"And my father?"

"His translation was: *Und Jimmy ging* zum *Regenbogen*, and that's what started our argument. I mean, you can't go *right up to* a rainbow, can you, and that's what the "*zum*" would imply? The rainbow: that's the symbol of beauty, truth, justice, universal reason and happiness, peace in the world—of all that's unattainable on earth, in other words. Which is why Kipling wrote: *And Jimmy went* to the rainbow's foot. To its *foot!* I was trying to render the spirit of Kipling's line by using the German preposition "*nach*," which means "toward," so that my version, which went "*Und Jimmy ging* nach dem *Regenbogen*," would mean "And Jimmy went toward the rainbow" or "And Jimmy followed the rainbow," and so would catch Kipling's sense more closely. But your father wanted to say "*Und Jimmy ging* zum *Regenbogen*," which would mean "And Jimmy went up to the rainbow," and that didn't seem right to me ... I don't know if you're following what I mean?"

"Yes, I know what you mean." My heart's beating so loudly, Manuel thought. I wonder if she's noticed? Is this the clue I've been looking for? Am I going to get a step ahead this time? "And so that's what you quarrelled about?"

"It was too ridiculous for words! I couldn't take it too seriously. But your father—for him, strangely enough, it was like life and death. It was really weird, you know ... he got completely worked up about it.

"Nach *dem Regenbogen*" is ugly, he said, clumsy, too long!"

"He said it was "too long?" Can you be sure he used those words?"

"How do you mean? I don't understand . . ."

"Did he say "*nach dem Regenbogen*" was "too long"?"

"Yes, he did."

"Are you quite sure?"

"Absolutely! I can still hear him saying it. But why is that so important? You look so pale all at once, Mr. Aranda. Are you not feeling well?"

29

The café was big, old, and dirty.

It was called "Eldorado," and was in the Praterstrasse. It was a gathering place for cardsharpers, whores, pimps, drunks of both sexes, pitiful and down on their luck, professional crooks and down-and-outs. There were police raids almost every night.

Manuel had driven as far as the "Eldorado," which was quite a long way from Yvonne's apartment, even though he had seen plenty of telephone booths near her house. It was important for him to speak to Commissioner Groll as soon as possible, but he did not want to endanger Yvonne any more than was necessary.

"What can I get you, sir?"

Manuel had hardly set foot in the dimly lit bar when he was approached by a giant of a waiter with a neck like a bull and a pockmarked face, who wore a stained white jacket and a crumpled shirt. He had two front teeth missing. It had suddenly gone quiet in the crowded café. The whores, pimps, and tipplers all had their eyes on Manuel, the pimps lowering their cards, the whores their tabloids and illustrated magazines. Sitting around with their pimps seemed to constitute their Sunday afternoon outing. The pimps and the girls were all dolled up in their finery. The tipplers were blind drunk, as always, whether it was Sunday or a weekday. The café was closed only between four and six o'clock in the morning.

"A cognac, please, and I'd like to make a telephone call."

"There's a booth at the back," the heavyweight waiter said. He escorted Manuel to the passageway leading to the toilets. "French?"

"French what?"

"Cognac."

"That'll be fine." Manuel disappeared into the booth, which stank of cigarette smoke and urine.

A young prostitute got to her feet and smoothed her hands over her thighs.

"What's the matter with you, Lucy baby?" her pimp asked, who was sitting at the next table.

"Didn't you see? A man on his own . . ."

The pimp patted her buttocks tenderly. "Sit down, honey. No need to let anyone hump you this afternoon. Such a good girl all week, in all that lousy weather, too."

Lucy baby sat down. She was touched.

"That's really nice of you, Schorsch!"

"And tomorrow we're going to get that red dress you've had your eyes on."

Lucy baby had tears in her eyes. "You mean it? You're too good to me, Schorsch."

"I just try to do what's right. Hard work deserves to be rewarded." Schorsch said.

". . . Praterstrasse, "Eldorado Café." He just went inside. Over." The man with the hand microphone in the white Chevrolet was wearing a duffle coat. His car was parked a few steps away from Manuel's on the deserted street. Today it was the Americans' turn to tail Manuel.

"Okay? Eagle Master," came a voice through the loud-speaker in the Chevrolet. It belonged to a man in the transmission room at the Hietzinger Quay HQ. "Can one of you go into the bar and take a look what he's up to?"

The man with the microphone looked over at his colleague behind the wheel. "Charley was in there already. Our friend's telephoning. One second! He's coming out! Getting in his car. Driving away. We're behind him."

"Okay, Eagle Master, report back soon. Over."

Eagle Master did in fact report back very soon afterwards: "Calling Stardust, come in, Stardust . . ."

"Receiving you, Eagle Master."

"Aranda drove over to the Security HQ. He's just going in. Now! On a Sunday afternoon! He must be on to something big. Be sure and tell the Chief, Stardust. We'll hang on here and wait for Aranda."

30

"The quotation's the one we were looking for!" Groll hurried over to Manuel as he entered the quiet office and helped him out of his overcoat. "Trans just called me."

"Who?"

"Trans—that's the Federal Police Coding Department. It's short for *translatio*, or translation."

"And?"

The silver-haired criminologist was extraordinarily depressed and uneasy. To hide his inner feelings he put on an exaggerated show of good cheer. If Manuel had not been so keyed-up himself, he would have noticed that Groll was trying to stall, to avoid having to come out at once with something he knew he was going to have to say. Of all people, why do I have to be the one who is going to have to inform Manuel, he thought. Well, he would do it slowly, carefully, step by step.

"My colleagues over at the Parkring decoded the whole text. They've got all sorts of tables to help them, machines and computers . . ." Groll led Manuel over to the desk, where he had placed the photocopies of the manuscript pages. The original was locked up in the safe at the offices of the lawyer, Stein. Groll pulled up his chair. How will the boy react, he was thinking; he's emotionally unstable, anything is possible in that state: despair, apathy, hate, aggression. Aggression and hate against all those who got his father involved in this affair. Against the Americans, the Soviets, and the French, in other words. Good God! And the boy only needs to take just one wrong step and he's done for. These people know no mercy. Aranda's life is in grave danger.

"Please sit down, Manuel—you don't have any objection to my calling you Manuel?"

"No, of course not . . ."

"Fine. So, let me explain the system to you. As long as we don't have the transcript from Trans we might as well . . . I mean, while we're waiting . . ." I'm stuttering now, to make things worse, Groll thought.

"Explain the system to me, please, Sir," said Manuel.

Groll wiped his hand across his brow.

"Something wrong?"

"Just a headache. The weather, I guess. Now, as I thought, it's a "Caesar," a twenty-five point Caesar, worked out according to the substitution method." Groll took a sheet of paper and a pencil. "I'm going to do a preliminary sketch first so that you can understand the method. First let me write down the German sentence that is the basis for the code."

UND JIMMY GING ZUM REGENBOGEN

He wrote it out.

"Now we write the appropriate number under each letter, counting according to the order in which the letters appear in the alphabet. Since there is no *A* in the quotation, the number *1* goes to the letter in the sentence alphabetically closest to *A*."

"That will be the B in *Regenbogen!*"

"Correct. So we put the number *1* under the *B* in *Regenbogen*. Now which letter in the sentence would be alphabetically closest to *B*?"

"The *D* in *UND!*"

"So we put a *2* underneath the *D*. The next letter?"

"*E.* In *Regenbogen*."

"Good."

"But that word has three *E*s!"

"Exactly. Otherwise it would be too easy to crack the code. Your father numbered the *E*s in sequence, Trans told me over the phone. They'd got far enough to know that much. Your father did the same with all the letters that appear more than once. So the first *E* is *3*, the second *E* is *4*, and the third *E*, *5*. Let's go on. The next letter alphabetically is the *G*. There are four of those in the sentence! So we get the numbers *6*, *7*, *8*, and *9* . . ." The pair continued to work until Groll's sketch looked like this:

U	N	D	J	I	M	M	Y	G	I	N	G	Z	U	M
22	16	2	12	10	13	14	24	6	11	17	7	25	23	15
			R	E	G		E	N	B	O	G	E	N	
			21	3	8		4	18	1	20	9	5	19	

"Now we write the beginning of your father's *coded* text underneath the numbers," said Groll. He continued the jottings:

U	N	D	J	I	M	M	Y	G	I	N	G	Z	U	M
22	16	2	12	10	13	14	24	6	11	17	7	25	23	15
E	I	Q	X	S	R	F	S	T	R	L	U	C	T	X
			R	E	G	E	N	B	O	G	E	N		
			21	3	8	4	18	1	20	9	5	19		
			M	N	C	R	Y	E	Y	B	S	X		

"But the coded text goes on for many more pages," Manuel said.

"True. But the Jimmy sentence is the key. Each time you get to the end of it, you start again. Just watch . . ."

And Groll wrote out:

U	N	D	J	I	M	M	Y	G	I	N	G	Z	U	M
22	16	2	12	10	13	14	24	6	11	17	7	25	23	15
			R	E	G	E	N	B	O	G	E	N		
			21	3	8	4	18	1	20	9	5	19		
			W	H	V	E	M	G	A	J	G	X		

"But, can you tell me what the decoded text says?" Manuel asked insistently.

"I don't know that myself yet," Groll lied. "That's what we're trying to work out. The beginning at least." And that will be more than enough, good God, yes, Groll thought. "It takes us infinitely longer than it would the boys at Trans. They have tables and a computer, as I told you. Your father had a table, too, to help him work faster. He probably threw it away when he had finished."

"Commissioner, *please!*"

"Yes, of course . . . So, now we write down the alphabet, in order, and twice, one after the other. That should be enough, I think." He wrote it down:

A	B	C	D	E	F	G	H	I	J	K	L	M	N	O	P	Q	R	S	T	U
V	W	X	Y	Z	A	B	C	D	E	F	G	H	I	J	K	L	M	N	O	P
Q	R	S	T	U	V	W	X	Y	Z

"Now let's see. The first letter in the *coded* text is an *E*. The first letter in the quotation the code is based on is a *U*. The 'U' has the number *22* under it. Next your father took the first letter of the first word he wanted to encode and counted twenty-two letters on in the *alphabet*. That's how he got the E in the *coded text*. We have to do it *backwards*. We have to take the letter *E* in our alphabets—using the second alphabet, I suggest, because 22 is a long count—then count twenty-two letters *back*. That brings us to ... *I!* So *I* is the first letter of the decoded text."

Groll wrote down the *I*.

They went on with the task. After seven minutes they had the first words of the decoded text, which were in German:

ISOLIERUNG UND WIRKUNG DES NERVENGIFTES AP SIEBEN
(ISOLATION AND EFFECT OF NERVE GAS AP SEVEN)

31

Silence. Absolute silence.

No reaction at all.

He is nearly immobile—his gaze is fixed.

Just as I imagined, thought Groll, watching Manuel attentively. He's beginning to see the light. Slowly everything's becoming clear to him. And it may even give him a certain amount of relief to see clearly. Relief, for a while, anyway. But let's wait. Let's wait ...

I knew the opening words, of course, I knew what it was all about before the boy got here. The fellows at Trans told me. I've been expecting something of the sort from the very beginning. Ever since I knew that the Americans, the Russians, and the French, all had been negotiating with the boy's father. Ever since I knew his father owned one of the biggest pesticide businesses in Argentina. And that was why I kept trying to get the boy to give up his search.

"Of course it had already occurred to me that it could be something of that sort," Manuel said in a flat, expressionless voice. "My father was a chemist, after all, and a biologist. Pesticides ... I thought ... but I just couldn't *imagine* ... I thought I knew everything about him and his work, our work ...I ..." He bent over. "Let's go on!"

"It's going to take forever by our method! Trans will be sending over the complete text in two hours or so at the most."

"And what shall we do during those two hours? Sit here and wait?"

It's no use trying to stall him any longer, Groll thought. Let's go on, then. Better now than later. Groll knew the next words in the text, but he went through the motions of decoding them with Manuel nevertheless.

AUFGABESCHEIN IN KUVERT AN MICH SELBST ADRESSIERT UND
POSTE RESTANTE POSTAMT 119 GESCHICKT
(RECEIPT MAILED IN ENVELOPE ADDRESSED TO MYSELF CARE OF POSTE RESTANTE POST OFFICE 119).

"What sort of receipt?" Manuel asked slowly and deliberately. He was staring directly at Groll, but Groll had a feeling that the boy did not really see him.

"I don't know," he said. "From what we've been able to learn your father sold this ... product ... to the Russians and the Americans. He had set up the coded manuscript for his third partner, the French."

"But why?" Manuel's voice was still devoid of emotion, his gaze still rigid.

"Perhaps he had trouble making a deal with them. Maybe he didn't trust them. My thought is the following: the French wanted the goods first, and to pay later. That was too big a risk for your father, who, as you learned from Yvonne, lived in constant fear for his life. No wonder, considering what he was up to! The Russians and the Americans would certainly have done everything to prevent him from selling to the French if they had found out that that was his intention. What we do know is that your father was planning to fly home on Friday morning. On Thursday he was poisoned. My assumption is that if he hadn't been killed he would have handed over the coded manuscript to the French before flying home, and then waited in Buenos Aires until the French came up with the money. Once in possession of the cash he would have given them the key to the code, and authorized a lawyer in Vienna to pick up the letter he had addressed to himself and sent to Post Office 119. Your father wanted to get out of Vienna more than anything else: it was getting too hot for him here. Where is his passport?"

"At the hotel."

"We'll drive by and get it. Meantime my friend Hanseder

254

can try to reach the Manager of the Post Office so that we can get the letter. Today is Sunday, and it's closed. It's quite a long way out, in the Pötzleindorfstrasse."

32

The envelope bore the coat-of-arms of the Ritz hotel. After a cursory glance at their identification papers, the manager of the suburban Post Office, an astonishingly young man, had handed it over to them with an ill-tempered expression on his face. Groll had literally got him out of his double bed. Manuel opened the envelope. It contained a light-blue piece of paper with the number 11568. LEFT LUGGAGE OFFICE VIENNA WEST in large black print, and a faded date stamp saying 2nd January 1969.

"That's the day my father arrived in Vienna!" said Manuel in a dull voice. "He must have taken something to the Left Luggage Office that same day . . ."

"At Vienna West, let's go," said Groll.

Groll got in behind the wheel of the roomy official car they had used for the drive. Manuel sat beside him. They drove the long stretch back to the Gürtel, then to the Mariahilfstrasse and the station. They had no escort, but Groll was carrying a pistol. He was quite sure, though, that nothing would happen. He said to Manuel, "It was a good idea to let all the parties concerned know that your father's manuscript is in a lawyer's office and that its contents will be published if anything should happen to you. Now they're all mightily concerned for your well-being."

As he drove along the deserted Gürtel—Vienna looking like a ghost town on this grim January afternoon—Groll repeatedly looked into his rearview mirror.

"Excellent. Excellent. Your protectors," he said. "Turn around and take a look. The white Chevrolet."

"How do you know that's the car?"

"It was parked in front of Police HQ, and has been following us ever since."

Groll shifted gears and stepped on the gas. The car shot

forward. The Chevrolet behind them accelerated immediately.

"See?" Groll said.

Manuel did not answer.

A number of down-and-outs, shabby and unshaven, hung around the Vienna West station to keep warm. Some were sitting on the benches in the upper hallway, others were sleeping or drinking from bottles. There were very few travellers to be seen.

The baggage window was between a large newsstand and a delicatessen. A few people were standing nearby. Groll turned around, aimlessly it seemed. A man in a duffle coat had come in through one of the glass doors, and as he felt Groll's gaze light upon him he wandered over to the tobacco counter and bought a pack of cigarettes. So here's one, thought Groll. "So, that's it, sir, if you please." The attendant had surfaced from the maze of luggage racks carrying a flat, square box about twenty by twenty inches. The box was secured with copper wire and lead seals. The attendant looked at the date on the receipt.

"It's been here since the January 2. Today is the 19th. That will be . . ." The man's lips moved as he added up the cost in his head. ". . . ninety schillings! It's a lot, but it's been here a long time and the daily charge is . . ."

"It's all right," Manuel said and paid the man. He took the box, and was surprised by its weight.

"What's in it, do you think?"

"Let's go to the car. I have a pair of pliers there. We'll soon see." Groll replied.

33

Dr. Raphaelo Aranda spoke in a pleasant, soft, low-pitched voice. He was speaking English, with almost no trace of an accent. It was the voice of a dead man. vibrant, clear, almost exaggeratedly distinct. Manuel sat listening to it, hands on his knees, motionless. He had listened to a dead person's voice once before: Valerie Steinfeld. And now. like a new reminder that these two, Valerie Steinfeld and his father, were inseparable, that they belonged together beyond life and death, that their lives had become as one, as one, as one . . . here was the voice of Manuel's father.

"We know," said the mellifluous voice, "that bacteriological and chemical weapons are infinitely more effective than hydrogen bombs. For one thing, the cost of manufacturing B-and C-weapons is not especially high; for another, the success quotient is millions and billions of times greater, especially with the B-weapons, and the attendant risk reduced to a mere fraction. In the case of the nerve gas AP Seven, which we have developed the success quotient is in the trillions of times greater . . ."

A drawing appeared on the silver screen of the small projection room in the basement of the Security HQ. A 16mm color film was running accompanied by magnetically recorded sound. The large reel had been in the black box which Groll and Manuel had collected at Vienna West.

"How did my father get this into Vienna?" Manuel asked when they had unpacked the box while still in the car. Groll had looked out of the window.

"You had a visit from a representative of the Argentine legation, did you not? They are worried. There are such things as diplomatic couriers, whose bags are not opened and searched at Customs. I could imagine that your father . . ."

"I see."

"He must have used a second print of the film."

"A second one?"

"Well, yes, for the Americans and the Russians," Groll had said.

The voice of Dr. Raphaelo Aranda came from the screen, agreeable and firm. It was explaining the screened diagram:

"In order to extinguish all human, animal, and plant life over an area of one square kilometer of land, at least ten tons of the American nerve gas *Sarin* would be needed, according to calculations by Harvard microbiologist Professor Meselson." A pointer followed the outline of the diagram. "A poisonous cloud would form at a height of four hundred feet . . ." The pointer moved across the black lines on yellow background, and the voice of Manuel's father continued. "For a hydrogen bomb, a kilogram would be needed. One-tenth of a gram for poisonous bacteria. A thousandth of a gram for poisonous viruses . . ." The voice rose in pitch and intensity: ". . . but for our new war weapon, the AP Seven,

257

the quantity needed *would not exceed one half-thousandth of a gram . . ."*

The diagram flicked off the screen. Groll could see beads of sweat glistening on Manuel's brow.

Next the film depicted a laboratory gleaming in white and silver. Ghostly figures were moving around clad in red-orange protective suits, protective boots, protective gloves, hoods, and gas-masks. In the middle of the room stood a breeder bull, its legs chained together. One of the ghost men pressed what looked like half a rubber ball over the mouth and nostrils of the animal. Tubing connected the rubber ball to an apparatus where a second ghost man sat at a set of controls. The next moment the bull keeled over, foam dripping from its mouth from which the rubber had been removed, its eyes rolled back to show only the whites. The animal was dead.

The voice of Manuel's father spoke the commentary in factual, friendly tones. "This bull inhaled 500 cubic centimeters of air, containing only 10 molecules of AP Seven. Inhalation of the gas caused instant circulatory paralysis, and with it instant death . . ."

Manuel shivered.

The picture on the screen changed. They showed air-pipes, ultra-violet rays for sterilizing the air, and other laboratories, with Manuel's father saying, ". . . AP Seven is the ideal aerosol, a substance as fine as dust that can be sprayed in particles the size of a micron, that is one-thousandth of a millimeter in diameter, from aeroplanes, rockets, or balloons. Particles of this size will penetrate the alveoli of the lungs within a few split seconds, as is shown in the following experiments . . ."

The picture became razor sharp: cages with dogs, birds, porpoises, rabbits; fish tanks full of fish.

The camera panned over the various animal pens. All the animals were healthy and lively.

The camera swung back. The animals were all lying dead in their cages and tanks.

". . . other spray experiments prove that AP Seven works just as quickly and effectively on all types of plants . . ."

A new picture: trees, grass, flowers, and grain growing in gigantic glass-covered greenhouses.

From one moment to the next the lustrous colors had gone, the trees were bared of their leaves, the flowers, the grass, and the grain faded, collapsed, blackened . . .

"... AP Seven is resistant to heat and cold and can therefore be used in all weather conditions ..."

Pictures showing more and different rooms appeared on the screen, more and different animals at the moment of sudden death. New masked figures and new glistening machines flashed across the screen ...

A close-up through a microscope showing tiny spherical organisms.

"... what you see is the bacillus *Clostridium venenatissimum*. I will not discuss the methods used for its culture or for the isolation of its toxin ..."

"No, we can read about that in the coded report," Groll whispered. *"Clostridium*—that is the species of extremely malignant bacteria to which the germs of tetanus and gangrene belong. And *venenatissimum* is self-explanatory: "the most poisonous" bacillus!"

"... at this point I will merely say the following: we discovered the germ in a species of Argentinian rodent. After isolating the toxin we tested it against every known protective substance and antidote. All were ineffectual ..."

Other rooms flashed on the screen, sterile, shining, clean, filled with monkeys and goats—alive one moment, dead the next.

"Where were these films made?" Groll asked. "Those must be secret laboratories . . . in some inaccessible. fenced-in area, no doubt. Have you any idea where, Manuel?"

"I've . . . no idea . . ."

"You told me once your father travelled a lot, was often away from home."

"Yes, that is true."

"Any idea where he went?"

"No . . . to outlying branch-plants, I always thought. He was never away for very long . . ."

"Could he have been travelling abroad?"

Manuel said something Groll did not understand.

"I beg your pardon?"

"I . . . I don't think so . . ."

"What's the matter?"

Groll saw Manuel suddenly cup his face in his hands and heard his loud sobs. "It's unimaginable . . . a monster . . . a beast . . . I am the son of a criminal . . ." More sobbing. Then Manuel lifted his head and stared at Groll. His voice wavered. *"But how my father must have suffered!"*

"What do you mean?"

"Who was putting pressure on him? Who was after him? Who was blackmailing him?" Manuel shouted, his voice breaking. He was gasping and weeping, tears rolled down his face. Groll could see him in the reflected light from the screen.

The boy still can't face the truth, Groll thought, shaken. He's fighting it. The criminal, the "monster" up there is his father after all. It's his father's voice he's listening to, and he's the son, and I'm scared to death he might panic and put his own life in danger.

I've been afraid of this all along. It's just what I wanted to prevent. But I failed.

And here we are.

34

The Black Plague. Smallpox. Splenetic fever. Meningitis. Dysentery. Gangrene. Yellow fever. Tetanus. Typhus. Botulism. Hepatitis. Bhang's disease. Q-Fever. About one hundred and sixty lethal diseases were being brewed for mankind in the laboratories of the East and West. Commissioner Groll knew that as well as Manuel Aranda did. They didn't have to talk about it. Just 30 grams of the Q-Fever germ, for instance, would be enough to infect twenty-eight billion people.

Two thimblesfull of *Botulinus* toxin, a poison closely related to AP Seven, would be enough to wipe out the population of half of Europe, and less than a pound would suffice to exterminate the entire population of the world. But that was a theoretical number, and an antidote had been discovered against *Botulinus* toxin. But there was no serum against AP Seven—if Raphaelo Aranda was to be believed—no defense at all . . .

And everywhere in the world such bacteria, viruses and toxins—B-weapons—were being researched and manufactured.

And everywhere in the world research was under way for chemical warfare materials designated simply as C-weapons.

In the East and West poison gases were being manufactured which were infinitely more effective than, for instance, the mustard gas deployed in World War I. These colorless, odorless gases could not be seen or smelled.

Nerve gases were being produced and tested—in the Yemen for example. by the Egyptians, and in Vietnam by the Americans—which set off whole trains of reactions, from mental dislocation through paralysis to death.

Crop-destroying substances were being manufactured and—had been tried out. in Vietnam, there were plant hormones and certain species of mushroom that lay waste the vegetation over long stretches of land and make the soil infertile.

Groll knew it, and Manuel Aranda knew it.

The silver-haired Commissioner and Manuel Aranda were now back in Groll's quiet office. Snowflakes drifted down past the windows. One window was half-open. The two men were silently reading two copies of the decoded manuscript, which a courier had brought from the Federal Police and handed over to Groll. Manuel sat next to Groll. The powerful desk lamp was on. The rest of the room was in darkness. Neither of the two men spoke a word.

From time to time Groll cast an anxious look across at Manuel. But Manuel had pulled himself together after his outbreak in the projection-room, though it had cost him enormous effort. and his face was now frighteningly rigid and expressionless. Groll was getting worried: the boy must not remain in that trance-like state, he thought. while he went on reading, horrified at what he read. He knew enough about biology and bacteriological warfare to realize: whatever had previously existed in that field was as nothing compared to the devastating effects of AP Seven . . . The two super powers are working feverishly on B- and C-weapons. Groll thought. Since 1961 America has quintupled its allocations for the development of such weapons. In 1967—now that he was on the Aranda case, Groll had refreshed his memory and upgraded his knowledge of the subject through the study of old newspapers. periodicals, and manuals in his large library—the annual budget in America for research and development of war poisons had reached nine hundred twenty million dollars. The Pentagon had disbursed four hundred million dollars for defoliants intended to blaze paths through the jungles of Vietnam. And just one month ago the U.S. Air Force had requested two hundred million dollars for the same purpose. The Americans had a seventy-five million dollar Research Center not far from Washington, at Fort Detrick. The British

261

research headquarters were at Porton Down. Russia and the countries of Eastern Europe kept the location of their research laboratories more secret. The West German microbiologist Ehrenfried Petras, who had defected to the East, had declared in an East German television interview in 1968 that the Federal Republic of Germany was also a participant in the development of B- and C-weapons, by contract with the Americans, and that the Americans were negotiating such contracts with *many* countries.

In the East the story was the same. The Russians were neck-and-neck with the Americans. American secret service reports showed that roughly one-sixth of all the weapons made by the Soviet bloc countries behind the Iron Curtain contained chemical war substances.

In spite of safety precautions seven hundred fifty accidents had occurred in the Fort Detrick complex since 1950. At least four research workers had died of infections invented for the war effort ... two of them of splenetic fever. The sudden death of a twenty-two year old soldier at Fort Detrick of "black lung" had caused a scandal that had been difficult to hush up. In Munich a mysterious epidemic of Q-fever broke out in 1967. Sixty-five hundred sheep were found dead on a lonely pasture in the American state of Utah—victims of a nerve gas that had escaped from a nearby research center and been wafted over towards the animals by the wind ...

Manuel groaned.

Groll looked at him, and saw that Manuel had lowered the manuscript and was staring across the room at one of the windows, behind which snowflakes were slowly drifting downwards.

"I can't stand it ... *I can't stand it* ... I'm his son ... the son of that swine ... my life is ruined ... I can't go on living ..." Manuel's voice was hoarse.

And what if he commits suicide or goes berserk, Groll thought? I've got to hold him by the hand, lead him, watch over him, and protect him from himself and from others. Aloud he said,

"At least we know now what happened, Manuel, and we'll find out why Valerie Steinfeld killed your father." His tone was warm and paternal. "Your father has paid for what he did. There's nothing in the world ... no utterance and no action by a human being that cannot be explained. We must examine all the circumstances closely ..."

"Yes!" said Manuel, straightening up. "Yes! And I must find this explanation, no matter what! I'm going to fly home. Now that I know all these things, there must be some clue in Buenos Aires I can track down. I must go back!"

35

"Cock-a-doodle-dooooo! Dammit! It's got to work sometime! Keep doing that! Harder!"

The redhead was crouched on the bed, naked. Before her stood Willem de Brakeleer, ruddy and massive, also naked and with a bundle of bird of paradise feathers sticking out from his backside. He was stamping his feet with rage and frustration while Yvonne did her best to help him, using both mouth and hand.

"Quaaa, quaa, quaa—quaaaaa!" Yvonne croaked out in the midst of her intense efforts, then asked, "What's the matter, sweetie? Don't you like me?"

"Cock-a-doodle-doooo!" squawked de Brakeleer. His eyes were filled with tears, as could be seen quite distinctly in the videotape machine. Nora Hill's closed-circuit television equipment worked excellently. The Dutchman was stamping his feet with fury, while Yvonne sucked and stroked and nipped—but all in vain.

The last picture flicked off the screen, which then became blindingly bright. Jean Mercier switched off the projector, and turned on the overhead light in the windowless back room of the first-class travel agency "Bon Voyage." The Frenchman hardly got a chance to sleep these days. He had received a powerful reprimand from his superiors, and cursed them roundly all the time. Was it his fault that everything had gone wrong, that that woman Valerie Steinfeld had gone and poisoned Dr. Raphaelo Aranda before they'd come to terms with him? The amount of money Aranda had asked for had been phenomenal, and Mercier's bosses had refused to pay it. Get him down, they'd told Mercier. And Mercier had tried to use Aranda's obvious state of panic to get him to lower his price. And I would have succeeded, Mercier thought bitterly, if only the Steinfeld woman hadn't stuck her nose in. And now it's me who gets the blame. Let those bosses of mine go to Santarin and Grant with their complaints—they were the ones who ruined everything. I did what I could—to save my own neck, at least.

There was a long silence in the back room. In addition to Mercier and de Brakeleer there were two Frenchmen present, burly, untalkative types who were leaning against a wall smoking cigarettes. Mercier had called them in for the discussion. You never knew what a man was capable of when he got upset. Willem de Brakeleer did nothing.

He sat there looking like a dead whale with blonde hair. His round little mouth hung open. His eyes were popping out of their sockets, his pudgy, pink hands were flopping like fins on his fat knees. His suit was too small for him, it was stretched tight over his massive frame. A clock beside the screen showed the time: 6:43 P.M. The Dutchman grimaced suddenly. Then he spoke in French and steeped in self-pity.

"I would never have suspected, never, never, that Madame Hill would stoop so low."

"Oh!" said Mercier with a wave of his hand. "You're greatly mistaken, Monsieur. Madame Hill has nothing at all to do with this film. She doesn't even know it exists. If she knew that we made it she would be furious."

"She knows nothing . . ?"

"Nothing at all." Mercier had his principles. One was to uphold the honor of a woman who had provided help. "She hasn't the faintest idea! What sort of woman do you think Madame is? Didn't she always try to accommodate you? Didn't she do everything in her power to try and satisfy you?"

"Do you swear that Madame Hill has nothing to do with this . . . with this film?"

"I swear it by the life and soul of my mother," said Mercier. His mother had been dead for thirty years. "It wasn't easy," he said, raising his eyebrows, "to get all the equipment inside and set it up without Madame noticing anything. It took us several nights. And one of the girls had to help us, of course."

"*Yvonne!*"

"No, not Yvonne. I swear to that, too. Another girl. You don't know her. Do you think Yvonne would be a party to anything like that?"

The Dutchman shook his head sorrowfully. "But why?" he

asked, plaintively. One of the bullnecked thugs leaning against the wall let out a short cackle.

"Why indeed, Monsieur, to be sure? Look, both of us are in a very unpleasant situation."

"How do you mean?"

"You represent an English firm that manufactures warplanes, especially fighter-bombers. You earn a lot of money. It goes without saying, I think, that you would be fired immediately if this film—several prints of it—were to get into the hands of your international business associates and your firm, the—" Mercier gave its name. "Would you agree?"

De Brakeleer groaned aloud. "What have I ever done to you? I don't even know you. Why do you want to destroy me?" The thug at the wall cackled again. He had a sense of humor.

Mercier's voice became gentle, almost ingratiating. "I don't want to destroy you, Monsieur, I merely wish to ask you a favor. At one time you worked for the police. You were in a position of authority. You had Interpol rank as Chief of the burglary squad in the Netherlands."

"Where did you find out about . . ."

"We made our inquiries, of course, Monsieur. We were looking for a man like you. Only you can help us. You gave up your police work five years ago, because you could make a lot more money with the—" Once again he mentioned the name of the aircraft factory. "But you are still in contact with your former colleagues, you're still an expert in that field, and you know who's who."

"This is a matter of espionage, isn't it? And you're a French agent!"

"What makes you think that, Monsieur? Please don't ever say anything like that again. Never. Not to anybody. Otherwise the copies of the films go immediately to—"

"All right, all right. So you're not an agent. So what is it you need?"

"A film," said Jean Mercier.

"Another film?"

"It's a complicated story, Monsieur de Brakeleer." Mercier continued in a sad voice. "Many films play a role in it. Films of every imaginable kind. This sort of film,"—he pointed to the projector—"and many others. And apart from the film, there's a manuscript I need. The manuscript is in the care of an attorney. In a safe with a seven-digit combination."

"Seven digits!" De Brakeleer repeated, horrified.

"We're told it's seven digits. A problem, a big problem. The film is also in a safe, probably the same one. If it's not in the same safe, then the manuscript will say where it is. But I am not able to open a safe with a seven-digit combination, and nobody I know could. But it has to be done, Monsieur, and soon . . ."

"Oh, I see!" said the Dutchman, his face turning purple. "And you thought *I* would know who could . . ."

"That's what I think, yes."

"But that's crazy! Even if I did know of such a person, what could I tell him?"

"Tell him to come to Vienna and open the safe, that's all. We'll pay him whatever he asks. I have the cash. Half in advance, the rest after the job's done. Now what about it?"

"Seven digits . . . it's madness! As far as I know, there's only one man who would be able to crack a safe like that . . ."

"Fine, wonderful!"

"But this man retired four years ago. He's not working any longer. He's German, a rich man, lives in Bremen."

"No man ever has enough money. He'll do another job, if the money's big enough. It's up to you to persuade him! Appeal to his artistic ambition! Do whatever you think is right! You have three days to get this man to say he's willing, otherwise—"

"Stop threatening me! Don't you think I *wouldn't* do what I can? My God, all this just because I . . ." De Brakeleer broke off and sank his head into his pudgy hands. He was very unhappy. "It won't work the way you imagine, Monsieur! The expert will have to know what sort of a safe it is so that he can make his own plans and get down to the job. It's more delicate than a brain operation!"

"I know."

"What the cracksman needs is *details:* what model safe it is, who made it—because every safe manufacturer has its own peculiarities—where the safe is kept, whether it's built into the wall, what alarm systems it has, what street and which house and which floor it's on, and so on."

"That's why your first job is to go and see him right away. Let him tell you exactly what he needs to know. I'll get him all the information he wants, photographs, floor-plans, everything . . ." Mercier said, thinking: It's Sunday evening now. If Inspector Schäfer puts the ad in the *Kurier* tomorrow as we suggested, it will appear the day after tomorrow. We can have made our deal with Schäfer by Wednesday. Mercier had no doubt that the Inspector would give away the address of the attorney to whom he had taken the manuscript—for a lot of money, of course. What a stroke of luck that Schäfer's wife has multiple sclerosis and that he is running out of money! He said, "Go and talk to your expert. Get him to do the job."

"But what if I can't . . ." De Brakeleer stammered out in a whine.

"Then it will be very bad for you. You've just got to get down to it, old boy. But I'm sure you'll pull it off. Then come back to Vienna and I'll get you all the necessary information which you can take back to your genius. And as soon as he has all he needs to know, he is to come here . . ."

36

It had become a little warmer toward evening, and now it was snowing again, in thick, soft flakes.

Ernst Seelenmacher had six guests in his small bar. As usual, he wore his gray-green loden suit and a white shirt open at the neck. He was seated at a small table playing slow, melancholy melodies on his zither. He was not singing this evening. His weather-beaten face had a far-away look: his thoughts were elsewhere. His friend Groll had telephoned to say Manuel Aranda was on the way out to the bar, and that the young man was in a perilously disturbed state of mind. He had just discovered that his father had been an unscrupulous criminal.

Around nine o'clock Manuel did in fact appear, accompanied by a young woman who looked equally solemn-faced and downcast.

"He has made a date with the niece of Valerie Steinfeld," Groll had told his friend on the telephone. "Be nice to the two of them. Keep an eye on them, and watch especially that the boy doesn't drink too much. He needs a clear head right now. In his place I'd probably feel like drinking myself silly, too."

Manuel Aranda and Irene Waldegg were sitting by them-

267

selves in one of the four small rooms that were all white-washed and connected to each other by arched passageways. An empty wine siphon and glasses stood before them. Irene's eyes seemed especially large and strangely damp this evening. Her brown hair shone in the light. She was wearing a gray outfit with a purple turtleneck pullover, and a little make-up. Her pale cheeks seemed rosy, her bloodless lips were carmine red. The pair sat side by side on a wooden bench, listening to Seelenmacher's playing. Manuel gazed at Irene for a long time as though seeing her for the first time. She returned his gaze with a serious expression. Her voice wavered slightly as she spoke:

"So you're flying home. When . . ?"

"Tomorrow evening, eleven-thirty. I could have got on a morning flight, but I have to wait for Cayetano."

"Who is he?"

"The General Manager of Quimica Aranda. My father's Deputy and confidant. His friend. Mine, too. Or so I always thought, and I still hope so. Cayetano and the attorneys are arriving in Vienna tomorrow at noon, and will fly home with me. I'm not going to say anything to alarm or alert them during the flight. Especially since I have to assume that Cayetano knew all about this whole affair . . ." Manuel pressed both hands to his head. Irene watched him with compassion. He seemed to sense it, for he dropped his hands and said, with some effort, "The wine's good, isn't it?" Then softly: "May I . . . may I call you Irene, now that I'm leaving?"

"Yes, Manuel," she said. Then hastily, "That's a beautiful song."

He beckoned to a pretty young waitress dressed in a dirndl.

"Yes, sir?"

"The song Herr Seelenmacher is playing—I've heard it here before."

"He plays it a lot, the boss," she said. "It's not really bar music at all. It's his favorite song. By Bach, I think."

"Would you ask him to sing it for us?"

"Of course." The girl went over to Seelenmacher and whispered to him. The winegrower nodded across, plucked a few transitional chords, and began the tender, melancholy melody again, this time singing in his soft, deep voice:

"If you, my love, would'st give me thy heart,
    Pray tell no soul right from the start, ̠
    That no one else may know our will . . ."

Manuel and Irene were sitting in complete silence, not looking at each other. Seelenmacher sang the second verse:

"Lock up our love that it bloom the best,
   Its greatest joys within thy breast . . ."

"Its greatest joys." Manuel repeated. He stared down at the wooden top of the table. "Our greatest joys . . ."

"This will pass," Irene said. "Everything passes. When Valerie died, I thought the world was coming to an end. It hasn't."

Manuel raised his head. "The secret is out. The Americans and the Russians know it. Isn't that enough?"

"But you can make sure no other countries get hold of it. You can—"

"Yes, yes, yes, yes!" He said, desperately. "I can, I will ... what good is it going to do? Of course I've got to do it. Now, as quickly as possible. And the state has got to help me, it will help me. My country cannot risk getting involved in an international scandal. But my father was not alone! A job like that requires teamwork, so there must be a lot of others in the know, working in secret factories somewhere—I don't even know where. What is going to happen to *them?* Can they be executed to make sure they never talk? Can they be put behind bars for the rest of their lives? No, that's impossible! How many of them have already told all they know?" His expression was wild, helpless. "I'm too young, Irene, too young for all these things that are happening. I'm all alone. I don't know what's going to happen now. All I know is that I have to go home at least to try to prevent worse things from happening than my father had started, that damned criminal . . ."

At that moment he looked like a schoolboy, and Irene was afraid he was going to burst into tears. His lower lip was trembling, and he was holding the glass in both hands as he drank. His hands trembled.

"Cayetano will help you." Irene said.

"And what if he doesn't? What if he was in it with my father?"

"I can't imagine that."

"Why not?"

"Why did your father choose Vienna as the place to make his deals?"

He looked at her, his glass still in his hands. "You're right . . ."

"Why didn't he do everything from Buenos Aires? No! He did it here, secretly and with all sorts of precautions. There must have been a reason. And perhaps the reason was that Cayetano knew nothing about it."

"It's possible. It's possible . . ."

"Your father was perhaps the only one who knew the whole picture. You said yourself it took teamwork: so perhaps the men who worked with him knew only a part of the project . . . always only the part *they* were concerned with, just a small portion of the whole . . ."

Manuel livened up. "That's all the more reason why I must get home as fast as possible!"

37

At the same time, 9:55 P.M., an inspector from Security HQ, was in the act of handing a flat, black box to the attorney, Dr. Stein at his villa in Döbling.

Groll had telephoned Dr. Stein to tell him of Inspector Alfred Kernmayr's impending visit.

"The box must go into the safe right away, Dr. Stein. I'm sorry to bother you with this on a Sunday, but it's really extremely important."

"My dear Commissioner, I'll be glad to take it into the city. The only thing is, I can't go right away, we have guests. But I'll leave as soon as they have gone."

"Fine," Groll had said. "I would have preferred to have sent Schäfer out to you, but he's with his sick wife today. So Inspector Kernmayr will be over with the box. He'll show you his I.D. Thank you very much."

The box was sealed with copper wire. Inside it was the reel of film and also a copy of the decoded text of the Aranda manuscript. Groll had burned the other copy.

After Kernmayr had handed over the box, Dr. Stein drove through the snow to his law offices on the Kohlmarkt, escorted and guarded by six officials in three Security HQ cars. He locked the box into the giant safe in his private office. The safe was built into the wall, and took up half the wall. Thirty minutes later Stein was back at home. His wife knew him too well to comment. Theirs had been a long and happy marriage. She did not ask him why he had gone out, or what it all meant. She knew her husband and Commissioner Groll were good friends; her husband often did inexplicable things after a conversation with Groll.

"If it keeps on snowing like this, traffic will be at a standstill all over the country by tomorrow," said the attorney.

"Yes, dear, it's really snowing very hard," his wife replied.

38

"What's the matter?" Manuel asked, staring at Irene.

"I'm tipsy! At last!"

"Nonsense! What have you been up to? What was it you just said?"

"Nothing special ..." Irene leant back. "Do you have a cigarette? Thanks!" She exhaled a cloud of tobacco smoke. "I wouldn't have mentioned it, but since you asked about my fiancé ..."

"I just asked about him because, well, because it occurred to me he might not think it right for us to be sitting here together. I didn't want to ... and then you said—"

"I said I threw him out," Irene replied calmly.

"I don't follow ... your engagement ..."

"Is over, finished. It lasted almost a year. And I'd known the man almost three years. At least, I *thought* I knew him. I was wrong." Irene puffed anxiously at her cigarette, her voice shaking. "I was very much in love with him. I ... yes ... I loved him! We had planned to get married this year." Irene shrugged. "Now it's over. Finished. Past. It doesn't even hurt any more."

"What did he do to you?"

Irene gave a short laugh. "He's an attorney with the state, a public prosecutor. Very ambitious, very successful. The trouble had started earlier, when Valerie poisoned your father and then herself."

"What trouble?"

"He had the biggest scare of his life! It was known that we were engaged. What a scandal! He was engaged to be married to the niece of a murderess and a suicide! Someone involved in a mysterious criminal case. Someone who'd been a suspect herself. So my boyfriend said he'd have to stop seeing me for a few days. I was supposed to think everything over till the weekend and see him again on Saturday. I did, and told him what I thought of him, and he turned very sour, really sour. It was a pretty ugly scene." Irene raised her glass. Manuel filled it, and she drank.

"I told him that I had expected him to stand by me in this situation, that I had depended on him. I did not want such a temporary separation. He twisted and turned and came up with a thousand and one reasons why we simply *had* to keep apart until some grass had grown over the affair. Then suddenly—have you ever experienced this, Manuel?—suddenly I realized that I didn't love him at all anymore . . . that he was like a complete stranger sitting there . . . a repulsive, vain, arrogant, unfeeling, career-obsessed man. Not the man for me. And I threw him out." She stubbed her cigarette out and laughed uncertainly. "That's why I wasn't free to see you those two evenings. Now you know. But it's all over now. So you see, I, too, had a story to tell you."

"Not a nice one."

"Well, yours wasn't, either."

"Irene . . ." he began.

"Yes?"

"Nothing." He bowed his head.

"It's all right," said Irene Waldegg. "It's all right. It's all right, Manuel."

"No, it's not!" he replied.

"Of course, it's not," Irene agreed calmly.

After that they sat in silence for a long time, looking down at their glasses. They started when they heard Seelenmacher's voice.

"I don't want to intrude, but you both look so miserable I thought maybe I'd better come over and talk to you a bit. My friend Groll told me you have big worries, Mr. Aranda, and that you are going to leave us."

"I don't want to, God knows, but I *have* to!"

Ernst Seelenmacher had brought along a new carafe of wine and three fresh glasses.

"May I join you?"

"Of course. But what about your guests?"

"They've all gone home. When you came here for the first time your situation was very similar, Mr. Aranda. In my office upstairs, remember?"

Manuel nodded.

"You're both unhappy. Neither of you knows what to do. I know what a disaster has befallen you, Mr. Aranda. Now you are adrift looking for an explanation and finding none. You don't believe in chance, but neither can you find any reason in what has happened. The time will come when you will realize that behind everything that happens there is ... not logic so much as *fate*, because we're all mortals, caught in the web of human destiny. May I tell you a story about an old friend of mine, a rabbi?"

"Yes, do, please," Irene said.

Ernst Seelenmacher looked down at his big, rough hands. Then he cast his gaze around the spacious room in his ancient wine house, where for more than four hundred years men had sought and found protection from other men.

"This is a story recorded by Martin Buber. According to Buber, the famous Rabbi Elimelekh in Czarist Russia once sat down to the Sabbath meal with his pupils. When one of the servants placed the soup bowl before him the Rabbi took it up in so awkward a fashion that it tipped over and the soup splashed all over the whole table. A pupil by the name of Mendel—who later became the Rabbi of Rymanow—called out in horror, 'What do you think you're doing! We'll all be thrown into the dungeons!' and the others all laughed at these stupid words. They would have laughed a lot louder but for the presence of the venerable Rabbi, who was not laughing at all. He just nodded over to the young Mendel and said, 'Do not be afraid, my son.' "

"Yes," said Manuel. "And then what happened?"

"A short time later it was learned that on that very same Saturday a new law had been submitted to the Czar proposing severe measures against all the Jews in Russia. All that was needed was the Czar's signature. He had begun to sign several times, but each time he was interrupted by some trivial event. Finally he signed the law. Then he reached for a box to sprinkle some writing-sand over the document, but in his nervousness he took up the ink-bottle by mistake and poured the whole of its contents over the paper. After that he tore it up and forbade his ministers ever again to submit such a decree to him."

Seelenmacher's voice grew lower. "Rabbi Elimelekh was a long way from the Czar when he knocked over the soup bowl. An apparently senseless incident, but coinciding with an incident of great historic significance—did they not belong together somehow in the web of life? Did not one provoke the other? Were they not in reality one and the same? Coincidences are governed by magic, and they are connected magically with one another . . ."

Silence fell over the three people at the table, and not one of them looked at any of the others. Outside the snow continued to fall, soundless, incessant, inexhaustible, king over city and country, while at the same moment in a villa in Anfa, an exclusive residential section of Casablanca, a little girl named Janine Clairon was smiling happily in her sleep, as she dreamed of running across the lawn of their garden into the arms of her beloved father, home at last from his long journey.

39

Manuel stopped in front of the house in the Gentzgasse, turned off the windshield wipers and switched on the parking-lights. Irene and Manuel looked through the windshield at the thick, swirling snow. The engine throbbed gently; it was warm inside the car.

"So this is good-bye," he said.

"Maybe I could come to the airport tomorrow?"

"No," said Manuel, shaking his head. "Commissioner Groll doesn't think that would be a good idea. There'll be agents at Schwechat, too. I'm afraid we're seeing each other for the last time now." How pathetic that sounds, he thought.

"You won't come back to Vienna?" she asked after a pause. The car windows were almost completely covered with snow.

"Yes, of course, that is, perhaps later on. I don't know what awaits me at home."

She turned to face him with a sudden swift motion. "So, Manuel . . ."

"I just have one thing to ask you," he said shyly. "Not a kiss—that would be silly, wouldn't it? What I really would like is a photograph of you."

"What for?"

"To remember you by, what you look like."

"What good would that do you?"

It was so dark in the car that all he could see was her silhouette. "I . . . I don't know. I'd just like to have a photo."

"Valerie kept all the photos we had in a big box. You can have one of me with pleasure, if you want."

"May I come up?"

"Yes," she said.

"Thank you." He turned off the engine.

They waded through the snow to the house entrance. The old elevator creaked and groaned as they rode up in it. Irene unlocked her apartment door and led the way into the living room in the center of the apartment, turning on all the lights. The curtains had not been drawn, and Manuel saw the snowflakes endlessly cascading through the light towards the courtyard below.

"It's right here," said Irene. She stood in front of a row of bookshelves, trying to pull a heavy mahogany box out from between two bulky volumes.

"Let me help you!" he said and rushed over to her, but it was too late. With a sudden jerk the box shot out from the shelves, slipped from Irene's fingers, and crashed to the floor. The top flew off and an avalanche of photographs, large and small, streamed out over the carpet.

"That was clever of me!" said Irene, kneeling down to pick up the pictures. Manuel knelt down beside her to help, gathering up photo after photo. He was looking for one of Irene, but could not find a single one among all those he had in his hand. Men, women, a woman . . .

"That's a picture of your aunt, isn't it?"

She looked at it and nodded.

He had never seen a picture of Valerie Steinfeld before, but she was very much as he had imagined: an oval-shaped face, bright eyes, very light hair that might possibly have been bleached, smooth skin, a large mouth with full lips, a small nose, ears flat and easily visible beneath her short, carefully cut hair. The photograph portrayed Valerie Steinfeld's face as solemn, controlled, and closed. She was looking directly into the camera.

"Yes, that's Valerie. Two or three years ago."

275

He looked at the photo again.

Valerie Steinfeld. A person with a secret. That was how she looked in the picture. But she had taken her secret with her to the grave.

Manuel picked up a few more photos. There was Valerie again, decades younger, blonde, laughing happily, at the side of a big, dark, laughing man. And another one, and another, and still more showing her with the same man—Paul Steinfeld, of course. Then there were photographs of a boy, her son in all probability. And a picture of Martin Landau at twenty. And then a picture of—

"What's this?"

"Which?"

Irene was holding a sheet of paper in her hand. The paper was yellowing with age, and covered with writing in a broad hand.

"Pasteur 1870 ..." Irene read uncomprehendingly. "I've never seen that before. How did it get in here? It must have been right at the bottom. I haven't had this box in my hands for ages ..."

"Let me see!" Manuel had glanced at the paper and suddenly felt his heart beating wildly. He almost tore it out of Irene's hand.

Written on it, in thick pencil, were the words

Pasteur 1870: silkworm epidemic
Germs: microbes
What about insects?
Could *viruses* be used as germs?
If so: insect invasions (gypsy moths, locusts, etc.)!
The same experiment with diseased rodents (cf. distemper, foot and mouth disease, etc)
Reference works!
AND/OR
Bacterial *toxins*
(Tetanus! Ransom 1898: the motor nerves!)
Pesticides?
Specific effects?
Reference Works!

Manuel was suddenly aware that the dizziness he had not felt for a long time was attacking him again. The room seemed to be spinning around. He let himself sink to the carpeted floor and stared at Irene blankly. She had been reading the lines over his shoulder, aloud. Her face had gone pale, and she was wide-eyed.

"Do you understand that?" Irene asked. "And where did it come from? That stuff about viruses, about toxins ... what does it all mean?"

"It means we still don't know a thing, not a thing. What am I going to do now? What the hell am I going to do?"

"What do you mean?"

"I can't go home now. Now I have to stay right here in Vienna, whatever happens."

"How come, why?"

"Because that writing there—and there's no doubt about it, I recognize the wide Hs, the inverted Ms and Ns—is my father's," said Manuel Aranda.

40

The trumpet solo from "Fidelio" came on full strength. Gradually the music faded away.

A man's voice proclaimed: "Freedom is on the March!" The trumpets re-emerged, jubilantly.

A second man's voice joined in: "With the Armies of our Allies in Europe and Africa!" The trumpets again, muted this time.

Then the first voice again: "Allied pilots over Germany and Italy!" Fanfare.

The second man's voice: "Enslaved millions waiting for their hour to come!" Fanfare.

First voice: "With the armies of workers, taking up arms in the new and the old world!"

Second voice: "Freedom is on the March!"

Once more, the trumpets sounded the music of freedom on the march. . . .

When the sound of the trumpets had died down, the first man's voice spoke again: "And that is the end of our weekend news round-up. Don't forget to listen in next week at the same time. Listen to our call . . ."

The second voice: *"Awakening Germany!"*

The first voice: "Don't forget . . ."

The second voice: *"The day will come!"*

The first voice: "Because England is on the attack—and youth is on our side."

Then the jubilant trumpets were back, triumphant, wonderful . . .

Valerie Steinfeld was listening with a happy smile. The first man's voice, the one that had had the last word, that was Paul's voice. Paul's voice! She had heard it again. He always spoke on this "news" broadcast by the BBC. Valerie listened to his voice almost every evening. He must be one of the most important newscasters, Valerie thought. She turned off the 'Minerva 405' after returning the tuner to the Vienna wavelength. Then she wriggled out from under the heavy blanket that she had draped over herself and the radio. On this evening, as always, Valerie had mistaken a stranger's voice for her husband's. She stepped out of the tea-room into the stacks and called out, "Martin! You can come in now!"

Then she walked back into the crowded room, which was lit only by the desk lamp with the green shade, and took a boiling kettle off the gas stove. She brewed a pot of tea, then fetched cups, spoons, and a bottle of brandy from the wall cupboard. Martin Landau surfaced from the back of the stacks, wrapped in an overcoat with the collar turned up, wearing a hat. He took off his topcoat and rubbed his hands.

"It's freezing back there," he said. "Tea, thank God!"

"Let it brew a minute."

They had closed the shop at 6:30 P.M., put out all the shop lights, and counted the day's receipts. Then it had been time for Valerie to listen to London, and as always Martin Landau had disappeared into the back of the stacks. Coal was in short supply, and the weekend was upon them, so they had let the heater in the stacks go out at noon. That was why Martin Landau had put on his hat and overcoat before disappearing to the back. He had even wound a scarf around his neck; he now took it off and threw it on the couch. Whenever he moved the Party badge on the lapel of his double-breasted suit flashed in the light. The gentle, withdrawn man had changed. He seemed full of energy and impatience.

"Come on, come on, let's get going!" said Landau, rummaging among the piles of documents on the desk for a pencil and a clean sheet of paper, moving aside the old Remington. "You'll have to have everything together before you go back to the lawyer. And tomorrow we've got to write to all

278

the churches and registries about the documents for yourself and me. You say Dr. Forster maintains we'll have to document our ancestry back to our great-great grandparents?"

"Yes, to our great-great grandparents. The tea will be ready now," said Valerie, filling the cups. "Two saccharines?"

"Yes, please. I loathe this saccharine stuff, it's got a filthy taste."

"What else can we do? Sugar's rationed, and you like your tea sweet." Valerie sat down.

"First let's make an outline, then you can type out the final version," Landau said. He folded his hands around the cup to warm them, then took a large swallow, scalding his mouth. "Ouch!" he said, putting the cup down quickly. For a moment he grimaced as though about to shed tears, then pulled himself together and said, touching his lips, in a rough voice, "Dammit!"

"How should I start?"

"Get right to the point! Write: I, Valerie Steinfeld, *née* Kremser, born—"

"I don't like the style!"

"Come on! You're not writing a novel. '. . . born March 1904 in Linz . . .' Got that?"

". . . in Linz . . ." Valerie repeated, taking it down. Landau leaned back, thumbs hooked behind his lapels, his slim chest expanded. His pale face had reddened. His voice suddenly sounded like the voice of a drill sergeant.

"Fine. When did you get married? It was in the Church of St. Dorothy, I know, I was there. But when was it? October 1923, wasn't it?"

"October fifth 1923. Do you want to write that in the first sentence?"

"Let's get it right in! So: born March 1904 in Linz, married October 5, 1923 in the Church of St. Dorothy, Vienna, to the Jew—no, wait, that's too obvious."

"I think so, too." Valerie took a sip from her cup. "It's all right, you can drink it now."

He drank, and shuddered. "I'll never get used to that saccharine. No, I'm going to change that . . ."

I, he said *I*, thought Valerie, suddenly cheered. Freedom is on the march.

"Here's what I suggest: 'in the Church of St. Dorothy in Vienna, against my family's will . . .,' that's better, isn't it?"

"Very good, Martin!"

". . . against my family's will, to Paul Steinfeld, born . . ."

"June Eleventh 1895 . . ."

"Period. 'My parents, who loved me very much, were afraid that I would not find happiness with a Jew whom they considered to be an unreliable person and to whom they had taken an instant dislike.' That's the right tone, don't you think? Restrained, but emphatic! You're not saying anything bad about Paul directly, and it's obvious you're trying your best to be objective. The strict truth, without exaggeration or understatement, just what you have to say and nothing else. The parents didn't like him from the start, that's important! They were against Jews in principle. You can swear to that without misgivings, your parents have been dead a long time. Why are you looking at me like that?"

She was really staring at him, open-eyed at the spectacle of this transformation from coward to hero.

Because you're doing such a wonderful job, really first-rate, Martin!"

Well, after all . . ."—he couldn't get those two words out of his system—"it's not so simple, after all. It's important to strike the right note! Keep writing. 'It was not long before I was forced to realize . . . hum, hm . . . to realize how right my ood parents'—no, cross out the 'good' . . . 'how right my p rents ad been, when they had tried to prevent me from m rrying Paul Steinfeld.' "

". . . prevent me from . . . marrying Paul Steinfeld."

"N vertheless . . . now listen hard, Valerie darling." 'Darling!' He had said darling!' He had never before dared call her that ever! Just listen how I phrase what's coming next. It's all psychology. That's the basis of the whole case, after all. W must think clearly about the psychology of it. You re unhappy with Paul, and you betrayed him with me. But *Paul.* Paul must have loved you. Otherwise he wouldn't have married you! And he wouldn't have been suspicious later and jealous of me—am I right?"

"A solutely, Martin."

"So et's go on: 'Although Paul Steinfeld loved me, he did not nderstand the sort of person I was, nor did I understand him.' That'll give them exactly what they want!" Martin Landau was beaming at Valerie like a little boy. He had stuck his thumbs into the armholes of his waistcoat. "Let me see . . . Paul sent you to Dresden at the beginning of 1924, didn't he?"

"Yes. To see Kokoschka. He was professor at the academy

280

there, and I wanted to study under him. I was crazy about painting. I kept going to lectures on art history at night until I got pregnant. That was so sweet of Paul! I know how Kokoschka means to you. I'm going to send you to him, he said. But not for too long! One month at most. I can't stand it without you longer than that!"

"That's precisely what I'm thinking about. Write this down, darling: 'After a series of severe quarrels I separated from Paul Steinfeld in April 1924 and went to Dresden, where it was my intention to study under Oskar Kokoschka. I was seriously interested in the history of art.' Dammit!"

"What's the matter?"

"Kokoschka is on the forbidden list!" he said angrily. "Degenerate art. We'll have to scuttle him. Who else was there at the Dresden Academy in those days? Let me think ... Flechner! Perfect! Heinrich Flechner! A real, shit of a naturalist painter!" Valerie shuddered. She had never heard that word before from the lips of Martin Landau. She was beginning to be a little bit afraid of him. "And he became a big wheel with the Nazis, one of the Führer's favorite painters! And he kicked the bucket in 1940, lucky for us! It was *Flechn*er you wanted to study with, of course! Cross out Kokoschka. Write 'study under Heinrich, no, better, under *Professor* Heinrich Flechner.'" Landau opened the brandy bottle and poured another shot into his cup, drinking from it while dictating, beating time with his other hand. "'But very soon afterwards Paul Steinfeld followed me to Dresden, and begged and implored me to return to him ...'—now we're going to put in something really beautiful, darling—'I had neither the strength to resist him nor the courage to go through with a divorce after so short a time. I was only twenty years old, and completely helpless. I was afraid of going back to my parents, because I had defied them by leaving them ...' Good, heh?"

Landau filled his cup half with tea and half with brandy, then disgustedly threw a lump of saccharine into the mixture. "When I'm tipsy—I can't take a lot, you know that—that's when I get my best ideas," he said. "Here comes the tricky part."

"Here's where you come in," said Valerie.

"Right. So, take this down: 'I returned to Vienna and resumed marital life with Paul Steinfeld. A quiet period followed. There were'—this is how we'll put it!—'two reasons for that. The first was that Paul Steinfeld was very often absent from Vienna on long journeys. The second was that during the frequent periods I was alone for a long time I renewed my friendship with a man I had met before I knew Paul Steinfeld. I met him on the premises of the Albertina Art Galleries in Vienna. The man in question was Martin Landau, born November 12th, 1903 in Vienna, the owner of the bookstore where I am presently employed . . .' "

Valerie was suddenly on fire. She was writing everything down and talking at the same time. " 'We had got into conversation over some Rembrandt drawings, and met frequently thereafter in the galleries. This acquaintanceship, limited at first to the exchange of purely artistic and spiritual ideas, later developed into a deep and genuine friendship . . .' "

"One second! '. . . friendship, which was forced into the background when I got to know Paul Steinfeld and fell in love with him . . .' Now we'll turn it around! '. . . but during the period following my forced reconciliation with Paul Steinfeld'—reconciliation in quotes—'when I had to live through my husband's many long absences from Vienna, the meetings between myself and Landau became more frequent, the old friendship between us grew stronger than ever, and because of my helplessness and my marital disappointment with Paul Steinfeld, who not only did not understand my artistic interests but also made fun of them and mocked them—' yes, write it down, it's important!—I have to go through with it. I have to. Heinz must be saved. Paul wants it—" '. . . the friendship that had been platonic for so long became intimate. I'm sorry, darling, but it all has to be said."

Valerie looked at Landau. His face had gone red and his voice was catching with embarrassment. He began to rub his hands together, symbolically. He suffered acutely from his own lies. Valerie replied, her face also red, "It's all right. Of course it has to be said. And we've got to put in those details that Dr. Forster mentioned, too." She pulled off her jacket. "I'm so hot all of a sudden."

"One second, let me get a hanger!" said Landau, jumping to his feet. As he was flipping the coat onto the hanger a folded sheet of paper fell to the floor from one of her pockets. He bent down to pick it up.

"Give it to me!" Valerie's voice sounded nervous. She had got to her feet.

"But what's the . . . why do you look like that?" he stammered. He unfolded the paper and read the words on it out loud, uncomprehendingly. "Pasteur 1870: silkworm epidemic . . ."

41

"Germ: microbes . . ."

"One moment, Mr. Landau." Manuel had to swallow before he was able to talk. The frail elderly bookdealer sat facing him in the drawing room of his hotel suite. He had appeared punctually at 3 P.M. as agreed. The date was Monday, January 20th. Landau had been telling his story fluently before Manuel had interrupted him.

" 'Germs: microbes.' *That was written on the paper?*"

"That or something like it, yes. Something about Pasteur and viruses and bacteria. It's possible the wording was a little different. I can remember the text fairly well, because I read it twice, and Valerie was quite worked up about it and wanted it back right away and wouldn't say where she'd got it or what it meant. We had a real scene. She became completely hysterical! But I didn't understand a word! I still don't to this day. What's the matter? Is something wrong?"

"It's all right." Manuel was gasping. He tried to take a deep breath, but could not. "That was a long time ago, twenty-seven years. Do you think . . . would you . . . do you think you would recognize the paper if you saw it again? The paper, and the handwriting?"

"Perhaps not the paper. After all, it's been twenty-seven years, as you said yourself. But the text, yes. Pasteur, microbes, such strange sentences. And the handwriting . . . the handwriting—"

"What about it?"

"That I can remember exactly! It was extremely strange! Very unusual! The Hs and the Ms were rounded off at the bottom and pointed at the top."

Landau started, because Manuel had pulled out his wallet and in a flash had unfolded a sheet of paper he took from it. It was the paper that he had found the night before in Valerie Steinfeld's photo box. Hoarsely he asked, "Is this it?"

For ten seconds or so there was no answer. Landau sat there staring at the paper as though in a trance. "Where did you get it? Where did it come from ... how did you come to find it?"

"I'll explain that later. But first, is this the same sheet of paper that fell out of Frau Steinfeld's jacket pocket twenty-seven years ago? Is the handwriting the same?"

"Yes, it's the same handwriting. And yes, it's the same piece of paper," Martin Landau whispered.

"Are you sure?"

"Absolutely!"

"Can you explain how this piece of paper came into Frau Steinfeld's possession?"

"No, of course not. She didn't tell me even then—"

"Or why she happened to be carrying it around on that particular day?"

"No idea, I've no idea, Mr. Aranda! I'm just telling you about something that happened so long ago and is over and done with, and you shove this piece of paper under my nose and—"

"It's not over and done with!" Manuel broke in passionately. "There's not the slightest doubt about that any more. This paper here is the proof that Valerie Steinfeld—" He stopped. He could not go on. He couldn't talk like that to Martin Landau, who didn't know what had happened, what it was all about. Manuel's heart was beating wildly. He was on to something! He had been on the right track from the beginning: it kept leading him back to Valerie Steinfeld, as fantastic as that seemed.

"Proof that she what, Mr. Aranda?" Landau whispered. He was shocked, but curious.

"I can't tell you that, unfortunately."

"Has it something to do with your father?"

"Yes."

At that moment, something quite different occurred to Manuel.

Why didn't I think of it sooner, he thought to himself bitterly. Why didn't I ask Landau about it long ago? I'm too young for this game. I just don't have the hang of it.

"Mr. Landau, do you know whether Paul Steinfeld had a brother?" Manuel asked.

"Of course, he had a brother, Daniel."

"Did you know Daniel personally?"

"Hardly at all. We met two or three times. Paul and he didn't get along."

"Why not?"

"I can't say. I really don't know. The brothers saw each other very seldom. even though Daniel lived in Vienna."

"In Vienna, here?"

"Yes. But he emigrated in 1937."

"Where to?"

"Prague. He was lecturing at the university there."

"At the university . . ." Manuel could hear his own voice as if it belonged to some stammering idiot.

"He was teaching here, too. He was a professor."

"What department?"

"In the Institute for Chemistry Studies."

Manuel's fingers gripped the arm of the chair. *"Where?"*

"At the Institute for Chemistry Studies in the Währingerstrasse." Martin Landau replied. watching Manuel worriedly. "Is something wrong, Mr. Aranda? What's the matter?"

"Nothing . . . nothing. Paul Steinfeld's brother was a chemist?"

"Yes, a professor of chemistry. That's what he . . ."

42

". . . taught. Chemistry. Biochemistry, if I'm not mistaken," said the voice of Martin Landau, coming out of the small, hypersensitive loudspeaker that was connected to the telephone on the desk in Count Romath's expensively furnished office.

"How long did Daniel Steinfeld teach in Vienna?"

"For many years, I presume."

"And he must have been doing research, too, in the laboratory, experimenting?"

"Yes, he did."

"How do you know?"

"Valerie told me once. I don't understand anything about chemistry. I don't know what he was doing or what experiments he was conducting. It had something to do with insects."

"With insects?"

"Yes, with destroying insects. I think he researched pesticides, if I remember rightly."

"Pesticides?!"

"Oh, and the paper—"

"What about that paper?"

"Oh well." Landau sounded offended.

"What do you mean, oh well?" Manuel asked.

"Well, after all, it's very mysterious, isn't it? Perhaps you feel that there are certain things you mustn't explain to me."

"Nonsense! I really don't know myself what it all means, Mr. Landau! Tell me what happened next, please."

"All right, fine. Valerie calmed down again after the episode with the paper, and we continued. If you remember, she had insisted that we include in the protocol what the attorney had suggested. At first I didn't understand what she meant, and asked her about it and she replied, very embarrassed, 'Now come on, I . . .'"

43

". . . told you already, at lunch." Valerie smoothed down her blouse, and looked over at the crackling stove in the corner of the tearoom.

"Oh, yes, I remember! Hum. After all. Yes, of course, it does have to go in." And Martin Landau stood up, took a water glass from the wall cupboard and filled it with the cheap brandy. He drank and shuddered. Then he laid a hand on Valerie's shoulder.

"We must do it. Otherwise none of it is of any use. But it's all just *lies*, Valerie, *lies* that have nothing to do with your love for Paul or my friendship with him. He would say the same. So, write it down: 'My married life also suffered from the fact that Paul Steinfeld and I failed to get along with each other not only in spiritual matters but also in our sexual relations . . .'"

Valerie took the glass from Landau's hand and began to dictate herself: "'Apart from the very first period of intimacy

286

between us shortly before and for a short time after our marriage, Paul Steinfeld forced me to—' "

"Won't do. What do you mean 'forced?' No woman can be forced to do something like that. You let it happen because you were desperate anyway and believed your life was a mess."

"But how to put it into words? Really Martin, it's awful!"

"Just stick to the facts. Don't let it affect you. It's a lie that doesn't have anything to do with you, darling. Have another drink. That's a good girl. Here's what we say: 'Apart from the very first period *etcetera, etcetera,* he *preferred*'—you understand? *Preferred!* That's important! He must have had sexual intercourse with you normally as well, otherwise he could never have believed for one minute that Heinz was his son."

"Yes, yes, of course. Go on, Martin, *go on!*"

" 'Paul Steinfeld preferred a particular method of sexual intercourse which ...' " Landau began to stammer. " '... which was painful to me and ... failed ... failed to satisfy me and ... deeply repelled me. Shame, despair, my youthful inexperience, and the knowledge that I had severely damaged, if not completely destroyed, my parents' love for me when I married Paul Steinfeld against their express wishes—oh, and *one other thing!*—'along with the general decline in morals and virtue everywhere at that time, made me feel the need for support, and I turned for solace and help to Martin Landau.' "

"Good God," Valerie said. "It's enough to make you sick."

"If it didn't make you sick we wouldn't have done a good job," said Landau, with deliberate brusqueness.

"On! 'During this period I went to Martin Landau, and I confess—and I wish this admission to be understood as one of the hardest things I have ever had to do in my entire life—that I had sexual relations with him on a number of occasions.' One moment: when was Heinz born?"

"On May 27, 1926."

"Nine months back would be April, March, February, January, December ... August 1925."

"Write this down: 'my husband was away very often in 1924 and 1925. During his absences in these years the occasions of sexual intimacy with Martin Landau were numerous.' Don't look at me like that, keep writing! " 'Paul Steinfeld and I were then living at—' "

"The housing shortage, Martin!" Valerie interrupted.

"I have it in mind. '. . . were then living, with the housing

287

shortage in Vienna very severe, at the outskirts of the city in Dornbach, with a certain Hermine Lippowski, from whom we sublet one floor of a small villa. That is where Martin Landau and I secretly—' why are you not writing?"

"Frau Lippowski . . . ," said Valerie in a whisper.

"We have to give her name. She'll be subpoenaed as a witness for sure."

Valerie leaned back in the old armchair and stared into space.

"I'm afraid, Martin," she whispered. "I'm afraid!"

44

"There you are! Right on the dot! What a pleasure to see you again, Frau Steinfeld! Please come in, please!" Frau Lippowski was exuberant. She had hurried out through the bare, scraggly garden at the front of her house to open the gate for Valerie, embracing the young woman warmly in greeting. She was all alone and on her own, unfortunately she explained as she escorted Valerie through the sorry garden.

"I have to do everything myself. I do have a charwoman twice a week, but she's lazy and not very clean, but what can you do, you have to be glad to get anybody these days to do the cleaning, and it's getting worse, it's enough to make you despair!"

Valerie listened uneasily. She was shocked at the way Frau Lippowski had changed. She had been no beauty nineteen years before, but she had been trim and graceful, with a pert little face—black hair, black eyes, and a melodious voice. But now the Lippowski woman was as round as a ball, her gray hair, was untended and stringy, her eyes were dull and half-hidden beneath their lids, her lips thin, her face a mass of wrinkles. Valerie had thought: if this woman was around forty in 1923, she can't be more than sixty now. But she looks older than seventy.

"I'm in trouble, Frau Lippowski, big trouble. That's why I'm here."

"Trouble? What sort of trouble? Tell me all about it."

On the floor above them a baby was crying, and other children were running back and forth. Valerie told her story, sometimes fluently, sometimes hesitantly, but towards the end the words were sticking in her throat, her uneasiness had grown stronger and stronger. She finished with these words:

"So when you are asked in court, Frau Lippowski, I would ask you very earnestly to testify in the way I have just described to you."

"You want me to say that I saw Mr. Landau coming here often, especially when your husband was away on journeys, and that your husband and you were always quarrelling and had a terrible marriage?"

"Yes."

The woman with the straggly hair sat there motionless, without replying.

"Please, Frau Lippowski, please! You know now what's at stake. You are a person I can trust. You told me once that you were married to a Jew who was killed in the First World War, in 1918. I'm sure you understand the situation I'm in. You must remember my husband very well still."

"I do remember your husband very well."

"And you understand my situation?"

"Yes, Frau Steinfeld, I do understand your situation. I understand it perfectly."

"So can I count on you to testify on my behalf?"

"No," Hermine Lippowski said. She was wearing a black, high-necked, old-fashioned dress with sparkling glass buttons and old, high clogs.

"No, Frau Steinfeld. You can't count on me. I won't testify for you."

"Is it that you don't want to lie? You don't need to have any scruples. I really did deceive my husband! Our marriage *was* on the rocks! You *must* have heard our fights! And seen Mr. Landau coming in to see me!"

"I didn't hear any quarrels, ever. So far as I know, your marriage was fine. And Mr. Landau was never more than a friend of yours, and of your husband's." The fat, black monster raised one of her pudgy hands. "All that wouldn't matter a damn, not a damn. I'm no Nazi. I'm a monarchist. I'd enjoy lying to that mob."

"But then, why won't you?"

"Your husband was a Jew," the old woman said, an expression of hate, insane hate, firing her dull eyes. "Your hus-

289

band is a Jew. I didn't know that until today. He registered as a Protestant."

"It's true, he was baptized, and his parents before him!"

"But a Jew just the same! If I'd had any idea, even the slightest suspicion, I would never have taken you in, Frau Steinfeld! I would never have let you live here in my house!"

"But, but why not?"

The flabby, black-clad woman replied in a voice brimming with passion: "Because I hate Jews, that's why, Frau Steinfeld!"

"You!"

"Yes, I hate Jews! More than anything! In this one point I agree with the Nazis. But anti-semitism is older than the Nazis, it's thousands of years old. Six thousand years! And rightly so! The Jews are scum. The bottom of the barrel. The biggest liars, the foxiest, meanest, filthiest, most depraved and unscrupulous vermin! Yes, it's true, don't stare at me like that!" Frau Lippowski struck the table with her fist. "There's nothing filthier than a Jew! Nothing more irresponsible! Nothing more repellent!"

"Frau Lippowski ... Frau Lippowski!" Valerie was shocked, but an idea had come to her nevertheless. "Look, that's why my marriage was so bad! Because I married a Jew. What do you think I went through!"

Hermine Lippowski had become as quiet as a tomb. "It won't wash, Frau Steinfeld. You think old lady Lippowski lives somewhere at the other end of the earth and has no idea what's going on, but you're wrong. I do have an idea what you're up to, especially in a case like yours. I knew a woman in Munich who tried the same."

"What do you mean, the same? What is it I'm trying?"

"To cheat the Government, to cheat the court, to pull off a lawsuit that's a bunch of lies, all because you're scared for your little Heinzi. You want to save your boy, so you try to set everything and everyone up and get people to lie for you and commit perjury—just so nothing happens to Heinzi, dear little Heinzi, who's a Jew, too!" she finished viciously.

The din from the first floor continued.

Valerie took a deep breath. It's no good, she thought. The old cow's out of her head. "Well, forgive my disturbing you, Frau Lippowski. No, no, please don't bother, I can find my way out. I know my way around in this house, after all." She walked toward the door. Suddenly Frau Lippowski shot by her like a cannonball and crashed against the door. She stood against the door blocking the way, her face distorted, her words tumbling out in an excited rush.

"Go if you want to! But there's one thing I want to tell you!"

"Let me through!"

"Listen to me first! I had a Jew for a husband myself!"

"Yes, I know. And he died in the First World War."

"That was a lie!"

"A lie?"

"Yes, yes, yes! My husband was *not* killed in 1918! He survived the war! Right in his hometown! Never budged! Had it well organized. Got *rich* by 1918. And after 1918 still richer, the filthy cheat. What do you think he pocketed during the inflation! We were married for seventeen years." The Lippowski woman was gripping Valerie's arm in an iron hold. "Seventeen years! The best years of my life, I gave to him! And what does he do? In 1922, he suddenly comes and says he wants a divorce."

"A divorce . . ."

"Yes, to marry a girl nineteen years younger than me and twenty-three years younger than him! His secretary! They had been carrying on for a year already, she was pregnant, and he wanted to marry her in a hurry."

"But you could have refused to divorce him."

"I did! But then his attorneys came down on me—Jews, of course—and threatened and intimidated me and drove me completely crazy, and said he would leave me anyway because I had cheated on him, too and he was going to file suit."

"*Had* you been unfaithful?"

"A stupid little affair once in 1912 with an army officer! There was no comparison. But I was scared at the thought of being the guilty party in a divorce, and being cut off without a penny of support, and so I gave my blessing to everything and he got to marry her, that young, lascivious Jewish pig!"

"*She* was Jewish?"

"Yes, of course Jewish! That bunch of swine like to keep to their own sty! He bought the house for me, during the inflation, for next-to-nothing, he bought all sorts of houses then. And he had to pay a monthly alimony—a ridiculous amount considering his income and riches. He shoved me off here to Dornbach, and because nobody knew me here I invented the story about our great love and his death in the war. I didn't want anyone to know about the disgrace I'd gone through—

off with a young bitch after seventeen years of marriage!"
Hermine Lippowski shook her fist at the ceiling. "But God is
just! He doesn't let something like that go unpunished! No,
He doesn't! It didn't bring Viktor any happiness, his sinning
against me, no, it didn't!"

"Why? Was your husband—"

"Yes, in 1938. One of the first. They got him just before
he could get out. The Jewish bitch finished herself off first,
just in time, and their Jewish boy, too. It was in March.
Good riddance to them! God avenged me with her, too!"

"And your husband?"

"Was put into a concentration-camp, I heard. Those Nazis
clean up all right, I'll say that for them!"

45

"I'm scared, Martin, I'm so scared!" Valerie whispered that
evening in the bookstore tearoom. "The Lippowski woman is
half-crazy with hate and hurt and loneliness. God knows
what she'll do if she's called as a witness. Dr. Forster won't
call her, that's for sure, but the prosecutor will, you said so
yourself!"

Landau got to his feet, and filled his glass with brandy.
Then he said in a firm voice, "Don't drive yourself crazy,
darling. Even if she says it's all lies, she doesn't know anything. Forster will put the squeeze on her. She *has* to admit I
was out at your place a lot during that period, because it's
true, I was. And the noise of your fights? Well, she just didn't
hear them. Forster can be as mean as she: he can mention,
for instance, that she was married to a Jew. Do you think
she'll like that? So pull yourself together. Where were we?"

"'. . . were living at the time . . . of a certain Hermine Lippowski, from whom we sublet . . . where Martin Landau and
I secretly—'"

"'. . . had our meetings,'" he dictated. "Well, come on,
write!"

She wrote it down.

He continued, "'When I discovered that I was expecting a
292

child by Martin Landau, I told him at once. He was determined to talk to Paul Steinfeld and tell him the truth.' Period." Landau took another drink and then shouted out at the top of his voice, "Jesus-Christ-Almighty, what a complicated mess!"

Valerie had picked up the thread again. " 'More than anything else he wanted Steinfeld to agree to a divorce, to insure that the child be recognized as his, Landau's. He loved me and wanted to marry me immediately, but I wanted to remain at the side of Paul Steinfeld and take upon myself all the suffering the relationship had caused for the child's sake. Paul Steinfeld's immediate reaction to the news of my pregnancy was one of anger, because he did not want to have a child. But it was too late for me to have the abortion which he suggested—' "

"Splendid! Sounds really Jewish!" Landau commented.

" '—and so he was obliged to come to terms with the state of affairs. Over the years he took as little notice as possible of my son and gave him no affection whatsoever. This feeling of instinctive dislike was reciprocated by my son, as he grew older. On the other hand, he began to feel more and more drawn toward Martin Landau, whom I invited to my home as often as possible even before the child was born, in order to see him as often as was practicable.' "

"Paul must have become suspicious, of course!"

"I'm coming to that now! 'Paul Steinfeld never really accepted Martin Landau completely. He was suspicious, and often expressed his suspicion that Martin was the father of Heinz. He frequently went into fits of jealousy, in connection not only with Martin Landau but also with various other men who used to visit us socially, always harping on his doubts about being Heinz's real father. In such fashion we had many years of marriage in name only—Paul Steinfeld went his way and I went mine. Together with Martin Landau I worked at night schools—' "

"That's really true, we did! Valerie, it *can't* fail!"

" '—where we gave lectures and courses in art appreciation. And so I built a world for myself that centered around my beloved son' " Her pencil flew across the paper.

" 'Paul Steinfeld's flight in 1938 was my salvation, even though he left me with virtually no means of support. In this situation Martin Landau showed himself to be a true friend. He immediately offered me a position in his bookstore, and he wanted to pursue the legitimization of our son, but I resisted—' "

"Why?" Landau asked.

" '—because the conditions for Heinz were favorable at the time," Valerie replied, writing it down. " 'He was placed on the same footing as Aryans and I hoped to raise him without having to rake up the past and go the route of a difficult law suit. I hoped to be able to give my gifted son a good education to prepare him for a profession and to make him a worthy member of our society.' " Valerie was writing more and more quickly. " 'But things developed counter to my plans. Hence, my decision now to make application for the legitimization of our son, an action which Martin Landau wanted to initiate as early as 1938.' "

46

The desk of the little tearoom, the old couch, and the floor all were covered with papers and documents. They lay on the radio set, the rocking-chair, and the gas-heater. It was Sunday evening. Valerie and Landau had been working since morning. It was tedious work. They had to produce for themselves the so-called "Proof of Aryan Descent," fully documented without gaps. It was a major undertaking.

In the case of Paul Steinfeld, the court needed evidence that he himself, his parents, and his grandparents were "Jews and of Jewish descent." Fortunately, his parents had had Paul baptized in the Protestant faith, and were themselves converted for purely professional reasons. A restriction had existed in Prussia before the turn of the century on the number of Jewish attorneys admissible by law.

Martin Landau already had most of the documents pertaining to himself. But Valerie had only those papers that Heinz had had to produce at school. Valerie did not even possess the baptismal certificates of her grandparents; she had, therefore, written on her own behalf to the various parish and registry offices concerned, painstakingly working out which ones to write to on the basis of the few documents she did have.

"This Pavel Matic, your second great-grandfather on your mother's side," Valerie expounded, tapping on a document, "married your second great-grandmother on your mother's side on September 25th, 1772, in the old Church of St. Borromeus in Prague. Your great-grandfather was also *baptized* in the same church. It says so here, but it doesn't say when."

"So what?" Landau asked, irritated. "We'll just have to write to this Borromeus Church in Prague and ask for my great-grandfather's baptismal certificate."

"We won't get it," said Valerie.

"What do you mean?"

She looked at him uneasily.

"What's the matter? Say something!"

"Martin, don't be angry with me! I wouldn't have mentioned it. You know I never tell you anything about—"

"I don't understand a word."

She looked over at the radio set.

"The BBC?" he asked, starting.

She nodded.

"What did they say?"

"I just know it, let's say."

"From the London radio?"

"I just know it, so stop! You'll have to listen to what I'm telling you. Remember when the Czechs killed Heydrich?"

He nodded.

Reinhard Heydrich, Chief of the Security Police and of the Security Service, Deputy Chief of the Gestapo, the thirty-eight-year old, long-nosed, ice-cold inventor of the "Final Solution," in his greed for more and more power, had had himself appointed "Reich's Protector for Bohemia and Moravia." On the morning of May 29th, 1942, he was driving in an open car from his country seat to the Hradschin, his official headquarters in Prague. A bomb was tossed into the car. The assassins were two members of the Free Czech Army in England, Jan Kubis and Josef Gabčik, who had parachuted into the country from an RAF plane. The two were supported by the Czech resistance movement.

Heydrich died on June 4th. The Germans wreaked terrible revenge. The Jews suffered the most: thousands of them were executed immediately in the concentration camps. According to Gestapo reports, 1,331 Czechs, among them 201 women, were also put to death on the spot. The village of Lidice, near Prague, made headlines all over the world: the Germans executed all the men by firing-squad, separated women and children, dragged them off and slapped them into concentration camps, then razed Lidice to the ground.

"The SS pillaged the church and set fire to it, and completely burned down the rectory. It's almost certain that the old baptismal records no longer exist," Valerie said, with a catch in her voice.

For a long time Martin Landau said nothing. Finally he hissed, "Those pigs, those damned swine! Then we won't write to the church, o.k.?"

"Oh yes, we *must!* Because what the Nazis did in Lidice is supposed to be a secret. If we let on we know about it they'll say we must have been listening to the BBC."

"But what's the point of—"

"Our own safety! We've got to act dumb!" Valerie sighed. "We're going to have quite a cross to bear with this Pavel Matic, I tell you. But first we write to the Church of St. Carl Borromeus. They will reply that they can't help us. It's possible they had the old baptismal records stored somewhere else. We'd be in luck then! Otherwise we'll have to find where Pavel Matic died and when and who made out his death certificate. The date and place of his baptism will be entered on the death certificate." Landau sat down on the rocking chair and swore like a trooper.

"Stop that!" Valerie said. "There's no other way. We'll make it." She squeezed his hand. "You'll see. In a few weeks we'll have everything we need."

Valerie was wrong. Thirteen months later they were still three documents short, thirteen months later they would still be writing pleading letters to rectories, registry offices and cemetery administrations, requesting authorized copies of documents they needed to prove the Aryan descent of people who had been dead for one hundred fifty, one hundred sixty, or one hundred eighty years.

They worked through the whole afternoon. Valerie insisted on speed. She had overcome the sense of despair she had felt the day before, and her face was marked with energy, strength, some would say ruthlessness. She typed letter after letter. On! On! She had to push on! There was no time to lose!

47

"I don't believe a word you're saying," said Dr. Karl Friedjung in a cold, ugly voice. He sat behind a large desk in his office on the first floor of the State Institute for Chemistry Studies. It was a dismal November day: outside the rain was coming down in sheets. The wind was whipping the rain before it.

"I don't believe a single word you're telling me, Frau Steinfeld, let's get that clear right from the start, you understand?"

Valerie bit her lip. She sat facing the Director on an uncomfortable, hard chair. Dr. Forster, tall and slim, sat next to her.

"But I'm telling you the truth! Director, I—"

Friedjung made a scornful gesture. "Lies! Nothing but a pack of lies! If I had known that's why you wanted to see me, I wouldn't have received you."

His thin face was pale and contorted with anger. Why is this man so angry, Forster was wondering, and then remarked quietly, tugging at his right ear, "You would have had to receive us, Director!"

"You think so!"

"I'm sure of it. We've been to see the Regional Commandant on this matter. He received us without any fuss, and without this kind of negative reaction, Director."

"You saw the Regional Commandant?"

"Of course." Filthy slob, Forster thought. Damned Nazi swine. He laughed politely. "It is my duty to inform you and the Regional Commandant personally that in my capacity as Frau Steinfeld's legal representative I have registered an action in the Regional Court of Vienna to the effect that Heinz Steinfeld is not a Jewish half-caste of the first degree but is descended from pure Aryan ancestors. The action has the number 25 Cg 4/42."

"I'm not interested in the number! It's nothing but a Jewish trick!"

Forster stood up. "Director Friedjung, I am a qualified attorney. I am also an Aryan like you. You will apologize to me for those last words. Otherwise I will sue you for defamation of character."

That worked. Friedjung twisted his face into a grimace of a smile. "I didn't mean it like that. All right, Dr. Forster, I apologize to you. To *you*, you understand. And now, please be seated again."

Forster sat down without a word.

A bell rang through the school. A few seconds later there were sounds of doors being flung open, steps running along the corridors, and a host of youthful voices shouting and laughing. It was an interval between classes.

In a firm voice Valerie said, "The Regional Commandant assured us that so long as the suit is in progress no steps would be undertaken against my son. We were requested to inform you."

Friedjung clenched his fists on the desk top. He seemed—as Valerie reported later to Martin Landau, who was not present—to be scarcely able to control himself.

Is the man prone to fits of rage? Forster was wondering uneasily. What is it that gets him so upset when Valerie Steinfeld says anything, or even when he just looks at her? Is there some quarrel between them? Forster made a mental note to ask his client about it when he got her alone.

Friedjung's voice came out in strangled tones as he said, "No steps will be undertaken, heh? Good. Very good. Excellent! Brilliantly thought-out. And how long will the suit go on?"

"No one can say. It could be a long, drawn-out process—"

"Oh, really?"

"—or it could be over quickly, and settled in favor of Heinz. establishing the truth once and for all."

"What truth?"

"That he is an Aryan."

"*Aryan!*" Friedjung squealed, so shrilly that even Forster shivered. "Let me tell you something, Frau Steinfeld! Your son is *not* Aryan! Your son is a Jewish half-caste!"

"Director, for the last time—" Forster broke in.

"And you! You should be ashamed to stand up in court for a case like this one. Complain to the Regional Commandant if you like. He knows me!" Friedjung leant over his desk and screamed directly into Valerie's face, "I can't stop you twisting the law. No, I can't do anything about that! But there's one thing I can do, because *I'm* the boss here. Just make a note of this: what your son has done is unforgivable, understand? I'll never forgive him for it! The dignity of the school will not permit it." His voice became softer, and he bent still further across the desk. "So you're going to bring a paternity suit, heh? It remains to be seen what the result will be. It's going to depend on luck and on how good a liar you are—"

"Director!" said Forster, jumping up.

"—and whether you're a good liar or a bad one, and whether your lies are believed! And I'm telling you, Frau Steinfeld, that Jewish lout—"

"That's enough!" Forster shouted. Maybe it will help if I shout back, he thought. It didn't.

"Enough? Then get out. This is *my* office, understand? Here I say what I think. And I say this: that Jewish brat is not going to come to my Institute any more, and you can lie till you're black in the face, and I don't care if you're lucky and win the case and manage to fool the court! He's not getting back into this school, is that clear?"

Friedjung was gasping for breath. He had turned very pale. Forster could see Valerie's hands trembling, her lips changing color. He took her by the arm.

"Let's go, Frau Steinfeld, it's no use wasting our time and breath here. I know how to protect you and myself from his behavior." (If only I did, Forster was thinking. This man is not responsible for his own actions! What is there between him and Frau Steinfeld? Even the wildest Nazi wouldn't behave like that.) Forster looked over his shoulder.

Dr. Karl Friedjung was sitting behind his large desk staring at Valerie with an expression of pathological hatred. He was still panting, his mouth half-open, his hands clenched so tightly that the knuckles protruded like white stones beneath the skin. In the outer office where two secretaries were typing busily, Forster helped Valerie into her coat. Then he put on his own, took his umbrella and his hat, bowed crisply, and left with Valerie.

The corridors and stairways of the school were crowded with young boys in white lab coats running around talking and shouting happily. The odor of chemicals pervaded the whole area. As they reached the foyer, Forster stopped, and, putting up his umbrella, asked, "Have you any explanation for Herr Friedjung's insane behavior, Frau Steinfeld?"

Valerie's face was expressionless. "None."

"But it wasn't normal! I ask you, my good lady!"

"That's the sort of person he is. A person to be feared. I . . . I am afraid of him. Terrified."

"But why?"

"Because of the way he is, because he was always—"

"What do you mean, always?"

"Ever since I've known him."

"And how long is that?"

"What do you mean?" Valérie whirled around, her eyes were unsteady. "Why, since Heinz has been going there. What did you think?" Pointless, Forster thought. Either she's telling the truth, or she's trying to keep something from me. That would be bad. But there's nothing I can do about it.

48

"What happened, Mommy? What did he say?"

With these words Heinz Steinfeld came rushing into the large living room. His thick, black rubber raincoat was dripping wet, the mechanic's overalls he had on beneath it were sopping, as were his shoes, and he was spattered with mud from head to foot. His blond hair and thin, freckled face were wet. It was 11:30 P.M. Outside, it was still pouring. The Department of Labor had reacted with great speed, and Heinz had been obliged to accept a job as a reel-runner. He left the house every day at 3 P.M., and never returned before 11:30 P.M., often later. The movie theaters between which he had to transport the films were in Mariahilf in District VI, which meant he had a long trek to his work. Usually Heinz was too tired to eat when he finally got home. But on this night he was in a fever of excitement. His wet, exhausted face lit up when he saw Martin Landau was there as well as his mother.

"Hello, Father!"

"Hi, my boy," Martin Landau replied in an uncertain voice.

"So, Mommy, tell me what happened! I'll bet Friedjung's eyes nearly popped out of his head when you walked in with the attorney, heh?"

Valerie was in her dressing-gown. "Yes," she said, smiling. "His eyes were popping, all right, Heinz! That was some surprise for him!"

"I guess he never expected anything like that, heh?"

Martin Landau mopped his brow. Valerie had asked him to stay with her until Heinz got home. She didn't have the courage to wait by herself.

"No, he never expected anything like that. Go and change, Heinz, you're wet through to the skin. There's something for you in the oven. Agnes made something special for you tonight. Come on, let's go to the kitchen."

"In a moment, Mommy, in a moment." Heinz was very excited. "I knew he'd back off when you turned up with a lawyer. The cowardly dog! I guess you really got him to back down, didn't you?"

"Yes, Heinz." Valerie was still smiling.

"And it's all clear that I can go back to my studies once we've won the law suit, right?"

"Completely clear," said Valerie. "We discussed that, naturally. Friedjung was . . ." She had to stop for breath. Martin Landau saw that Valerie could not speak. All she could do was hold her smile.

"That's right, my boy," said Martin Landau. "He had given the matter a lot of thought. It's really a big embarrassment for him, the whole thing. The lawyer really told him off, you can imagine that, can't you?"

"And how!" A puddle was forming around Heinz's feet. No one noticed. "The idiot! That'll be something when I march back into that school again as an Aryan! What do you think of that, Mommy?"

Valerie nodded, still smiling.

Martin Landau said slowly, "It's going to take a while, Heinz. Quite a long time, perhaps. Law suits like this one are not won in one day."

"I know that!" the boy shouted. "The suit can take as long as it has to, for all I care! Everyone knows by now that I'm not a half-Jew! Friedjung, the Regional Commandant, the court! That's the main thing! What's the matter, father?"

"Your new job—I was just thinking how hard that must be for you."

"*Hard?* Not at all! At first it was, and sometimes when the weather's as bad as today, it's not too pleasant then! But I've got used to it already! And even if I do get home late, I can sleep late the next morning. I could never do that before!

301

And you meet such interesting people, you know? And I always get to see part of a movie when I'm waiting for the reels, always the same bit from the same reel, never the whole film—weird, don't you think? No, you don't need to worry about that!"

Heinz, dirty and wet as he was, rushed over to Landau and his mother, embraced and kissed them both. "Thank you! Thank you! I'm so grateful!" Then he said, a little more calmly: "I'm going to put on some dry clothes. I'm even hungry now, and not a bit tired! Will you two come into the kitchen while I eat? I want to hear all about what happened with that swine Friedjung!"

"We'll come," said Valerie, her smile frozen to her lips. Heinz blew her a kiss and disappeared. A long silence followed.

Then Landau said, "We couldn't tell him the truth."

"No, we couldn't." Valerie's smile had vanished. She looked totally exhausted. "Who knows how long this suit is going to last? Who knows what's going to happen to us all, to the world? As long as Heinz believes that he'll be able to study again, he's happy. It's vital he stays that way. He mustn't be in despair when he goes to court, he must have hope. And if we manage to win the suit, I will *force* Friedjung to take him back into the Institute."

How do you force a man like that? Landau was thinking, but he kept silent and merely nodded.

"Those are tomorrow's worries. We'll have to deal with them one by one. The first thing is the law suit. That's the most important. And we will win it . . ."

"Touch wood," said Landau, drumming his knuckles against the table.

Valerie got to her feet. In a voice that sounded distant, mechanical, completely foreign, and devoid of human warmth, she said, "Let's go to Heinz. He'll be in the kitchen by now."

He was not in the kitchen.

They found him in his room, completely undressed except for underpants and tee-shirt. His wet top clothes lay scattered around the room. Heinz had sunk into his bed and was asleep. The fatigue he dragged home with him every night had caught up with him.

"Poor kid," Landau said.

Valerie hurried over to the bed. She pulled the blanket out

from under her son's body and spread it over him. Martin stepped closer. Heinz lay with his head on the pillow, his hair and face still damp with rain. He was sleeping deeply.

49

The telephone rang.

Martin Landau gave a start in his armchair, a frightened, sick old man. He gestured helplessly, as though to say: you see, even the telephone can scare me half out of my wits.

Manuel got to his feet and walked across the honey-colored carpet and the Chinese scatter rugs to the little table on which the telephone stood.

"Hello?"

"A call from Paris for you, Mr. Aranda, one moment please." Then came a man's voice speaking Spanish. Manuel recognized it at once.

"Cayetano!"

"At last! I've been waiting almost five hours for this call to go through!" The Managing Director and Deputy of the Quimica Aranda had a loud, nervous way of talking. "My dear Manuel"—he had known Manuel since his childhood—"we're stuck here."

"Where's here?"

"Orly Airport. There's a snowstorm. You can't imagine how bad it is. I'm calling so that you shouldn't worry. We're okay, the lawyers and I. But we'll have to wait till the storm's over and they can clear the runways."

"How long will that be?" Manuel could feel a tugging at his heart. Cayetano and the attorneys held up in Paris. The discovery of a scrap of paper with notes in his father's handwriting. The cancelling of all flights for that night. Was it all some sort of omen? Was he meant to stay in Vienna?

He had to! With every hour that passed he was learning more about the mysterious link between Valerie Steinfeld and his father. If today he had not listened to this puny bookdealer—he would never have learned that Martin Landau too had seen that scrap of paper with his father's specu-

303

lations about viruses and toxins. The paper that had fallen from Valerie Steinfeld's jacket pocket in 1942 . . .

"They say it will take until tomorrow morning at least."

"Don't worry. I'll see you when you get here."

"Have you managed to find out anything about your father's murder?"

"Yes, but I can't discuss it over the phone. I'll expect you sometime tomorrow, then."

Manuel put down the receiver and turned to Landau. "Forgive me, please . . ."

"Not at all. It's late and I have to leave anyway. I'll come again of course, but after all, you understand, Tilly . . ."

"Mr. Landau, tell me just one thing: did you ever find out why Director Friedjung spoke so brutally and cruelly to Frau Steinfeld?"

"No, never."

"And she never offered any explanation, either?"

"She had none. I mean, she *said* she had none."

"Do you think she was hiding something?"

"I don't know. She was terribly bitter about Friedjung. But when I think back on it, I can't help feeling that she knew he had acted as he did *not without reason*. Yes, he must have had his reasons."

The telephone rang again. Manuel shrugged and picked up the phone. He recognized the deep, slightly hoarse voice at once.

"Good afternoon, Madame."

"Are you alone?" Nora Hill asked.

"No. What can I do for you?"

He heard her throaty laughter. "It's been days since I've heard anything from you, my friend. I was getting worried. Are you all right?"

"Thank you, yes."

"You've probably made many discoveries in the meantime."

"You could say that."

"So, my prediction was correct. I have something interesting to show you. A surprise."

"You have a surprise for me?"

"Yes. Can you come and see me?"

"Of course. When?"

"Just one moment. Do you have travellers' checks with you?"

"Travellers' checks?"

"Travellers' checks."

"Yes." he replied, baffled.

"In large denominations?"

"Yes."

"Bring what you have with you. The surprise is going to cost you money. Five thousand dollars. But I think it's worth the price."

"Five thousand dollars?"

"This evening at ten o'clock?"

"All right. But listen—"

"I look forward to it. So long, my friend," said Nora Hill, breaking the connection.

Nora Hill . . .

Manuel stood by the window, deep in thought. Was it mere coincidence that she had happened to ring at this particular moment? Or was it intentional? Planned? She was involved in this whole affair: was she trying to lure him into a trap? Couldn't he: everyone involved knew by now that his father's manuscript was in a lawyer's safe. What kind of surprise?

50

The bar at the Ritz was about four feet above the floor of the main lobby. To get into the bar, one had to climb a short flight of steps.

A group of American businessmen were sitting around the bar. One of them was doing most of the talking, with the others dutifully laughing at his jokes. The booths were all occupied. It was a busy night for the head mixer and his three assistants.

"I'm so glad you agreed to have dinner with me, Irene," Manuel said. He was sitting next to her in a corner booth. Irene looked very beautiful this evening, attracting second looks from every man who walked by.

"And I'm happy you're not flying home right away," Irene answered softly. Then she added after a short pause, "When do you think you will be leaving?"

"I don't know yet. After what we discovered in the box, and what Landau told me—"

"Yes?" The question was almost breathless.

"Well, I mean, everything is different now! The situation has changed completely. If it's at all possible, I'd like to stay here. I'm pretty sure now that I'm more likely to find what I'm looking for in Vienna than in Buenos Aires. But of course I want to hear what Cayetano has to say. And Nora Hill, too."

"She must be a fascinating woman, I suppose, in spite of her . . ." Irene paused.

"What nonsense," said Manuel, feeling himself grow warm. "If anybody's fascinating, it's—" Embarrassed, he broke off. They looked into each other's eyes, and Irene smiled for the first time. She opened her handbag.

"I brought you something . . ."

"Good evening, madam, sir," Count Romath's voice broke in. Manuel looked up, and Irene lowered her handbag. The man with the snow-white hair and the black suit bowed low as Manuel introduced him to Irene. Romath looked cheerful and carefree. Nobody would have guessed that he was about to keep a secret and dangerous midnight rendezvous. He complimented Irene on her beauty, made certain that they were being properly served, then said,

"All the best, Mr. Aranda, all the best."

"Thank you. But I have put off my departure, so we shall no doubt be seeing each other again."

"I didn't mean it that way."

"How then?"

"You have so many—the lady is involved in the case herself, so she knows what I am talking about—you have so many worries. May they disappear soon, and may you again be happy and carefree, both of you," said the Count, then bowed and walked away with an old man's mincing gait.

"He's nice, isn't he?" said Irene.

"Yes." Manuel watched Romath walking away. A page entered the bar carrying a small blackboard on the end of a stick. In white letters was printed TELEPHONE CALL FOR: and beneath it, written in chalk, MR. MANUEL ARANDA. Manuel got up.

"Excuse me a moment!" Manuel manoeuvred himself out of the booth.

"Mr. Aranda? Cabin Five," the page said.

Manuel hurried across the foyer to the passageway which led to the Café. A row of telephone booths was situated there. Manuel went into Number 5 and lifted the receiver.

"Yes? Aranda here."

"Thank Goodness I've reached you! I'm in luck. This is Martha Waldegg. Can I talk? Are you alone?"

"Yes. Good evening, Frau Waldegg," Manuel said.

"My husband is with friends. Have you seen Irene?"

"A few times. She's at the bar right now. We were going to have dinner together."

"For goodness' sake! She mustn't know that I—Mr. Aranda, you promised me that—"

"I won't say anything to her. And I haven't said anything to her so far. You're calling to tell me when I can come see you, I presume."

"Yes."

"When?"

"The day after tomorrow. Wednesday."

"At what time?"

"You can't come by car. The Semmering pass is snowed in. You'll have to take the train."

"That's fine."

"You leave from the Vienna South Station. The best train is the "Venetia Express," which leaves Vienna at 8:05 in the morning and gets to Villach at 13:29. You can get a train back from Villach at 16:26, arriving in Vienna at 22:05."

"Sounds fine. Nobody will know anything about it. I'll invent some excuse."

"Thank you, Mr. Aranda! You'll have three hours stay here, I'll have time to tell you everything. Make a note of the address: Fliederstrasse 143. Our villa is fairly secluded, and I've given the housekeeper the day off, so we'll be alone."

"Till Wednesday afternoon then, Frau Waldegg."

As Manuel walked back to the bar through the lobby he wiped his brow with a handkerchief. Irene watched him coming.

"Cayetano. From Paris," he said, sitting down again.

"The snow's worse than ever." He noticed that Irene had her hand covering something on the table. "What's that?"

"It's what I brought for you," she said.

It was a photograph of her, in color, showing only her head. She was laughing. Her brown eyes and brown hair were shining, her beautiful teeth glistening.

"Oh!"

"You wanted a photo of me, and last night, in all the excitement we forgot it."

"Thank you, Irene." Somehow he felt depressed. A few

minutes ago I was talking on the phone to your mother, he thought. And I had to promise her not to tell you. Manuel suddenly felt like a cheat. He said:

"But you have to write something on the back for me!"

"I've done that already," she said.

He turned the picture round and read:

It was no accident the Rabbi upset the soup bowl. S••'enmacher doesn't think so. And I don't think so, either.

Irene Waldegg

51

The farm-house room had a wooden floor. Bulky furniture painted in bright colors decorated the room, the windows were hung with checkered curtains, and there were two pictures on the walls, one showing a stag in a clearing, the other high mountains in the red glow of sunset.

In the center of the room stood Yvonne Werra. She was wearing a corset, rough woollen stockings, and wooden clogs. She had a heavy rope in her right hand. Next to her stood a goat, a large bucket under its nose from which it occasionally drank thirstily. And behind the goat, half bent over her, stood a slender, muscular man wearing only a Tyrolean hat. His naked skin was very white. The man had dark hair, dark eyes, and a face contorted with excitement. He was performing coitus with the goat; the animal seemed to have no objection; from time to time it brayed contentedly.

The man was panting.

Yvonne slashed the cord across his back with all her strength. It was no nylon whip. The lashes hurt, and were meant to. Dark weals swelled up on the man's white back.

In one corner of the room was a tiled stove and a bench, on which was a tape-recorder, switched on. A quartet of mixed voices was singing and yodelling, "On the grass of the fields, you don't care who yields ..." The goat lowered its head and drank from the bucket.

Yvonne lashed out again.

"Harder!" the man panted. "Harder! Yes, like that! Like that!"

His body twitched and jerked. The goat chewed its cud nonchalantly, untouched by the proceedings. Yvonne screamed at the man, "Don't you feel ashamed, you pig, you miserable sod? Yesterday I caught you with the duck! Are you going to stop now?"

"No, no, I can't stop," the man stammered.

"You filthy lump of shit! The poor goat! I'm going to report you to the pastor! You should be locked up! It'll be the horses next!"

The quartet yodelled away happily.

The goat brayed.

The man groaned: "The horses! What do you mean, the horses! Goats are my favorite!"

"You God-forsaken swine! Take that! And that!" The cord slapped down across the muscular white back. The man wearing the Tyrolean hat howled and leered at Yvonne's naked parts, licking his lips lasciviously.

"That's enough, I think," said Nora Hill, and switched off the TV in her living-room. The picture of the farm room faded, the yodlers went silent.

"I'm always happy to offer you some entertainment. And I wanted you to see the man. Who knows? Some day it might be important for you to recognize him."

Manuel had taken Irene Waldegg home after their dinner at the Ritz, and then had driven out to see Nora Hill.

"What do you mean it might be important for me to recognize him? Who is he?" Manuel asked.

"Easy now. I told you, I have a surprise for you. But make us a couple of drinks first, my friend."

Nora Hill watched attentively as Manuel filled the glasses at the bar cart which stood next to him, pouring in whisky and soda water over ice cubes. The fire crackled in the fireplace.

"Thank you." The cigarette holder she used on this particular evening was extra long and gold. She blew a few smoke rings.

"Poor Yvonne," she said in her deep voice. "She really does end up with that type a bit too often. They're all crazy about her. She can't work completely naked tonight. Had a little accident a couple of nights ago. Still has some blue bruises on her body. That's why she's wearing the corset."

"An accident?"

"A professional risk! There's always the danger of something happening. It wasn't anything of interest. But the man I showed you is interesting. A regular customer for a long time now. Three years. That's how long we've had Emma."

"Who?"

"Emma the goat. We keep a whole farmyard of animals in one of the small houses behind the villa. We have geese and rabbits and hens, even a donkey, Hugo. You need all sorts of things in this trade. We bought Emma when this gentleman asked for a goat. He promised to keep coming, and he pays fantastic amounts. So what can you do? As you saw, he's very . . . delicately built. And so, if Emma's the only one who can make him happy, what can you do?"

"I agree, I agree."

"Everybody's happy—the man, ourselves, even Emma."

"Emma, too?"

"Yes, Emma, too. Emma loves beer. There's nothing she likes better! So every time we use her we give her a whole bucketful of beer. You just saw it."

"Doesn't she get drunk?" Manuel asked politely.

"Completely drunk, in the end. But that puts her in an especially good and happy mood and she lets Mr. Penkovic do whatever he likes."

"What's the man's name?"

"Vasiliu Penkovic. That's what he calls himself, at any rate. A Roumanian, supposedly. From Temesvar. Makes a lot of money."

"Doing what?"

"Special missions. He works for both East and West as a sort of private detective. His specialty is tailing and shadowing people. Mr. Penkovic is an artist at his job. He has rendered quite outstanding services to all his clients. But he seems to be going through a bad time right now."

"What makes you say that?"

"He offered to sell me something that someone had commissioned him to get. It's not his usual style to go in for such double-dealing. He must be in urgent need of money. And he's well-informed, as always. He already knew when he came to visit me, that I know you for instance. He showed me what it is he wants to sell, because he thought it might have some value for you. I shared his opinion, and so I bought it. That's why I asked you to bring travellers' checks in the amount of five thousand dollars. You did bring them, didn't you, my friend?"

"Yes, but I don't know what you so kindly bought for me—or why?"

"Because Penkovic does not want to deal with you personally."

"Then you took a risk."

"I don't think so, my friend."

"Five thousand dollars is a lot of money. I can expect a lot for that!"

"And you're going to get it! I'm sure I wasn't over-hasty. Penkovic is expensive, but he delivers first-class goods."

"Can I see them?"

"Of course." Nora got up, hobbled on her crutches over to a small writing-desk, took out an envlope, and swung back over to Manuel.

"There you are."

Manuel opened the envelope.

Six colored photographs fell out. They were all of the same three people: depicting them on the street, in a lonely quarry, on the edge of a wood, and always deep in conversation. The photos must have been taken in summer, in bright sunshine. All three people were wearing light clothing. Two of them Manuel knew, but not the third, who was small and thick-set, bald-headed, and with bulging eyes. Of the other two, one was a man, the other a woman.

The second man had a swarthy complexion, almost olive-colored, hands covered with black hair and black hair on his head. He was Ernesto Gomez, the little man from the Argentinian Embassy, who had visited Manuel at the Ritz and practically ordered him, with veiled threats, to abandon his inquiries in Vienna and return to Buenos Aires.

And the woman—Manuel recognized her immediately, from the many photos he had seen the night before—was Valerie Steinfeld.

52

"Valerie Steinfeld and Ernesto Gomez from the Argentinian Embassy!"

"Right, my friend."

"And the other man?"

"If Penkovic is to be believed, and I don't see why not, then he is a certain Thomas Meerswald. A remarkable man. He—"

"What do you mean, remarkable? What does he do?"

"Let me finish! Goodness, you really are impatient! Penkovic says the photos were taken in the summer of 1966. At that time Meerswald happened to be in Vienna."

"Happened to be? Where is he normally?"

"Penkovic says that at the time the photos were taken Meerswald owned a factory just outside of Vienna with offices in the city. But one saw him rarely because he was always away on journeys, most of them in South America, and especially in Argentina. That's remarkable, don't you think?"

"Yes. What sort of factory was it that Penkovic spoke of?"

"He said that Mr. Meerswald was manufacturing pesticides."

"But that's . . . that's . . ."

"Calm down, Mr. Aranda. Have another drink. Did I promise too much? You see. Nora Hill never promises too much. Is five thousand dollars too high a price for these pictures? I don't think so."

"But what do they mean? What had Valerie Steinfeld to do with these men? She must have been up to her neck in this nasty business! It gets worse all the time!"

"Mr. Aranda! Please take five travellers' checks and countersign them for me. I like you. Really. I wanted to have travellers' checks because once they're in my hands I know you can't stop them at the bank."

"Incredible," said Fedor Santarin, laughing admiringly while rubbing his diamond ring on one of his sleeves. "Simply unbelievable. Nora's really precious! Penkovic told me he sold her the pictures for four thousand dollars. She's the most amazing woman I know."

"Why does she do such things for you, Santarin?" Jean Mercier asked.

"Oh, just as a favor. I'm doing her a favor too, you know," the Russian said, smiling. He was sitting with the Frenchman in the room decorated as a little girl's room, with dolls, dolls' clothes, and children's underwear.

A microphone hidden in the chimney over the fireplace in Nora's living-room transmitted the conversation between her and Manuel Aranda for them. The speaker was next to a picture of Snow White and the Seven Dwarfs, above the head-board of the bed on which Santarin sat.

"The photos are doing just what we wanted," Jean Mercier said. He was sitting on a small red wooden chair. "They're just what was needed to convince him that he must stay in Vienna now. Santarin, you're a rogue, but you're also a genius."

"I know," the Russian said. He opened a book of fairy tales that lay on the night table by the bed. The book was a fake, hollowed out inside. It contained an assortment of condoms. The Russian took one out, rolled it down between two fingers, then blew it up like a balloon. He held the opening tight shut so that no air could escape and contemplated the inscription written on the contraceptive in capital letters: I LOVE YOU. "Charming," said Santarin. Everything was going according to plan in Nora's living-room, Mercier and Grant both knew that. Santarin, who had known Penkovic for a long time, had sent the Roumanian to Nora with the photos, under orders to ask four thousand dollars for their purchase. And Nora had in turn been advised by Santarin to pay this price for the photos, then to inform Manuel Aranda at once and tell him the story she had just told him.

"Tell Aranda you bought the photos on his behalf and want to get your money back. I'll advance the four thousand dollars. You can give them back to me when Aranda pays you."

"And what if he doesn't buy?"

"He'll buy, don't worry," Santarin had said.

"Four thousand dollars—why so much?"

"The photos *have* to cost that much, so that Aranda will think they're especially important. People are strange."

"Why were the pictures made in the first place? These are just prints. And why did you have Penkovic follow the Stein-feld woman two years ago? And what do you hope to gain from all this now?"

"Don't," Santarin had said.

"Don't what?"

"Don't ask so many questions, please. Penkovic doesn't ask any. Just do what I say and that's all. Do we understand each other?"

"We understand each other," Nora had answered.

"Madame, I thank you," Santarin had said, kissing her hand . . .

"Yes," the Russian said now sitting on the child's bed,

313

slowly letting the air out of the contraceptive, then tossing it away. "I think Aranda will stay now. The danger's over. You were really upset at the thought that he might leave Vienna, eh, Mercier?"

"So were you and Grant, weren't you?"

"Yes, we were," Santarin admitted. He pulled a long bag of candy from his gray suit pocket and offered them to Mercier, who took a long time choosing.

"And we'll find out, too, what it was that upset Aranda so much," Santarin said confidently.

"If *you* get behind it," said Mercier politely. You can be too clever, he thought, and over-confident. You, my dear fellow, have taken care of making sure that the young man stays in Vienna—which means that the manuscript and the film will stay in the attorney's safe. Mr. de Brakeleer has flown to Bremen to talk with the expert safe-cracker. And this morning Inspector Ulrich Schäfer handed in the ad that will appear in tomorrow's *Kurier*. One of my people was in the classified ad offices waiting for Schäfer to show up. Schäfer brought in the text about the violin teacher we had given him. As soon as the ad has appeared we will get into touch with him. Let them all take me for an idiot—it's the best thing that can happen to me.

You *bet* I'll find out what upset Aranda so much, Santarin was thinking. I'll find it out tonight. When Count Romath goes over to Gilbert Grant's, I'll be there too. I'm only staying here to see if everything goes smoothly, then I'm off. Romath will tell us what he knows and he'll do what I tell him to do. But all that's no business of yours, you French fleabrain!

"If this Meerswald fellow manufactures pesticides, was he at the Congress, too?" Manuel's voice came in over the loudspeaker.

"At the Congress?" Nora questioned, her voice rising doubtfully. "I don't know. His firm does business all over the world, it's true, but it isn't one of the major manufacturers, you know. The name was unfamiliar to you, after all, was it not?"

"Yes, it was, Madame. Can I . . . may I . . ."

"What?"

"I really should make a telephone call, but—"

"But you're afraid somebody might be listening in, eh?"

"Nora! Nora!" said Santarin, delighted. He blew up another contraceptive, with the text CHERIE, JE T'AIME. The

314

Russian laughed. "Look at that, Mercier! I wonder if they have it in all languages? What a house!" He poked around in the fairy tale book-box. "Where are the ones for Russian guests? Ah, there's one!"

"Of course I am," Manuel's voice answered. "I don't really know why. It's not hard to figure out whom I want to call."

Nora Hill, stretched luxuriously in the comfortable armchair.

"Groll, of course."

"Right. So, I might as well . . ."

Half a minute later Groll was at the other end of the line: "Good evening, Manuel. You want to talk to me?"

"Yes, very urgently, sir. Do you know a certain Thomas Meerswald?"

"Certainly. What brings you to him?"

"And a certain Vasiliu Penkovic?"

"That pig? Of course! Tell me, Manuel!"

"What do you know about those two?"

"Not over the phone. Where are you?"

"At Nora Hill's."

After a short surprised silence, Groll laughed out loud.

"Sir, I've made another discovery. When can we meet?" The six photos lay in front of him on the little smoking-table, next to the telephone. "I can come over right away. I——"

"No good. We've been interrogating a lovers' lane murderer since this morning. I can't get away yet. Come to my apartment after midnight. Porzellangasse——"

"I know the address, I'll be there. And thank you, Commissioner."

"But call me first from a telephone booth. I'll have to unlock the door for you."

"I'll call you again." Manuel hung up and took his briefcase to put in the six photos. As he opened it the folded sheet of paper he had found in Valerie Steinfeld's box slipped out onto the floor. He grabbed for it quickly, but Nora Hill was faster.

"What sort of old paper is that?"

"Give it back to me this minute!"

Nora half-opened the paper and read aloud:

"Pasteur 1870: silkworm epidemic . . ."

In the little girl's room Santarin jumped up from the bed.

"That's it! I told Nora to take note of everything Aranda had with him!"

315

"Please, Madame, give it back to me!" said Manuel's voice, loud and urgent. Steps were then heard.

"Ouch! What's got into you? I'm going to give it to you! You're hurting me!"

"Excuse me, please. I'm sorry."

The sound of steps again.

"Pasteur 1870, silkworm plague ... old paper ... could *that* be it?" Mercier asked. He had also got to his feet.

"It's quite possible," said Santarin, nodding. "When Nora comes to see you later, make her describe the paper exactly."

"Of course."

"Today, it's your turn to tail Aranda. Go tell one of your radio cars outside to drive over to Grant's apartment and give him all the details of what's been happening."

"Why Grant's apartment?"

"Because I'll be there, too. I have to know what's going on as it happens. I still have another meeting to go to tonight."

"Who with?"

"I'll tell you that tomorrow. Just do as I say!"

"Yes, of course, right away," Mercier stammered, taken aback by the unusually sharp tone of Santarin's voice.

In Nora's living-room Manuel was getting to his feet.

"You're not going, are you?"

"I ..."

"Where to? It's only ten-thirty. What are you going to do till midnight?"

"I don't know. All this is so upsetting ... I'm sure you understand ... that Valerie Steinfeld ... that woman seems to be at the center of everything."

"Then I had better tell you some more of my own story, and some of Valerie Steinfeld's at the same time. What do you say? Since you're here anyway, and I promised I would tell you everything I knew about Valerie Steinfeld and what I went through with her."

Manuel sat down again.

"Good." Nora smiled. "But I have only an hour. I'm expecting a visitor at eleven-thirty and you'll have to excuse me then."

53

On April 7, 1766, The Austrian Emperer Joseph II donated twelve thousand acres of wooded land, formerly a Hapsburg hunting preserve, to the people of Vienna. Here, they were to be able to "ride, drive, walk and indulge in lawful pursuits of pleasure."

The area filled up quickly with puppet theatres, shooting galleries and pavilions where food and coffee were served. The "Wurstel Prater", a huge amusement park, opened officially in 1852. In 1945 it was totally destroyed during the heavy fighting between the SS and the advancing Red Army. A few years later, the "Wurstel Prater" was rebuilt. Back came the shooting galleries, puppet theatres, boat rides, swings and mini-cars and back came—completely restored—Vienna's ancient landmark, the Giant Ferris Wheel.

January 17, 1943 was a cold, sunny day. The city had been blanketed by snow for weeks. But the Giant Ferris Wheel, as yet untouched by the ravages of war, was going around and around. In one of its cabins, two passengers sat huddled side by side. Nora Hill had been in Vienna for a week. She had let some days go by before calling up Valerie Steinfeld to arrange a meeting with her.

"At the ferris wheel tomorrow afternoon at two-thirty. By the box-office."

Valerie had arrived punctually. She was wearing her Persian lamb coat—a 1937 Christmas present from Paul!—a small black hat and a black suit. She was delighted to see Nora again.

The wheel had scarcely begun to turn when Valerie asked for news of her husband.

"He is fine and very happy about your decision to go through with the law suit. He sends you all his love."

Brilliant sunshine pouring in through the windows of the cabin shimmered in Valerie's blonde hair, which curved out from under her hat.

"Is he in good health?"

317

"Perfect."

"And his liver?"

"Fine. You needn't worry. He has a lot of friends who are looking after him."

"That's good. I was afraid he might be very lonely in London."

The cabin, as large as a tramcar, was quite high up. The houses, people and streets down below became smaller and smaller. More streets came into view, churches, the Danube canal, the river, the bridges across it. The cabin swung gently, soundlessly. Huge iron girders supporting the wheel moved past the windows.

"When are you flying back to Lisbon?"

"At the end of the month. Your husband is naturally anxious to know how the suit is going. Is everything all right?"

Valerie looked at Nora. "Couldn't be better!" she said, beaming.

"And how about Heinz?"

"He's thrilled!"

"I knew he would be. He hates his father."

"Yes," Valerie said. "It'll be different once the war's over, of course; the boy's just brainwashed. But he's a good boy. When we're all back together again and happy, he'll be just as fond of his father as he was before 1938, I'm sure. Have your friend tell my husband that, please."

"Certainly."

"And have him say that Heinz is doing very well at school," Valerie continued in a happy voice, "and that the Director is treating him in an *especially friendly* way now that he knows I've filed suit."

"He *knows* that?"

Valerie nodded eagerly. "I went to see him with Dr. Forster—who's a wonderful lawyer, by the way!—and told him. I went to see the Regional Commandant, too. Their eyes almost popped out of their heads! And they outdid each other trying to be polite!" Valerie laughed heartily. "Especially Friedjung, the Director of the Chemistry Institute! Incredibly polite! He had been expecting something of the sort, he said. He just couldn't imagine Heinz wasn't Aryan, he's too good at gymnastics!"

"He said that?" Nora was watching Valerie carefully.

"Yes!" said the slender blue-eyed woman. She was talking with great verve. I wonder what makes her eyes glisten so, thought Nora—excitement, joy?

318

"The Director's handling Heinz with kid gloves. As long as the suit lasts, and it can drag on for a long time, Forster says, nothing will happen to the boy. I don't have to worry about him. It was a wonderful idea of my husband's."

The cabin floated up and up, the sunshine flooding it more and more.

Valerie opened her handbag and rummaged around inside it. "This is really an ideal meeting place. Nobody can listen in on us here. And I want to show you everything. Look! Carbon copies of the application. That's how it began. This was the suit he filed." She passed a bundle of thin sheets over to Nora.

Nora read the pages over quickly. "To the Regional Court, Vienna I, Courthouse. Plaintiff: Heinz Steinfeld, minor . . . represented by his mother, Valerie Steinfeld, appointed official guardian in court resolution no. 6 G 503/42 at the County Court of Währing on November 26, 1942. Frau Steinfeld represented by Dr. Otto Forster, Attorney-at-Law, Vienna I, Rotenturmstrasse 143 (Power of Attorney dated 24 October 1942). Defendant: a Public Prosecutor to be appointed to uphold legitimacy of birth and blood descent. SUIT disclaiming legitimacy of birth and blood descent . . . Costs of Action Reichsmarks 2,500."

"We've turned the whole truth upside down and claimed that our marriage was bad from the very beginning—but that's what Paul wanted! If he could read this he would have a good laugh!" said Valerie, laughing herself. She pointed with her finger. "Here, for instance: "the incompatibility of the two spouses." There's a lot in that style. A masterpiece, don't you think?"

"A masterpiece," said Nora. She saw that Valerie's hands were trembling, and Valerie noticed that Nora had noticed. She laughed again.

"I'm so nervous and excited because everything is going so well! And the judge we're getting is anti-Nazi, too, Forster says. How lucky can you get?"

Now the cabin had reached the highest point in its climb, and stopped, swinging gently. Every cabin stopped at this point for five minutes. The city was spread out down below, people were no longer visible, the houses were dwarfed, the mountains of the Vienna Woods looked like gentle hills, the Danube like a brook.

"I must congratulate you," said Nora.

"Me, why me?! I'm very happy about everything, of course.

319

But *Paul!* It's Paul who's going to be the happiest, isn't he? When will your friend be flying back to London?"

"Very soon after I get back."

"My God, have him tell Paul everything exactly as I've told you! How well everything's going ... please don't leave anything out!"

"I won't, not a single word," Nora said, and went on reading, her eyes flying over the pages. "... in both his nature and his external appearance Paul Steinfeld possessed, in easily recognizable form, the typical characteristics of the Jewish race. Proof: numerous photographs, testimony of witnesses ...

"... the plaintiff is completely free from all these characteristics so that it must be assumed as beyond all reasonable doubt that he is the issue, not of the legitimate marital intercourse between the two spouses, but of the intercourse with Martin Landau."

Valerie handed further papers over to Nora. "Then came the first hearing, which lasted until December 18. I was not there. Forster wrote to me." She gave Nora a new sheet.

"At the first hearing the public prosecutor, Dr. Kummer, was awarded an adjournment until January 15, 1943 in order to establish the case for the State."

"And Dr. Kummer is anti-Nazi too, Forster told me. Incredible luck, don't you think?" Valerie was beaming.

"Yes," Nora said dully. "Really incredible. A miracle, almost."

Valerie rummaged in her handbag again. "Dr. Forster gave me a copy of the prosecutor's brief, too," she said. "Here it is." She handed Nora a sheet of paper.

"I refer first to the documents on which the suit is based, but which have not yet been submitted. I contest the plaintiff's claim to be the issue not of Paul Steinfeld, as the said documents presumably will show, but of Martin Landau, so long as the plaintiff has failed to file the proper documents in support of his claim, the onus of proof being upon the plaintiff ..."

"It's just a lot of legal jargon that the man has to write for the record, Dr. Forster says," Valerie said nervously as she saw Nora examining the last sheet more carefully than the others. "You don't have to read it all!" she said.

"But I want to," Nora replied gently.

"I reserve the right, in the event the plaintiff submits documentary evidence to support his suit, to order anthropological and genetic examinations of the plaintiff, as well as reports by authorized experts to establish whether the hereditary characteristics of descent from the non-Aryan begetter are present or excluded. In my capacity as public prosecutor, insofar as my case against the suit was held valid in principle at the first hearing, I hereby request summary dismissal of the suit with costs."

Doesn't look good at all, Nora thought, and said, "But it says here—"

"I know, I know! I was shocked at first, too. But then Forster told me the public prosecutor *had* to include that paragraph in order to *protect* himself!" Valerie shrugged her shoulders, laughed, and stuffed the papers back into her handbag. "People must always protect themselves from each other, mustn't they? It has no special significance."

The toy houses were getting bigger now, and dwarf-like figures could be seen in the streets once again. Nora looked at Valerie.

"And what if they do a blood test?"

"Let them do it!"

"You're so optimistic. The blood test can ruin everything."

"No, it can't," said Valerie, laughing again as the people, the houses, the churches, and the tramcars grew bigger and bigger. The ground seemed to be rushing up to meet them.

"How can that be?"

"Forster knows a doctor with a serological lab. For safety's sake *we already had our blood-groups tested.* Martin, Heinz, and myself! The doctor's absolutely dependable: he won't say a word." Valerie was lying fluently. "There's no danger at all! According to the tests, it is *possible* that Martin Landau *could* be the father."

"Splendid," said Nora, impressed.

"Please take this with you!" said Valerie, and pressed a very small object into Nora's hand. It was a deer fashioned out of lead, smaller than a penny.

"On New Year's eve, 1937. We were invited out ... just two-and-a-half months before Paul had to leave. After midnight we pulled fire-crackers. In the one Paul and I pulled we got this, a miniature deer. We were really happy about it because Paul had always called me "little deer." I was always so slim. He said it would bring us good luck, the little deer, and I should keep it. It has brought *me* good luck here, and I want it to protect *him* now!" Valerie was suddenly talking like a bashful young girl. "I want *him* to have it now. Please

321

take it with you to Lisbon, and have your friend take it to London with him! To give to Paul. Will you?"

"Of course," said Nora Hill, and put the tiny lead figure in her pocket. Then she stood up.

"We won't be seeing each other again, but you'll hear from me after I get back. Let me get out of the cabin first. You get out afterwards and stay here a few minutes. We don't know each other."

"Thank you, Miss Hill. You and your friend. God will reward both of you for your goodness."

Valerie was still smiling. She walked away in the opposite direction from Nora into the heart of the Prater. Her walk became slower and slower, the smile evaporated from her face, and suddenly she staggered, managing to reach a bench before she collapsed.

She was panting for breath, as though she had just gone through a great exertion. Her mouth hung open, her lips were drained of blood. Her hands were shaking, and her whole body quivered. She sat on the snow-covered bench, and suddenly felt sweat running down her spine in spite of the cold. She could only think of Paul. He must be reassured. I had to lie. I just hope I lied well. I hope Paul will be reassured. Oh Paul, I love you. The deer is on its way to you . . .

54

"Come in!" shouted Nora. She had just entered the spacious drawing room of her apartment on the first floor of the infamous circular house. There had been a knock on the door. Now there was another.

"Come in!" Nora called out once more. It was 4:40 P.M. and dusk was falling. It had taken Nora almost two hours to get home.

The door to the living room with the huge fireplace, in which a roaring fire blazed, opened and the chauffeur, Albert Carlson, entered. The lamps had been turned on and in their light Carlson's lean, hungry-looking face with its piercing eyes and heavy brows appeared livid and ghostly, like a skull.

"Oh, Carlson. What's up?" Nora threw her coat over a chair. The chauffeur was wearing a business suit. He stared at her without speaking.

"Carlson! What is it you want?"

"You!" he said hoarsely.

She looked at him coldly. "Have you gone out of your mind? Get out of here! Out!"

"I wouldn't dream of it," said Carlson, approaching her.

Nora had quick reflexes. She wheeled around and reached for the telephone. But before she could lift the receiver, he had grabbed her hand.

"Just leave that be, got it?"

"I wanted—"

"To call the guard at the gate, I know."

"No. Konrad." Konrad was the butler.

"He's not there, baby." He was standing so close to her now she wanted to recoil, but he held her hand in an iron grip.

"There's nobody here at all. The entire staff has the day off until midnight. The Chief won't be back until late. I'm supposed to fetch him at nine o'clock. The only man here is the one at the gate—and the gate's a long way away. We have enough time. There's not a soul in the house. Only the two of us . . ." His eyes had a glassy expression.

Nora had moved away from him bit by bit. Now she was backed up against a wall. He placed a hand upon her breasts.

"Stop that or I'll scream!"

"Go on, scream!" Carlson grinned. "Scream away, you whore! Scream your head off! There's no one to hear you."

"Take your hand away!"

In answer he ripped open the upper part of her brown dress. Her breasts were covered only by a black silk slip, their contours clearly outlined through the thin material.

"Quite a luscious feast," he drooled, stroking and pinching both breasts through the black silk. "Why should the Chief have it all to himself? Why can't I have a share?" He pressed his body against hers and she felt his arousal.

"You . . . you . . . I'll report you to Mr. Flemming!"

"The hell you will, you whore. Remember your first rendezvous with the Steinfeld woman? In the bookstore, and afterwards in the Church of St. Stephen?" He was stroking her breasts constantly with one hand, gripping her arm tight with the other. She was rigid with fear. "You know exactly what I'm talking about, don't you?"

"Not the vaguest idea—"

"No idea, she says! You really didn't see me?"

"That was you? So it wasn't just—" Nora bit her lips.

"Dreamed up by that bookdealer of yours, that's what you were going to say, weren't you?" He laughed, his breath blowing sourly all over her. "Now you've given yourself away. No, he didn't dream it up. I always wore the blue overcoat and the Homburg when I was on your tail." He nipped at one of her nipples. She gave a muffled squeal.

"Always?"

"Yes, always," said Carlson. "For a year."

"But why?"

"Because I want to fuck you. Just keep that trap of yours shut, will you? At first I didn't know enough. Meantime I've asked around about that Steinfeld dame. Followed her, too. To an attorney called Forster. And to the county court in Währing. I played it dumb and asked a few straight questions. She's bringing a suit, the lady is. About her brat. Claims he's no half-Jew. Steinfeld, her husband, is a Jew. He's in England."

"That's not true!"

"Oh, yes, it is. I have my friends. Here and there. At the Courthouse, too. And where were you today? At the Prater! With the Steinfeld woman again. You were all by yourselves in one of those cabins, gabbing away all the time—"

"That's nonsense."

"It's not nonsense. You're in Lisbon all the time. He can get news through to there, that Jew. You bring it to him. Then you bring it to Vienna. It's the same the other way 'round. It took me a while to figure it all out, but now I've got it down pat. Take your clothes off."

"What . . . what?"

"Come on! That's enough talk! Now I'm going to have you. I must have you. I'm mad about you. Have been ever since the first day. And you, you treated me like dirt, as though I were not even a man—"

"That's not true!"

"—but now things are different. I'll keep my mouth shut if you let me screw you. Otherwise the Chief hears the whole story. And once that happens you'll be whipped off to a concentration camp quicker than you can say *boo*. Now get on with it!"

Concentration camp? Nora's mind was working feverishly. Maybe not, because Flemming's in love with me, so maybe

324

he'll send *you* to camp you swine. But *Valerie Steinfeld!* If Flemming finds out what she's planning. then she's in danger, and so are her son and Martin Landau. They're just strangers as far as Flemming's concerned. He won't care about them! And once he finds out that Jack is the connection to London, he'll never let me go to Lisbon again. Oh, to hell with it, Nora thought, let that filthy pig have his five minutes. There's too much at stake.

"Please, serve yourself," said Nora scornfully. The next moment Carlson gave her a mighty slap across the face. She screamed in pain.

"Go on, scream! Let it rip! I like it! I'll serve myself, all right, you arrogant bitch. But in my own way. I'll do my own thing!"

Carlson stretched out his hand and with a single tug tore Nora's dress from her body. He looked at her gray stockings and her black panties. He lunged at her again, panting.

"What are you after?" Nora protested. "I'm letting you ... I'll do anything ... I—"

Once more he slammed her in the face, this time across the other cheek. The blow stung. The man was losing control of himself rapidly. Nora's horror was growing: the man was mad, mad!

"*Help!*" Nora screamed, and ran towards the door of the bedroom, hoping to escape him. She feared for her life. The fear was stronger than thought. He stuck his foot out in front of her and she crashed to the ground. With two strides Carlson was at the door and had locked it, then he jumped back to Nora.

"Be reasonable," she begged him. "You can have me—" Carlson bent down and drove both fists hard into her stomach.

"That's the beginning of my thing, understand?"

Nora forgot every consideration. She was utterly terrified by this man with his dishevelled hair, glassy eyes, and sweat-covered features.

"*Help,*" she screamed. "*Help! Help!*"

"Scream! Scream! Keep screaming!" He yanked at her black slip, which tore with a loud ripping sound. Carlson stared as though in a trance at her white breasts, which were heaving as Nora gasped for breath.

"You whore, you wanted to drive me crazy, completely crazy, with your lah-dee-dah ways! I'm really crazy about you. You'll see in a moment just how bad it's got me ..."

"But I'm letting you! Why are you hurting me?"

"Because I enjoy it." He dragged his trousers down and leapt on Nora, who resisted desperately. In a flash he loosened his silk tie, wound it around her neck, and knotted it. Nora, choking, gasped for breath, her body arched. He slackened the tie.

"That's what I've dreamed of, that's how I want it . . . tried it on myself . . . leaves no traces, it's silk, the luscious thing." With one hand he pulled her panties down over her thighs. The panties tore.

"Please . . . please . . . come . . . do it . . . but don't—" The knot tightened again. Carlson slumped down on Nora's naked body, his elbows pinning her upper arms so that she could not move them. They were lying on a thick carpet in front of the fireplace.

"Open your legs!"

Underneath him she squirmed.

"Get those legs . . . open . . . you beast," Carlson grunted, tightening the knot. Nora was fighting for breath and getting none. Her mouth was wide open, her head jerking in all directions. She opened her legs.

An instant later he was inside her, savage and brutal. Her throat rattled as the pain jabbed through her. Carlson was raving like a lunatic.

Nora felt herself pass out. She felt fire between her legs, the man was rapt in true delirium, bucking and stabbing like a merciless machine.

"Aaaaaah . . . now!"

Nora lay still. She had lost consciousness.

When she came to again, she was alone. She had no sense of how long she had been lying there on the floor, naked, bruised, spattered, her limbs spread-eagled. The room was illuminated only by the glow of the fire. Moving her sore body with great caution, Nora inched herself upright. But when she tried to walk, she collapsed instantly.

It was some time before her strength had returned sufficiently for her to stagger across the living-room and switch on the light.

She examined herself in a mirror. Her face was chalk-white. Make-up was smeared all over her features. She raised her head to look at her neck. Not a trace, as Carlson had said. Nora stood there, naked, stockings hanging half-off, barefoot, then she let herself sink back onto the bed. Panting she stared up at the ceiling.

"That's how we'll always do it!"

The words buzzed in her ears. She pressed both hands to her head. I was scared to death, really to death. It was horrible, she thought. If I knuckle under now, if I don't do something against Carlson at once, he'll be back time and again wanting to do it his way again and again. And what if he gets into such ecstasy one day that he pulls the knot too tight? I can't take that, not even once more.

But what can I do? If I fight him off he'll rat on me. And then what will happen to all those people involved? Nora buried her face in her hands, her naked arms on her naked knees. She tossed it back and forth in her mind, in despair . . .

An hour and a half later, when Carl Flemming—big, tall, handsome, with short, wiry, graying hair—came home, he hurried straight to Nora's door, knocked and entered. She was sitting by the fireplace with a glass in her hand.

"My darling!" The chief of Vienna's "Flemming Group" of the Berlin foreign office hurried over to Nora and kissed her tenderly. "Forgive me please for taking so long today. I had to have dinner in the city—"

"Carl."

Something in her voice made him listen. "What's wrong?"

"I have to tell you something. Please sit down."

"Right away?"

"Right away, yes," said Nora Hill, draining her glass and putting it down.

"What's the matter, Nora? What is it you have to tell me?" He sank into an armchair next to her.

"A lot." Nora answered. "It concerns a woman by the name of Valerie Steinfeld . . ."

55

"What did you tell Flemming?" Manuel asked, staring across at the woman with the paralyzed legs, amazement in his eyes.

"*Everything*," said Nora Hill. She lifted her cigarette holder, inhaled, and blew the smoke out through her nose.

"After thinking about it for a long time. it seemed the best way. I told him the whole story here, in this very room, in front of this fireplace."

"You betrayed Valerie Steinfeld?"

"I just told you. Valerie Steinfeld and Martin Landau, plus their whole plan for the lawsuit—everything."

"And Flemming? How did he react? What happened then?"

There was a knock at the door.

"Yes!" Nora Hill looked toward the door. George. long Nora's lover, confidant and deputy, came into the room. His dinner jacket was immaculate as always, his pleated shirt-front spotlessly clean.

"Please forgive me, Madame, but it is a quarter to twelve. The gentleman has been waiting for half an hour. He says he would very much like you to come at once."

"Really a quarter to twelve already?" Nora looked shocked. "How time flies when you're telling a tale! It's easy to forget the present, eh, Mr. Aranda?"

In reality, Nora Hill had not forgotten the present for one instant while she had been telling her yarn to Manuel. A hidden button near her seat, beneath the lapis lazuli-tiled mantel-piece enabled her to signal George to come in at any time. On this evening he had been standing by waiting for her call. And Nora had pressed the button at the moment she was telling Manuel how Carl Flemming, twenty-six years before. had stepped into that very room.

"Tell the gentleman I'm sorry and will be over immediately, George."

"Certainly, Madame."

"And take Mr. Aranda to his car."

"Yes, Madame."

"But listen, you can't just . . . not when——" Manuel had leapt to his feet.

Nora took her crutches and hoisted herself out of the chair. "I'm sorry, my friend."

"Please tell me at least what happened after you confessed everything to Flemming!"

"I really must break off our session now. I told you I was expecting an important visitor—remember?"

"Please! Please, just five more minutes!"

"It's impossible."

The manservant gripped Manuel by the arm.

"Let go of me!" Manuel swung a fist at him.

328

George grabbed his arm and gripped it tight. "Don't, sir," he said with a smile. "I advise you not to. Let's go, I'll take you down."

"Madame, Madame! Surely your other business can wait just a few more minutes! Please!"

"*No*. Now you're annoying me, Mr. Aranda. I'm telling you: come back again sometime. I have a lot to tell you still. And don't forget Commissioner Groll. He'll be waiting for you after midnight. It's almost midnight now. You're going to be late yourself: you couldn't stay even if I did have more time for you. The photos are the most important thing at the present time, are they not?"

Manuel gave up. "You're right."

"But give me a call! Come back again!"

"I certainly will." Manuel shrugged his shoulders and left the room at the side of the manservant.

She waited a moment, then swung on her crutches into the passageway with the many doors and the Forty-Nine Positions of Giulio Romano. Manuel and George were just disappearing round a bend.

She waited a few more seconds, then swung down the hall. The lights were on over many of the doors, including the door to the 'Little Girl's Room,' which she entered without knocking.

Jean Mercier got up from the small red armchair. Nora slammed the door closed behind her.

"Magnificent, Madame, magnificent!" the Frenchman exclaimed.

"Santarin gone already?"

"He left just half an hour ago. Up till then we both listened to everything you told young Aranda. Santarin would like to thank you sincerely. He is as gratified as I am. A stroke of genius to end your story just where you did! Beautiful! Aranda will come back, all right!"

"Yes, I think so," Nora Hill said, thinking: if only these damned swine didn't have me in the palm of their hands. Aloud she asked with a smile: "Did the film help you with the 'Flying Dutchman?'"

"More than expected, Madame. I very much appreciate your help. And now tell me quickly, please, what was that paper Aranda's carrying around with him? Old, Pasteur ... silkworm epidemic ... Santarin would like you to tell me. He did talk about all that with you, didn't he?"

"Yes," Nora sighed. "Now listen ..."

56

Commissioner Groll was wearing his old dressing gown and slippers; he had already taken off his tie and opened his shirt at the neck. He was standing in front of the purring samovar in his library, filling two cups with tea. He put one on his desk, which was piled high with books and manuscripts, and handed the other to Manuel, who was sitting in a deep armchair.

"Well, anyway, you've had plenty of time," Manuel said.

"What for?"

"To think about what you would have to tell me. Or was it too much all at once?"

"Yes," said Groll, "it was. How that scrap of paper got into Valerie Steinfeld's hands I really don't know. I can't give you any enlightenment there. It's ... it's uncanny! And as for the photos—"

"Yes? Yes?"

"There are some cases which can't be solved. I'm afraid this is one of them."

"But how come? In my opinion we're getting closer to a solution every day."

Groll sighed.

"You do know the three persons on the photographs? You said earlier you did—right?"

Groll sighed again. "That's what I said, all right. And the description you gave of the man you saw in action at Nora Hill's would certainly fit Vasiliu Penkovic."

"Then why did he take those photos?"

"I really have no explanation, none that makes sense."

"Then *ask* Penkovic! Have him come to your office."

"That's impossible, unfortunately."

"Why?"

"Penkovic has already done a few things in this country that badly needed explaining, and still do. Then, every time we thought we had him by the collar, the Ministry of the Interior received a hint from the Soviets—always polite, you understand? Just a request—the idea being we should leave Penkovic in peace. If we didn't, the Soviet Union would regard it as an unfriendly act."

"So Mr. Penkovic will be left in peace forever after!"

"Manuel!" Groll ran his fingers through his graying hair. "After everything you've experienced up to now with the Austrian authorities, and after all I've told you about the Austrian situation, can you still really believe that anyone here would dare to do anything that might upset the Soviets? That's the worst damned problem in this whole affair! I know Penkovic well. We've had this sort of thing before: photographs taken by him and then siphoned over to someone else. We've had a few conversations with him, asking him *politely* to help us."

"And?"

"He was always ready with a sincere apology—he was sorry, but he had no idea what we were talking about. We do know more or less definitely that Penkovic carries out missions for the Soviets, shadowing people and photographing them. He's brilliant at it. These here might come from one such job of his. The only difference is that this time he seems to have made two difficult deals with them." Groll pointed at the photographs Manuel had bought from Nora Hill.

"Why would the Soviets want to have these three persons shadowed?"

"Well, perhaps they wanted to find out whether the Americans had made any contracts for the development of "B" and "C" weapons. Could be they were further ahead and already suspected your father of experimenting on his own. After all, they *knew* it later, and your father sold his invention to them *and* to the Americans—"

"I don't understand one word," said Manuel.

"You will soon. This Embassy attaché, Ernesto Gomez, had been working for a long time with Thomas Meerswald, we do know that."

"What do you mean, they had been working together?"

"Meerswald succeeded in winning over Gomez. Perhaps he gave Gomez money. Or perhaps Gomez is an idealist. At any rate, he is an exception. Because I've never heard of any other Argentine legation abroad involving itself in investigations of that kind."

"*What?*"

"Look: there are many German companies in Argentina that have highly qualified specialists! Maybe there are some

331

disguised munitions factories among them, I don't know. But it's pretty well known that there are large numbers of Nazi war criminals working undercover in these firms. Gomez helped Meerswald hunt out nests like that."

"Why? What could Meerswald do?"

"Meerswald was a fanatic." Groll looked at the small, thick-set man with the protruding eyes and the bald head in the photographs. "He owned a pesticide factory in Vienna. But that was only his cover."

"I've lost you again."

"In reality Meerswald was one of the biggest headhunters in all of South America. He went after wanted persons and hidden plants that manufacture weapons of mass destruction. He was always travelling all over the world, apparently on business; in reality, he was on the hunt. He had a lot of collaborators. But once a scent got hot, he followed it himself."

"Why do you always talk about him in the past tense?"

"Because he's dead."

"Dead?"

"He was found on the morning of November 24, 1966, shot dead in his hotel room in Buenos Aires. The assassin was never caught. That same day a firebomb went off in his office where he kept all his records. The office and all his files and documents were completely burnt out, and an armored safe melted in the heat. It was the perfect crime, carried out in two parts and on two continents. We never found any clues here in Vienna, either," said Groll.

"Then there can only be one explanation for Valerie's presence in these photographs," Manuel replied excitedly, "She was involved! A collaborator of Meerswald, perhaps! Possibly she even knew what my father was doing—she killed him, after all. That's what it looks like!"

"Sometimes something looks like one thing, then turns out to be another," Groll said. "Valerie Steinfeld—a woman— kills your father because he manufactures a nerve gas? Manuel!"

"Have you any other explanation?"

"No."

"So!"

"If Valerie Steinfeld had known anything, Gomez would have known it, too—and your father would have been called to account by the authorities in *Argentina*, and not by an old woman in Vienna. It's unreal!"

"These photos are real! Neutrality can be overdone, Commissioner! If the activities of Gomez and Meerswald were known to you, then why didn't you, in November 1966, when Meerswald was murdered—" Manuel broke off.

"—interrogate Valerie Steinfeld?" Groll said, finishing Manuel's question. "You just answered your own question, don't you see? At that time we had no idea that she was connected with these two men. I learned that only tonight, from these photographs. And we can't ask Valerie Steinfeld now."

"My goddamned father," Manuel said. The cup he was holding scraped against the saucer. He stared at the police chief.

"Why?" he asked. *"Why?* Why did Nora Hill speak of Meerswald as though he were still alive?"

"Probably she had to lie. Somebody's been putting the screws to her for some time now, I expect."

57

One hour earlier . . .

"A sheet of old paper," Fedor Santarin said.

"Brittle and yellow with age," Gilbert Grant added.

"Written by hand."

"First line reads: 'Pasteur 1870, silkworm epidemic!' "

"Second line: 'Germs: microbes.' "

"Then something about insects."

"And about bacterial toxins and pesticides—or something along those lines."

Grant and Santarin were describing the paper in Manuel Aranda's briefcase as exactly as Nora Hill had been able to describe it to Jean Mercier, and as he had described it to the men in one of his radio cars, and as the man in the radio cars had in turn described it to Grant—shortly before midnight.

"No," Count Romath said. "I've never heard of this piece of paper. Aranda did not discuss it with Landau."

"You're lying, you old bugger," Grant said, his words slurring. His face was very red, his bleery eyes bloodshot. He was holding a glass of bourbon in his hand.

"I'm telling the truth." Romath fingered the pearl tiepin on his tie. No, he thought, no. I've had enough.

"Count Romath." Santarin said with an ingratiating smile. "Why do you deny it? You heard this afternoon that we have a second man in the hotel. And this man maintains that Aranda and Landau did discuss the paper, *extensively*."

"So if that's what he maintains. why do you bother asking me?" I knew it, it's all bluff, they don't know a thing, Romath thought to himself.

The three men were sitting in the living-room of Gilbert Grant's apartment. He occupied one floor of a villa, furnished in ultra-modern style. The room was a mess: newspapers, magazines, and clothing lay scattered everywhere. Bottles, glasses, and an ice-bucket stood around on the table and on the floor. The ashtrays were all spilling over.

"Because our man did not hear everything, only a small part. He was interrupted. But you had the chance to hear *everything* in your office. Count!" Santarin tugged at the small silk handkerchief in the breast pocket of his jacket.

The truth was that the house electrician, Alfons Nemec, a willing, able, and cheap worker with decidedly criminal inclinations, who was always in financial difficulties because of his habit of playing roulette in Baden, had in fact often plugged himself in whenever Manuel had a visitor. He could not do it for long, however, without running the risk of being seen. During the past few days he had been repairing a complicated electrical circuit in the outer office of the main hotel switchboard. When the girls were very busy it was easy for him to put on headphones unnoticed and listen in for a while to the conversations being held in Manuel's suite. Nemec was working for Grant, who in turn was acting on orders from Santarin. Santarin trusted nobody in the world, not even himself.

The house electrician was to keep a check on Count Romath and his reports to the radio car. Nemec had picked up a few snatches of conversation relating to an old scrap of paper and something about silkworm epidemic, and had gathered from Landau's excited tone that it was important. Nemec had immediately written down what he had heard. He had then quickly passed his notes to the man in the white Chevrolet parked behind the hotel. Grant's HQ was informed immediately, and Count Romath was summoned to see his boss ... Grant and Santarin knew too little. and they had to know everything. The Russian became even more courteous.

"You are not answering, Count. I assume you are deliberating about what is more important: the money Aranda is paying you to misinform us, or your personal freedom. That is no real choice, Count: freedom is always more important."

"I am not getting any money from Aranda! I am keeping silent because I will not answer your suspicious insinuations."

"Oh, won't you?!" said Grant, refilling his glass. "You will *beg* to be allowed to answer, you shithead!" The American's hands were shaking; he let an ice cube fall to the carpet. He pointed to a cupboard. "In there are statements by two pages, both under sixteen, that you've been buggering, you swine."

"And don't forget the statement from the third boy," Santarin said in a friendly voice, "the apprentice in the Ritz flower shop."

"Sweet little Karl the Blossom," Grant said. "That was your nickname for him, wasn't it? Fourteen and a half he was then, tsk, tsk."

Santarin kept up his façade of unwavering charm as he said, "The three boys are still in Vienna even though they're working in other hotels now. What little angels they are, and they're blackmailing you, Count. And you're paying them."

"With our money," said Grant. "We're giving you the money. And if we stop giving it to you. and hand it to the kids directly with a bonus on top, they'll go straight to the police and swear you tried to buy their silence with money."

"You kept after Karl the Blossom," said Santarin, dipping into his bag of sweets, "until the poor kid couldn't stand it any more! He talked it over with the other poor kids, and they came to the common decision that it was their *duty* to report you."

Romath clenched his fists.

"It's too bad," said Santarin, "that the police have known for years that you are a pervert."

"A law-suit against you in 1963," said Grant, "was quashed only because you had some good lawyers who managed to make it look as if a group of minors had conspired to put the squeeze on you."

"It will look like that again," said Santarin, "except that no one will believe you this time."

"You'll be convicted this time," Grant went on, "and spend your old age in prison. Perhaps for the rest of your life. It'll make a fine scandal! The Director of a Vienna luxury hotel. Last scion of one of Austria's best-known families. An ancient line of ass-divers!" Suddenly his voice rose to a scream.

"You do what we tell you or you'll be put away, understand?" Romath shuddered.

"Gently, gently," Santarin said. "You really shouldn't frighten the Count like that, Gilbert. Look at him, he's going to be sick. A drink, perhaps, Count?"

"No . . . what . . . what is it you want?"

"The paper," Santarin said.

"How do you expect me to get it?"

"Oh, so you do know about it all of a sudden!" Grant exclaimed.

"Only because *you* keep talking about it—"

"Don't get fresh or I'll smash you in the kisser!" Grant raised his fist.

"Gilbert!" the Russian broke in admonishingly. He turned to the Count. "Aranda is still carrying the paper around with him in his briefcase. He'll be home late tonight. You get back to the Ritz right now, and take that with you." The Russian placed a small glass vial filled with tiny silver globules.

"What's that?"

"An extraordinarily strong sleeping-aid, that has the advantage of not being in the least dangerous. Once it's done its job, there's no trace of it left in the body."

"But—"

"You reported to us that it's Aranda's custom always to order a whisky in his room before he goes to bed, is that correct?"

"That is correct . . ."

"Where does he order the whisky?"

"From the waiter on his floor."

"Perfect. Then what you do is this: first wait until Aranda is back in the hotel. Then go up to the fourth floor, where Aranda has his suite; go to the floor-waiter's stockroom, and make an unannounced spot-check. That sort of thing is quite usual, is it not?"

"Yes, certainly."

"Keep the check going until Aranda orders his drink. When the waiter has poured the drink, distract him somehow."

"How?"

"Any way you like, dammit! Ask him something. Or complain about something. Or drop something. The waiter only needs to let the glass out of his sight for a moment or two. You take the chance and tip six to eight grains from this vial into the drink. They melt instantly. That's all. An hour and a

336

half or two hours later, when you're sure Aranda's sleeping soundly you go up to his suite."

"That's impossible! The door will be locked from the inside, with the key in the lock inside!"

"We told you not to rent the adjoining suite. It's vacant, is it not?"

"Yes."

"So." Santarin popped another sweet into his mouth. The diamond on his finger flashed red, green, and white as he moved his hand. "Aranda sleeps with the window open, we know that. You come in from the outside, over the balcony. He'll be sleeping like the dead. Get the paper—you know what it looks like by now, and what's on it—and bring it here tomorrow morning."

Romath sat motionless.

"You won't do it?"

"What choice do I have? You've got me where you want me," the white-haired hotel director replied, and looked at the Russian without expression.

"I knew you'd be reasonable, my dear Count."

"Yes, reasonable," Romath muttered, putting the glass tube into his pocket.

"Here." Grant handed the Count a full bottle of whiskey which he took from a wall bar. "Small gifts help keep friends."

"Thank you."

"Now get out, go!" said the American brutally. "There's no time to lose. Get going!"

"Gilbert, please!" Santarin grimaced and apologized for the American, then escorted the Count into the hallway, helped him into his coat, and wished him good luck. He waited at the top of the staircase until Romath had reached the front door, then pressed the buzzer. The door opened and closed again and soon afterwards there was the sound of an engine starting up.

Santarin returned to Grant's living-room. The massive American was stretched out in an armchair, glass in hand. He said, "We're going to pull it off this time, dammit."

"Let's hope so." Santarin gave his colleague an earnest look. "This dreadful boozing of yours is killing you! It's awful for me to have to stand by and watch you going down the drain!"

"I can't leave the stuff alone, you know that."

"Then you'll have to take a cure."

337

"I can only stand it with whisky."

"How come? What's happened?"

"It's *people*," said Grant thickly. "I feel sorry for people."

"That's just a lot of drunken nonsense."

"No, Fedor, it's not . . ." The American had tears in his eyes.

"You of all people feeling sorry for your fellowmen! That's a joke," Santarin said. "Did you feel sorry for them when you were a collector for the Chicago syndicate and used to beat them half to death if they didn't pay up?"

"No, that's true, I didn't . . . but I was a lot younger then . . ."

"And what about later? In Los Angeles? When you were the big brain of the gang? And shot the nightwatchman of a bank you robbed?—"

"That was an accident, Fedor. I hadn't figured on killing the man, I just wanted to get him in the knees so he couldn't sound the alarm. I—"

"Yes, yes, yes, I know it all by heart. He died from a slug in the belly. He had a wife and children. And did you feel sorry for him? Not one shit! You never felt the teeniest twinge of guilt, I know, I asked you often enough! And when the guys came to you and made you a little proposition, you took it right away, didn't you—with pleasure, just to save your own skin? Answer me!"

"That's true, yes . . ." Grant moaned.

"And were you not suddenly the main witness for the prosecution, and you got off scot-free? Okay, Okay. Then afterwards . . . it's twenty-three years you've been working for them now, is it not, and you've done a great job, right? Have you felt sorry all those twenty-three years for the people you've sent up?"

"Yes, I have felt sorry for them. Not at first. Not at all then. But six or seven years ago, that's when it started. That's when I began to hit the bottle, too. And it got worse and worse and worse. It's real bad now. Clairon. Romath. Aranda. But it's not only them I'm sorry for, Fedor, it's everybody, the whole damned world! Because that's who we're working against, that's true isn't it, Fedor? We're working *against* them all, *against* mankind, and we're not *for* anyone. And that's what kills me when I'm sober and think about it."

"Good God," said Santarin, shaken to the core. "That's bad, that's really bad."

"And the case we're on now is the worst of the lot," Grant

338

hissed, suddenly hurling his glass against a wall, where it shattered, splashing whisky all over the carpet; then his voice rose to a shriek. *"AP Seven!* That's on *our* conscience! That's something *we* created! We did it, we, we—and no use claiming orders from above or any other excuse—*we* were the ones who handed the military crowd the means to kill every single human being on this earth!"

"You are a security risk, Gilbert, if it's really got you so bad!"

"And you have decided you must relay that to my superiors at once."

"Yes."

"And will you?"

"No."

"Why not? That's the reason I spilled it all out to you! To finish the whole caboodle once and for all!"

"But it's not going to be finished. I don't want any other partner. I like you, Gilbert, and we understand each other. So why should I stab a friend and colleague like that in the back? No, I won't do it!"

"Then I'll do it myself!"

"You'll never do it, never. You know what will happen to you if you just once mess up a job on purpose, let alone if you go and point the finger at yourself. You're too much of a coward to load that on yourself."

Grant gaped at the Russian. "By God," he said. "You're right!"

At that moment Count Romath was just arriving at his home. He lived alone in a bungalow he had bought five years before. The bungalow had an adjoining garage, and Romath steered the car into it through the heavy snow.

He was already beginning to feel the effects. As soon as he had reached the end of the street in which Grant lived and had turned on to the Lainzerstrasse, he had stopped the car, pulled a plastic beaker from the glove compartment, emptied into it half the contents of the glass tube, then filled the beaker with whisky. He had seen the silver grains dissolve immediately, and had then drunk the whole beakerfull at one swallow, tossing the tube into the gutter afterwards. As he drove he continued to drink, this time straight from the bottle, driving through the Fasangartengasse, the Wattmangasse, and Feldkellergasse, where he threw both bottle and beaker as far as he could into the deep snow of a vacant plot. It had to look like an accident, that was the most important thing.

He turned out the light in the garage. His headlights were still on, the motor purring softly. Romath walked over to the metal door, that had swung upwards to open, and pulled it down. The catch clicked into place. Good gate, he thought. Nice gate. Closes well. It will suffice, I'm sure. He was beginning to feel the effects of the unusually large amount of whisky he had swilled down on top of the sleeping pills. He got in behind the wheel, rolled down the window on his side, and looked into his rearview mirror. He could make out the white exhaust fumes quite clearly as they rose from behind the car. Count Romath switched off the headlights and listened to the purring of the engine. He was now sitting completely in the dark. He rapidly became drowsier and more lethargic. That can't be the carbon monoxide yet, he thought, it must be the sleeping pills. They really are strong.

How clever of me to have removed the transmitter from the slot behind the "Masked Supper" in my office before I left the hotel. I took the microphone out of Aranda's suite, too, from above the door the drawing-room. To cap it all I took the speaker with me, too, the miniature one that can be connected with my phone. I took everything with me when I left, and threw it all into the river from the bridge near Schönbrunn Castle. The water's deep there, and it wasn't frozen over. It'll be spring or summer before those things are found, if they ever are.

The Count lifted his arm and draped it over the steering wheel. Already it felt as heavy as lead. Romath smiled a little. It's going splendidly, he thought, it's as easy as pie. Another hour and it's all over. What luck that Santarin gave me the pills and Grant the whisky. A man can't ask for better luck, all things considered.

58

"Yes, that was a difficult time we had with the Nazis, but everything turned out all right in the end, the worst didn't happen! We lost the war like nobody else in the world had ever lost a war, Hitler was done away with, and the good Master was able to come back from London! We were all so happy then! And the Master and Madame were together again and both worked, Madame in her bookstore and the Master on the radio, and what pleasure we had with Heinzi! Famous, he was, Professor at the University and giving lectures all over the world, truck-loads of respect for him everywhere and all the students pushing to be in his classes!"

Agnes Peintinger had spoken at a gallop, her face a picture of childlike glee, the wrinkled, leathery face of an old woman. Next she clapped her big, scrawny hands and smiled at Manuel Aranda. She was smaller than he had imagined her, and truly resembled what she had become in old age: a child.

"It's good of you, Agnes, to tell Mr. Aranda everything so nicely," Irene Waldegg said. "He is very interested in learning what happened in those days. Could you think back a little and try to tell him just a bit more—about the lawsuit, for instance?"

Agnes laughed. "The lawsuit, oh, my goodness me! We really did pull the wool over the eyes of those fellows in that one, and how! I can't remember the details any more after such a long time, though my memory's pretty good otherwise. Anyway, they did a lot of twisting and turning, but in the end they had to say Heinzi was a pure Aryan. That was 1950, I think . . . no, 1951, I do remember it after all, exactly, 1951, in the summer."

It was 9:30 A.M. on Tuesday, January 21. At 6:45 A.M. Manuel had driven through the snow to Gentzgasse to pick up Irene, then with her over the slippery streets, to the Vienna East station to meet a man neither of them knew. Jakob Roszek was due to arrive in Vienna that morning on the "Chopin Express" bringing an important message from Paul Steinfeld's brother Daniel. It had been ice cold on the train platforms. The wind had howled through the huge halls. A large indicator kept announcing trains, delayed by the snowstorms.

"The 'Chopin Express' was now scheduled to arrive at 13:45 hours—another six hours."

"We can't wait here all that time," Irene had said. "Tuesday's the day Valerie or I always used to visit Agnes in the Old People's Home. Shall we go and see her?"

So they drove over to the Home, which was in a quiet sidestreet off the Josefstädterstrasse. On the way Manuel had stopped at a toyshop, at Irene's suggestion.

"Agnes loves stuffed animals. She has a whole collection. Let's take her a new one."

They bought her a small zebra.

Agnes now held it in her hands, looking at it with an enraptured gaze. She had already forgotten what they had just been talking about.

"*A zebra!*" Agnes lifted it up and pressed the soft fur to her cheek. Then she scurried from her bed to a large carton that stood near a closet. Crouching down, she began to throw stuffed animals over her shoulder, with the boisterous exuberance of a small child—an elephant, a crocodile, a sheep, ducks, ravens, monkeys, rabbits, giraffes, animals large and small, until the whole floor was covered. Agnes hooted excitedly in a high, reedy voice, "Isn't that nice? Do you like it?"

"Very nice," Manuel replied, looking helplessly from Irene, who was shrugging her shoulders, to a short, heavy-set man who stood next to Agnes. Father Ignaz Pankrater was seventy-six years old, but looked no more than sixty-six, a sturdy peasant of a man with gray hair cut short into a crew cut, sparkling, tiny blue eyes, and, like Agnes, a broad face, broad nose, big mouth, and heavy hands.

Father Pankrater visited Agnes several times a week, and today was one of his days. Irene and Manuel had found him already there in the overheated and crowded little room, which smelled of apples (there were some on top of Agnes's cupboard). Irene explained to the pastor who Aranda was. Pankrater offered his condolences in the rough, throaty speech of his home region, and then listened to Agnes's story in silence.

"And Madame went with the Master to America," the elderly cook declared while still on her knees among her toy animals. She was talking to Aranda.

"America?"

"Yes. They went visiting somebody in Canada."

"How do you know that, Agnes?" Irene asked.

"Well, the last time Madame came to see me, she said good-bye and said, Agnes, it's going to be a few weeks before I can come again, maybe even longer, I'm going to Australia with my husband."

"Oh!" said Irene. "Yes, of course."

"And that's why you're here to visit me, Miss Irene! It's so kind of you to take care of me the way you do! I'd like to come to the Gentzgasse again, but I'm afraid to set foot on the streets these days, with all that traffic and the trams and

342

such crowds of people, you know?" Agnes said, looking at Manuel, who nodded.

"Reverend Mother says I shouldn't go into the city if it really frightens me so much, and I've got everything I need here, Miss Irene is there, and Madame comes, and the Reverend." A sudden idea made Agnes giggle with pleasure. "Do you think I should, Miss Irene? Show your friend the wonderful animals I have?"

"Yes," Irene replied calmly. "It's a good idea. Build your zoo up, Agnes."

Agnes became as bashful as a small child.

"Then you've got to wait outside till I've finished! I'll call you!"

"All right, we'll wait outside in the corridor," Pankrater said.

The three visitors left the room. The corridor was long, with many windows, a stone floor, and a number of small tables and brightly painted chairs.

"Let's sit down over there," Pankrater said. Old men and women, some in dressing-gowns, many of them on the arms of nurses, shuffled by constantly, murmuring greetings and looking at the group inquisitively.

"A lot of them know me here," Pankrater commented, returning the greetings. The old priest offered Manuel some small, cheap cigars.

"No, thank you," Manuel said.

"I don't have any cigarettes, I'm afraid. May I smoke, Miss Waldegg?"

"Of course!"

Ignaz Pankrater lit up an evil-smelling cigar, nodded his hard, square head, and said, "You came because you were hoping to learn something from Agnes about the lawsuit, I presume, Mr. Aranda?"

"I'm afraid you won't get anywhere with her. She's gone senile, mildly and mercifully. She's happy, she still recognizes a few people, but she mixes everything up and really doesn't remember anything any more. Well, you heard it yourself." Manuel nodded. "The animals have become her whole life and joy. What a blessing from God it is to forget! I sometimes wish that had happened to me." The old priest blew out a cloud of the evil-smelling tobacco-smoke. "But my memory is intact. I'm doomed to remember everything about those horrible times. God, what suffering I saw in those days! What grief I had to hear! And I can't get it out of my mind, can't

343

forget one thing. Yes, yes, I know what you're going to ask me, Mr. Aranda. Of course I remember the lawsuit, of course I remember Agnes coming to me. She wanted to tell me everything in the confessional—just imagine, in the empty church! If someone had heard her ... Anyway, I stopped her right away and told her it wasn't the right place, and asked her to come to my office that evening, as late as possible so that she would be one of the last and I would have time for her. There were always so many there in those days, unhappy, desperate people, all seeking help and advice—from me, a little priest in a small church in Ottakring. Poor people, good people, most of them women.

"Well, anyway, she did come to my private office that evening, and told me the whole story, with all the details she knew. She was the last one, so I had plenty of time to listen to her ..."

59

Agnes talked and talked.

Ignaz Pankrater sat opposite her in his office at the other end of a long table. Rain drummed against the windowpanes. The shades were down.

"... of course I'll have to testify at the lawsuit. And I'm going to say everything the way Madame wants me to, we've got to save Heinzi. But it's all a pack of lies what they want me to say, Reverend, and perjury is a deadly sin, so what am I going to do? Help me, please help me, please tell me if I should do it!"

Her voice penetrated Ignaz Pankrater's mind less and less. Bitterly he wondered, What would be the normal thing to do in such a case? I would go the route of *forum externum*, that is, I would ask Agnes to bide her time patiently for two days while I submitted the case to the Vicar General of Vienna for guidance. The Vicar General—a decent man, I know him—would in turn put the case before the Archbishop of Vienna, Cardinal Innitzer. I know him, too. He is an impassioned Nazi.

Yes, Innitzer is a Nazi!

If he were not a Nazi, he would say to the Vicar-General: call up this parish priest and tell him I can make an exception in this case. We are living in an unjust state. In these circumstances perjury does not have its usual meaning. The priest should advise the woman to lie to the court and to swear to her lies, and you can tell her she will not thereby be committing any sin. I, the Prince of the Church of Vienna, will assume the responsibility. That's how a decent archbishop would act. But Innitzer, he had displayed the swastika on the Cathedral of St. Stephen when the Nazis marched in in 1938. Perhaps he thinks differently now, but who knows?

Pankrater's thoughts were bitter: How terrible the true faithful are! And how happy I must be that they still exist!

"Agnes!" he said aloud, "God does not wish evil to grow more powerful than good. Good always conquers in the end, even if sometimes it takes a long time. So we must resist evil, Agnes, and support the good. Every one of us, each in his own way. That is why, Agnes, in your case doing good is *more important* than the oath you take, and saving a family or the life of a fellow human being is *more important* than perjury."

"That means . . ."

"That means you may lie. I hereby give you the permission. I, your father confessor! I hereby cleanse you from all the consequences of perjury. *For it is not an act of perjury* in this case, Agnes. Not in these times, not before people such as these. You *must* bear false witness. It is *necessary*."

"Oh, Father, Father!" Agnes sprang to her feet, and before Pankrater could stop her had kissed his hand.

He drew it back quickly.

"Agnes! You know that is not allowed!"

"But I'm so happy! And Madame will be so happy!"

"Easy," the priest said. "Easy, Agnes. Be careful. What you and Frau Steinfeld and Mr. Landau are planning to do is dangerous, you are risking your lives, you included."

"Me included?" Agnes shuddered.

Why am I a parish priest, Ignaz Pankrater thought, if I do not do all I can to help in such a case? And he said, "Yes, Agnes, it's dangerous in the event that the Court—it probably will not happen this way, certainly will not, but in theory it *could*—has you arrested for perjury. The punishments for that offense are very severe."

"Yes?" Agnes asked nervously.

"Very severe. And therefore I say to you: If that should happen to you—and it won't, I'm sure *(I truly hope not,* he was thinking, *I truly hope not)*—then you must tell the Court that *Father Pankrater ordered* you to bear false witness!"

"That you . . ." Agnes sank back down on her chair heavily, shocked. "I could never do that!"

"You *must* do it. Someone has to take the responsibility in this case. You came to me for advice, and I advised you, so the responsibility is mine. If it's me—" he paused, his voice sticking in his throat, and thought: I'm no hero. If only we all possessed more courage, dear God. But if we were more courageous, this scourge would never have descended upon us. Then he continued, "If it's me, those people won't be able to lay their hands on me as easily as they would you." Alas, he thought, they can do it just as easily, but I mustn't let that influence me.

60

"She resisted for a long time, but eventually she did swear to it, in front of the crucifix and the burning candles," the old priest said, stubbing out his evil-smelling cigar in an ashtray. Men and women were still shuffling along the endless corridor of the Old People's Home, bent, bowed, some supported by nuns.

"You're a great man, Father," Manuel said after a while.

"Nonsense!" Pankrater said. "What else could I have done? Would you have done anything else if you'd been in my place? So there."

"But I am not a priest."

"But you're a human being," said Pankrater. "A *human being.* And that's what I was, first and foremost, for Agnes, for a lifetime, almost. I'm the person she trusted most in the world. I could not let her down, I could not disappoint her."

"Father," said Irene, "do you know how the lawsuit ended? And what became of the boy?"

The little man shook his head. "Unfortunately, no. In autumn of 1943—with no decision in the lawsuit—I was close to being arrested, because of my sermons. I'd been shooting my mouth off from the pulpit, you know, and the Gestapo were getting ready to haul me off. Luckily we got wind of it in time, and my superiors got me out of Vienna at the last minute. I lived in hiding, near Salzburg. I'm ashamed to confess it, but I forgot all about Agnes at that time."

"But she didn't forget you!" Manuel exclaimed.

"No, she looked for me, everywhere, for years. But couldn't find me. I had been working in Hallein for a long time before I was pensioned at last, and even then I continued to help out in another Salzburg parish before coming back here. But when I did return to Vienna I remembered Agnes and looked for her. I found her, too, but she was already senile. She couldn't tell me anything, she got everything jumbled up, just as she did with you now. I tried to make contact again with Frau Steinfeld, but she asked me politely not to visit her." Pankrater lifted his hands and lowered them again. "It's a big mystery, a terrible mystery that has its roots in those frightful times some fools think are behind us for good . . ."

Pankrater's last words aroused Manuel's curiosity, and he asked, "Don't you think so?"

"No, I don't, Mr. Aranda. The dreadful spirit of the Third Reich, the arrogance, the intolerance, the baseness and the sadism of Hitler and his crew—all that is still alive in here!" And he pounded his breast. "And can break out again any time, in another form, in another land, anywhere in the world. We're only human, all of us, and we each bear our own Hitler within, at all times."

61

"There were three-and-a-half million Jews in Poland before the War," said Jakob Roszek. "When Hitler's exterminations and the War were over, about 25,000 were left. In 1967, following the Israeli's Six Day War against the Arabs, anti-semitism flared up again in Poland, systematically stirred up and organized by the State, for the purpose of driving out the few remaining Jews. Last year about 10,000 of them abandoned their homes and made their way to Israel via Austria." Jakob Roszek was puffing jerkily at an American cigarette Aranda had offered him. It was his fourth. The foreign cigarette and the sense of freedom to talk worked like a drug on Roszek. He was a tall man with a very broad, very pale face. He wore dark glasses.

His wife was sitting beside him, quiet and hunched up. During the past half hour she had barely spoken ten words. Their daughter, a beautiful young girl with blonde hair and blue eyes, was the only person at the table who was eating anything. She was tucking it away hungrily, excited at a hearty lunch. They were in a restaurant at the Vienna East station, a gigantic concrete slab of a building. The girl was wide-eyed with amazement and curiosity about the new faces and the new world around her. Roszek noticed Manuel looking at the young girl.

"It's all so new for Ljuba. My wife and I know it already. It's the second time for us."

"You speak German like a Viennese," Irene said.

"I come from Vienna! My wife, too. We fled to Prague when Hitler came. Then from Prague we fled to Poland. In Poland we both landed in the same resistance movement. That's where we met. Later we were with the partisans, and met Daniel Steinfeld there. He, too, had ended up in Poland by way of Prague. We were incredibly lucky, all three of us. We survived," said Roszek after a pause.

The time was 2:20 in the afternoon, and snow was still falling.

The "Chopin Express" had arrived at Vienna East, more than six hours late, its windows iced over, icicles hanging from the tops and sides of the coaches. A group of about thirty Jews, mostly elderly persons, had descended from one coach, and were received by two waiting men.

Irene and Manuel recognized Jakob Roszek immediately from Daniel Steinfeld's description and from the bulky volume he was carrying under one arm—Shakespeare's *Collected Works* in Polish. The mother and daughter both wore, as Daniel Steinfeld had advised, fur coats, with white silk scarves wrapped around their hair ...

"Mr. Roszek!" Manuel had hurried toward the man in the thick-rimmed dark glasses. He was standing in the midst of the group of Jews. They all looked helpless and a little overwhelmed by what had happened to them. They waited there in the heavy snowstorm, their suitcases, briefcases, and bundles beside them in the snow.

Jakob Roszek pushed his way through the group and a moment later he was standing right in front of Manuel and Irene.

"Who are you?"

"You were expecting to be met, were you not, Mr. Roszek?" Irene asked.

"Yes, but by an elderly lady, not by two young people. Valerie Steinfeld, she's called."

"Valerie Steinfeld could not come," said Irene, astoundingly calm and collected. "I am her niece. The letter from Daniel Steinfeld came to me."

"What has happened?"

"That's what we're going to tell you."

Ten minutes later the Roszek family were sitting with Irene and Manuel in the station restaurant. They had received permission to stay on condition that Manuel brought them to the camp afterwards.

Irene and Manuel took turns reporting what had happened. Roszek and his wife were so shocked they could not eat, and ordered only coffee. The young girl had a healthy appetite, and was going through a big menu. Ljuba spoke only a little German, and understood only fragments of the conversation. She asked no questions; she simply sat there looking around as though she had landed on another planet . . .

62

After the Six Day War (Jakob Roszek told them) all the Eastern countries, especially Russia condemned Israel as the aggressor. Diplomatic relations were broken off, embassies, legations and consulates shut down. There were anti-Jewish demonstrations everywhere. In Poland the demonstrations degenerated into a relentless "clean-up" campaign . . .

"People were bounced out of their jobs," Roszek reported, "and many had to face rigged lawsuits for treason. More and more Jews began to realize that it was the end of their exis-

tence in Poland, and that their only hope was to emigrate
..." At this point the Israeli aid organization "Jewish
Agency" stepped in with help, paying the costs of one-way
journeys to Israel, the money being remitted not to the Jews,
but to the Polish state. Every Jew who wanted to leave Poland had to pay five thousand Zloty to the Polish government,
cash on the barrelhead.

"Five thousand Zloty are about five thousand West German marks or thirty thousand Austrian schillings," said Jakob
Roszek while his wife stared down at the tablecloth and his
daughter, as though in a trance, looked all around her as she
ate.

"It's a fact that every Jew who emigrates—and remember
that my wife, I myself and Daniel Steinfeld were given
medals after the War and declared honorary citizens of Poland in recognition of our service in the resistance movement
and with the partisans—it's a fact that every Jew who emigrates has to renovate his apartment for the next tenant; it's a
fact that he's allowed to take with him only a minimal
amount of luggage, and may not take with him any certificates, diplomas, references, books written by himself, or
manuscripts. The punishments for any infraction of these regulations are severe. As far as the Viennese are concerned, we
are merely in transit and do not come under the authority of
the immigration authorities, except if one of us asks for political asylum. And very few do that. Most really do want to
go to Israel, just as we ourselves do."

"There could be another war down there at any moment,"
Manuel exclaimed. "The Arabs have a lot more weapons
than before."

"We're aware of that," Roszek said.

"But you still want to go there?"

"Yes," said Roszek. "Where else can we go without fear of
the same thing happening to us as happened in Poland?
Which country likes to let Jews in? If we're in Israel, at least
we can't be deported."

"And Daniel Steinfeld?" Irene asked. "What about him?
What was my aunt supposed to do for him?"

"Your aunt ... If he had any idea ... if he knew ... It's
terrible, what's happened."

"What's happened to you is terrible, too," Irene answered.
She has become strangely hard lately, Manuel thought. He
looked at her. Irene placed a hand on his shoulder.

"Daniel ... Daniel is not in good health, you know. He

350

can put in a good day's work as well as the fittest, but he has to keep to a strict diet. He just got over an attack of hepatitis ... lost forty pounds from it ... and now he's afraid he wouldn't be able to get his strict diet in the refugee camp. And sometimes it takes weeks before we're out of the camps, they say! He would never live through that. Exceptions are made—in cases of sickness, or if the refugee has relatives in Vienna. Then all he has to do is report to the "Jewish Agency" once a day. But special treatment has to be applied for from Vienna; you can't do it from Warsaw."

"What you're saying is that Daniel Steinfeld wanted to live with my aunt during his stay in Vienna, and he wanted her to make the necessary applications here."

"Yes. But now that your aunt is dead ... and he doesn't know that. There's an old cook, Daniel said, she could see he gets the right diet."

"The old cook has been in a home for the last four years." Now Jakob Roszek, as well as his wife, looked down at the tablecloth.

"But I know another woman who can cook for him!" Irene continued quickly. "And he can live with me, it goes without saying. I'll apply immediately for the necessary permissions, and write to him."

Roszek raised his head again.

"Thank you. I thank you, Miss, on behalf of Daniel."

"When does he want to come?"

"All he's waiting for is news from you, and he's ready to go. As soon as he knows he can be accommodated privately, he'll leave the same day. He's already on the list."

"I'll talk to the people from "the Agency" and send him a telegram right away. How old is Daniel Steinfeld?"

"Sixty-nine."

"And he still wants—" Manuel broke off, feeling ashamed.

"He *has to!* And he wants to, too, he's had enough, he can't breathe there any more!" Roszek said. His broad, pasty face was twitching. "None of us can bear it any longer. I'm no spring chicken myself, I'm sixty-one. But what choice do we have?" Roszek gave the appearance of nonchalance, but his struggle to keep calm was becoming noticeable.

"I've been doing my newspaper since 1947. It's a good paper, really, and I've had a lot of pleasure with it ..." He ran his hand over the fat volume of Shakespeare's *Collected Works*.

"I'll have to see what can be done in Tel Aviv about get-

351

ting it going again.". He looked at Irene and Manuel with a smile, a smile that acknowledged a thousand years of exile, persecution. pain. torture, and fear.

"And Daniel Steinfeld?" asked Irene. "What's his line?"

"He was a chemist, a biochemist," Roszek said. "Professor at the University. Thev built him his own institute in the country, just outside the city. He stayed there for months on end sometimes, working, then coming back to Warsaw. He was a very distinguished scientist over there, honored everywhere—until September 1967. Then they threw him out. He was not allowed to set foot in the University again, nor in his Institute. They accused him of treason. of serving Israel as a Zionist and America as a secret agent! He was tried, but he was acquitted. Nothing happened to him. But these upheavals didn't help his health any, and he just got sicker. The accusation that he was an American agent, by the way, was based on the fact that he had a friend who was always travelling all over the world. including America."

"Who was that friend?"

"Not a Pole. A Viennese, same as the rest of us. The man visited him often during the past years. They were working together on something, I don't know what. In 1966 his friend, whose name was Thomas Meerswald. was killed. In *1966!* and in *1968* the Attorney General's office declared him to have been a spy. He was supposedly Daniel's contact man to the Americans—"

63

About six hundred miles southwest of Buenos Aires. in the province of La Pampa and on the northwest rim of a large salt-lake basin, lies the town of La Coppelina. The salt lake is fifty miles long.

In 1952 the southeast end of the flats swarmed with life. A year later, there were factory-buildings, warehouses, some large low-slung buildings and a runway that accommodated transport planes. In La Coppelina the story was that the firm *Quimica Aranda* was putting up a branch manufacturing plant after scientists had examined the salt in the lake and discovered that it contained huge quantities of certain substances eminently suited for the production of pesticides. The government had given *Quimica Aranda* permission to exploit the virtually inexhaustible reserves of these materials. Since the chemicals under manufacture were equally poisonous to human beings, the entire factory complex was surrounded by tall barbed-wire fences. Guards and dogs kept watch night and day, there were watchtowers with searchlights, and security controls were extremely strict. The inhabitants of La Coppelina were pleased about the new plant, because the city benefited from the influx of new residents—the families of chemists and engineers working at the southeast end of the lake—as well as from the additional tax income and the boom in business enjoyed by the local shopkeepers, restaurants and inns. But, on the other hand, the presence of so strange an industry, of the thunderous planes, and the constant hum of the machines, quite audible in the town when the wind was right, truly sent shivers up and down the spines of the more primitive natives. But there was no doubt that enthusiasm for the economic benefits was the stronger feeling. The children of the chemists and technicians went to a school in La Coppelina that had been built especially for them, and lived with their mothers in newly constructed bungalows. The men spent weekends with their families, having lived during the week in prefabricated dwellings at the plant. Only men worked in the factory—two hundred fifty-three in all.

Then came the terrible day.

On Tuesday, January 14, 1969, about noon, the earth under La Coppelina trembled, and the sound of powerful detonations rent the air. Panic-stricken, the townspeople rushed outside. They saw thick black clouds of smoke belching skywards at the southeast end of the lake where the plant was located, and orange-colored flames licking out from the center of the smoke. The people had scarcely recovered from their initial shock when the earth shook again and dark smoke mushroomed upwards again into the sky. The entire rim of the lake was now one huge blaze, and it looked as though the bare, hard soil was on fire. The black clouds spiralled towards the radiant blue sky like giant towers. Police, firemen, and the desperate families of the men who had worked at the plant ...

"... rushed toward the scene of the tragedy. But they could not get to within less than a mile and a half of the plant, for the blaze was still raging everywhere, the air was a poisonous mess of fumes, soot, and smoke, and the temperatures created by the main blaze were enormously high," Juan Cayetano reported. He sat facing Manuel at a small table in the circular expresso bar on the Cobenzl. To get there they had driven up the winding mountain road, whose twists and turns were now visible beneath them. From where they sat they had a view over all of Vienna, which looked like an ocean of houses, palaces, and churches, the Danube and its bridges, and the countryside beyond. Manuel had listened to Cayetano with mounting excitement. Now he spoke.

"That happened on the 14th. I left on the 13th. It's the 21st today. Why didn't you call me up long ago to tell me all this? And why didn't you mention it when you called from Paris?"

"I was forbidden to do so," Cayetano said. He was a large, heavy man in his fifties, there were dark bags under his eyes. The café was overheated, but he felt cold.

"You were *forbidden* to tell me?" said Manuel. "Who was it who forbade you?"

"The police. We've had their officials sitting at our main office ever since the disaster. I have been interrogated, we've all been interrogated. All hell's been let loose, I can tell you, Manuel."

"But why?"

"Let me go on. The people of La Coppelina couldn't do a thing, not a thing, except stand there helplessly watching the blaze. The investigation later showed that napalm bombs had been used, timed to go off in a certain order to make sure that nothing at all would be left of the plant."

"Go on! Go on!"

"Buenos Aires was alerted. I was called up. The Ministry of the Interior got involved, then the Ministry of Defense!"

"The Defense Ministry? I don't understand . . ."

"I had alerted them."

"You? But why?"

"All in good time. I'll tell you in a moment. The Government took the matter very seriously."

"But why?"

"Let me talk! They dispatched three planes with selected high officials, officers, fire experts, detectives, and representatives of the Government. I flew with them. It was the first time I had ever been in La Coppelina."

Can that be true, Manuel wondered. You, my father's deputy, were never in La Coppelina? The development center for the nerve gas AP Seven was at La Coppelina, I'm convinced of that. It must have been destroyed by secret agreement between the Soviets and the Americans. They had got what they wanted. My father was dead. Now all his co-workers and everybody who might have shared his knowledge had to go. The whole plant had to go. Yes, Manuel thought, napalm: generates enough heat to destroy everything down to the last microbe and last particle of poison gas. Napalm. A good idea. Makes for a clean job.

"Now listen," the heavy-set man said, "I can see you don't trust me."

"Really Cayetano, I—"

"Just a moment. I don't know what you found out while you've been here in Vienna. You're not telling me. All right, then, I'll tell you!"

"You will?"

"Yes, *I* will." Cayetano put one fist on the table. "*I* will. You have found out that your father had been experimenting with B weapons, that he brought his invention with him to Vienna and offered it to representatives of foreign powers for money."

"How do you know that?"

"I know it from those bastards at the Defense Ministry, who haven't let me out of their sight lately. And they got it from Vienna! The Embassy keeps them up-to-date on what you're doing here! I can understand you, Manuel. It's a rotten twist to be told that your father was a criminal, a bandit, a swine, and it's pretty rotten for me, too. But it's the truth!"

"And how does our Defense Ministry know what my father was doing?" Manuel asked quickly. Cayetano was in a very excited state. Perhaps he would give something away.

"How come?" The heavy man slammed his fist against the table top. "Your father, the *Quimica Aranda,* got a secret assignment to develop B weapons from our Ministry of Defense!"

Manuel stared at Cayetano. He swallowed hard and managed to choke out a few words. "The Ministry of Defense gave him an assignment?"

"Yes! The only ones in the know were your father, myself, the chemists, and the technicians at La Coppelina. And we all had to take an oath of absolute silence."

65

"... the early photographers taught him—and he in turn taught the photographers—what surprising effects can be achieved by singling out one small portion of a picture and showing it from a special perspective, such as looking down on it from above at a steep angle, as in this painting of a ballet dancer, or viewing it from below. Just look at the incomparably sophisticated composition!" The tall, slim man with the impressive head and piercing eyes of a surgeon was standing motionless in front of a painting on an easel. He had beautiful, strong hands; the hands of a surgeon. He was wearing an extremely formal dark suit. But if instead he were wearing a white doctor's coat, rubber gloves, and a white cap over his gray hair, he could easily have been mistaken for a famous surgeon. In the jails where he had spent eleven years of his life his fellow prisoners had always called him "The Professor."

And in fact his own profession had required the same qualities of ultra sensitivity, painstaking care, concentration, and absolute mastery as were displayed by the great surgeons of his day.

A Rhinelander by birth, Anton Sirus had been living in Bremen since 1965, a wealthy man of sixty-one, a man who put his money to work or invested it in paintings of the famous "French School." Anton Sirus was a great admirer of the fine arts, and his greatest love was for the Impressionists.

He had bought a great villa on the Findorff-Allee, an exclusive residential street adjoining a beautiful old park.

His neighbors knew nothing about Anton Sirus. They thought he was a highly successful, respectable businessman who had retired and was enjoying life in the lap of luxury, surrounded by hand-picked servants, driven about in a huge Bentley, and filling his leisure with golf, travel, and the acquisition of new paintings for his superb collection.

The paintings were hung on the walls of a very large room on the first floor. Sirus had converted three rooms into one, protected by the most sophisticated burglar-alarms. There were works by Cézanne, Picasso (from his Blue Period), Degas, Modigliani, Gauguin, Renoir, and Toulouse-Lautrec. The ex-jailbird millionaire, still one of the best cracksmen in Europe, spent several hours every day in this room, lost in the contemplation of his treasures.

On the morning of January 21, 1969 he had flown back from London. On January 16 he had bought Degas' "Ballet Dancer" for a tremendous price at an auction at Christie's. He had then personally supervised the transportation of the picture to Germany, which had cost him time and nerves. But Anton Sirus was a man of strong and steady nerves, unlike the ruddy, flabby, blonde-haired Willem de Brakeleer, who was sitting in an armchair and growing rapidly more and more restless.

"Professor . . ." The Dutch police, Interpol, and de Brakeleer also had been honoring Anton Sirus with this nickname for decades.

"Yes, what is it Baas?" Sirus looked at the Dutchman in a daze, slowly coming back to reality from his wonderful world of art. Addressing de Brakeleer as "Baas," the Dutch word for "Master," was a gesture of habit and affection, a remembrance of the honorary title respectfully bestowed on de Brakeleer by his colleagues and by the criminals he hunted.

"I share your enthusiasm, Professor. Incomparable, truly incomparable, this painting. But can we—I mean, won't you tell me at last what you think of my proposition?"

"No," Sirus replied.

"What do you mean, 'No?' "

"Your proposition does not interest me, Baas."

Oh, my God, de Brakeleer thought, feeling suddenly sick. I've got to bring him around . . . that damned film . . . Mercier will send it to the aircraft company . . . that's the end of my job . . .

The ruddy Dutchman forced himself to smile. "Don't say

357

no right away! As I said before, money is no object for this job. You can name your own price."

"I have all the money I need."

"Mr. Sirus ... Professor ... I beg you! You're the only man in the world who can do this job! You'll have all the support you want! Just say what you need, and it will be provided. You'll have every protection. Do it, I implore you! For my sake! Remember 1947? The Peoples' Bank in The Hague? I knew it was you, I knew all the time!"

"You knew nothing, Baas."

"I did!"

"So why didn't you have me arrested?"

"Because I—even then I admired you, Professor. I thought you were a genius ... and I—"

"Oh, stop that! That's a lot of bullshit. You didn't know a damned thing."

Sirus sat down. He cupped his beautiful fingers and leaned his chin on them.

"You're being blackmailed, Baas, right?"

De Brakeleer answered with a nod.

"Bad?"

"Very bad."

"Hn. And your friends need what's in that safe very urgently?"

"Extremely urgently, Professor!" de Brakeleer felt a surge of hope. "They'll accept any conditions you make, any."

"Are you sure?"

"Absolutely sure!"

"All right then," Sirus said. "We'll see if you're right."

"Yes? Yes?" de Brakeleer was shaking with excitement.

"What fascinates me about Monet," Sirus said, "is his unique gift for creating atmosphere through light, and through the interplay of mist, sunshine, and water. There's one painting of his, "The Poppies," done in 1873 ... I'm mad about it. It's my dream to possess it ... I simply *must* have it. I have to have it. You understand what I'm saying, Baas?"

"Of course, of course!" de Brakeleer's words came stumbling out. "You want the painting! Wonderful! You shall have it!"

"Easy, easy," Sirus said. "There must be a reason why I don't have the painting already if I like it so much, wouldn't you say?"

"I guess so ..." de Brakeleer's hopes sank again.

"I can't get it. Not at any price. I've tried everything, but it can't be done. The painting's in Paris, in the *Musée de l'Impressionisme*. It's not for sale." Sirus's voice grew more excited: "But if I don't get "The Poppies" I'm going to go out of my mind. So there's your chance!" His voice returned to its normal, soft, cultivated tones: "You are here on behalf of the French, correct?"

"I told you already. The French absolutely want—"

"They absolutely want, yes, yes. If the French absolutely want me to do their job, Mr. de Brakeleer, then they'll have to arrange for the *Musée de l'Impressionisme* to sell me "The Poppies." I'll pay. I'll pay whatever price is asked. But I've got to be allowed to buy, you understand? The painting has to be released."

"And if it is released, would you then be prepared—"

With restrained emotion Anton Sirus said, "In that case I would do another job, yes. It would be worth it to me."

66

"We owe you an apology, Mr. Cayetano—the gentlemen had no choice."

"An apology? I don't understand—"

"The officials investigating the case in Buenos Aires did not tell you the truth, nor did the representatives from the Ministries. You were intentionally being lied to and misinformed in the interests of furthering the investigation," said the Argentinian ambassador. He had a heavily lined face, angular cheekbones, steel-gray eyes, and was a descendant of one of the oldest and most distinguished families in Argentina. He had his emotions under perfect control, but he nevertheless did show a few signs of tension and nervousness, as did all those present in the large drawing-room of the Embassy building in Vienna. The one exception was Manuel Aranda. He had suddenly gone cold as ice. Sitting around the low smoking table were the massive Cayetano on Manuel's left, and the attaché Ernesto Gomez on his right, with his black curly hair and olive skin; facing Manuel sat the Ambassador,

359

flanked by the two attorneys who had arrived with Cayetano.

"You will understand in a few moments, Mr. Cayetano. Dr. Aranda told you he had received a secret contract from our Defense Ministry for the manufacture of B weapons."

"Right."

"You and all the scientists working on the project had to take an oath of absolute silence."

"Yes! Two top officials from the Ministry—" Cayetano broke off in mid-sentence, then continued. "I've been asking time and again to be given a meeting with those two! My request has not been granted. Why not?"

"Because those two men—traitors, we must assume—have disappeared without a trace."

Cayetano blurted out breathlessly, "That means—"

"That means that neither the Defense Ministry nor any other agency of our Government *ever* entrusted Dr. Aranda with a secret contract of that nature. We do not manufacture any A, B, or C weapons, nor do we have any intention of so doing. Together with his two accomplices, who were no doubt very handsomely compensated, Dr. Aranda staged these theatrical cover-ups for the benefit of yourself and all the scientists working on the project, so that you and the others would continue to collaborate without any scruples on something which Dr. Aranda—entirely on his own, I declare that in the name of my Government—was determined to complete."

So my father lied to everyone, even his closest colleagues, in order to develop his invention, Manuel thought. He was astounded at his own calm.

The last will and testament of Manuel's father contained no surprises. Manuel was the sole heir. Manuel's father had made the special request that Manuel appoint Cayetano as General Manager of *Quimica Aranda* for a term of years still to be determined. There followed guidelines about capital planning, the development of the individual branches, and the general business policies of the firm.

The tension relaxed as the attorney read out the lengthy will. At the end Manuel said, "Every detail has my full agreement and approval. I am especially happy to name Mr. Cayetano as General Manager, with immediate effect." It surprised him to see tears come to the eyes of the big, strong man. Cayetano embraced Manuel impulsively and kissed him on both cheeks.

"Thank you for your confidence, my boy," he whispered, "I won't disappoint you . . ."

And even if you do, it won't shake me any more, Manuel thought, and shuddered at the idea. Could it really be that he mistrusted *everyone* now? Cayetano was one of the people he had known longest in his life, he was a friend. I've got to pull myself together, Manuel thought.

Soon afterwards the meeting broke up. The good-byes were polite and cool.

Back at the Ritz Manuel took Cayetano aside.

"Will you do me a favor?"

"Of course, with pleasure. What is it?"

"If anyone asks for me tomorrow, tell them I'm at the Embassy. I'll leave the same message at the desk. In the event anyone asks you, which is not probable but it could happen—"

"You're thinking of that young woman, Irene Waldegg?"

"Yes," Manuel nodded. "Her especially. Tell her, too, that I'm at the Embassy. It'll take until late in the evening."

"What will?"

"The trip I have to make. I'm going to Villach tomorrow, and Irene Waldegg must not find out."

67

"You're sure?"

"Quite sure. I'm sick all the time. I've missed my period three times now. My breasts are getting bigger and harder. And I'm having dizzy spells again. A second child, Martha! I'm scared to death of having another baby! And I'm not *supposed* to have one."

"But you're never going to find a doctor to help you out. They've all got to keep strictly to the regulations these days."

"Yes, I know."

"Have you told anyone? Agnes, I mean, or Martin Landau?"

"Not one word. And I chose Sunday to come and see you so that Martin wouldn't get suspicious. I told Agnes and Heinz you had something you wanted to discuss with me . . ."

This dialogue between Valerie Steinfeld and her sister Martha Waldegg took place on the afternoon of June 17, 1938 in the living-room of the small, yellow villa in Villach. Behind the house was a large, wild garden full of fruit trees and bright flowers. It was midsummer, the sun blazed down, and the air flickered above the mountain forests surrounding the town. The house, built at the turn of the century, had been inherited by Martha's husband Hans Waldegg, a career officer in the Army. Soon after the annexation of Austria Major Waldegg was transferred to command a battalion in a garrison near Berlin, and his wife had been alone for two months, The Waldeggs's house lay in a very secluded spot. Martha had a woman in on weekdays to help her with the housework. But today, on Sunday, the help was not there, leaving Martha and Valerie alone. The two sisters, both trimly built, resembled each other strongly. Both had shining blonde hair and light, beautiful skin. Martha was two years younger than Valerie.

"Oh, my God in Heaven," Martha said softly. She kept staring at her sister.

"I can't see it through, Martha," Valerie said. *"I can't see it through!* Two weeks ago I had to give Heinz the papers for his Aryan I.D. card—his class teacher kept insisting and insisting. I had to tell the boy that Paul is Jewish, and that he is therefore a half-caste. You know what I had to go through after that . . ."

"You wrote to me about it."

"The boy nearly went crazy! He made a terrible scene; really terrible! Screamed and howled and spit at me! In his eyes I'm the one who's to blame! Then two days ago they threw him out of the Hitler Youth."

"That, too?"

"Of course. It was to be expected. Since then he hasn't been speaking to me." Valerie gripped her sister's arm. "Two children, in these times! The Nazis could start something against the half-Jews any day, start treating them as Jews, who knows? And I'm all alone! I have to see that I get Heinz through! But if I have another baby now, it's impossible, Martha, it's impossible!" Valerie gasped for breath. "It must have happened just before Paul fled, the afternoon I brought him to Vienna West station. I even had a feeling . . ." Valerie pressed her nails into her sister's arm. "You've got to help me! Please help me! I beg you!"

"But *how?*"

Valerie spoke pleadingly, but with great urgency in her

voice. "You've been married eleven years and have no children even though you've always wanted them! Your husband is very unhappy about that, he told me so, and you told me the same! Your husband is not here, and won't be back from Berlin so soon. Not before the end of the year anyway. And that would be enough, Martha, that would be enough."

"You mean, you would . . ." her sister stammered.

"I have to! I have to! Please Martha, help me! You . . . you'll be helping yourself at the same time! Think how happy Hans would be if you had a child after all this time!"

"Of course he would be happy. And I'd be happy with a child, too. But Valerie, you . . . you . . . it would be *your* child. Do you think you could stand it?"

Valerie nodded and said nothing.

"It's madness," Martha said, her voice choking. "It's madness. But then again, when I think . . ."

"Yes?" asked Valerie. "Yes?"

". . . how happy Hans would be, and me, too. A child . . . our marriage would be as it used to be, as it was at the beginning."

"Well, then!"

"But—and I'm not thinking of you now, Valerie—but there are so many problems. We need a doctor."

"You've got one! Old Dr. Orlam! You've been going to him ever since you were married. He knows everything about your marriage. And he's not a Nazi, you told me."

"No, he's not a Nazi. Just the opposite. But all the same, all the same, Valerie, think of what he's risking!"

"It's his duty not to say anything. Let's talk with him. He can only say no. Come on, call him!"

"Now, on a Sunday?"

"Sure, I have to get back to Vienna. Tell him it's urgent. Please, Martha!"

68

"There's no doubt about it," said Dr. Josef Orlam two hours later in his quiet examining room. He was an elderly man with kind eyes, steel-rimmed glasses that kept slipping down his nose, and slim hands that had brought many hundreds of children into the world.

"There isn't the slightest doubt, Frau Steinfeld. You're pregnant. In the third month."

He had examined Valerie. Dressed again, she was now sitting next to Martha in front of Orlam's desk. The two sisters had confided fully in the experienced doctor as soon as they arrived. Orlam had bent over listening without a sign of shock or rejection. He lived in the center of town, on the Nikolaiplatz, opposite the church. The window of his office looked out on the slow waters of the River Drau and the bridge across the river leading to the square. The bridge and the square were both deserted, as usual on Sundays. The doctor lived alone, and today being a holiday his office staff was not there. His housekeeper, too, was away, on a visit to friends.

Valerie asked, with almost unnatural calm, "Would you be willing to help me with my plan, Doctor?"

"Frau Steinfeld," Orlam answered, "I'm afraid you think it far too easy."

"Too easy for you?"

"No, for *yourself*," Orlam said. "If you carry out your intentions, then according to the law and the baptism, but above all according to a personal commitment that *you* must enter into, your child will become your sister's child."

"I know that."

"I'm afraid you only think you know." The doctor was buttoning and unbuttoning his white apron nervously. "At this moment you want your plan to go through. But just wait a little while, until your mother-instinct asserts itself, as it does with every woman who's expecting a baby. And then what will happen? And especially once the child is *born*. Have you any notion how strong your love, your longing, and your yearning for your own offspring are going to be *then*? What you will want to do *then* but won't be *able* to do without risking a catastrophe? Have you any idea—"

"Doctor," Valerie interrupted, her voice rising excitedly as she spoke, "you are right, I haven't any idea. And perhaps I can't even imagine it. But I do know what it is to live in fear day in, day out, without any hope that it will end! To be called into the Gestapo and be screamed at and threatened and intimidated every week, week after week! To have lost a husband who, might be dead for all I know, and whom I might never see again!" Now she was shouting. "And to have one child who's exposed to the sadism of these hounds, and to have to tremble for this child every minute of every hour of every day and night. *I do know that.* And nothing I might have to face if I go through with this plan could be as bad or as painful as what I'm having to suffer now! I don't want this unborn being to have to suffer, too! I want this child to be able to grow up in peace!"

"You are desperate and panic-stricken, helpless—"

"Is there anything you can do about that, Doctor?" She shook her head. "No, there isn't. Nobody can do anything about it. That's why I am sitting here and asking you: Will you help us?" She noticed that her sister had her hands folded in prayer.

"I will help you," said the doctor after a pause. "We'll have to be careful, that goes without saying. On the other hand, everyone in town—everybody here knows everybody else—is aware that Frau Waldegg has been coming to me for years trying everything to have a child, and that I've been doing my best to help her. So that would all be to our advantage. My treatment turned out to be successful, understand? Frau Waldegg has got pregnant at last, I would confirm it, she could talk about it around town a bit, keep coming to see me regularly. Her home is in a pretty secluded spot, that's good, too ... I'll have to give her instructions on how to act like a pregnant woman.

Martha seemed suddenly to have forgotten what was being planned. "If you are really going to help us, Doctor, then I'll write to my husband tomorrow and let him know that I'm expecting a baby—no, it's all right, no need to worry, they won't let him leave his regiment. They're working like crazy. He wrote that he wouldn't get any leave for months. Maybe they'll let him go for a few days once the child is born ..."

"I would come to Villach in October and live with my sister in order to help her at the birth," Valerie said. "In Vienna everything can be taken care of. Martha and I have already discussed it. And you could examine me in Martha's house, Doctor—officially, of course, it would be my sister you're examining. Nobody would notice anything. What's the matter? Is something wrong? Don't you want to do it after all, Doctor?"

He gave no answer.

"Please, Doctor, please, you said yes once!"

365

"And I will keep my word," Dr. Joseph Orlam answered slowly. "My heart is with the weak and the helpless, probably because I'm weak and helpless myself. But there isn't a lot I can do for you."

"You can do an immeasurable amount!" Valerie exclaimed. Orlam shrugged his shoulders.

On December 17, Hans Waldegg arrived in Villach. He had been given leave over Christmas. The major found a gay Valerie and a solemn Martha, who was in bed holding a loudly crying infant in her arms. She broke into tears when he went down on his knees and kissed her over and over again, whispering, "Thank you, thank you! I thank you, my darling . . ."

In the dim light at the other end of the room Valerie Steinfeld stood motionless, a smile on her lips. The same smile could be seen on her face on December 21, 1938 as she stepped before the vicar in the Church of St. Nicholas with the snuggly blanketed baby cradled in her arm. Outside, its high waters almost bursting its banks, the River Drau swept by. At the beginning of the baptismal ceremony, that is, before the entry of the child into the Kingdom of Light and of Life, the vicar wore a violet surplice.

"Peace be with you," said the vicar. "How shall this child be named?"

Outside the river roared, and the ice-cold north wind howled.

"This child shall be named Irene," Valerie answered in a clear, loud voice. Major Waldegg and his wife had chosen the name. It was a name borne also by three saints.

The vicar spoke, "Irene, what dost thou want from the Church of God?"

Valerie heard a suppressed sobbing from Martha, who stood behind her, then heard her husband calming her with tender words. Valerie answered in a voice as clear as a crystal bell:

"Faith."

"And what does Faith vouchsafe Thee?"

"Eternal Life," Valerie answered.

"If thou wouldst enter into Life therefore," said the Vicar, "then keep the Commandments. And love the Lord thy God with all thy heart, with all thy soul, and with all thy life, and love thy neighbors as thyself."

You too will never know, Paul, my beloved Paul, Valerie was thinking, nobody will know except for myself and Martha and Doctor Orlam, and God Himself if there is a God. No, nobody shall know.

THE MEANING

To solve the labyrinthine quest
I spun out the thread guiding me best:
Did you feel the sense in the tale I told,
That I'm not just one but double-souled?

1

In the quiet room full of old-fashioned furniture in which Manuel held his conversation with Martha Waldegg, the screeching whistles of passing trains and the rumble of their wheels formed a backdrop of sound . . .

"You know everything now, Mr. Aranda," the voice of the sixty-three-year-old woman sounded hoarse. "Now you know the secret. My husband and I love Irene! She means everything to Hans. It would break his heart to find out the truth after all these years. That's the reason I was so terrified. Can you understand that?"

"Yes," Manuel said quietly.

"I have told you everything in confidence, Mr. Aranda. Please don't break this confidence. My husband and Irene must never know the truth—that was Valerie's wish, too."

Manuel looked at his hostess, strangely embarrassed. "I'll never say a word about it to Irene," he said. "I promise you that."

"Thank you. I thank you from the bottom of my heart. You see, I had a lot of heartbreak with her in the last few years . . ."

"Heartbreak?"

"Well, yes, you see . . . as Irene grew up, I began to push the deception out of my mind. Finally I really felt toward her as I would toward a child of my own, and my husband did, anyway. And Valerie kept her part of the bargain."

"That's just what I wanted to ask," Manuel said. Wheels rumbled by again, and a whistle tooted and screeched on the railroad tracks some distance away.

"Did Frau Steinfeld ever try to get her child back after the war?"

"No, never! You didn't know my sister. Once she gave a promise she stuck to it, she was incapable of a wrong deed."

Incapable of a wrong deed, Manuel thought. She poisoned my father. And even if he deserved to die a hundred times for what he did, who gave Valerie Steinfeld the right to take

371

his life? The words came with difficulty as he said, "It must have been a terrible psychological burden for Frau Steinfeld to see her own child growing up as someone else's."

"The greatest psychological burden of all was giving me the child in the first place," the trim-figured Martha Waldegg replied. "But she possessed superhuman self-control, and was always able to cover up her real feelings. Only inside her ... it must have been grim, that's for sure. Especially at the beginning, when the child was born, and for the first few years after that ... but she never once showed it, not once! She never complained, and was always merry and gay when she met with my—her—daughter, here or in Vienna. She kept our secret to the time she died. Right up until her horrible, puzzling, grisly death."

"Her death is a puzzle to you, too?"

"Completely, Mr. Aranda, completely! My husband and I were thunderstruck when we learned about it. There's simply no way to explain it."

"You said before you'd had a lot of heartbreak with Irene these last few years. Why was that?"

Martha Waldegg shrugged helplessly. "Just life! It was nobody's fault, certainly not Valerie's. But when Irene was eighteen and started her studies in Vienna, she went to live with Valerie, and stayed with Valerie all the years she worked in the pharmacy and then after she took over the business. The pharmacy had belonged to her uncle, my husband's brother. His wife had been constantly sick. Irene could not have lived with them. She loved Valerie, and I ... well, I became jealous! It's grotesque, I know, but everything changed completely. The two went on holidays together, travelled together. Irene came to visit us less and less often. Home for her began to mean more and more the Gentzgasse, Valerie. More and more we became strangers to her."

Manuel remembered Irene's words at the Civic Cemetery, the day they had met for the first time: "Valerie ... I loved her so much! More than any other person ... yes, even more than my mother! I'm very fond of my mother, I really am ... but ever since I've been living in Vienna *Valerie* has been my mother ... more than my real mother ... and she became so more and more ..."

Martha Waldegg had turned her head away and wiped her eyes. Quickly he asked, "And the lawsuit ... how did it end?"

"It never did." Martha Waldegg had pulled herself together again and was looking straight at Manuel.

"What do you mean?"

"It was still running when the war ended. It never was concluded."

"Your sister told you that?"

"Yes, Mr. Aranda. When we finally managed to get together again after the war, in February of 1946, she told me."

"February 1946? I don't understand . . ."

"My husband was wounded in the summer of 1944. Very seriously. He was in an Army hospital in Breslau. For a long time it looked as though he would die. I got permission to go and be with him—officers' wives could still get those permissions at that time."

"So you took the child—who must have been almost six, I suppose?—to Breslau?"

"Yes. We rented a room there and I stayed with my husband. Slowly, very slowly, his condition improved. The front was coming closer every day. There were air raids all the time, it became impossible to get mail to or from Valerie, letters got lost . . . And then, in February 1945, we had to take to the streets because the Russians were coming. We were driven west, then north in a truck, constantly under fire from low-flying aircraft, in ice-cold weather. Little Irene, my sick husband. Finally we got to Lüneburg. Hans had to go into hospital right away—the strain of the journey had been too much for him; he suffered a total collapse. The old wounds began to fester, he had to be operated on again. He was in the hospital the whole of 1945. I worked in the hospital as a cleaning woman."

"Could you not go back to Austria then?"

"My husband was not well enough to risk the journey until the end of the year. Travelling in those days was pretty rough! We came via Vienna in winter . . ."

"And it was then you saw your sister again?"

"Yes, I saw her. She was like a walking ghost, more dead than alive. It was shattering, Mr. Aranda! She'd gone through so much! Her husband had been killed in an air raid in London—a British officer had brought her the news. Her husband, with whom she'd so much wanted to be reunited after the war, and be happy with again! But not only that Heinz . . ."

"Yes?" Manuel sat up.

"Something really bad. That ghastly lawsuit had completely alienated him from his mother."

"Why?"

"I don't know exactly. There had been quarrels. He had blamed her for everything. It just wasn't possible to get a clear account from Valerie about what happened. She'd gone down in weight to barely ninety pounds and seemed on the verge of collapse. At any rate, her son, whom she'd managed to get through the Nazi time with so much effort, had run away."

"*Run away?*"

"To the country somewhere. He was working for some farmers. He didn't want to live with his mother any more, and was just biding his time until Canada would accept more immigrants. And in 1947 he did in fact emigrate, and was killed a year later in Quebec in a car accident. If anyone has had a hard life, it was Valerie. And then to end up this way, it's really terrible! What other secret was Valerie carrying around with her? What can it have been? What, what?"

Yes indeed, what?

2

"*Please don't ask why I'm leaving,*" the small hotel orchestra was playing when he entered the bar at the Ritz. Irene Waldegg was sitting in a booth, waiting for him. She watched him walk toward her with some embarrassment. Her big, brown eyes glistened in the light, her chestnut hair flowed in soft, wide waves over her shoulders.

Manuel had found some messages at the reception desk including a note from Cayetano. Manuel had known that Irene would be in the bar. Nevertheless, seeing her was a shock, even though her presence filled him with pleasure.

Irene! Valerie Steinfeld's daughter!

He knew it since this afternoon, and he would never forget it. The young woman looking toward him with such a bashful smile knew nothing about it, and should never know, no, never. Would it shake her, he wondered, as he walked toward her, or would she have been overjoyed and proud if she knew?

"Good evening, Irene," he said, bending to kiss her hand. "What a wonderful surprise!"

"You're not angry with me?"

"Angry? What an idea—"

"It's almost eleven thirty, and you've been working until now . . . your Director told me you spent the whole day at the Embassy, and stayed on after he left."

Cayetano had said the same in the message he had left for Manuel. He had been in the hotel when Irene arrived at 10 P.M. He had told her that he, Cayetano, and the two attorneys would have to go back to the Embassy still.

"It's all very important and urgent, I suppose?" Irene asked.

"Yes, very. Cayetano has to go back to Buenos Aires, and there's a lot to settle before he leaves . . ."

"I telephoned you during the afternoon and again this evening," Irene said, "but you weren't there of course. I could have called again later, but somehow . . ."

"What?"

"Somehow I . . . I just couldn't relax. It's too stupid! I got dressed and drove over here, I felt I simply had to see you before the day was over. We haven't seen each other for a whole day now, and it was making me fret. I'm not usually like this, really I'm not, but today . . . and with you . . ." Irene lowered her gaze. "I'm a silly little girl," she said softly. "I . . . I had a feeling all at once that you were in some danger, and that something had happened . . ."

He was looking at her intensely, his heart thudding. We're falling in love, he thought. Perhaps we're in love already. I love the daughter of my father's murderer. She loves the son of the man her mother killed. What a situation . . .

Manuel, who had sat down next to Valerie, said, "It was the same for me. All day long there was one thing I couldn't get out of my mind: I wanted to see you today still, to drive over tonight, if you allowed it . . ."

"Really?" She raised her head. Her eyes were huge.

"Really," he said, and thought to himself: And it's true, it's really true.

"Good evening, Mr. Aranda." The head bartender bowed. "What can I get for you?"

"What are you having, Irene?"

"Cognac."

375

"Then two cognacs, please."

"Very good, Mr. Aranda." The bartender hurried away smiling and looking busy. All the staff are smiling and look busy, Manuel thought.

"Bianca Barry called," said Irene.

"Bianca Barry . . ."

"The painter's wife, Heinz's childhood sweetheart. The one who told me that the story she told in front of her husband was a pack of lies!"

"Oh, yes, I remember!"

"She tried here first, but couldn't get you."

The bar was empty except for two couples at the counter. Music wafted in softly, sentimentally. Manuel was thinking: The mouth. The nose. The ears. On the photos Valerie Steinfeld has a similar nose, similar ears, a similar mouth. Is it possible Irene has never noticed the resemblances? It's fantastic, utterly fantastic. The daughter of Valerie and Paul Steinfeld is sitting here next to me, talking to me, smiling at me because she absolutely wanted to see me . . .

"Manuel!"

"Yes?" He said, with a sudden start.

"Why are you looking at me like that?"

"You're . . . you're so beautiful, Irene. More beautiful than any woman I've ever seen before."

"Oh, come on! There are lots of beautiful girls in Argentina. You must have known many."

"Not many . . . a few . . . but none like you, none."

She looked down at the tiled tabletop.

"This Bianca Barry . . ."

"Yes?"

"She wants to see us again and tell us the truth, she says."

"When?"

"Tomorrow afternoon. She'll have time then. Her husband is leaving in the morning to go to Linz. He won't be back until late in the evening."

"Tomorrow afternoon is good. I still have some work to finish up with Cayetano and the lawyers. And there was a message at the desk saying that Forster had called and is expecting me at eleven o'clock tomorrow morning."

The waiter brought their two drinks.

"A toast to the most beautiful woman in the world," said Manuel.

"You shouldn't talk like that!"

"To the most beautiful woman in the world," he repeated,

lightly tipping up her chin. "To the hope that she may enjoy happiness and laughter again, myself along with her."

"No," Irene said. "Let's drink to Valerie. Let her be happy, wherever she may be."

"To Valerie then," Manuel said. They drank. "Where will Bianca Barry meet us?" Manuel asked.

"At the main entrance to the Civic Cemetery," Irene said.

"What's the significance of that? What does she want to do there?"

"I don't know. I asked her, but she said she had to be quick, she could hear her husband coming and had to hang up."

"At the entrance to the Civic Cemetery . . ." Manuel murmured, baffled.

"At three o'clock."

He kept his gaze fixed on Irene. Valerie's daughter. Valerie's daughter. The thought obsessed him, pounded at his brain.

Valerie's daughter.

"At the main entrance. That's where you and I met for the first time."

"Seven days ago. Just seven days ago," Irene said.

"Eight. Almost eight now. I didn't trust you."

"You hated me!"

"Oh, no!"

"Oh, yes!"

"Eight days . . . they have been like eight years," he said. "I feel I've known you for eight years, Irene. Don't you feel the same?"

She looked at him silently, then nodded.

"Listen!" He straightened up. "The orchestra—the piano, I mean."

Slowly, melodically, and softly the old man at the piano in the ballroom was playing *If you want to give me your heart . . ."*

The pianist looked over at Manuel and Irene through one of the large windows in the wall of the bar, and nodded his head with a smile. The other four musicians, who had lowered their instruments, bowed also.

"It's our song," Irene said.

"Charlie!" Manuel called discreetly. The barman came over immediately. He too was smiling.

"It's about the way Mr. Wawra's playing, right?"

"Yes. Where—"

377

"It's a really odd story," Charlie said. "He told me about it, Mr. Wawra did, the pianist."

"What?"

"The experience he had. He was on the Graben this morning. There's a big sheet-music store there, which specializes in old and secondhand sheet music. Mr. Wawra is a collector, you know. Anyway, he was just rummaging around, with a salesman helping him, when a man who'd also been leafing through the secondhand stuff butted in. He said he'd gathered from the conversation that Mr. Wawra worked at the Ritz. Next—and he didn't give any name—he slipped out the music to the song Mr. Wawra's playing right now, and said: "Please play this song when you see a certain Mr. Manuel Aranda, who's a guest at your hotel, sitting with a young lady with brown eyes and brown hair." The man described you perfectly to Mr. Wawra, Madame. He must know you."

"Yes, he knows us," Manuel said.

Charlie bowed and returned to the bar.

The pianist began the song again.

Manuel placed his hand on Irene's.

She placed her other hand on top of his.

And the old man at the piano outside kept on playing the slow melody, his eyes fixed on the music, and Manuel wished it would never end and Irene wished the same, and both knew what the other was thinking but neither of them said a word for a long time.

3

"Valerie Steinfeld ... An unusual woman, that's for sure," said Commissioner Groll. He was pacing up and down in his office to relieve the slight breathing difficulties he experienced with his half lung. The high-intensity lamp on his desk was burning, one window was half-open, and the radiators exuded warmth. Everything was as always. For the past hour heavy snow had been falling on Vienna. The time was close to two o'clock in the morning. Manuel had taken Irene home, then gone on to Groll's office.

He had given an account of his meeting with Martha Waldegg while Groll walked up and down. When Manuel was finished, Groll stood still at the window for some time looking out at the swirling snow. Then he began to talk about Valerie Steinfeld.

"The more I hear about her, the more I admire her." Groll stopped and swallowed some pills. "I expect that you feel the same way, despite everything, don't you?"

"Yes," said Manuel. "I do." He saw Groll taking off his tie and opening his shirt collar.

"Don't you feel well?"

"Not very. But no need to panic. Happens to me a lot when the weather's like this. My diaphragm presses against my heart. Stabs like hell." Groll reached into his pocket, brought out a little bottle of Underberg, unscrewed it, and drank. "I always carry one with me," he said, then let out a thunderous rumbling belch.

"Sorry, but I needed that. I'll feel better now in a moment. OOPS, there goes another, sorry! Aaah!" He sat down in his desk chair and took a deep breath.

"It's a relief. If you ever get the blahs yourself down there, let me know, I can always spare you a bottle!"

"Listen, Commissioner, shouldn't you take a rest? Maybe get some sick leave?"

"And who'll do all this garbage here? It's out of the question," said Groll. "Besides, once you get yourself certified as sick and put into bed, that's the end, that's when you really *do* get sick! No, no, I feel fine again. Don't look at me so scared, my boy. You're absolutely right: your Irene—I hope you don't mind my referring to her like that, you go red when I just mention her name—it's best if your Irene doesn't find out anything about it."

There was a knock at the door, and Inspector Schäfer came in. "Yes, Chief?"

"Leave the building as conspicuously as possible with Mr. Aranda and drive him to the Ritz. Act like his bodyguard. Ham it up a bit, you know what to do. In front of the hotel entrance, too. You'll have a whole posse on your tail. I want those types to get the *impression* that we Austrians are watching over your welfare from now on at least, Manuel. And I really will assign a plainclothes man to you now and again, on my own head! But it's especially important tonight. I know I can rely on you, Schäfer."

"I'll take care of it, Chief."

"Afterwards take a taxi back here and drive home in your Volkswagen. You can reach me at home if you need to. But I'm counting on you, Schäfer."

"Yes, Chief. I won't let you down."

4

Ulrich Schäfer "hammed it up," as Groll had asked. He stood at Manuel's side for a short while in front of the main entrance to the Ritz, then looked up and down the Ring, discovering in fact several cars that had followed them and were now parked behind trees along the Ringstrasse. Nothing moved. Manuel and Schäfer were standing in the bright lights of the hotel entrance. They shook hands and Manuel went into the Ritz, while Schäfer turned up his coat collar—getting some snow down his neck, and walked off quickly toward a taxi-stand some distance away. A single vehicle stood there. But before he could reach it he was overtaken by a second taxi driving in the side lane of the Ringstrasse. Schäfer whistled to it: he wanted to get out of the cold and the snow, so why walk all the way to the taxi-stand if there was no need?

The taxi that had driven past him stopped. The driver, a broad, burly man in a flat cap, bent over the back seat and opened the right rear door. Schäfer climbed in. "Berggasse. Police HQ."

The driver turned into the Ring at the next cross street, and drove along it toward the Town Hall and the Burg theater. The snowstorm was so blinding that he had to proceed slowly, headlights dim. Visibility was less than ten feet. The driver pressed a button on the dashboard.

Schäfer gave a tremendous start when a voice with a strong French accent came over a small loudspeaker in the back of the car:

"Good evening, Inspector Schäfer. You took our advice and placed the ad in the *Kurier* just the way we had told you to . . ."

"What is this?" Schäfer exclaimed.

The driver showed no reaction. He seemed to be deaf. He kept his eyes on the road. More words from the loudspeaker:

"We are very sorry that your wife is so ill. She needs special care in the sanatorium. You know that." Schäfer swallowed. The taxi crept on through the blizzard, the driver behaving as though he could not hear a word.

"We offer you two hundred thousand schillings in return for a small favor. On the evening of January 16th you took a bundle of documents out of the Hotel Ritz and to an attorney's office." Schäfer clenched his fists.

"That we know. But we do not know which attorney. You will give us his exact address. Write it down on a piece of paper, in your own handwriting. Underneath it write: one hundred thousand schillings received. Write the date and your signature. We are watching you. At the first opportunity a man will hand you one hundred thousand schillings—have no fear, nobody will see it. You may count the money before you give the man the information. When we are convinced that you gave us the correct name and address you will receive the other hundred thousand schillings in the same manner within ten days. You will give a receipt for that amount also. We warn you not to give us false information. We are in possession of the paper bearing your signature. It would go straight to your superiors. That is all.'"

The voice went silent. The driver switched off the tape recorder. He was just driving by the House of Parliament. A snowplough rattled by them down the Ring. Inspector Schäfer sat motionless in the backseat of the car, his face devoid of expression. They reached the Burg theater. The driver slowed down even further, then asked in a cold voice, without turning his head: "So?" His gaze fixed on the swirling white flakes sweeping into the windshield, Schäfer asked, "Do you have the money on you?" The driver flicked on the right turn signal, edged into the right-hand lane of the Ringstrasse and stopped. He switched on the light in the back of the car, and handed over an envelope. Schäfer tore it open. It was stuffed with banknotes.

"Count it," the driver said.

Schäfer counted it. There were one hundred one-thousand schilling notes, some old, some new. Schäfer's hands suddenly began to tremble convulsively. The money almost slipped down onto the wet, dirty floor of the cab. Schäfer had only one thought: I have to do it. I expected something like this. It doesn't come unexpectedly, I'm not unprepared. If I don't do it, I'll cause Carla even greater suffering, even worse pain, just dreadful misery. Carla, my Carla . . .

"What's wrong? Doesn't it add up?" the driver asked.

"Yes, it's okay . . ."

Without turning around the driver handed him a sheet of paper and a ballpoint pen.

"There's a large book on the seat next to you. Use it to write on," he said. "And write clearly."

Schäfer had to wait until his hands were trembling less violently. Then he wrote:

Dr. Rudolf Stein. Kohlmarkt 11

And underneath that:

100,000 schillings received

Ulrich Schäfer
23 January 1969

He handed the paper and the pen back to the driver. The driver took both, glanced at the paper, then switched off the light inside the car.

"That'll do," he said. "Now get out."

"What?"

"Get out. I'm not taking you any further. You'll get another taxi over there."

Schäfer got out. The taxi sped away, all its lights out. In a second it had disappeared into the thick snow.

Inspector Schäfer stood at the curb, motionless. He noticed he was still holding the envelope containing the money in his hand, and put it into his pocket. "Miracles can and do happen, my dear Mr. Schäfer. Sometimes the disease comes to a halt, even clears a little. The patient can then live a long time, a very long time . . . and who knows, a cure for the disease might be found in that time. New cures are being discovered every day, every single day . . ." The doctor's voice echoed in Schäfer's ears.

I can only hope they'll keep their word and pay me the other one-hundred-thousand schillings, he thought.

5

"The girls in my office have turned up another section of the file," Dr. Forster said. "It's still not all there is, but we'll have everything together before long."

Manuel, who was sitting in the old man's living-room, suppressed a yawn. Manuel had got to bed very late, and risen early. Dr. Forster continued: "Here are the minutes of the first hearing. It took place on March 20, 1943. The hearing was public, but nobody was interested, and the benches for the spectators were empty. There was just a judge and a court stenographer. I remember her very well: Herta Bohnen was her name, there it is. And the judge was called Gloggnigg, Heinz Gloggnigg. One of the fiercest Nazis in the whole judicial system! And a real sadist."

6

"So your husband preferred a particular method of sexual intercourse?"

"Yes."

"Which was painful to you and failed to satisfy you?"

"Yes."

"I am merely reading out what you yourself wrote in your statement. According to what you state, this particular method of sexual intercourse with your husband, the said Paul Israel Steinfeld, deeply repelled you. That's on page three of Frau Steinfeld's statement, gentlemen, at the top of the page."

"Your Honor—"

"One moment, Counsel, *I'm* asking the questions right

now! A "particular method of sexual intercourse"—I find that extremely vague. Could you define it a little more precisely, please, Frau Steinfeld?"

"My God, for me that's—"

"You're in court here! You are under oath to tell the truth and nothing but the truth. And you are the one who initiated this suit. The purpose of my question is to establish the facts." Or do you think I'm asking them merely for my own entertainment?"

"Of course not."

"Then explain yourself more clearly."

"An abnormal method of sexual intercourse . . ."

"Abnormal. Abnormal covers a lot of things. Be more precise, please!"

"He . . . my husband . . . didn't like the normal channel, he—"

"I've had about enough now, Frau Steinfeld! If you don't want to use direct language, I'll have to put some direct questions: did Paul Israel Steinfeld prefer sexual intercourse through the anus?"

"Your Honor, I beg you to consider a more delicate way of questioning my client!" said Forster, springing to his feet and tugging excitedly at his right ear.

"You will have to leave that to my judgment, Counsel. I will spare her feelings as much as possible. You don't want to prevent me from establishing the facts of the case, do you?"

"Of course not, your Honor."

"None of us here are little children. I don't think the questions are going to give anyone present any psychological shocks."

Public Prosecutor Dr. Hubert Kummer giggled.

You God-forsaken dog, Forster thought, staring fixedly at the District Court Judge Dr. Fritz Gloggnigg. You deserve to get your teeth kicked in for the way you're torturing this poor woman, who stands pale and trembling before you. And as for you, he thinks, whirling his head around to stare at Public Prosecutor Kummer, who was still chuckling, as for you, you dirty ass-licking scum dredged up by the tide of the times, you're oh-so-thrilled by this inhuman inquisitor of a judge that you can't even keep your rapture under decent control. How I'd like to smash your face in! I just hope Frau Steinfeld can hold up. She's as pale as wax.

"Won't you please sit back down, Counsel?" Forster sits back on the hard, straight chair and rubs his ear. The three long benches for spectators on the other side of a barrier are completely empty. They are made of the same dark wood as the chairs and the two large tables for Forster and Kummer. The attorneys sit facing each other. Behind Forster are three large windows. Spring sunshine, warm and bright, slants across the room. The day is beautiful—for others. Next to Forster is an empty chair for Valerie to sit on when she is not on the witness-stand. At the moment she is on her feet before the judge's table, which is raised up on a podium. District Court Judge Dr. Gloggnigg, a short, bulky man with brown hair and cold, glittering eyes, looks down on Valerie as from a throne. Herta Bohnen sits at the short end of the table, a dull, young stenographer with mousy hair and no make-up, her eyes glazed and her face vacant. She hardly ever looks up, apparently (and probably in fact, thinks Forster) uninvolved, bored, emotionless and indifferent. An outsized picture of Hitler decorates the wall behind Judge Gloggnigg. The District Judge leans toward Valerie, eyeing her the way a scientist examines his laboratory rabbits before an experiment. The glitter in his eyes sharpens.

"Frau Steinfeld, I asked you a question. Would you be good enough to answer it?"

"Not through the anus," Valerie answers, suddenly completely in control of herself. Her face has gone white, her lips are bluish. She is wearing a dark blue suit and shoes with wedge-shaped heels. The floor beneath her feet feels as if it's slipping away, but she knows it's not. She clenches the fists of both hands so hard that the fingernails dig into the flesh.

"May we learn how the particular method of sexual intercourse was performed?" Judge Gloggnigg leaned over still further, fingers interlocked, forearms leaning on photos, documents, and geneaological charts.

It's not me standing here talking, Valerie thinks, not me at all. It is some stranger to whom I am lending my voice to enable her to do whatever necessary to save my boy. In a monotonous, flat tone she says: "As a rule he performed the sexual act by inserting his penis between my thighs, but not into . . . not into—"

"Go on, go on!" Gloggnigg prods.

"Your Honor, I beg you—" Forster starts out, jumping to his feet.

"Don't interrupt the lady, Counsel," Gloggnigg says in a threateningly ingratiating tone. "She's quite capable of speaking for herself. So, Frau Steinfeld, but not into the . . ."

"But not into my vagina," says Valerie.

"You see, we're making progress." Gloggnigg looks down at Valerie again. "So that's how your husband had sexual intercourse with you."

Watch it now, Forster thinks. We've discussed all this. She mustn't make any mistakes here.

"Not only," Valerie says.

"How else?"

"The normal way. Only he always pulled back too soon."

"You mean *'coitus interruptus?'* "

"Yes."

The Public Prosecutor livens up. "Your Honor, may I ask one question in-between?"

"Go ahead, Dr. Kummer."

"Frau Steinfeld, if everything is as you describe—"

"It was exactly as I describe it," says Valerie, her lips now a grayish blue.

"—then your husband can never have believed for one moment that your son Heinz was spermed by himself." Kummer looked down at his papers. "In your written statement, however, Frau Steinfeld, you declare ... on page five ... that your husband did in fact give voice later to doubts concerning the paternity of the boy—but I do not see any reference anywhere to the fact that he contested it from the very beginning. How do you explain that?"

"My husband preferred to have intercourse with me in the manner I have described"—Forster notices to his consternation that Valerie's temples have hollowed out, and bluish veins are throbbing in the sockets—"but *not exclusively.*"

"But that means therefore that impregnation by Paul Israel Steinfeld *cannot be excluded!*" retorted Gloggnigg in a flash.

"My husband, at least, believed it could not be excluded, your honor. I have explained this in detail in my statement."

Thank God, Forster thinks. She didn't forget anything.

7

"Mr. Landau, we have now heard your testimony. You insist that you are the father of Heinz Steinfeld."

"Yes, absolutely!" The skinny little bookdealer, dressed in a dark suit, sticks out his chest and lifts his head, jutting out his chin. His words come out loudly, quickly, and aggressively. Valerie has never seen her old friend like this. In a loud voice Landau proclaims, "Furthermore, I request the Court to declare me the legal and legitimate father of the boy."

Gloggnigg has been boiling inwardly with rage during the entire testimony of this quarrelsome, lean individual at the brazenness, yes, brazenness was the word, with which the fellow behaved. Now he roars:

"Don't push your luck too far, Mr. Landau! You have no right to request anything of this Court. You're being heard here as a witness. We are not answerable to your private wishes. It's a bit too early for them anyway, in my opinion."

The Public Prosecutor chuckles dutifully.

"Let's wait for the suit to be settled, all right?"

Martin Landau tosses his head. "What is there to wait for? As far as I can see, it's as clear as day!"

"Your opinions are not required here, Mr. Landau. The matter is by no means as clear as day. This is not the first such suit that has come before me." Rage is beginning to get the better of Gloggnigg. "And how do you think this case looks? Your own sister, subpoened by the Public Prosecutor, sends us a doctor's certificate to say she can't appear because she had two teeth pulled yesterday!"

"Well, so what? She's in bed, in great pain."

"Your sister got notice that she was to testify two weeks ago: why did she pick now to go to the dentist?"

"She had an acute infection!"

"That's what *you* say! But don't think your sister will get out of testifying so easily."

"I've told her that!" It's true, Martin is thinking, Tilly deliberately did wait until yesterday to have her teeth pulled.

387

She didn't want to come. I knew it wouldn't do her any good.

"You've told her that?" Gloggnigg inclines his head.

"Your Honor!" Everyone in the room flinched, even the dull-witted stenographer for Martin Landau at the top of his voice, and in as savage a tone as he can muster: "Your Honor! I am a Party Member! Are you trying to insinuate that a Party Member is lying?"

Judge Gloggnigg almost chokes over his words before answering. "There'll be no shouting here, Mr. Landau, you understand?"

"It's your attitude that's getting me so worked up!" Landau exclaims. "I am afraid you are prejduiced—"

"I am not prejudiced at all!"

"The charge is ridiculous," the Public Prosecutor croaks out from behind his table.

"And you're the same!" Landau exclaims, wheeling around. A different person, someone totally unknown to her is standing there in front of Valerie. She rubs her eyes, and hears this stranger bellow: "I've been aware of it all along. I stand before you as the protector and representative of good German blood—"

"Mr. Landau!" the Judge shouts. "We want no speeches from you here!"

But Landau is furious now: "—as a convinced National Socialist, for whom the purity of race is of preeminent importance! The seriousness of this case does not seem to have dawned on you yet—"

"Witness Landau, control yourself!"

"I will *not* control myself. I will lodge a complaint in Berlin about your persistent efforts to influence and intimidate me—"

"Nobody has tried to do that!" replies Gloggnigg, raising both hands. (Berlin! The fellow is capable of it! He will rake up a lot of muck!)

"Yes, you did!" Martin Landau's shout is now a battle-cry. He can feel the blood coursing more quickly through his veins, throbbing with warmth. He feels strong, free, and happy, completely fearless . . . for the first time in his life! "And you're accusing a Party Member of lying!"

"We are not!"

"Of course you are!"

Forster's mouth has shut tight. With grim satisfaction he notices that the Public Prosecutor has begun to tug at the collar of his black legal robe. I know that dirty bastard, he

388

thinks, that cowardly bully. He's starting to shit his pants.

"Mr. Landau, you must calm down, you're getting too excited," Kummer mumbles. It's really true, Forster thinks, pulling at his ear, the only way you deal with these swine is to stand up and yell back at them!

"You misunderstand us. We're just as interested as you are in establishing the truth in this case. You can be sure that I and His Honor—I mean, His Honor and I—have no preconceived opinions or prejudices ..." (Berlin, Kummer thinks. Trouble with the big shots, after all I've built up for myself ...)

"It doesn't look that way to me!" Landau answers the Public Prosecutor, giving him an ugly look. "I at any rate am being treated here in a manner which I can no longer accept!"

Judge Gloggnigg shouts: "That's enough! Kindly respect the dignity of the court, Mr. Landau. I told you at the beginning of your cross-examination that as a witness you might have to testify under oath, and should therefore tell the truth, pure and simple."

"Yes, and ... ?" Landau crows.

"After the scene you just made and your inappropriate behavior, I *will* put you under oath," Gloggnigg says softly, a foxy tone in his voice, picking up his cap. "Raise your right hand. Repeat after me, just the final words."

"With pleasure, your Honor!" Landau raises one hand. Everyone in the courtroom stands up.

Gloggnigg intones the oath. "I swear by Almighty God that I have told the truth, the whole truth, and nothing but the truth, to the best of my knowledge and conscience, so help me God."

"I swear it, so help me God," Martin Landau replies.

8

Heinz is wearing his first suit with long trousers. His mother had got an old tailor to alter one of Paul Steinfeld's leftover suits: dark gray, with broad, padded shoulders. Heinz also wears a white shirt and a blue tie, although ties and buttoned-up shirts are a horror to him. He is tall and straight, with his mother's blonde hair, blue eyes, and slim face, his skin full of summer freckles. He carries himself well. His voice is loud, clear, eager, courteous, impassioned, and capable of sudden, wild hysteria.

There he is in front of the judge standing so straight, my boy, my little Heinz, to whom I gave birth, whom I brought up and took care of and must continue to take care of—there he is, standing up for himself before the judge, the Public Prosecutor, and Dr. Forster.

There he is saying, "No, your Honor, I never could stand my father. And he couldn't stand me."

And later, "I was never really close to my father. I always felt he did not really understand me, and did not like me. And I never understood him, either. He said so many things I did not understand, or if I did understand them they disgusted me."

"Disgusted you? How?"

"His talk was so cynical. So destructive. All he did was make jokes about everything, drag everything through the mud."

"What, for instance?"

"Our Fatherland, for instance, your Honor. And also concepts like Faith and Loyalty and Honor and Comradeship . . ."

Oh, Heinz, how well you and Paul got along in the early days when you were just a child, just a little boy, before the Nazis came! How you talked for hours! How you admired him! And now all that's left in you is hate. Terrible!

"Wonderful," Doctor Forster whispers to her. "The boy is making an impression on those two." He really is.

An amazing boy, Gloggnigg finds, who has a boy of his own. He could be my son's brother, the way he looks, talks, carries himself . . .

"No, your Honor, I did not know that my father, this *man*, I mean, I didn't know that he's Jewish. I didn't find out until I had to apply for my Aryan I.D. at school. My mother told me then. I was very unhappy, I really was. I hate the Jews. They're the most poisonous race on earth. I am convinced of that . . . In the Hitler Youth? I was one of the best and keenest, my corps commander can tell you that . . . The worst day of my life? Well, of course, the day I found out my father is a Jew. I understood then why we never got along with each other ..."

Keep on like that, Heinz, keep on ...

"Mr. Landau? I *always* got on well with *him!* I could *talk* to him! He is a good German, a decent man, really ... The happiest day of my life? The day my mother told me Mr. Landau is my real father, not that other ... not the Jew."

Going through the Public Prosecutor's mind is the thought: no more hand-holding with the judge! He's got to get through on his own. I've got to behave correctly, strictly correctly all the time.

"So you hate your father, Mr. Steinfeld?"

"My *so-called* father! Yes, I do hate him, your Honor. More than anything else in this world, I hate *him!*"

That's the stuff, Heinz, very good, keep on like that. Oh, God!

"How I would feel if I heard he was dead? I *wouldn't feel a thing!* He's not my father, after all! Mr. Landau is my father!"

This Landau fellow is giving me such dirty looks, the Public Prosecutor thinks uneasily. He's plotting revenge. I'll have to do something right away.

"Your Honor, if I may allow myself the interjection ... we have all parties here before us. Paul Steinfeld only in the form of photographs, of course—but the photographs do exhibit, in my estimation, numerous unmistakable characteristics of the Jewish race. The young man here, your Honor, seems to me to be absolutely free of such characteristics. Absolutely! Under these circumstances, I would like to propose that we call upon experts in the fields of genetics and anthropology, and—"

"That sort of decision is for me to make, is it not, Counsel? I am in charge of this hearing."

The agony of being a lawyer in the Third Reich! If only they'd at least say exactly what they wanted, and which law one should support!

"I really did not wish to anticipate you, your Honor, but I do think I will submit the proposal ..." The Steinfeld woman is smiling at me now for the first time. Smile back, go on!

Why are those two smiling at each other? Does that shithead Kummer know something I don't, Gloggnigg is thinking? Does he already know what the tests will show? Then I'd be the one to get shafted if I keep shouting here. It's all a comedy of course, but the boy really does look Aryan, and if the blood-groups really turn out to be compatible, well . . .

"Mr. Steinfeld, please sit down."

"Yes, your Honor." The boy clicks his heels and marches up to the witness stand, looking at his mother solemnly on the way. She's thinking, 'Please,' the swine said! 'Please!' To our boy! 'Please sit down!' Paul, Paul, keep your fingers crossed now, Paul, my love!

9

". . . it was hell, your Honor, real hell, I swear it! Nothing but trouble, night and day, when he was at home—Mr. Steinfeld, I mean. Often he was away for weeks on end, even when he wasn't on a trip. He had other women, lots of other women, I swear!"

Agnes, wearing her best black dress, a bonnet over her hair, but without overcoat, which she has taken off, is in a state of tremendous excitement, and would like to just keep on talking.

"Why did you stay on in such a household, witness?"

"I stayed on for the sake of Madame, who's so kind and so good, and for Heinzi's sake, little Heinzi. They needed me, after all. They wouldn't have had anyone except me and the good Mr. Landau. If there hadn't been the two of us, goodness, I think Madame would have done away with herself, she was so down and so unhappy sometimes, I swear your Honor."

"Were you aware that there was an intimate relationship between Frau Steinfeld and Mr. Landau?"

"Yes, I can swear to that, too—"

"Please stop saying 'I can swear to that.' What's it supposed to mean? Answer my question!"

"I'm saying, I can swear to it—"

"Witness Peintinger!"

"Because Madame confessed it to me one day in her despair."

"When was that, witness?" "Right after the birth, when

392

Mr. Steinfeld began ranting and raving at her that it was not his boy and that something was going on between her and Mr. Landau. So that's it, gentlemen, I swear it to you, Madame told me so!"

I won't have this rabble leading me around by the nose, thinks Gloggnigg and rumbles: "You're at it with that swearing again, witness!"

"Yes, your Honor! Please excuse me, but I really want to—"

"Ah, ah! And why?"

"So that you will believe me, your Honor. It's important that you believe me! I'm telling you about all the fights and squabbles and how glad Madame was when the Third Reich came and Mr. Steinfeld had to flee the country. He always treated me like dirt. Workers and domestics, they were dirt to him, he had no social feelings at all, you understand, your Honor, Counsel? Jewish, typically Jewish, I swear!"

"Witness Peintinger!"

"Whereas Mr. Landau, so kind, so good ... a real gentleman. And always friendly! And the boy was always so fond of him, even as a small child. And Madame, so happy whenever Mr. Landau came, and he came a lot, the one bright spot in her unhappy married life, I swear—"

"Miss Peintinger, I—"

"You're going to let me swear to it, right?"

"Wrong," said Groggnigg, slowly and deliberately.

"*What?*"

"I'm not going to have you swear to it."

"Why did she have to overdo it like that?" Forster whispers into Valerie's ear. "What's the matter with her?"

Valerie replies in a whisper, "The priest, you know ..."

Forster nods his head.

"Well, yes, and now she wants to *absolutely!*"

"Unfortunate. Very unfortunate. And the Lippowski woman next ... Don't Madame, keep calm! Everything will be all right. I can see that Kummer is getting cold feet already. He'll submit his proposals all right, and we'll be a giant step forward."

Meanwhile Agnes and Judge Gloggnigg have been talking together, both of them heatedly.

"But I don't understand why you don't want to swear me in, your Honor. It's the only way you can be sure I'm really telling the truth! And you must know the truth, right?"

"Yes, I must know the truth. But I'm not going to get any

nearer to it by swearing *you* in. You'd be perfectly capable of swearing to perjury!"

"Perjury? *Never!* Why should I—"

"To help Madame, whom you love so much, and little Heinzi, dear little Heinzi." The flaming anger inside Gloggnigg flares up, getting the better of his caution. "The whole show is a fix, planned and agreed-on beforehand. You're all play-acting!"

"Your Honor, I won't stand for that! I, as a Party Member—" Martin Landau has sprung to his feet.

Gloggnigg gestures him to sit down. "I don't mean you."

"Then whom do you mean, your Honor?" This time it's Forster who is on his feet.

"You know exactly whom I mean, Counsel! Don't go too far! I'm warning you! It's well-known all over Vienna that you of all people should avoid dishonest suits such as this one like the plague!"

"Your Honor!" Forster shouts back in reply, "that is an incredible statement! I will complain to the President!"

"Complain, I don't care. You won't get far. By all that's holy, I'm going to see to it—"

10

Everyone is wearing their Sunday best, including the fat Hermine Lippowski, now standing before the Judge, her straggly hair unkempt, her wrinkled cheeks clumsily powdered and too heavily rouged, dark circles under her eyes, bent, breathing stertorously, a wreck, not yet sixty, but looking older than seventy.

Hermine Lippowski has not looked at anyone when she came into the room, and now she looks only at Judge Gloggnigg, only at him, and not even always at him. Her breath comes in wheezes. The room has suddenly gone quiet. Valerie and Forster and Martin Landau are burning her back with their eyes, because this one witness is going to bring everything tumbling down that's already been built up, the witch, the damned witch!

"Frau Lippowski, Mr. and Mrs. Steinfeld lived in your house, did they not?" the Judge begins.

"Yes, they did," says the black monster.

"And what were the dates of their residence?"

"From November 1923 until October 1928."

"You remember your tenants well?"

"I remember them very well, yes." Valerie's fists are clenched once more, her lips drained of blood, Forster watches her anxiously.

"I remember both of them, and the baby that came, and Miss Peintinger . . . I remember them all. It's a long time ago . . . so, here we meet again." She pauses to gasp for breath. "I am happy if I can perhaps still help."

Valerie shudders and looks at Forster, who blinks rapidly. Easy now, easy.

"Help? How do you mean that, witness? What do you mean, help? Help whom?"

"Poor Frau Steinfeld," the monster said, without moving her head, her hair sticking out every which way, her breath rasping. "It's about her husband, isn't it?"

"Yes. And her son, too."

The Lippowski woman nods grimly. "Her son, too. What Frau Steinfeld had to go through because of Heinzi! It'll be good for him to listen to what I have to say about his father, miserable, rotten scum."

After that the room goes quiet again, so quiet that Lippowski's panting is clearly audible.

"Miserable, rotten scum?" Judge Gloggnigg says questioningly.

"You heard me right, your Honor," wheezed the fat old woman. "He was a crooked, slick bum. All he did for his wife was torture her and put her on the rack. You listen, Heinzi! Miss Peintinger has probably said it already, and I expect you've known it yourself for some time now, Paul Steinfeld wasn't your real father. Mr. Landau's your real father, you do know that, don't you?"

"Yes," Heinz replies.

The gavel sounds so loud that everyone shudders again. "Address the bench, witness! Not his real father? Mr. Landau is his real father? How do you know that?"

"Poor Frau Steinfeld told me once when she was feeling really down and desperate, when Heinzi was still very small and her husband was going around with other women all the time. And he was always shouting at her, nothing she ever did was right for him, he cursed her all the time. I could hear it through the ceiling, it came right down into my apartment below, the man's yelling and screaming and this poor woman's crying."

She looks grotesque, the old woman, her skin won't take the powder, she needs sleep and care, but Valerie, Forster, Agnes, and Martin Landau are having trouble keeping their seats, they feel like rushing forward and throwing their arms around the old crone, this woman Hermine Lippowski, as she tells her story to Judge Gloggnigg, whose brow furrows doubtfully while she describes to him the kind of devil Paul Israel Steinfeld was and how *she* really was responsible for bringing Valerie Steinfeld and Martin Landau together, properly as it were, by dropping hints here and there, keeping both eyes closed on the occasions he came when Paul Steinfeld was away, especially in the summer of 1925 when Martin Landau must have got Valerie Steinfeld pregnant, her husband was absent for months with just two or three brief visits in between.

"Witness Lippowski, are you willing to swear on oath to what you have just said?"

"Of course, your Honor."

Everyone stands up while Gloggnigg runs through the standard phrases of the oath, and Hermine Lippowski, who just a few months before had screamed in Valerie's face that she wouldn't lift a finger to help her, repeats the Judge's concluding words: *"I swear, so help me God!"*

Afterwards, dismissed, she seats herself at the extreme other end of the witness bench, as far as possible from the others. With her hands hanging, she sits there slumped over, staring at the floor with a tragic expression on her face. The witnesses next to her, Forster, Valerie, look at her furtively, shaken.

What has happened to the woman? *What?*

Judge Gloggnigg, struggling with a sudden attack of heartburn, is rummaging among the heap of papers on his desk.

"Incomplete ... the ancestral tables are still absolutely incomplete," he mumbles.

"We have not yet received all the documents, your Honor," says Forster, getting to his feet. "We will hand them in as soon as they are in our hands."

"If we still need them then," growls Gloggnigg.

There is a knock at the door.

396

"Come in," the Judge calls angrily. This affair is not going at all to his liking. Not at all ...

The door opens. And there, in a spring coat with a fur collar, a broad brimmed hat on her head, dark eyes, narrow lips, a handkerchief pressed to her swollen right cheek, is Ottilie Landau.

"Tilly!" her brother calls, jumping up.

"Sit down," she says. Then, loudly and a little indistinctly to Gloggnigg, "I am Frau Landau. I received a summons to appear at this paternity suit. A clerk outside told me not to wait but to make my presence known at once."

The Public Prosecutor Kummer's eyes are almost popping out of his head.

Valerie stares at Tilly. Everybody is staring at Tilly except for Hermine Lippowski, who is no longer taking the slightest notice of what's going on around her.

"But you sent us a medical certificate that you couldn't come," says Gloggnigg, his arrogance visibly shaken. "You're sick. You weren't supposed to be able to come."

"It was not easy, your Honor," Tilly replies. "I still had very bad pains this morning. But I took some aspirin and it got a little better. I said to myself that I simply had to come." She looks at her brother, who shudders. "The occasion is simply *too* important, I *must* give my testimony."

"Damn and blast!" Forster whispers.

Valerie looks at Tilly, her eyes wide with fear. It's the end, she's thinking. Tilly's a fanatic. She's going to tell the truth, and swear to it too ...

11

"And that is really the truth, Frau Landau?" Judge Gloggnigg asks.

"I can't change a thing, your Honor, that's how it was." Tilly is standing straight up in front of the judge's table, her handkerchief still pressed to her cheek.

"Your brother ..."

"Confessed *everything* to me. Correct."

"When? Tell me again!"

"In the early fall of 1925, after it was established beyond doubt that Frau Steinfeld was pregnant. He came to me and told me he was her lover and had been for some time, and now he was the father of her unborn child."

"And you, what did you say?" Gloggnigg is furious.

"I was horrified!" Tilly Landau retorts. "For one thing—I have somewhat old-fashioned moral principles. And I never could stand Valerie Steinfeld."

"But you've come here nevertheless, and even though you're sick, to testify in her behalf?"

"Not in *her* behalf, your Honor! In my *brother's!* I don't want you to think he's a liar. He is not. *He is incapable of lying.*"

"Frau Landau, are you prepared to swear on oath to the truth of your testimony? All of it?"

"Of course, your Honor. I will swear to every word."

12

"... in consideration of the facts and the testimony of the witnesses named in the foregoing, together with the express request of the Public Prosecutor Dr. Hubert Kummer, the Court will admit as evidence—are you getting it all down, miss?" Gloggnigg asks, having rattled out the dictation in an irritated voice at breakneck speed.

"—will admit as evidence," from the bored, dull-witted female at the narrow end of the table—Herta Bohnen the stenographer—scratching the back of her neck with one hand.

"—comma, as requested also by Counsel for the Plaintiff, Dr. Otto Forster ..." I can't just ignore all that testimony, Gloggnigg is thinking; if I do I'll be in trouble with the President,

"... an anthropological, genetic examination, to establish the racial classification, and whether and how far the possibility can be excluded that the plaintiff Heinz Steinfeld was fathered by Paul Israel Steinfeld ..."

Valerie is looking at Forster, who smiles and nods and tugs at his ear.

". . . and secondly: a blood test, to establish whether the fathering of the plaintiff by Martin Landau can be *excluded beyond doubt* as a possibility—do you have that, miss?"

". . . excluded beyond doubt as a possibility," the bored stenographer repeats.

"Period. New paragraph." (I can't do a thing in the face of so much sworn testimony. I'll have to be careful. I'm up for promotion. My reputation is good in Berlin. Keep it correct now. I'll nominate a really sharp expert. That'll settle their hash. And nobody can blame me.)

"As the expert witness for the first point, the Court appoints SS Lieutenant Dr. Kratochwil, Lecturer at the Anthropological Institute of the University of Vienna." (He's the *sharpest* of the lot! They're in for a shock!)

"As the expert witness for the second point the Court appoints Professor Dr. Schmalenacker, Physician and Chairman of the Institute for Forensic Medicine at the University of Vienna."

13

The sun was bright. People hurried past the little group just emerging from the Courthouse. Trams clanked along the Museumstrasse with bells ringing, cyclists rode by, army vehicles passed.

"I'm so happy! So happy! That really went well, didn't it, Mommy?" Heinz Steinfeld pulled off his tie and opened his collar: they had been torturing him long enough. "Only the tests now, and then—"

"Not here," Forster broke in. "Come with me." He hurried in the direction of a small park near the Courthouse. Valerie and Martin Landau found themselves suddenly alone with Hermine Lippowski, in her all-black outfit.

"I thank you from the bottom of my heart," Valerie said.

"And so do I," Landau said, still tensed from the hearing.

"No need for you to thank me," Frau Lippowski replied,

399

wheezing, words and breath coming with difficulty in spurts. "I got a piece of news. Yesterday. Through some friends. From the concentration-camp at Sachsenhausen."

"Good God! About your husband?" Valerie asked.

"Yes, about my husband," the flabby woman replied, looking at Valerie through swollen eyes. "He's dead. They murdered him, the beasts. My husband. The one man in the world I ever loved. Even after he left me . . . today still . . . I still love him, still! It all became clear to me yesterday in a flash. That's why I committed perjury under oath for you and your husband and your son, Frau Steinfeld. Your good fortune came from my bad fortune." And Hermine Lippowski nodded once again, briefly and desolately, then shuffled away, without a word of farewell, without turning her head, completely immersed in her own deep grief.

Agnes said softly, "God holds his hand over all good people who are in trouble and need him, my priest told me that. And perhaps I will still be allowed to take the oath, the good attorney says. Come on now, Heinzi, your Mommy and your father must get back to the shop."

Valerie looked up at the clock on the corner. Anxiously she called: "Martin, we have to be quick! It's twenty to one!"

"Well, and so? We're closed until—oh, of course," he said as he remembered. The BBC, of course, she wanted to listen to the BBC again at one o'clock!

When he got back to the shop a quarter of an hour later he found Valerie under the blanket, her head on the desk top, fast asleep. The radio was on. A Czech announcer was reading the news. Landau switched the radio off quickly and turned the tuner to a local station, then bedded Valerie down on the old sofa and covered her up carefully.

That was how Heinz had fallen asleep once, on the night it all began. Martin Landau looked at Valerie Steinfeld. A blissful smile lit up her face . . .

14

"... at that moment it was the face of a very young girl, Mr. Landau told me, I remember now," said the ageing attorney Dr. Otto Forster, talking to Manuel on the top floor of his villa in the Sternwartestrasse. He placed the papers he had been leafing through on the table.

"Martin Landau had the courage to tell you he let his assistant listen to the BBC in your shop?"

"Courage! Once, after we'd come to know each other very well, he was present when Valerie told me she listened to the BBC. That was when he described how he had found her on the day of the first hearing."

He looked at the paper and laughed. "Everything was well organized at the courts in those days!"

Manuel read a listing at the end of the typed minutes.

Court Adjourned	: 12:30 P.M.
Length of Session	: 5 Half-Hours
Fee	: 21.40 Reichsmark
Two Copies of Minutes	: 4.80 Reichsmark (2.40 RM each)
Total	: 26.20 Reichsmark

"The minutes typed by Herta Bohnen, Gloggnigg's stenographer," Forster said. "I see her sometimes. She has three grown-up children now. Wife of a President of the Senate."

"No!"

"I'm telling you! Married in August 1945 to a very nice, respectable judge."

"Doctor Forster, even though the first hearing went so well, your own thoughts were preoccupied with the seriousness of the situation. Can you say why exactly?"

"Because I knew there was no turning back. A paradoxical reaction. Everything was moving. But if anything went wrong, there was no predicting the consequences—for any of us."

"And how did the tests go?"

"That's precisely what I don't know any more. They must have been held in May sometime. All I remember is that there was a new judge at the next hearing. It wasn't Gloggnigg any more."

"Why not Gloggnigg?"

"He was promoted soon after the first hearing and transferred to Berlin. Rumor has it that he really terrorized everyone there."

"Do you know anything about his career after that?"

"Disappeared at the end of the war. Dead perhaps. Or perhaps he went underground. I never heard from him again."

Manuel quickly pulled his father's photograph from his briefcase and placed it in front of Forster. It was the same picture he had shown to Nora Hill and Martin Landau. They had declared that they had never met any man resembling Manuel's father as he appeared in the photograph, but Manuel continued to show it, and was determined to miss no opportunity to do so.

"That's your father?" Forster asked.

"Yes. Does the picture remind you of anyone you knew during the war here? That sadist Gloggnigg, for instance?"

Forster was looking at the photo carefully.

"Why are you silent?"

"It's enough to drive you crazy," the attorney murmured. "I've seen this face somewhere before . . ."

"*What?*"

"But it's not Gloggnigg, I'm sure of that."

"Who does my father remind you of, then?"

Forster thought for a long time. Then he handed the photograph back, shaking his head. "I'm sorry, I don't know."

"But it does remind you of someone you knew?"

"Yes," said Forster. "Yes, I do, that's for sure."

"Of whom, Doctor Forster? Of whom? Please try to remember!"

"For the life of me," Forster said, "I just can't remember."

15

WARSAW + 22 + 1 + 2030 HOURS ++ IRENE
WALDEGG GENTZGASSE 50A + VIENNA 18 + AUS-
TRIA ++ SINCERE THANKS FOR PROMPT HELP AND
TELEGRAM ++ VERY HAPPY TO BE ALLOWED TO LIVE
WITH YOU + ARRIVING ON CHOPINEXPRESS 27TH JAN-
UARY + GREETINGS DANIEL STEINFELD +++

16

Bianca Barry was wearing a beige, tailored mink coat, tan boots, and a scarf around her hair. She was standing at the curb in front of the main entrance to the Civic Cemetery. It was not snowing that afternoon, but there were dark clouds covering the sky, and an icy east wind was blowing.

"There she is," said Irene. She sat next to Manuel, who was driving the blue Mercedes. Irene was also wearing boots, a headscarf, and her Persian lamb coat.

"We're on time," said Manuel. It was exactly three o'clock on the afternoon of Thursday, January 23. Manuel stepped gently on the brake and let the car roll to a stop in front of the painter's wife. She opened the rear door quickly and moved next to Irene.

"Good afternoon," Bianca Barry said hurriedly. "Keep driving, please."

"Where to?"

"Straight ahead," Bianca offered her hand to Irene, who had half-turned toward her. "You were probably very surprised when I picked this spot for our meeting, but the Civic Cemetery is directly on the way."

"To where?" Manuel asked.

"To . . . I want to show you something . . . It's a long way still."

The man next to the driver of the gray Peugeot that followed Manuel's Mercedes at some distance spoke Russian into a hand microphone. "Calling Lesskov . . . Calling Lesskov . . . this is Tolstoi . . ."

"We read you, Tolstoi," a voice said from a speaker beneath the dashboard. Today the Soviets were guarding Manuel. "What's up?"

"They're driving toward the airport."

"Follow them, Tolstoi, wherever they go. If there are any incidents, alert us at once and intercede."

"Understood, Lesskov. Over."

In Manuel's car Bianca Barry had lit a cigarette. She smoked nervously.

"Now calm down," Irene said, "Your husband is not in Vienna!"

"You've no idea how jealous he is. He might even have hired someone to follow me."

"Nonsense!"

"Yes, I know, it's nonsense. I was very careful. Nobody followed me. This whole story has got me so worked up. And then you came along, and I had to invent a bunch of lies for you. Believe me, I've been longing for the day I could see you again and tell you the truth about Heinz and myself."

Manuel had driven through the center of the town of Schwechat, which was surrounded by industrial plants, and as he came onto a new, straight highway he increased his speed. The landscape was flat. Suddenly there was a thunderous roar. Manuel glanced up quickly. An aircraft was flying over the road, huge and very low, just a few seconds before touchdown.

"There's the airport," Bianca said. Manuel saw large buildings, hangars, and parked aircraft all under snow.

"Still further?" Manuel asked.

"Yes," Bianca replied. She had become more relaxed. "What I want to show you is still quite some distance away. It's a place that—oh, it sounds so pathetic and ridiculous to talk like this—but for me it's an unforgettable place. You are the first people I've ever told what happened there. You've heard about the lawsuit that was held in those days. Now you're going to find out what Heinz and I did together at that

404

time, what . . . what happened in that place. But I'll have to
tell the story in proper order. The crucial thing didn't happen
until summer 1943. Before that, at the end of 1942 and in
winter 1943, at the start of the year, everything was still fine,
just wonderful . . ."

17

"I wish you a very happy Christmas, Heinz."

"And I wish you the same, Bianca."

"And let's hope everything goes well!"

"Of course everything will go well. We'll celebrate the next
Christmases properly. You can come to my place, or I'll
come to your family. Everything will be over by then, the
lawsuit finished, I'll be an Aryan, and your father won't be
angry with me any more!"

These words were whispered, yes, whispered, mouth to
mouth, at around 7:15 P.M. on December 20, 1942. Bianca
and Heinz were standing close together under the arcades of
the ancient Church of the Minorites. Bianca and Heinz had
been meeting there three times a week for more than a
month, always at the same time. It was a meeting-place
where they could be in almost total darkness, and without
fear of being disturbed by anyone.

Two coincidences had helped them.

Heinz Steinfeld had been transferred from the Sixth to the
Ninth and First Districts to do his reel-running. For his em-
ployers the transfer had been purely an exchange measure,
but for Heinz it meant happiness! Bianca had been en-
rolled in a training-course for Group Leaders by the Head
Girl of her section of the League of German Girls. It took
place in a building near the church of the Minorites. The few
minutes that Heinz and Bianca managed to steal for themselves under the arcades of that church in darkness, cold, and
often in rain, represented the most precious and beautiful of
their daily lives. They whispered oaths of loyalty and love in
each other's ear, embraced, kissed, and stroked each other.

"I've brought a present for you," Heinz whispered and
handed Bianca a small package.

405

"And I've brought one for you," she replied, giving him a slightly larger package. "Don't open it now, wait till later!"

"The lawsuit's been filed already," Heinz pronounced happily.

"And you think . . ."

"What, then? Don't you? *Of course* everything will go well. I'm just furious that my mother didn't start the suit earlier."

"It's hard for your mother, Heinz."

"Yes, I know. I don't say anything to her. Oh, Bianca, how wonderful that we can see each other again! Every night I look at your photo, the one you gave me, before I go to sleep."

"I do the same, Heinz, with your photo. I keep it well hidden away, always."

"Me too, of course."

"When I'm not at home I carry it around with me."

"That's taking a big risk! If it should fall out of your pocket . . ."

"It won't fall out of my pocket. Do you want to know where I keep it?"

"Yes! yes . . ." He pressed himself closer to her, felt her hot breath on his cheek as she spoke.

"Put your hand in my blouse . . . right inside my bra, the left one . . . Yes . . . there . . . yes . . . oh, Heinz!"

The Church of the Minorites had been partially destroyed over the course of the centuries. A corner of the roof was missing and so was the uppermost part of the tower, which had been shot off during a siege by the Turks. Countless lovers had etched their initials into the stone of the walls beneath the arcade. Heinz had done the same. At about eye level, there was a primitively carved heart, inside it the initials B.H. and H.S., beneath them the year 1941, followed by a horizontal arrow pointing to the mathematical sign for infinity, a horizontal figure eight.

Heinz stroked Bianca's nipples. She moaned softly, her hands running through his short blond hair.

"No, Heinz, don't do that! Please, don't . . . yes, yes . . . do it!"

"I can't stand it much longer. Bianca, I want—"

"Do you think I don't? When you touch me I go half-crazy!"

"When, Bianca, when?"

"The winter will pass . . . When it's spring again, and warm . . ."

406

"Yes, yes . . ."

"Then, Heinz, then . . ."

"I have to go."

"So do I."

"We won't see each other again before Christmas Eve. You don't have school any more."

"No, but on the twenty-eighth again."

"I'll be here as usual. And Bianca, on Christmas Eve, at this time, I'll go out of the house and look up at the sky. You do that too, please. Perhaps it will be a clear night, and there'll be stars."

"Yes, Heinz. Then we'll see the same stars and think of each other."

"And if there are clouds, we'll see the same clouds."

"Dear sky, dear clouds, dear stars, dear Heinz!" They embraced and kissed again, for a long time. Then Bianca hurried off, and Heinz turned his heavily loaded bike and started off in the opposite direction through the arcades. Now he really had to dash! He whizzed like a racing cyclist through the dark streets to the movie theater in the Ninth District. He made it in time, as always. The projectionist took the reels from him in his little room.

"Just wait a few minutes and I'll give you the next two reels. One of them isn't quite run out." The voices of the film actors resounded from out of the movie house. The left projector was humming, and the man spooled a new reel into the right-hand machine. Heinz sat down on a small bench and opened the package Bianca had given him. There was a gray, thick woollen scarf with fringes, a pair of thick, gray woollen gloves, a small twig from a pine tree, and an envelope. Heinz tore it open, took out the letter, and read: "My darling. You are always working outdoors at night, and it's so cold then. That is why I chose these gifts for you. I knitted them myself—secretly, at home, before going to sleep. The scarf was easy, but the glove fingers weren't! All my love is in them. Happy Christmas, my beloved Heinz, your faithful Bianca." Underneath was the postscript: "P.S.: I long for you."

At that same moment, Bianca Heizler sat, with three dozen other girls, in a large room in the building where the League for German Girls had its meetings. At the front of the room there was a swastika flag and a plaster bust of Hitler. A somewhat older girl stood there, on a small platform. She was reciting a poem from a leather-bound book. Her voice throbbed with enthusiasm.

> *"My Fuehrer, see, we knew about the hours untold*
> *In which your arms our burden's weight uphold,*
> *In which, with loving father's hands, you feel*
> *Our wounds, the wounds you've come to heal . . ."*

Bianca turned sideways. Slowly, carefully, she opened the small package Heinz had given her. It contained a box. Bianca pried off the lid and found, embedded in yellow cotton batting, a silver ring with an enamel square like a flat stone. It shimmered with a fantastic design in red, green, white, yellow, black and purple.

There was a small card in the box. Bending over, Bianca read what Heinz had written, while the girl on the platform went on chanting the hymn to the Fuehrer:

> *"That's why our love for you is so profound—*
> *Oh, Fuehrer— let our gratitude abound!"*

"My darling Bianca! We first saw this ring a few months ago in a shop, and you liked it so much. That's why I put a deposit on it right then, and now I've got it all paid off at last . . ."

I wonder where he got the money, Bianca was thinking. Oh, well, probably he saved it from his miserable pay.

> *"Our Faith in you is true, and without restraint . . ."*

bawled the Leader of the League of German Girls. ". . . save the ring, hide it, I know you can't wear it now except perhaps when you come to meet me. But just be patient a little while longer, and you will be able to wear it always, if you love me as you are loved by your Heinz."

> *". . . The work of our hands and minds is based on*
> *gratitude to you."*

the Leader of Girls proclaimed, concluding her recitation.

With a smile, Bianca Heizler pushed the ring onto a finger of her left hand . . .

". . . and I'm still wearing it, look, here it is," Bianca Barry said, twenty-seven years later, holding up her left hand. Manuel took his eyes briefly from the road in order to take a quick look. Irene gazed at the ring in a more leisurely manner. It was still snowing.

Manuel noticed that the road was narrowing. They were coming to a small village. A sign gave its name as Fischamend. They crossed a bridge over a frozen stream. Immediately beyond was a gate leading to a high tower with battlements.

"We're almost there," Bianca said. "Stop over there."

They were in a large square, with small houses on all sides. Manuel swung to the right and stopped the car.

"Let's get out," said Bianca.

They stepped out. The air was very clear and cuttingly cold. As Manuel locked the door on his side, a grey Peugeot containing two men came through the gate and drove past them, then stopped some distance away. Nobody got out. A trap? Manuel thought briefly. Or was it one of the cars that followed him all the time?

"This is a very old place," Bianca said. "The tower over there dates back to the eleventh century."

She was staring at a certain house. Its ground floor was a grocery store.

"Frau Barry!"

She turned her gaze away from the shop with reluctance and pointed toward the north. "Up there is the railroad station. And behind the station is a paint factory—that was where Heinz was sent at the beginning of summer in 1943 to do war work, as a manual laborer."

"A manual *laborer*? But he knew a lot of chemistry!"

"Not organic chemistry. Or at least, not enough. He had to work here like the forced laborers, like the prisoners."

"*Here?*" Manuel stared at Bianca. "But it's—"

"A long way from the Gentzgasse, by God! Heinz had to

get up at five every morning and travel by tram, the city line, then the Hainburg line. The situation was critical at that time. Goebbels had declared total war. Women had to work in factories, too. Nobody could choose where to go."

"Is that the factory where Heinz . . ." Irene asked.

"Yes," said Bianca Barry. "The factory's been rebuilt. It was hit in a heavy bombing raid and was blown to smithereens. Over there"—she pointed with her hand—"is where Heinz was killed. But of course I didn't bring you all this way just to tell and show you that. Come with me. You will understand in a minute."

19

A landscape of meadows all white, white, white: ancient trees, willow trunks, underbrush. It was a frozen world, eerie and fascinating, with not a trace of wind.

They were walking side by side, Bianca in the middle. She was looking around her like someone gazing at a road that leads back into youth.

"They've cleared this road," Bianca said. "The fishermen used it to go to and from the river with their motorbikes. In those days the old men who lived here went on foot. I recognize everything again . . . every tree, every pond, every bush . . ."

Irene and Manuel looked at each other over Bianca's head. She didn't notice. She was sinking more and more into her memories.

"It was summer," Bianca said. "The beginning of June, 1943. Boiling hot. It was a Sunday, and Heinz was on air raid duty at the factory with a few others. It was routine work, everyone did it in turns. Vienna wasn't being bombed at that time. The men had nothing to do, so nobody cared if one of them played hooky for a while . . ."

We must be near water, Manuel was thinking. I can smell it.

"It was wonderful for Heinz and myself. We had been meeting in many new places: tramway underpasses, lonely parks, churches. And we always needed new excuses and new alibis. I had a girl-friend who helped me a lot. Inge was her name. Inge Pagel. She helped me in Vienna and here, too."

"How?" Irene asked.

"In previous summers I had often gone up the Danube to Klosterneuburg with Heinz," Bianca said. Then she turned to Manuel and explained, "That's north of Vienna. But it so happened that in June of '43 my father was away on a lecture tour, all through Austria. I was alone with my mother. I told her Inge and I would be going to Klosterneuburg together on that particular Sunday. Inge had a boy-friend, too, and she really did go to Klosterneuburg with him. I took the Hainburg line and came out here. My holidays were due to begin in a month! Then I would be able to meet Heinz here more often, much more often . . . He could see to it that he had air raid duty on Sundays, maybe even taking other workers' turns for them! We had it all worked out. But that particular Sunday, June 6, was the first time we met here. I arrived at about ten o'clock in the morning. Heinz did not pick me up at the station, but waited for me on this road—he had told me exactly how to get here. We wanted to make sure nobody saw us. Then we walked, holding hands. It was a beautiful day with not a cloud in the sky . . . and when we got to the river, there was a fisherman's boat, roped to a peg in the ground . . .

"My God," Bianca said, "Look, there's another boat . . ."

Manuel and the two women had walked through frozen bushes and were standing on the banks of the Danube, watching its gray, lethargic waters flow sluggishly past. Less than sixty feet away, directly opposite them, was a narrow island, overgrown with bushes and trees, completely white and covered with snow, blocking the view across to the other bank of the river.

"We took the boat and rowed across," Bianca said, her voice sounding breathless and her gray eyes darkening. "We didn't see a soul, not a soul . . . I was more aroused than ever in my life. And Heinz, too, he was just as aroused as I . . ."

20

The old boat slithered crunching a short way up onto the bank of the island. Heinz jumped out and helped Bianca climb out of the boat. She was carefully carrying a bag that held some picnic food for the day and her bathing suit. Bianca wore a sleeveless blue dress, Heinz short pants, sandals, and a white shirt. He was carrying his bathing trunks in his hand. He dragged the boat far up onto the sandy shore of the island. In the underbrush the grass and the leaves shone green, and the leaves on the ancient trees glistened silver. Bianca could now see the further shore with its meadows, woods, chimneys and factories, all a long way off, under the blazing sun of the day.

"Come on, let's go over there," Heinz said, leading the way through the sand to a spot where the grass grew tall. She followed him, her heart beating high in her throat.

"It's nice here, very soft . . . and no one can see us." He trod down a spot until it was flat, then straightened up. She was standing close to him, her eyes searching for his. He blushed.

"What's the matter? We're going to go swimming, aren't we?"

"Yes, of course. But . . ."

"But what?"

"You'll have to turn around while I undress."

"Yes," Heinz said. He turned around, unbuttoning his shirt as he did so, then pulled the shirt over his head. He slid out of his trousers, his underpants, his sandals.

Bianca undressed also. She could sense her hands trembling as she unhooked her bra, took off her panties and slipped off her shoes. Her heart was thumping away so hard, so *hard!* Impulsively she whirled around, and at the same instant Heinz turned around to her. They stood facing each other, both naked, the sun glinting off their bodies. Eyes aflame, they gazed at each other. Heinz let his look caress her whole body, her full breasts, then up and down, drinking in every detail. And Bianca looked at him, saw his erection and felt a shudder run along her spine.

"You're beautiful!" Heinz stammered. "So beautiful ..." He stretched out his arms and pulled her to him. She felt his body. Her knees gave way and she wrapped her arms around him.

"Bianca!"

"Heinz ..." She sank into the grass with him. She was on her back, with Heinz over her. She whispered, "I ... I'm afraid ... I've never ... it hurts, they say ..."

"It doesn't hurt!"

"How do you know? Have you already—"

"No, it's the first time for me, too, you know that. I only love you, there aren't any others."

"Then it will hurt. Heinz, please, Heinz!"

"Don't you want to?"

"Just as much as you."

"Then don't be afraid," he said, stroking her breasts. "Don't be afraid, Bianca, my love, my darling. I've been reading how to do it ... I know exactly ... if we're careful and do it slowly ... we have plenty of time ... we have all day ..." She saw him taking something out of a paper wrapping.

"What are you doing?"

"We have to take precautions, Bianca. I'll be careful, very careful. Take your hands away there. Relax, relax! I'm not going to hurt you, for sure."

She sighed, closed her eyes, and let herself sink back. He began to cover her whole body with kisses, her lips, eyelids, forehead, shoulders, arms, breasts, belly, then gently pushed her thighs apart and knelt down between them and kissed her there.

"Heinz, Heinz!"

"Take your time, and don't be afraid. I know what to do, it was all in the book." He went quiet and aroused her again, carefully and gently.

Suddenly Bianca opened her eyes wide. "Come, now!"

He slid on top of her. Bianca wriggled and moaned a little as he entered her, then immediately moaned again. He stopped, disconcerted.

"Does it hurt? Very much? Shall I—"

"No ... no ..." She pressed him closer to her. "It's done already. You did it wonderfully! It doesn't hurt any more. Slowly, do it slowly, slowly. Now it's wonderful, really wonderful ... Oh. yes, yes, yes ..." Bianca had her head turned to one side. Heinz lay with his head in the curve of her neck. She could see the deep-blue sky above and a few tall blades of grass, but nothing else. Then she felt something inside her beginning to twitch and throb, she felt as though she were floating, flying, as though her entire being were suddenly concentrated in one spot, more, more, and ever more. And then it came—she didn't know what was happening to her, she had never experienced anything like it, nothing so inexpressible. She wrapped her thighs around his hips, and pressed her arms against his back.

"Yes, Yes, like that, do it like that! Just like that!"

He did not answer, and his movements remained the same.

"Now ... now ... there ... there!" She screamed out loud. He crushed her lips with a kiss as she began to gush forth with a stream of orgasms that never seemed to end—another, and another. and another, and yet another. I could die now, thought Bianca, and still be the happiest person on this earth. How beautiful it is, how indescribably beautiful, and I was so nervous about it, so afraid. Oh Heinz, Heinz, my beloved Heinz ...

21

And so it began.

And it continued, with pauses while they lay still and gazed at each other, or ran down naked into the water.

They sat close to each other, her head on his, and looked over the waters of the river glittering in the sun. They kissed. They became aroused again, and sank down into the grass, and were in heavenly bliss, together.

Then they lay together, passions spent for the moment, smoking, talking softly ...

"I'll never forget this day even if I live to be a hundred years old."

"Nor will I, Bianca, nor will I ..."

"Nobody would have been as ..."

"Nobody loves you as much as I do ..." He bent over her.

"Everything is as we always wanted it. It won't be much longer now."

It was nine-thirty in the evening and quite dark when they finally put their clothes back on. The moon was shining, the stars sparkled, and the air was still warm. He helped her into her clothes, and she helped him, kissing and caressing each other as they did. Slowly they walked across the sandy soil of the island to the spot where they had moored the boat. They had their arms wrapped around each other. Suddenly Heinz noticed something.

"Shhh!" He put a finger to his lips, ducked down, then raced off. By the light of the moon Bianca could just make out a man kneeling by the boat, trying to push it into the water. He did not succeed, for Heinz hurled himself at him and knocked him to the ground.

Bianca ran up. Heinz! Heinz! If anything happened to Heinz . . .

But nothing happened to Heinz. The man he had swept to the ground was lying on his back, a small, thin man with a bony face and the fear of death in his eyes. His hair was short, his cheeks so caved-in that the cheekbones stood out sharply. His miserable face was pale and unshaven, and the greenish-gray rags he wore were filthy. Yes, rags—a pair of trousers, a jacket, a shirt without a collar, and boots with soles full of holes. The man had put a shabby overcoat and a grimy provisions' bag into the boat.

Heinz knelt down on top of him. The man seemed to know only a few words of German: "Don't do it! Please . . . I good, Sir. Please leave me . . . please leave me alone . . ." He sounded desperate.

"Heinz, who is it?" Bianca had caught up.

"Lady, help me . . . I good. Poor . . . weak. Man hurting me." Heinz was gripping the man's arm. "Aaaah! No . . . no no . . ." The man rolled over on his back, his jacket slipping up. The letters SU were painted on his back in oil colors.

"A prisoner-of-war!" said Bianca, pressing her hand to her breast.

"A Russian!"

"Yes." His voice, so wheedling a moment ago, was cold now. "Escaped. Bust out. Hid away here."

"Oh God, here, on the island . . ."

"Slept . . ." The half-starved man was panting, his words indistinct. Heinz held his arm in an iron grip.

"All day in the bushes . . ."

"Don't lie, you swine!"

Bianca shuddered. She seemed to be hearing a different person, not Heinz.

"Slept, walk at night . . . always only at night, understand . . . day too dangerous . . ." The man groaned. "Foot . . ."

"What's wrong with your foot?" Heinz saw he had a board in his boot, fastened to the leg with a cloth.

"Not good, sick. Tread on stone, fall . . ."

"Sprained or bruised," Heinz said. "You escaped, right?"

"Yes . . . yes . . . please, Sir . . ."

"Where from?"

"Steyr, big camp there . . . factory."

"How long have you been walking?"

"Weeks . . . two weeks . . . friends dead . . . police, understand? Only not me."

Heinz did not answer. Quickly he searched the pockets of the man on the ground.

"No weapons," he said, after looking into the provisions' bag also. He released the Russian, who rolled over and sat up. His eyes were burning with a frantic fire: Fear! Fear! Fear!

"How did you get onto the island?" Heinz asked. His voice, Bianca thought again, his voice! It's quite different, he is completely different, it's a stranger kneeling there. Heinz, my lover, what has happened?

"I swim."

"With that foot? Don't lie!"

"No lie! With the foot, yes! Hide, understand?"

"And now that it's night and dark, you wanted to take the boat and get away! Across to the north bank, and on from there. Across the border. Right? The Czechs would understand you, and hide you . . ."

"No, no, I—"

Heinz hit the Russian across the face.

"Heinz!" Bianca called out, horrified.

"Be quiet," he hissed back.

"I home, wife, children . . . three children . . . don't know if they're dead. War not good . . ." The Russian got to his feet with a sudden movement, then dropped to his knees before Bianca and embraced her legs. He looked up at her, tears streaming down his lined face.

"Please, woman, tell man . . . let me go . . ."

Bianca tried to free herself, but the man was holding her in an iron grip. He was trembling, she could feel it.

"So far already, and now, good woman ... good man ... you let me go, yes?"

"Yes," Bianca said, her voice choking.

"Thank you ... thank you ... *spassiba*—" A flood of words in Russian rushed out. The prisoner of war kissed Bianca's hands. He was still kneeling at her feet, his injured leg badly twisted.

"Let go!" Heinz dragged the Russian off Bianca, and the man fell over sideways into the sandy soil. He raised his arm over his face to protect himself. Heinz jumped to his feet. "Come, Bianca!"

"What will happen to him?"

"You'll soon see." He pushed the boat into the water. The Russian began praying aloud in his own language, his hands clasped.

"Climb in," Heinz shouted to Bianca.

"But what about the man?"

"He stays here!"

"How is he going to get off the island?"

"He won't!"

"What?"

"Come on, come on, get in!" Heinz dragged Bianca into the boat. Then he pushed the Russian back with a curse, for the man had approached him on his knees. The Russian fell down, his strength gone.

"You can see, he doesn't have any strength left. He'll never be able to swim back to shore, and even if he does manage it, he won't get far."

"We've got his overcoat, and his provisions' bag!" Bianca shouted.

"Of course. We need them to take with us!"

"Take with us where?"

"To the police station," said Heinz, rowing resolutely. His voice sounded choppy. "Don't look at me like that, Bianca! I'm only doing my duty!"

The oars were cleaving the water deeply. Bianca looked back. The Russian was still standing on the island. With a gesture of absolute despair he let himself sink slowly to the ground as though in slow motion, then lay on the white sand, a helpless, defenseless, miserable heap of human flesh.

22

The path from the riverbank to the village of Fischamend looked unreal and fantastic in the moonlight. It shone. It gleamed. The still-water ponds sparkled. Frogs croaked. The branches, twigs and leaves of the ancient willows, the linden trees, the chestnuts, and the white trunks of the birch trees, all were agleam.

Heinz was walking quickly. He carried the Russian's torn overcoat provisions' bag. The overcoat had the SU sign painted on it too. Bianca had trouble keeping up with Heinz' pace.

"You won't do it, Heinz—"

"Of course I will do it!"

"Please don't! The man is wounded, starving—"

"We're at war with Russia! It's a life-and-death war! Have you forgotten that?"

"But you . . . but you . . ."

"What do you mean, 'but you?' " He stopped and looked at her so angrily that she began to tremble.

" 'But you half-Jew—that's what you were going to say, weren't you? 'You half-Jew, it's not up to you?' That's what you wanted to say, is it not?"

"No, Heinz, no! Dear, good Heinz, I never wanted to say that, never!" she shouted, feeling desperate.

"No? Never?" He looked her up and down, his lips tight shut. Was this the same man in whose arms she had lain for hours, the first man in her whole life?

"Then it's all right. Because I'm not a half-Jew! I'm an Aryan like you—not a sub-human like him over there!" He pointed with his chin to where they had just come from, then said, in a suddenly quiet, penetrating, trembling voice, "And I am going to go the road that I must take!"

"What road is that?"

"The *straight one!* My mother has ruined her life by not going the straight road, but that won't happen to me! Not to

418

me, Bianca! There is only one honorable, right road now—to the police station!" And with that he hurried on.

She ran after him.

The walk was a mile-and-a-half. And for a mile-and-a-half Bianca begged and implored Heinz to change his mind. But after a while he did not even answer her. Upright, with his head thrown back, he marched toward Fischamend.

The first houses. The main street. The end of the meadow path.

Heinz turned in the direction of the market-place. Bianca was still hurrying at his side, in a last effort to stop him.

"If you love me, don't do it. The poor soul's done-for if they catch him, and they will catch him! He can't get anywhere without a boat, with his foot! Heinz! Heinz, listen to me! They'll put him against the wall, they'll shoot him!"

"Stop that crap!"

"What kind of talk is that? Of course they'll kill him!"

"And what if they do? What are his people doing to our soldiers?"

The main street was deserted, not a soul in sight. They reached the market-place. It was empty and dark. Just one blue lamp was burning, above the entrance to a shop with boarded-up windows.

That was the building in which the police station was located. Heinz knew that, and had told Bianca.

"Heinz!" Bianca had taken his arm once more. "Don't do it!"

He looked at her, his eyes and his mouth were mere slits. "I'm going to! And nobody's going to stop me! Not even you! Nobody! I am only doing what every good German must do."

"If you go in there, Heinz, if you go in——" Bianca had to break off, panting for breath.

"Yes? Yes? What then?"

"Then I can't love you any more!" She called out in a paroxysm of despair. It was the worst threat that came into her mind. I don't really mean it, she thought desperately. But perhaps he will believe me, perhaps . . . he's looking at me . . . differently from before. He's opening his mouth, trying to say something, no words are coming out. He's swallowing. Heinz managed to croak out, his voice catching, his face twitching, "All right. Then you must make your choice."

"What? Choice between what?"

"You must choose between the Russian and me."

"I don't understand."

"It's simple." Heinz was now standing very straight and tall. "Either I go in there and report the Russian, and then everything stays the same between us, forever. Or . . ."

"Or?"

"Or the Russian is more important to you. Fine. Then I will not go in. Then I have not seen him."

"Heinz! Heinz!"

"But then I will leave you. Now, this instant. I will go back to the factory. And it's all over between us . . ."

"Heinz! Have you gone mad?"

"Not in the least. Then it's over between us. If you demand *that* of me—fine, I will do it. But I cannot continue to love you. I cannot live with the thought of you any more. I do not want to have anything to do with you anymore."

They looked at each other, almost touching, they were so close.

"Well?"

Almost inaudibly Bianca whispered, *"Don't go in, Heinz."*

Without a word he handed her the old, dirty overcoat and the provisions' bag belonging to the Russian. Without a word he wheeled round and walked across the square towards his factory.

"Heinz!" she called out softly, overwhelmed. "Heinz! Heinz, please!"

She stood alone now on the hard soil in front of the house with the blue lamp; still following Heinz with her gaze. He was disappearing into the darkness. Only his footsteps could still be heard, becoming fainter, and fainter, and fainter . . .

23

"That was the last time I ever saw Heinz in my life," Bianca Barry said twenty-six years later, standing on the very same spot in the market-place of Fischamend. "I never saw him again, never again . . ." Manuel and Irene, who were standing next to her, kept silent.

Finally Bianca looked at them once more. "That's where

the police station was, over there," she said. "Where that grocery store is today. I used to come here often after the war. I always wandered down to the river and looked over at the island, our island. I never went back across."

"And how about Heinz, did he ever try to get into touch with you after that?" Irene asked.

"No, never." A strange pride filled Bianca's voice. "I tried everything, everything! My girl-friend got letter after letter through to him, in which I begged and implored him for a rendezvous. But he never came. And she also tried to reason with him, to make him change his mind. It was all no good. He had given me a choice at that particular moment. I made my choice. And he stuck to the rules. That's all."

Another silence followed.

Then Bianca said, "Do you understand now why I brought you here? Why I wanted to show you the island when I told you about Heinz and myself?"

"Yes," Irene said.

"It was the most important, the most beautiful, and the most terrible day of my life," Bianca said. "Now you know my secret. There has only been one man whom I loved without reserve, madly, and beyond all bounds. I wanted you to see where it all happened on that Sunday afternoon in June, I wanted you to see for yourselves. I don't suppose it helps you very much in your search, Mr. Aranda, does it?"

"Yes, it does, it helps me a lot," he said, feeling helpless and deeply moved. "Now I understand everything that happened in those days much better . . . the despair . . . and the happiness . . ."

"It was wonderful how he behaved on that day, wasn't it? Just wonderful." Bianca said.

Manuel could only nod, but Irene said loudly, "Yes."

"The choice he gave me . . . he was a unique individual, and I will never, never be able to admire, respect, and love another man as I did him, no, never. Heinz has become a symbol of perfection for me, my dream, my whole life, my eternal lover."

24

At the very same time the attorney Dr. Rudolf Stein was listening to the impassioned complaint of a certain Victoria Rayo. His client, a very attractive and elegant Viennese woman of twenty-eight who had chosen Dr. Stein, she said, because of his fine reputation in such cases, was telling him the following story: for five years she had been the constant companion and fiancée of a wealthy manufacturer in Innsbruck. During this time the man, who was many years older than she, had had to undergo two serious operations to have tumors removed, so that their marriage, was delayed several times. Her fiancé had, however, given her his solemn promise that in the event of his death she, Virginia Rayo, would be his chief heiress, leaving his sister, with whom he was on bad terms, with only a minimum legal portion. One week before, on the evening prior to his hospitalization for a new operation, the rich man had allegedly dictated a Last Will and Testament to his sister, who also lived in Innsbruck, and then had signed the typed copy she had made, writing with his almost paralysed right hand. The stipulations of the will were precisely as promised, but the sick man had somehow failed to have the document countersigned by two witnesses, a necessary measure when the will was not written by hand. Victoria Rayo found this glaring omission very peculiar on the part of a canny businessman.

Her fiancé died on the operating table. Immediately after the burial his sister took the will, without consulting anyone, to the District Court, where it was at once declared invalid. The sister was named sole heiress. Stein's client now wished to file suit against this decision. She expressed her suspicion that the sister had herself written the will, and had then added a scratchy and shaky signature that would look like the hand of a sick old man. Virginia Rayo had reached this particular point in her narration when suddenly the screams of several girls and the roaring of one man, could be heard through the padded office door. It was a very large office, with heavy, old furniture. The heavy curtains opening onto the Kohlmarkt were closed and the lights were on, causing a mild glimmer to reflect from the silver-gray door of the safe, which was as tall as a man and built into the wall behind the desk of Dr. Stein. The outside, chromium-covered wheel on the armor-plated door glistened.

"Excuse me a moment, Miss Rayo. I must take a look at what's going on out there. I'll only be a moment." Stein hurried out of the office, closing the double-doors behind him. In the outer office, where four girls were employed, a huge, drunken man was running amok, chasing the screaming secretaries around the room, sweeping files and papers from the desks to the floor, raising a chair above his head and smashing it to bits on the floor. As soon as he caught sight of Stein, he hurled himself upon him with a hoarse cry. "You swine, you stole my money!" he yelled. Stein, taken by surprise by the sudden attack, fell to the floor. The drunk, who reeked of schnaps as though his clothes had been soaked in it, fell on him and started to hit him and tried to strangle him. He cursed and shouted, blowing his evil-smelling breath into the attorney's face. Stein's partner, Weber, emerged from another door. The girls were screaming for help at the top of their lungs, and one of them was trying to call the police. Young Weber took a run and leaped on the drunk, who proceeded to display phenomenal strength. The three men were rolling on the floor, and the telephone from which the girl was trying to reach the police crashed to the ground and split in two. Other occupants of the house came rushing in and tried to help, but they were clumsy and only got in each other's way. The chaos was complete . . .

Meanwhile, the elegant young woman calling herself Virginia Rayo had taken a camera with a flash-cube from her handbag. Calmly and quickly she began to photograph the office and the safe, as the noise of the fighting, the curses of the men, and the screaming of the girls reached her from the outer office. Once the first flash-cube was used up, after four pictures, the woman put it into her suit pocket and took out another one. She went right up to the safe door and took close-ups of it from every angle, especially the cone-shaped combination knob above the large chromium wheel, the circle of digits and fine, white lines surrounding the cone, and the trademark of the manufacturer which was placed near the floor in the bottom left hand corner of the wall safe and included details of the year of manufacture, model, and serial number.

Outside everything had gone suddenly quiet.

Virginia Rayo got to her feet without haste, sat down again, lit another cigarette so that the fumes of the used flash-cubes would not be noticed, and crossed her shapely legs.

In the outer office Weber and Stein got to their feet. The drunken giant had suddenly wriggled out of their grasp, beaten a path through the goggling spectators, and rushed out into the street as fast as he could.

"How did the bastard get in?" asked Stein, smoothing down his hair and tightening his tie.

"Came in just the way he went out," one of the dazed girls answered. "Banged the door open and went for us! The one phone is done for, but we have another. Shall we call the police?"

"You should have done that earlier! They'll never catch up with him now!" Dr. Stein shouted angrily, then returned to his office, where he apologized to Virginia Rayo and explained what had happened.

"It's never happened before. No need to be alarmed, Miss Rayo, everything is in order again," Stein said. "Now, let's see, your case . . . I wouldn't like to rouse any false hopes. Your chances are not great! But there are several possible avenues of approach that could be successful if . . . Where can I reach you? In the next few days?"

"I must return to Innsbruck to get my things out of the villa. After that I shall come back to Vienna. I'll be here again in five or six days."

"I probably won't have accomplished anything before then, with the weekend in-between."

"I'll be happy to come whenever you need me," the young woman said. She had not the slightest intention of ever setting foot in the attorney's office again.

Tonight at 11:30 P.M. I'll be back in Graz, she thought. This camera is wonderful, it's never let me down. Mercier will be satisfied.

25

"You just can't imagine what they used to do in an anthro-pological examination! What they examined! They took the craziest measurements! And what a panoply of instruments they had." Martin Landau paused to take a deep breath. "Prescribed by the Reich Office of Racial Purity, and laid down in decrees and guidelines on tests and examinations to establish racial ancestry, in paternity suits, ancestry suits, and to clarify the question of whether a person belonged to the Nordic, Aryan, Master Race, or to some inferior race of slave peoples or sub-humans, suitable only for hard labor, or perhaps best eradicated from the face of the earth—ac-cording to the will of such fat swine as the pornographer and Jew-hater Streicher, the drunkard Dr. Ley, that little squirt Dr. Goebbels with his clubfoot, that morphine addict Göring, Hess, who was half off his head but nevertheless the Führer's Deputy, fat-necked square-heads, psychopaths, perverted noth-ings with glandular imbalance like Himmler, and human cari-catures like Rosenberg and Ribbentrop!"

"If they had not been so degenerate and malformed, per-haps they would not have been so fanatical about their dream of the magnificent, blonde, blue-eyed, super-race," said Man-uel Aranda. He and Landau sat at a window-table in the glass pavilion on the Cobenzl. Landau was eating his second piece of cream tart while describing the tests demanded by the Court at the end of the first hearing. He was drinking coffee, as was Manuel, who, thinking of Bianca Barry's story, asked, "And when did those anthropological tests take place?"

"In May 1943. May 10th. Might have been the 11th or 12th, I don't remember the exact date. It was hot, steaming hot. Summer came early that year."

Yes, Bianca had said the same ... "And when were the blood tests taken?"

"About a week later."

"We were called in one at a time," Landau recounted.

"Heinz was first. It took ages. Valerie and I sat in a huge waiting-room. She was terribly nervous, as you can imagine. There were two other people in the waiting-room besides ourselves. They were very polite. Whispered all the time, and smiled at us from to time. But nevertheless, because of them there was almost a catastrophe."

"How so?"

"One of them was a young woman, almost a girl still, very slim, pretty, tall, brown hair, bright eyes . . ."

26

. . . and next to her sat a Japanese gentleman, dressed despite the heat in a very correct formal black suit with waistcoat. He was at least two heads shorter than the girl, very dapper and delicately built. His face was olive-colored, with high cheek-bones and dark, slanting eyes, behind round, steel-rimmed spectacles. The little man had black, gleaming hair. He held a black hat on his knees in his delicate, olive-colored hands. On entering the room he had bowed and smiled in greeting. He had then handed copies of two summonses to a young girl assistant in a white lab coat, just as Valerie and Landau had done before him, bowing again as he did so to show his cooperation and courtesy. The Japanese gentleman—he was of indeterminable age, he could have been twenty-five or forty—smiled whenever he chanced to look over at Valerie and Landau, but he seemed worried. And he whispered anxiously to the young woman who was so much taller than he.

Valerie wore a light summer dress, Landau a light suit. He watched her unhappily. She was getting more and more nervous, restlessly shifting about on the bench, crossing and recrossing her legs, and dabbing her damp forehead with a handkerchief. She's thinking of Heinz, of course, Landau thought. Of Heinz, who is standing behind one of these doors, naked or half-naked in front of SS doctors and SS professors, being weighed, measured, and sized-up from head to foot . . .

Landau tried several times to make conversation, but Valerie did not answer. Her face was pale, and she could not keep her hands still. Then, after more than an hour, she blurted out all at once, her voice trembling with fear and anger, "How long do they need? It's enough to drive you crazy!"

"Valerie!" Landau succeeded in silencing her just as a very big, strong man flung open a door and entered the waiting-room. He had very short blonde hair, scars on his angular face, and he wore a white doctor's coat. But one could see that he also wore black uniform trousers, boots, and a brown shirt with a black tie. The doctor took no notice of Valerie and Landau, but turned directly to the small Japanese. "Mr. Yoshida."

The Japanese jumped up and bowed, smiling. His companion looked anxious.

"At your service," said the Japanese gentleman softly. The doctor introduced himself, "SS Lieutenant Dr. Kratochwil. Heil Hitler!"

"SS Lieutenant Kratochwil? You are the Director of the Institute?" The little Japanese spoke German with a heavy accent.

Valerie and Landau were listening attentively.

"The Executive Director, yes." Dr. Odilo Kratochwil, Lecturer at the University of Vienna, spoke in a chopped, guttural voice. He was holding two papers in his hand. "Got here late. Important meeting in the Regional HQ. Found your summonses on my desk. A mess-up. A real mess-up!"

"A mess-up? I don't understand, what do you mean?" Mr. Yoshida whispered.

Kratochwil flexed his knees a few times. "A few blockheads have fouled up again. Have already bawled them out. The summons was addressed to you at the Japanese Consulate-General?"

"Yes, Doctor. I not only work there, I live there, too. Fräulein Wiesner received her summons the same day. We are very worried. After such a long engagement . . . We informed the authorities, nobody has any objections. The banns are up, and now it seems we must go through tests."

Valerie's lips were a single thin line, her eyes half-closed.

"That's the point!" thundered Odilo Kratochwil, who combined uniform and doctor's smock so nonchalantly. "You were summoned because some addle-brained thickhead at the registry office got too eager and reported you to us, and we

427

still have a few idiots here who don't know what we owe to our allies in this war!"

"I don't understand."

"Mr. Yoshida and you, my dear lady, were summoned here wrongly. You do not need any racial certification in order to get married. By decree of the Führer! The heroic Japanese race is equal in all respects to the Nordic-Aryan race!"

The young woman leaped to her feet. "So we can get married?"

"Of course you can get married!" And SS Lieutenant Kratochwil bowed charmingly.

Valerie clenched her fists. Landau watched her, horrified. Those two can get married, Valerie was thinking, her mind in a whirl. That little slant-eyed Japanese and the tall German girl. They can get married! And my Heinz gets thrown out of school and must get up at five every morning to toil like a laborer, just because he kissed an Aryan girl. ". . . ancient Samurai tradition, a proud and heroic race," she could hear the man in the white smock, that uniformed sadist, saying to the couple, while her own thoughts raced on: the little Japanese can't help it! But what sort of racial laws are these? What sort of criminal fraud is this? Just because Japan is fighting on our side in the war, the Japanese are as fine as the finest Aryans! Despite the fact that they belong to another world, have a different culture, and look completely different from ourselves, despite the fact that they fought *against* us in the last World War!

"An axis of steel—Tokyo, Berlin, Rome!" Kratochwil bowed before Yoshida and his fiancée.

"But that's—" Valerie began, her face white as snow, her whole body trembling with rage. Like a flash Landau seized her arm and pressed it as hard as he could. The pain brought Valerie halfway to her senses. She groaned. "Ouch!"

The man in the doctor's smock wheeled around, his eyes full of malice. "Is something wrong?"

"No, nothing, nothing," Landau stammered. "Frau Steinfeld, is it not?" The voice of the SS Lieutenant sharpened. "You said something! I heard it! What was it? An objection, perhaps?"

"For goodness' sake!" Landau exclaimed.

"Then what else? I'd like to know! Speak up, Frau Steinfeld, what was it?" Kratochwil insisted.

Summoning up her last strength of mind and will, Valerie

428

answered, "I just said we have been waiting now almost an hour and a half."

"And you'll have to wait a lot longer. Your son is not through yet. We are very here. Please be patient, Frau Steinfeld. *Please!*" Kratochwil threw Valerie a contemptuous look, then turned back to Yoshida. "All the best, my friend. Don't know Japan, unfortunately. But have a round-the-world study trip waiting for me after the Final Victory! Until then, *Heil Hitler!*" Kratochwil jerked his arm upwards.

"*Heil Hitler!*" said Mr. Yoshida.

"Heil Hitler!" said Fräulein Wiesner.

27

"It was four-thirty in the afternoon before we had all been tested and examined and were allowed to leave," Martin Landau said. While telling his story he had ordered another cup of coffee, with an extra-large portion of whipped cream on top.

"Heinz was in an exuberant mood, Valerie close to a breakdown. Me, too. All the underlings treated us just as their boss did. Heinz didn't seem to notice that. We were dirt to them, even I, with my Party badge!"

"And nothing was said about the results of the tests?"

"Of course not. They only talked with us when it was absolutely necessary. 'Raise your arm, turn your head, breathe in, breathe out'—no more than that. The young lady doctor in the Sensengasse was much more friendly!"

"The young lady doctor where?"

"In the Institute for Forensic Medicine. What's the matter? Why are you looking so—oh, I know, because your father also—"

"Yes," said Manuel, "because my father also ..." Full circle, he thought, this affair has really gone full circle. And now the circle's closed. Closed around a secret.

"It didn't take long to get the blood to determine our blood groups," Landau continued. "They took the blood from our fingertips." He turned around in consternation, for someone

429

had gripped him by the shoulder. It was his sister. She was wearing her Persian lamb coat again, edged with mink, and her Persian lamb hat with the mink trim.

"Caught you!" she said softly. "At last!"

"Who told you?"

"Nobody," Tilly Landau said. "But I've been noticing lately how nervous you were in the evenings when I picked you up, so today I kept watch and saw you leave the bookstore. I had the car."

"My dear lady!" Manuel said, getting up, "please forgive me! It's entirely my fault! I have been putting pressure on your brother, coaxing him, intimidating him, nagging him, to persuade him to—"

"Tell you about Valerie and us and the past. I thought as much," Tilly Landau said quickly. "Martin, Martin, what did you promise me?"

"Tilly, you heard Mr. Aranda, he says himself he—"

"I heard him. Why didn't you tell me? Put pressure on you? Blackmail you? Threaten you? I'd have told him something all right! He would have learned something, and still will. I'm not going to stand for that, he can't just push himself into our private lives! I will—"

"You won't do a thing," Manuel said, who found Tilly completely intolerable.

"Won't? Well, we'll see about that! Come on!" she said, dragging her brother to his feet. "That's enough here! And you and I will be talking again, Mr. Aranda!" Panic was in her voice as she turned to her brother. "Have you forgotten what I told you? Do you absolutely want to be done in, too, in this business?"

"Done in . . ." Landau stammered.

"You're being watched, just so that you know—two hoodlums in a huge car in the parking lot. They had binoculars on you when I arrived. And then one of them took a telephone receiver in his hand as I was getting out of my car and talked over a radio transmitter."

"Over a radio!" Martin Landau went pale. "Oh, Tilly, if they do anything to me . . ."

"It's a bit late to think of that, now!" Other guests had turned their heads to look, alarmed by the loud voices.

"We're going! Come on!" Landau gestured sadly with his hands, as though to say, What can I do?

Manuel stood silent. His face was red with anger. But what can *I* do? he thought. Nothing, nothing at all. He watched

430

helplessly as Tilly pulled her brother through the café. And then, all at once, the little man turned around and called out to Manuel, loudly and defiantly: "The results of the blood tests were published in June."

"And?" Manuel shouted across. The café guests gaped at him.

"Keep your mouth shut!" Tilly hissed.

But this time her brother took no notice. "Dreadful!" he shouted back. "The blood-groups excluded mè as father! One hundred percent! It was all over!"

28

"It's all over," said Valerie Steinfeld. She was wearing her black sales smock and looked terrible. Her face was pale, there were deep shadows beneath her eyes, she spoke without hope. "What's going to happen now? The suit will be dismissed at the next hearing and Heinz will be branded as a half-Jew for good. What will they do to him? And what should I tell my husband? I'm scared to death about that. But we have to tell him something, Miss Hill. But what? The truth—"

"Slow down," Nora Hill said. "Take it easy, Frau Steinfeld. Exactly when were the results of the blood tests given to your attorney?"

"Five days ago," said Valerie. "On June 16."

"Does Heinz know about it yet?" Nora asked.

"No. But he'll have to know, of course. I keep putting it off, I just don't have the heart. And what's going to happen to all those witnesses? The Judge is a rabid Nazi, Miss Hill, and the Public Prosecutor's a spineless bootlicker. I lied to you that day on the Ferris wheel."

"I suspected it."

"I only wanted to relieve Paul's mind! Now ... now I don't know what to do ..." Valerie raised her head and looked at Nora Hill.

"What does Forster say?"

"Dr. Forster's a good man. He's trying to find a way out, he's racking his brains ... tells me to keep calm ... Martin too, all of us. That's the most important thing right now, not to lose our nerve."

Nora Hill sat up straight. "You really mustn't lose your nerve, Frau Steinfeld!"

"Easily said! But in my shoes—"

"I can put myself in your shoes very easily! There must be a way out! There always is."

"Not this time."

"There *must* be! And we'll find it!"

"How?" asked Valerie desperately. "Given the fact that the blood tests have *absolutely* excluded Martin Landau as the father? *Absolutely!* Miss Hill, the tests are very scientific and exact, there's no mistake, no slip-up."

Nora laid one hand on Valerie's hand. "Give me a little time. Just a few days. I will have to talk with my friend. This Carl Flemming is an extraordinarily smart man."

29

"Hold it! One moment!"

Manuel had got up from the deep armchair by the fire-place in Nora Hill's living-room. "Now I don't understand anything any more! Carl Flemming? You told Frau Steinfeld you were going to talk with your boss Carl Flemming, of all people, that out-and-out Nazi, about finding a way out?"

"Yes."

"But how could—I mean, that was sheer madness!"

"It wasn't madness at all, my dear friend." Nora Hill was wearing an evening pants-suit of light silk, cream-colored, with a print design of large flowers and petals in green and rose, and a deep décolletage. The pants were broadly flared at the bottom.

An old clock on the wall showed the time as 10:35 P.M. After his conversation with Martin Landau had been so rudely interrupted, Manuel had first driven to the Möven Pharmacy to see Irene. From there he had telephoned Nora Hill and asked her if he could come to see her that same evening. She had agreed.

"I'm always glad to see you, my dear friend . . ."

After the call Manuel had visited Groll at Police HQ, eaten a late dinner at the Ritz, then driven out to Nora's villa. There were many cars parked outside the fantastic round building; business was brisk that evening. Nora Hill escorted Manuel up to her apartment, and after he had mentioned the negative outcome of the blood tests, she had immediately responded with an account of her meeting with the desperate Frau Steinfeld.

Now the beautiful woman with the paralyzed legs said, "When you were here last time, we had to break off our conversation because of my appointment with the tax inspector, who was waiting, do you remember?"

"Yes, yes, of course."

"I told you that Flemming's chauffeur raped me in this very room, and that when Flemming came home I told him everything because I was too scared to do anything else, told him all about Valerie Steinfeld and about what Carlson had done to me. You remember?"

"Yes, I remember, you told me."

"You were horrified at my disloyalty, my friend. You couldn't understand me." Nora smiled. "I had thought about everything carefully. I knew Flemming—he was a Nazi, a careerist, but he was no fool. No, indeed not, he was no fool."

"What do you mean by that?"

"Sit down again. You're making me nervous."

"Madame, please!"

"I'm about to continue the story, my friend. On that evening in January Carl Flemming listened to everything I had to tell him without saying a word. He drank and I drank, just as the two of us are drinking now, in the same room, twenty-six years later. And when I had finished, he stood up . . ."

30

. . . and paced up and down the room in front of the hearth where there was a roaring fire. He had a long narrow face and distinctive features, intelligent and at the same time fiery eyes, bushy, black eyebrows and black, wiry hair cut close to the head.

Nora watched him, tensely. His silence frightened her anew. Had she made a mistake? She lit a cigarette. The Director of the "Flemming HQ" leaned against the same bookshelves in which Manuel Aranda, twenty-six years later, was to see a built-in closed-circuit tv. Flemming gazed at Nora broodingly, then began to whistle the *Marseillaise*.

"Carl! Say something!"

Flemming stopped whistling and shrugged his shoulders. "We have two problems to solve, darling. An easy one and a hard one. The hard one is my chauffeur."

Nora looked at him, filled with grudging admiration. "What are we going to do with Carlson?" she asked.

"Slowly. Let's talk first about the easy problem. I love you too much to start throwing reproaches at you. It would only take time, and time is what we don't have to waste just now. I always thought you were capable of something like this. You're the type. You're capable of more, too. Of being a double-agent, for instance."

"Carl! You don't seriously think—"

"Well now, sooner or later the possibility has to be considered, darling." Flemming took her right hand and kissed the palm. "And considering how little useful information you bring, and how much useless, false stuff, from this Jack Cardiff—"

"Cardiff is really on our side!" she shouted. "He's betraying his own country in order to help Germany, out of conviction! It's not his fault if the material he delivers isn't always correct or useable."

"He can't help it?" Flemming gave a friendly smile.

"He's doing what he can! Perhaps he's being watched, he's been under suspicion for some time now." Nora was making it all up in a wild rush of fantasy. "Perhaps they're giving him false information on purpose. Who knows, he might be in danger!"

"Darling, darling!" Flemming replied, shaking his head. "Just one mild observation from me, a truly *reasonable* observation, and you go\off the deep end, as though ... as though you were in love with this man Cardiff."

"I ..."

"Enough of that. You don't love him, I know. You love me." Nora stared at Flemming. Did he mean what he was

434

saying? Had he guessed the truth? Had he known it for a long time? All through their relationship Flemming was to remain a mystery for Nora. She never succeeded in seeing through him completely.

"You are *not* a double-agent of course, you're working only for me and only for Germany. And you know as well as I do that Germany has already lost the war. I'm right at the source, I don't fool myself. The period immediately after the war is not going to be a pleasant one for me, if I live to see it."

"It won't for me, either," she said quickly and helplessly.

"Oh, for you!" He gave a short laugh. "You're a woman. It's different for a woman. The winners love women, and women love winners. And besides, your position can't be compared with mine. I have exposed myself much more, unfortunately. There's nothing to be done. Ambition, darling, ambition! Now I'm its victim. It's vital now to think of the future and do some good deeds—as you are doing, for instance."

"Good deeds?"

"Well, in this Steinfeld affair, for instance." He took a cigarette, too. "You are brave enough to do a truly good deed there. It will stand to your credit later, and that's why I'd like to do the same as you."

"Which means?"

"That you can count on my silence, my sympathy, and my cooperation." He grimaced. "No bursts of emotion, please. You understand now why I'm being so magnanimous. I have to try to find some other good causes. In order to have some friends when I'm on trial before an Allied tribunal. And there's my condition: that Frau Steinfeld in such an event be willing to make a statement in which she describes with gratitude and in detail how wonderfully I acted for her in her time of need. I imagine she would go along with that, wouldn't she?"

"Of course, Carl, of course!" Nora nodded. Quite a man, this Carl Flemming, quite a man, she was thinking.

"Now on to the bigger problem, darling: Carlson, that filthy swine!"

"He's not normal, Carl! He must be sick in the head."

"Not exactly pleasing news, if you're right. And I'm afraid you are right," Flemming said. "What are we going to do about him? I could charge him, report him, have him arrested, have him sent to the front as punishment. I have the power to do that. I could even get him into a concentration-camp—Kaltenbrunner would help me there, I'm sure. But that's all too dangerous, because the filthy dog would shoot his mouth off everywhere about you being mixed up in the Steinfeld affair and my covering up for you." Flemming suddenly began to whistle and pace the floor again, then he walked over to Nora and kissed her on the forehead, "Go and get some sleep, darling. I have to think about this thing." He kissed her again, then left the room.

31

Carl Flemming's apartment housed many treasures: antique furnishings, tapestries, icons, old carpets, and a very large glass case containing a collection of Chinese porcelain from the Ming dynasty. His desk had a door at one side that was fitted with a special lock. Flemming opened it with a key and took out a pile of documents. He switched on the bright desk light and pulled a miniature camera out of his jacket pocket. One by one, he pushed nine documents under the spotlight of the lamp and photographed them. He worked slowly and calmly.

After he had photographed the papers he returned them to their shelves and bent down. At the bottom of the side compartment was a small box. Flemming opened it. In it, bedded on cotton batting, were a number of glass capsules. Flemming often gave some to his foreign agents to take with them. Now he picked one out, closed the box again, and clicked the lock back into place. He put the capsule and the camera into his pocket, then picked up the receiver of his house telephone and dialled a two-digit number. After a while the sleepy voice of Carlson answered.

"I'm sorry, friend, to disturb you so late," Flemming's tone was kind. "But it has to be. Get dressed. I've just had an urgent call: one of our people is flying to Athens, and I have to get some files to him."

"Very well, Chief." Carlson's voice sounded uneasy.

Flemming spoke without changing his expression. "Come

up to my office. There's a whole stack of files. Some of those vertical binders, too. You'll have to help me carry them."

"Very well, Chief, I'll be over as soon as I can."

"Good," Flemming said. He replaced the receiver, walked over to a wall bar, and took out two glasses and a bottle of cognac. Holding the capsule, he broke it very carefully and let its contents, a fine-grained powder, pour out into a brandy-glass. Then he took a pair of scissors and shredded the two halves of the capsule, crushing them until they were fine splinters. He then shook these into the glass. He walked into the bathroom, where he washed first his hands and then the scissors very thoroughly, afterwards replacing the scissors on the desk. He took a few Leitz binders from the desk, and piled them up on a chair. He was still busy with them when the knock came at the door.

"Come in!" Flemming called.

Carlson, dressed in his chauffeur's uniform, came in hesitantly. Terror, scarcely suppressed by a great effort of will, shone through his eyes.

"Come on in!" Flemming called, apparently preoccupied with the vertical binders on the chair.

Like an animal braced to flee, the chauffeur came cautiously toward Flemming, remembering what had happened just a few hours earlier. Had Flemming been with that whore in the meantime? Had she told him something despite all his threats? If so, what was Flemming planning to do now? Carlson went hot with fear. He licked his dry lips.

Flemming turned and looked at him with a smile. "There, that's the lot!" He looked Carlson up and down. "What's the matter with you?"

"Nothing, Chief, nothing ... I ... I'm a little queasy." Carlson was still not quite sure of himself.

"Feeling a little queasy? Then let's have a little pick-me-up before you go!"

Flemming walked over to the bar and poured Cognac into the two glasses. The powdery substance in the one glass dissolved, and the pulverized glass of the capsule became invisible.

"Thank you, Chief, that's very thoughtful." So that sweetie of a whore kept her trap shut, Carlson was thinking. Good for her. Got her head screwed on the right way. Is thinking of that pretty neck of hers. So we're all clear. The old man doesn't suspect a thing."

"But if I have to drive—"

"Oh, come on!" Flemming said, handing Carlson a glass. "You're not going to get drunk from one swallow! Good health!"

"Your health, Chief," said the chauffeur Albert Carlson. They were his last words. After he had downed the contents of the glass in one hefty swallow (all the better, Flemming thought, now he's got the crushed glass in his mouth as well), the rest followed quickly. Carlson's face went greenish-white, his lips bluish, he croaked, gripped his throat, and began to stagger about the room. The glass fell from his hand, and he crashed down on the carpet. There was a short but terrible death struggle. Carlson's body twisted and turned, foam frothed from his mouth, his eyes bulged from their sockets, his throat rattled.

Flemming stood leaning against the desk. Calmly he lit a cigarette, reached for his glass and drank contentedly as he watched the man writhing and thrashing before him, dying in horrible pain. Their eyes met. Flemming smiled. At the instant of his death Chauffeur Carlson recognized the truth. He stretched out a hand and tried to get up. But the effort was too great. The next second he collapsed and lay still on the floor. He was dead. The scent of bitter almonds pervaded the room. Still whistling, Flemming bent down to the man he had just murdered and picked up the glass, which was not broken. It had fallen on the soft carpet. Flemming examined the glass carefully. A few bits of the capsule were still stuck to the inside. Flemming went into the bathroom once more and fished the bits out one by one, then drained them down the sink. He washed his hands again, went back to his office, and laid the glass back down where it had fallen. He took the tiny camera from his pocket, carefully wiped it clean with a handkerchief, and pressed the dead man's fingers against its metal surface. Then he took a duplicate key to the file compartment of his desk and pressed Carlson's fingers against that, too. He didn't touch the two objects again with his bare hands, but kept them wrapped in his handkerchief. He then quickly left the office and hurried downstairs.

Carlson's room was in the basement of the villa. Flemming pressed the door handle with his elbow, holding camera and key wrapped in his handkerchief in one hand, and using his other handkerchief-covered hand to turn on the light. He looked around for a moment, then climbed on Carlson's bed, the headboard of which was by the barred window. The curtains were closed. They were on runners, hidden by a val-

438

ance. There was a small ledge between the ceiling and the rod, and Flemming carefully pushed the camera and the duplicate key onto it, using the handkerchief still. He jumped down from the bed, put out the light, and closed the door from the outside with his elbow. He put both his handkerchiefs back in his pocket while hurrying back to his office on the first floor. He stepped over the corpse to his desk, took a sip from his glass, then dialled a number on his outside phone.

The Gestapo HQ answered.

"Flemming," he said in his roughest voice. "Who is the ranking officer on duty?"

"Major Englert."

"Connect me with him, please. It's urgent."

"Yes, sir!"

The Major came on the phone a few moments later.

"Horst? I'm glad it's you on duty."

"What's up?"

"It's my chauffeur, Carlson."

"What about him?"

"Have suspected him for a long time now, but never had anything concrete. Today I found the papers in my desk arranged differently from the way I had left them. Got home late. Called him up to see me, pretended we had to drive somewhere. A bluff. Didn't want to alarm him, you know."

"Yes, and?"

"Gave him a drink. Then confronted him with it. He denied it. I told him I wanted to search his room. With some of your boys. That's when he did it."

"What?"

"Put something in his mouth very quickly and bit into it. Thirty seconds later he was dead. Cyanide. Stinks of prussic acid here. Come out as quick as you can. I'll wait for you."

32

"And Flemming *told* you all that?" Manuel looked at Nora Hill in astonishment.

"Yes," She answered, and nodded. The huge emeralds on her ears gleamed in the light of the fire.

"Not right away, of course. I awoke—I really had fallen asleep after all the excitement—when the Gestapo people arrived. They brought the homicide squad from the Criminal Investigation Department, too. That was around midnight. The staff and house guests were just getting home, one by one. It was really chaotic! Searches, interrogations! The key and the camera were found in Carlson's room."

"Didn't anyone think that was a pretty primitive hiding place?"

Nora shook her head. "Everyone thought Carlson had merely hidden the two objects in a great hurry when Flemming called him up, and was intending to put them in a more secure place, but couldn't get to it in the short time. He had the camera and the duplicate key with him that evening because he had done some photographing earlier, knowing the house was almost empty. Sounded logical, don't you think? Flemming suggested this version subtly to his Gestapo friend Englert, and the Criminal Investigation Department had a lot of respect for the Gestapo. The police doctor established that death had been caused by cyanide. Spies often carried capsules of poison while on a mission, that was normal practice. Remnants of crushed glass were found in Carlson's mouth. That same night the film in the camera was developed, and was found to contain pictures of the documents that Flemming had photographed. Then there were Carlson's fingerprints on the camera, Flemming's statement that he had suspected the chauffeur for a long time. It seemed an open and shut case . . ."

Santarin, Grant, and Mercier were sitting in the little girl's room, listening in to the conversation in Nora's living-room. The speaker was still on, and the little girl's room was booked until further notice.

Santarin, wearing a gray suit with a silver sheen, said, "One, at most two visits more, and Nora can get to the point."

"Yes," Grant nodded, hip flask in hand as usual.

"We'll be ready by then."

Nora's voice continued:

"All of us were questioned, but couldn't say anything, of course. They kept at me for an especially long time, since I had been alone in the house with Carlson during the afternoon."

"And?" said Manuel's voice.

"No 'and.' I'd had a lie-down in bed, I said, because I hadn't felt too well. Flemming came up to see me briefly, then went over to his own apartment. What I'm telling you is the truth, I assure you. Englert and Flemming were very close friends, on first-name terms with each other. There was never any shadow of suspicion that there'd been foul play. Over the next few days attempts were made to establish for whom Carlson had been spying and what he'd passed on so far, how long he'd been an agent, and where he'd been taking his photographs: after all, he had virtually free access to files all over the city in the offices of Flemming's staff—but all the investigations led to nothing. Nevertheless, the conviction stuck that Carlson had been an agent, and the proof was his suicide!"

Santarin, fingering his bag of candy, said, "What Aranda can't get from Nora or anyone else in Vienna he will presumably learn from Daniel Steinfeld. Steinfeld's arriving Monday, we've managed to establish that." Santarin looked across at Mercier. "One of our people works in the post-office from which the Daniel Steinfeld's telegram was delivered to Irene Waldegg."

"Congratulations." said Mercier. What he thought was: you shit-head, you're so obsessed by your own smart-aleck antics, but I've got Anton Sirus arriving Monday afternoon. He'll be flying home again on the first plane Tuesday morning. If he really can open the safe—and he will, he told de Brakeleer so after the Dutchman had brought him all the stuff he needed—then I'll have what I want out of that safe on Monday night. But, Christ, what red tape I had to unravel! Getting the French Ministry of Culture to release Monet's "Poppies" from the Musée de l'Impressionisme, so that Sirus could buy it. We are an ancient cultural nation. But we also want the best B-weapon in the world . . .

In her living-room Nora Hill was saying, "As for your first question: Flemming told me everything once the excitement had subsided. We were alone together one evening. I just asked him and he admitted everything right away."

"He must have trusted you completely," Manuel said.

"Trusted me!" Nora laughed. "He'd shit in his pants, I told you already. And by the way, I haven't told anyone this story, right up to the present day, not even Cardiff."

"And Frau Steinfeld?"

"Frau Steinfeld? Oh, you mean because Flemming said he

would keep quiet and help her if she testified on his behalf after the war?"

"Yes."

"Well, I told Frau Steinfeld exactly that and no more except the news that Flemming's chauffeur had poisoned himself with cyanide."

"Why did you tell her that? I assume the incident was hushed up."

"Of course it was. That sort of thing was always hushed up. I told Frau Steinfeld because she was still afraid I was being followed by the man in the blue overcoat and the Homburg hat. Flemming's opinion was that the best thing was to tell her that Carlson had been that man so she needn't be afraid any more on that score. And it did in fact relieve her a lot. From that time on she trusted me and believed everything Flemming said."

"And what did he say?"

"At first he just gave her advice. I kept him up to date on what was going on. He became really active only after Frau Steinfeld had given me the news that the blood tests had turned out negative, proving that Martin Landau could not possibly have been Heinz's father. I told all that to Flemming right here in this very room. It was on a beautiful summer evening, it stayed light for a long time . . ."

33

. . . and gradually the sky to the West became pale blue, rosy, then dark red.

Flemming had listened in complete silence while Nora recounted the unhappy turn of events in the lawsuit. He was smoking a pipe. For a long time he sat thinking, then went to the window and looked out into the gathering dusk. Nora waited patiently. Finally the big man turned around.

"I can see only one way," he said, "which perhaps, *perhaps*, could be successful."

"Yes?" For as long as Nora had known Flemming, the man had aroused a mixture of hate and admiration in her.

442

"It's not an easy way, and it's not a safe way. It will take strong nerves. Frau Steinfeld's nerves are quite strained already, are they not?"

"To the limit. But to save her boy, she would stand anything! There's only one thing she wants: to get the boy through. Now tell me what you've been thinking of."

"Of a corpse," Flemming answered.

"Of *what?*"

"The father must be dead."

"I don't get it."

"The alleged father of this boy," he said, softly and patiently. The sweet song of a nightingale wafted over from the park. "Frau Steinfeld must have known a man—well, as well as she knew Landau—who is now dead. An Aryan. A lot of people are dying these days, aren't they? At the front, for instance, although it would be better still if the man in question had been dead for some time. But the witnesses must all have known him—or there must be witnesses. I mean, people who are willing to testify in court. The original witnesses would be the best, that goes without saying." He contemplated the clouds of smoke.

"A dead father," Nora said breathlessly. "You're a genius! That's the answer! A dead man can't go through anthropological tests! You can't make blood tests on a dead man!"

34

"Nora Hill was the one who made this suggestion to you?" Ottilie Landau asked. She looked pale and exhausted, her pointed nose seemed to stick out even more conspicuously than usual, her cheeks were hollow, her thin lips drained of blood. Ottilie Landau could not take heat too well, and this June 23, 1943 was inhumanly hot. Nor did the evening bring any relief, especially not in the center of the city. The heat had penetrated into the little tea-room of the closed bookstore. It hung there, mercilessly sweltering, impossible to dispel now that the four-foot-thick walls were warmed through. There are too many people in here, Tilly thought, mopping her face with a slightly faded lace handkerchief. Valerie, Martin, Agnes, myself. There's not enough air ...

"Yes. Nora Hill came here and said she thought it was the best idea."

Valerie had dark circles under her eyes, and her hair was stringy. She had only confided to her old friend Martin that the idea actually was Flemming's and that they now had him on their side.

"Given the circumstances, I find the idea excellent."

"Given the circumstances!" Martin Landau, who was sitting in the broken rocking-chair, let out a pitiful laugh. In the last few days he had been tilting his head to one side again, and his shoulders hunched, even when seated. "Given the circumstances I would regard *any* idea as excellent that saves me from being accused of perjury!"

On this evening Valerie was supported by Tilly. "Well, that's what could be accomplished!" Tilly exclaimed.

"What?"

"If we present the court with a new father, you're off the hook!"

"How am I off the hook?"

"Oh, come on! After all, Valerie *could* have betrayed her husband with another man besides you, couldn't she?" Tilly was behaving as if she welcomed the new development. On her way to the bookstore, she had been in an ugly temper. Now she felt relieved, and was thinking: I thought Valerie wanted to drag us all deeper into this crazy quagmire. But no, she's got hold of a proposal that pulls us all out of the mud!

"I would be prepared to swear to it to help Martin. And you too, Valerie," Tilly said.

"And Frau Lippowski?" Martin Landau asked, his head sloping to one side. "After all, do you think she would?"

"I'm going to go see her tomorrow. But I'm sure she will," Valerie said quickly.

"Then we will all be together again," Tilly said. "What does Dr. Forster think?"

"He listened to it all without moving a muscle of his face. He has to behave as though he believes every word I say. But he's willing to go along with it, he let me understand that, indirectly. The anthropological report arrived at his office, too."

"What?" Landau said. "When?"

All eyes were on Valerie. "Today."

"Well? Well?" Agnes exclaimed.

"Four pages of jargon that not even Forster could make head or tail of," Valerie said, "but then, in the summing-up, there it is, black on white!" She produced a sheet of paper. "I wrote it down word for word." She read aloud from the sheet: " 'Racially, the anthropometric external attributes and appearance of the plaintiff'—that means Heinz—'exhibit no features that would lead to the conclusion of Jewish descent, although'—*although*, just listen to that!—'although the legal father of the plaintiff, in the photographs submitted, displays Jewish characteristics *to an especially extensive degree!* "

A silence followed.

"Jeesus H. Bald-headed Christ!" from Martin Landau.

"Martin!" Tilly exclaimed, horrified.

"It's enough to drive you crazy! A really first-class report! Heinz looks like a real, pure Aryan! We'd be through, we'd have won the case, if only it hadn't been for those damned blood tests."

"We can't do anything about them," Valerie said, "but the Court has to recognize and *acknowledge* what is in the anthropological report. It was prepared by SS-doctors, after all! It makes it all the easier now for me to say I made a mistake and it wasn't Martin who was the father, but Ludwig Orwin." Valerie was speaking more slowly, formulating her words as she intended to deliver them in court.

"Ludwig Orwin, the well-known sculptor, a friend of mine since the days of my youth. His works are in all the best German museums, in parks, in front of public buildings. An artist of great reputation ... was always in and out of our house. Martin and he were good friends."

"And both of us slept with you," Landau said dismally. His sister threw him a sardonic look, but he did not notice.

"Yes," Valerie said, "I slept with both of you, but neither of you knew of the other. I did not want to destroy your friendship."

"Ludwig Orwin, of all people. He was *really* my friend, after all," Martin Landau murmured.

"Pull yourself together!" Tilly said to him crossly. "We don't have anyone else."

"And what if the Court—after all, what if the Court rejects this second version?" Landau asked.

"The Court will not reject it! It cannot!"

"Wishful thinking! To say it cannot! That miserable Nazi of a judge! That I'd like to see! It will give him special pleasure to be able to say, that's the end, I won't listen to any more lies!"

"We have Dr. Forster!" Valerie said. "And we have that Public Prosecutor, who was already half on our side the first time!"

"He's not likely to be now!" Landau groaned.

"Now that Germany is being clobbered on all fronts: you bet he'll be on our side, the coward!" declared Valerie, but thought to herself: Martin's right, it is wishful thinking, that's all. And to Martin she said:

"What's wrong with you? You've been such a fighter up to now, so brave! And now, all at once—"

"I was never brave," the little man said softly. "I just screwed up all my courage like crazy. But now ... now I feel like a balloon that's had the air let out of it."

"You'll feel something else if you don't go along now and the Party hits you with a perjury charge," Tilly said sharply.

He shuddered. "Yes," he stammered, "yes, that's true ... I ... I don't have any choice ... I have to keep playing the game ..."

35

"... I'm sure you can imagine how difficult it is for me to tell you all this, my boy," Valerie said, searching with much effort for the right words. "But the blood tests have shown that Uncle Landau cannot be your father. So it must be Uncle Ludwig who's your father. You do remember your Uncle Ludwig, don't you? He always brought you toys and read fairy-tales to you when you were still a little boy ..."

Heinz Steinfeld did not answer. He was sitting on the edge of his bed, in his pyjamas, looking at his bare feet. His face was completely expressionless. Valerie sat beside him. Heinz always went to bed soon after he got home. He had to get up very early to get to the factory on time.

"Don't you remember Uncle Ludwig?" Valerie's voice had the sound of urgency.

"Oh yes, yes, I remember him," Heinz said without looking up.

446

"Uncle Martin is just as hurt as you, now that I've told him that I . . . that I . . . that Uncle Ludwig and I . . . but you don't know how terrible my marriage was, Heinz. Nobody knows that. It was hell, sheer hell!"

"You mustn't shout so much, Mommy," Heinz said. Now he was looking at his fingernails. "And don't get so excited."

"Of course I must!" Valerie had the feeling she would burst into tears at any moment. Oh, she thought, oh, I can't cry any more. I wish I could, the way I used to. But I've forgotten how to cry. "Uncle Martin and Uncle Ludwig, they were the best of friends, and I deceived them both."

"And your husband, too." The boy's voice was suddenly hard.

"What do you mean? Of course."

He was looking at her now, coldly and matter-of-factly.

"What is it, Heinz? Don't you believe me?"

"You really did deceive him then, your husband?" Heinz put the question slowly and deliberately.

"Yes. Yes."

"Can you swear to it—I don't mean in front of some judge, but on my life?"

"I swear it on your life, Heinz, yes."

He was looking at her still. She could hardly hold his gaze, but she forced herself to bear it. I've sworn a false oath on the life of my son, was what she thought.

"Oh, well," said Heinz.

"What's that supposed to mean? What's the matter?"

"Oh, Mommy, you know I'm no idiot. And if a man is not an idiot, then he asks himself in a situation like this one: 'Isn't the woman lying?' ('The woman,' he calls me, Valerie thought, horrified) 'and committing perjury because she wants her son, who's really a half-Jew, to be an Aryan?' It's natural to ask oneself that! Every judge would ask himself the same question."

"But it's not so, Heinz," Valerie exclaimed. "It's not so, Heinz, I've sworn to you it isn't."

"Don't" he said softly.

"Don't what?"

"Don't shout like that. And don't get so excited."

"I can't help getting excited! Do you think it's easy for me to stand here and say these things to you? What must you think of me?"

His lips scarcely moved as he spoke, and his voice sounded

447

to Valerie like the voice of no one she had ever known. "I do not want to talk about what I think of you."

"Heinz!"

"No. I don't want to."

"Why not?"

"Because it's not important."

"Not important? But it is for me!"

"But not for me. There's only one thing in the world that's important for me. I don't give a damn about the rest."

"What are you talking about?"

"The Jew. I am not his son. You swore to that. Uncle Martin is not my father, Uncle Ludwig is my father. Okay, either way, I don't care. I'm glad you found a substitute so quickly. I might otherwise have got used to thinking of Uncle Martin as my father. A mistake, a small mistake, can happen. It's only human to make mistakes."

That's how an SS-Commandant must speak, Valerie thought, horrified, someone like Himmler, or Kaltenbrunner! And it's my boy who's talking, my own son! She shuddered as she listened to Heinz's next words.

"The one thing in the world that's important to me is that the Jew is not my father, and *that I am Aryan!*"

36

"So that was how your son reacted," Nora Hill said three days later in the bookstore tea-room.

"Yes. All he said then was that he had to go to sleep, it was late . . ."

It was a hot day. Nora Hill wore a cornflower-blue dress of light silk, white gloves, white shoes, and a large, wide-brimmed white hat.

"It's all very hard for you, Frau Steinfeld."

"It's all right." Valerie smoothed down her smock. "It has to be all right. It will be all right!"

Nora knocked on wood.

"No, no, I mean it! The anthropological report is first-rate! All my witnesses are prepared to testify again, including Frau Lippowski. I'll be seeing Dr. Forster again tomorrow. I had already mentioned a second man during my very first visit to his offices, he says. It's in the minutes, he looked it up."

"How come? Did you have the same idea yourself even then?"

"No! I was totally terrified. He frightened me with the idea that it might turn that Martin Landau could not be the father, and so I threw something in about another man. It must have been instinct, nothing else ... It's a real blessing now, Dr. Forster says, because he can refer to it now. No, no, you need not pity me. I feel really great, because I have new hope now!" Valerie leaned forward: "Oh, something really important, Miss Hill. When are you flying back to Lisbon?"

"Very soon, in about ten days. We'll see each other again, of course. Herr Flemming wants to be kept up-to-date. Maybe he can help you with some advice. He has to be careful, of course. And you must never give him away!"

"Never!" Valerie raised two fingers, like a child. "And after the war I will show my gratitude, he can rely on that."

"He is relying on it. There was something important you wanted to tell me, Frau Steinfeld."

"Yes. Two things really. First: please tell your friend that everything's going well here in Vienna, slowly but well. And that the blood tests indicated that it was *possible* for Martin Landau to have been the father. Please, Miss Hill, lie for me, please!" Nora felt her hands suddenly seized in Valerie's ice-cold ones. "Not even your friend must know the truth. So that he cannot make any slip-ups when passing the message on to my husband! I'm thinking of Paul's health! Tell your friend it may take a long time, but we're all in good health and spirits. You'll do that for me, won't you?"

"Yes," Nora Hill said, filled with compassion, "I'll do that, Frau Steinfeld. And what was the second thing?"

"The second thing ..." Valerie took a deep breath.

"Herr Flemming's chauffeur committed suicide with cyanide capsules, did he not?"

"Yes, why?"

"And you said secret agents and such people all carry those capsules, it's nothing out of the ordinary."

"Yes, that's true."

"Then Herr Flemming must have some, too! Don't deny it! He must have some for sure!"

"I'm not denying it. Don't be so loud!"

"I want to beg him, beg him from the bottom of my heart, to let me have two of those capsules."

"You don't want—my God, Frau Steinfeld!"

"No, no, what an idea! Only in case of absolute emergency, extreme emergency." Valerie whispered urgently. "Nobody can know what may be around the corner! And you and Herr Flemming might not be there to help, and they'll come for us, Heinz and me, and take us somewhere, I don't know where. I mean, I *know* that could happen, *precisely* that! And you know it, too! I ... I don't want to go through all kinds of torture, and I don't want them to torture Heinz, he's still a child." Valerie gripped Nora's hands again.

"I promise you I will only use the capsules if it is *absolutely* necessary! Will Herr Flemming let me have two? Do you think he will?"

"I think so," Nora Hill said, shaken.

"He's a good person," Valerie murmured. "Truly a good person ..."

37

Three rust-colored squirrels with dark tails. Two gray-brown squirrels. And two black ones. They were squatting on a path from which the snow had been cleared away in the Türkenschauz Park, around the edge of a small, solidly frozen lake, nibbling at hazel-nuts, which they held between their tiny paws. They sat upright, their thick-tufted tails elegantly erect, quite tame, quite close to Irene and Manuel, who were feeding them. They had bought the nuts in little bags from a coin-machine in the park.

It was Saturday, January 25, at about 2:30 P.M. Manuel had spent the morning with Groll, and had told him of his conversation with Nora Hill the night before. She had not been able to say what had been the outcome of the second paternity suit, and had once again broken off her narration ...

"But the attorney will know for sure, my dear friend."

"I have an appointment with him tomorrow afternoon."

"I see. And when you know what happened, come and tell me ..." With this exchange the conversation with Nora had come to an end.

"There's just one thing . : ." Manuel had said later to Groll.
"Yes?"

"The poison capsules. Frau Hill told me Flemming gave
them to her when she asked for them, and she passed them
on to Frau Steinfeld, who kept them for twenty-six years!
She kept those cayanide capsules for twenty-six years.
Right until this year, this month, right until the ninth of January. Yes, they were what Frau Steinfeld used to kill my father and herself."

"Well, at least that point's cleared up at last," said Groll. It
was Saturday morning, and they were in his office. He was
tracing the outline of the silver-green gingko leaf under the
glass of his desk. He let the tip of his finger glide along the
stem and around the edges of the leaf, then back down the
stem.

"But why didn't Frau Steinfeld resist throwing away the
poison in all those years? Why did she keep it? *Was she saving it for my father?*"

"We don't know," said Groll.

"We don't know *yet!* But I'll find out! I'll find everything
out, you'll see, Commissioner! Down to the last detail."
"Surely," Groll replied, his finger tracing the leaf.

The Möven pharmacy closed early on Saturday afternoon.
Manuel had taken Irene to lunch at the Ritz, and afterwards
they had driven out to the huge park, leaving their car in the
Gregor Mendel strasse.

They went for a long walk. It was a very cold day. Irene
wore her sealskin coat and boots. Manuel had told her everything he had learned. Then they had walked silently, side by
side. And behind them walked two men, some distance away,
hands in their pockets, stopping when they stopped, continuing when they walked on. Today the French were watching
Manuel ... Irene had discovered the squirrels by the little
lake. At first two of the playful animals had come hopping
across a snow-covered meadow, then a third, and now there
were seven. They seemed to be having a nibbling contest.

Manuel looked at Irene as she strewed a handful of hazel-
nuts across the path. "What are you thinking of?"

"Of the boy," she replied.

Of her brother, he thought. Of her brother, whom she will
never know as her brother, if I can help it. How strange that
after all I told her, he is the one that occupies her thoughts.
Strange? "And what do you think?" he asked.

451

"That he had a terrible fate," she said.

"A terrible fate?" he repeated, surprised. "If anyone is to be pitied, it's his mother. Think how the boy's reaction must have hurt her when he talked to her the way he did. Was someone who could act that way worth all that—the suffering, the lying, the excitement, all that trouble?"

"You *can't* ask such a question!" Irene countered vehemently.

"And what about the way he behaved with Bianca? And with that Russian, just because he considered himself an utter 'German?'"

"But that's precisely what I call a terrible fate," said Irene, scattering nuts for the squirrels, who were not at all disturbed by the sound of human voices.

"Terrible? How do you mean?"

"The soul, the character of the boy were so twisted and all his feelings so confused and perverted. He absolutely wanted to be like the others, like the 'good' Germans, the 'decent' Germans, like the—"

"He absolutely wanted to be a part of the establishment—that was what he wanted," Manuel said angrily, and thought, even while he spoke: Irene is his sister. The sister is defending her brother, without knowing why. She takes his side automatically.

"Yes, on the side of the Aryan establishment!" Irene said. "What do you think the Nazis were trying to do with the faith, courage, and candor of these half-grown young men? If the youth of a country is on your side, the future is yours. Youth and future, those were their key words; they are the key words of all dictators! To fit in with the ideal that was being held up to them, that was what the young people wanted. What do you expect from a seventeen-year-old who has been kicked out, defamed, and outlawed? Critical reasoning? Reflection? Resistance against the regime and love for his father, who is the cause of all the ills he's had to suffer?"

"But—" Manuel began, but she interrupted him.

"Wait! I'm trying to say that I *understand* Heinz. He acted as he *had* to act under the circumstances. Do you know that there were countless cases of children reporting their parents for listening to London or cursing Hitler, just because their teacher, their respected teacher, had told them they had to be on the alert and report all and everyone who was against the State? Do you know what Fascism did to the souls of some of our best and most worthwhile young people, and what

452

they then did, out of dedication to a terrible evil which they loved?"

Her brother, Manuel thought. She's defending her brother while speaking of an entire generation.

"You were not here! You have not had to go through anything like that! You can't imagine it!" Irene said.

"I've been told that a few times. May I say something now?"

"You have no conception how ... What is it you want to say?"

He put his arm around her shoulders and pulled her to him. "I love you," Manuel said softly, as if not even the squirrels should hear. She did not answer, but when he put his lips on hers, they parted and her mouth became soft and sensuous. Suddenly she flung her arms around him. The kiss lasted an age.

Seven squirrels sat before the motionless pair and gaped. The eyes of the little animals shone.

38

Dr. Forster seemed changed to Manuel, almost frighteningly so. His disfigured face was pink and lively, he walked with a springy step, he spoke fast and in an animated voice, and his eyes sparkled. On this occasion Anna, his housekeeper, had served the afternoon snack on a table in his work-room, which was crowded with tools and ships' models and pervaded by the smell of glue and paint. A big stack of files rested on another table.

"Now have another piece of streusel cake, Mr. Aranda, it's superb—I've now got most of the documents together, but meanwhile you've learned so much from Frau Hill and Mr. Landau. You've been quicker on the draw than I!"

"But there's a lot I don't know yet."

"Then my efforts have not been in vain." Forster laughed. "Don't think I haven't noticed how you're staring at me, Mr. Aranda! I'm so excited, so confused, my blood pressure must be two-hundred!"

"What's happened?"

"What's happened?" Forster rubbed his hands, beaming. "Mrs. Demant has died! In the Bahamas. The widow of the department-store tycoon. Diamant was his real name, a Viennese. I helped him get out in 1938, and got his fortune to a safe place, too. The Demants had no relatives and the widow named me in her Will as sole heir. Crazy, don't you think? Unbelievable? But you *must* believe it, it's true!"

"So you're a rich man now!"

"Yes, I am. A very rich man. I can't take care of the business of course, but neither could Mrs. Demant. She had her authorized representatives, and so will I."

"You're going to move to the Bahamas?" Manuel had understood at last.

"Of course!" said Forster, beaming. "That's the wonderful part! It's like a fairy-tale! I can get out of Vienna! My dream all these years! Now it's going to be fulfilled!" He leaned across the table and looked up at Manuel. "All at once I believe in God again. I don't know if I will live in the Demant's residence. It's a huge property, probably too big for me. So I'll sell it and buy myself a small house. In the Bahamas, Mr. Aranda, in the Bahamas!"

"And your family . . . what do they say to this news?"

"They're happy for me! Not only about the money, but also about the fact that I can get out of this city at last. I'll go by ship, of course," Forster blinked, his eyes sparkling.

"And you won't be homesick?"

"Homesick? For *Vienna*? No."

"I'm happy for you," Manuel said.

A few minutes later they were sitting at the other table. Forster was leafing through files.

"We've found everything now, you see, the report on the blood test, the anthropological report . . ." He pushed yellowed papers towards Manuel, who quickly read a few sentences. "A first-rate report! The boy came out of it a veritable Nordic showpiece! Those doctors—idiots!—discerned strong resemblances with the mother and the alleged father, Mr. Landau." The attorney sighed. "A dream report! The blood test results were all the more crushing after that!"

"Frau Steinfeld told you she had had sexual relations with a second man . . ."

"Yes, she did."

"You had been expecting her to say something of the sort if the blood tests didn't work out in her favor?"

454

"Of course. I had to think of two things, you realize. Firstly, the boy had to be brought safely through the war. So my first duty was to try and see that the case dragged on, whatever happened. That was the first consideration. And secondly, I had to make sure that the witnesses, above all Mr. Landau, came to no harm. They were not in a very good situation in those days. Fortunately, that bloodhound Gloggnigg had been transferred to Berlin, as I told you. The new judge was called Arnold, a completely dedicated and assiduous man, almost too much so, to the point where he lived in constant fear he might make a mistake somwhere. And another stroke of luck was that my friend from Berlin, Peter Klever, came to visit Vienna again in July 1943, just at the right moment. We saw each other, of course. And of course he reproached me about the way I acted, told me the Vienna Bar Association was getting more and more annoyed about it, and then of course he helped me again in the end, good old Peter!"

<h1 style="text-align:center">39</h1>

"It is a special pleasure for me to be able to tell you how satisfied we in Berlin are with your work, Judge Arnold. As Regional Court Judge you are indeed the perfect replacement for your predecessor and colleague, Judge Gloggnigg!" Dr. Peter Klever twisted his broad face into a smile, his bushy eyebrows jerking up and down. The big, heavy man from Berlin, wearing his uniform and boots, his flat cap on his knees, sat in the courthouse office of chubby, ruddy, undersized Dr. Englebert Arnold. It was routine for Kleber to visit any newly appointed judge he had not met before during his stay in Vienna. But this conversation was not routine. What Klever was saying was not true. The activities of Dr. Arnold as Regional Court Judge had so far failed to attract the attention of anyone in Berlin. But at the request of his good friend Forster, Klever was buttering up Dr. Arnold, who reminded him of a human pudding, with a few well-chosen lies. He did not feel too comfortable with the task, but was thinking, of course I'll keep on helping Otto, stupid ox that I am. A little more than a year later, Klever was to be hanged in a horrible way after the abortive attempt to assassinate Hitler.

The human pudding radiated rapture. "A man does his best, Dr. Klever! I'm trying all I can to fill the shoes of my great predecessor, but it's not easy. Such a message is therefore all the more welcome!"

"Your unflinching integrity is what is respected most in Berlin," Klever declared. "In a State based on the rights of man, like ours, it is essential that each case must be looked at and examined from every angle. We must never let it be said that German justice is either frivolous or subservient to the interests of the Party. That must not happen at any price, Dr. Arnold!"

"It must and will not happen. I agree. That is my principle, too. I am a Party member, of course, and a faithful follower of the Führer. And it is for precisely that reason that I always pay the most assiduous attention to the proprieties in any case that comes before me—even if it appears dubious and weak from the outset, my principle is: no verdict until the *in-all-probability* guilty party has been given every chance to prove his innocence."

"Bravo! That's the right spirit," Klever said in his strong Prussian accent, thinking: you miserable little asshole, you. "If I am not mistaken, you must deal with a great many racial origin suits."

"Yes, Dr. Klever, with quite a number. You mention that because it's an especially sensitive area, I assume?"

"Now we've got to where we want to be, Klever thought, and replied, "Especially sensitive, quite right, my dear man. I travel throughout the Reich—"

"Indeed!"

"—and throughout the Reich such lawsuits are being brought to the courts—"

"Indeed!"

"—not masses of them, but large numbers, large numbers. You cannot imagine the irresponsibility that is sometimes displayed in conducting them—with the best of intentions, of course! The judges tend to assume that the suits are fakes trumped-up by mothers to make their half-Jewish brats into Aryans. But that is *not always* the case! Not always by any means, as we have discovered. A friend of mine in the Reich Office of Racial Purity told me that in such cases the most meticulous care and attention to detail is essential, and any

456

shadow of a doubt must be removed before a verdict is pronounced."

I don't have any friend in the Office of Racial Purity, Klever was thinking. My God, Otto is going to fall on his face one of these days with these affairs. And you can't talk to him about it.

"You must bear in mind, Party Member Arnold, that it *could* possibly be an Aryan standing before you, that the mother and the witnesses *could* possibly be telling the truth, even though the stories they tell might sound fantastic, as they often do. The Reich Office of Racial Purity does not wish to have any wrong decisions in such cases, because a mistaken verdict can thrust a good, worthwhile Aryan down into the morass of Jewry. These particular lawsuits, my dear Arnold, are watched with the maximum care in Berlin!"

"Very kind of you to tell me that, Dr. Klever." Judge Arnold made a slight bow from his sitting position. "Truly most kind. It is, after all, important to know what the high-ups in Berlin regard as top priority. Here in Vienna I am only a Regional Court Judge—"

"No false modesty! Vienna is the second city of the Reich. And as for mere Regional Court Director—I've heard some talk about a State Supreme Court appointment."

"Oh, really?" Arnold's small, round mouth dropped open. A mouth like a—oh, well, Klever thought, as he said smilingly, "But keep that to yourself . . ."

"Of course, Dr. Klever!"

"I don't know when it'll go through . . . Could take a while yet." I'll just have to fix that in Berlin, Klever thought. A promotion, my goodness! I can certainly swing that.

"Keep it up, my dear fellow, keep it up!"

40

"So that was how my old friend set up the judge for us," Forster said. "Arnold was a real bum. The first hearing after the medical reports were in, with him presiding, did not take place until September 10, 1943."

"Why so late?"

"The courts were closed for vacation!" Forster handed Manuel several sheets of paper that had been clipped together. "The minutes of the hearing, prepared by that pasty-faced zombie Herta Bohnen again. She survived, Frau Bohnen did," Forster said. "Here, take a look: 'Court called to Order at 9:35 A.M.'"

Manuel read on. "'Under the new presiding Judge, the hearing will be resumed according to Paragraph 412. The evidence will be repeated, the minutes of the first hearing will be read, and the reports resulting from tests and examinations ordered at that time will also be read, by agreement with all parties ...'"

41

"Hmmm," mutters Regional Court Judge Arnold, bunching his sausage fingers together and fixing Valerie with his stare, "that settles that aspect of the case, Frau Steinfeld. Mr. Landau cannot be the father of your son. Nobody can ignore the result of scientific examinations."

Picking her nose spasmodically as she writes, the sloppy stenographer Herta Bohnen occupies a seat next to the ruddy-faced Judge Arnold, her facial expression a dull void—but she's an Aryan, an Aryan, thinks Valerie, an Aryan who is allowed to sit next to the judge. Valerie herself is seated beside Dr. Forster, behind a desk to the right of the Judge. The Public Prosecutor, Dr. Kummer, is seated facing them. Kummer had seen a slim, weak-looking man in the corridor outside Hearing Room 29, as though expecting to be called. The sight of that man, who reminded him of someone, made Kummer cautious. Easy now, easy, you never know, never ...

"Frau Steinfeld!" Arnold repeats, having received no answer from Valerie, who is staring disconsolately at nothing.

"I ... I ..." she begins, but at that moment Forster rises to his full height. He addresses the court in carefully balanced tones.

"I wish to inform the Court that my client visited me after the results of the blood tests were received and told me that

458

at the period in question before the birth of her son she was engaged in a sexual relationship with another man."

It's a lie, of course, Judge Arnold thinks, but something new at least. I never heard that one before. Careful, careful, don't get carried away. Stay correct and matter-of-fact. What was it Klever said? In the Reich Office of Racial Purity they consider these cases of great importance.

Public Prosecutor Kummer is thinking: I knew this Forster fellow had something up his sleeve. It's a trick, of course. But he's a tricky customer, all right. And I personally don't give a shit whether the kid's Aryan or not, or whether he gets to be one honestly or through some hanky-panky! It looks grim at the fronts. The bottom's going to drop out, it's bound to. And if I start shooting off my mouth too much now, what will happen to me afterwards? Easy, easy. I'm not going to mess up my future because of some squirt of a half-Jew.

The presiding judge, ruddy-faced, asks politely, "Who is the second man in question, Counsel?"

"Ludwig Orwin, your Honor."

"Orwin? Orwin? Wasn't there a sculptor called—"

"That is the man, your Honor."

"But he has been dead a long time!"

Forster is looking Arnold straight in the eye. "He was killed in a train accident near Hamburg on August 24, 1934."

Wow thinks the Judge, if this is not the truth, it's an excellent invention.

My word! thinks the Public Prosecutor, a really brilliant idea, have to give them credit.

"Frau Steinfeld," the Judge says, in an almost fatherly tone—at least he thinks so—"Would that be your new testimony, then?"

"Yes, your Honor."

"You know that you must tell the truth here, and nothing but the truth."

"I know."

"Why did you not say anything before about your intimate relationship with Mr. Ludwig Orwin?"

"I was absolutely certain that Mr. Martin Landau was the father of my son!"

"But according to your own statement, you had been having sexual intercourse with Mr. Orwin as well."

It's amazing how calm I feel, Valerie is thinking, and says,

"That is correct. Our relationship was very intense. For

459

several months in the fall of 1924. And again when my husband was away for such a long time in August 1925, we became intimate again . . ."

"On just one occasion?" the Prosecutor breaks in. One has to do something, or else they'll think I'm neglecting my duty.

"On three occasions," Valerie answers. "The relationship with Mr. Landau was much more frequent, and we were not careful, but neither was Orwin always. But that's the reason I thought that Martin Landau must be the father of my son, and . . ." She breaks off and stares at Judge Arnold until he actually blushes.

Forster gets to his feet. "Your Honor, I beg you to consider how terribly embarrassing this whole procedure is!"

"I realize that, Counsel." Arnold's voice is as soft as velvet. "But after all, *she* is the one who filed the suit. We do have to establish the truth, don't we? That's the most important thing, is is not, Frau Steinfeld?"

"Yes," Valerie says. "It certainly is. And I do see now that I should have mentioned all these circumstances from the very beginning. But I was too ashamed. Now I have no other choice. I beg the Court's forgiveness for having given incomplete information. *Incomplete,* not *untrue.*"

"You will agree, I think, Frau Steinfeld, that this changes the situation completely!" the Public Prosecutor shouts.

Valerie nods.

Judge Arnold looks at the Prosecutor and observes, "But now that we do know about it, we have to take a look at this new situation, correct, Dr. Kummer?"

"Of course, your Honor, of course. I only meant, we'll have to begin again at the beginning, to all intents and purposes."

"Then we'll simply begin at the beginning. Frau Steinfeld is introducing new facts, and I am of the opinion, especially after such a positive anthropological report, that we must test and evaluate them properly."

"Does Mr. Landau know anything about it?"

Forster stands up again. "I have taken the liberty of asking Mr. Landau to be present so that he can be questioned without delay. He is waiting outside."

So that's Landau outside, the Prosecutor thinks. Now I remember. Good thing I kept my mouth shut. Especially with this new judge.

"Very thoughtful of you, Counsel," says the judge.

"It may not be completely in accordance with legal procedure, but since he's here already. No, no, Frau Steinfeld, please wait. I must swear you in again now. Raise your right hand and repeat after me ..."

All present stand. Valerie raises her right hand.

42

"Mr. Landau!"

The little man flinches. The dash and aggressiveness he showed during the first hearing are missing today. He is nervous and his mind is elsewhere.

Valerie watches him, her heart thudding.

"Pardon me, your Honor! I did not hear the question."

"I asked: it was therefore known to you that Frau Steinfeld had an intimate relationship with Mr. Orwin as well as with yourself?"

Oh, Valerie, what a mess you have stirred up! "That was known to me, yes, your Honor." Dreadful. "But I only found out after the birth of the boy, during a private conversation between Ludwig and myself."

"Ludwig: you mean Orwin?"

"Yes, Ludwig Orwin. He and I were very good friends, your Honor. And when Heinz was born, I felt proud and happy. I wanted Frau Steinfeld to get a divorce and marry me, so that I could acknowledge the child as my own legally. Well, one day I was in Ludwig's studio and we were drinking a lot, and I can't take too much, and I spilled the whole story to him about me and Valerie ... Frau Steinfeld."

"And?"

"Ludwig became quite upset and told me that he too had relations with Frau Steinfeld."

"Was *still having* or *had had*?" Arnold interjects quickly.

"No, no, had *had!* But it seemed to have been an intense relationship. They were still close friends, but Orwin had met a young woman and had fallen in love with her. That didn't last long, but his intimacy with Frau Steinfeld had been interrupted and was at an end. After this conversation with me Orwin became very withdrawn, and it was the end of our friendship, too, your Honor."

461

"And did you confront Frau Steinfeld with the situation?"

"Yes, your Honor."

"And?"

"She cried and . . . and . . . admitted that she had slept with both of us."

"But *you* did *not* break with her."

"No!" Landau livens up a little. "I suffered for a long time, it's true, but I was too fond of Frau Steinfeld, and much lonelier than Orwin. I had trouble getting to know people. Orwin was quite different . . . and then there was the little child . . . I kept telling myself Heinz was mine, and I've kept telling myself that until now; until the blood tests. Now I must come to terms with the truth: Heinz is not my son, but Ludwig Orwin's."

"Hmmm," Judge Engelbert Arnold says after a pause, during which he thought about that Berlin big shot, Klever, or about the Reich Office of Racial Purity, his promotion, and the praise he had received for his magnificent handling of certain court cases.

"In that case . . ."

The room goes deadly quiet.

". . . in that case we must proceed to have you take the oath, Mr. Landau."

43

"And so this hearing, too, ran its course," Dr. Otto Forster said, twenty-six years later in the hobby room of his snowed-in villa in the Sternwartestrasse. He handed Manuel a few more pages of the court records.

"So Frau Steinfeld succeeded in having the suit continued," Manuel said.

"Yes, she had succeeded in that." Forster nodded. "Everything went well when the witnesses testified. It was only with Fräulein Peintinger that something almost went wrong—I'll have to tell you about that when I've refreshed my memory a bit. I remember it only vaguely. But my son called to say he'll be at the office this afternoon and will personally search for the last few files. He's sure he will find them. If you'd like to come and see me again tomorrow ... I mean, I assume you want the information as soon as possible, don't you?"

"Yes," Manuel said. "And I expect you want to be leaving Monday and will be getting ready for your departure."

Forster smiled. "How happy I am, you just can't imagine. So shall we say tomorrow morning at ten-thirty?"

"Excellent."

"Then I'll tell you how the story ended insofar as I was involved. I was involved right until the very end, because I was thrown into prison in July '44 and the suit was still in progress."

"Still?"

"I know that for a *fact*. And something else: it was still in progress even though the second anthropological report, ordered by Arnold to show whether Ludwig Orwin could have been Heinz's father, was absolutely, brutally unfavorable and negative."

44

"Mr. Aranda?"

"Yes?"

Manuel was sitting in the drawing-room of his hotel suite. He had just telephoned Nora Hill and asked her if he could see her that evening. As soon as he had put the receiver back on, the phone had rung again.

"Ottilie Landau here," said a voice somewhat bashful in tone, a voice that until now had always been hard, aggressive, and imperative.

"I'd like to apologize to you, Mr. Aranda, for my behavior yesterday afternoon on the Cobenzl. And for my behavior in general ..."

He didn't answer. What's all this about? he wondered.

"... hope you'll understand, Mr. Aranda! I'm afraid, terribly afraid. The whole business is so uncanny! But I've had a long talk with Martin and I realize that we must help you find out the truth. None of it is your fault, you are totally innocent! And so I have decided to tell you what else happened."

"You?"

"Yes. I'm not the way people say I am. Everybody thinks I'm cold and heartless, but that's not true, Mr. Aranda! It's just that I have to take care of my brother. He's helpless, he would be lost without me. I'll come over and tell you what I know."

It's going in circles, everything keeps going in circles in this affair, Manuel thought. He said, "No, better not meet me at the hotel. Besides, I have an appointment this evening, I'm not free, anyway."

"And tomorrow?"

"I was just going to suggest that. Tomorrow afternoon: is that all right? About four o'clock? In the espresso bar on the Cobenzl again?"

"Splendid," said Ottilie Landau. "I'll be there."

Two hours later Manuel was sitting in the living-room of Nora Hill's apartment. It was snowing hard again, a storm had come up, and Nora's house was filled with loud, noisy guests. It was Saturday night. There were many cars in the parking lot. The sound of laughter, voices, and music floated into the living-room. Nora was in her armchair beside the fireplace, with Manuel opposite her, watching her partly through the flames of the crackling fire. Both were drinking whisky. Manuel was thinking that all his conversations with Nora Hill had taken place in the same manner and place, ever since he had met her for the first time: always the same fireplace, always the same, small portable bar at hand, and always Nora's crutches leaning against the fireplace . . .

"I know," said the amazingly young-looking woman. "Flemming's idea worked. The suit was taken up again by the courts, and was still running when the invasion began, and dragged on, and on. In August 1944 I flew to Lisbon for the last time. Flemming—no longer the man he'd once been—Flemming told me he'd make sure I have to stay in Lisbon for a long time."

"For how long?"

"Until the end of the war. The idea was I should not come back. He himself had to stay behind at his HQ, of course."

"What became of him?" Manuel asked.

"The Russians caught him in April 1945. He was deported to the Soviet Union. I found out from . . . from my Russian clients here later. They told me Flemming was kept alive in a prison-camp for two years, then shot." Nora shrugged her shoulders. "Too bad!"

The sound of loud laughter broke across the room from outside.

"An Italian," Nora said.

"I beg your pardon?"

"There's an Italian downstairs who's been introducing a new game: every guest has to describe the most comical coitus of his life. I listened in for a while before you arrived. But to get on with my story. Nobody at the German Embassy in Lisbon wanted to go back home, and they left me alone. Everything was chaotic, even there. I had a beautiful time with Jack for months. Twice he had to go to London. He was able to put Steinfeld's mind at rest: the lawsuit was dragging on and on and there was no end in sight. The war would be over soon, and I planned to move to England with Jack. That's what we talked about that night ... the February 12, it was, 1945. And balmy, a balmy night on the beach at Estoril ..."

45

Stars twinkled, the full moon shone, and the foamy crowns of the lazy waves shimmered like the lights of the luxury villas above the beach and the candelabra of the gambling casino.

The sand was very pale, and against it the long pier on its heavy wooden piles leading far out over the water gleamed black. Jack Cardiff and Nora Hill had made an excursion to Estoril, as they had so often before. They had dined, played a little roulette, and then walked down to the beach where they changed and went for a swim in the swirling waters.

Now they were sitting on the sands, Jack Cardiff's leather attaché case between them. They had taken glasses from it, then ice-cubes from a thermos flask, and poured two whiskies. Nora spoke softly and longingly of the life that lay before them.

"I'm already dreaming of our country inn, Jack, really! I can see it! I do see it in my dreams, again and again! It probably looks quite different in reality, but I can see the house, the trees all around, the big poplars ..."

"Yes, darling," said Jack Cardiff. Sunburned, bright-eyed, he seemed strangely uneasy. He kept looking around him, at the Moorish villas in their gardens, the fishing-village of Cascais, the old palm trees, the forests of giant pines. He poured two more drinks. Then he lit two cigarettes and handed one to Nora. She took it and smiled at him. "We'll decorate it in our own way, won't we?"

"Yes, darling."

"When do you think the war will be over?"

"In two or three months at the most."

"Then we'll be there in May! In May! Oh, Jack! And we have enough money! You're marrying a rich woman! All my jewellery, my gold coins, my furs, my stones, I got them all out and they're here! We'll never need to worry about money! Doesn't matter if it takes two or three years before our pub is making any profit."

"Nora ..." Somehow she didn't notice that his voice was catching in his throat.

"Yes?"

"There's something ... there's something I have to tell you."

"Then tell me!"

"I should ... I ought to have told you long ago, right away ... at the beginning. I ... I'm a swine, Nora."

"Is this some joke?"

"No, I wish it were."

"Well, what—"

"I haven't been telling you the truth." Cardiff was speaking with great effort. "I've been lying to you. From the very beginning."

"Lying to me? But how?"

"I can't go back to England with you and marry you."

"You can't? But why not? Please don't talk like that! You're just pulling my leg!"

"Nora, I'm married ... have been for nine years ... and I have two children," Cardiff said. Then he emptied his glass and refilled it. Nora watched him. He was drinking straight whisky.

"Give me one, too," she said. "Neat."

"What I've done is unforgivable, but when I saw you, I

just lost my head ... I've been wanting to tell you, Nora, really. Time and again I've been on the verge, but I never had the nerve when it came down to it. It was such a beautiful time we had together."

"Yes, wasn't it?" said Nora. "A really beautiful time. Here's mud in your eye, darling."

"Don't talk like that, please! And don't drink so fast!"

"But I'm thirsty! Come on, give me some more! A lot more! Fill the glass to the top! You were never stingy, at least!"

"Nora, please!"

"Not a miser. Just a liar. A liar out of love. That has to be considered." Nora was sipping at the whisky as she spoke. "That has to be a mitigating circumstance. Also the fact that you're telling me the truth now after all. I suppose it would have come out anyway, but you could have just split ... No, you're behaving like a gentleman."

"Nora, really, you're drinking too much—"

"And I'm going to drink a lot more after such a happy piece of news! That deserves a toast! And your wife, she knows nothing about me, I suppose?"

"No. Look, Nora, I—"

"Is she pretty?"

"I ... please!"

"So she is."

"She looks quite different from you!"

"Of course she looks quite different from me. That was the attraction. A blonde, right? I can see it in your eyes, I've guessed it! How exciting! A blonde in London, a brunette in Lisbon."

"Nora, stop that please! Please believe me, I lost my head! I swear to you, I sincerely—"

"If you say it, Jack, I'll smash this glass over your head, and it's a heavy glass. Which I'd like you to fill up for me again."

"No!"

"Oh, yes, I'm going to have another glass!"

There was a brief struggle for possession of the bottle, then Nora had a full glass of whisky again.

"The children are sweet, I'll bet," she said. "I drink to the sweet children, and your sweet, blonde wife, and to your sweet, happy future together!"

Cardiff watched her, feeling helpless.

"Don't make such big eyes, Jack. I'm not going to make a

467

scene. Everything's okay again. Just a little shock at even-time. A shitty German woman is fair game for that sort of trick any time. After all, you're at war with us! *C'est la guerre, voilà!*"

"Nora, please, please! We can stay good friends!"

"Of course, sweet friends!"

"... and I'll always be there ... if I can do anything for you!"

"You can."

"I can what?"

"You can do something for me!"

"What?"

"Come swimming with me again, right now!" she shouted, jumping to her feet.

"No! Don't! You've had too much to drink!"

"I want to have a swim! And you, you say you'll do any-thing for me, so come and swim with me!"

He tried to hold her back by one leg, but she twisted out of his grip, ran toward the wooden pier, then up and along it.

"Nora!" he yelled, running after her.

She had reached the end of the long pier. The water was deep there, and she dove into it head-first. A few seconds later Cardiff dove in after her, and tried to catch up with her.

"Come back!" he screamed. "Come out of the water! Nora, be reasonable, dammit!"

Her laughter swept across the waves to resound in his ears. She was swimming with a crawl stroke now, as fast as she could, constantly turning her head towards Cardiff and laugh-ing. She was swimming in a big circle. He was not far behind her. But she had in fact drunk too much and too quickly, and suddenly she felt it, powerfully. She lost her sense of direc-tion, her breath began to come in short gasps, and the sea and sky spun before her eyes. But she continued her crawl stroke, swimming straight toward the pier.

"Nora!" Cardiff shouted. "Look out!"

She took a quick glance ahead of her and caught sight of the black, massive posts and the planks of the pier looming up in front of her. Stretching her hands up, she reached the end of the pier and using the extra strength her drunkenness gave her, she dragged herself up out of the water, got to her feet on the pier, and began to race unsteadily across the slip-pery wooden planks.

"Nora! Nora! Stand still! Stop!"

Cardiff had climbed up on the pier after her. She heard

him behind her and turned around, losing her balance as she did. She fell and her back struck the pier with tremendous force. She felt a stabbing pain at the base of her spine, then lost consciousness.

The stars and the moon were the first things she saw when she came to. Then she saw Jack Cardiff beside her and noticed she was still lying on the wooden boards of the pier.

"Hi," Nora said weakly.

"Do you feel anything wrong? Have you hurt yourself?" She turned on her side and vomited a quantity of water that smelled of whisky. Then she moved her limbs and felt herself all over.

"No," she said, "everything seems Okay." She touched her back and gave a low scream, saying, "Jesus, that hurts!"

Cardiff bent over.

"Any damage?"

"I don't see any."

"So, I'm in luck," Nora said. "In luck *again*. My God, what an evening. Just one big stroke of luck, luck, luck!"

46

The next morning a letter was brought up to Nora's hotel room with her breakfast. The letter was from Jack Cardiff. He wrote that by the time Nora read these lines he would be on a plane to London, he had been recalled urgently to home base and was taking the first available morning flight. He did not think he would be coming back to Lisbon. He begged Nora from the bottom of his heart to forgive him. He would never be able to forget her.

Nora read the letter twice, then tore it to shreds. Her back hardly hurt any more. She felt like committing suicide, but was extremely hungry and so decided to have breakfast first. After she had breakfasted, she no longer felt like killing herself.

She moved to get out of bed and go to the bathroom, and discovered to her horror that her legs would not carry her. She could hardly move them. Three days later Nora's body was paralyzed from the hip to toe.

47

The greatest specialists in Lisbon, Rome, and Paris operated on Nora Hill a total of eleven times, performing major surgery on each occasion. Subsequently she spent an entire year in Paris in the private clinic of the French neurologist Professor Fleury. It had been established at the outset that the paralysis was caused by injuries sustained when she fell on the wooden boards of the landing-pier at Estoril.

The eleven operations were totally unsuccessful. Nora Hill could neither stand nor move her legs. So that she would not have to lie on her back the whole time, she received a specially constructed wheelchair. The nurse who looked after her during those two years, a young French girl, pushed the chair out onto the balcony of Nora's room whenever the weather was good. Later Nora was trundled through the parks of the clinic by the young nurse. She was an unbelievably agreeable and cooperative patient.

After the eleventh operation Professor Fleury, a white-haired man with a white pointed beard, told her, "Mademoiselle, it's no use, you have to hear the truth, and I know you will be able to bear it: we have tried everything in our power; but the truth is—"

"—that I'll never walk again," Nora Hill said calmly, interrupting him in mid-sentence.

Professor Fleury nodded.

48

Nora Hill took this final verdict with astonishing calm. In the summer of 1947, after undergoing massages of every kind, she began with superhuman determination to prepare herself for a life on crutches. Every day she practiced until she was exhausted. Only crutches were possible for her: as a result of the far-reaching paralysis of the nervous system, any other form of support for her legs was ruled out.

By the end of 1947 Nora Hill could propel herself on her crutches without help. She was still in possession of large fortunes in jewellery, was still a rich woman. She had a new wardrobe designed for herself in Paris. The British Embassy in Paris looked after her as solicitously as had the British embassy in Lisbon. After all, she was a woman who had risked her life for Great Britain during the war! And in 1948, on January 3, she was flown to Vienna in a British military plane.

The villa near the Lainz Zoo had been requisitioned by British officers. It came under the general heading of 'German Property,' and therefore belonged to the Austrian government. All the officers had been prepared for the arrival of Nora Hill. She found her apartment on the first floor exactly as she had left it two and a half years earlier. The British placed a jeep and a driver at her disposal. Later, after negotiations between the British Military High Command and the Austrian Authorities, Nora Hill received the clearance to buy the circular house. Now the villa belonged to her.

The English officers remained with her as her guests until 1950, and she gave many parties and held many discussions and conversations with them. She became the black-market queen of Vienna. She dealt in German Army material, scrap metal, and Marvel cigarettes, sometimes even with people. Her connections with the various secret services dated from those days, too. By 1950 Nora Hill had multiplied her fortune several times, and she knew exactly what lay in the future . . .

Soon after she had bought the villa, Nora remembered Valerie Steinfeld, and on March 17, 1948 she had herself driven through the devastated, rubble-filled, dismal city to the Kärtnerstrasse—once the most glamorous street in Vienna but now resembling the main street of a Polish village—then to the Seilergasse and the Landau Bookstore. She asked the sergeant at the wheel to wait, then swung herself on her light metal crutches toward the shop, dressed in Canadian mink, draped in jewellery, and wearing a pair of long silk pants. The metal sign still hung over the entrance, weatherbeaten as always. The glockenspiel melody sounded as she entered, *Take joy in life. . . .*

49

And there stood the bear with the basket of books in its paws. The basket was empty. Nora looked around. Lights were on, as they had been formerly in the frosted glass globes that hung from the high ceiling. The bookshelves were half-empty. Nora swung herself down the narrow passageway, where secondhand crime novels during the war had been stored. Now the shelves were empty, covered with dust and cobwebs. Light from the lamp with the green shade fell across the passageway out of the tea-room.

"Frau Steinfeld!" Nora called.

"Yes," answered a toneless, tired voice.

A moment later Nora reached the tea-room and saw Valerie, sitting at desk. She had turned at the sound of Nora's voice. She was wearing a smock—just as she did then, Nora thought, just as she did then. Her face was pale, she seemed to have aged greatly. Her blonde hair was combed upwards. It had lost its sheen. Her blue eyes, once so radiant, were dull.

"I'm Nora Hill, Frau Steinfeld!"

"Of course, Miss Hill. I recognized you at once. How nice that you come to see us. Please sit down." Valerie had got to her feet. Her hand was like a piece of ice, Nora noticed. Carefully but quickly she lowered herself into the defective rocking chair. Valerie did not resume her seat until Nora was seated. Her gaze was not only dull, but strangely fixed. She seemed to stare at something slightly above Nora's right shoulder. Her thin hands were clasped in her lap. She was smiling. She's like a blind woman, Nora suddenly thought. Yes, like a blind woman.

"Did this happen in an air raid?" Valerie asked with a serious face.

"No, at a different time."

"Terrible."

"There are worse things," Nora said, looking around. Everything was as she remembered it.

472

"And you?" she asked. "What happened with you?"

"It was a difficult time," said Valerie in her toneless voice. "But now it's past . . ." She was twiddling her thumbs as she kept her hands clasped in her lap.

"The lawsuit! Your boy! What happened to him? We haven't seen each other for such a long time, Frau Steinfeld! Tell me, please, what happened?"

Valerie answered softly, "Heinz is not here any more."

Nora felt a shock. "Is he . . ."

"No, he's not dead, Miss Hill," Valerie answered, looking and talking like a wax figure with a built-in talking-box. "He's alive. In Los Angeles."

"How did he get to America?"

"He was invited to study there. You remember that he wanted to be a chemist, I suppose?"

"Yes, of course. When did he . . . ?"

"He left me about a year ago. All we did was quarrel at the end, you know." During the entire conversation Valerie did not once look at Nora directly, but gazed past her all the time, her thumbs twiddling continuously.

"Quarrel? What about?"

"It was my fault. I've been too strict with him. The lawsuit made me so hard, I'm not the woman you remember. Heinz couldn't stand it with me any more. He's good boy. I've made mistakes, bad mistakes, I see that now. Nevertheless, I was hurt, of course, when my husband divorced me."

"Your husband . . ."

"Yes, Miss Hill. Right after the war. He's married again now, in London, has been for some time. A young woman, younger than I. He met her during the war. He's all right. He writes to me sometimes. I mustn't be too bitter about him. It was too long a separation, was it not?"

"But—"

"Yes, it was, yes, it was. And the times! The war should not have lasted so long. You didn't marry the man you loved, either."

"How do you know?"

"Would you be here otherwise? He left you, am I not right?"

Nora Hill nodded.

"The men leave their women. The women leave their men. One person is always leaving another, sooner or later."

"But the lawsuit! How can your son leave you, how can

your husband divorce you, after such a lawsuit?" Nora exclaimed.

Valerie's thumbs were twiddling at an accelerated pace.

"The lawsuit," she said, "was never concluded, it was still going on when the war ended . . . and now all that is past and over and unimportant and uninteresting . . ."

50

"Grisly," said Manuel Aranda, shuddering.

"Yes, the whole visit was grisly," Nora Hill answered.

Laughter rolled into the living-room once again from the hall where the guests were swapping their coitus anecdotes.

"I drank tea with her. Landau joined us, but said hardly a word. We just sat there looking at each other without talking."

"Did you have the feeling that Frau Steinfeld was mentally disturbed?"

"Not mentally disturbed. Just . . . confused. Landau was, too, though not so much. The woman had had a bad time, I told myself, after all. She asked me to come again as we were saying good-bye, and I invited her to visit me. But I'm sure she had the same feeling I did: those were just the usual empty courtesies. I had become a complete stranger to them, an embarrassment, even. And to be honest, I felt the same. They never called. And I never went back to the bookstore."

"Which means you were seeing those two for the last time, is that correct?"

"Yes, Mr. Aranda, that's what it means." Nora Hill smiled and showed her fine teeth. "It also means my story is at an end."

"But *my* story is not at an end! I still do not know the truth."

"Of course not. You'll have to talk to Dr. Forster again."

51

Outsize snowflakes were coming down in a veritable blizzard on the morning of January 26, 1969, when Manuel rang the bell at the garden gate of the villa in the Sternwartestrasse, punctually at ten-thirty. The buzzer sounded and the door clicked open. Manuel walked up the snow-covered gravel path to the house, the front-door of which was just opening. Anna, Forster's plump, round-faced housekeeper, appeared at the door, wearing her black dress but not her white apron.

"Yes?" Anna seemed completely distraught.

"What can I do for you?"

"My name is Manuel Aranda. You know me! Dr. Forster is expecting me. Good morning, Frau Anna."

The woman burst into tears.

"Anna! Has something happened?"

"It's the old gentleman ..."

"What about him?"

"He's dead!" Anna called out.

Manuel stepped back. "But . . . I . . . I was with him yesterday afternoon. He was bursting with life, and so happy about his big move. He was going to go to the Bahamas . . ."

"That's it," the housekeeper sobbed. "That's it, the doctor says. Must have excited him too much. His blood pressure, his heart, he wasn't well. It was the happiness killed him, too much happiness all at once."

"How did it happen?" Manuel asked, feeling a recurrence of his dizziness coming over him.

"During the night as he slept. His heart just stopped beating. He can't have felt a thing. This morning, when he didn't come to breakfast, I knocked at his door, then peeped into his bedroom. He lay there in bed, quite peacefully, smiling . . . yes, smiling with happiness . . ."

52

"Did you see Ludwig Orwin often, witness Peintinger?"

"Well, of course, your Honor, very often indeed. Mr. Orwin, God bless his soul, came to see Madame all the time when the Master was away on trips or just out of the house."

"The 'Master' you mention, that's Paul Steinfeld?"

"Who else?"

"Refrain from that tone, witness. What is wrong with you, anyway? Why do you talk so loudly? Why are you so red in the face? Don't you feel well?"

"I feel very well, your Honor," Agnes Peintinger said. The strong-willed woman with the broad, peasant face and long beak-like nose, was standing before the desk of the Regional Court Judge Dr. Engelbert Arnold. From time to time she swayed, but it was hardly noticeable. And she did in fact talk very loudly.

It was the morning of November 10, 1943, a dismal autumn day. In Hearing Room 29 Judge Arnold was continuing the new hearing set up by himself. Hermine Lippowski and Ottilie Landau had already testified under oath. They were sitting in front of the spectators' benches which were empty. The two women had testified that Valerie's relationship with the deceased sculptor Ludwig Orwin had been known to them, and that Valerie had told them that Martin Landau and Ludwig Orwin had had a violent quarrel on her behalf which had ended their friendship. Public Prosecutor Kummer was putting almost no questions. So his first impression had been right! This fellow Forster was obviously prepared to go to any lengths! A cunning manipulation with the object of getting the boy declared an Aryan despite the negative outcome of the blood tests. And it was going to be successful, Kummer had the feeling. So keep your mouth shut, Hubert, he thought to himself, think of the future.

Similar thoughts were in the mind of the ruddy-faced, rotund, presiding judge, Dr. Engelbert Arnold. He let his mind wander back time and again to the visit of Klever, the big-shot, from Berlin. But the witness before him at that moment was making him more and more nervous every second.

"But Mr. Landau also visited the house when Frau Steinfeld was alone, did he not?"

"Both men came, but not at the same time, of course. One after the other," said Agnes, trumpeting it out. Her eyes were glistening a little.

"Which of them came more often?"

"I don't remember that any more. Mr. Orwin. No, Mr. Landau. No, Mr. Orwin."

"Witness!"

"What period are you talking about, your Honor?"

"The summer of 1925."

"Then it was Mr. Landau who came more often. But Mr. Orwin was there, too, again and again. I'm sure of it!"

"And what happened when Mr. Orwin came to visit Frau Steinfeld?"

"The same as happened when Mr. Landau came to visit her."

"And what was that?"

"Your Honor, surely you can *imagine*!"

Arnold had difficulty restraining himself.

"Please answer my question, witness Peintinger!"

"Then I can only tell you what I *think* happened!"

"You are not here to say what you *think*, but what you *know*, understand?"

"Yes, your Honor!"

"Why is she behaving like that?" Forster whispered to Valerie. "If she keeps that up, we can get in trouble. The woman is always so sensible otherwise . . ."

Meanwhile Arnold had asked her, "So what do you *know*?"

"I know that Madame always sent me away when Mr. Orwin or Mr. Landau came! She always said she would make the coffee herself. And that's my job after all, don't you think, your Honor? But no, I had to go, rain or shine. When the weather was nice I used to go walking to the farm in the woods, and sit there for hours . . ."

"For *hours*?"

"Well, Madame always said I should stay away three or four hours." Agnes became very loud. "That was fine when the sun was shining. But when it was cold or *raining*! The

477

only thing I could do was go to the movies. And do you know how far the nearest moviehouse was from us?"

"Heavens!" Valerie whispered. "She is drunk."

"What!" Forster was horrified.

"I can tell by the way she's rattling on. Her speech is thick, too. She must have been drinking this morning, probably because she was so excited. I'm sure I'm right . . ."

"That's all we need," Forster said softly.

"And what did you find when you came back from your outings, witness? And please, talk *only* in answer to my question, understand?"

"Of course, I understand, your Honor. All right, then. Well, when I came home, Madame"—Agnes turned her head, swayed all the more precipitously as she did so, and looked through slightly glazed eyes at Valerie—"Forgive me, Madame, but I have to tell the truth here . . ."

"Witness Peintinger, for the last time! Look at me when you talk and leave out the side remarks!"

"At your service, your Honor. Madame was often in her dressing-gown."

"In her dressing-gown?"

"In her dressing-gown and her underwear. And twice I went into the bedroom and the bed was all messed up, like. Madame said she hadn't been feeling well and had had to lie down for a while."

"Witness, are you really telling the truth?"

"The truth by God, your Honor!" Agnes sobbed. "I adore Madame, I really do, she's the best woman in the world. But the itch . . ."

Valerie was staring at Agnes open-mouthed. Forster was tugging at his ear as though he wanted to pull it off.

"What sort of itch, witness?"

"Your Honor, you know what I mean!" Agnes put on an embarrassed look. "The poor soul. She can't help it."

"Help what?"

"Having the itch so, your Honor. I feel sorry for all women who have the itch so bad they need to—"

"Witness!"

"—but what else can they do? The itch is stronger than they are! Your Honor, I'm so glad that the itch has never bothered me so in my life! I can thank my Creator for that mercy!" Agnes had become very loud.

"Witness, don't shout like that in court!" Judge Arnold was

478

breathing heavily. "Are you suggesting that your bread-giver exhibited nymphomaniac tendencies?"

"*What* kind of tendencies?"

"That she was constantly looking for and finding male companionship?"

"Not constantly. But that which I saw was quite a lot already, don't you think? The Master, and Mr. Landau, and Mr. Orwin." Agnes looked across at Valerie again. "I beg you to forgive me, Madame, but the truth has to come out, is that not so?"

"Yes, it does have to come out," Judge Arnold exclaimed. He'd had just about as much as he could stand from this witness. If what this obviously half-wit said was true, then it would be impossible to say who the father of the boy was—the husband, or her lover Orwin, or even some other man—it was like looking into an abyss!

"Witness Peintinger, are you prepared to swear to your statements under oath?"

Agnes's face lit up. This time we've done it, Father, she was thinking.

"Of course, Director!" And a few moments later she was repeating the words of the oath, solemnly and ceremoniously, her right hand raised.

"*I swear it, so help me God!*"

53

"Her face was radiant when she took the oath, Valerie told me later," Ottilie Landau reported. She and Manuel sat at a window table in the large, circular, espresso bar on the Cobenzl. They had been talking for the past half-hour.

Manuel, still shaken to the core by Forster's sudden death, heard the woman's voice as if coming from a long distance away. Ottilie, hard-faced and tight-lipped, was elegantly dressed in a somewhat old-fashioned outfit. Manuel felt dazed, and had a headache. Forster's dead, he was thinking. The city from which he wanted so badly to escape would not let him go.

Manuel had told Tilly of Forster's death. She had been profoundly shocked. For the first time since Manuel had known her her voice sounded gentle, warm, and womanly.

"So everything went well. Now a new report had to be submitted to the court. We had won another round. And we had gained time, time! After the hearing Valerie reproached Agnes, naturally. She was merry, my God, really merry, and replied. 'Yes, I had a little drink! I said to myself, this time the judge has really *got* to let me take the oath! But without the schnaps I would never have had the nerve to let such things cross my lips about Madame. But in this state I didn't care about anything or anybody! And it worked, didn't it? I was sworn in! I was allowed to take the oath!'" Tilly Landau said, "That was what she wanted so much, you understand?"

Manuel nodded.

"And so," Tilly continued, "the lawsuit dragged on and on. Valerie had until the end of October to submit to the court the proof of Aryan descent for Orwin, and as many photographs of him as she could rake up. As it turned out, there were plenty of photographs—Orwin had been a fairly famous man—but several of the necessary supporting documents just could not be traced. It was January 1944 before she had them all together. Then all the material was sent to the Anthropological Institute. The next hearing did not take place until May of that year."

"With the catastrophic report," Manuel interjected.

"Yes," Tilly continued, "the report was a disaster. The SS-physicians presumably said to themselves: 'it was our so *positive* first report that was decisive in the court discussion to have this case prolonged. We want to make sure that does not happen again.'"

"And they succeeded?"

"There were two further hearings. The verdict was pronounced at the beginning of June. It was several typescript pages long. But in a nutshell, the case was dismissed. Valerie almost had a breakdown, but Dr. Forster said: 'Now we'll appeal to the Reich Supreme Court in Leipzig!.' It was really incredible, how Forster continued to stick his neck out for her . . ."

480

54

Exhausted, his legs heavy as lead, Heinz Steinfeld got out of the No. 41 tram at the Währingerstrasse—Martinstrasse stop around 7 P.M. on September 11, 1944, and walked the short distance to the Gentzgasse. He walked with the shuffling step and hunched shoulders of a manual laborer. As he opened the door of the apartment he heard voices coming from the large living-room. He went in and saw his mother, the two Landaus, brother and sister, and Agnes. They all fell silent as he entered the room and stared at him. Over the radio, a so-called 'People's Receiver,' came the sound of the ticking clock from the air raid warning transmitter.

"Good evening," Heinz said.

Immediately he was encircled by the persons present, who embraced and hugged him. His mother and Agnes kissed him.

"My boy," Valerie said, "my little boy . . ."

"What's going on here?" Heinz felt suddenly revived. "Is there news from Leipzig?"

His mother dangled a sheet of paper in front of him. "Yes, Heinz, yes! From Dr. Burkhardt." Dr. Burkhardt was an attorney in Leipzig whom Forster had requested to represent him when he lodged the appeal. Valerie's voice sounded uncertain, her sentences came out haltingly. Her eyes were shining.

"And from the Reich Supreme Court also!" She held up a second sheet.

"The verdict?" Heinz asked.

"Yes," Martin Landau exclaimed. "It's the verdict!"

"And?"

"You can see," said Tilly Landau, "Agnes has baked a cake, we've brought two bottles of wine: we've got something to celebrate!"

"So the Reich Supreme Court . . ." Heinz's voice caught.

"Yes," Valerie replied, her voice shaking, "the Reich Supreme Court overturned the Vienna Court's decision. The five Judges on the Leipzig bench have formulated a new disposi-

481

tion in the case, according to which you are now an Aryan. We have won the suit!"

"Heinzi, Heinzi!" Agnes called out. "Heinzi, isn't that wonderful?!"

The slender youth did not answer. His gaze went right through the people standing before him and soared beyond, into the far, far distance. The clock of the air raid warning transmitter ticked on relentlessly. Without looking at anyone, Heinz intoned in a flat voice, "At last."

Landau had uncorked a bottle of wine and filled some glasses. He handed them around. "Now let's drink a toast to the happy result!" Martin Landau said. Valerie was looking at her son worriedly. He was not really there, she thought, Everyone clinked glasses and drank. Just as they drained them, the sirens began to howl, a long, drawn-out moaning sound.

"It's been a long wait. But now everything will go fast." Heinz now smiled as he spoke.

"What will go fast, Heinzi?" Agnes asked.

"My getting into the Army," the boy answered. "I had my physical a long time ago. They turned me down. Not draftable! That's all changed now!" He laughed happily. He was not looking at anyone, and so failed to notice that the adults were staring at him with renewed fear, shocked and terrified expressions on their faces.

"But I'm not going to wait until they come for me. Tomorrow I'm going to volunteer for the armed SS!"

A glass crashed to the ground and exploded into pieces. It had slipped from Valerie's fingers.

55

"The armed SS!" Manuel Aranda exclaimed, horrified.

Tilly Landau nodded. "There was no talking to the boy anymore. Whenever we just got a few words out, he started to scream and rage like a madman. No, there was nothing to be done. My brother and I left soon afterwards . . ."

"What was Frau Steinfeld's reaction?" Manuel asked.

"She had many quarrels with the boy during the next few days, fight after fight after fight! That was when the two started to grow away from each other. The split between them began then." Tilly sipped her hot chocolate. "But he got his way. He received his draft call at the end of September. He wouldn't let anyone take him to the train. He had to go to some place near Pressburg for training. Valerie was on the verge of a complete breakdown. She'd had a tremendous to-do with her son at the end, and they had parted very bitterly."

"And what happened to the boy?"

"After his training period they sent him to the front. Hungary."

"And he lost his life—in the last few months of the war?"

Tilly looked up in astonishment.

"Lost his life? No. Why?" She shrugged her shoulders. "The danger was great, of course. You can't imagine how Valerie suffered. Heinz hardly ever wrote, and even some of the few letters he did send were lost in transit, but no, no, he was lucky, he survived and even escaped being taken prisoner. His unit was transferred to Upper Austria, back beyond Vienna. And when the Americans marched into Upper Austria, Heinz took refuge with some farmers and stayed in hiding for a while. Valerie heard from him in June. He did not want to come home anymore."

"Didn't want to come home?"

"No. He and his mother were bitterly estranged, as I told you. None of us really knew what the times and the lawsuit and all this miserable business of Aryanism had done to the boy's mind. He didn't want to return to Vienna either, because the Russians were here, and he was afraid of being taken prisoner. So he went to work on a farm, and when the Canadians said they were accepting immigrants, he applied right away. He wanted to get out of Austria, and out of Europe! Valerie begged him to stay. At that time there were a lot of people on the road who were willing to carry letters with them. She implored him to come to his senses. He answered with bitter remarks. His whole world had fallen apart. He had identified himself so intensely with the German side, and become—it's a terrible thing to say, but it's true—an outright, fanatical Nazi. Heinz! And then Valerie made the big mistake."

"Mistake?"

"She told him the truth. Wrote to him that everything had

been nothing but lies. That he really was in fact a half-Jew."

"She wrote and told him that?"

"Yes, Martin told me. Everything I'm telling you I learned from Martin. He was always with Valerie in the shop in those days, remember? I didn't see her for months, I had to look after the house in Hietzing. And I got sick, too. Martin was the one who told me what went on ..." Tilly spooned whipped cream onto her cake. "Valerie's truth-letter made something snap in the boy's mind. He wrote back that he didn't want to have anything more to do with her or any of us! And then he emigrated to Canada, on one of the first boats. Frightful for Valerie, all that, just frightful! A year later Heinz was killed in an automobile accident in Quebec. When that happened Valerie almost ceased to be a human being. Everything she had done and suffered was wasted, everything wasted ..."

Always. Always the different stories about what happened to the boy, Manuel was thinking. What's true and what's a lie? Valerie Steinfeld herself told Nora Hill that Heinz had gone to Los Angeles to study. And that her husband had married another woman in England ...

Manuel asked, "And what about Paul Steinfeld? What happened to him? Do you know that, too?"

"Yes," Tilly Landau replied. "I know that, too."

56

Wydalo mi sie, ze swiat—obojetny dotad na moje sprawy—zwrocil ..." said a woman's voice over the loudspeaker of the large 'Minerva-405.' Valerie Steinfeld was sitting on the sofa in the tea-room, without a blanket over herself and the set. She had turned the BBC up very loud. In the shop up front, Martin Landau was making a lot of noise. It was the lunch-hour, and the bookstore was closed. The time was 1:20 P.M. on May 18, 1945, and Vienna had had two months of glorious springtime, with trees, bushes and many varieties of flowers sprouting forth between the ruins and the rubble. The battle for Vienna had run its final course and the corpses of civilians, German and Russian soldiers, and piles of horses, had had to be buried with great haste, as they decomposed very rapidly. Valerie had become very thin, and her back was slightly bent.

"... *sie nagle ku mie*," the young woman's voice continued, then became fainter, and another voice was superimposed, the man's voice that Valerie had been listening to for years with a thudding heartbeat, the voice that had been bringing Paul to her, her one and only consolation in the dark and difficult years that lay behind her and were still with her today, living as she was without news from Heinz, not knowing whether he was still alive, or was wounded, captured, or dead.

In this BBC broadcast many voices spoke, in many languages. Reporters had been to Germany, and had interviewed two dozen of the millions of refugees and escapees now flooding the country roads.

Someone knocked loud and long at the locked outer door of the shop. Valerie ignored it. She continued to give her undivided attention to the voice from London, which was translating what the young Polish woman was saying: "Heaven was no longer far-off. With loving fondness it had returned to Mother Earth, casting light upon Her vastnesses and shadow upon Her homelands, following the flight of the birds, and wallowing within the cups of the flowers. Its name was Freedom ..."

As the last words were being spoken Valerie had heard steps approaching. Now she looked up, to see a Russian officer standing in the entrance to the tearoom.

The Russian took off his flat cap and bowed. He was scarcely forty years old, and had a solemn face with large, dark eyes.

Valerie turned down the volume of the radio, until the voice from London was quite soft, then stood up.

"The major insists on speaking with you," Martin Landau said, standing behind the Russian wringing his hands, his head tilted to one side, his left shoulder hunched. "He says it's very urgent."

"Yes, it is urgent." The Soviet officer spoke fluent German with a Russian accent. "My name is Mossyakov, Frau Steinfeld. I worked in the German Section of Radio Moscow. Now I am with Radio Vienna, as Officer in Control. We are rebuilding the network. I was just in Salzburg, and spoke there with a few American and British radio officers, and with several newsmen from the BBC."

"And?" Valerie's face was as immobile as a mask.

"One of the BBC people was called Gordon White. Do you know him?"

"No."

"But he knew your husband. He asked me to come and see you during my next stay in Vienna ..." Mossyakov took a step forward, as though wanting to be near enough to steady and support Valerie. "It grieves me greatly, Frau Steinfeld, but there is something I must tell you. You will be given the news officially as soon as the Allies get to Vienna. The Red Cross cannot cope. Please forgive me for being the one to bring you the news, I . . ."

"What news?" Martin Landau exclaimed.

"Paul Steinfeld is dead," replied Major Mossyakov.

"What?" Landau fell back against a shelf.

Valerie was staring at the Russian as though she could not see him.

"Dead, yes," Mossyakov said.

"But when . . . and how . . ." Landau stammered.

"He died a week ago, on May 11. He had liver trouble, Gordon White told me." Mossyakov was speaking very quickly. "About a week ago Mr. Steinfeld collapsed in the studio after a broadcast. They rushed him to the hospital, but it was too late. Your husband died of an internal hemorrhage, Frau Steinfeld. Gordon White asked me to assure you that he could not have suffered. His death was a gentle one . . ."

"Valerie!" Martin Landau exclaimed. "Valerie!" He brushed past Mossyakov. "Valerie, keep calm, I beg you! It's a terrible piece of news, but you must not . . ."

"Rest assured," said the blonde young woman to Landau. Then she turned to Mossyakov, her feelings under complete control, and said, "There must be some mistake, Major."

"I fear there is no mistake, Frau Steinfeld."

"But there must be!" Valerie turned up the volume on her radio. A muffled voice was speaking in Yugoslavian and a German was translating:

". . . I have survived the holocaust. I am on the way to Sarayevo. If God helped them as he helped me, then my wife and my son will be alive and well, and I shall see them again, and we shall all be together again . . ."

"There!" Valerie Steinfeld exclaimed, as the voice went on translating. "There! How can my husband be dead when you can hear him speak this very instant!? That's the BBC, Major! I've been listening to the BBC all through the war! My husband used to be a radio announcer! I know his voice—it's his voice you're listening to now!!"

The Russian had been biting his lips. Now he replied, "Those are the interviews with Displaced Persons, are they not?"

"Yes," Valerie nodded. "Why?"

"They are made long before they are broadcast, Frau Steinfeld. You must understand that these interviews took place earlier. Your husband must have spoken the commentary for this broadcast several days ago, shortly before his death ..."

"But what about the other broadcasts I heard during these last few days with his voice?"

"Was he reading the news?"

"No, not that. Commentaries and suchlike ..."

"You see."

"You mean, they were all recorded?"

"All on records!" Who knows whose voice it was this woman actually hears, thought the Russian wearily.

"Major," Valerie Steinfeld said. "Thank you for coming." The Russian squeezed her hand, bowed, and left. Valerie locked the outer door again.

"My God! This is awful! Awful! You must lie down. You look like death, come, quickly ..." Martin Landau had hurried after her.

Now they stood facing each other by the old Baribal bear at the entrance.

"I don't have to lie down. I feel all right," Valerie said in a voice that sounded strangely childlike. "So Paul is dead. And it was a recording I was listening to ..." She never finished the sentence. She slid to the floor without a sound, and lay there motionless, in a dead faint.

57

"A collapse," Ottilie Landau said. "She had suffered a collapse. Martin ran for a doctor, who came right away and gave her an injection. Valerie regained consciousness. The doctor made her stay lying down on the sofa in the tea-room. By evening he had arranged for an ambulance—an almost insoluble problem in those days! Valerie was taken home in it, and had to stay in bed for a week, with the doctor coming to see her every day—Martin and I, too, of course. Agnes looked after her. During that week Valerie spoke to nobody. Then, eight days later, she was on her feet again and back in the shop."

"She must have had tremendous self-control."

"Yes. You cannot imagine the strength this woman possessed. But there was one thing Valerie never did again."

"What was that?"

"She never listened to London again. She gave the radio to Martin. You know Martin a little by now, don't you? He didn't want to give the radio away and that's why it's still in the tea-room." Tilly shrugged her shoulders. "We spent a lot of time with Valerie in those days. But she remained closed-mouthed forever. During all the years that followed she scarcely ever mentioned her husband. British officers brought the death certificate in the summer of 1946. The BBC bought a grave for Paul Steinfeld and paid for his burial. They also assumed responsibility for maintaining the grave, and it has been kept up at their expense right up to the present day."

"Frau Steinfeld never went to London to visit it?"

"No, never, Mr. Aranda. She ... she was an extraordinary woman, and during the years through which she and all of us grew older she became very inward and silent, even with us and with Agnes. Irene Waldegg was the only person towards whom she showed any warmth." Tilly shrugged her shoulders. "Nobody knew what was really going on inside her, what she was thinking. She must have been leading a complete double life!"

"A double life?"

"How else can you explain what she did at the end? We can't find any explanation! And that's why we're so afraid! And that's why I wanted to prevent our getting involved in it at any price!"

"I understand," said Manuel Aranda.

58

The powerful flashlight beam wandered slowly over the dark, ancient wall, scanning innumerable dates, initials and symbols scratched into the hard stone.

"Leave it now," Irene Waldegg said. "You'll never find it!"

"I'll find it," said Manuel Aranda who was holding the flashlight.

"Let's go," Irene said. "I'm freezing!"

"There!" exclaimed Manuel. "There it is!"

The light beam settled on a heart scratched into the stone, weatherworn and partly crumbled away. Inside it, as Manuel and Irene were able to pick out, were the initials B.H. and H.S., under them the year 1941, and a horizontal arrow pointing towards a figure eight lying on its side, the mathematical symbol for infinity, or 'eternity.' Bianca and Heinz had met in 1941, and wanted their love to last into eternity.

"You found it!" Irene felt her heart skip a beat.

"Here is where they stood in December 1943," Manuel said. "Exactly on this spot, where we are standing now. That's why I wanted to come here with you."

"Why?"

He faltered. "Well, I thought . . . I imagined . . . oh, I'm a stupid idiot!"

Irene gently took the flashlight from his hand and switched it off. In the pitch darkness she moved close to him, put her arms around his neck, and found his lips with hers. He hugged her tight. The kiss lasted long. They stood in utter silence, pressed close to each other, motionless. He took his lips from hers and whispered, "May I come to your place?"

He felt her body go suddenly rigid. "No," Irene said, "please don't, Manuel."

"Forgive me," he murmured.

"Don't be sad," she said, stroking his cheek. "I . . . I . . . I want to as much as you, but—"

"But what . . . ?"

"It's everything," she said, taking his face in her hands,

"everything that's happened. All the terrible things that have happened, and the weird things that are still pursuing us. I've no peace of mind, Manuel, no peace of mind at all. Please be patient with me. I'm so fond of you. Let's ... let's save that for when everything is behind us, when we know the answers, the truth, the sense, when there's no more mystery. Can you understand me?"

"Of course I can." He kissed her hands. "I understand perfectly. And I will wait—however long it takes. Come now, I'll take you home ..."

Hand in hand they left the arcade, meeting-place of lovers throughout the centuries, which now lay dark and deserted behind them.

59

The woman who took care of the building Kohlmarkt 11 lived on the ground floor of the neighboring building. She was responsible for two apartment houses. On Monday January 27, 1969, at 9 P.M. precisely, she pulled the lever controlling the house lights so that the lamps in the halls and stairways would not burn constantly, but would go on for a period of sixty seconds only when someone pressed a light switch. Then she locked the old, green main entrance door to No. 11 and walked quickly through the driving snow back to the next house, locking its door from the inside.

Ten minutes after 9 P.M. two men were standing in front of the entrance to the law-offices of Dr. Rudolf Stein and Dr. Heinrich Weber. They were wearing felt slippers. Their shoes were in their coat pockets. The two men were Jean Mercier and the tall, slender Anton Sirus, the legendary king of safecrackers. This man, with his massive head, sharp eyes, fine, sinewy hands worthy of a surgeon, this passionate amateur and collector of French Impressionist art, had spent the last two hours waiting with Mercier in the drafty, ice-cold attic of the office building. The Professor had opened the lock of the attic door with two flicks of the wrist. He had arrived in Vienna at noon, and had spent the afternoon in

490

a back room of the Travel Agency Bon Voyage. The two men had then come to the building separately. Mercier had to be present during the operation, because he had to decide which papers in the big safe were of value to himself and his superiors.

His hand shaking with cold, Mercier aimed a flashlight at the Yale lock of the door to the law-offices. The "Professor" worked with three wires which reminded Mercier of roulade skewers, except that these wires had sharp teeth and indentations at their front ends. Sirus seemed to be a man completely free of nerves. On the floor beside him he had placed a large bag of the type formerly carried by doctors. After six minutes the lock snapped open. It took the Professor four minutes more to open the second lock in the door. The two men stepped into the dark office. Anton Sirus closed the door and re-locked it. Treading soundlessly from room to room he assured himself that the curtains in each room were drawn, then he climbed on a chair in the outer offices and opened a little black box hidden behind a filing cabinet. The Professor had found what he was looking for. With a few deft movements he disconnected the burglar alarm. Next he walked with Mercier into Dr. Stein's private office, where he snapped on the high-intensity desk lamp, turning it so that its light was directed at the huge, softly gleaming door of the wall safe.

The two men took off their coats, Sirus his jacket as well. It was very warm in the office. Mercier sat down in an armchair in front of the desk. Like Sirus, he was wearing black crêpe gloves. The Professor had brought him a pair.

"There'll be no fingerprints this way. I use only crêpe and never rubber. With rubber you lose the feeling in the fingers, and you need that."

Mercier watched in silence as the big man opened his bag. On top was a white surgeon's gown, which he quickly flung on over his head. He tightened it to his body with two knots behind his back. Then he handed Mercier several gauze pads.

"You'll have to wipe my forehead from time to time."

Mercier nodded without speaking.

Next the Professor pulled a stethoscope from his bag and hung it around his neck. Then he spread a cloth over the desk and placed upon it at least three dozen thin, long strangely shaped steel tools. The whole thing looked like a set of surgical instruments. The Professor took out a white surgeon's cap and put it on.

"Retains the sweat from my scalp," Sirus said. Then he stepped forward, contemplating the safe broodingly as though examining a patient, then turned around again and took a writing-pad and a pencil from his bag. The task Anton Sirus faced was a formidable one—Mercier had received a brief explanation of its dimensions as they had waited together on the roof, so he had a fair idea.

At about chest height the wall safe had a chromium-plated steering-wheel. Above the wheel, at about shoulder height, was a cone-shaped knob roughly four inches in diameter, about four inches in depth, and notched all around the sides. This snub-nosed knob was encircled around three-quarters of its rim by a silver band. The upper left quarter segment was missing. Digits were engraved into the silver band. The first digit was 00. There followed nine equidistant slashes, then the number 10, and so on around the cone up to the number 90, which marked the end of the three-quarter circle. The cone had a single-line black pointer painted on it.

"00, 10, 20, 30 and so on are the tumblers for the digits 0, 1, 2, 3, and so on," the Professor had explained. "The cone can be turned to the right and to the left, in normal position or in pulled-out position—it pulls out about a quarter of an inch. The seven-digit combination is put together in irregular sequence from digits that have to be clicked into the tumblers by turning the knob to the right and left, in normal and in pulled-out position. But a turn one single stroke too far locks the whole system automatically, and you have to start all over."

"What do you do then?" Mercier had asked.

"The combination lock has to be released again."

"How?"

"By reversing every single turn to the right and to the left, in normal and in pulled out position, and continuing until the lock is released."

"But that means you have to remember every turn you make exactly!"

"That's why one has to take notes all the time. A mistake at the beginning is not too tragic. But on the sixth or seventh digit it can be really tough."

"Oh, God."

"Don't say Oh, God yet! That's only the beginning. Even with the entire seven digit combination, only the tiny doors on the safe wall open, and can be swung out . . ."

The tiny doors he mentioned were situated above the

492

cone-shaped knob and the chromium-plated steering-wheel, and were half an inch in height each, 1½″ wide and 4 inches long.

"Behind each of these tiny doors we then face two times two openings leading into the safe. Every one of the openings contains an eight-inch key. Once the combination is set right these reserve keys can be withdrawn. The safe must still, however, be opened up on top and at the bottom, which means cracking the two locks at the top and bottom."

"How is that done?"

"You'll see," the Professor had said. "The steering-wheel can be turned only after those two locks are released. Turning the wheel causes steel shaftings in the roof, sides, and floor of the safe to slide out of their groundings and back into the armor plating. After that a tug on the steering-wheel opens the safe."

"And you think ... I mean ... you really think you can do all that?"

Anton Sirus had merely looked at Mercier without saying a word ...

He now put the stethoscope to his ears, pressing the rubber mouth at the end of a long red tube as close as possible to the cone-shaped knob and the encircling digits. He said,

"From now on I have to ask you to be absolutely quiet."

Mercier sat motionless, scarcely daring to breathe.

The Professor worked without a trace of nervousness. After twenty-six minutes he turned suddenly around, removing the stethoscope from his ears.

"That one's dropped all right," he said calmly.

"The first digit?" Mercier leaped to his feet.

"Not so loud! It's only the first digit! *Eight.*"

"So we have one out of seven already!" Mercier was suddenly excited. "With luck ..."

The Professor raised a hand, tapping the desk with the knuckles of his other hand.

"Never say that word again," he said severely.

"I'm sorry," Mercier stammered.

"Any idiot can find the first digit."

60

Daniel Steinfeld said:

"I saw Valerie for the last time in July 1948. I had come to Vienna for a few days to attend an international reunion of former resistance fighters."

The sixty-nine-year old looked around the large room, where he and Irene and Manuel had settled. He was a frightening sight. His suit hung baggily on his large frame. His yellowing skin was stretched tight over the bones of his emaciated face with its bloodless lips and sunken cheeks. His weary eyes were yellowish, too, as was the skin of his bald head, flecked with brown spots. His bony fingers were yellow. Daniel Steinfeld still spoke with a Viennese accent. The "Chopin Express," on which he had travelled to Vienna, had arrived very much behind schedule at 3:45 P.M. at Vienna East.

They had eaten in the dining-room, Steinfeld his special diet, prepared by Irene. After supper they had returned to the living-room to have tea. Steinfeld was allowed to drink tea, and it was his main pleasure in life. And as he sipped at his tea, hunched over, the ghost of a man who, as his suit showed, had once been strong and powerfully built, he had begun to tell his tale . . .

". . . 1948 it was, yes, in July. She looked bad, Valerie did, really terrible. Like an old woman. And she wasn't old at all! She had been such a beautiful girl once. But now she had completely immersed herself in her grief. She told me everything then . . . that Paul had died in London just before the end of the war, of internal bleeding. It was a big shock for me, too, to hear it, even though Paul and I had never hit it off too well."

"Why not, Uncle Daniel?"

"Just call me Daniel, please, Irene."

"Happy to . . ."

"Why not, indeed? We just didn't get along, not even as children. We were always fighting about ridiculous little things. Our parents were very unhappy about it, but there

494

was nothing they could do. Paul was the older. I firmly believed my parents loved him more than me—all nonsense of course, but that's what I thought." The old man, who was still determined to travel to the distant land of his ancestors, raised his hands. "And then there were the girls . . ." Steinfeld smiled. "There was one I was madly in love with. She got to know Paul, fell in love with him, and he took her away from me . . . that sort of thing happened time and again. He was already successful in his profession and I was still struggling with exams . . . and I was envious and impatient, yes, I think I was to blame for the bad relationship between us." Steinfeld sipped his drink and continued. "I was very immature and couldn't take setbacks. It took a long time for me to learn that a man who wants to live his own life must be able to withstand its vicissitudes. A man has to know that things will be good for him sometimes, and sometimes bad. And only that man is worthy of respect who is grateful for the good and knows how to bear the bad." Steinfeld took another sip.

"Wonderful tea," he said. "When our parents died, in 1919 and 1920, one after the other, Paul and I started to grow away from each other. If there were still moments when we acted like brothers, they were moments created by Valerie, our good angel. Now she is dead, too; in 1948 she was sitting here with me—it's so long ago! It must have been her very worst time. Then there was the business with her boy, young Heinz. She found out everything about him in December 1945, from another boy, I've forgotten his name . . ."

61

His name was Erwin Traun, he was a year older than Heinz Steinfeld, and they had been friends in the armed SS. They served in the same detachment of the same company, were both from Vienna, and Heinz greatly admired the strong, hefty Erwin. Erwin in his turn admired Heinz's intelligence and daring, which bordered on the foolhardly.

March 15, 1945 was a warm, beautiful day with sunshine and a blue sky. There was new grass growing in the fields, and the snow had melted. Large units of various SS Divisions had been hastily moved to line of defense west of the Danube blockaded by trenches, tanks, barbed-wire fences, and mine-fields. Having taken Budapest in February, the Soviets were ready to attack Vienna. They were massing their forces, ready to advance on both sides of the Danube.

On this morning of March 15 all was quiet in the detachment to which Erwin Traun and Heinz Steinfeld belonged, no fighter planes ripping through the sky, no rifle shots from snipers, no artillery fire. Everyone knew it was the lull before the storm. Erwin and Heinz were squatting in a hastily dug trench behind a heavy machine gun, keeping their eyes fixed on the opposite bank of a narrow river. Its waters were clear, and along its banks there were visible brightly washed stones and dark, jagged, flotsam and jetsam. The terrain sloped down sharply from the defense lines across fields and meadows to the river. Beyond the Raab was a dense forest, from which, it was clear that the Soviets would shortly appear to launch their offensive.

"Man," said Erwin Traun, pushing his steel helmet back from his forehead, "once hell breaks loose around here we won't be able to hold them more than half a day, I hope you realize that."

"We've *got* to hold them!" Heinz Steinfeld, behind the heavy machine gun, spoke vehemently. "We'll be getting rein-forcements."

"Reinforcements my ass," Erwin said. "Where will they come from, do you suppose?"

"From the north. A whole Army division. The Danube Division."

"Heinz! North of here the Russians are already at the Danube. You couldn't drive a pig through there any more! Your Danube Division doesn't exist!"

"It does exist! The Old Man said so last night! And the Old Man doesn't lie! They beat the Russians back in the North! And when they get here, there'll be all hell to pay! Why else do you think the Russians keep waiting? Why do you think they're still hiding in the forests over there and not coming across the river?"

"That's bullshit!" Erwin cursed. "We've been betrayed and sold out down here, that's what, and we're going to get our asses shot off and if we don't all croak here we can thank our lucky stars!"

"Shut your dirty mouth, you yellow swine!"

Erwin swung round, and looked at his friend in utter surprise.

"What sort of talk is that?" Heinz hissed. "Have you gone nuts? We *must* win this war, otherwise it will be the end of Germany! The end of the West! But we will triumph! The new wonder weapons are about to be deployed! Once we start with them, the world will hold its breath! And you, you stupid bastard, you're babbling about getting your ass shot off! That's . . . that's . . ." Heinz paused to wipe froth from his mouth and murmured, "I'm sorry, I didn't really mean it that way! Say something! Say you're not angry!" Heinz's face was that of a child under the steel helmet. "Erwin, please! I've got something for you! Chocolate! You're crazy about chocolate, I know! I've got a whole bar . . . here, wait, you can have it!"

"Aw, shit. That's okay."

"No, I want you to have it." Heinz straightened up to reach for his ration kit, which hung from a tree stump behind him. As he did so his head bobbed up over the edge of the trench. An instant later there was the thud of a mortar gun going off.

Erwin Traun flung himself to the ground and dug his face into the damp soil. The mortar shell, fired off from the opposite bank of the river, exploded split-seconds later in the air directly above them. Erwin heard the swish and hum of shrapnel and burrowed down into the dirt. Suddenly he felt his comrade's body close beside him. "You lousy dog," Erwin cursed. "Why did you have to go sticking your nose in the air? Well, we got off lucky that time." He sat up, then let out a stifled cry. *"Heinz!"*

Heinz Steinfeld lay on his back, his eyes wide open, teeth bared, blood gushing from his mouth with every breath. Blood, more blood, a terrifying outpouring of blood came seeping through his shredded uniform from above the chest on the left side, reddening the ground and in the blood that streamed from him and soaked the earth lay a piece of chocolate . . .

"Heinz . . . Heinz . . ." Erwin Traun knelt down by the side of the wounded man, then shouted as loudly as he could, "Medic! Over here! Quick! Hurry up, you bastards! Steinfeld's been hit!"

Voices answered from nearby. Erwin bent over Heinz. "They're coming, boy, they're coming, they'll be here in a jiffy . . ."

Using a roll of bandage he tried to stem the tide of blood heaving from Heinz's breast. The cloth was immediately soaked through. Heinz must have been hit by a large piece of shrapnel. His breath was coming in slow, shallow puffs now, the blood pouring from his mouth was bright red. His face was white.

Erwin Traun put his hand on his friend's forehead, mopped the sweat away, heard Heinz say something, but it was incomprehensible, choked by the constant flow of blood.

"Don't talk, Heinz, don't talk, Heinz . . ."

"Germany," Heinz gurgled suddenly and distinctly. He raised his head and looked at his friend through vacant, staring eyes. "Germany will . . ." His head fell back.

Erwin Traun heard the tramping of boots. The medics, he thought, tears rolling down his cheek. They're too late. He's dead. Heinz Steinfeld is dead . . .

62

"The Russians attacked the next day. I got the hell out of there while everything was confused during the first skirmish. Got as far as the Tyrol." said Erwin Traun on December 12 in the tea-room of the Landau Bookstore. "I've been back in Vienna since yesterday. Heinz told me a lot about you, Frau Steinfeld, that's how I knew where you worked . . ."

Erwin Traun, thin, in mechanic's coveralls that didn't fit him, sat freezing with cold on the tattered couch, and looked anxiously at Valerie Steinfeld. Behind Valerie stood Martin Landau, holding one hand over his heart and stammering, "Horrible . . . really . . . horrible . . ."

Erwin Traun began to feel uneasy in the presence of the slim, blonde woman with the expressionless eyes. Why did she not say anything? Why did she not break down? He had expected and feared and steeled himself for her breakdown. But not for this silence, this immobility.

"Heinz cannot have suffered, he died immediately. Believe me! Please believe me!"

"I believe you," Valerie said. "I knew that Heinz was dead."

"What?" the boy on the sofa exclaimed.

"What?" Landau exclaimed. "How do you mean, you knew? Since when?"

"Ever since the Russian officer came to say that Paul had died. That day, I had a sudden flash of intuition before I lost consciousness, and I knew for certain that Heinz, too, was dead. And ever since then I have been living with this certainty . . ."

"But the grenade that killed him—" Erwin began, but was interrupted by Valerie, who said, "It was not a grenade that killed him."

"I don't understand . . ."

"It was not a grenade that killed my son," Valerie Steinfeld said, her eyes fixed on the two volumes that had been the start of a big adventure, so many years ago . . .

63

" 'It was something else that killed my boy," Valerie said. "Namely, a man. There's a man who has my boy on his conscience!"

Daniel Steinfeld held out his cup to Irene, who refilled it with tea. "Thank you, my child. Yes, that's what happened to Heinz. And that's how Valerie heard the news, in December 1945, from Heinz's comrade. And that's what she told him—she told it to me three years later, in 1948, when I visited her."

A long silence followed Steinfeld's words.

After a while Manuel said, "So it was all for nothing, everything that Valerie did to save her boy."

The sick old man nodded as he replied, "For nothing, absolutely for nothing. But the story didn't end there for Valerie! Oh, no! She became slowly obsessed with one fixed idea. Nobody could get her off it. It was the idea that a man, and not a grenade, had killed her boy."

"Who, Daniel, who?" Irene shouted.

"That Professor Friedjung, Director of the Institute for Chemistry Studies."

"Friedjung?" Manuel stared at Steinfeld.

"Karl Friedjung, yes. Everything had started with him. He was the one who had thrown the boy out of school and reported him to the Nazi authorities. He was the reason Valerie filed that lawsuit, a suit which at first she did not want to bring at all, but which she finally did fight—and win!"

"I understand her thinking," said Irene. "It must have gone something like this: if Friedjung hadn't done what he did, there would have been no lawsuit, then Heinz would not have been sent to the front, and that means he might have survived the war—as so many other half-Jews did . . ."

"That's what she thought, yes," Steinfeld said, sipping his tea. "Her mind was in a complete whirl. What had been right once was wrong now. What had once meant salvation now meant disaster, unhappiness, the end. And the person to blame for all this misery, misfortune, death, and waste was, in Valerie's mind, Karl Friedjung. She just couldn't stop thinking of him, day-in, day-out, always. What's wrong, young man?"

"But Friedjung was dead, too!" Manuel exclaimed. "She must have known that if she was so interested in him!"

"She knew. She had been told. She was shown his death certificate and all the other documents to prove it," Steinfeld answered. "But it changed nothing. Her fixed idea grew more and more obsessive. And besides: a man doesn't have to be alive to be believed responsible for something."

Manuel stood up, rubbing his forehead. "Was Martin Landau present when the young soldier brought the news?"

"I told you he was!"

"And he was also present when the Russian officer came with the news of Paul Steinfeld's death. Apart from Valerie he is the only person ever to have learned the real truth. Once, when I asked him if Frau Steinfeld had won the lawsuit, he replied, 'She won it, and she lost it. When you have heard everything, you will understand what I mean.' I understand that now, he was right. But there's something else I don't understand."

"What's that?"

"Frau Steinfeld was constantly spreading new versions of the death of her husband and her son." The old man nodded. "Why did she do that, why, Mr. Steinfeld?"

The sixty-nine-year old Jew from Poland, formerly from Vienna, exiled from Warsaw and on his way to Israel, answered, "You can only understand that by thinking yourself

500

right into Valerie. And probably that's impossible. A woman—Irene!—will perhaps be better able. You see: Valerie did have just *one* happy moment: when the news came from the Reich Supreme Court in Leipzig that she had won the case."

"But the happiness was all over that very same evening, when Heinz declared he would volunteer for the armed SS," Manuel interjected.

"Absolutely right! Valerie must have suffered a terrible shock at that moment. After all she and the others had risked, that was the pay-off. That was how their anxious waiting was to be rewarded, that was how her son thanked her."

"And what followed were fights and quarrels with Heinz ..." Irene looked at Steinfeld.

"One thing led to another," Steinfeld said. "Fear for Heinz's safety followed on the heels of her despair. For weeks she didn't have a single line from him. Valerie began to reproach herself: if only she had not brought the lawsuit! But she had had no choice—and all because of Friedjung! He was the one who was to blame for everything. But how far was she to blame, herself? She started accusing herself, more and more vehemently. Then came the news of her husband's death. Another blow! Paul—dead! Then the news of the boy's death. That was the climax. She couldn't take it. Do you understand that? *She was incapable of bearing the truth!* The truth had to be not true. Because even if Friedjung was to blame, so was she. She told herself that day and night. And she didn't *want* to be to blame! She could not *bear* that!"

"And for that reason she began to lie," Irene said.

"Clumsily, awkwardly, telling one person one thing, another something else. Lies to prevent herself from feeling blame. Yes, I can understand that. Valerie was not to blame if her husband was killed in an air raid, if he divorced her and married another woman. And no blame could attach to her if her son emigrated to America or Canada and died there in an automobile accident! She was not to blame for that! She was not to blame! Her sense of guilt, her desire to liberate herself from it, obsessed her. That was what made her lie, and keep on lying. Can't you understand that, Manuel?"

"Yes," he said. "I think I can."

"Only Valerie and Martin knew the truth, and Martin never gave her away!"

"Agnes, too," the old man said. "Agnes knew the truth,

too. Those three. And the three held together and kept silent."

"There were four persons who knew," Manuel said. "You knew, too, Mr. Steinfeld."

"Yes, I knew, too. I . . . I" Steinfeld was speaking hesitantly, "I even know what happened, once, between Karl Friedjung and Valerie . . ."

64

Zierleiten is the name of one of the most beautiful footpaths through the southern slopes of the vineyards at the foot of the Vienna woods. The path is narrow, ancient, with weatherbeaten, centuries-old "Virtrer's" madonnas, sculptured in stone, standing at intervals by the side of the pathway. The Zierleiten starts at the Western edge of the Vienna woods and cuts directly through the vineyards in an easterly direction. Walking along it one always sees the city in the valley below.

On the afternoon of June 25, 1922, two young people were wandering over this enchanted path, over which, in places, blackberry and elderberry bushes formed a leafy roof. The bright sunlight flashed from a hundred thousand windows, and gleamed golden on the domes of churches and the cornices of old palaces. It was warm, very warm, and the leaves of the vines all around were thick and green. Bumble-bees buzzed and hummed through the air. The two young people were deeply immersed in discussion.

"In 1918, after a heroic struggle that lasted four years, we were disastrously defeated. Two great countries—Germany and our own Fatherland. Tragedy had struck."

It was Karl Friedjung speaking, in an excited, emotion-ridden voice, a youngster of eighteen, tall, slender, with thick, brown hair, brown eyes and an open, appealing face. He wore a white shirt, knickerbocker trousers, heavy walking shoes, and a windbreaker.

Valerie Kremser was walking close beside him, for the path was narrow. She wore a dirndl. Her blonde hair shone dazzlingly in the sunlight. She was the same age as Friedjung, almost exactly the same age, in fact. Both youngsters were due to take their final exams in just a few weeks.

"But there's one thing," Friedjung said, "that could have turned this tragedy into a blessing!"

"What's that, Karl?"

"I'll explain it to you, Valerie." He laid his arm around her shoulder. They had known each other for about six months. Valerie, who was living with her uncle's family because her parents wanted her to attend an especially good high school in Vienna, was weak in mathematics and chemistry. Friedjung was the best in his class in these subjects, and tutored his classmates in them, because in these times of inflation it was not easy ever to get enough to eat. Karl Friedjung's pupils, among whom was Valerie, paid him in groceries, which he handed over to his parents like a good son. Karl Friedjung made a great impression on Valerie because of his intelligence, his idealism, and his knowledge. And his behavior was impeccable. He had never once, during a lesson or on one of their walks, taken advantage of a situation. He had not even kissed her once, even though she had been expecting it.

And yet . . .

And yet there was something about Friedjung's fanaticism, his political involvement, that frightened her, however much she admired him for it. There were times when she actually felt afraid of him. And she had never told Martin Landau, the man she had met in the Albertina, of her friendship with Friedjung. An instinct warned her not to. Martin Landau—that was a different kind of man, living in a different world. So Valerie kept her friendship with Friedjung a secret. Despite her liking for him, she was uncertain of her feelings toward Friedjung. She could admire him, be fond of him, but *live* with him? No—that she would never be able to do, not any more. Because now . . .

She tore herself out of her own thoughts and listened again to his voice:

"The German-Austrian Republic was not only to unite us with Germany but also to embrace all German territories of the former Empire in the Alps and the Sudetenland, remember? That was what was planned, remember? And then came that vicious Treaty of St. Germain! September 1919!" Friedjung kicked a stone from the path. "Article 88! Annexation attempts of any kind are forbidden! The designation

503

'German-Austrian' is forbidden! They lied to us, Valerie, betrayed us, sold us out! Do you see that?"

"Yes, Karl, yes." What he was saying seemed reasonable to her, and she shared his feelings. And yet ... yet there was something that made her shudder when he spoke in that vein. She said, "The consequences of the Peace Treaty bear out what you say."

"God, God!" said Friedjung, his eyes staring into the distance, but he saw neither the gleaming city nor the beauty of nature all around him. He strode along taking no notice of the road, hitting at the bushes along the path with a branch he had cut from a tree.

"Czech soldiers have occupied the defenseless territories of the Sudetenland, right? And are oppressing our brothers there! The southern Tyrol is occupied by Italian soldiers all the way to the Brenner! Styria occupied in the south by Yugoslav troops! It must not be allowed to continue, Valerie! We must fight for the Annexation! The workers have to understand that! And that is our mission, to explain it to them, to prove it to them!" Friedjung had stopped and was standing still, whipping the air with his branch.

"Loyalty! Faith! Honor! Self-sacrifice! Courage! Decency! Duty! Patriotism! All these concepts have been dragged through the mud since the war. They're laughed at now by our fine conquerors, those double-dealers, and by the scum of our own people! It's up to us, to *us*, to see that these words begin to make sense again, that they take on a meaning for values worth fighting for, yes, yes!" He noticed that the girl was watching him, fascinated, half in admiration, half in fear. "What is it?" he asked her.

"Nothing, nothing, Karl."

Suddenly he flipped his branch away and stepped up close to her. All at once his voice lost its cocksureness, he found himself groping for words, a bashful teenager.

"Valerie ... I ... please forgive me if this comes as a surprise, but—"

"What do you mean, surprise?"

"... but I don't know another soul in the whole world with whom I can talk this way, not another single soul. I ... I love you, Valerie. Do you think you can love me, too?"

"Oh, God," Valerie said.

"What?"

"My poor Karl." Valerie stroked his cheek. "I'm fond of you, really I am. Very fond ..."

504

"Fond. Oh. I see."

"No, you don't see." Valerie bowed her head. "I've met a man, Karl. He's older than I am. We've known each other for some time now. I should have told you. But I didn't know that you . . ." She couldn't go on.

"Another man." Friedjung applied pressure with one hand under her chin, so that she had to raise her head. "What sort of other man?"

"He loves me very much."

"And you love him," he said dismally.

"Perhaps. He is so good to me, so human. I'm really sad for you. This man and I, we're going to be engaged."

"What?"

"Yes. As soon as the exams are over. I have to introduce him to my parents. They haven't met him yet."

"That means you'll marry him?"

Valerie nodded.

"And what's his name? This man's name?"

"Paul Steinfeld."

"The journalist?"

"Yes, Karl."

Friedjung spoke his next sentence softly: "But this Paul Steinfeld's a Jew!"

"That's true. I don't understand what that—"

But he interrupted her, and now was almost screaming. "Have you gone mad? The filthy pigs who've got us into this mess, who've destroyed everything, who've caused all the misery we're in now—*it was the Jews!* And now *you* want to become *a Jew's whore?*"

A split-second later Valerie had slapped him across the face with the flat of her hand as hard as she could.

65

"Karl Friedjung never forgot that blow," the ageing Daniel Steinfeld went on. "The relationship between them was finished of course, and hate took over where love had left off. Finished, I said? No . . ." Steinfeld shook his head. "No,

505

that's wrong. I think that it would be more true, in a deeper and different sense, to say that the relationship between the two never ended, never. Because what is hate if not the other, darker side of love?"

"Valerie told you about this incident herself?" Irene asked. It was 11:15 P.M. A beautiful antique clock with a horizontal four-ball pendulum behind glass showed the time.

"Yes, in 1948, when I visited her," the old man said. "She had never said anything about it to anyone else ever before, not even to her husband or to Martin Landau. Nor had I myself any idea in 1929 that the young instructor at the Institute for Chemistry Studies, who later worked for me, that this young Dr. Karl Friedjung knew my brother's wife. He never said a word about it to me."

"Friedjung was your assistant?" Manuel exclaimed.

"Yes. Right up to the time of my emigration. An outstanding biochemist, he was. But even in 1929 his political views were those of a fanatical Nazi, and grew more and more so."

"What was his attitude toward you?"

Daniel Steinfeld shrugged his shoulders. "My collaborators and I were a team. There were Jews, Catholics, Atheists, Nazis, and Communists among us. I had forbidden any and all politics in my department. So the working climate stayed tolerable. And then we were all too taken up with our work to indulge in petty squabbles and fights. I do believe I can claim that peace reigned in my laboratories longer than anywhere else ... A top-notch scientist, he was," Daniel Steinfeld said. "Very gifted. And with a strong pedagogic talent."

"He became Director of the State Institute for Chemistry Studies, after all," Irene said.

"Yes, he did." Daniel stroked a bony hand over his bald skull. "Actually not until a year after Heinz came to the Institute. Valerie told me that. She got the shock of her life! She would never have sent Heinz there if she'd known. But when she first registered Heinz, the Director was an elderly, tolerant man whom she trusted completely. But because of his age and tolerance he was pensioned off a year later and Friedjung put in his place."

"Who at first behaved with absolute correctness toward Heinz," Manuel said.

"At first, yes. He was waiting. Time was on his side. He knew his chance would come during the four years Heinz still had to spend at the school. The chance to revenge himself on the boy for the humiliation he had received. He was ap-

506

parently one of those totally convinced Nazis. But what does "Nazi" mean anyway? A certain type of person . . . A certain kind of regime. There have always been Friedjungs, and always will be, and no one should be arrogant enough to say 'that couldn't happen here!'" Steinfeld sighed. "Well, anyway, as soon as Friedjung had a chance to show his claws with right and the law on his side, he grabbed it. He revenged himself on Valerie by taking it out on her son, the son of a Jew. He wanted to destroy Heinz! If he could not destroy Valerie and her husband, then at least the mother should lose her child. Heinz must be sacrificed! And he achieved his purpose, though differently from the way he had planned . . ."

"And he died himself in the process," Manuel said.

"But that is precisely what Valerie would not accept," Daniel Steinfeld said.

66

"He's alive!" said Valerie Steinfeld.

"He's dead!" said Daniel Steinfeld.

"He's not dead," Valerie Steinfeld replied.

"Good God, you're just imagining that! It's a fixed idea you have! You don't have the slightest evidence that Freidjung is alive."

It was July 12, 1948. The day was a scorcher.

Valerie and Daniel Steinfeld were sitting in the shade of an old tree on a bench in the Volksgarden, near the Burgtheater. The gardens all around them were ablaze with blooms. Bomb craters and shrapnel holes had been filled in and planted with new grass, new flowers and bushes, so that even while hunger and misery still prevailed in Vienna, the city's parks blossomed and sparkled, a refuge for exhausted people and a playground for laughing children with their balls and old tires.

"No evidence?" said Valerie. "I have mountains of evidence!"

"What, for instance?"

"I have spoken with people who were there when the Chemical Institute was bombed. All of them say the same thing: the bodies were so disfigured they could be identified only by the papers found on their persons."

"But Friedjung was identified by his wife! *And* by students of the school! *And* by his colleagues!"

"Yes, from his papers!"

"How can you be so sure? Have you talked to all the witnesses? And to his wife?"

"To all except his wife. She won't talk to me about it. I've tried several times. No use."

"Why won't she?"

"Friedjung must have told her about me and Paul and the boy. She refuses to see me. She hates me."

"Valerie!" Steinfeld took one of her hands. "You have to pull yourself together. This woman doesn't hate you. Why would she? She just doesn't want to be reminded of her husband's death. It's *you* who's doing the hating! *You* hate Friedjung! You *want* him to be still alive!"

"He *is* still alive," Valerie said stubbornly.

"He is *not* alive, he's *dead*. Yesterday I took the trouble of going to the magistrate's offices and looking at his Death Certificate. Then I went to the graveyard in the Ettinghausenstrasse, and took a look at Freidjung's grave. Valerie, *please!*"

"When the air raid started a lot of people came into the Institute from off the streets for shelter. Students and professors have all told me that. And when the bombs started hitting the building, they were all trapped in the dark cellars for a long time. Friedjung dressed a corpse in his clothes, put his papers in the dead man's pockets and when the rescue squads arrived he sneaked off and disappeared."

"You think that was the way it happened because that's the way you would have liked it to have happened!"

Valerie continued, "Friedjung had a girl-friend. I know that for sure. I've investigated that, too. She lived in the Siebensterngasse. She had a baby. An illegitimate baby. The housekeeper swears to that. The woman's name was Spiegel. She was twenty-seven years old at most. Friedjung kept coming to see her. He was her lover and the father of her child."

"Says the housekeeper."

"*Yes!* Yes!"

"How does she know it was Friedjung who was visiting the young woman?"

"I described him. She recognized him from my description."

"The other way around would have been more interesting."

"A week after the raid on the Chemical Institute the Spiegel woman and her child disappeared. At night! A car came to pick them up. She left everything behind, took only one suitcase with her. It was a large car with a chauffeur. And he was sitting in the back. Friedjung."

"The housekeeper saw all that? In the middle of the night? In pitch darkness?"

"There was some light inside the car." Valerie did not let herself be distracted. "Friedjung picked up his mistress and went underground."

"Where to?"

"Anywhere. Germany. Abroad. He was a Nazi big shot! Anything was possible for those people just before the collapse. He's alive, Daniel! Friedjung's alive! And I'll find him . . ."

He said nothing, feeling uneasy. It's all senseless, he thought. This woman's grief has completely muddled her mind.

"And once I find him . . ." Valerie did not finish her sentence. But her white hands clenched into tight fists.

67

As quick as lightning Anton Sirus's hand turned the cone back. He muttered a curse under his breath. Mercier, who was standing next to him and had been mopping the Professor's brow from time to time, jumped aside, frightened.

"What was that?"

"A close shave. Almost a catastrophe." The Professor was breathing heavily. "Half a space beyond the right number. I could hear the reserve mechanism getting ready to snap shut."

Mercier went pale.

"Good God! We have four digits already." He looked toward the desk and the sheets of paper covered with notes and calculations. At the top of one sheet were the combination numbers found thus far: 8 4 1 9.

"In twenty minutes it will be midnight," Mercier said. "And you would have had to start all over again."

The Professor merely nodded. He was back at his post at the cone-shaped knob. He turned it millimeter by millimeter toward the number he had passed. All at once he stopped and took the stethoscope from his ears. "The fifth digit is 3." He wrote it down, then made a note of all the movements of the knob he had made, forward and back, normal and pulled-out, in order to find the 3.

"This is a profession that can teach a man to pray," Mercier said.

He had scarcely spoken the last word when the whooping of a siren sounded from the streets below, coming closer.

"Light out!" the Professor hissed, softly.

Mercier rushed to the desk lamp, switched it off. The office was now in total darkness. The Frenchman fumbled his way across to one of the windows and peeped out from behind the curtain. A patrol car came hurtling down the deserted, snow-covered street, blue roof-light turning, siren whooping, and skidded to a stop directly beneath the window.

"Police," Mercier said breathlessly.

He received no reply, but was so petrified he didn't notice. He kept staring down into the street. Two uniformed policemen had leaped out of the car and started running. Mercier did not see where they went. Minutes passed. Mercier started to pray, silently. If things fouled up now, at the last second . . .

Suddenly the police came into view again. They were dragging a raging drunk, who was shouting like a madman. With some effort they got the man into the car. The car doors slammed. The blue light started to rotate, the siren whooped, and the patrol car drove off.

Lights had gone on in a number of windows across the street, and people were leaning out to catch a glimpse of what was going on. It must be the same on this side, too, Mercier thought. Oh, well, no matter. In luck again. He let the curtain fall back into place, groped his way to the desk and switched the lamp on. He got a shock: Anton Sirus had disappeared!

I'm losing my mind, Mercier thought. That's impossible, he thought, just impossible. He can't simply have dissolved into thin air. Then he saw him.

The Professor was sitting in the lotus position, his legs folded under him, on the carpet. His face had taken on a gentle, rapturous expression. His gaze was fixed on the open book shelves packed with legal books. He was motionless, and apparently in utter bliss. He reminded Mercier of a statue of Buddha. The only difference, Mercier reflected, is that the Professor's hands are in his lap, peacefully and relaxed. The Buddha always has one hand upraised.

"Mr. Sirus!"

No answer, no reaction.

"Sirus, what's wrong?" Mercier exclaimed, mildly panic-stricken.

The Professor didn't bat an eye. He was gazing past Mercier at the bookshelves.

"Sirus! Sirus! I beg you, say something! One word! Just one word!"

But Anton Sirus said nothing, and Mercier flopped down into an armchair. He's not dead, he thought idiotically. Dead men don't sit upright like that. He must have gone mad, the mental strain and the shock must have been too much for him. Mad, yes, that's what he is. And here am I, trapped in an office I can't get out of without his help . . .

68

One day at the beginning of September 1966 two men were sitting in a modern chemical laboratory located at the back of a large building. An old park was visible through the windows. The Institute was situated twenty-two miles south-west of Warsaw, and was a branch of Warsaw University. In this lab Professor Daniel Steinfeld, and a hand-picked staff of colleagues, were engaged in research on new forms of pesticides. Steinfeld had a Chair for biochemistry at the University, but often spent long periods at the lab. Despite his age, he possessed enormous vitality. His face was that of a fifty-year-old, his cheeks ruddy, his eyes sparkling, a band of hair wreathing his massive, scholarly head.

The second man in the bright laboratory was bald-headed,

his eyes bulged, and he exhibited an impressive corpulence. He panted as he spoke. Thomas Meerswald suffered from a touch of asthma. He and Steinfeld had known each other for many years. A close friendship bound the two men together; Steinfeld the celebrated Polish scientist, and Meerswald the Viennese who had built up a collection of documents which enabled him to track down Nazi war criminals and secret arms câches all over the world. On this mild September day Steinfeld had had no inkling that in just a year he would be expelled from the university, divested of all his offices, and accused of being a "Zionist and American agent." And Meerswald had no idea that he had less than two months to live . . .

"I've found out a little about that man Karl Friedjung," said the Viennese. Steinfeld had arranged for him to have access to the huge Polish archives in which tens of thousands of German war criminals were listed systematically and with full documentation. Steinfeld was Meerswald's contact-man to all the official agencies, and the two men had been working together since the end of the war.

"The files show that Friedjung had worked on secret research projects under the Nazis, in addition to his job as Director of the Institute for Chemical Studies in Vienna. That job was just a cover. The research projects were coordinated out of Berlin: they were on poison gases."

Meerswald's breath came in rattling wheezes. "Here in Poland I have found conclusive proof of Friedjung's experiments with concentration-camp prisoners. At least sixty people died through him."

"Everything you say is true, I'm sure, Thomas," said Steinfeld, standing up. "But Friedjung is dead! Killed in an air raid on the Institute for Chemistry Studies. I was in Vienna in 1948 and saw the Death Certificate with my own eyes. I also visited his grave and talked with his widow. The man is dead."

"Your sister-in-law doesn't think so."

"Valerie?" Steinfeld sighed. "Hasn't she calmed down yet?"

"She came to me two months ago and told me her story."

"Thomas," Steinfeld said nervously, "don't let her drive you crazy. The poor woman has suffered terribly . . ."

"I know."

". . . and she was completely confused when I saw her last. We haven't been in contact with each other for an age. She never writes to me. I thought she was doing it purposely in order to forget all the horrors she had gone through, to avoid being reminded . . ."

"And that's true. She told me I should not tell you about her visits to me, because you would simply say she wasn't quite right in the head."

"*Visits?* Did you see her several times?"

"Yes. And with her came a man from the Argentinian Embassy in Vienna. Gomez was his name. My man for Argentina. We used to meet at a different spot each time—in his position Gomez has to be careful."

"Why was Valerie present?"

"I wanted Gomez to hear what she had to say, too. He knows his way around in his own country. I was hoping he might be able to identify Friedjung when Valerie described him exactly and told him all she knew about him."

"And?"

"We drew a blank. Gomez had a few people in Argentina checked out, but the results were all negative. No trace, not the slightest, of Friedjung."

"That's what I've been trying to tell you!" Steinfeld was getting excited. "Why won't you believe me? There can't be any trace of Friedjung, he's dead, dead, *dead!*"

"Then why was I being shadowed whenever your sister-in-law and I met with Gomez?"

"You were being shadowed?"

"I have a nose for things like that, you know. We were followed all the time. Cleverly, very cleverly."

"Thomas," Steinfeld said, "is that the first time you've been shadowed?"

"Of course not!"

"So? A man like you is tailed all over."

"Sure, when I'm travelling. But not in Vienna! That's the first time I've been tailed in Vienna! And your sister-in-law was with me every time."

Steinfeld got up and carefully studied a dark-red fluid bubbling in a glass cylinder. A long cooling spout was attached to the neck of the cylinder, and from it dripped a colorless distillate. Steinfeld said, "You're not only after war criminals, Thomas, you're after scientists, too, who are producing new weapons somewhere in the world. You have been seen with Valerie Steinfeld. The people watching you must know what happened to her. They know about me. I could produce B- or C-weapons, too, if I wanted to. So I'm a man who's very interesting to the West, am I not?"

"That's true. And if Friedjung were still alive . . ."

"Oh, stop harping on that, please!"

"In a moment. If he were still alive, Friedjung would be interesting to the West and to the East, assuming that he has continued his researches. He was a fanatical Nazi. Germany lost the war. If Friedjung were still alive he would, I'm sure, keep on working and then sell the results of his researches to the Americans for example, out of hatred for the East. Am I right?"

"He's dead, Thomas, he's dead!"

"But just supposing he were *not* dead! The revenge motive would be colossal, would it not? Could be that I'm wrong, and it's the *Americans* he hates! After all, they, too, were fighting against Germany. Then he would put the results of his work at the disposal of the East. Both possibilities are real . . ."

69

"So help me God," the Professor said, tugging the cone-shaped knob on the wall-safe to the pull-out position. "I'll try it like that now."

8 4 1 9 3 5.

These numbers were written side by side on one of the sheets of paper on the attorney's desk. The Professor had found the sixth digit during the past three-quarters of an hour.

It was 12:46 A.M. on Tuesday, January 28, 1969. The Frenchman, so exhausted he was ready to drop, was standing next to Sirus, who showed no signs of fatigue; Mercier mopped the safecracker's face from time to time.

It had been the most strenuous night of Mercier's life. He could still feel the chill in his bones that had shuddered through when he had first caught sight of Sirus sitting motionless, staring fixedly at the bookshelves. The Professor had remained in his Lotus position for six endless, horrible minutes, hands in his lap, his face gentle and enraptured, as still as a statue, while Mercier stood by the desk gnawing his knuckles and alternately cursing and praying under his breath. Then, so suddenly that Mercier let out a soft cry, Sirus got to his feet with a graceful movement and smiled at the Frenchman. He radiated a sense of infinite peace.

"What ... what was the matter with you?" Mercier stammered. "What were you down there on the floor, in Heaven's name?"

"Yoga," the Professor said, flexing his fingers to loosen them up.

"What?"

"I'm an old devotee of yoga. It's the most wonderful thing on earth. The spirit is liberated through meditation, concentration of the mind, and complete mastery over the body. At difficult moments in my work, when, just like now, a catastrophe has been narrowly averted, I always sit down like this."

"So it was not the siren that disturbed you?"

"What siren?" The Professor sounded perplexed.

"You didn't hear anything?"

"I can't remember."

"But you remember my switching off the light?"

"You switched off the light?"

Mercier merely groaned and made a gesture of resignation. The Professor, refreshed and possessed of energy, had gone back to the safe.

The knob, now in pulled-out position, turned, infinitely slowly. Mercier couldn't bear to look, and cast his eyes to the side. An instant later he heard the Professor say:

"We have the seventh digit. It's 2."

Mercier whirled round. "The whole combination?"

"We'll know in a moment." The Professor stripped off his stethoscope and reached for the tiny door above the cone-shaped knob. It swung open on its hinge, revealing two keyholes. From the lower one protruded a steel rod.

The Professor bent down.

The second tiny door swung open, too.

From one of the keyholes in the lower lock Sirus drew a steel rod about eight inches long and a quarter of an inch in diameter, with strange serrations at one end. After that he pulled the second rod from the upper lock.

"The bars come out," he said. "So the combination must be right." He laid the two rods on the cloth he had spread over the desk. "Now we still have to open the two locks."

"How?"

The Professor held up a steel rod very similar to the two he had just removed from the safe. It had a holder and a number of bent steel pins projecting from it.

"This is one of my own little inventions. With it I . . . well, I suppose it won't harm to blow my own horn a bit . . . I became world-famous." The Professor moved one of the tiny pins. To Mercier's amazement, a single notch from the serrated end of a key, about one millimeter thick, slid out of the smooth end of the rod. He saw now that this end of the rod had a succession of fine slits. The Professor nudged a second pin. A second steel edge, bizarrely cut, emerged from one of the slits.

"You follow the system, I suppose?" Sirus said. "I introduce the steel rod with all the individual key-notches still inside it. Then I start trying it out, going through every conceivable combination of notches until I find the one that fits the lock. If I don't get the right one with one rod, I move on to the next rod. As you can see, I have about a dozen of them here. They're all for this type of safe. That's the reason why I had to know in advance what type of safe we're dealing with."

"You have tools like that for other types of safes?"

"Of course. The collection as a whole represents a fortune, as you can imagine."

"And once you have managed to open the locks, are you able to lock them again?"

The Professor looked at Mercier with raised eyebrows.

"Of course," he said. "Or do you prefer me to leave the safe door wide open? If so, you would have done better to have hired somebody else. When I am finished the safe always looks exactly as it did before I started. Anton Sirus leaves no traces . . ."

70

"I feel obliged to object to this question most vehemently!"

"Now come on, it's not all *that* extraordinary!"

"Oh, yes it is! I'm going to tell you something, Paul: what

we're doing at the Institute is basic research, pure and simple, theoretical research."

"Sooooo."

"Yes, basic research, pure and simple! We base what we do on work that's already been done, of course! And we take into consideration, therefore, what Ransom wrote as early as 1898 about the effect of bacterial toxins on the motor nerves, and we are aware of the possibility that our investigations might have some practical results—in the area of pesticides!"

"Aha! And in the area of military—"

"No! Never! That is absurd! That is completely impossible! Nothing but the hare-brained notions of a journalist!"

"For goodness' sake, stop it!" Valerie Steinfeld exclaimed unhappily. "You don't see each other for ages and then you do nothing but yell at each other!"

This conversation took place on evening towards the end of November 1936.

The brothers were sitting opposite each other in the living-room of the apartment in the Gentzgasse, and they were quarrelling. Valerie had jumped up from her chair and was trying to calm the men down. She looked very young, charming, and very beautiful in the company of the two brothers, who resembled each other strongly despite the differences in their temperament. Both were tall and slender, with thick black hair and black eyes, tall foreheads, high cheekbones, and swarthy skin. The younger brother, Daniel, was the one more given to outbursts of temper, while the older brother, Paul, had a bent for irony and was in the habit of raising his eyebrows sharply and mockingly.

"Forgive me . . ." Daniel turned to Valerie and kissed her hand. "But I just can't help getting excited. Paul always gets me worked up! That's one of the reasons you see me so seldom here: I prefer to avoid scenes like this. But I *had* to come today! Your people from the radio have been snooping around our labs!"

"All they did was ask a few questions."

"I call that snooping! And why did nobody ask *me* any questions?"

"But you always refuse to give interviews!"

"Yes, because they make me sick! But when I hear that you intend to let loose against the Institute over the radio with an inflammatory story that it's *war materiel*—the idea alone is incredible—that it's war materiel we're really trying to produce, well, then it's a different cup of tea! Then I *do*

517

give interviews! In my capacity as Director of the Institute! And I even come to you so that *you* can interveiw me!"

Paul stroked Valerie's thigh. "Sit down, darling. And keep completely quiet. You know us two by now. We're a couple of old fighting cocks. I am a journalist. I have my professional ethics. Daniel is a scientist, and he has his. If he convinces me, really convinces me, that his researches cannot some day be used for purposes of warfare, then I will never maintain that they can. But I have to be *convinced*."

"I've been telling you: it is conceivable, just conceivable, that with the aid of our researches methods will be developed for the control and destruction of vermin."

"The only question being, what sort of vermin," Paul said.

"Please!" Valerie begged. "Not again!"

"What's that supposed to mean?" Daniel exclaimed.

"There will always be people for whom other people are nothing but vermin," Paul said.

"What you're saying is that our work might some day be used for the development of chemical or bacteriological warfare weapons, aren't you?" Daniel took a deep breath. "You really have gone out of your mind!"

"Well, poison gases were used in the last war, after all."

"But nobody can develop poison gases from what we're working on!" Daniel put his hands to his head, then rummaged in his jacket pockets. "Don't be afraid, Valerie, I'm quite calm. I'll explain it to Paul in detail. My assistant, Friedjung, wrote a few key words down on paper for me, if I can find it . . ." Valerie had given a little shudder at the mention of the name Friedjung, but it had gone unnoticed.

She said, "I don't understand anything about it. But if Paul says poison gases were used in the last war . . . they were developed by chemists, too, weren't they? And the chemists who developed them may have had no idea what their researches would lead to."

"Really, Valerie, as you say yourself: you don't understand anything about it!" Daniel smiled at her. "Ah, there's the piece of paper!" He unfolded a sheet of paper and looked at Paul. "So listen. We began our researches with a world-famous man: Louis Pasteur. You know, I suppose, that epidemics can break out among silk-worms? Well, in 1870 . . ."

518

71

"Is this Herr Friedjung's piece of paper?"

Manuel Aranda had jumped up. He was holding up a yellowed scrap of paper he had taken out of his wallet while Steinfeld was telling his story. Manuel was thinking: It's a good thing I had Dr. Stein send me this piece of paper. I had a feeling I would need it when Daniel Steinfeld arrived.

Manuel put his question more urgently, "Please! Is this the paper?"

Steinfeld examined the scrap of paper. "Yes," he said in a hoarse voice. "Yes, that's it. Where did you get it? I guess I must have left it here that night after I talked to Paul. Did Valerie save it?"

Manuel's words came tumbling out. "Yes, she saved it! Perhaps she even deliberately took it from you when she learned that it was Friedjung who had written these notes."

"I don't understand . . ."

"And when she heard something about war and chemical weapons. Her subconscious must have been at work . . . she knew Friedjung was a Nazi. He had been her friend, and now he was her enemy. Perhaps she wanted to protect herself against him with this scrap of paper, in the event he ever tried to do anything to her."

"But that's crazy!" Steinfeld exclaimed.

"Unfortunately not, Daniel," Irene said softly. "Just think of all that's happened in the meantime."

The old man bowed his head. "We were blind, we scientists. We still are, even today. By the time we realize what's happening, it's too late. In 1936 I simply could not imagine that . . . Yes, that's Friedjung's piece of paper! My God, it's thirty years ago that he wrote it . . . thirty-three years . . . Where did you find it?"

Irene told him. Swiftly Manuel had pulled the photograph out of his wallet which pictured his father on the deck of a small yacht, sturdily built and thick-set, dressed all in white, suntanned, a pipe in one hand.

"And what about this man, Mr. Steinfeld? This man in the photo—who is he?"

"Oh, Almighty Lord," said the old man in a trembling voice. "That's ... that's him ... that's Friedjung, my former assistant!"

Irene came up beside Manuel and put a hand on his shoulder. "Are you quite sure, Daniel?"

"Absolutely sure ... looks older ... older than when I knew him, of course. But the lips, the nose, the forehead ... the smile ... that's Karl Friedjung, I could swear to it."

"You won't have to," Manuel said, his voice quiet and controlled. "The scrap of paper is enough. I recognize the handwriting."

"The man in the photograph—is that your father?" Steinfeld asked, suddenly speaking very softly himself.

"That was my father," said Manuel. He sat down. Irene looked at him for a long time. For a long while all was silent in the large room.

Then Steinfeld said, "So I did poor Valerie an injustice, she was right about all her suspicions and hypotheses ..."

"Karl Friedjung. So that was my father's real name," said Manuel in the flat tone of voice he had lately begun to use. "I am the son of the man who once loved and then hated Valerie Steinfeld. And my mother is that young woman who left Vienna in the middle of the night after the air raid on the Institute in 1945. She had a small child with her, and they disappeared with Friedjung ... And the small child, that was I. They fled to Argentina with me—that was possible for Nazi big shots, and he was an important man, my father! The Argentinian authorities let a lot of people like him into the country. He forged papers for us all, forged papers that said we were born in Buenos Aires ... and that our name was Aranda. So that's how it was ..."

Another silence followed.

Then the old man said, "But Valerie never found out that your father and Friedjung were one and the same. She never found out where he was living, what name he used, what had become of him—up until the moment he walked into the bookstore to buy a book of engravings, unsuspecting and completely by chance—Valerie had known nothing about Friedjung before that! Nothing at all!

"On the tape the police made at the scene, Valerie said she had been waiting a lifetime for that moment, and that he did not recognize her, do you remember, Manuel?" Irene asked.

"I remember," Manuel said, taking her hand. "If my fat..
had not gone into that bookstore, but into a different one, o.
none at all . . . if Frau Steinfeld had happened not to be there
on that day, my father would still be alive, nothing would
have happened . . ."

Daniel Steinfeld said, "But he *did* go into the Landau
Bookstore and not into any other. And Valerie did not happen to be away, she was *there*." The ailing old Jew nodded
his head slowly as he spoke, an old man, hunted and driven
from his home searching for a new one. Let us not pass
judgment on any man. Let us not say of anything that it is
impossible. For, there is no man who has not his destiny and
no thing that has not its hour . . ."

72

The same night, at 2:14 A.M., the Professor, who had been
kneeling before the safe working at opening the lower lock,
straightened up. Mercier was watching him like a man hyp-
notized.

The Professor gripped the chromium-plated wheel and
turned it to the right. Then he tugged at it firmly, pulling it
toward him. There was a whistling inrush of air as the powerful, eight-inch-thick steel door swung open. Inside the safe
neon-lights flickered on in the vault which measured four feet
square by eight feet high. There were shelves on the walls of
the safe and a table on the floor in the center. Packages, files,
papers and a variety of boxes filled the shelves and the table.

Fascinated, Mercier advanced. One step. Another step. He
entered the vault with the thought that this was the most
solemn moment of his life. Anton Sirus was thinking of
Claude Monet's painting 'The Poppies,' which still hung in the
Musée de l'Impressionisme, but which was now his. Both
men felt exceedingly happy.

73

Around 11 A.M. on January 28, 1969, the blizzard over Vienna ended with surprising suddenness, as the gray grew darker and darker in the west. The day was fading slowly.

Many lights were on in the elegantly furnished reception room of the 'Society for Austrian-Soviet Student Friendship' in the old Baroque palace on the Wollzeile. Fedor Santarin, immaculately dressed as ever, sat at a table facing Nora Hill, who wore a wine-red pants-suit. Her mink coat was thrown over the arm of her chair. George had driven his mistress into the city.

Fedor Santarin exhibited exemplary courtesy. "The work you did was excellent, Madame. We are very pleased with you. It may be assumed that we will be able to conclude the Aranda case within the next two days. The young man was at Miss Waldegg's this evening until long after midnight. I suppose Daniel Steinfeld had a lot to tell. We can expect that by now Mr. Aranda is completely informed. Call him up and ask him to visit you this evening. Grant and I will be there, as always. I think the moment has come for you to tell him what the little wish is that you want to express to him."

Nora wrinkled her forehead. "Why did you ask me to come here? Surely not to tell me I should invite Manuel Aranda. You could have done that by phone."

"Of course." Santarin opened his gold-leaf-wrapped bag of sweets.

"May I have the pleasure of offering you—"

"No, thanks."

The Russian chose a marzipan potato and ate it with obvious enjoyment.

"Well?" Nora had an uneasy feeling.

"I'll explain in a moment. But before I do, please tell me how you intend to present your little wish."

"Fine," said Nora, placing her hands on the crutches on either side of her easychair. "I will ask Aranda whether he knows everything about his father's death now."

"Let's assume he says yes."

"Then I will tell him that I have been approached with a request that I am supposed to pass on to him."

"Namely what?"

"Santarin, really, must we—"

"Yes," he said abruptly.

They looked at each other briefly.

"As you wish," Nora said. "The request is that once the case is cleared up, he get his father's documents and the film from the attorney's safe, destroy them, and go home." Nora was rattling off the words like a petulant schoolgirl forced to recite her homework. "There's nothing he can do about the two super powers already being in possession of his father's invention. Destroying all the papers and the film will at least eliminate the danger that a *third* power might get hold of the invention. I will appeal to his reason."

"And if he refuses?" Santarin asked, in the tones of a benevolent teacher.

You miserable swine, Nora thought. "Then I will draw his attention to the fact that his refusal is endangering the life of his friend Irene Waldegg. My principals have threatened to take care of her."

"Good. Everything has gone as I hoped. The young man has fallen in love with Irene Waldegg. But what if he still wants to play the hero and enlighten the whole world?"

"Then I will make my warning more urgent and explicit. Tell him that he is causing the death of his friend and that he himself will not live to give that press conference in the Swiss Embassy."

"What if he proposes to notify the Austrian authorities?"

"I remind him of all the experience he has had so far with the Austrian authorities, of the fact that they never interfere in cases like this, of the fact that even his own Embassy will not help him, and of the fact that the two super powers will soon publicly declare their renunciation of B- and C-weapons. And then whom will the public believe? Him—or the two powers?" Nora shrugged her shoulders and went on. "That should do the trick, I think. He will be reasonable."

"I'm quite sure he will," Santarin said, "and without our needing to use threats. The case would thus be completed. And it has to be, because Grant and I have another job for you."

Nora swallowed. So that was why Santarin had called her in. "What, me again so soon?"

523

"You again, Madame. You are irreplaceable. We need you constantly."

"So it's going to go on forever?"

Santarin nodded benevolently. "There's never going to be an end to it?" Nora's voice was rising.

Santarin shook his head benevolently.

"But I've had enough! I've had enough, I tell you! I—"

"Not so loud, Madame. You are an intelligent woman. You know very well that you have no alternative but to do as we ask." One quick, deft movement and Santarin suddenly had in his hand a Smith & Weston automatic, caliber 6.35, made in 1940, which Jack Cardiff had once given to Nora for self-protection.

"Do I really have to show you once again that we are in possession of your gun? You know that already."

"I fired in self-defense," said Nora Hill, but there was a tone of resignation in her voice. I'm never, never going to be free again, she thought. "That Hungarian had found out everything that goes on in my house, and he wanted money to keep quiet about it, a crazy sum. You know as well as I do! You were at the villa when it happened! You heard us quarrelling!"

"That is so, Madame. On November 21, 1962."

"You heard him rave, saw him begin to attack me physically. You know that it was sheer terror made me draw my gun—"

"I know it, Madame. You pulled out your gun, he laughed and tried to take it away from you, it went off in the struggle, and the gentleman fell down dead."

"Self-defense, pure self-defense, that's what I've been telling you!"

"You've been telling us that, yes. Nevertheless you came running to me and Grant for help, thinking the police might not believe you. And Grant and I put together a first-class alibi for you and arranged for the murder weapon to disappear—you remember that, of course, Madame."

Nora Hill looked across at the window in anger and frustration. Outside it was getting darker and darker. A sudden gust of wind rattled the window-panes.

"Answer me!"

"Yes! Yes! Yes! You helped me then."

"Helped you *very much*. Repeat that, please."

"Helped me *very much*."

"Thanks to our help the police did not arrest you, even

though everything pointed to you at first. Thanks to our help nothing could be proved against you. And that's how it will remain, provided you cooperate as splendidly as before. If ever you should cease to do that—which would incur my deepest regrets—this gun would go straight to the Austrian police. And Grant and I will not hesitate to destroy the alibi we built up for you at the time. You can still be accused of murder. Twenty years are not up yet, remember that. I hate having to talk in this way, but it seems that from time to time you must be reminded—" A telephone rang on another table. "Excuse me, please."

Santarin walked across the room and picked up the receiver.

Nora looked at him, her eyes filled with hate.

"Santarin!" The Russian spoke his name into the phone. "A call from Paris? Who could call me from—*Mercier*! What are you doing in—" Santarin broke off. Nora, watching him, saw him bite his lips as he listened. She kept her eyes on him, scrutinizing him carefully. She knew Santarin well. Something had happened. Something *bad* had happened. But *what*? Her heart began to thud wildly. Mercier in *Paris*?

"One moment . . ." Santarin's voice was hesitant. "I can't talk here. I'm going to take it somewhere else. Please hold on." He unplugged the telephone cable and walked quickly past Nora to a door. He smiled as he passed her. But it was a strained smile.

"I'll be with you in a moment, Madame."

"Of course," Nora said, deeply immersed in her thoughts . . .

Santarin hurried along a corridor to a steel door covered with wallpaper, and opened it with two keys. Quickly he entered a large room, illuminated by indirect lighting. In this room was the short-wave transmitter through which contact with the radio cars was maintained. Two young men were operating it. One of them spoke in Russian to a radio car. This room, too, was furnished with antiques and the walls were covered with silk hangings. There was a telephone outlet above a wall cupboard, underneath an old engraving. Santarin put the phone down, plugged it in, and placed the receiver to his ear. He spoke in French.

"Mercier? What's that you were saying? And how come you're calling *this* number? How did you get it, anyway?" The call had come in over a line fitted with a scrambler.

"I just know it, that's all." Mercier's voice sounded in Santarin's ear, quite close but completely changed—no longer depressed, but filled with a triumphant ring. "I've known it for some time now. Here in Paris we have a phone with the same scrambler, so nobody can hear us. I'm going to keep it short, Santarin: I had the attorney's safe cracked Santarin, during the night. I flew to Paris with the first plane this morning. I won't be coming back. All the material I found in the safe is now with my superiors. So we, too, have AP Seven now."

"You're bluffing," Santarin croaked.

"I'm not bluffing. The attorney's name is Rudolf Stein. Kohlmarkt 11. I found not only the film and the coded manuscript Dr. Aranda had made, but also the transliterated text decoded by the police. It's on the Trans letterhead. I'll read you a bit, so that you believe me . . ."

Santarin listened without moving a muscle, except for a slight twitch under his right eye. After a while he said, "That's enough. So you pulled it off, Mercier. Congratulations."

"Thank you. You're not angry with me, are you?"

"Angry? Not at all! What gives you such an idea?"

"That makes me feel a lot easier." Mercier cleared his throat. "That is, not completely easy, though. When that attorney, Stein, opens his safe—I had it properly locked up again—he's going to discover, of course, that the material is missing. He may have discovered it already. Perhaps he will discover it one hour from now. Perhaps in two hours. Perhaps not until tomorrow. What will happen then? Stein will call up Aranda. And what will Aranda do? Talk, I assume, loud and clear. In the Swiss Embassy, at an international press conference. I am quite sure he will talk once he has figured out that the material is now in *our* possession. And he has to figure that out, since you and Grant already *had* it. Puts you on the spot, eh?"

"You miserable—"

"Come, come! This is not the time for cursing. Now we really must stick together, in my opinion. I can't do anything from here, unfortunately. And it's really a matter of minutes now, you do see that, old boy, I hope—"

The Russian put down the receiver. The connection was broken.

74

"So now you know the whole story," said Wolfgang Groll. Seelenmacher, the winegrower, leaned back in the big wing-chair in Groll's study, looking silently at the carpet. Groll was wearing a pair of pyjamas, a dressing-gown, socks and slippers. While telling his story he had paced up and down between the bookshelves covering the walls, and past a half-open window through which cold air gushed into the over-heated room. Outside the darkness was gathering fast. Groll looked bad. During his account he repeatedly had to gasp for breath and swallow pills.

The day before, Monday afternoon, he had suddenly felt deathly ill while meeting with a police official. The police doctor had been called in. He had known the Commissioner was prone to these attacks for years. "You are going home immediately and straight to bed. Stay there for the next three days. You are totally overworked."

"Nonsense. I'm feeling fine again already," Groll rumbled.

"Feeling fine again! So you really want to plug away until you get a nice heart attack, do you? Is that what you want?"

"Yes," Groll answered. "That's what I want, doctor. And a fatal heart attack, of course. No speeches over my grave, ei-ther—"

"That's enough of that!" The doctor broke in vehemently. He insisted on Groll's taking a break, and promised to call on him daily. They argued. Finally Groll was ordered by his top-ranking superior to do as the doctor said. The doctor then drove him home (Groll did not own a car), buying various medications on the way. He waited until he had seen that Groll really was undressed and in bed, and had given him some medication.

"It's the same story every winter, Doctor!"

"Roll up your sleeves." The police doctor fumbled with a hypodermic, then gave Groll an injection, after which the older man quickly fell asleep. He spent a pleasant night, and next day the doctor called again.

"Now listen, doctor, I'm really fine now, I can go back to the shop."

"Over my dead body. You're staying in bed. I'll drop by again this evening. Woe betide you if you smoke or drink!"

"Why would I do that?" Groll had said. An hour later (in the meantime Groll had called up his friend Seelenmacher and invited him over to play chess), when Manuel Aranda arrived, Groll got up, delighted to have such a good reason, put on a dressing-gown, and went into the study with his guest.

"They told me Police HQ that you were at home. Forgive me for coming unannounced. But I have a lot to tell you . . ." Manuel had been visibly excited. He had hardly slept during the night. "Of course, if you're not feeling well . . ."

"I feel fine! The old pump sometimes plays tricks on me. You've seen it for yourself. Nothing serious. I'll live to be a hundred! Cigar?"

"No, thank you."

"But I will." Groll lit one of his favorite Virginia cigars. "Now, tell me your story, Manuel."

And Manuel recounted everything he had learned from Daniel Steinfeld, telling all he now knew. He talked for an hour without a break, with Groll pacing up and down and interrupting him only with an occasional question. Finally he said; "So that's the truth. I'm sorry for your sake, Manuel, really sorry."

"You don't need to be sorry. I know the truth, that's what's important."

"But that your father—"

"I'll get over it," Manuel replied.

"What are you going to do now?"

Manuel had seemed embarrassed. "I have a rendezvous with Irene Waldegg . . ."

Groll nodded. "I understand."

"I'll call you, Commissioner, and visit you again. Tomorrow perhaps?"

"Tomorrow is fine." Groll squeezed Manuel's hand warmly. "And all the best, my boy . . ."

Left alone, Groll had seated himself in the old, carved chair behind his desk, following with his gaze the smoke of a second cigar which now hung from his lips.

Seelenmacher appeared soon afterwards. Groll had brewed some tea and placed the samovar on the little table near the desk. Both men sipped at the hot, fragrant liquid as Groll told his friend of the latest events, walking up and down as he did so in order to breathe more easily. At last he had finished, and stood still in front of Seelenmacher.

"Now you know the whole story."

At that instant a bright flash of lightning zigzagged across the skies. Immediately afterwards there was a loud thunderclap. The storm came up rapidly. The window shutters were rattling, and Groll closed them hastily. Another flash of lightning, and another. The thunder rumbled incessantly.

"A winter storm!" The Commissioner looked down into the street. It had become almost pitch-black, cars and trams were driving with their lights on. "So that's why I felt so lousy yesterday. I felt the weather in my bones!" The words were hardly out of his mouth when hailstones began hurtling down with a deafening din, and so thickly that one couldn't even see the houses across the street. The hailstones plopped to the ground and bounced up high. People were running into doorways for shelter, all traffic had come to a standstill. Visibility was less than fifteen feet.

"The circle has closed," Seelenmacher said. "Dr. Aranda's chosen path took him halfway around the earth—back to the Landau Bookstore, to Valerie Steinfeld. He had no idea she was working there. And yet. And yet! You are a scientist. You often don't like the way I talk, especially when I say that everything's predestined and that there's no such thing as chance—"

"I don't like your kind of *explanation*," Groll replied, staring out at the storm. "You're a man of faith. I, on the other hand, try my best to keep everything that has to do with religion at arm's length. Faith just doesn't come naturally to me. I, too, have a theory about chance, but it's different from yours."

"Yes, I know. I believe that all coincidence is magic ... there is no such thing as a *real* coincidence ... You told me this Friedjung was once in love with Valerie Steinfeld."

"Yes."

"And she with him. These two, you see, are the lovers in this story—tragic and evil relationship, perhaps, but at the very core of events. Their hands touched even in death, even in death. It was *necessity* that brought those two together again, a metaphysical necessity. You don't like that sort of thing, I know, but nevertheless—"

A blinding flash of lightning lit up the room. The thunderclap followed immediately. Then the telephone rang.

Groll picked it up and spoke his name.

"Nora Hill here," said a woman's voice, scarcely audible. It was a poor connection, with a lot of static and interference.

"Good day to you, dear lady. To what do I owe the—"

"I don't have much time." There was an urgency in her voice. "Commissioner, I know you won't betray me, I have to tell you something. It's urgent. Very urgent."

"Talk."

Nora Hill's voice came through in fits and starts, broken up by the disturbances on the line.

". . . and you did put it into an attorney's safe, did you not?"

"Yes. What about it?"

"Call the attorney at once! Tell him to open the safe and check whether the materials belonging to Manuel Aranda are still there!"

"What's it all mean?"

"I've no time to explain, and can't."

"I thank you, my good lady. I will immediately . . . *hallo!*"

Groll rattled the recall button. The line was dead.

Nora Hill was in a telephone booth, balanced on her crutches. George was waiting in the car outside. Nora looked out into the storm. I've done what I could, she thought . . .

Groll, at his desk, had suddenly gone purple in the face as he hastily dialed the number of Dr. Stein's law-offices.

"What is it?" Seelenmacher looked at him anxiously. "Wolfgang! Don't let yourself get so excited!"

"I'll explain everything to you in a moment . . . Operator? *Operator!* This stinking weather! Yes, I can hardly hear you. Groll here. Connect me with Dr. Stein please." A few seconds later he had the attorney on the line. The savagery of the storm made it hard for them to understand each other. Groll had to shout. He shouted at Stein to open the safe immediately. Two minutes went by. Then Seelenmacher heard his friend: "Gone . . . everything . . . no, don't do anything, nothing at all. You'll hear from me again." He hung up and dialed another number.

"Wolfgang!" called the winegrower.

"In a moment. Everything's gone full circle again," Groll said. He was calling the Ritz.

"I'm sorry, Mr. Aranda is not in the hotel. No, we don't know where he went."

Groll called the Möven Pharmacy.

A girl answered.

"Mr. Aranda was here. He just left with Miss Waldegg, ten minutes ago."

"Where to?"

"I don't know. Somebody called. Then they suddenly—"

"Thank you," said Groll.

He dialed the number of Security HQ in tremendous haste.

"The documents have been stolen from the safe?"

"Yes! And Manuel has driven off somewhere with the Waldegg girl, nobody knows where, after they had a phone call."

"Oh, my God!"

Groll's exhaustion seemed to have been magically cured. Seelenmacher listened in amazement as Groll asked his Chief to authorize an all-out manhunt using every available car and man. He got the go-ahead. Just two minutes later the first squad cars were on their way out of Police HQ, with descriptions of Irene and Manuel and of Manuel's car. Groll had Inspector Schäfer on the phone.

"Get a car and pick me up."

"But you're sick, commissioner . . ."

"Sick, bullshit! Somebody has to coordinate things now! Pick me up, I tell you! Be here in ten minutes! I'll get dressed and wait for you in the street! No more arguing, just come!" Groll slammed down the receiver and hurried into his bedroom, where he began to get dressed. "The swine," he said as he was pulling his clothes on. "They mustn't pull it off, we have to be quicker than they are this time . . . we *have to!*"

At the same moment Inspector Ulrich Schäfer was already hurrying toward a patrol car in the parking-lot of Police HQ. He turned on the engine and guided the car out onto the street through the arched gate. The storm was so bad he could hardly see a thing, and had to drive at snail's pace. Suddenly he slammed on his brake. A man had loomed up in front of his car's radiator. Cursing, Schäfer rolled down his window to yell at the pedestrian, but the latter ran quickly around to the right-hand door, opened it, and slid in next to the Inspector. He had his hat drawn down over his face; from his pocket a bulging envelope, a sheet of paper, and a ball-point pen.

"Here," the unknown man said. "One hundred thousand schillings. No time to let you count them, but it's all there. Sign that you received the money." Fingers shaking, Inspector Ulrich Schäfer signed the receipt. The man tore the paper and the pen from his hand and jumped out of the car.

A second later he had disappeared in the dark. Schäfer sat holding the envelope in his hand. They have kept their word, he thought, I have all the cash. I can pay for the sanatorium again. And perhaps a miracle will happen, perhaps they'll invent a new cure, perhaps . . .

75

The wind howled around the car, buffeting and shaking it. Hailstones slanted through the air, crashed against roofs, house walls, and the streets; soon a thick hard crust had formed over the frozen snow. Manuel switched his windshield wipers on fast. The rubber strips swished back and forth over the glass at top speed, but did not help much. Manuel could scarcely see a thing. The constant flashes of lightning blinded him. The thunder following each time in their wake sounded dully through the loud drumming of hailstones against the car roof.

"We should have waited until the storm let up a little," Irene said as Manuel turned into the Rennweg.

"But she said we should meet her as soon as possible! She's waiting already," he answered, bent low over the steering-wheel. "And besides, look, it's brightening up over there."

"Crazy weather, in January, but I remember something similar three years ago, in the middle of winter . . ."

Forty minutes earlier the telephone had rung in the office of the Möven Pharmacy. Manuel had gone there straight from Groll's apartment. He wanted to have lunch with Irene.

The telephone rang incessantly.

Manuel gestured to Irene, who was standing at the cash register. There were about a dozen people in the shop, many of whom had simply dashed for cover when the storm broke. Irene hurried into the office and lifted the receiver.

"Möven Pharmacy!" A huge thunderclap followed on her words. Irene shuddered. *"Who?"* Her face brightened. "Oh, it's you. Good day to you Frau Barry!" Irene gave Manuel a sign. Manuel picked up the second receiver, which lay on the desk. Cracklings, hissing, and the noise of traffic reverberated in his ear. He could barely make out what the woman was saying.

"... already called the Ritz, but ..." The rest was lost in the noise.

"What was that?" Irene shouted. "I can't hear! What did you say?"

"... Mr. Aranda is not at the hotel," said Bianca Barry's voice.

"No, he's here, with me." A blinding flash of lightning zigzagged down. Thunder rumbled and roared. "What is it, Frau Barry?"

"Scared ..."

Crackling over the line.

"What?"

"I'm scared, so scared ... that's why I'm calling you ... please come ... please come."

"Where to? What has happened?" Irene exclaimed.

Communication was almost impossible, Bianca Barry's voice came through completely distorted and sometimes totally incomprehensible for several seconds.

"He wouldn't let me ..." The rest was drowned by noise.

"Who? What? I can't hear you!" Irene shouted. A few customers in the shop were looking at her. Manuel quickly closed the door.

"A man ... called me over the phone two hours ago ... Roman is away today and tomorrow ... the man must have known that ..."

"Are you at home?"

"No, not any more! I'm talking ... telephone booth ... in the city ... Schwarzenbergplatz ..."

"What are you doing there?"

"... this man saw us ... when we were in Fischamend ... I'm the one who's to blame ..."

"You? To blame for what ..."

"For everything ... I lied to you ..."

"You ..."

"Lied, yes! I simply *could not* tell you the whole truth."

"The whole truth about what?"

"About Heinz ... and his mother ... and Mr. Aranda's father ..."

"You know the whole truth about them all?"

"Yes ... yes! But I didn't tell you ..."

"Why not?"

"... too terrible ... too horrible ... was there myself ..."

Flash of lightning. Thunderclap. Flash of lightning. Thunderclap.

"... trying to blackmail me ... the man ... if I don't do what he says ... needs me ... must do it ... or you're in danger ... your lives at stake ..."

"But—" began Irene, disconcerted.

Manuel shouted into the phone.

"Frau Barry, you *must* tell us the whole truth. Do you understand? You *must* tell us!"

"That's what I want to do before I meet the man ... I want you to know everything ... come please, please come ... quickly ... he's expecting me in an hour ... till then ..."

"Where is he waiting for you?"

"In Fischamend ... at the Merzendorfer restaurant."

"How were you planning to get there?"

"... tram to the Civic Cemetery, then bus ... I'll tell you everything before I meet the man ... scared ..."

Manuel interjected quickly, "Where shall we meet you?"

"At the Cemetery, main entrance ... tram shelter ..."

"We'll come as fast as we can," said Manuel, replacing the receiver and looking at Irene.

"She lied to us! She lied to us! She knows the truth, *the whole truth*! Now we'll hear it at last!"

"But Daniel has told already us the whole story!" Lightning flash. Thunderclap. Lightning flash. Thunderclap.

"Perhaps he didn't really know it, either! Anyway, we've got to go to the Cemetery. Come on, quick, let's get going."

Irene, fired by his excitement, stripped off her white apron, pulled on her sealskin boots and her fur coat, then reached for her fur hat. They ran out through the shop, and a minute later were driving through the storm.

"Bianca Barry! So she knew the truth all along," Manuel said, steering the car carefully. "The whole truth. Why she of all people? And who is the man? What does he want from her?"

"I don't know, Manuel. Look out, a truck!" He wrenched the wheel around and missed a collision by inches. "Perhaps Daniel Steinfeld really doesn't know everything ..."

"The man saw us in Fischamend! Some of Santarin's men were watching us in Fischamend, too. Santarin phoned Groll especially to tell him, to reassure him. So who is?"

"Let's listen to what Frau Barry has to say. Don't talk now or we'll have an accident." And so they had hardly spoken during the long ride.

The Simmering Road seemed endless to Manuel. "Quarter past one. She must have gotten there a long time ago."

"We'll make it, Manuel, keep calm. The storm is over now,"

And, indeed, the storm had abated and the sky was brightening.

The houses were smaller now. On his right Manuel could see the long wall of the Civic Cemetery. The dirty piles of snow at the side of the road were covered with white hailstones.

"We're here," Manuel said, driving into the square in front of the massive main entrance. A few taxis were standing there, their drivers talking among themselves. Otherwise, there was not a soul to be seen.

"Where's Frau Barry?" Manuel asked. The glass shelter at the tram stop was deserted.

Irene rolled down her window and looked around.

"No sign of her," she said.

A man emerged from the porter's lodge to the right of the open gate and walked toward them with a broad smile, that revealed yellow teeth. Manuel stared at him.

"Who's that?" Then he remembered. "The gatekeeper. Remember him?"

"Yes," Irene said. "And he seems to remember us."

It was true.

"There you are, Miss! And the gentleman, too!" The little old gatekeeper touched his cap in greeting, bending over to the open car window as he did so. His sharp face was very white again, his ears and nose very red, as were his eyes. His walrus moustache was stained with nicotine. "I was keeping an eye out for you. You have an appointment with a lady, is that right?"

"Yes," Irene said. "How do you know?"

"Frau Barry, correct?"

"Correct," said Manuel. "Have you spoken to her?"

The old gatekeeper nodded.

"It was hailing cats and dogs when she got here. She ran over there into the tram shelter, I was watching. Then the weather cleared and she started walking up and down. All at once she came over to me and said that you two would be coming here, Miss Waldegg and . . ."

"Aranda."

"Yes. But that it might be a while yet before you got here. She was terribly nervous. 'I don't want to stand around here,'

535

she said. And asked me to tell you, be good enough to go over there. She's waiting for you there."

"She went to the grave?" Manuel leaned sideways across Irene to look at the gatekeeper.

"Like I said! She didn't want to wait here. Don't know why not. The storm was over. Do you want an entrance-ticket?"

"Yes, please."

An aircraft that had just taken off roared overhead, above the clouds.

The gatekeeper tore a ticket from his block. Manuel handed him twenty schillings.

"Thank you very kindly, Baron!" The gatekeeper saluted once again.

76

Crows croaked, squawked, squealed. They squatted by the hundreds in the bare branches of the old trees lining the walk big, horrible. Their hoarse screaming filled the air.

A new, grainy layer of ice had formed on the roads. Manuel had to drive very slowly. A lot more snow had fallen since he had first met Irene here. The snow lay like a blanket over graves and gravestones, shrubs and bushes, cypresses, plane-trees, oaks and elms. There it was again, the white, boundless desert of death . . .

Manuel was staring straight ahead as he said, "Irene . . ."

"Yes?" She too was looking straight ahead.

"I don't know what all this means and what we're going to have to face now, but there has to be an end sometime, there has to be a solution."

"Yes."

"And there's Nora Hill, too. She wants to ask me for something, I don't know what. And whether I can fulfill her wish is going to depend on what it is Bianca Barry has to say, and what we have to do after that . . . with this man in Fischamend, what happens there . . . but we'll have to count on our luck . . . we've always been lucky so far, have we not?"

"Yes," Irene said. "Yes."

There was not a soul to be seen.

"And once we know everything and can begin to forget it all—"

"I'll never forget it," she said.

"No," Manuel said, "nor shall I." For a while he was silent. "But since what happened did happen to us both," he then said, "and since everything that has happened and is happening affects both of us, would you, when it's all over ... would you ... would you be able to consider becoming my wife?"

She gave no answer.

"Please, Irene! I love you. I love you so much. When it's all over, I would like to leave Vienna with you, and live with you in my home land ..."

Irene remained silent.

Suddenly sunshine brightened the snow.

"Irene," said Manuel, turning the car into the path between Sections 73 and 74. "Please, Irene, answer me. Even if you have to say no. Even if you don't want to be my wife. Even if you don't want to come back with me. Please, Irene. Why don't you say something?"

Her voice was thick and caught in her throat as she said, "I can't ..."

He glanced quickly over to her, and saw that she was crying. "Irene! What's the matter?"

"Nothing," she said, with an effort. "Nothing ... I'm just so happy in spite of everything ... even though we don't know what to expect ... I'm so happy you asked me ..."

Manuel stepped hard on the brake. The car skidded to one side. He put the gear in neutral and turned toward her.

"That means ..."

"That means yes," Irene whispered. "Yes, yes, yes!"

He put his arms around her. Their lips touched. And in the sweetness of the kiss, uncertainty and fear, grief and pain, past, present and future sank away for both of them.

77

The mouth of the rifle poked out directly above the gilded letter 'U' in the word VOLUPTAS.

The rifle was an American "Springfield," model 03, caliber 7.62 millimeters, bullet length 75 millimeters, overall rifle length 1250 millimeters. The magazine held ten rounds and it was fitted with telescopic sights. Everything included, the "Springfield" weighed only ten pounds.

David Parker was wearing his rust-brown duffle coat again and heavy shoes. His outfit was exactly the same as it had been on the afternoon of January 16 when he had shot Louis Alphonse Clairon from the window of a nearby men's toilet with Clairon standing exactly where Parker was standing now, namely on a mound behind a gray marble monument, almost as tall as Parker himself, that was the gravestone of the Reitzenstein family and was located in Section L 73, among snow-covered shrubs and hedges. Above the massive stone was a pedestal supporting the lifesize kneeling figure of a weeping angel, with outspread wings. His hands were clasped over his face. The handle of a marble torch was fastened to his right thigh, its crown resting on the pedestal. On the front end of the pedestal, in large capital letters, were these words:

EST QUAEDAM FLERE VOLUPTAS

Under the angel's bent left knee the folds of his flowing robe left a triangular opening, blocked by snow which David Parker quickly cleared away, as once Louis Alphonse Clairon had done, to provide an embrasure for his "Springfield." He slid the barrel into the peephole until it rested securely on the left big toe of the marble angel.

David Parker's duffle coat was soaked through, and felt heavy. Parker had been waiting three-quarters of an hour. He had sat through the tail-end of the storm, cursing and freezing.

It was the only way. He didn't want to have to rush to the

scene at the last moment this time. Gilbert Grant had despatched him in plenty of time for once, immediately after Gerda had finished making her telephone call. He had driven Gerda, whom he never seen before, to a tram stop on the Simmering Road, and had waited for her to complete her call from a phone booth. Gerda was supposed to use the tram for the last stage of the journey, Gilbert Grant had made a big point of that, that drunken bum of a boss.

David Parker was well aware there had been some kind of major foul-up and that he must not fail. And I won't fail, he thought. I never have yet.

Parker had been in Vienna for some time now. Grant had called him in from New York.

"Just routine. We want to have you on the spot, in case. We don't expect to have anything for you to do, we're working out a peaceful solution to the problem. Having you here is merely a safety precaution."

Obviously a very prescient safety precaution, because suddenly, very, very suddenly, the problem couldn't be resolved peacefully at all, Parker had no idea why not. He never asked questions. He never asked questions because he knew his bosses would never tell him the truth.

Clairon really had found himself an ideal spot that day, the American was thinking. The best far and wide. I wonder if he's still here, under all that snow? Parker trod up and down a little, and had the feeling that his feet were touching a few uneven spots. I'm standing right on top of him, he thought. The idea amused him.

Parker looked along the path.

Still nothing.

Oh, well, the car would come sooner or later. Parker was happy that the sun was shining. He thought of the woman named Gerda, no longer a young woman by any means, talking with the Russian and the horribly bloated Grant in the little room with the steel door, where the two men had been very busy with the transmitter before Gerda, whose name was probably something quite different, began her telephone conversation.

A strange conversation. With a Frau Barry or something like that. Gerda pretended she absolutely wanted to buy a painting—Frau Barry, whoever she was, must be the wife of a painter and taking care of the business side of things. There was a lot of bargaining, then Gerda promised to visit the woman. She hung up.

"Was it long enough?" the Russian asked.

"Sure," Gerda nodded.

"Let me hear it!"

Then Gerda began to speak in a completely different voice, with the thunderstorm crashing in the background—she was, without doubt, imitating the voice of Frau Barry. Gerda seemed to be a specialist at imitating voices.

"Excellent! So get going! Stop at a telephone booth on the Simmering Road and call the pharmacy. Aranda's still there with the girl, our radio cars tell us. You know what to say?"

"Yes."

"If it works, tell Parker. He will get to the grave and take care of everything."

"But if this weather keeps up," Parker said, "Gerda can't simply march into the Cemetery. What do we do then?"

"The weather will be all right," Grant said, more calmly. "We have cars on the thruway by St. Valentin and by Pressbaum. St. Valentin has clear skies already. In Pressbaum it's only raining and very slightly. The storm is moving at a fair speed across the city and the Vienna woods to the northeast."

"Okay, fine, sounds all right to me."

"We have the cemetery surrounded by cars. If you have any difficulties at all, tell us over the radio. We'll keep the receivers open."

Well, Parker was thinking, no difficulties so far. Gerda had left the telephone booth—at the height of the storm—and told him to drive on.

So she must have imitated that Barry woman's voice well enough to fool these two people I've got to take care of, Parker thought. They had wished each other luck as they parted company, Gerda saying, "I'll go in through the main gate and out again through the third gate. You go in through the third gate."

"Okay."

Parker had watched Gerda again through the rear-view mirror. Hardly any make-up, slim, excellent figure. Can't be forty yet. Just my cup of tea, he thought. Looked terrific in the light mink and the light boots. She was holding an umbrella with both hands to keep it from turning inside out. The Barry woman must have a mink and boots like those, Parker thought. Gerda's job is to lure my customers to the spot. Before she goes into the cemetery she will pass the time of day with the gatekeeper and ask him to tell those two to come to the grave. They might well ask him how the woman had looked. Well organized. Grant's a drunken wreck, but he does a good job. He'd be lost without the Russian, of course . . . He heard a dull roar. A plane taking off from Schwechat airport, Parker thought.

The next moment he saw a blue Mercedes approaching. Parker looked at it through the telescopic sights. The number on the license plates was correct. So that's it, he thought. Everything hunky-dory. Slowly and deliberately he aimed his weapon, swivelling the barrel of the "Springfield" millimeter by millimeter so as to keep the left front door of the Mercedes constantly in his sights. Resting on the angel's big toe it was easy to keep the gun steady and controlled as it inched around.

78

"I don't see Frau Barry," Manuel said, letting the car roll to a stop between the fourth and fifth path in Section 74. He threw a hasty look at the cast-iron cross some distance away which he, together with Irene, had rammed into the frozen soil just twelve days ago—only twelve days ago!

"I don't see her either," Irene said. "What do you make of it? Do you understand this?"

Manuel had reached the fifth path off to the right, and stopped the car.

"Perhaps she's behind a tree," he said. "Wait a moment." He opened the door on his own side and got out. The noise of the climbing aircraft was deafening. The crows had ceased their croaking, the air shook.

"Frau Barry!" Manuel shouted, stepped forward and looked around. He had left his fur hat in the car. The Boeing was passing closer and closer overhead. Clumps of snow were already tumbling from the branches and the gravestones.

"Frau Barry! Frau Barry!"

They were his last words. An instant later Irene, who had stayed in the car, saw Manuel stumble forward and fall to the ground. Seized with sudden terror, she saw blood pouring from his right temple across the icy crust of the path and over the snow.

"Manuel!" she screamed. She leapt out of the car and ran to his side. The pool of blood around his head was spreading rapidly. Irene knelt down by the fallen man. Her boots, coat, and hands were stained with red blood as she tried desperately to turn Manuel over onto his back. Blood was gushing, an unending torrent of blood, from a gáping wound in Manuel's right temple.

Irene felt incapable of leaping to her feet, running for her life, or screaming. She was paralyzed by horror.

"Manuel," she stammered. "My God, Manuel . . ."

The aircraft whined and whirred overhead, howling and roaring as though about to burst apart. A shadow flitted over Irene, the shadow of the angel of death. Infinitely slowly Irene lifted her head. Directly above she saw the Boeing passing in a radiant blue sky, trailing its white jetstreams. The diabolical din came to a furious crescendo. The earth began to vibrate. Irene lowered her head, slowly, bit by bit. And there, before her tear-filled eyes, against the purple, black, and gray cloud banks of the departing storm was tallowed very wide, a shimmering, radiant rainbow. It seemed close enough to touch.